GRIMOIRE NOIR

GRIMOIRE NOIR

WRITTEN BY
VERA GREENTEA

ARTWORK BY
YANA BOGATCH

:01

First Second

NEW YORK

CHAPTER 1

THE EMPTY ROOM

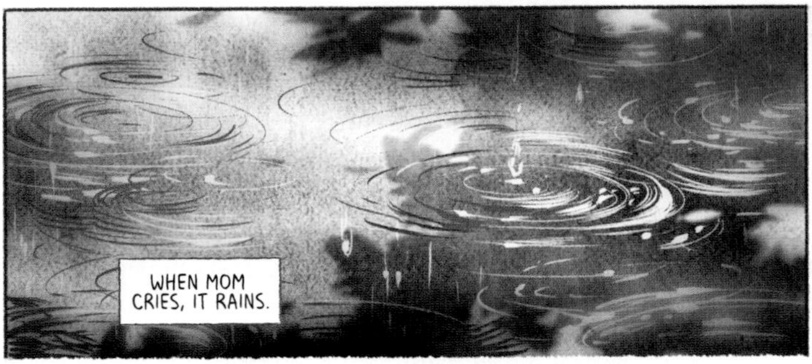
WHEN MOM
CRIES, IT RAINS.

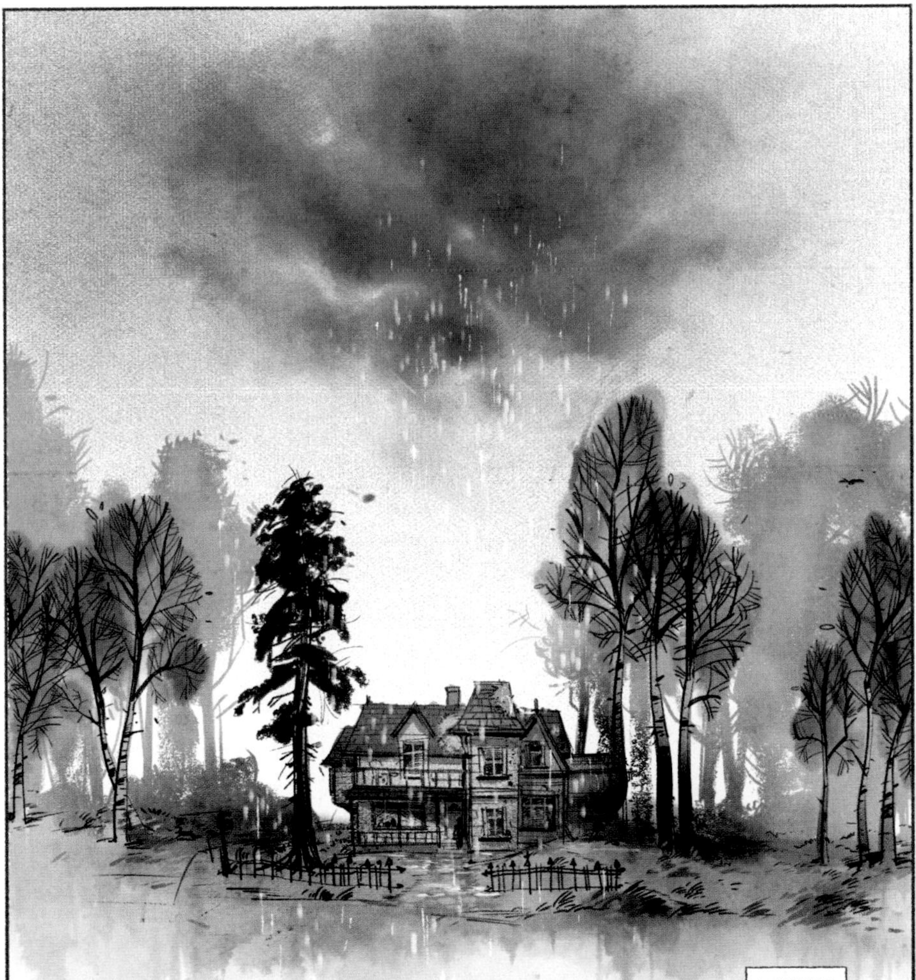
LITERALLY.

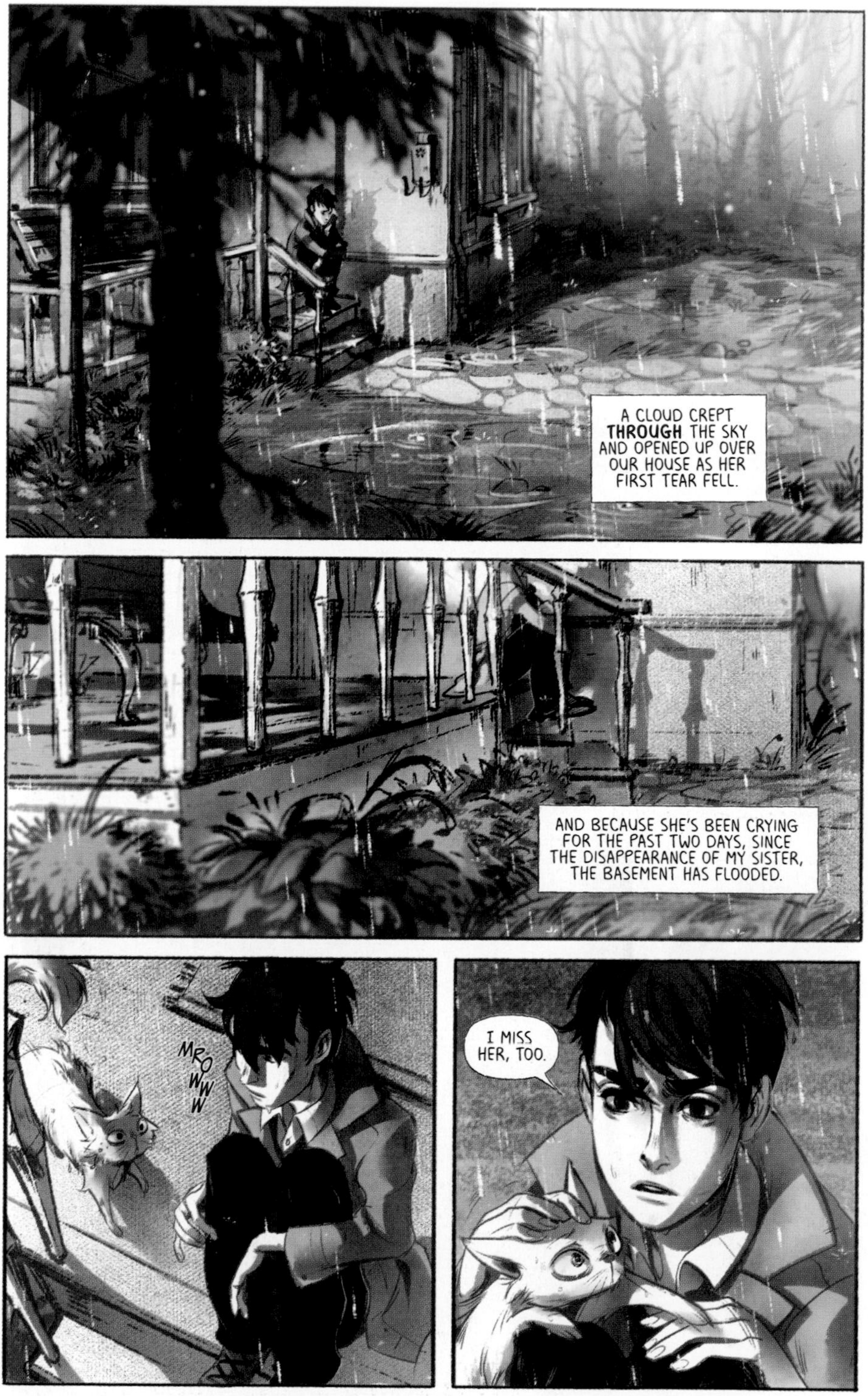
A CLOUD CREPT **THROUGH** THE SKY AND OPENED UP OVER OUR HOUSE AS HER FIRST TEAR FELL.
AND BECAUSE SHE'S BEEN CRYING FOR THE PAST TWO DAYS, SINCE THE DISAPPEARANCE OF MY SISTER, THE BASEMENT HAS FLOODED.
MROWWWW
I MISS HER, TOO.

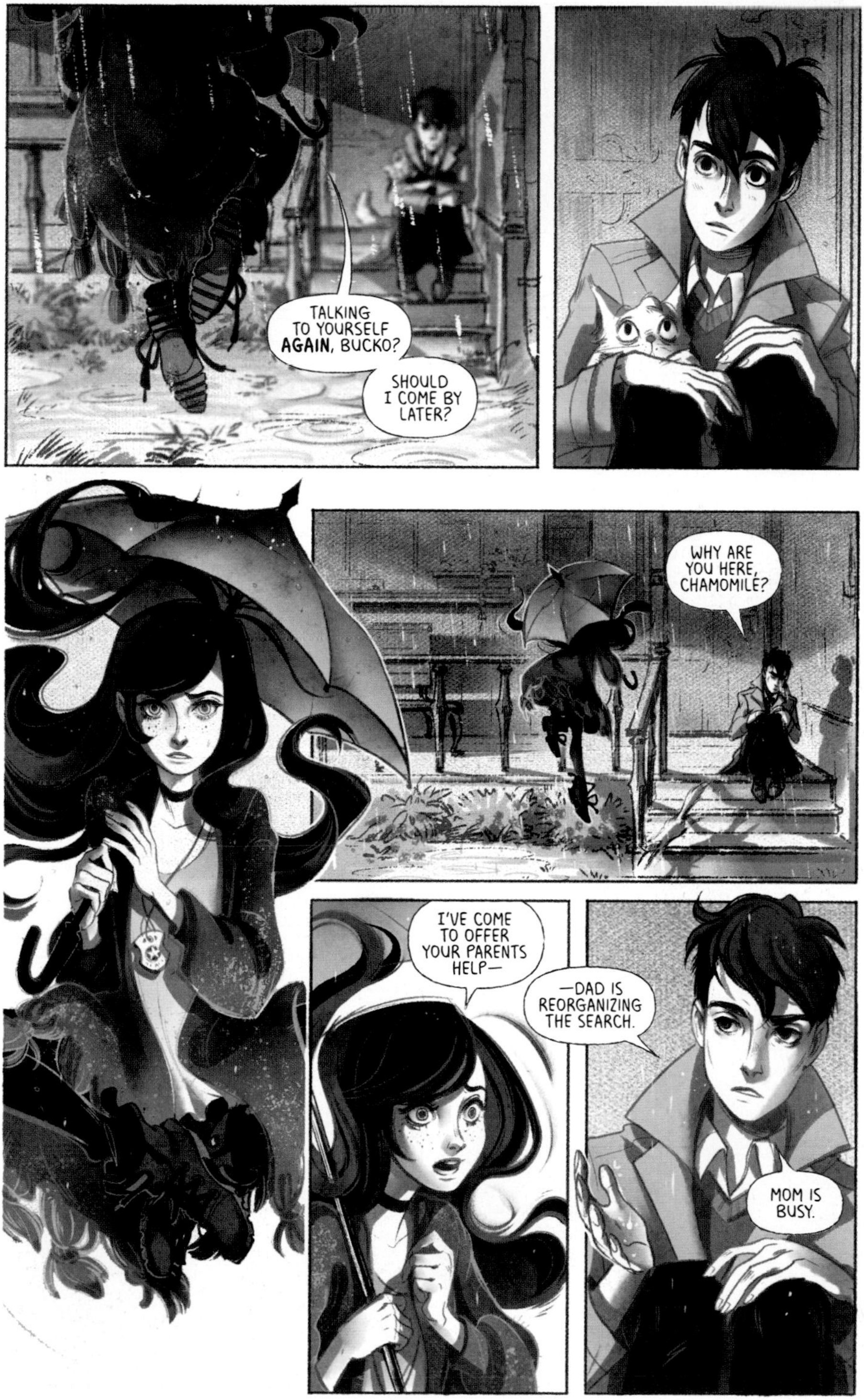
TALKING TO YOURSELF **AGAIN**, BUCKO?
SHOULD I COME BY LATER?
WHY ARE YOU HERE, CHAMOMILE?
I'VE COME TO OFFER YOUR PARENTS HELP—
—DAD IS REORGANIZING THE SEARCH.
MOM IS BUSY.

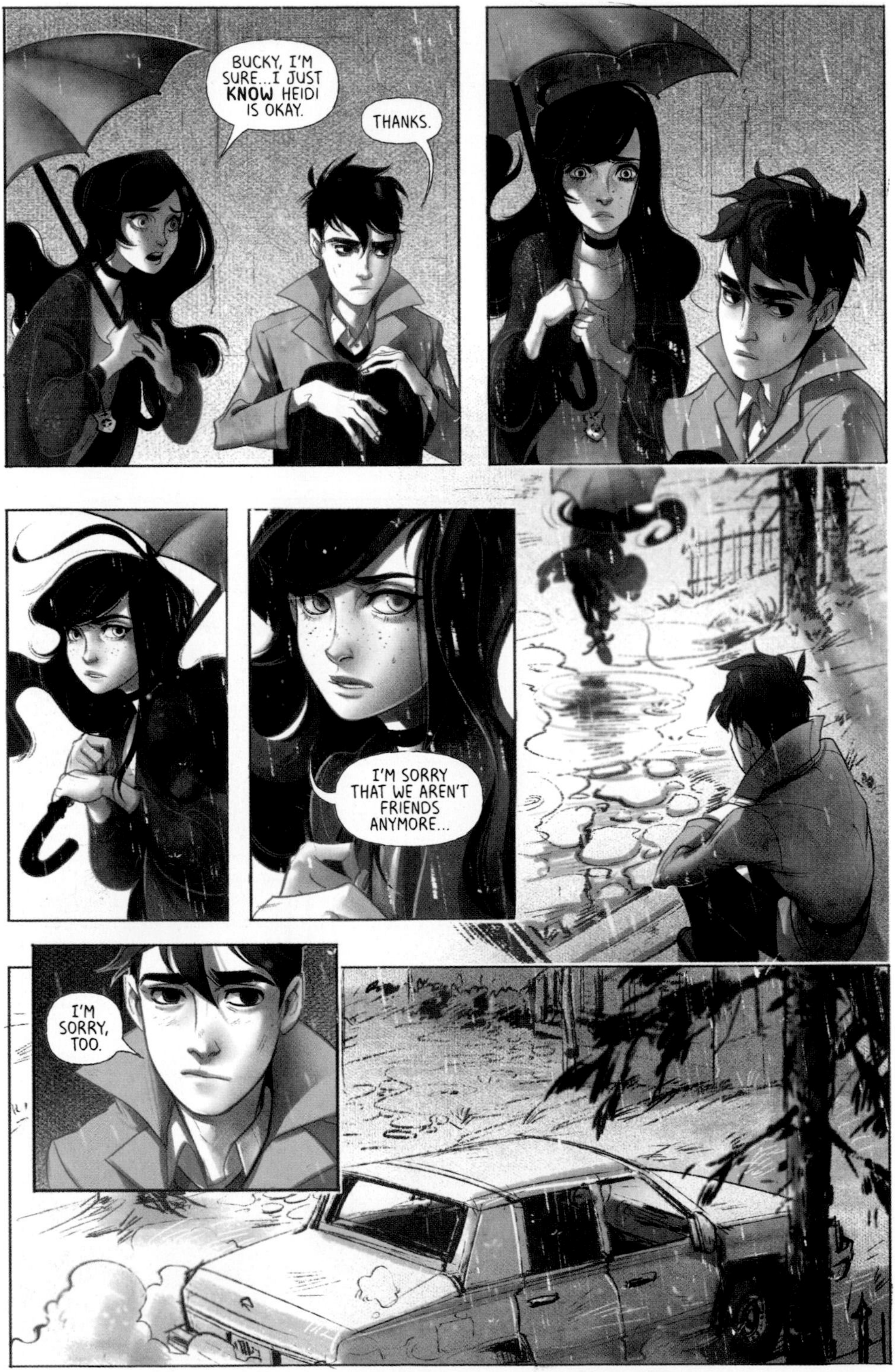
BUCKY, I'M SURE...I JUST **KNOW** HEIDI IS OKAY.
THANKS.
I'M SORRY THAT WE AREN'T FRIENDS ANYMORE...
I'M SORRY, TOO.

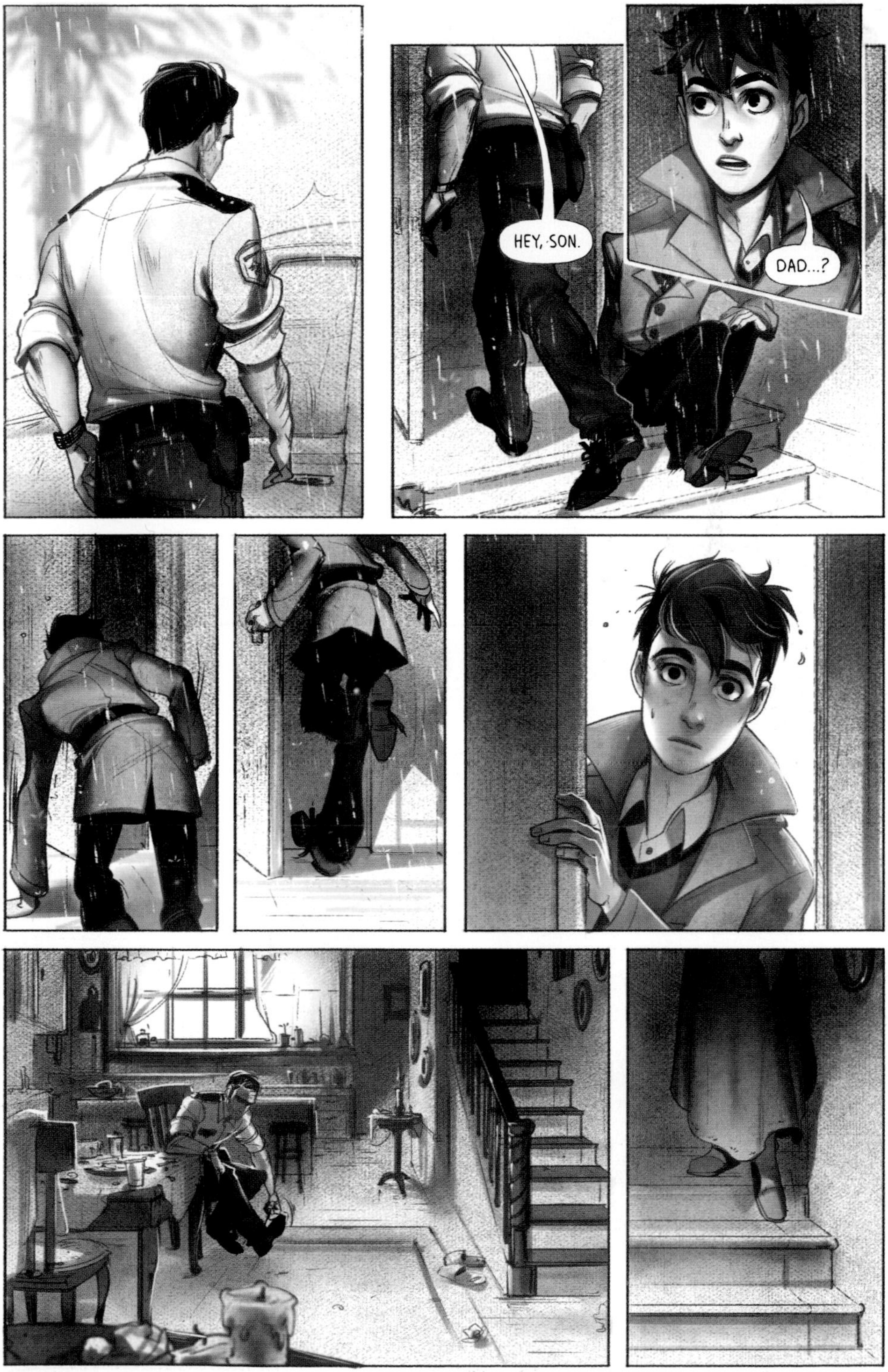
HEY, SON.
DAD...?

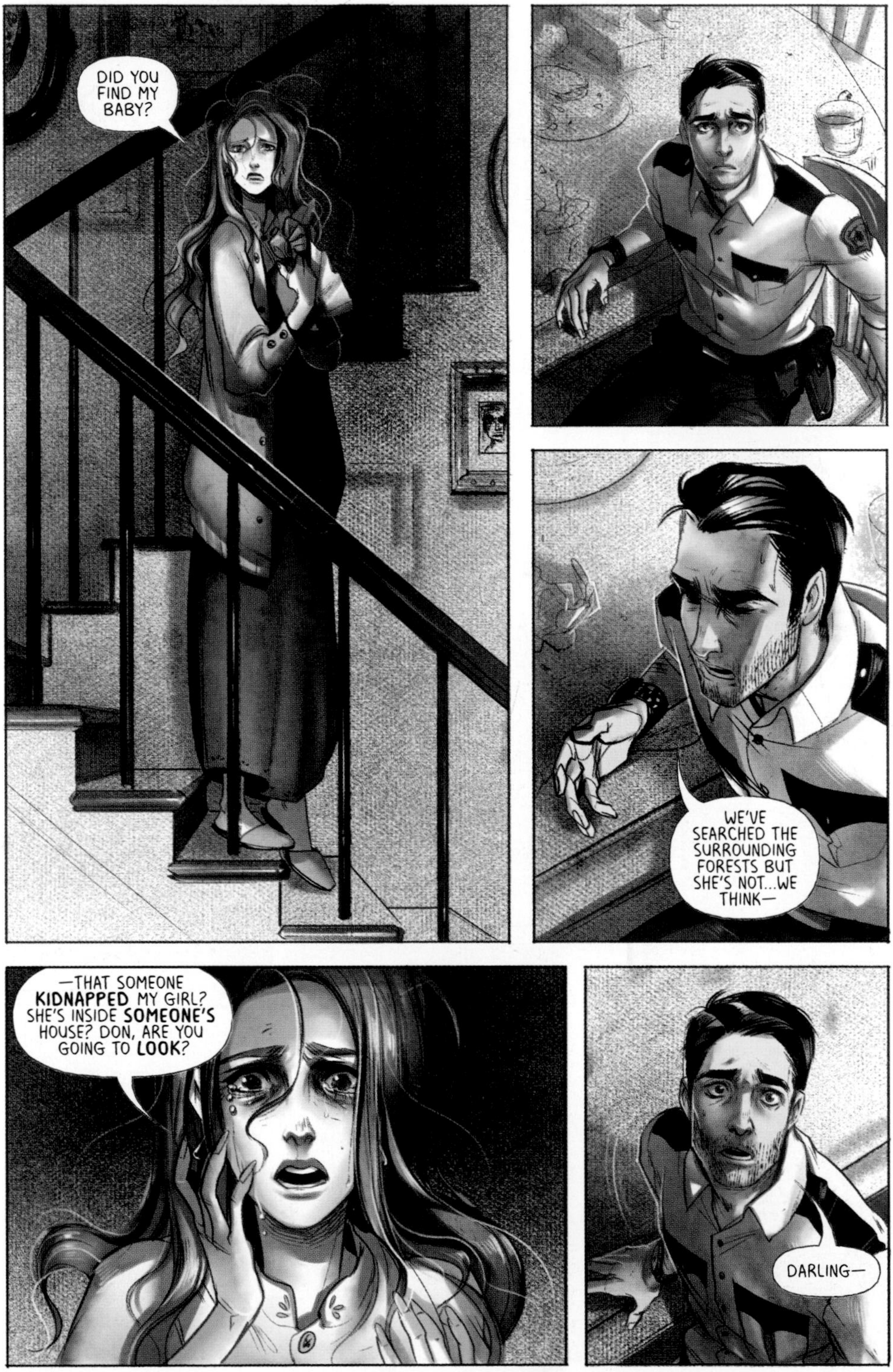
DID YOU FIND MY BABY?
WE'VE SEARCHED THE SURROUNDING FORESTS BUT SHE'S NOT...WE THINK—
—THAT SOMEONE **KIDNAPPED** MY GIRL? SHE'S INSIDE **SOMEONE'S** HOUSE? DON, ARE YOU GOING TO **LOOK**?
DARLING—

whoosh
YOU'RE THE SHERIFF, DON!
IF SOMEONE ABDUCTED HER, IT IS YOUR DUTY TO BRING THAT EVIL CREATURE TO JUSTICE!
YOU DO THAT FOR YOUR FAMILY!
CORDELIA... IT'S NOT THAT SIMPLE—
IT SHOULD BE THAT SIMPLE.
SLAM!
SIGH...

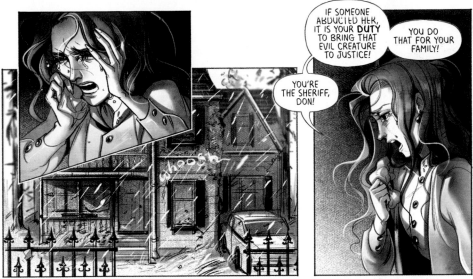

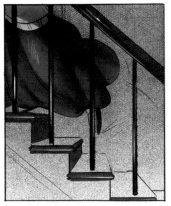

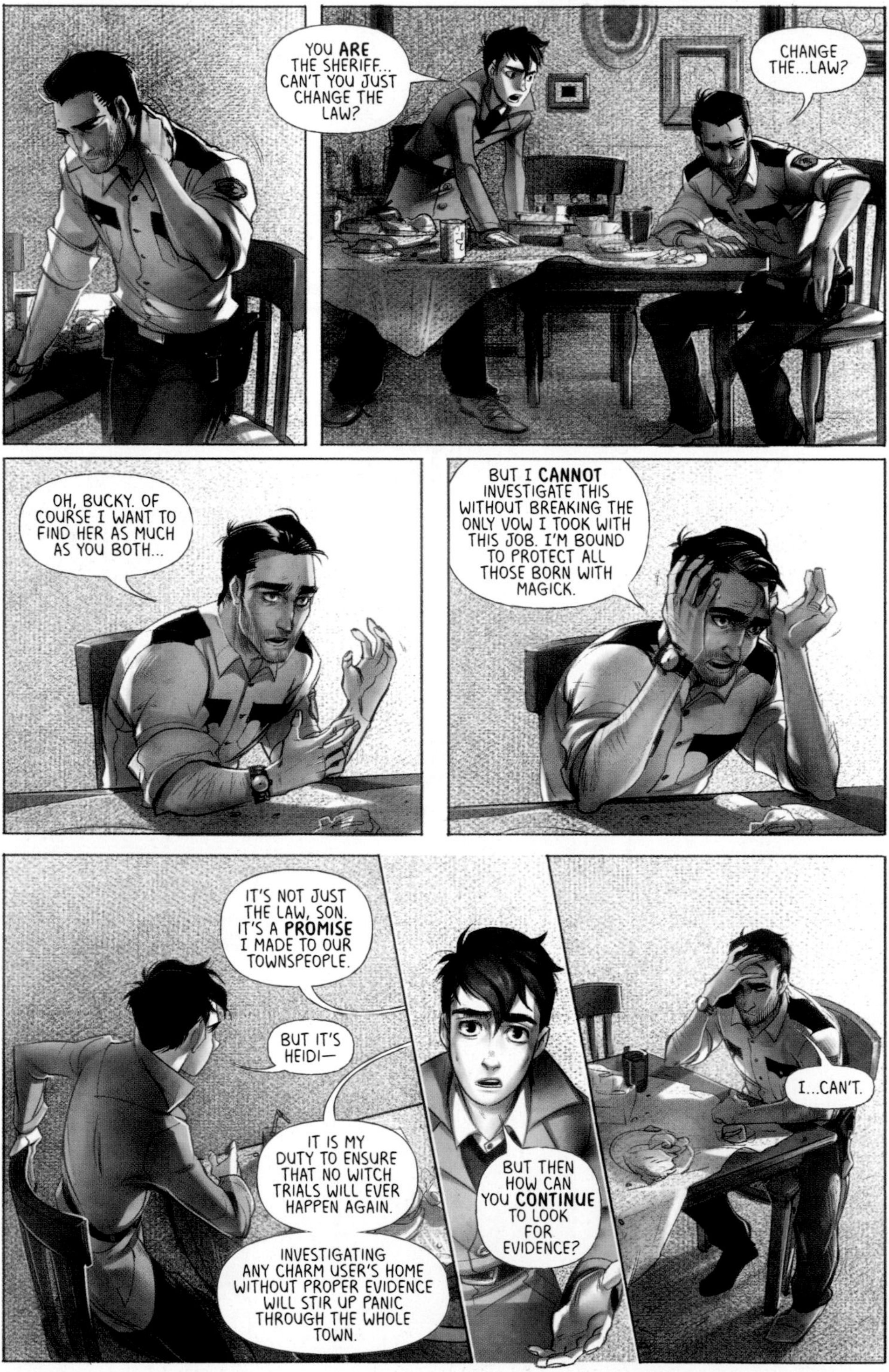
YOU **ARE** THE SHERIFF... CAN'T YOU JUST CHANGE THE LAW?
CHANGE THE...LAW?
OH, BUCKY. OF COURSE I WANT TO FIND HER AS MUCH AS YOU BOTH...
BUT I **CANNOT** INVESTIGATE THIS WITHOUT BREAKING THE ONLY VOW I TOOK WITH THIS JOB. I'M BOUND TO PROTECT ALL THOSE BORN WITH MAGICK.
IT'S NOT JUST THE LAW, SON. IT'S A **PROMISE** I MADE TO OUR TOWNSPEOPLE.
BUT IT'S HEIDI—
IT IS MY DUTY TO ENSURE THAT NO WITCH TRIALS WILL EVER HAPPEN AGAIN.
INVESTIGATING ANY CHARM USER'S HOME WITHOUT PROPER EVIDENCE WILL STIR UP PANIC THROUGH THE WHOLE TOWN.
BUT THEN HOW CAN YOU **CONTINUE** TO LOOK FOR EVIDENCE?
I...CAN'T.

HERE'S SOMETHING WE CAN DO, BUCKY.

TELL ME EVERYTHING LEADING UP TO HEIDI'S DISAPPEARANCE AGAIN. MAYBE WE MISSED SOMETHING THE FIRST TIME.

"THE INVITATION ARRIVED LAST SATURDAY..."

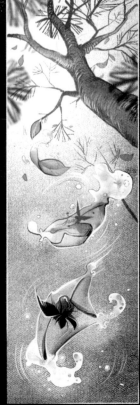

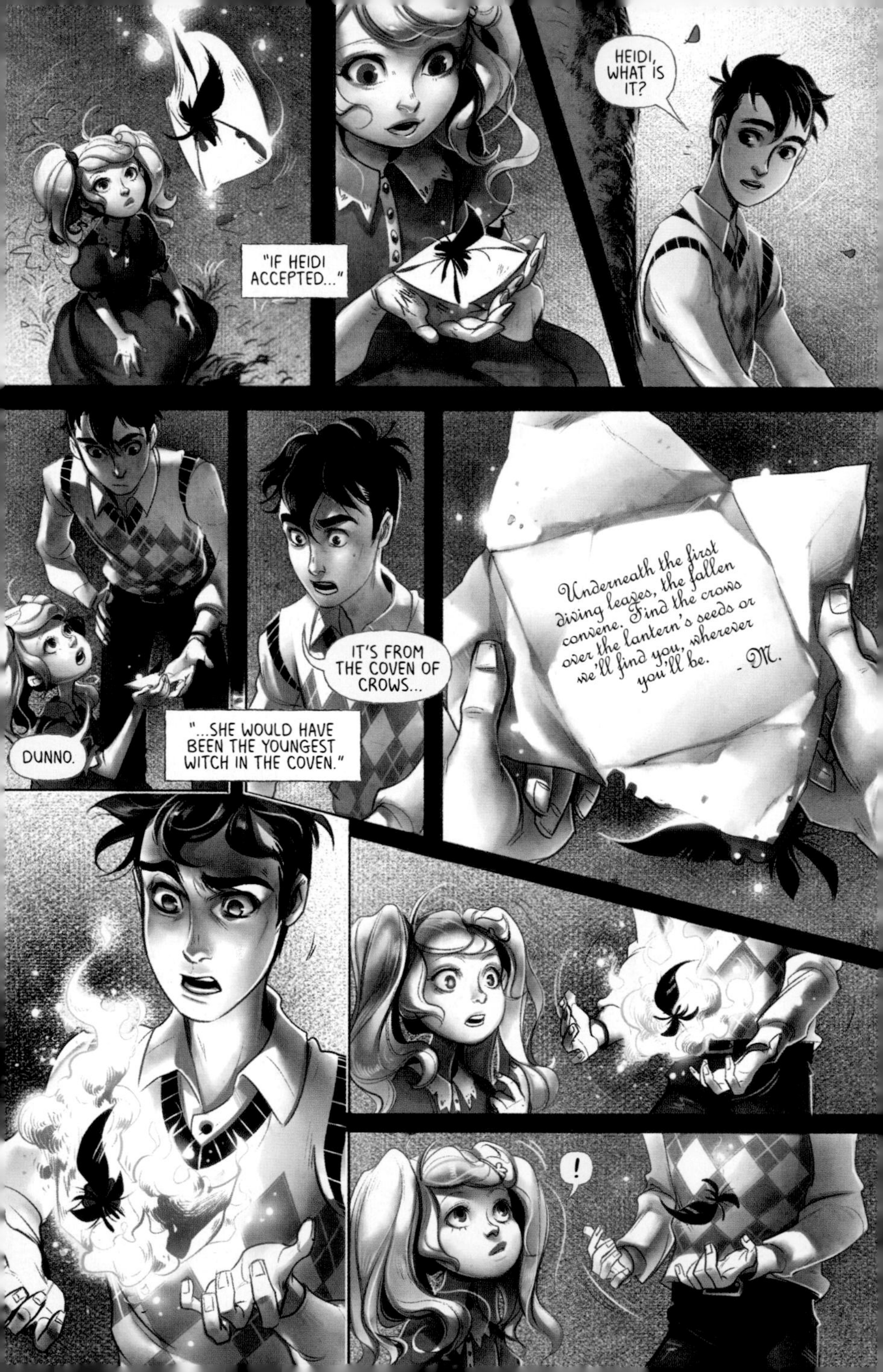
"IF HEIDI ACCEPTED..."
HEIDI, WHAT IS IT?
DUNNO.
IT'S FROM THE COVEN OF CROWS...
"...SHE WOULD HAVE BEEN THE YOUNGEST WITCH IN THE COVEN."
Underneath the first diving leaves, the fallen convene. Find the crows over the lantern's seeds or we'll find you, wherever you'll be. - M.
!

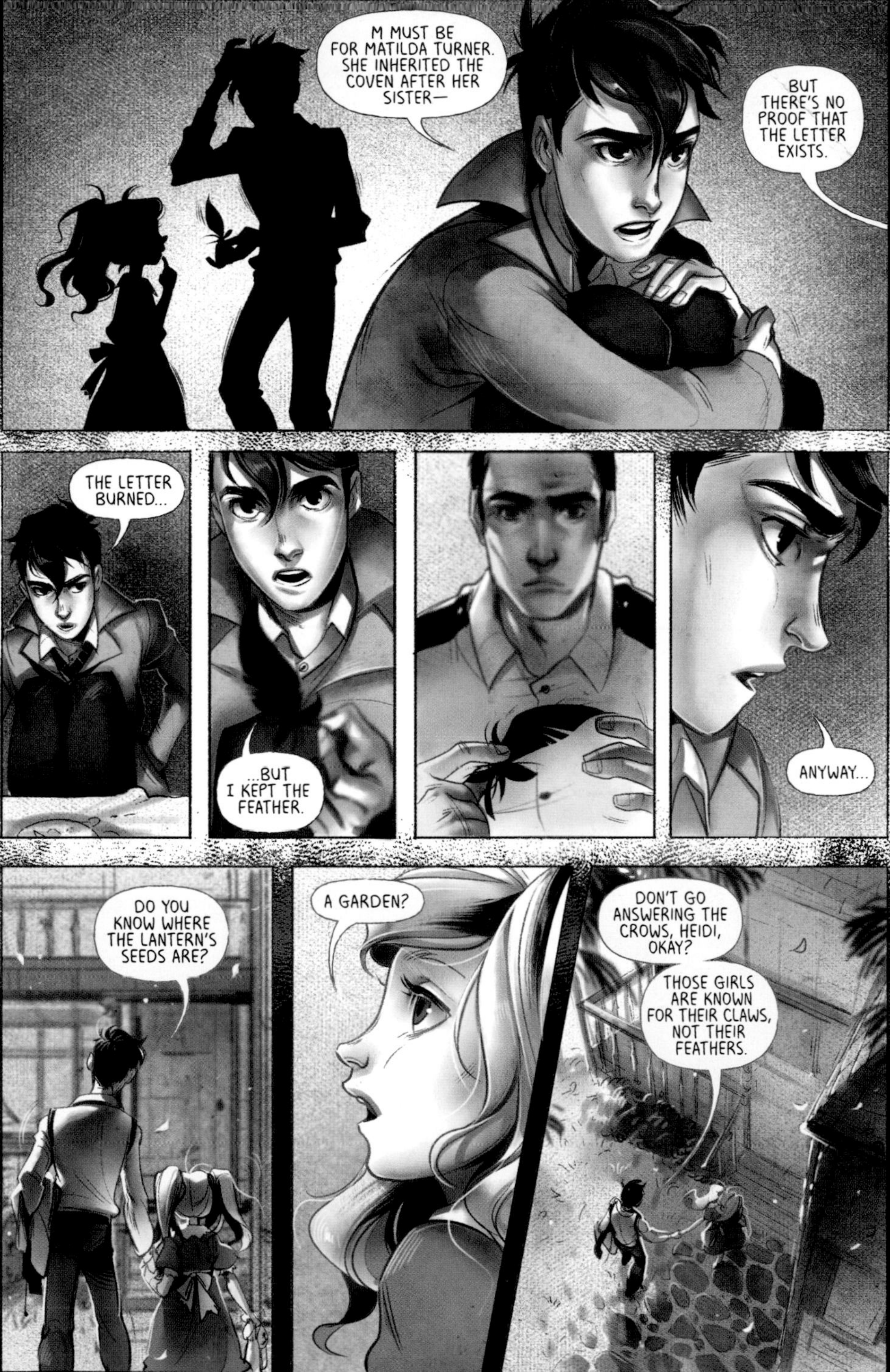
M MUST BE FOR MATILDA TURNER. SHE INHERITED THE COVEN AFTER HER SISTER—
BUT THERE'S NO PROOF THAT THE LETTER EXISTS.
THE LETTER BURNED...
...BUT I KEPT THE FEATHER.
ANYWAY...
DO YOU KNOW WHERE THE LANTERN'S SEEDS ARE?
A GARDEN?
DON'T GO ANSWERING THE CROWS, HEIDI, OKAY?
THOSE GIRLS ARE KNOWN FOR THEIR CLAWS, NOT THEIR FEATHERS.

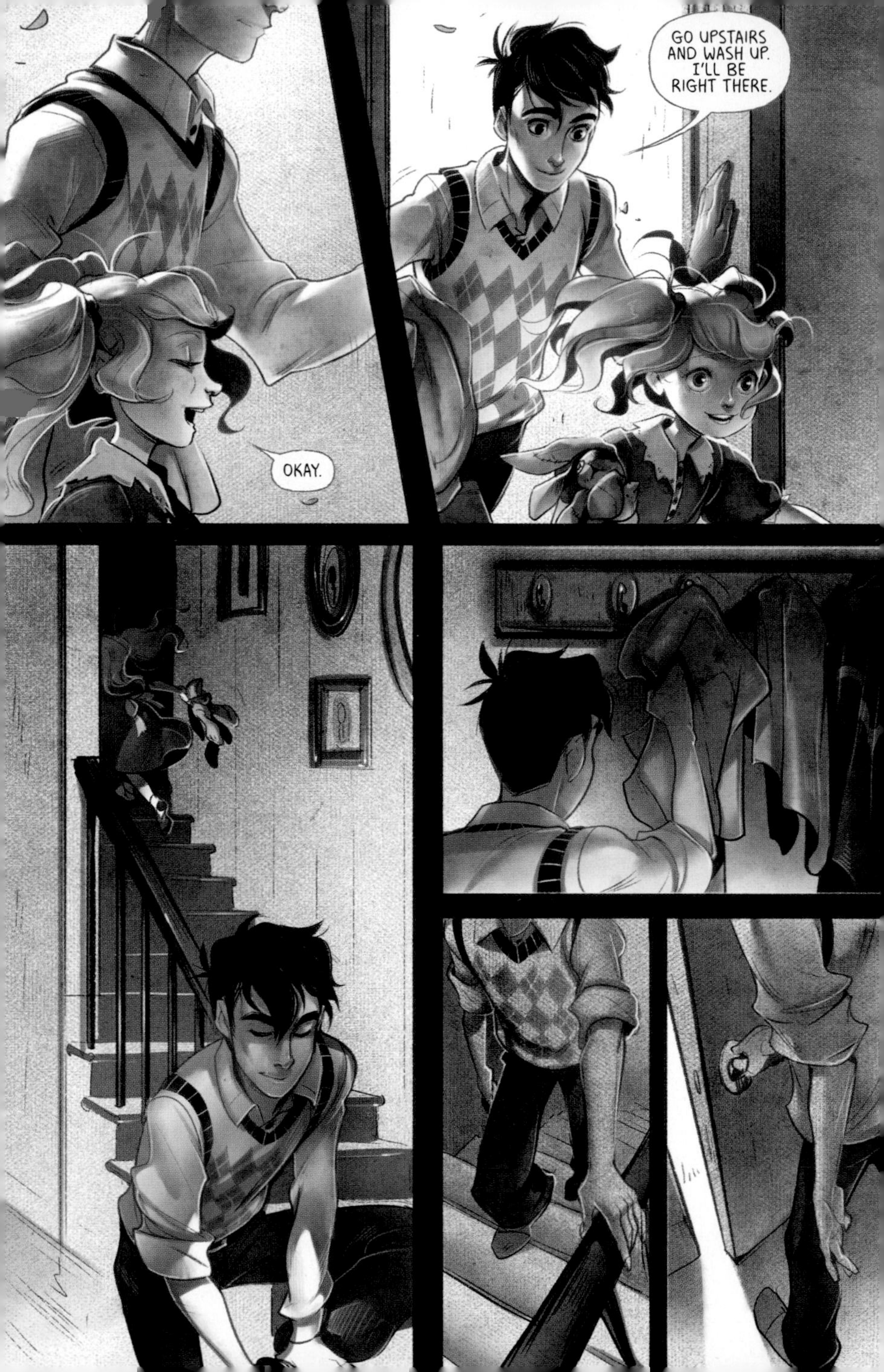
OKAY.
GO UPSTAIRS AND WASH UP. I'LL BE RIGHT THERE.

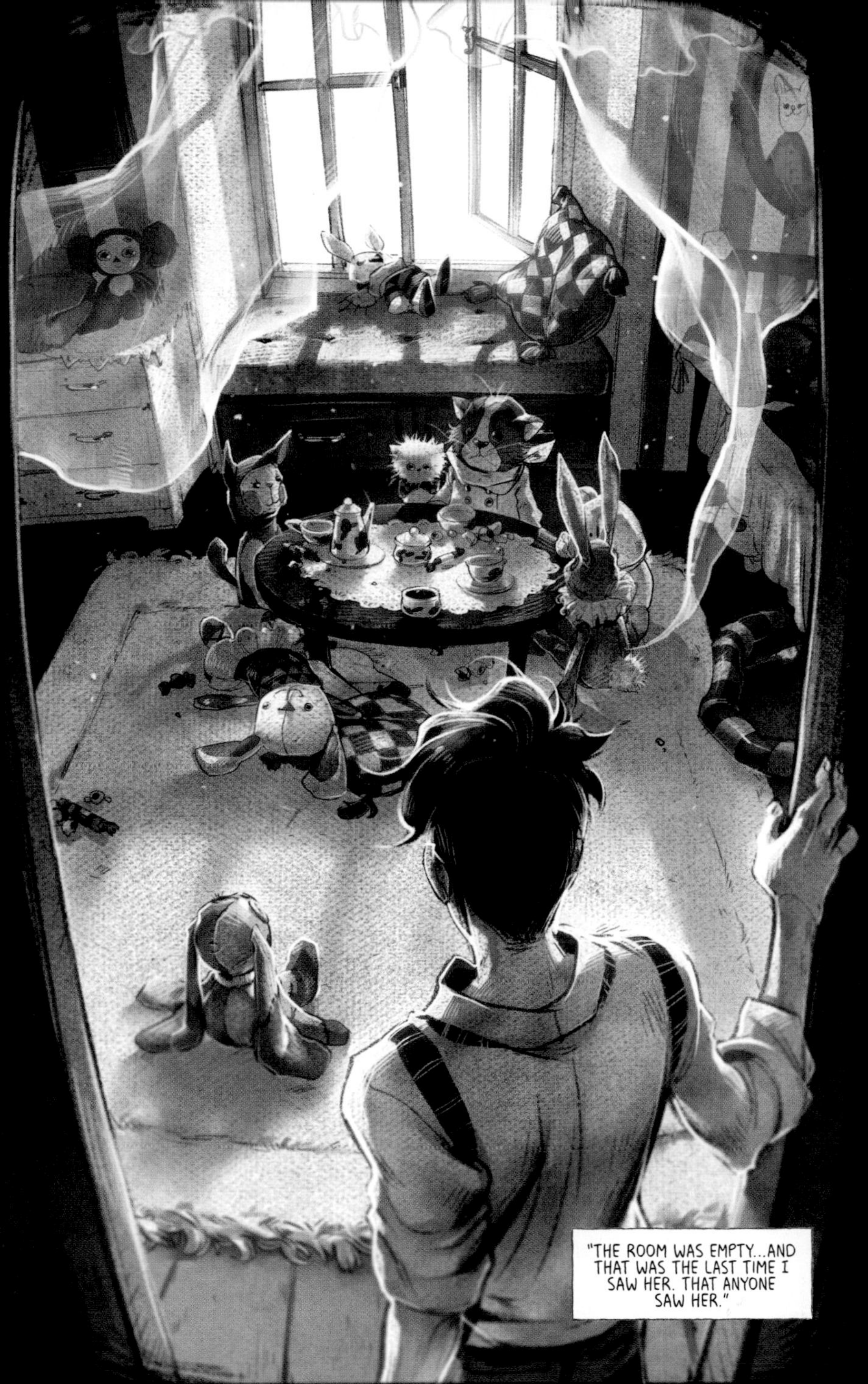
"THE ROOM WAS EMPTY...AND THAT WAS THE LAST TIME I SAW HER. THAT ANYONE SAW HER."

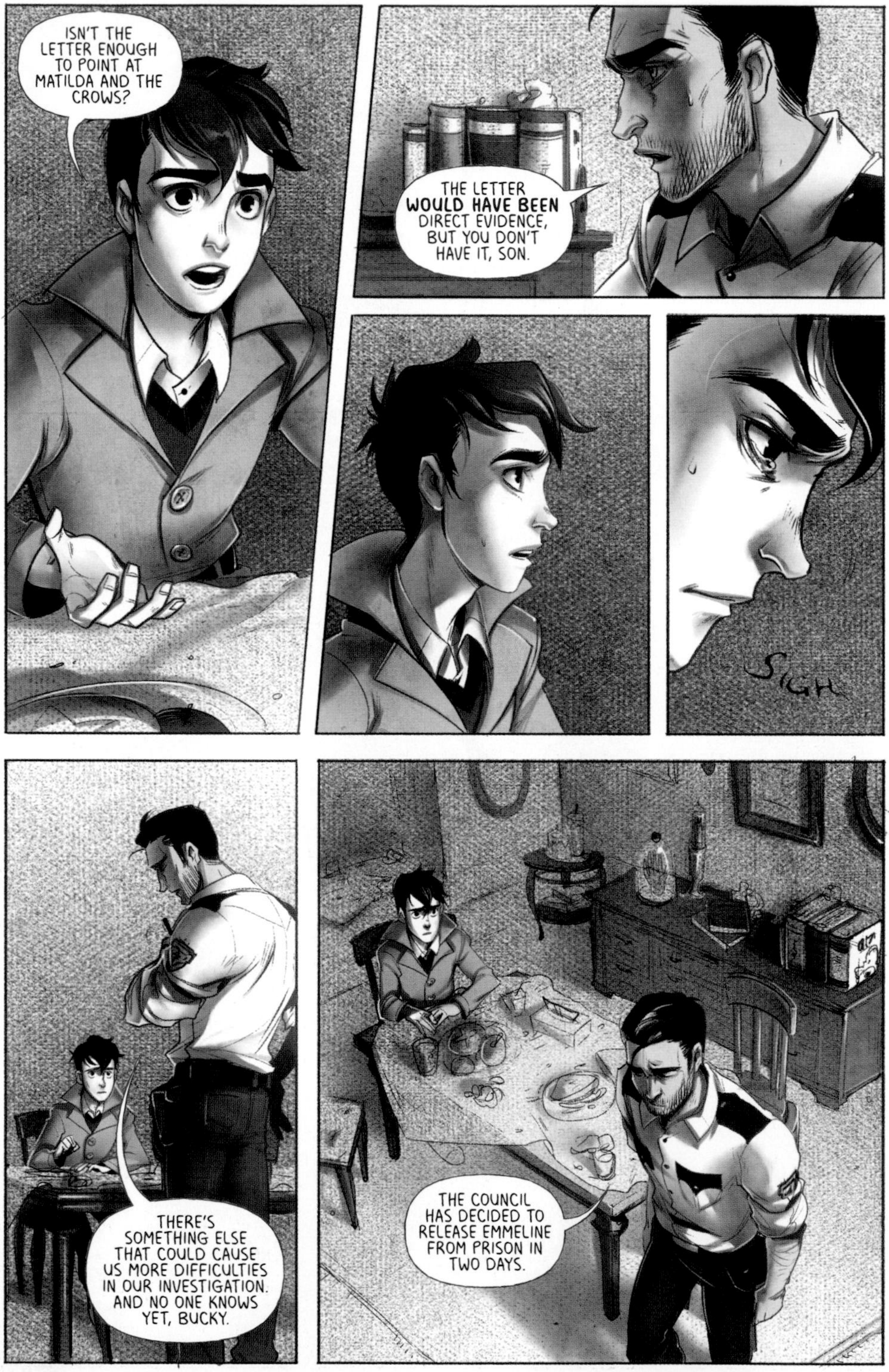
ISN'T THE LETTER ENOUGH TO POINT AT MATILDA AND THE CROWS?
THE LETTER **WOULD HAVE BEEN** DIRECT EVIDENCE, BUT YOU DON'T HAVE IT, SON.
SIGH
THERE'S SOMETHING ELSE THAT COULD CAUSE US MORE DIFFICULTIES IN OUR INVESTIGATION. AND NO ONE KNOWS YET, BUCKY.
THE COUNCIL HAS DECIDED TO RELEASE EMMELINE FROM PRISON IN TWO DAYS.

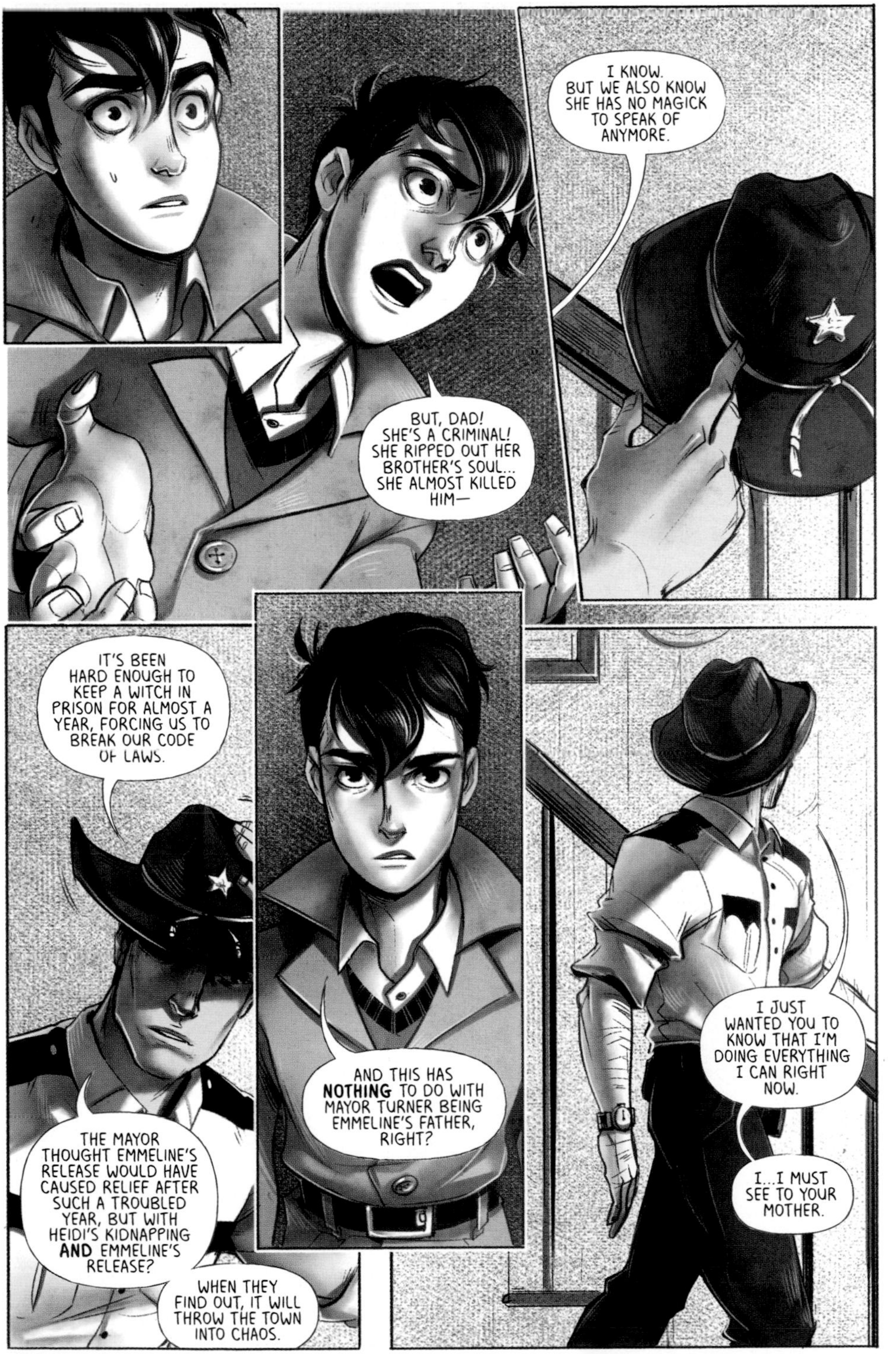
I KNOW. BUT WE ALSO KNOW SHE HAS NO MAGICK TO SPEAK OF ANYMORE.
BUT, DAD! SHE'S A CRIMINAL! SHE RIPPED OUT HER BROTHER'S SOUL... SHE ALMOST KILLED HIM—
IT'S BEEN HARD ENOUGH TO KEEP A WITCH IN PRISON FOR ALMOST A YEAR, FORCING US TO BREAK OUR CODE OF LAWS.
THE MAYOR THOUGHT EMMELINE'S RELEASE WOULD HAVE CAUSED RELIEF AFTER SUCH A TROUBLED YEAR, BUT WITH HEIDI'S KIDNAPPING **AND** EMMELINE'S RELEASE?
WHEN THEY FIND OUT, IT WILL THROW THE TOWN INTO CHAOS.
AND THIS HAS **NOTHING** TO DO WITH MAYOR TURNER BEING EMMELINE'S FATHER, RIGHT?
I JUST WANTED YOU TO KNOW THAT I'M DOING EVERYTHING I CAN RIGHT NOW.
I...I MUST SEE TO YOUR MOTHER.

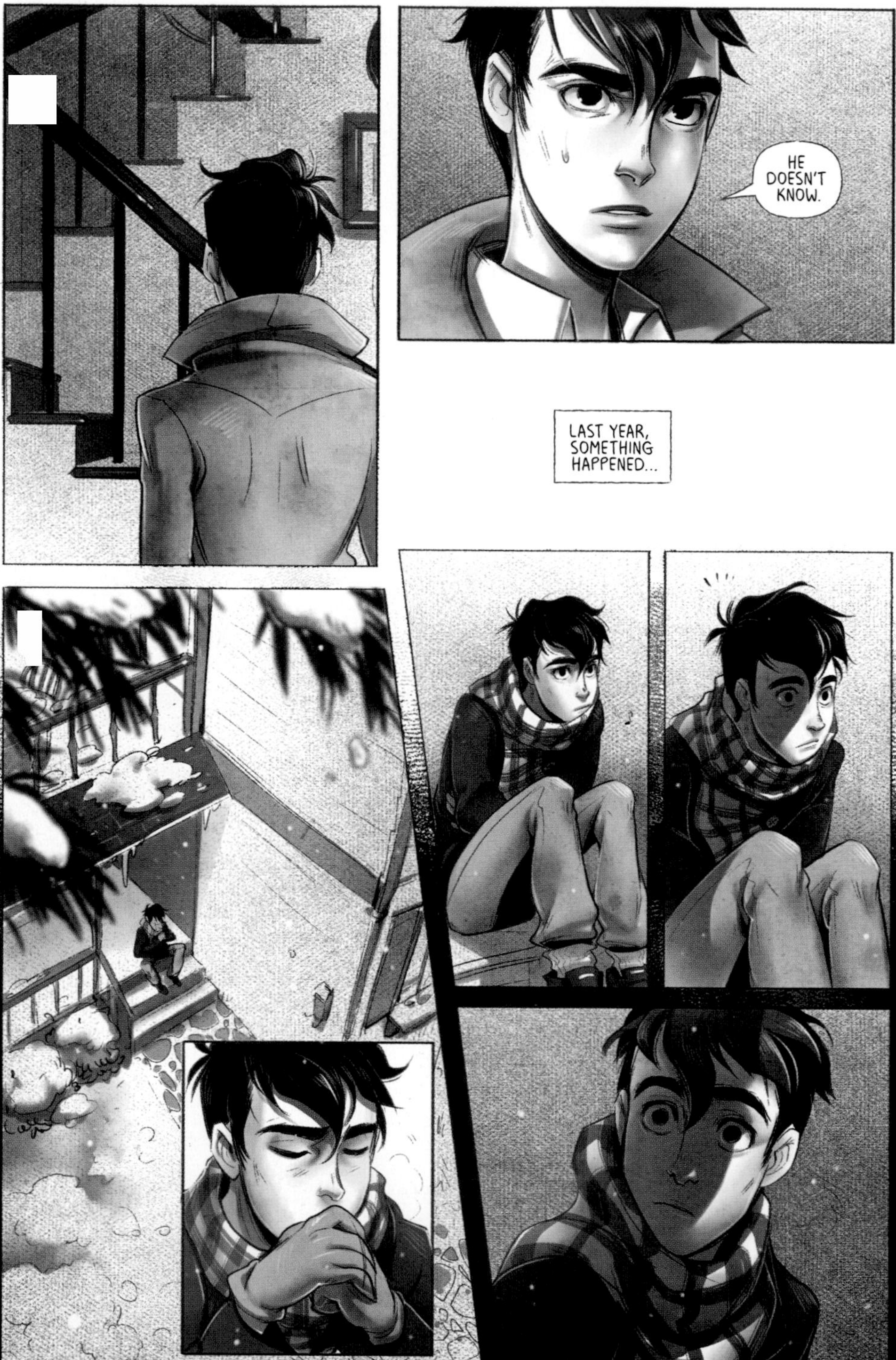
HE DOESN'T KNOW.
LAST YEAR, SOMETHING HAPPENED...

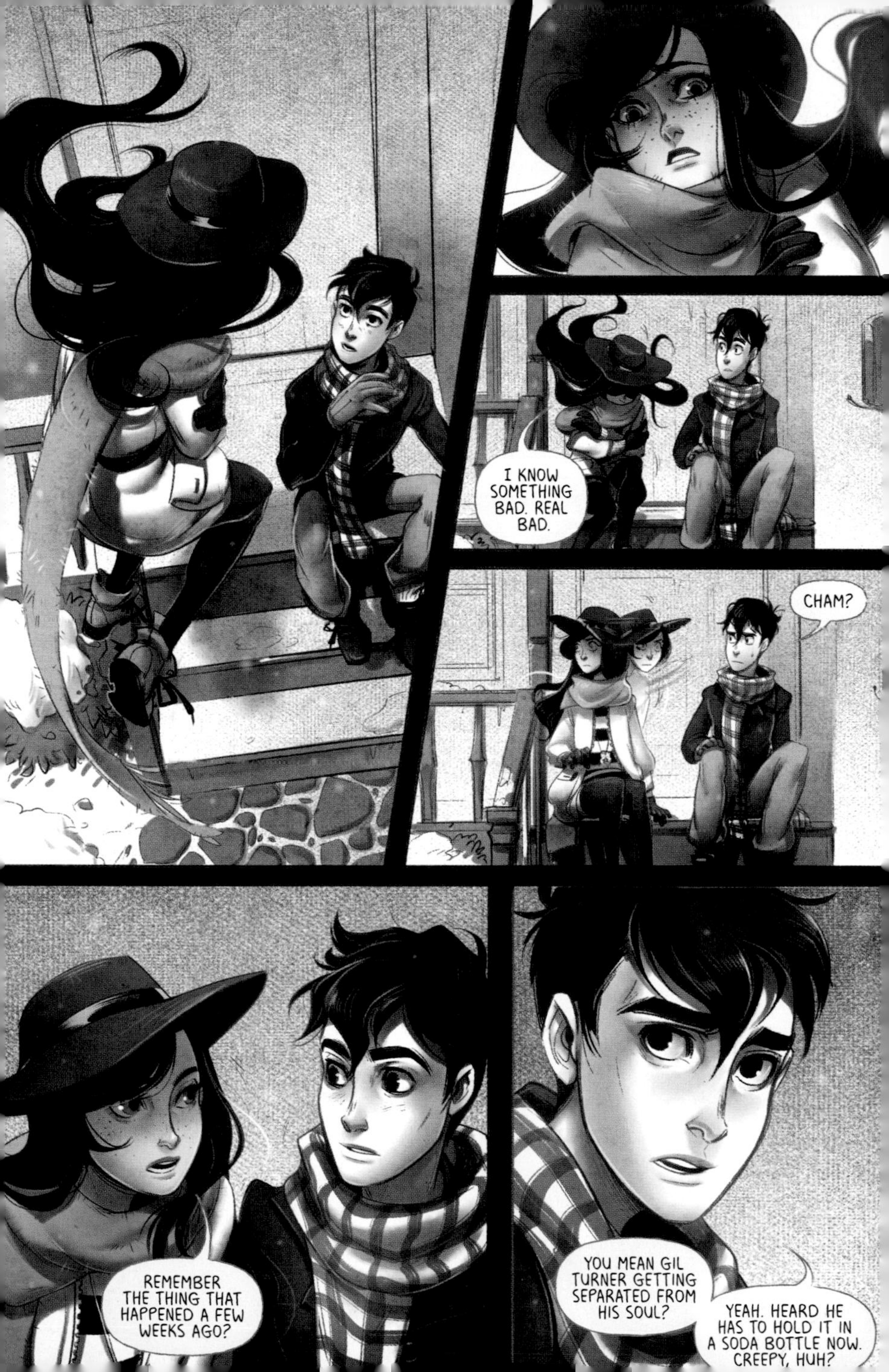
I KNOW SOMETHING BAD. REAL BAD.
CHAM?
REMEMBER THE THING THAT HAPPENED A FEW WEEKS AGO?
YOU MEAN GIL TURNER GETTING SEPARATED FROM HIS SOUL?
YEAH. HEARD HE HAS TO HOLD IT IN A SODA BOTTLE NOW. CREEPY, HUH?

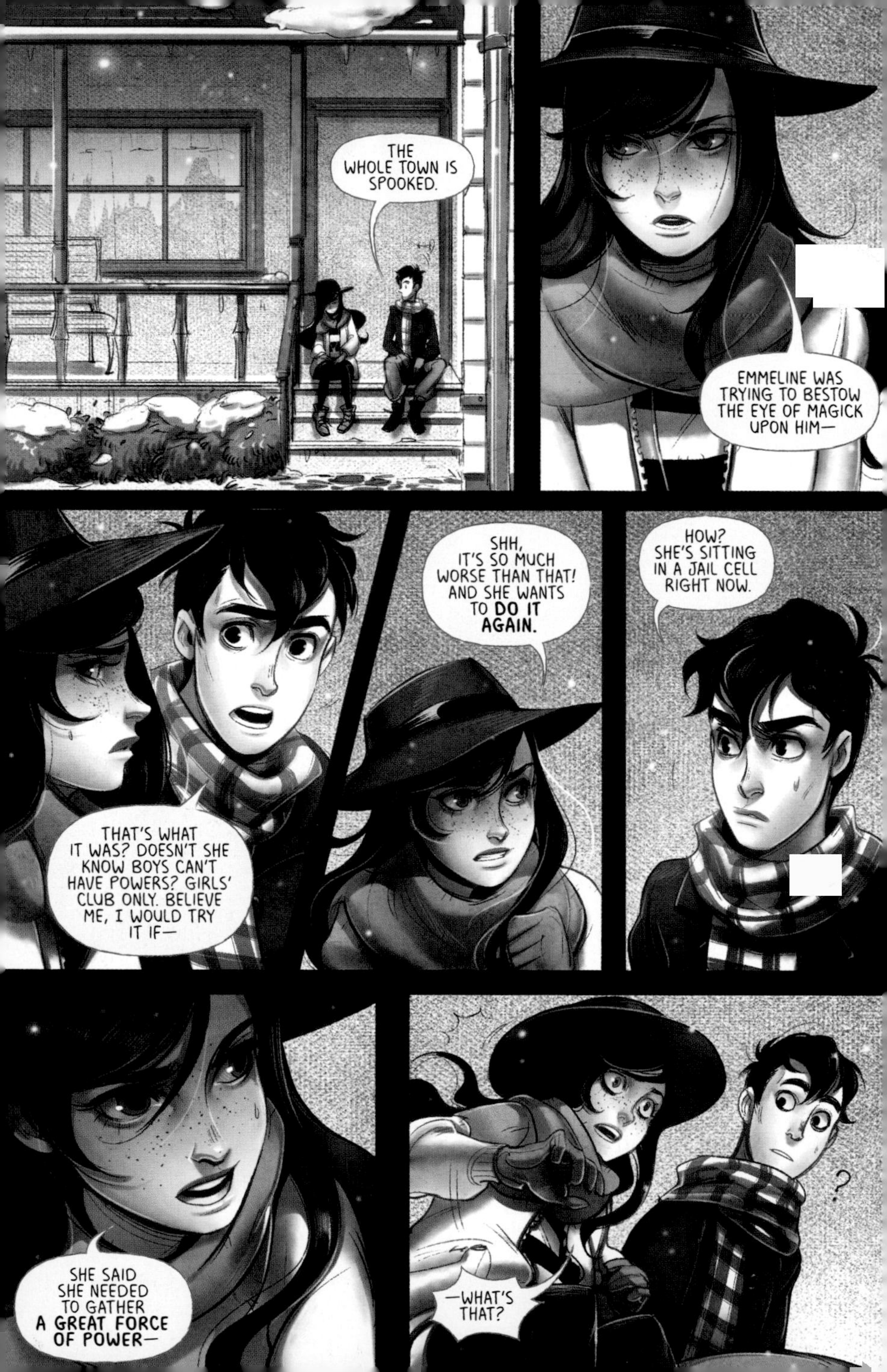
THE WHOLE TOWN IS SPOOKED.
EMMELINE WAS TRYING TO BESTOW THE EYE OF MAGICK UPON HIM—
THAT'S WHAT IT WAS? DOESN'T SHE KNOW BOYS CAN'T HAVE POWERS? GIRLS' CLUB ONLY. BELIEVE ME, I WOULD TRY IT IF—
SHH, IT'S SO MUCH WORSE THAN THAT! AND SHE WANTS TO **DO IT AGAIN.**
HOW? SHE'S SITTING IN A JAIL CELL RIGHT NOW.
SHE SAID SHE NEEDED TO GATHER **A GREAT FORCE OF POWER**—
—WHAT'S THAT?
?

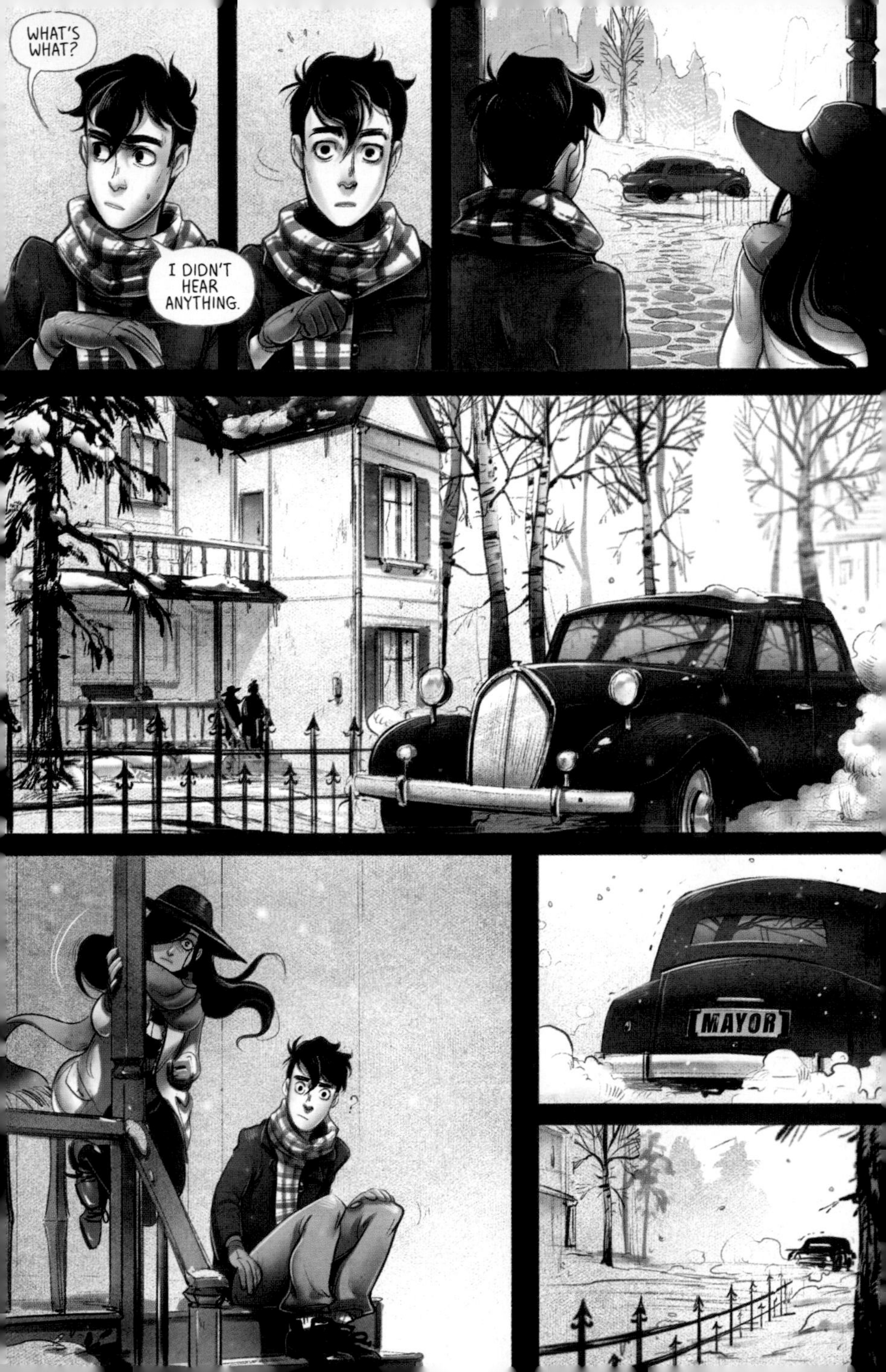
WHAT'S WHAT?
I DIDN'T HEAR ANYTHING.
MAYOR

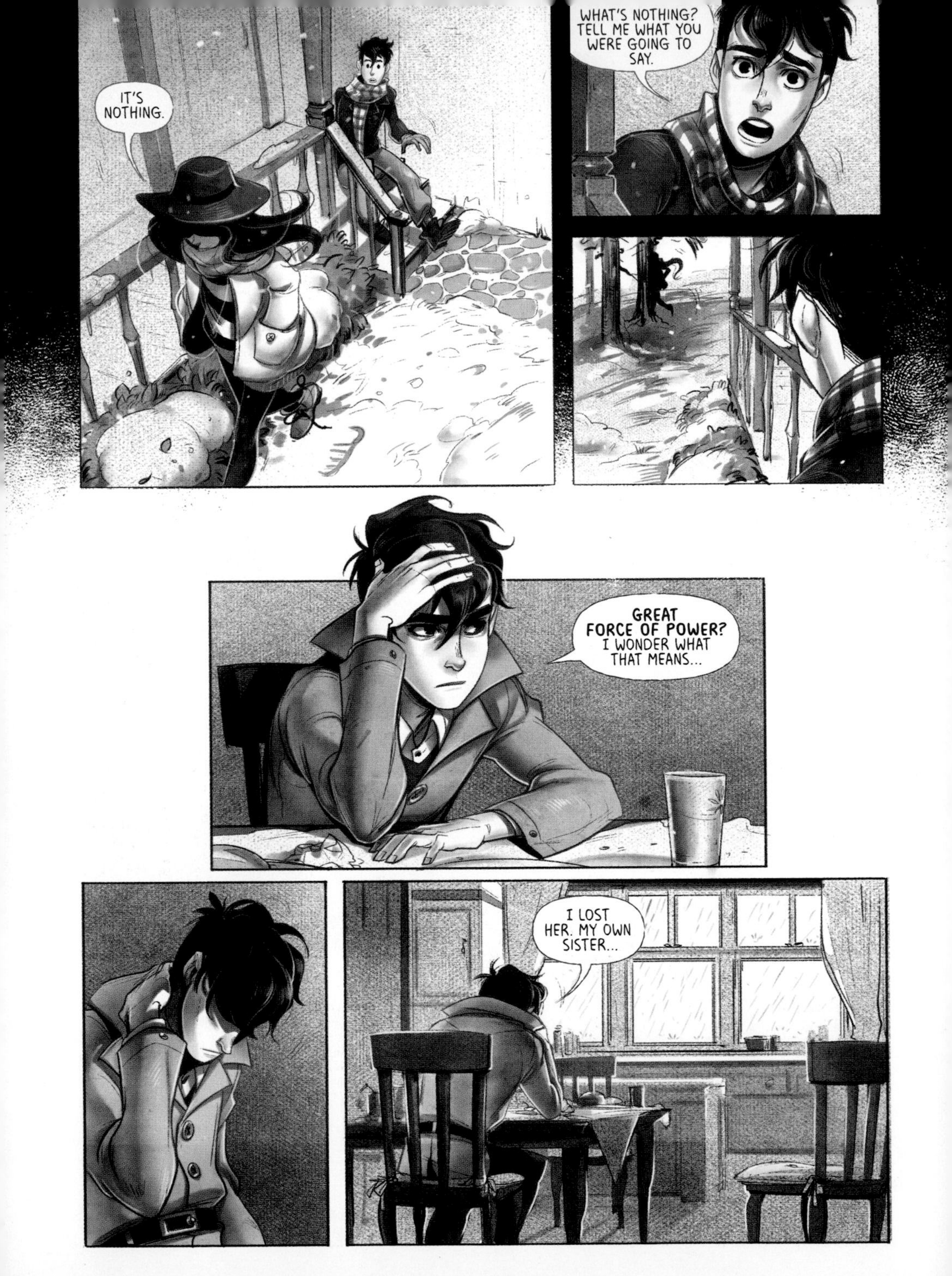
IT'S NOTHING.
WHAT'S NOTHING? TELL ME WHAT YOU WERE GOING TO SAY.
GREAT FORCE OF POWER? I WONDER WHAT THAT MEANS...
I LOST HER. MY OWN SISTER...

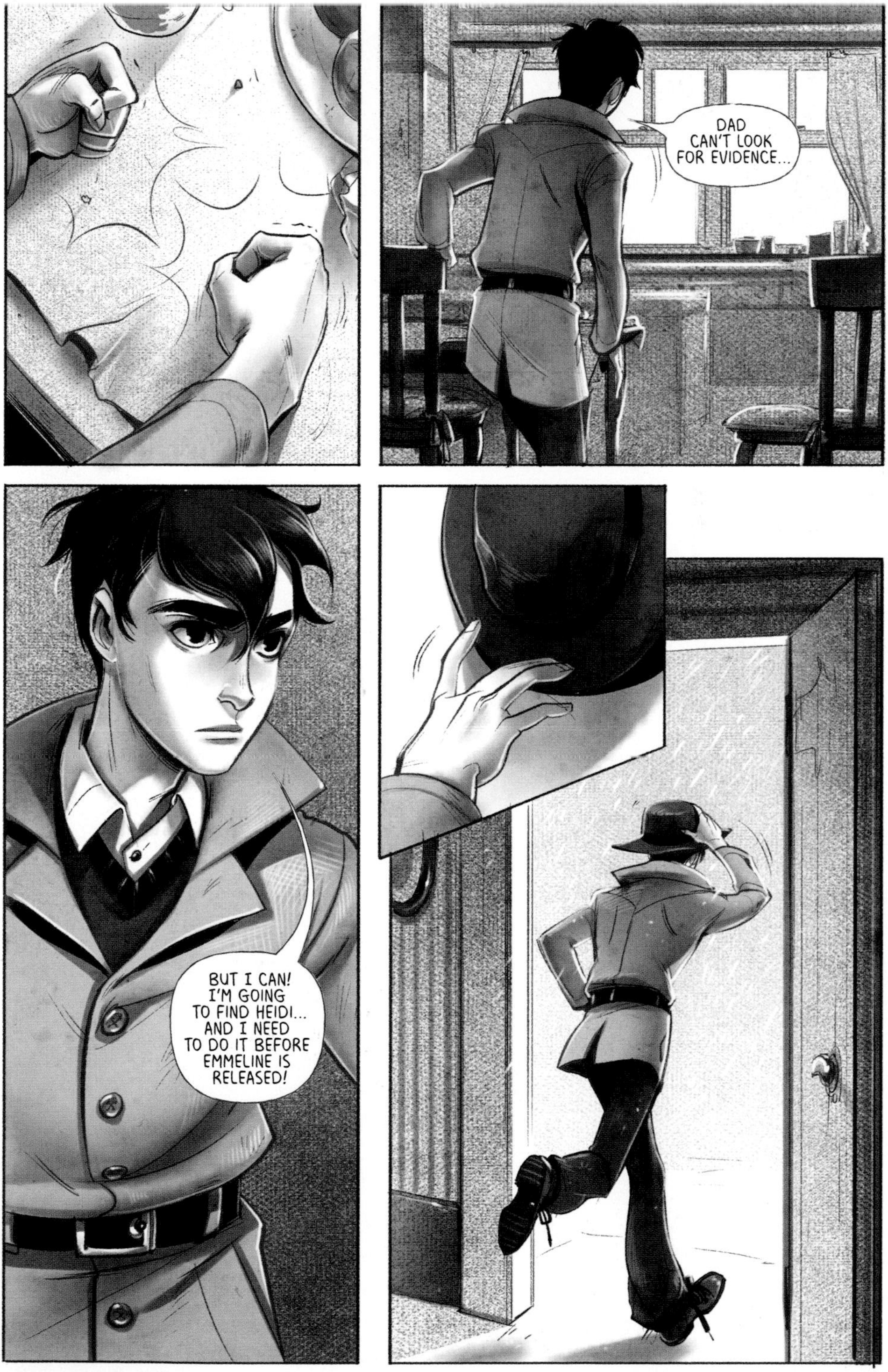
DAD CAN'T LOOK FOR EVIDENCE...
BUT I CAN! I'M GOING TO FIND HEIDI... AND I NEED TO DO IT BEFORE EMMELINE IS RELEASED!

CHAPTER 2

THIS TOWN
IS FULL OF
CROWS

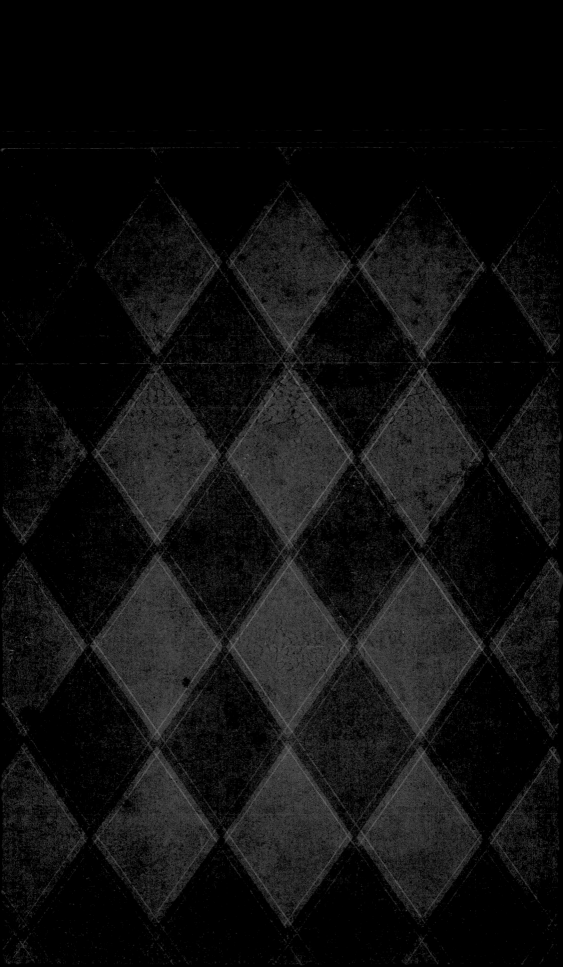

MAYBE CHAM WILL TALK THIS TIME—SHE **DID** OFFER TO HELP.

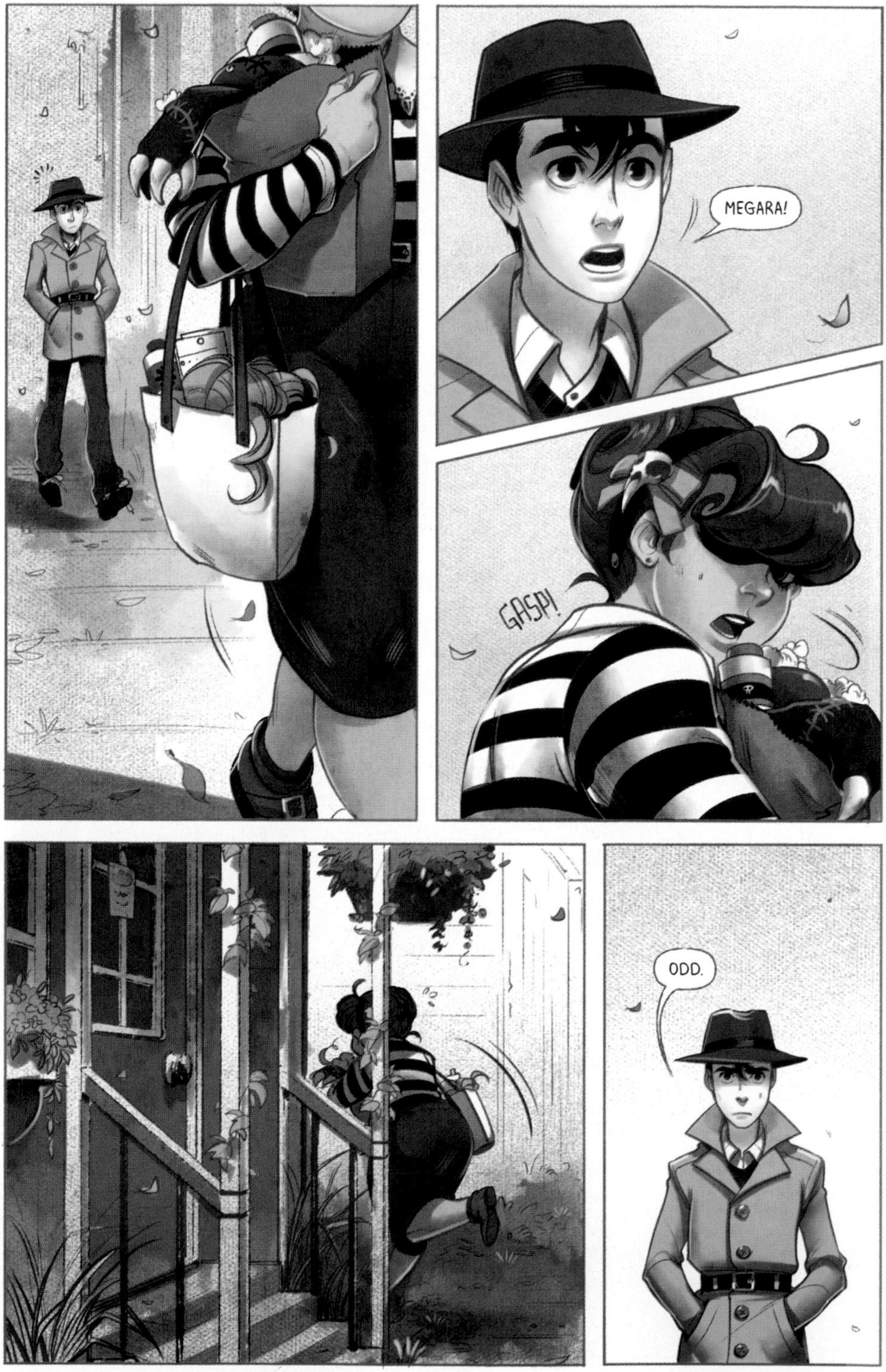
MEGARA!
GASP!
ODD.

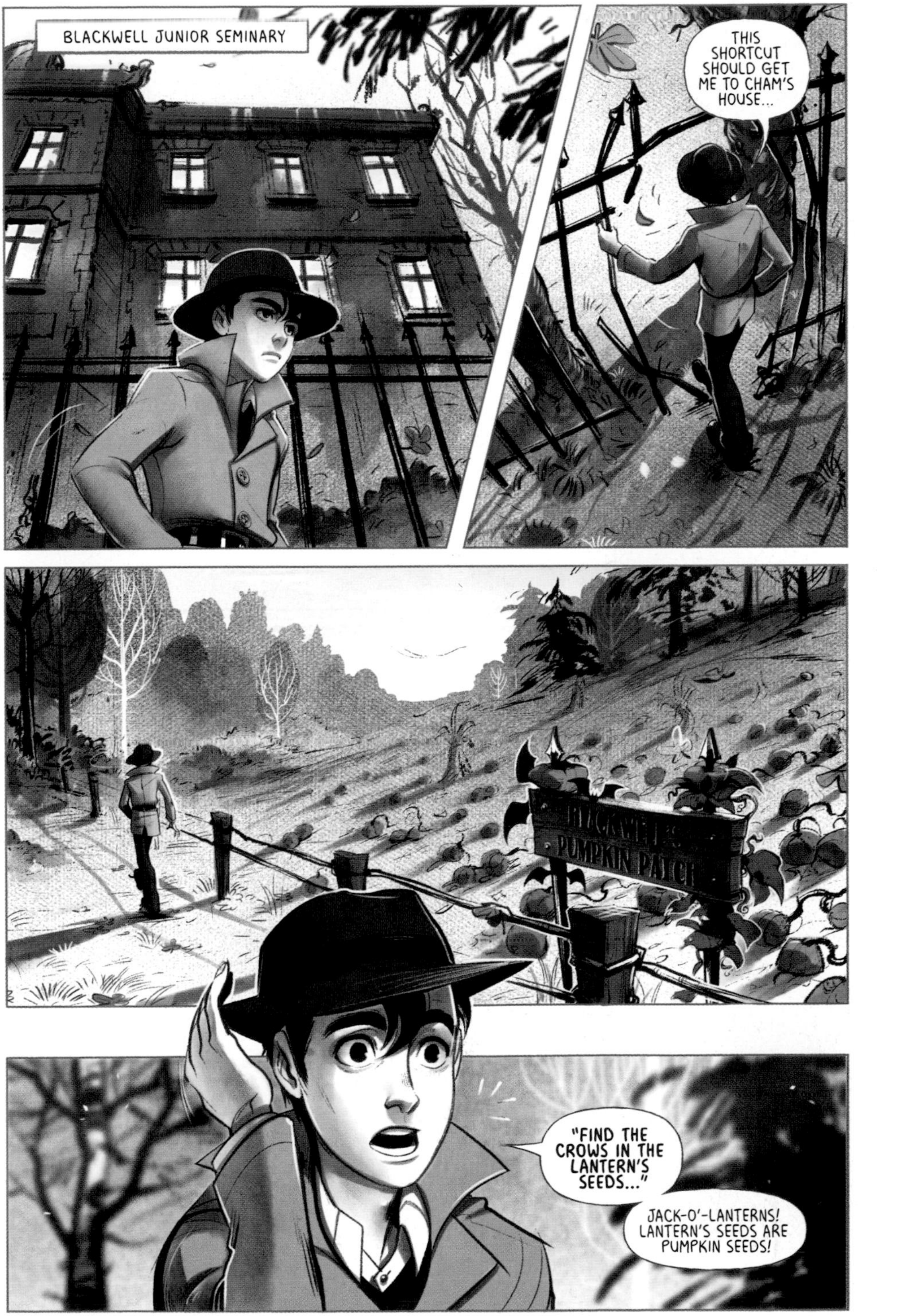
BLACKWELL JUNIOR SEMINARY
THIS SHORTCUT SHOULD GET ME TO CHAM'S HOUSE...
PUMPKIN PATCH
"FIND THE CROWS IN THE LANTERN'S SEEDS..."
JACK-O'-LANTERNS! LANTERN'S SEEDS ARE PUMPKIN SEEDS!

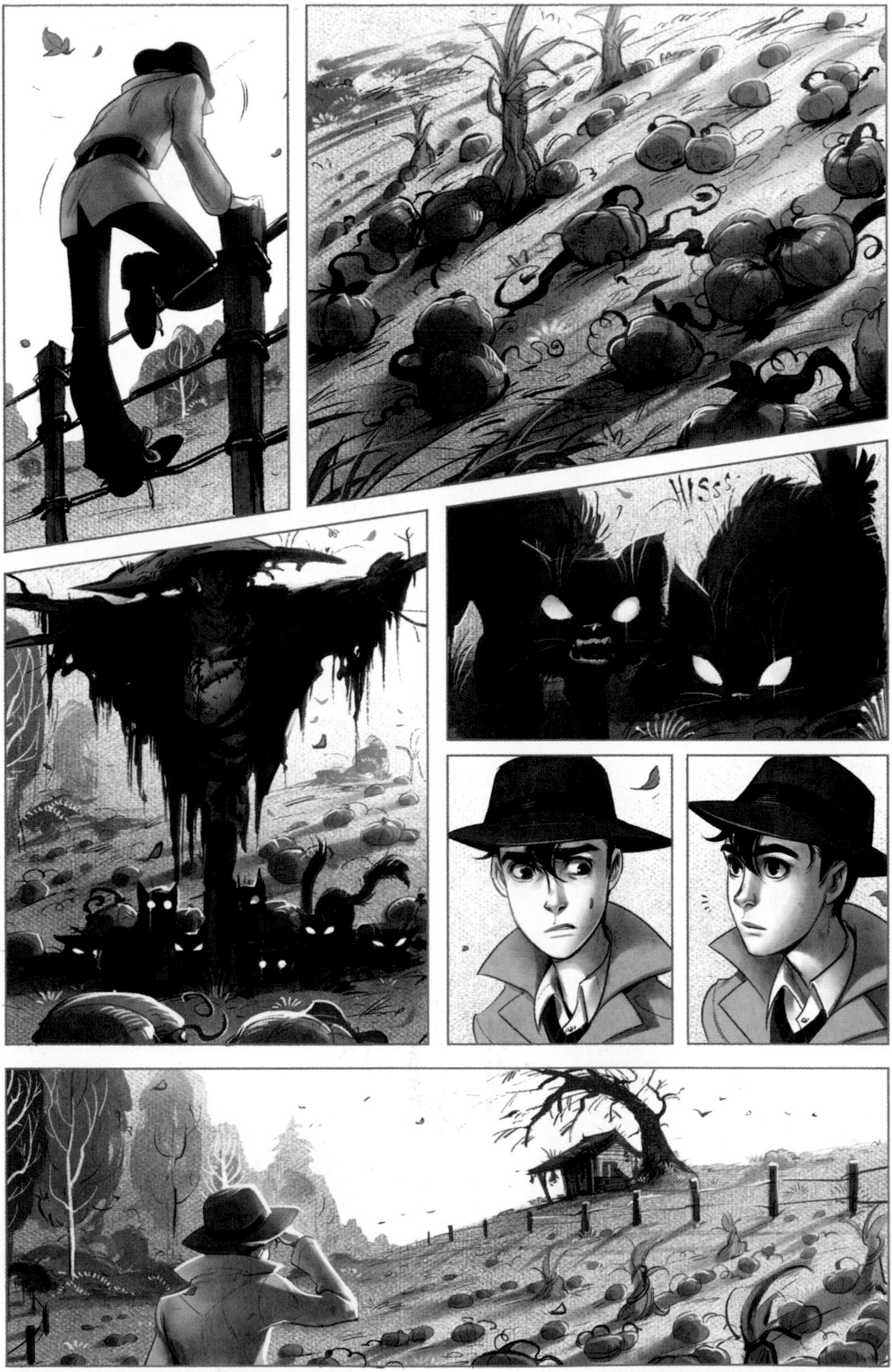
HISSS

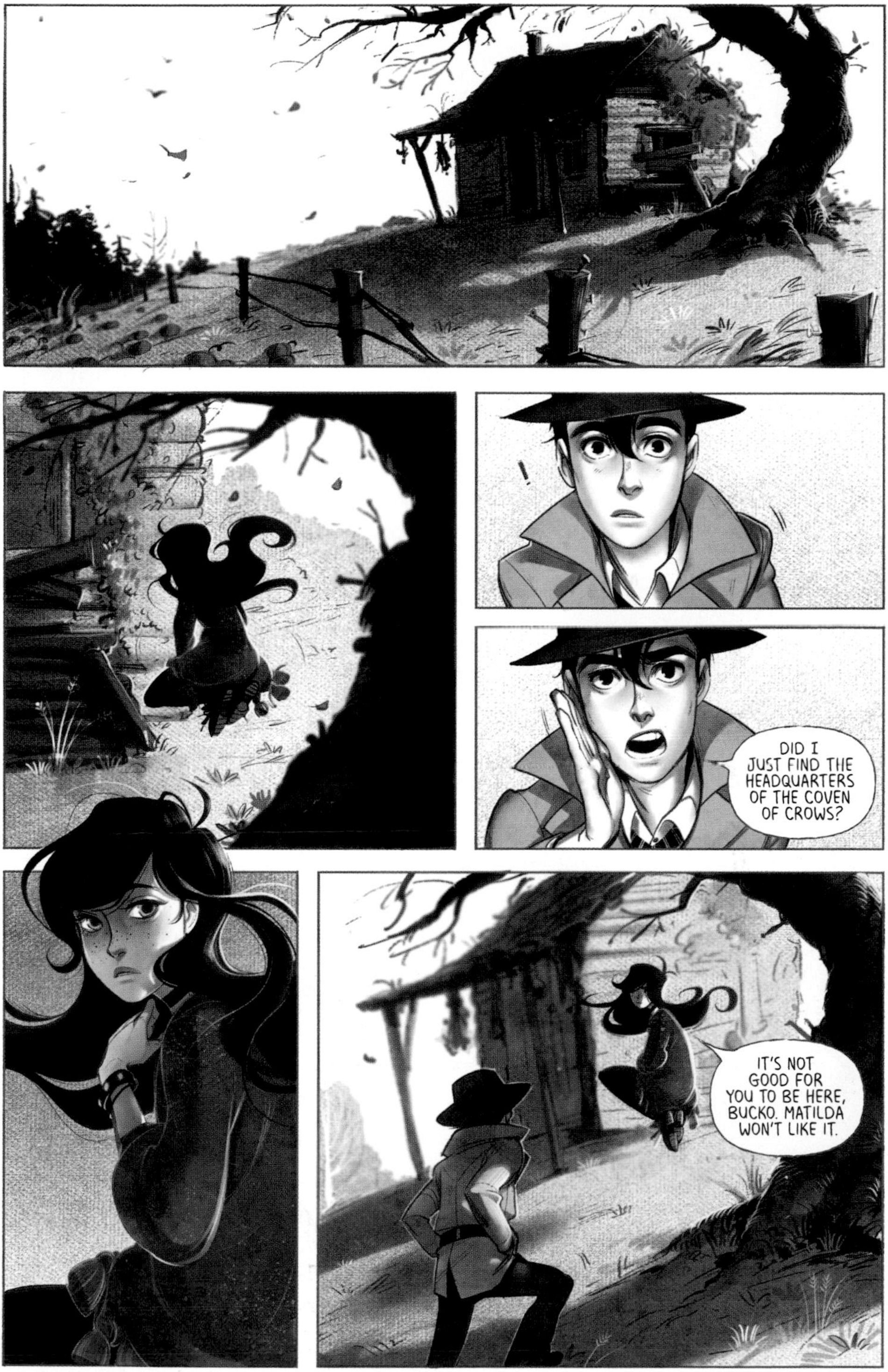
!
DID I JUST FIND THE HEADQUARTERS OF THE COVEN OF CROWS?
IT'S NOT GOOD FOR YOU TO BE HERE, BUCKO. MATILDA WON'T LIKE IT.

SO MATILDA TURNER REALLY IS THE NEW COVEN PRIESTESS?

I HAVE TO GO IN—

CHAM, WAIT! I NEED TO ASK YOU ABOUT SOMETHING YOU SAID BEFORE!

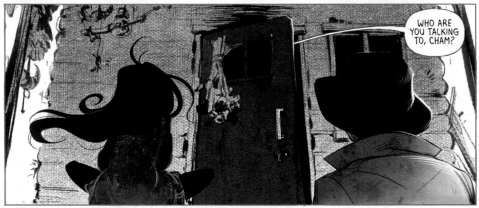

WHO ARE YOU TALKING TO, CHAM?

BRING 'EM IN.

SURE THING.

32

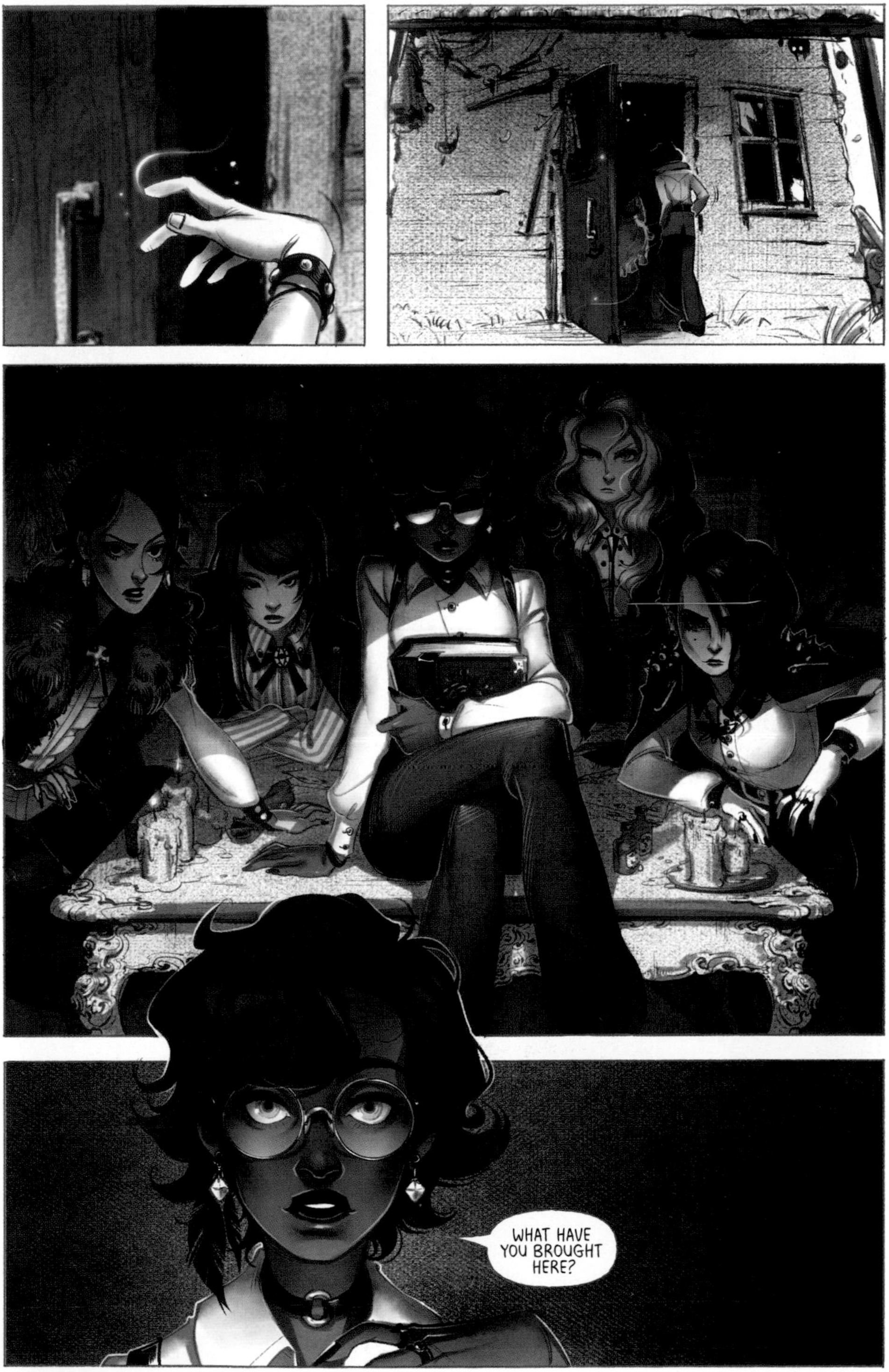
WHAT HAVE YOU BROUGHT HERE?

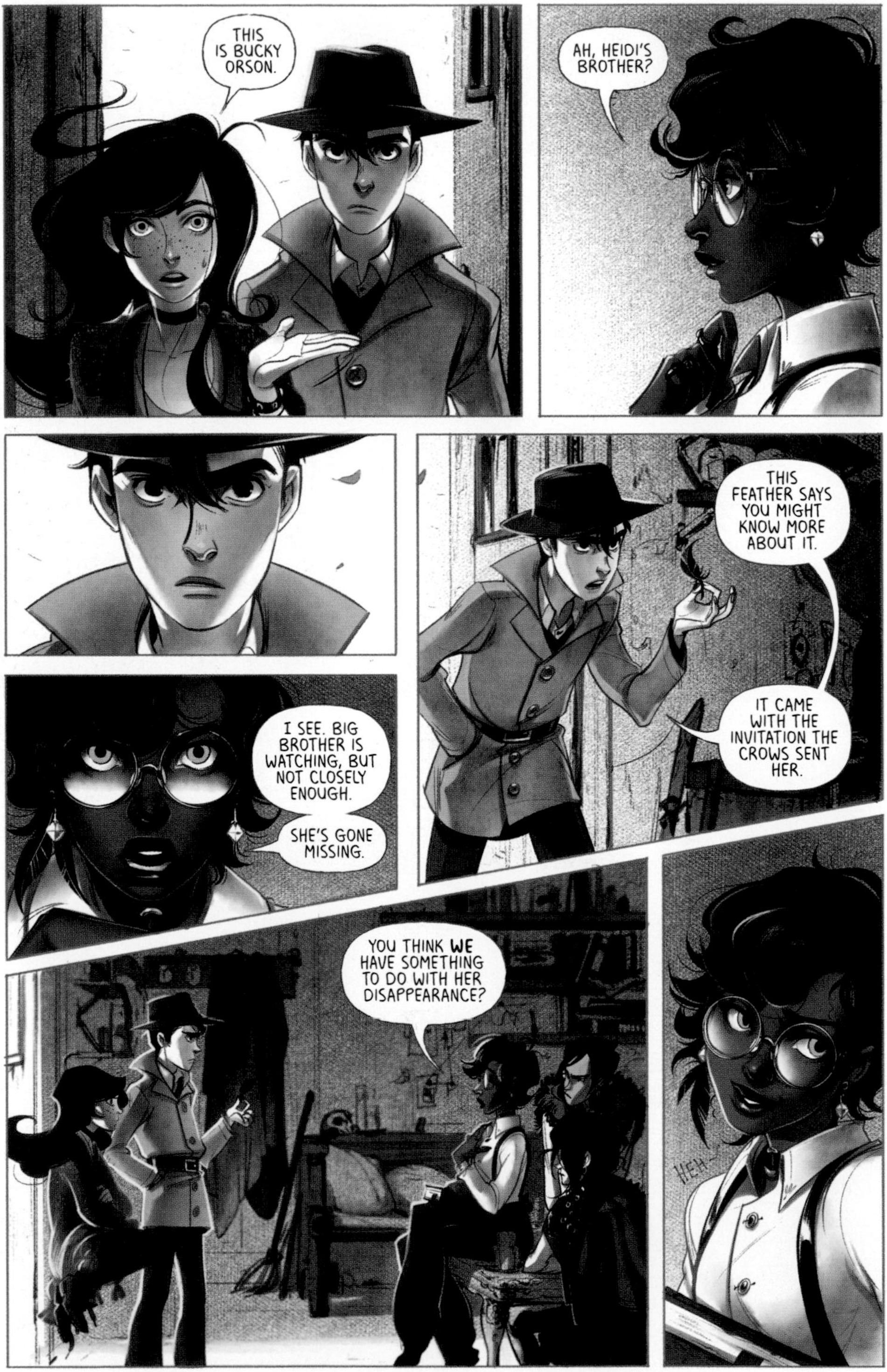
THIS IS BUCKY ORSON.
AH, HEIDI'S BROTHER?
THIS FEATHER SAYS YOU MIGHT KNOW MORE ABOUT IT.
IT CAME WITH THE INVITATION THE CROWS SENT HER.
I SEE. BIG BROTHER IS WATCHING, BUT NOT CLOSELY ENOUGH.
SHE'S GONE MISSING.
YOU THINK **WE** HAVE SOMETHING TO DO WITH HER DISAPPEARANCE?
HEH-

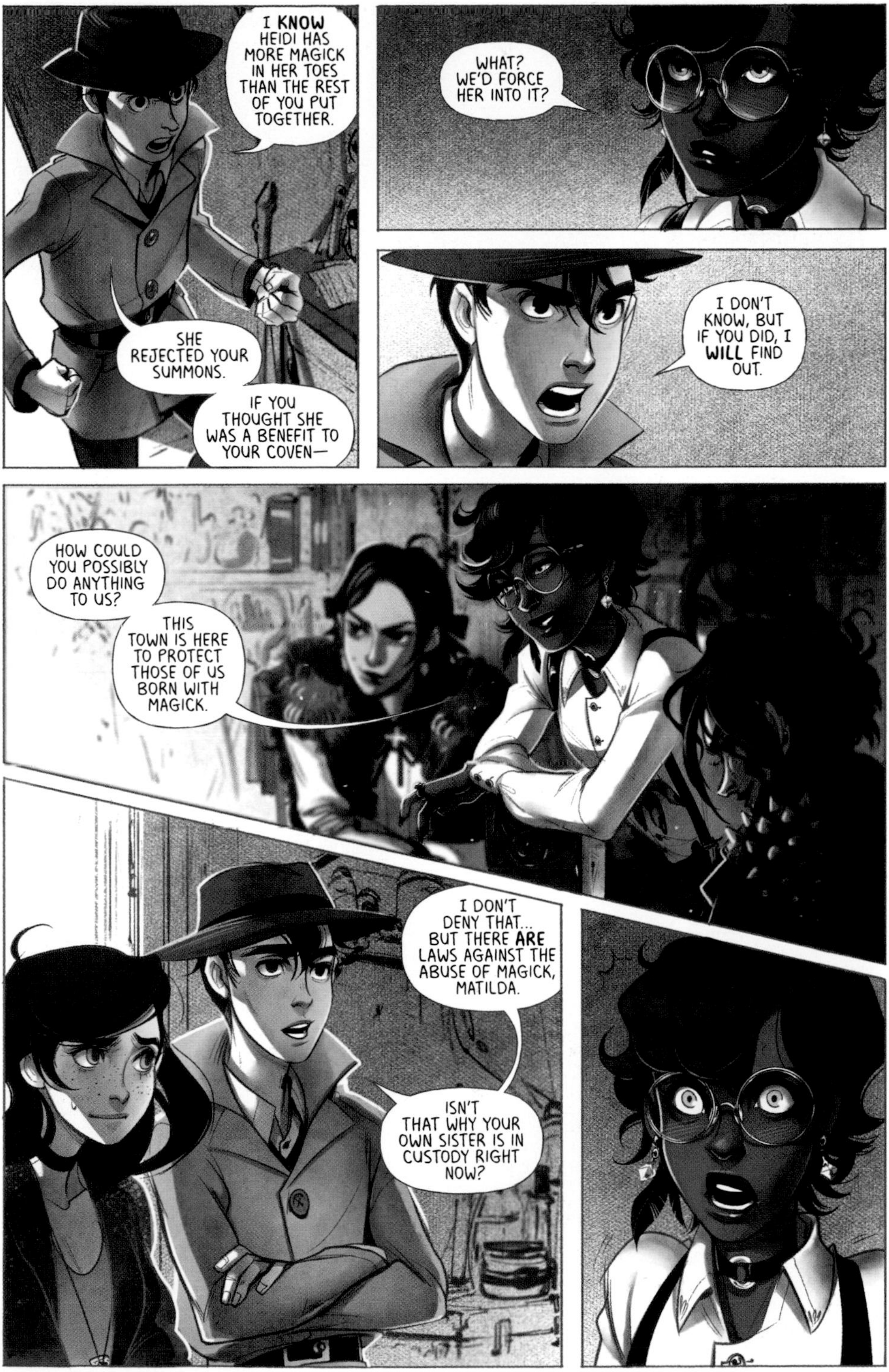
I KNOW HEIDI HAS MORE MAGICK IN HER TOES THAN THE REST OF YOU PUT TOGETHER.
WHAT? WE'D FORCE HER INTO IT?
SHE REJECTED YOUR SUMMONS.
IF YOU THOUGHT SHE WAS A BENEFIT TO YOUR COVEN—
I DON'T KNOW, BUT IF YOU DID, I WILL FIND OUT.
HOW COULD YOU POSSIBLY DO ANYTHING TO US?
THIS TOWN IS HERE TO PROTECT THOSE OF US BORN WITH MAGICK.
I DON'T DENY THAT... BUT THERE ARE LAWS AGAINST THE ABUSE OF MAGICK, MATILDA.
ISN'T THAT WHY YOUR OWN SISTER IS IN CUSTODY RIGHT NOW?

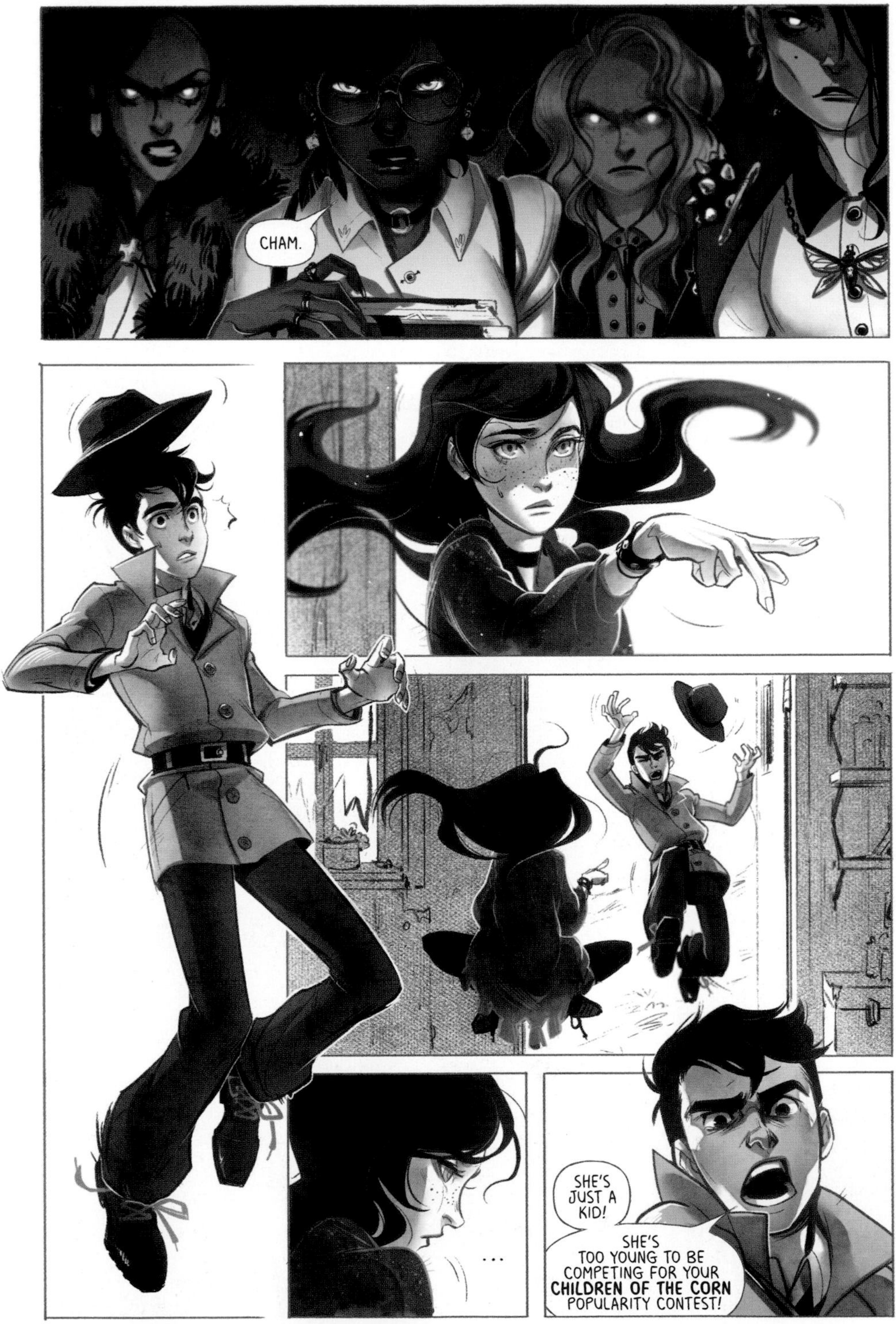

CHAM.
...
SHE'S JUST A KID!
SHE'S TOO YOUNG TO BE COMPETING FOR YOUR CHILDREN OF THE CORN POPULARITY CONTEST!

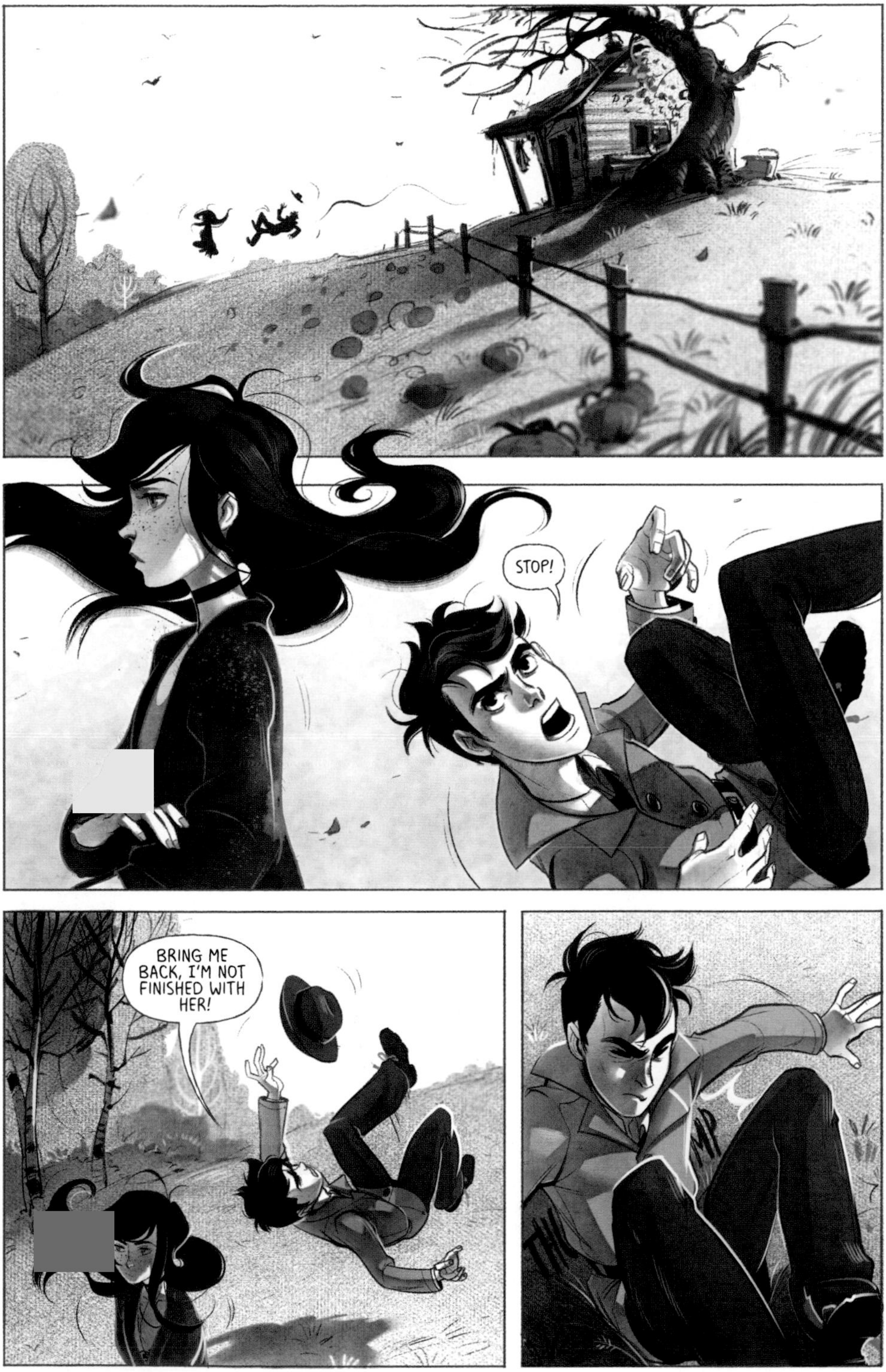
STOP!
BRING ME BACK, I'M NOT FINISHED WITH HER!

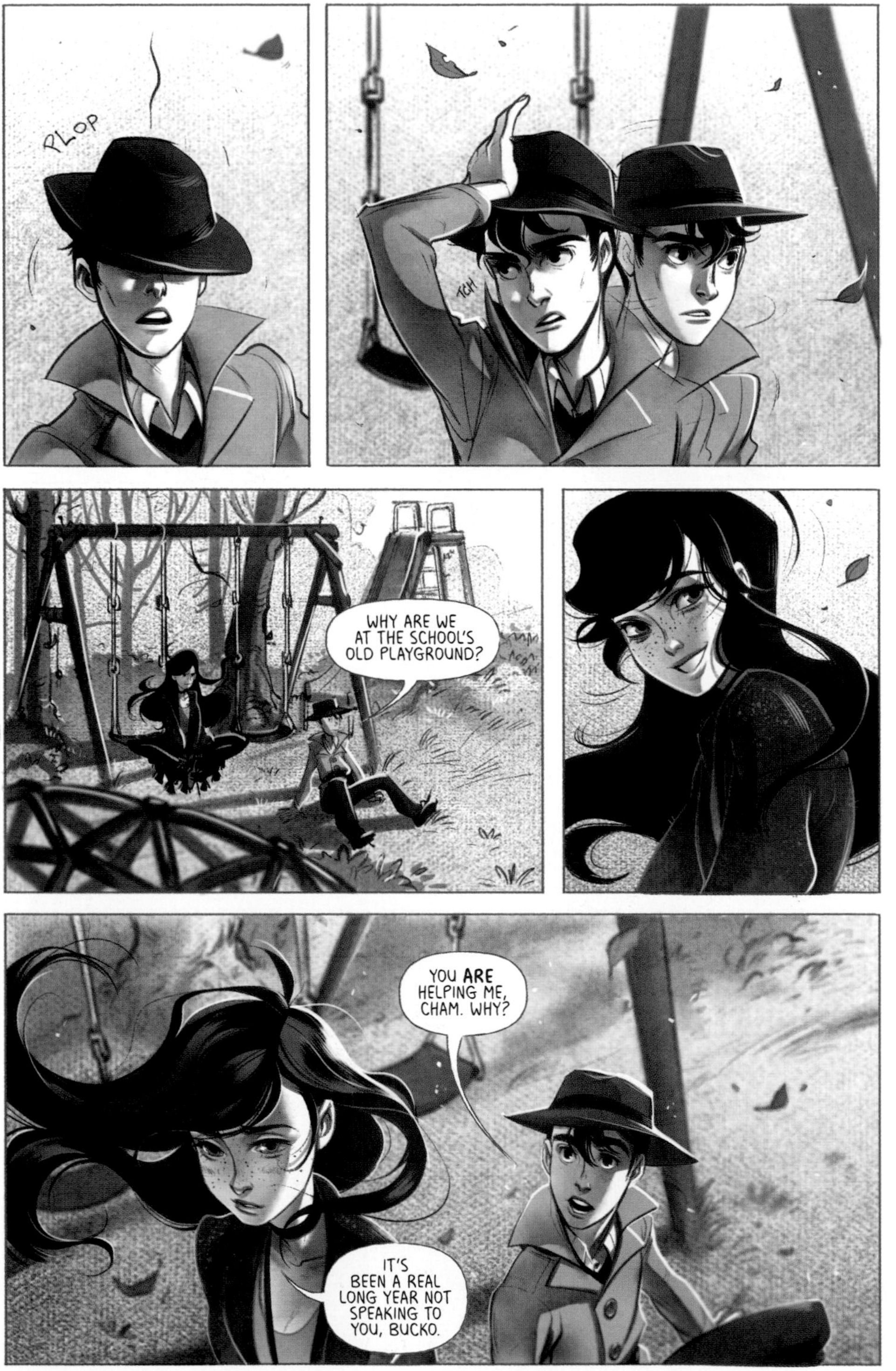
PLOP
TCH
WHY ARE WE AT THE SCHOOL'S OLD PLAYGROUND?
YOU **ARE** HELPING ME, CHAM. WHY?
IT'S BEEN A REAL LONG YEAR NOT SPEAKING TO YOU, BUCKO.

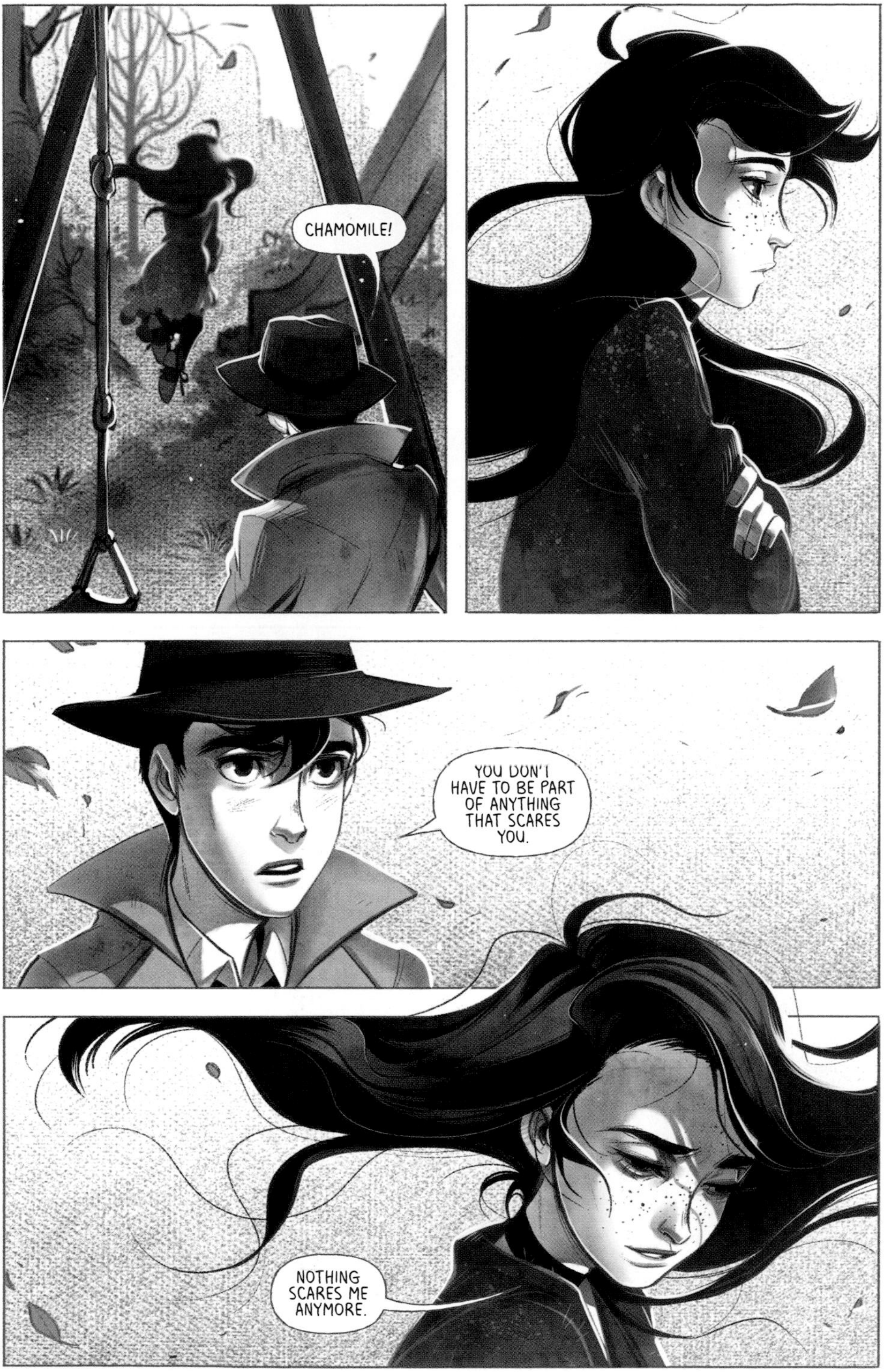
CHAMOMILE!
YOU DON'T HAVE TO BE PART OF ANYTHING THAT SCARES YOU.
NOTHING SCARES ME ANYMORE.

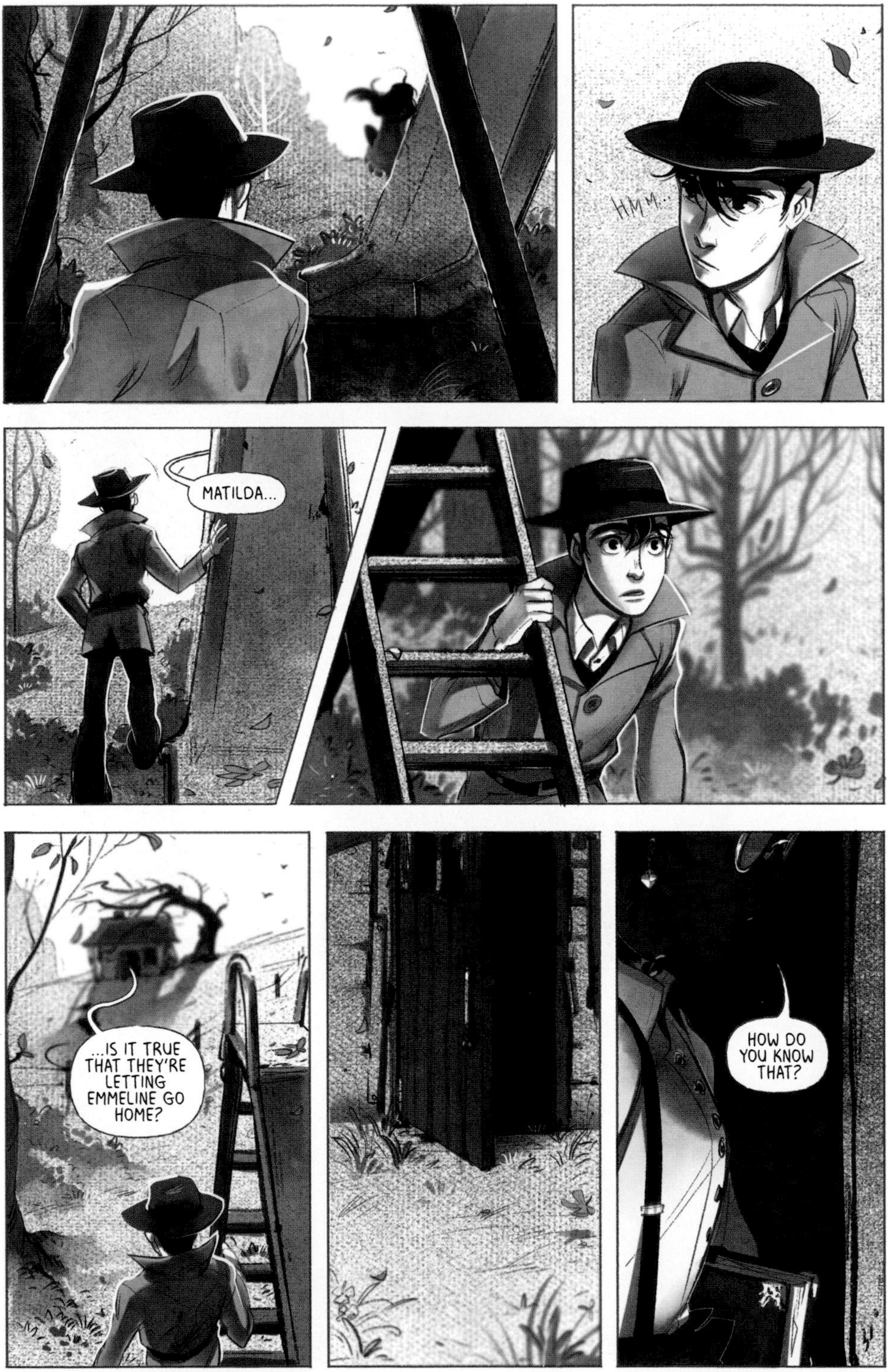
HMM..
MATILDA...
...IS IT TRUE THAT THEY'RE LETTING EMMELINE GO HOME?
HOW DO YOU KNOW THAT?

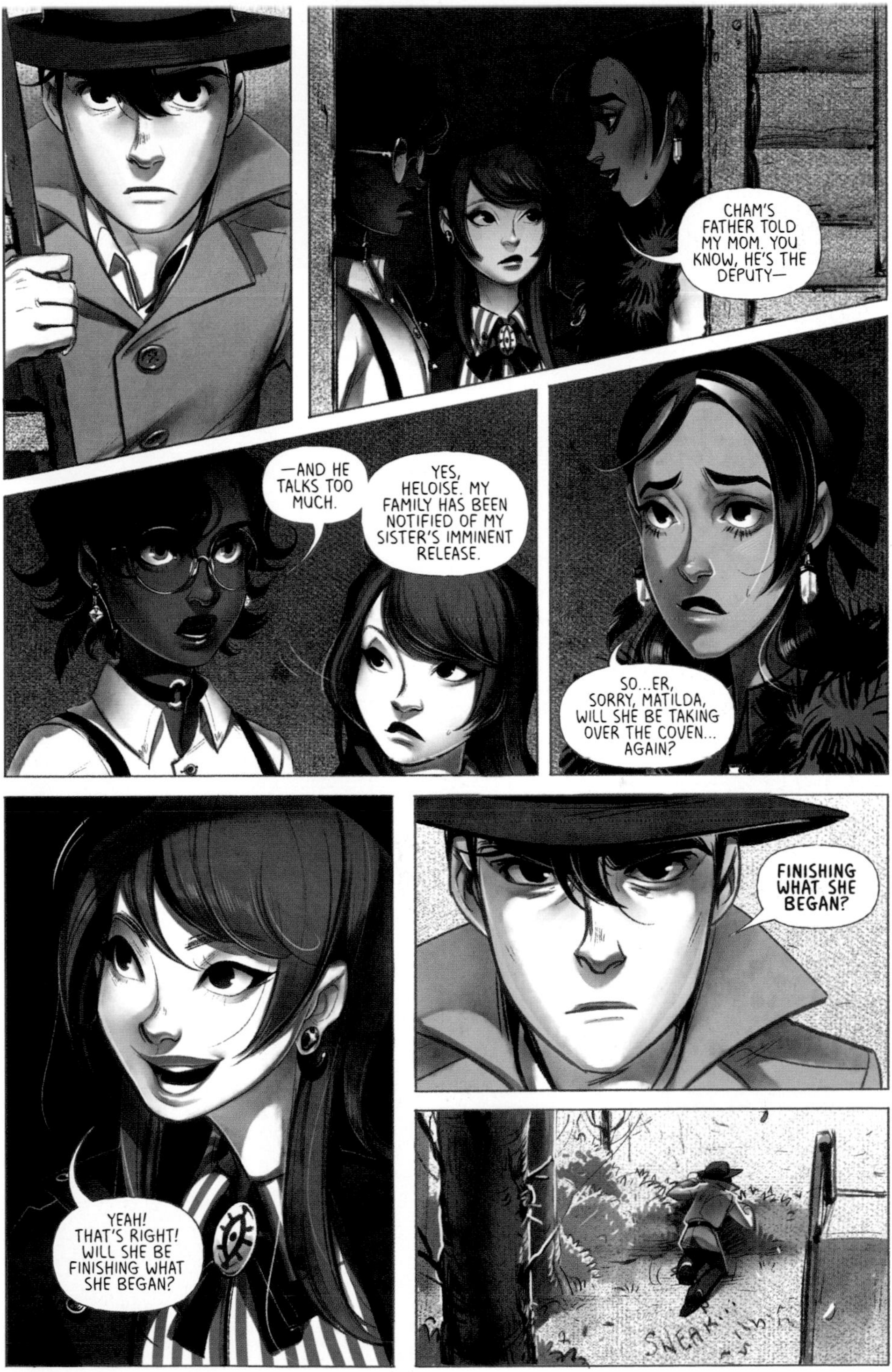
CHAM'S FATHER TOLD MY MOM. YOU KNOW, HE'S THE DEPUTY—
—AND HE TALKS TOO MUCH.
YES, HELOISE. MY FAMILY HAS BEEN NOTIFIED OF MY SISTER'S IMMINENT RELEASE.
SO...ER, SORRY, MATILDA, WILL SHE BE TAKING OVER THE COVEN... AGAIN?
YEAH! THAT'S RIGHT! WILL SHE BE FINISHING WHAT SHE BEGAN?
FINISHING WHAT SHE BEGAN?
SNEAK...

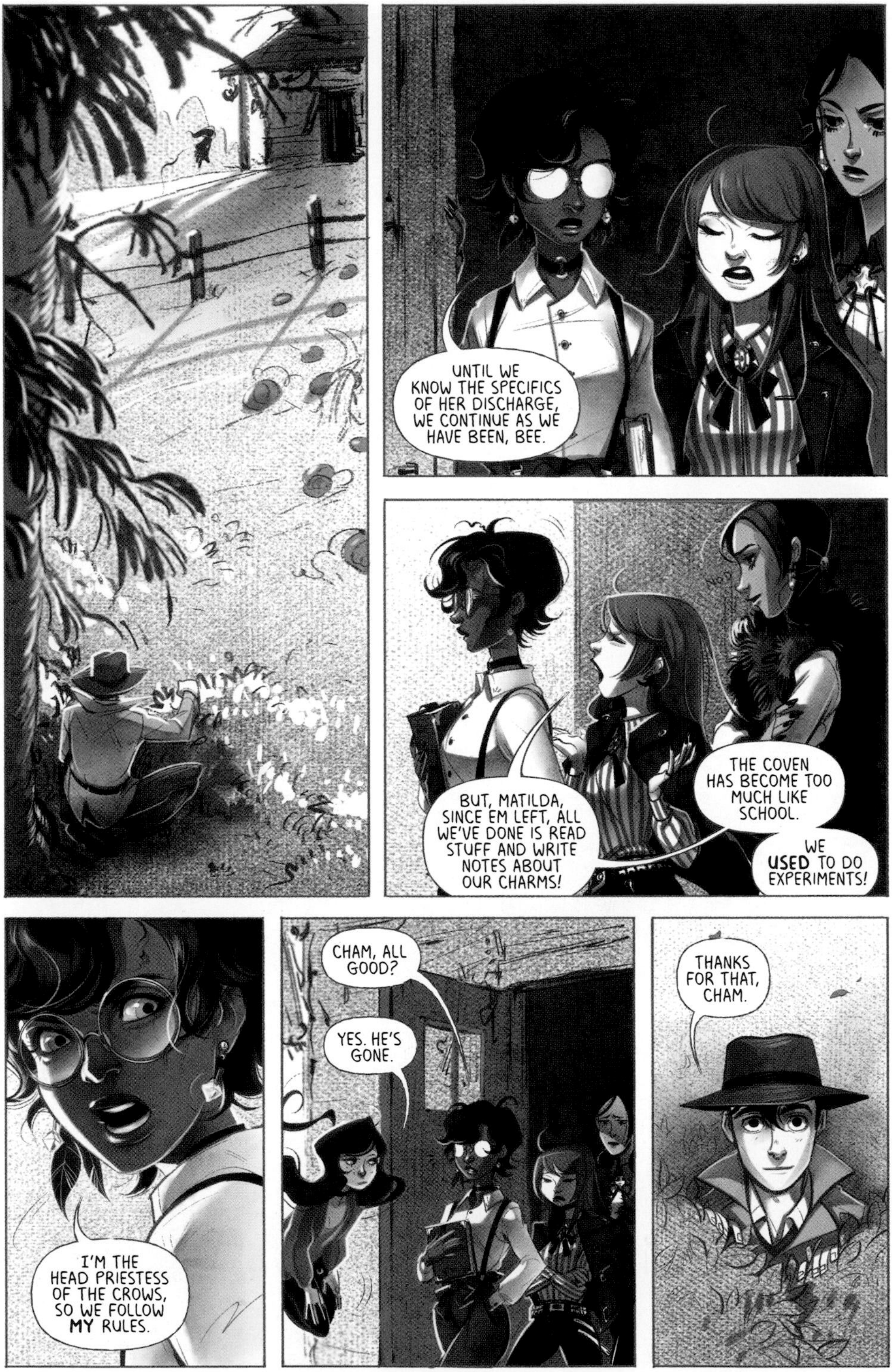
UNTIL WE KNOW THE SPECIFICS OF HER DISCHARGE, WE CONTINUE AS WE HAVE BEEN, BEE.
BUT, MATILDA, SINCE EM LEFT, ALL WE'VE DONE IS READ STUFF AND WRITE NOTES ABOUT OUR CHARMS!
THE COVEN HAS BECOME TOO MUCH LIKE SCHOOL.
WE **USED** TO DO EXPERIMENTS!
I'M THE HEAD PRIESTESS OF THE CROWS, SO WE FOLLOW **MY** RULES.
CHAM, ALL GOOD?
YES. HE'S GONE.
THANKS FOR THAT, CHAM.

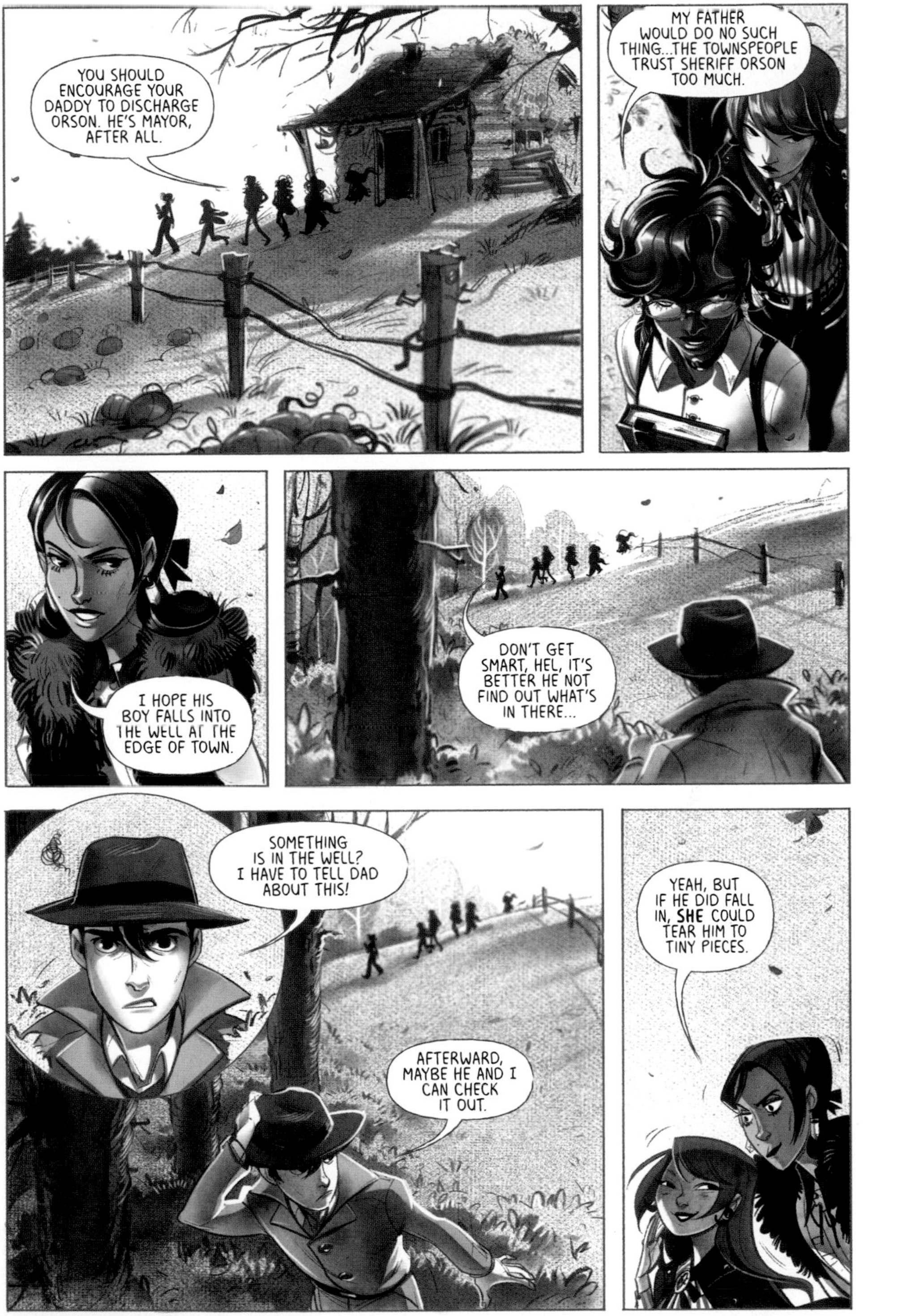
YOU SHOULD ENCOURAGE YOUR DADDY TO DISCHARGE ORSON. HE'S MAYOR, AFTER ALL.
MY FATHER WOULD DO NO SUCH THING...THE TOWNSPEOPLE TRUST SHERIFF ORSON TOO MUCH.
I HOPE HIS BOY FALLS INTO THE WELL AT THE EDGE OF TOWN.
DON'T GET SMART, HEL, IT'S BETTER HE NOT FIND OUT WHAT'S IN THERE...
SOMETHING IS IN THE WELL? I HAVE TO TELL DAD ABOUT THIS!
AFTERWARD, MAYBE HE AND I CAN CHECK IT OUT.
YEAH, BUT IF HE DID FALL IN, **SHE** COULD TEAR HIM TO TINY PIECES.

CHAPTER 3

SMALL TOWN
SHADOW

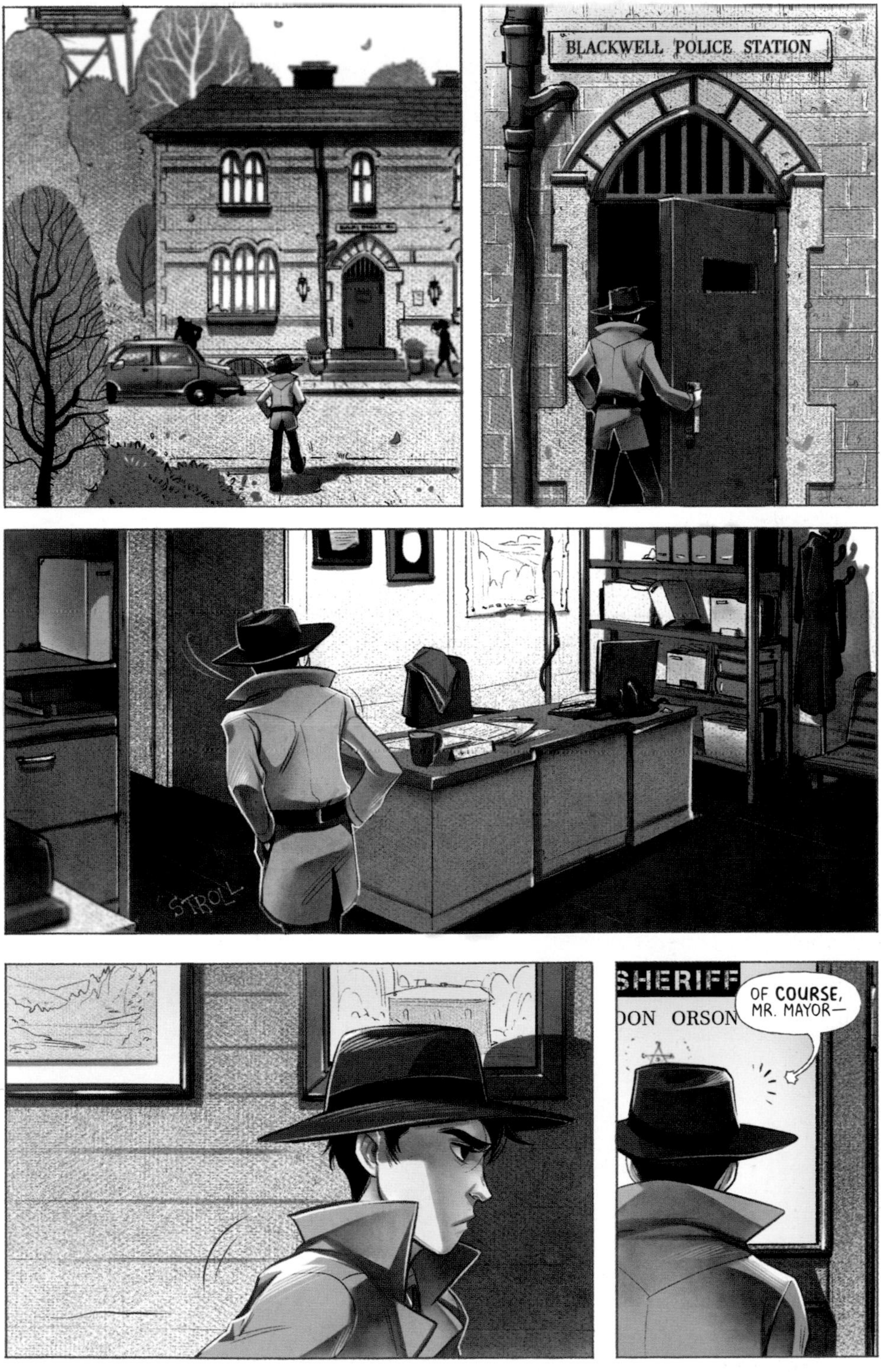
BLACKWELL POLICE STATION
STROLL
SHERIFF
DON ORSON
OF COURSE, MR. MAYOR—

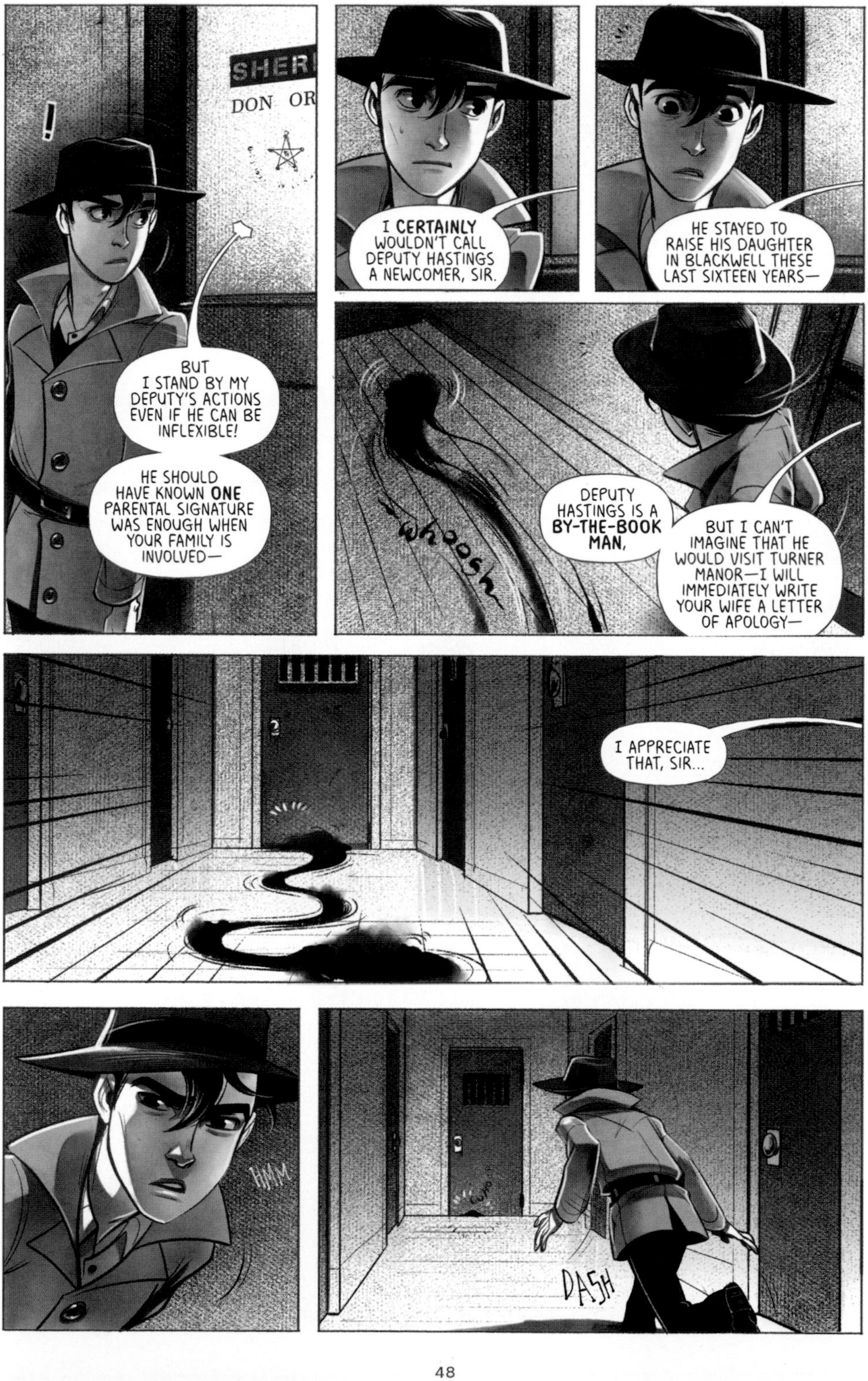
SHERI
DON OR
!
BUT I STAND BY MY DEPUTY'S ACTIONS EVEN IF HE CAN BE INFLEXIBLE!
HE SHOULD HAVE KNOWN ONE PARENTAL SIGNATURE WAS ENOUGH WHEN YOUR FAMILY IS INVOLVED—
I CERTAINLY WOULDN'T CALL DEPUTY HASTINGS A NEWCOMER, SIR.
HE STAYED TO RAISE HIS DAUGHTER IN BLACKWELL THESE LAST SIXTEEN YEARS—
whoosh
DEPUTY HASTINGS IS A BY-THE-BOOK MAN,
BUT I CAN'T IMAGINE THAT HE WOULD VISIT TURNER MANOR—I WILL IMMEDIATELY WRITE YOUR WIFE A LETTER OF APOLOGY—
I APPRECIATE THAT, SIR...
HMM
DASH

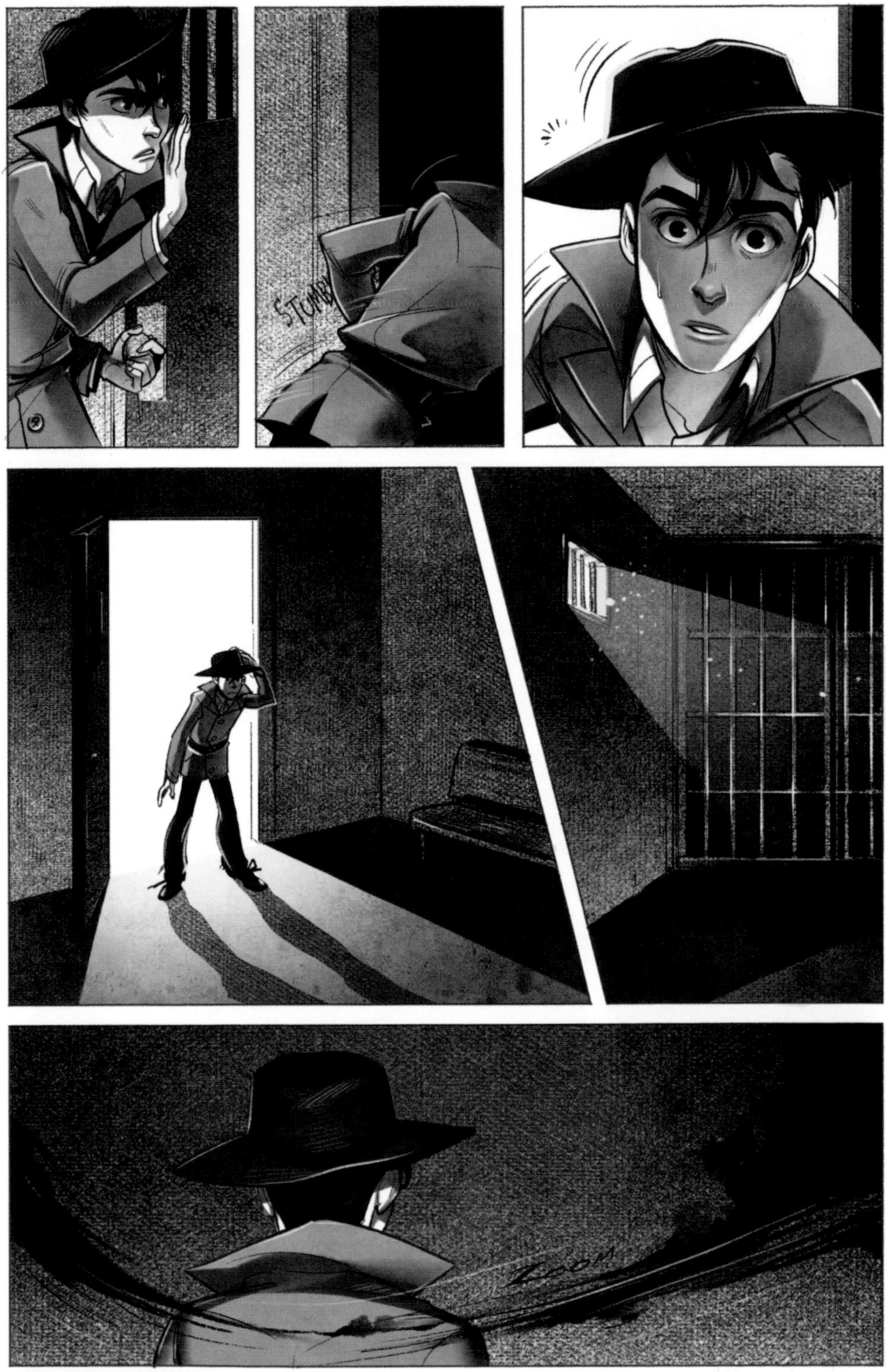

STUMB
ZOOM

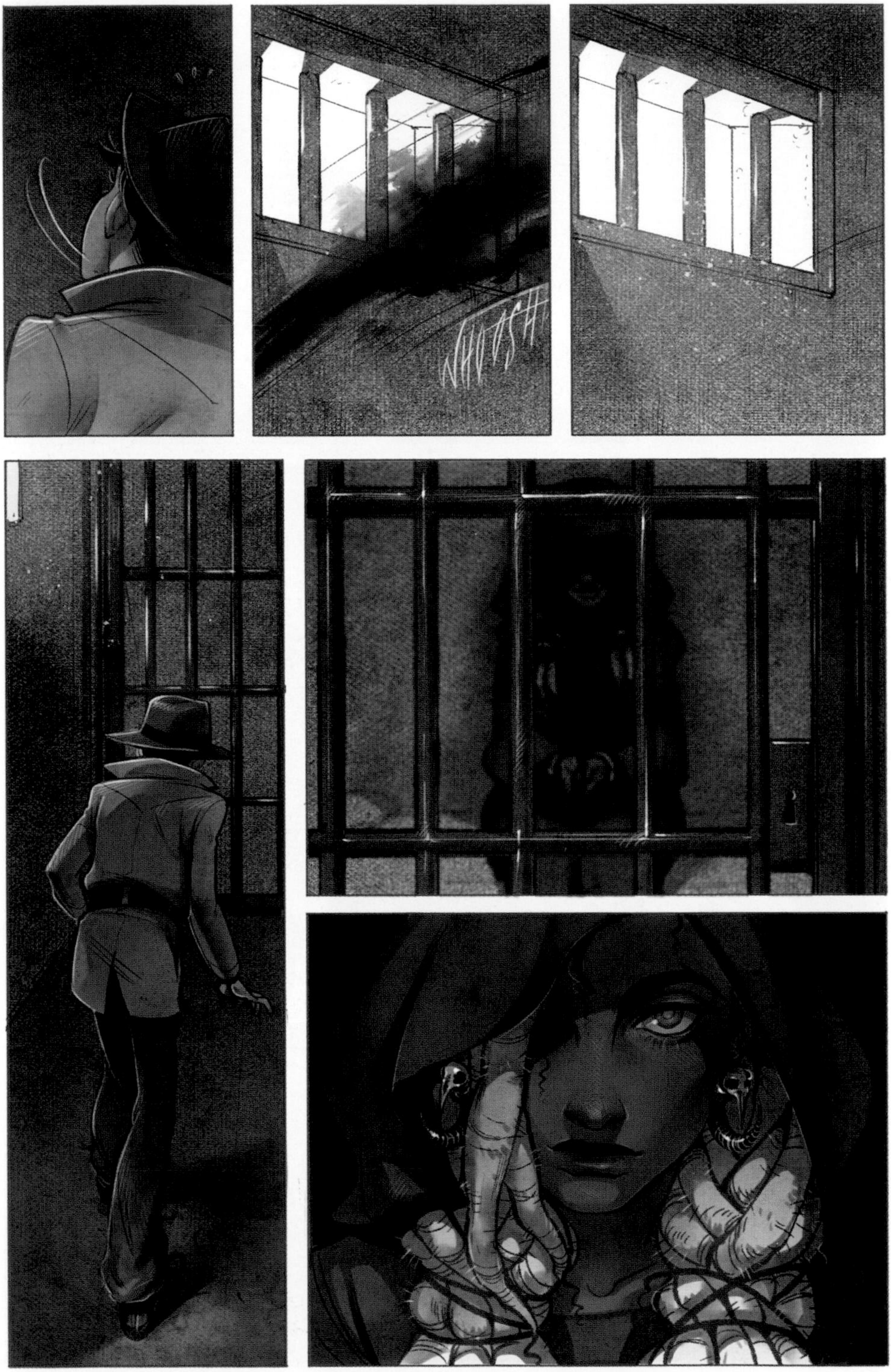
WHOOSH

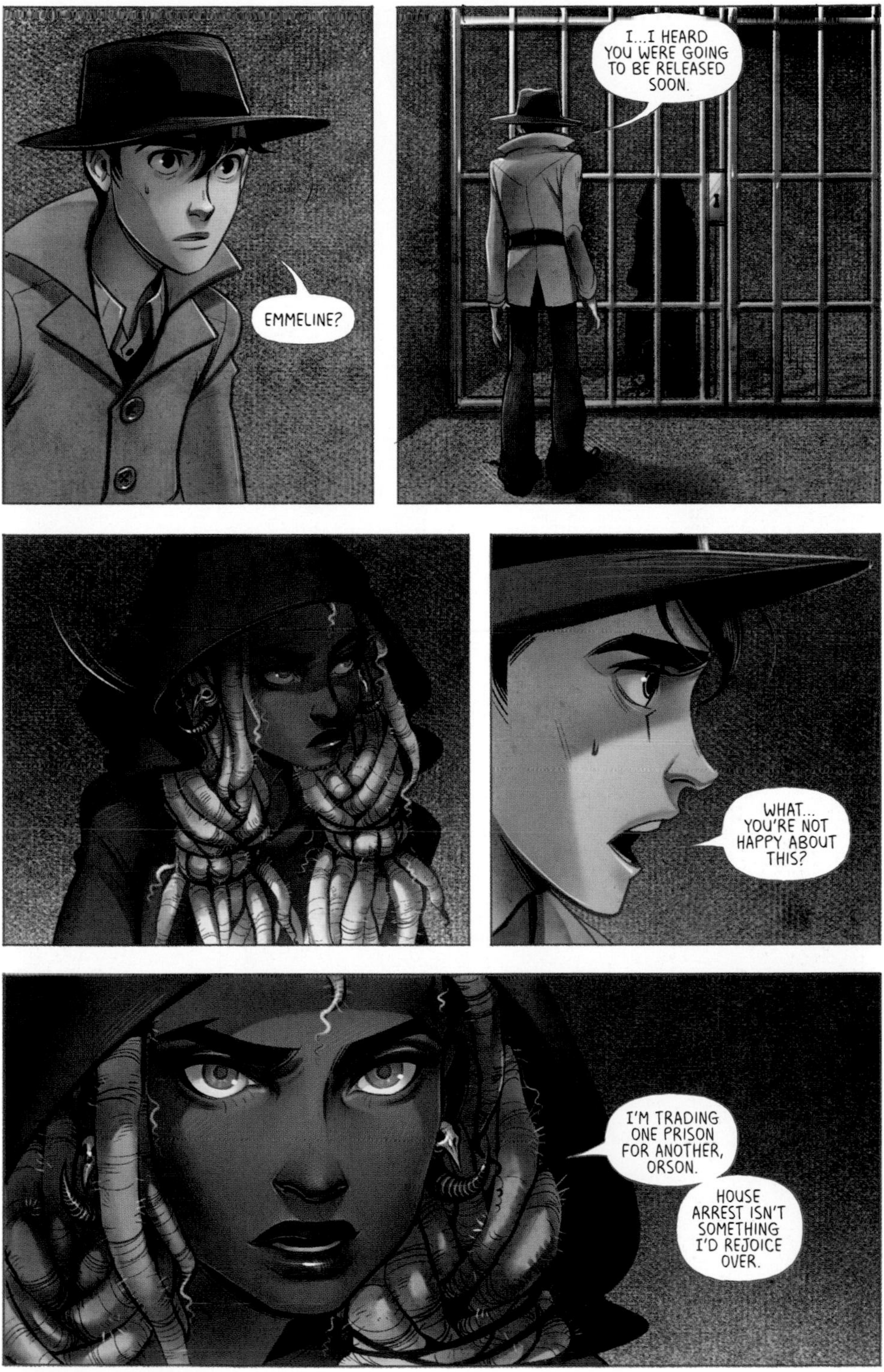
EMMELINE?
I...I HEARD YOU WERE GOING TO BE RELEASED SOON.
WHAT... YOU'RE NOT HAPPY ABOUT THIS?
I'M TRADING ONE PRISON FOR ANOTHER, ORSON.
HOUSE ARREST ISN'T SOMETHING I'D REJOICE OVER.

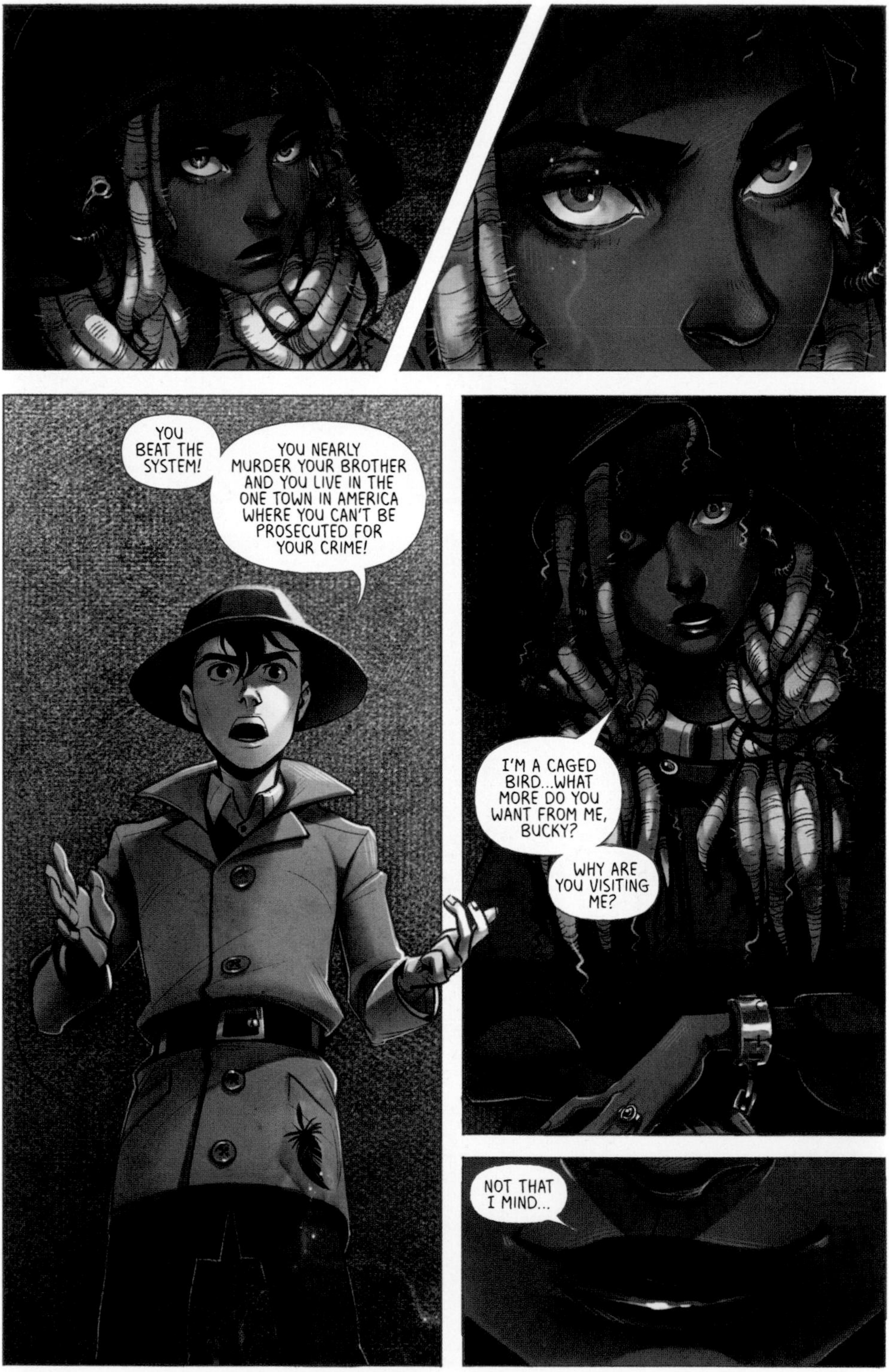
YOU BEAT THE SYSTEM!
YOU NEARLY MURDER YOUR BROTHER AND YOU LIVE IN THE ONE TOWN IN AMERICA WHERE YOU CAN'T BE PROSECUTED FOR YOUR CRIME!
I'M A CAGED BIRD...WHAT MORE DO YOU WANT FROM ME, BUCKY?
WHY ARE YOU VISITING ME?
NOT THAT I MIND...

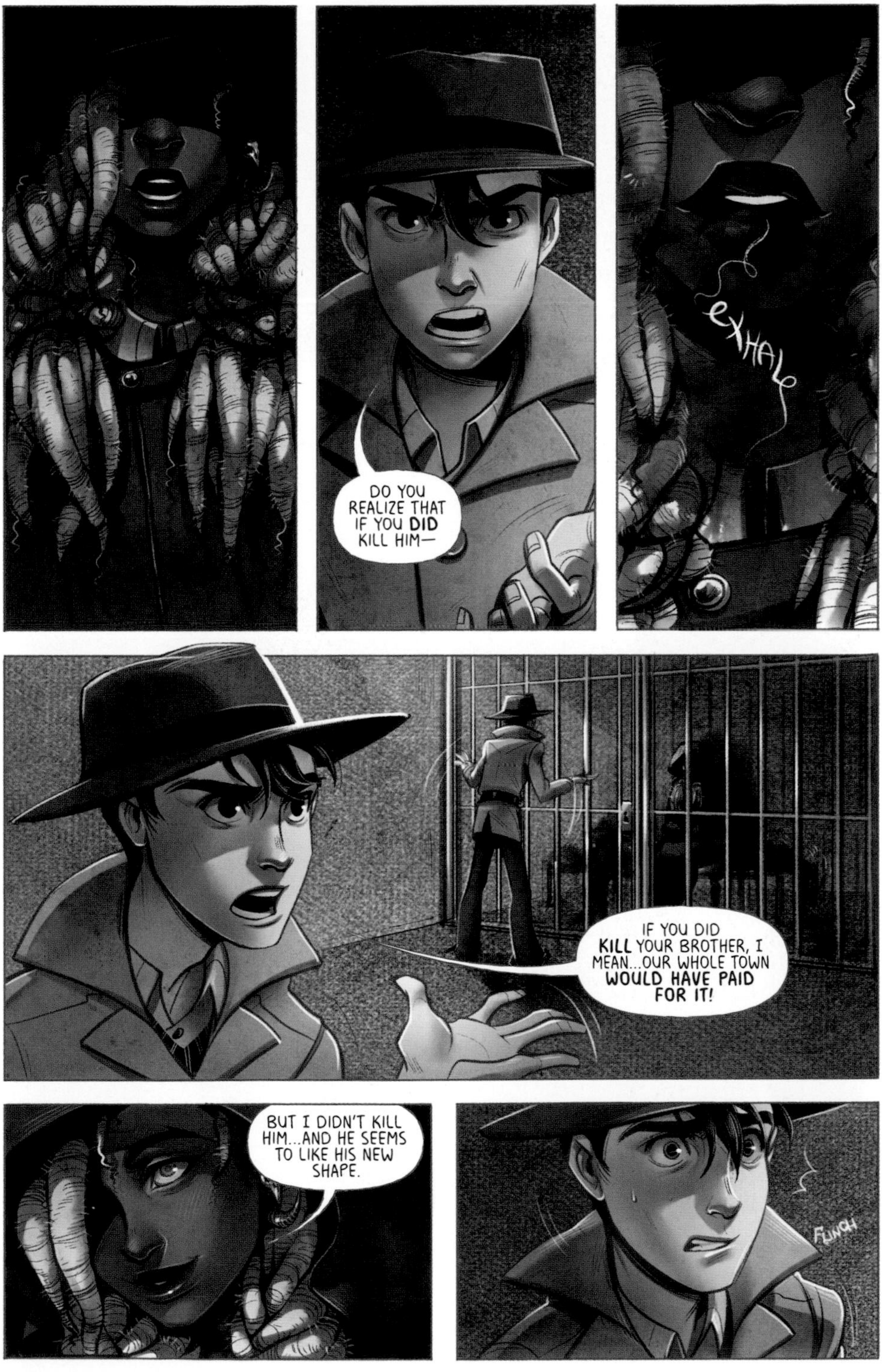
DO YOU REALIZE THAT IF YOU **DID** KILL HIM—
EXHALE
IF YOU DID **KILL** YOUR BROTHER, I MEAN...OUR WHOLE TOWN **WOULD HAVE PAID FOR IT!**
BUT I DIDN'T KILL HIM...AND HE SEEMS TO LIKE HIS NEW SHAPE.
FLINCH

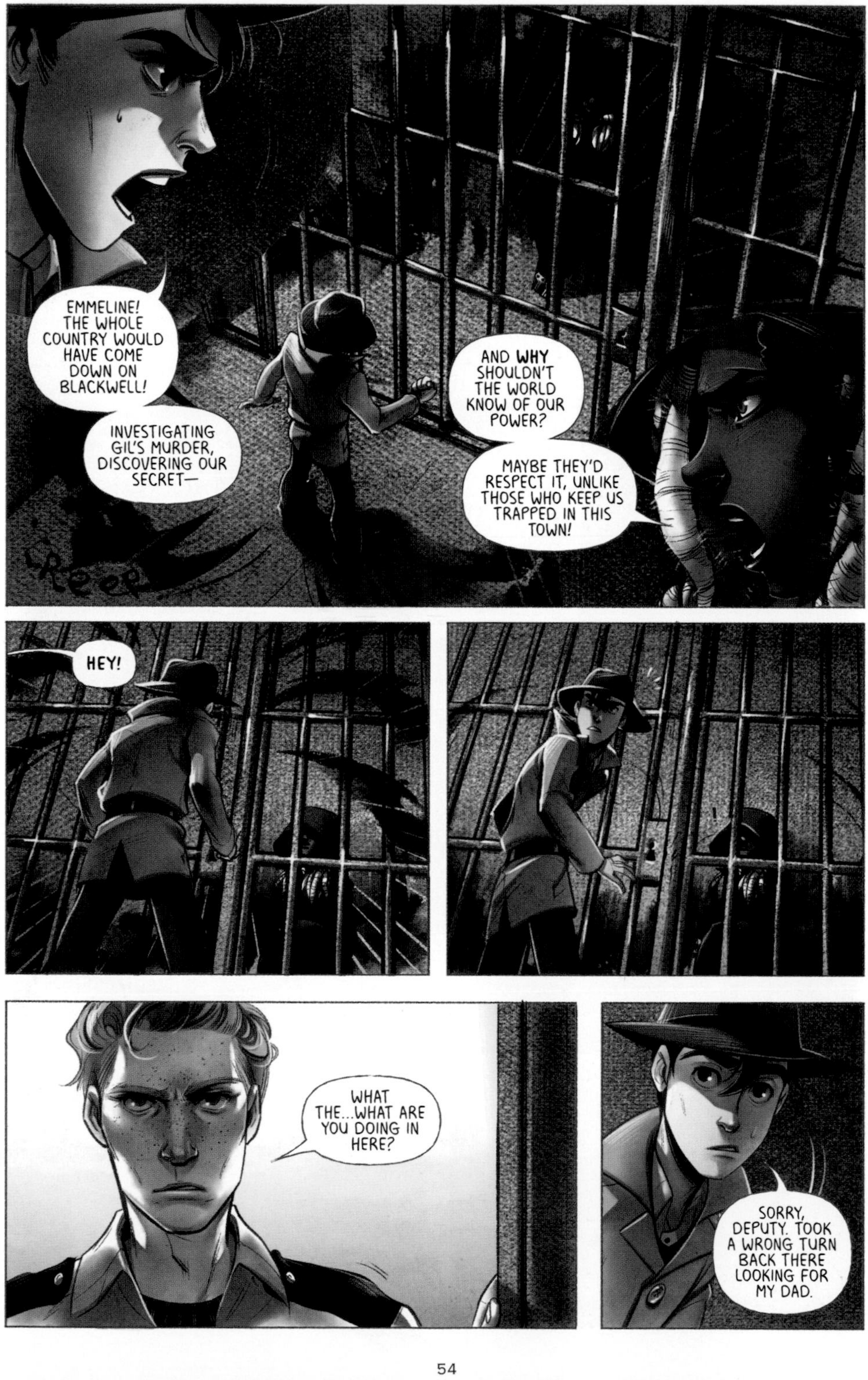
EMMELINE! THE WHOLE COUNTRY WOULD HAVE COME DOWN ON BLACKWELL!
INVESTIGATING GIL'S MURDER, DISCOVERING OUR SECRET—
AND WHY SHOULDN'T THE WORLD KNOW OF OUR POWER?
MAYBE THEY'D RESPECT IT, UNLIKE THOSE WHO KEEP US TRAPPED IN THIS TOWN!
HEY!
WHAT THE...WHAT ARE YOU DOING IN HERE?
SORRY, DEPUTY. TOOK A WRONG TURN BACK THERE LOOKING FOR MY DAD.

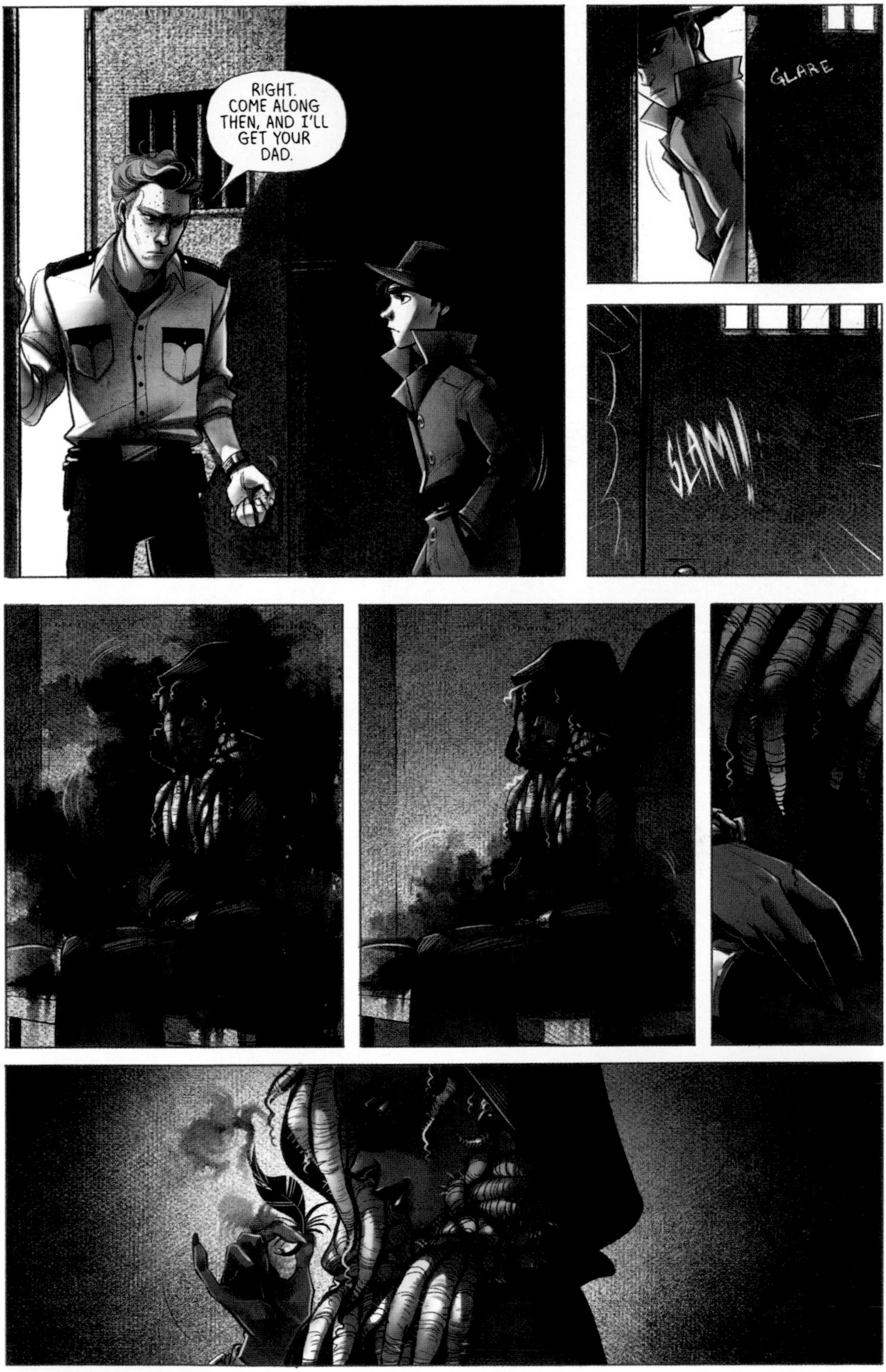
RIGHT. COME ALONG THEN, AND I'LL GET YOUR DAD.
GLARE
SLAM!

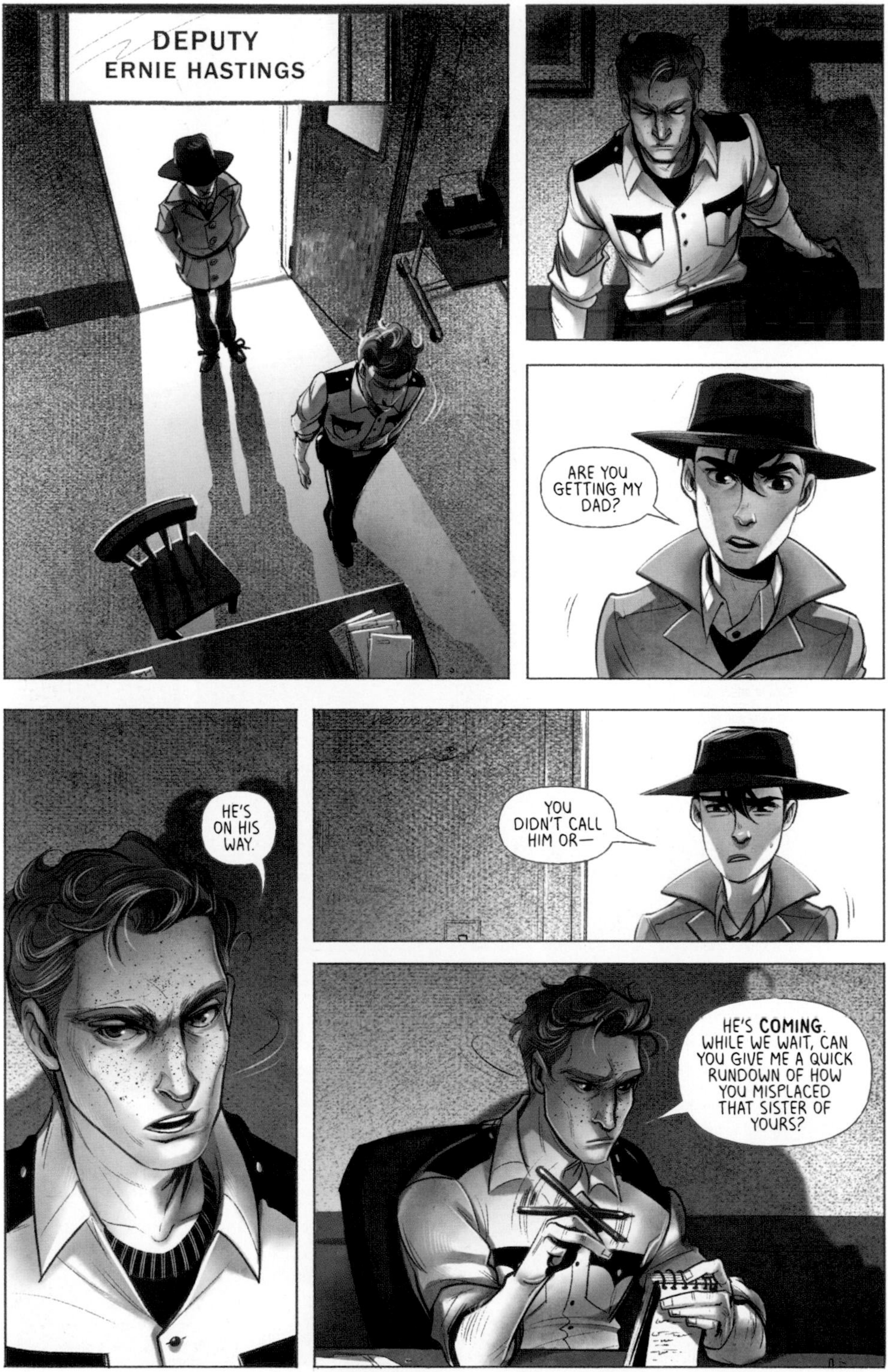
DEPUTY
ERNIE HASTINGS
ARE YOU GETTING MY DAD?
HE'S ON HIS WAY.
YOU DIDN'T CALL HIM OR—
HE'S **COMING**. WHILE WE WAIT, CAN YOU GIVE ME A QUICK RUNDOWN OF HOW YOU MISPLACED THAT SISTER OF YOURS?

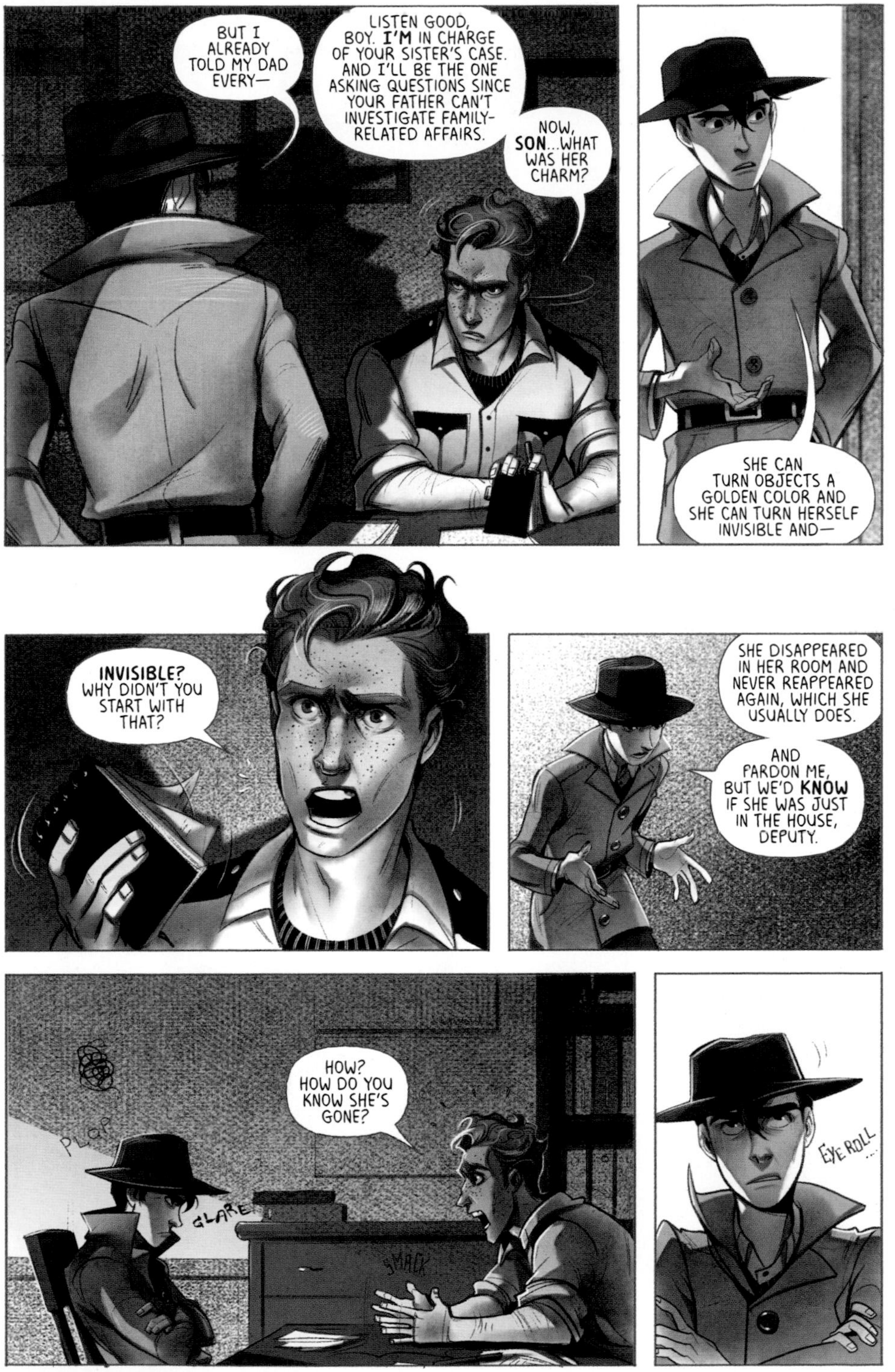
BUT I ALREADY TOLD MY DAD EVERY—
LISTEN GOOD, BOY. **I'M** IN CHARGE OF YOUR SISTER'S CASE. AND I'LL BE THE ONE ASKING QUESTIONS SINCE YOUR FATHER CAN'T INVESTIGATE FAMILY-RELATED AFFAIRS.
NOW, **SON**...WHAT WAS HER CHARM?
SHE CAN TURN OBJECTS A GOLDEN COLOR AND SHE CAN TURN HERSELF INVISIBLE AND—
INVISIBLE? WHY DIDN'T YOU START WITH THAT?
SHE DISAPPEARED IN HER ROOM AND NEVER REAPPEARED AGAIN, WHICH SHE USUALLY DOES.
AND PARDON ME, BUT WE'D **KNOW** IF SHE WAS JUST IN THE HOUSE, DEPUTY.
HOW? HOW DO YOU KNOW SHE'S GONE?
GLARE
SMACK
EYE ROLL...

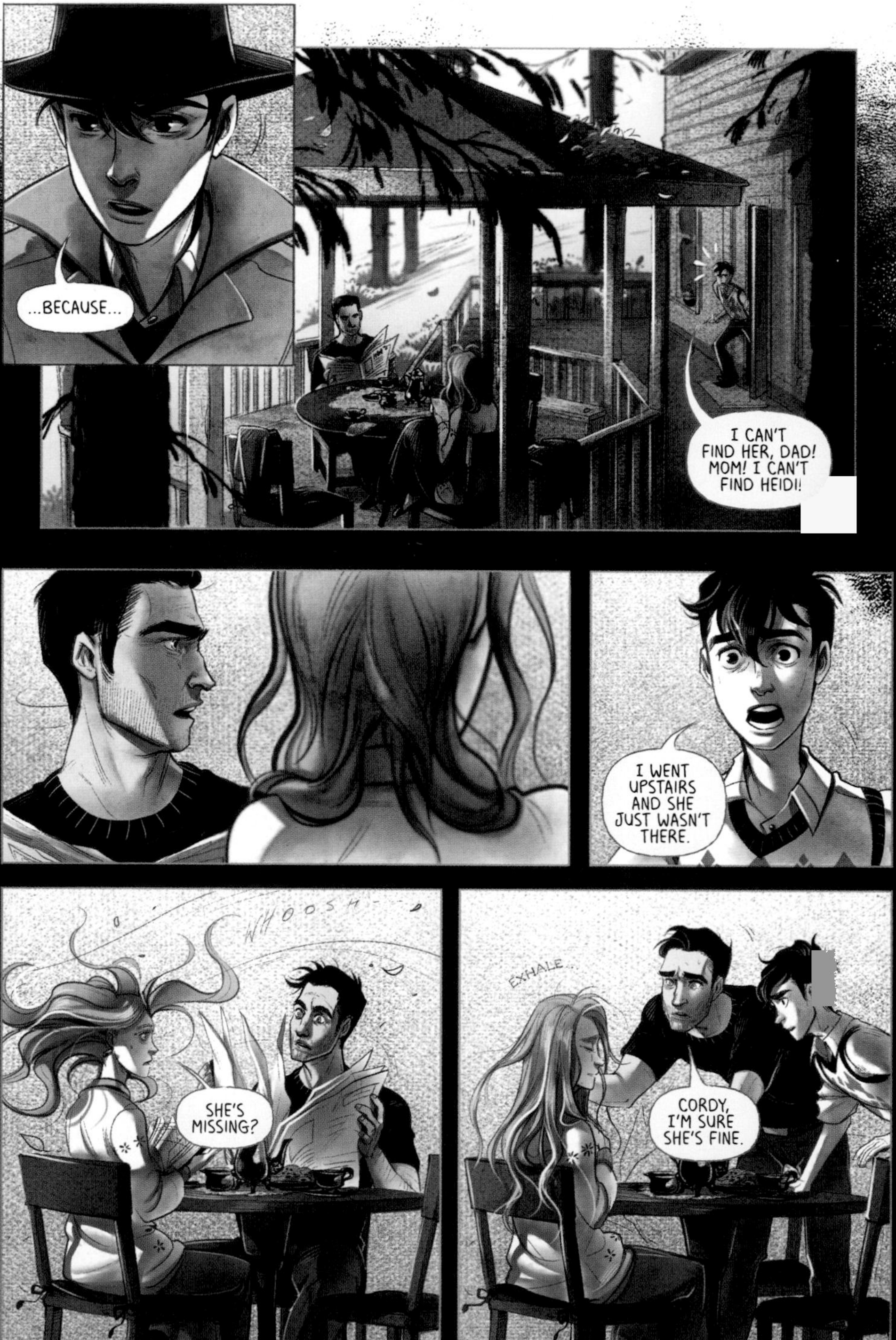
...BECAUSE...
I CAN'T FIND HER, DAD! MOM! I CAN'T FIND HEIDI!
I WENT UPSTAIRS AND SHE JUST WASN'T THERE.
WHOOSH
SHE'S MISSING?
EXHALE...
CORDY, I'M SURE SHE'S FINE.

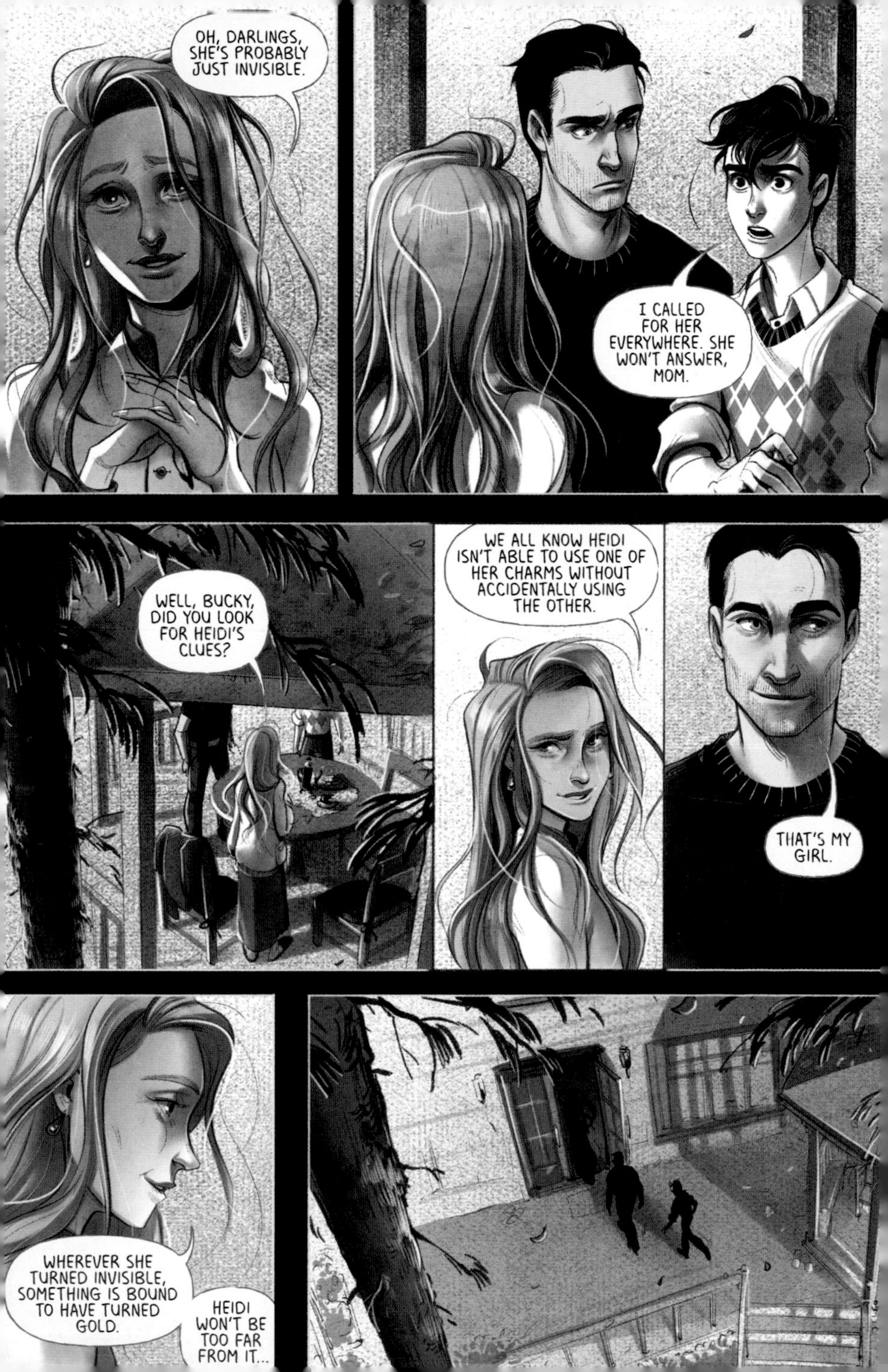
OH, DARLINGS, SHE'S PROBABLY JUST INVISIBLE.
I CALLED FOR HER EVERYWHERE. SHE WON'T ANSWER, MOM.
WELL, BUCKY, DID YOU LOOK FOR HEIDI'S CLUES?
WE ALL KNOW HEIDI ISN'T ABLE TO USE ONE OF HER CHARMS WITHOUT ACCIDENTALLY USING THE OTHER.
THAT'S MY GIRL.
WHEREVER SHE TURNED INVISIBLE, SOMETHING IS BOUND TO HAVE TURNED GOLD.
HEIDI WON'T BE TOO FAR FROM IT...

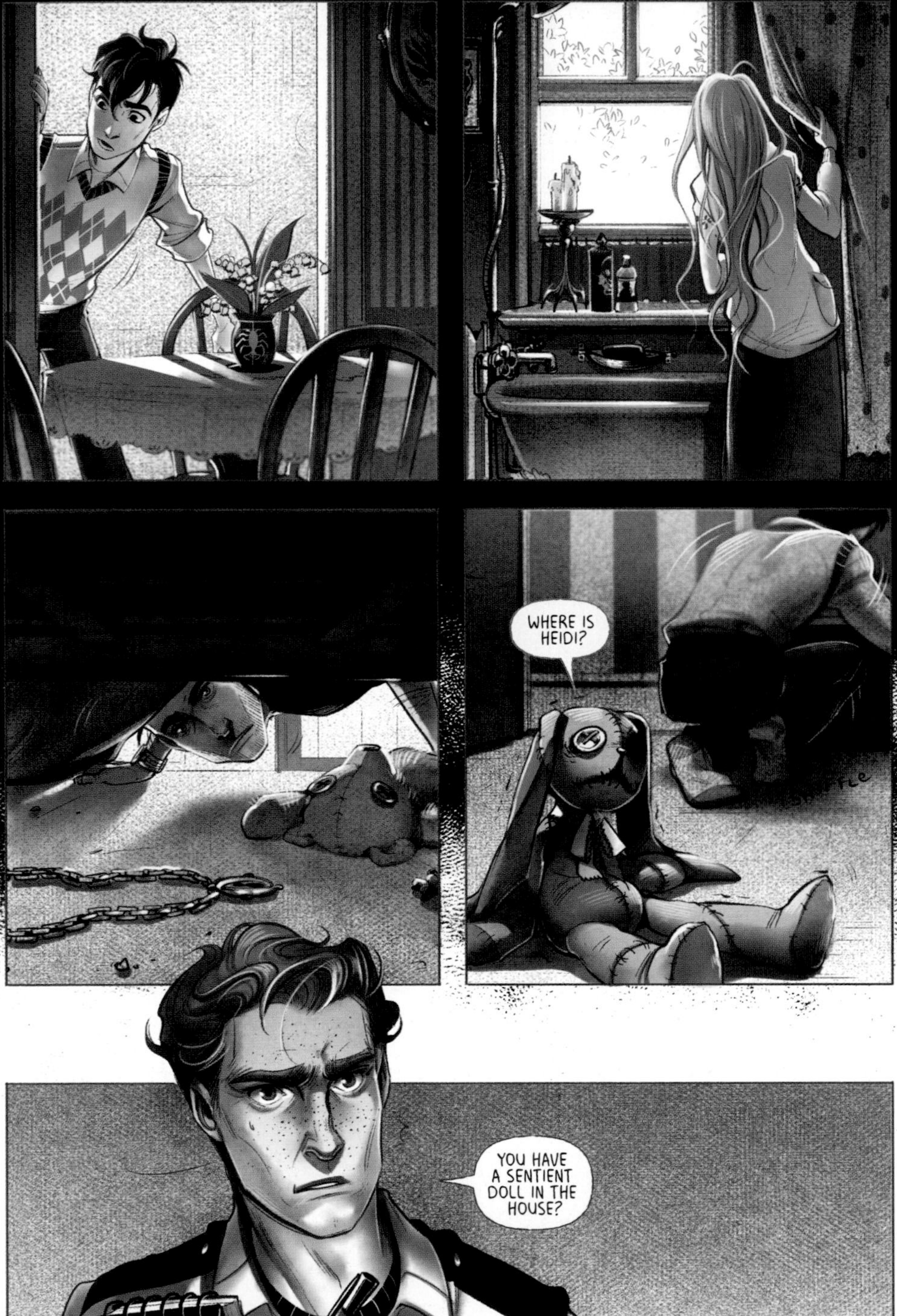
WHERE IS HEIDI?
YOU HAVE A SENTIENT DOLL IN THE HOUSE?

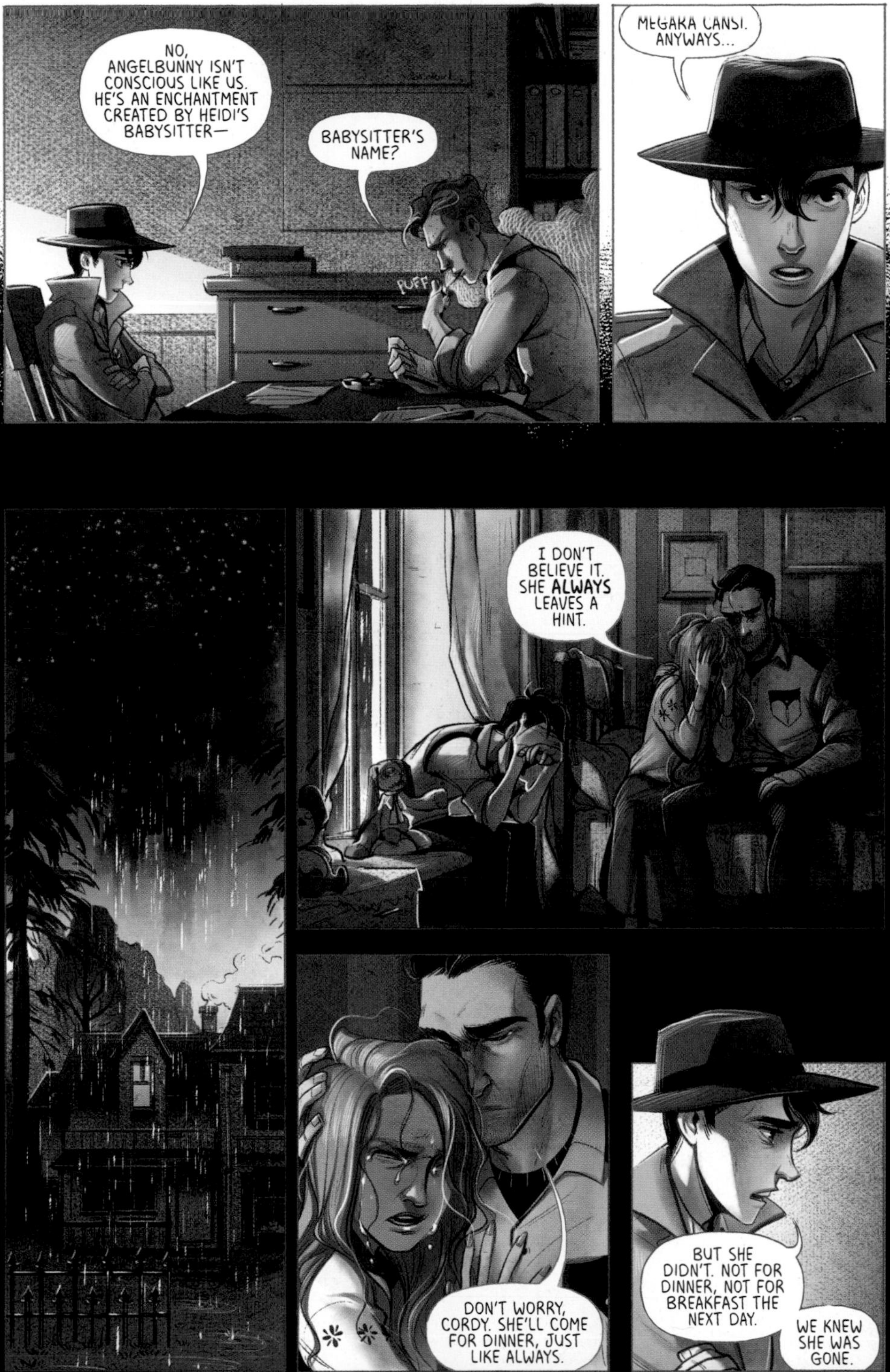
NO, ANGELBUNNY ISN'T CONSCIOUS LIKE US. HE'S AN ENCHANTMENT CREATED BY HEIDI'S BABYSITTER—
BABYSITTER'S NAME?
PUFF
MEGARA CANSI. ANYWAYS...
I DON'T BELIEVE IT. SHE **ALWAYS** LEAVES A HINT.
DON'T WORRY, CORDY. SHE'LL COME FOR DINNER, JUST LIKE ALWAYS.
BUT SHE DIDN'T. NOT FOR DINNER, NOT FOR BREAKFAST THE NEXT DAY.
WE KNEW SHE WAS GONE.

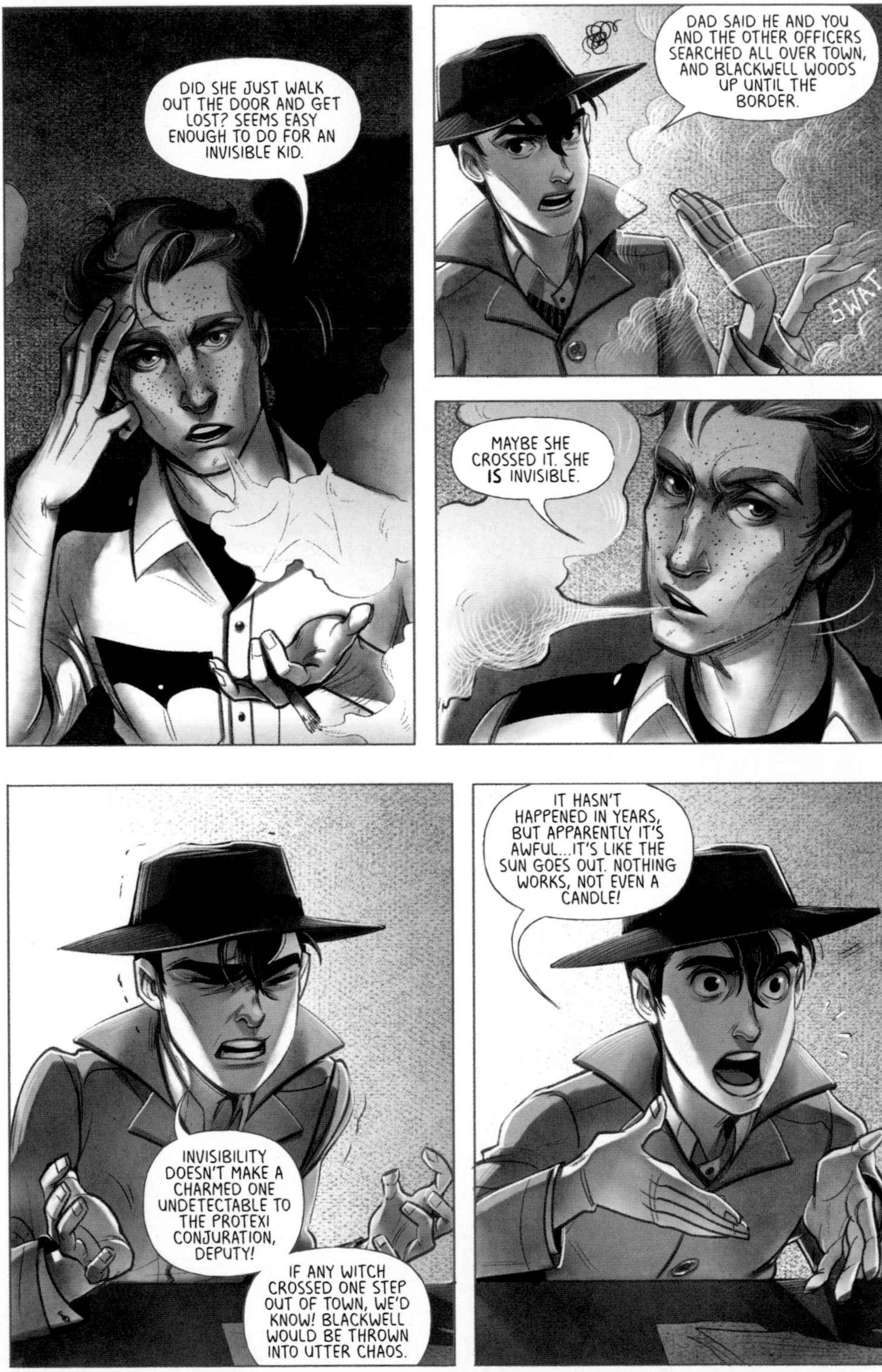
DID SHE JUST WALK OUT THE DOOR AND GET LOST? SEEMS EASY ENOUGH TO DO FOR AN INVISIBLE KID.
DAD SAID HE AND YOU AND THE OTHER OFFICERS SEARCHED ALL OVER TOWN, AND BLACKWELL WOODS UP UNTIL THE BORDER.
SWAT
MAYBE SHE CROSSED IT. SHE **IS** INVISIBLE.
INVISIBILITY DOESN'T MAKE A CHARMED ONE UNDETECTABLE TO THE PROTEXI CONJURATION, DEPUTY!
IF ANY WITCH CROSSED ONE STEP OUT OF TOWN, WE'D KNOW! BLACKWELL WOULD BE THROWN INTO UTTER CHAOS.
IT HASN'T HAPPENED IN YEARS, BUT APPARENTLY IT'S AWFUL...IT'S LIKE THE SUN GOES OUT. NOTHING WORKS, NOT EVEN A CANDLE!

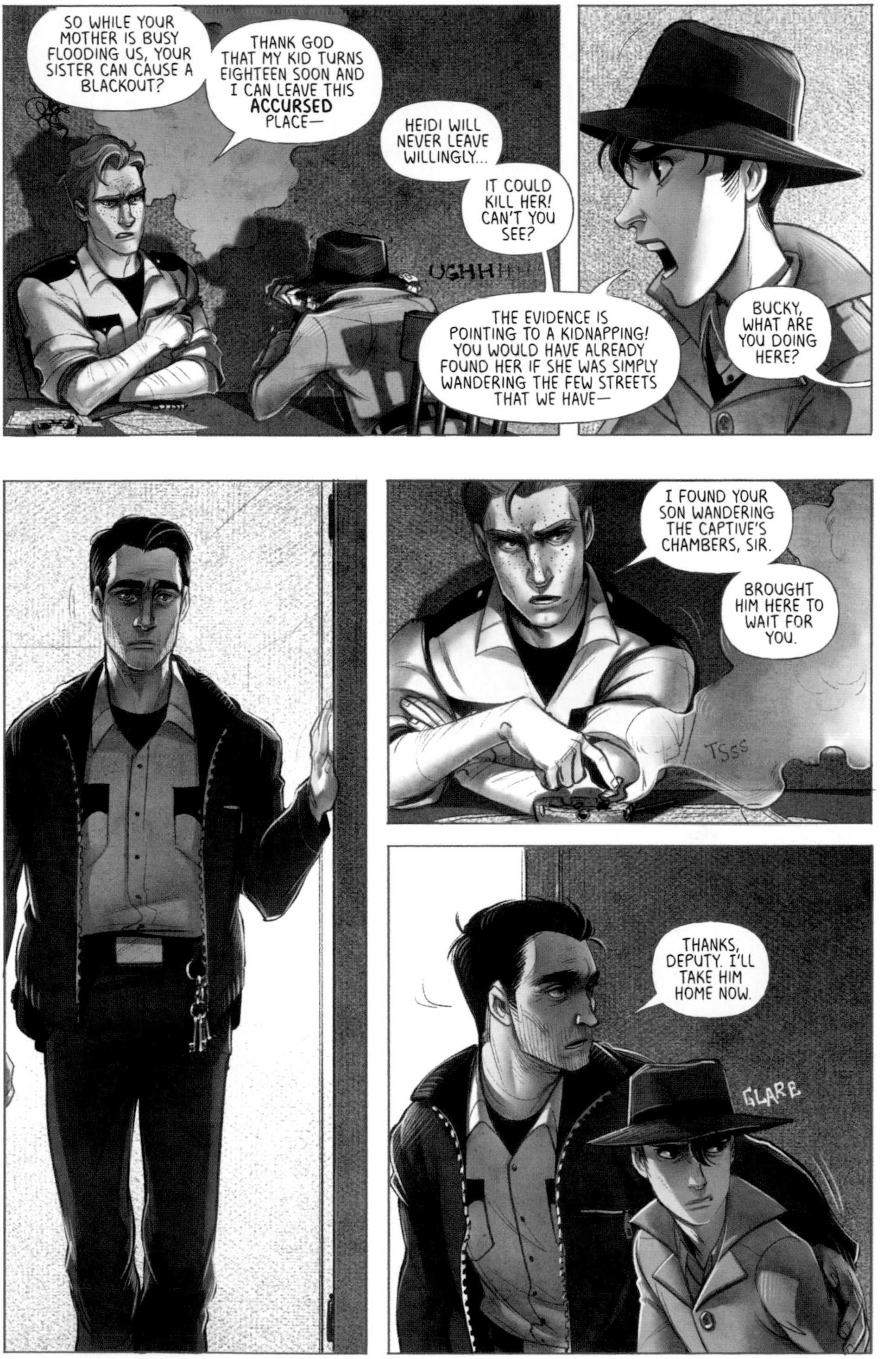
SO WHILE YOUR MOTHER IS BUSY FLOODING US, YOUR SISTER CAN CAUSE A BLACKOUT?
THANK GOD THAT MY KID TURNS EIGHTEEN SOON AND I CAN LEAVE THIS **ACCURSED** PLACE—
HEIDI WILL NEVER LEAVE WILLINGLY...
IT COULD KILL HER! CAN'T YOU SEE?
UGHH
THE EVIDENCE IS POINTING TO A KIDNAPPING! YOU WOULD HAVE ALREADY FOUND HER IF SHE WAS SIMPLY WANDERING THE FEW STREETS THAT WE HAVE—
BUCKY, WHAT ARE YOU DOING HERE?
I FOUND YOUR SON WANDERING THE CAPTIVE'S CHAMBERS, SIR.
BROUGHT HIM HERE TO WAIT FOR YOU.
TSSS
THANKS, DEPUTY. I'LL TAKE HIM HOME NOW.
GLARE

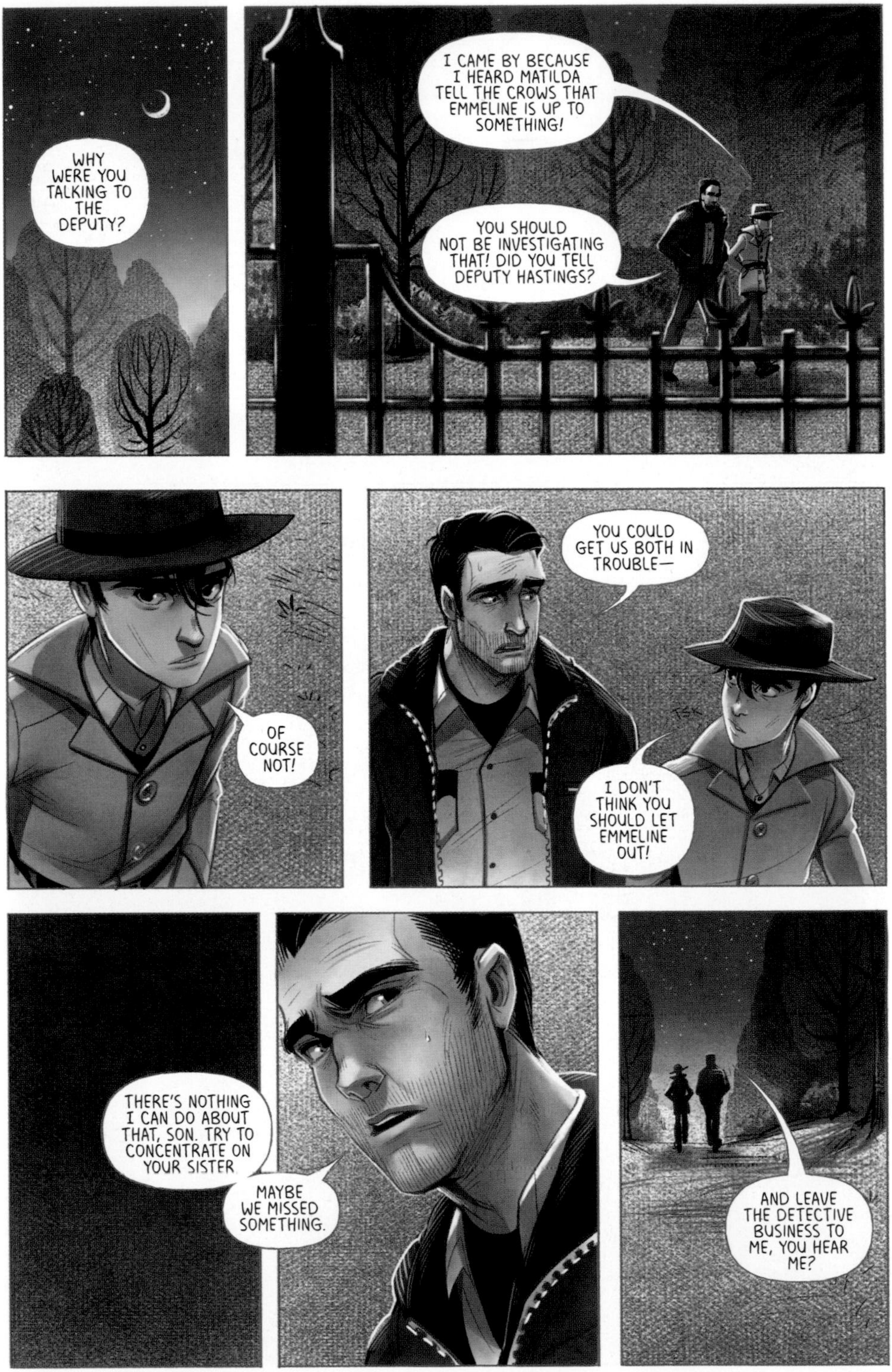
WHY WERE YOU TALKING TO THE DEPUTY?
I CAME BY BECAUSE I HEARD MATILDA TELL THE CROWS THAT EMMELINE IS UP TO SOMETHING!
YOU SHOULD NOT BE INVESTIGATING THAT! DID YOU TELL DEPUTY HASTINGS?
OF COURSE NOT!
YOU COULD GET US BOTH IN TROUBLE—
FSK
I DON'T THINK YOU SHOULD LET EMMELINE OUT!
THERE'S NOTHING I CAN DO ABOUT THAT, SON. TRY TO CONCENTRATE ON YOUR SISTER.
MAYBE WE MISSED SOMETHING.
AND LEAVE THE DETECTIVE BUSINESS TO ME, YOU HEAR ME?

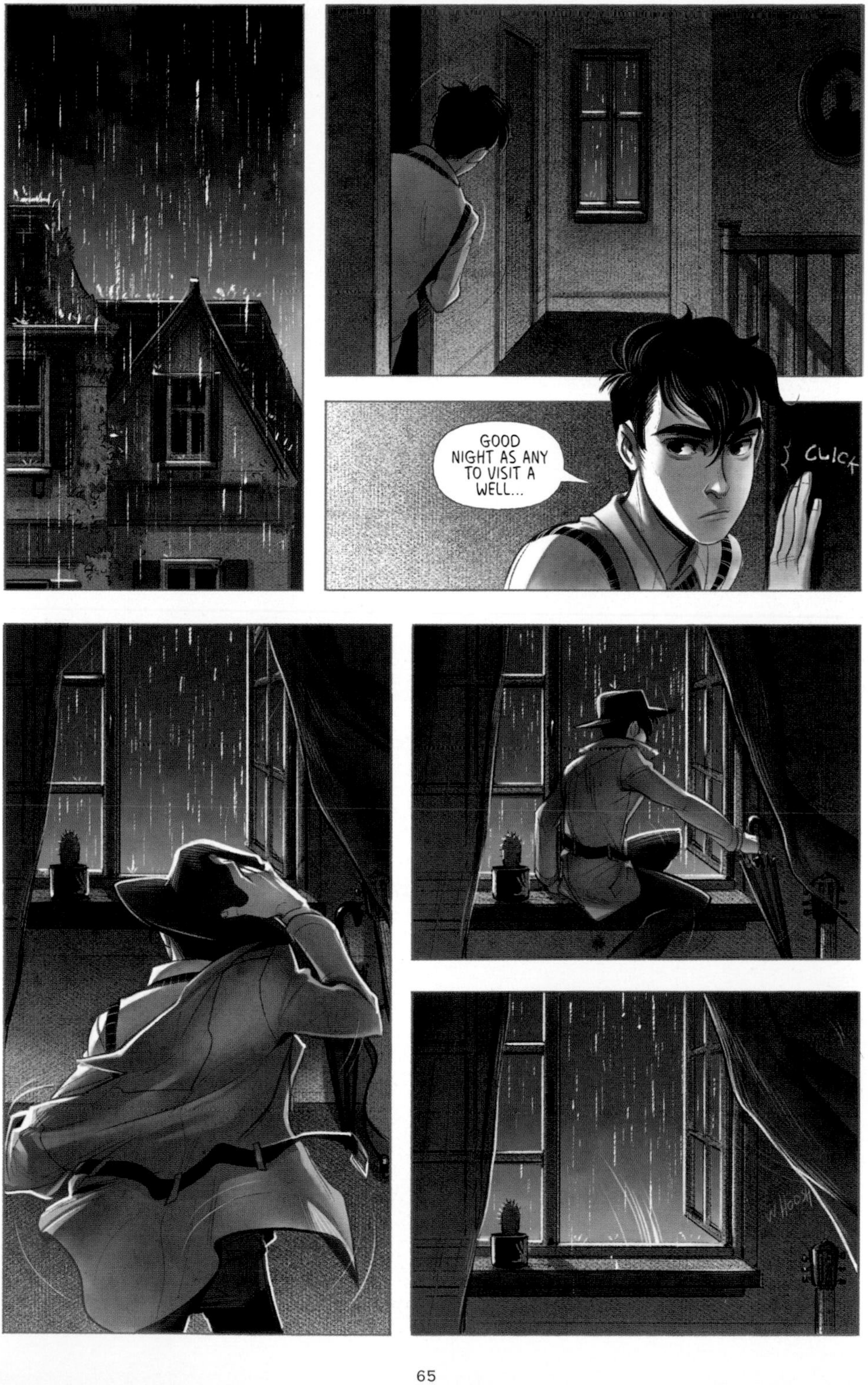
GOOD NIGHT AS ANY TO VISIT A WELL...
CLICK
WHOOSH

CHAPTER 4

OLD GHOSTS ARE SO SPOILED

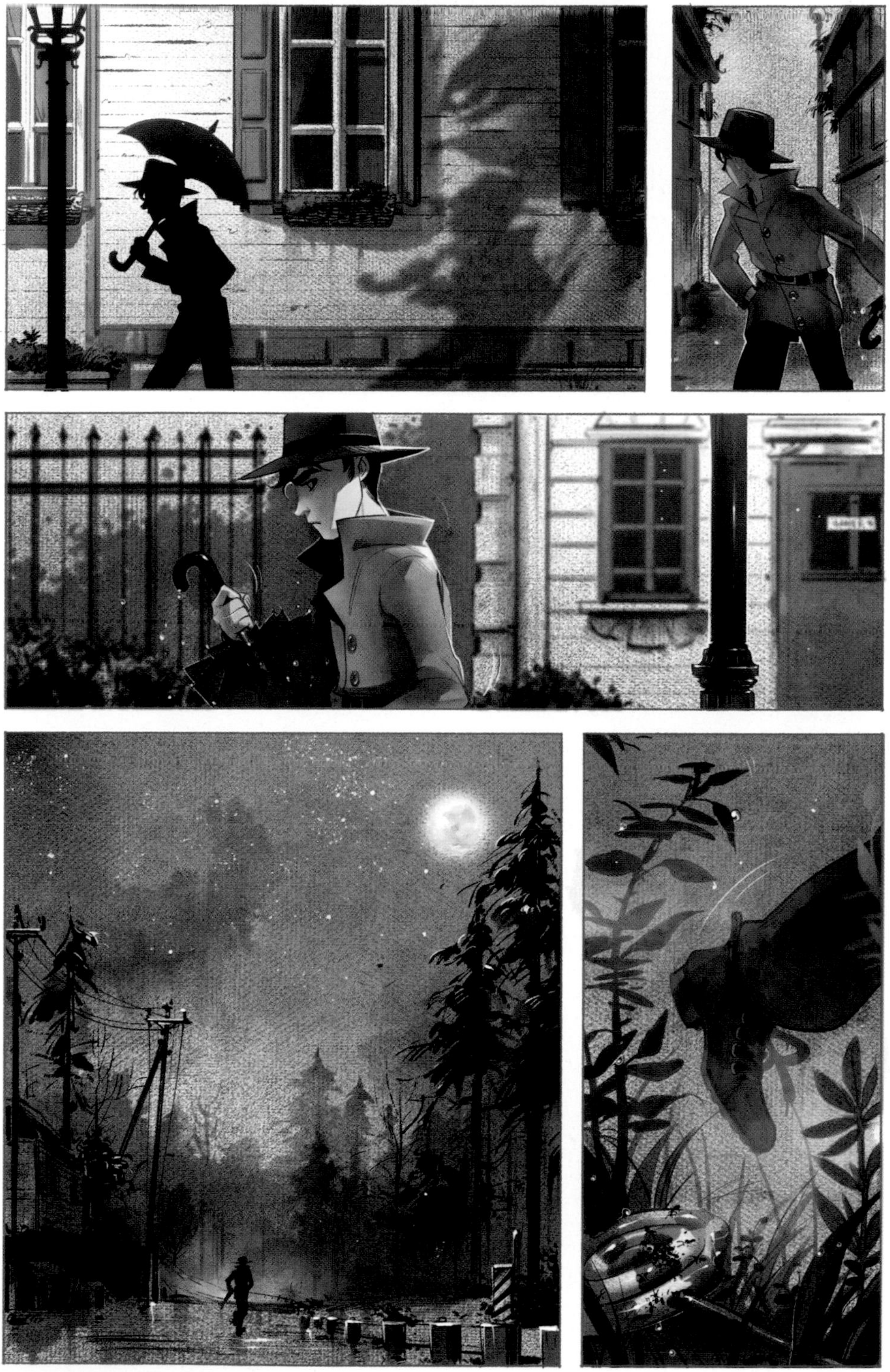

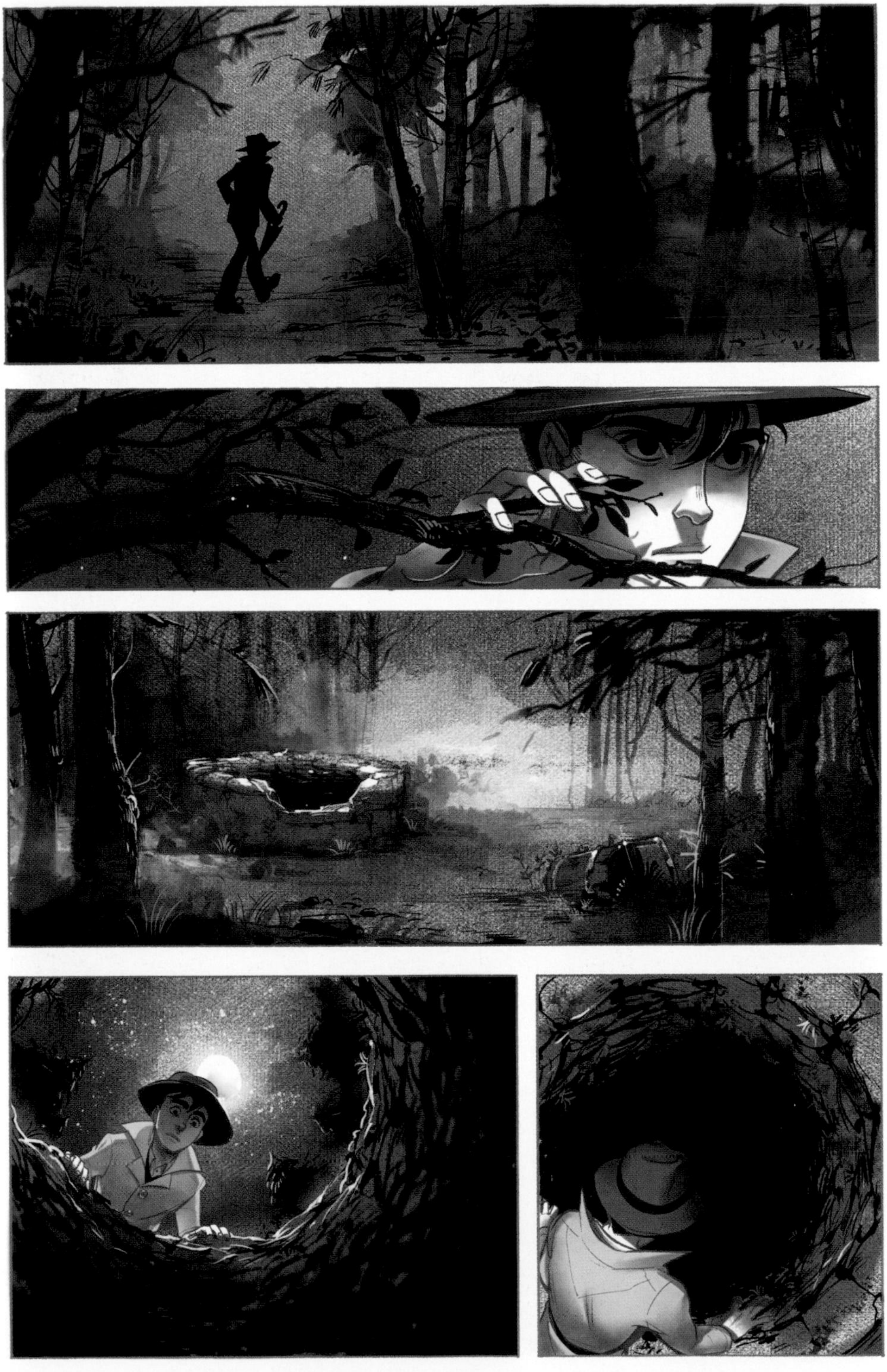

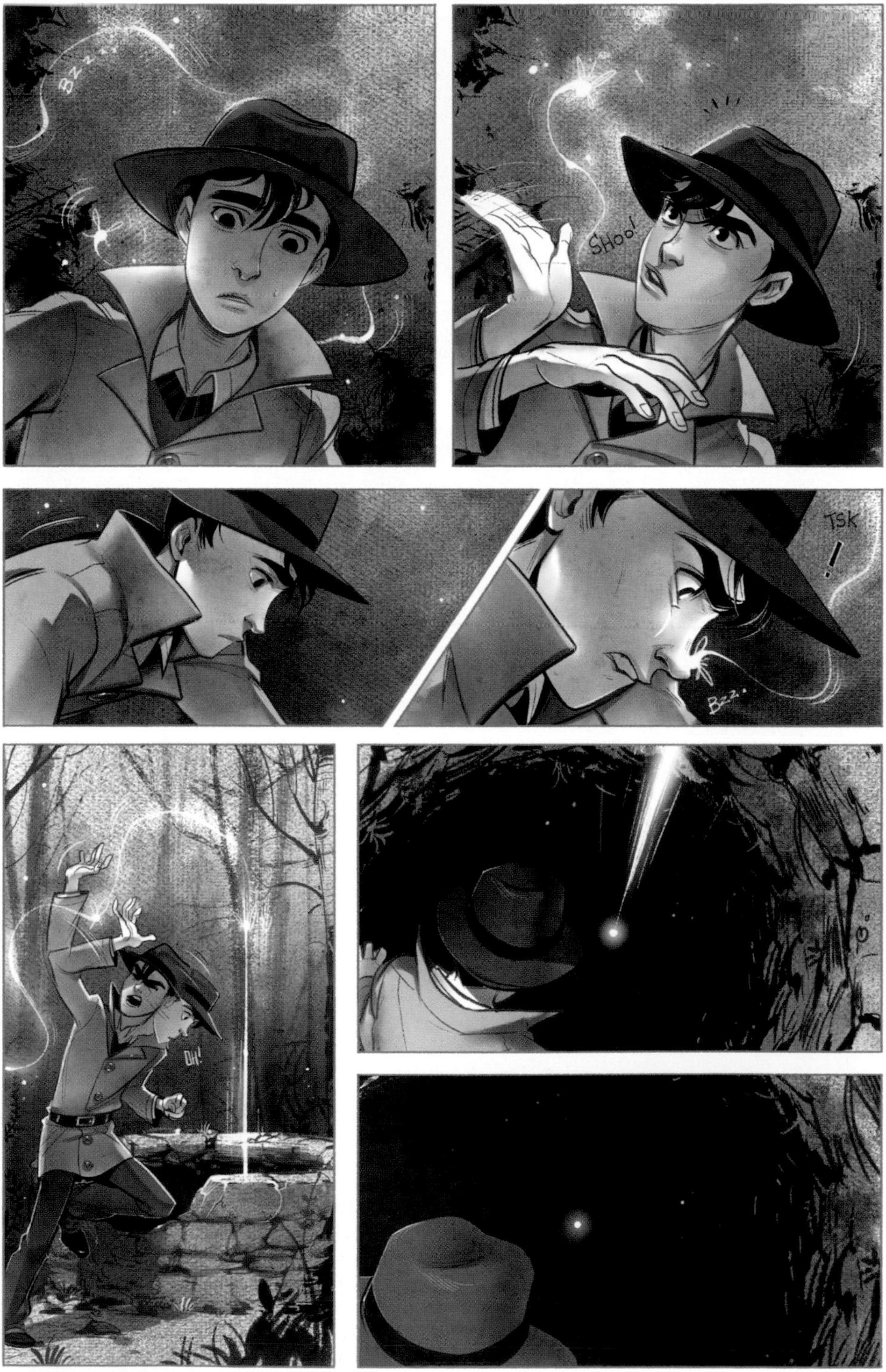
Bzzz
SHOO!
TSK
!
Bzz
OH!

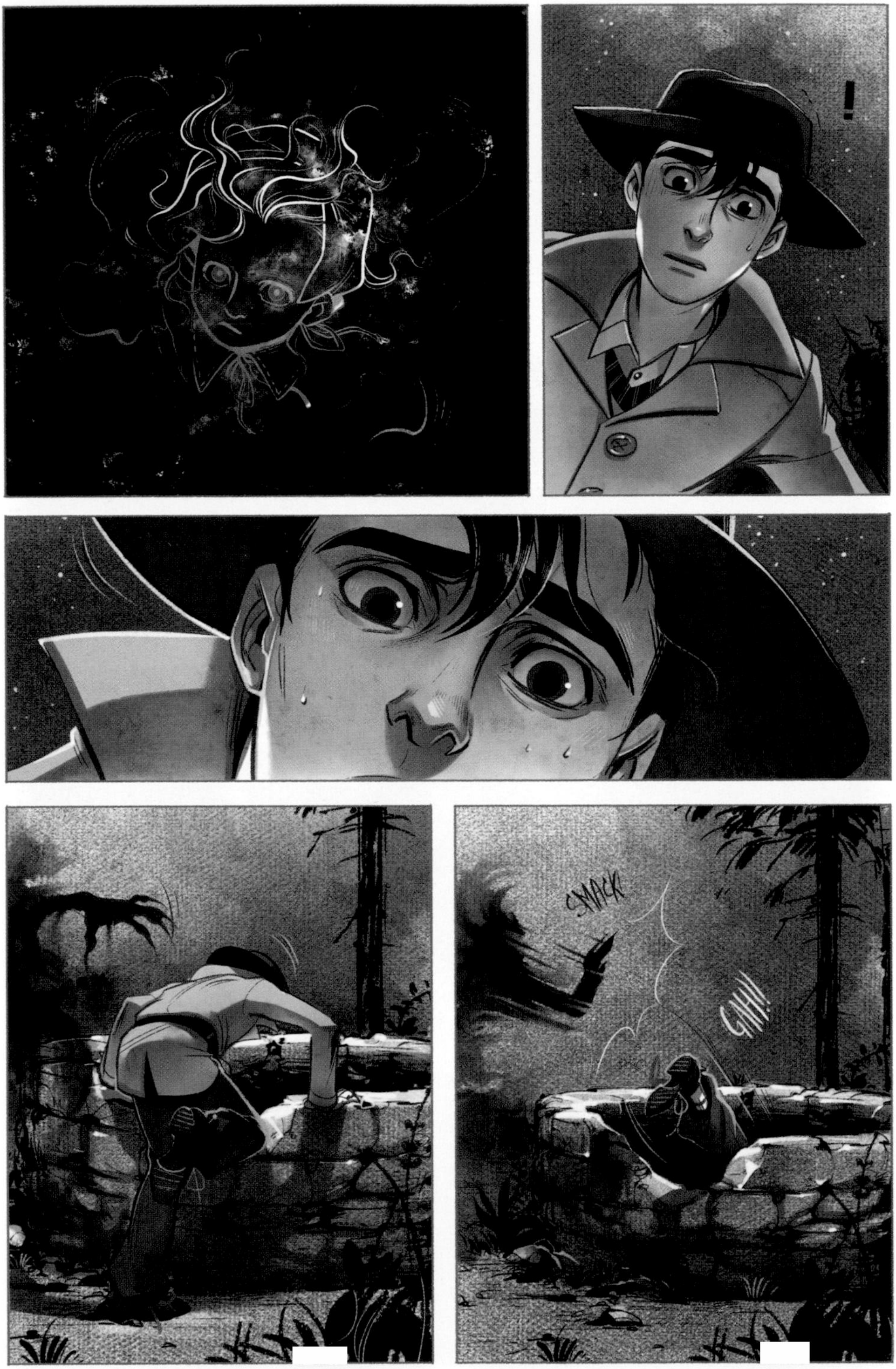
!
SMACK!
GAH!!

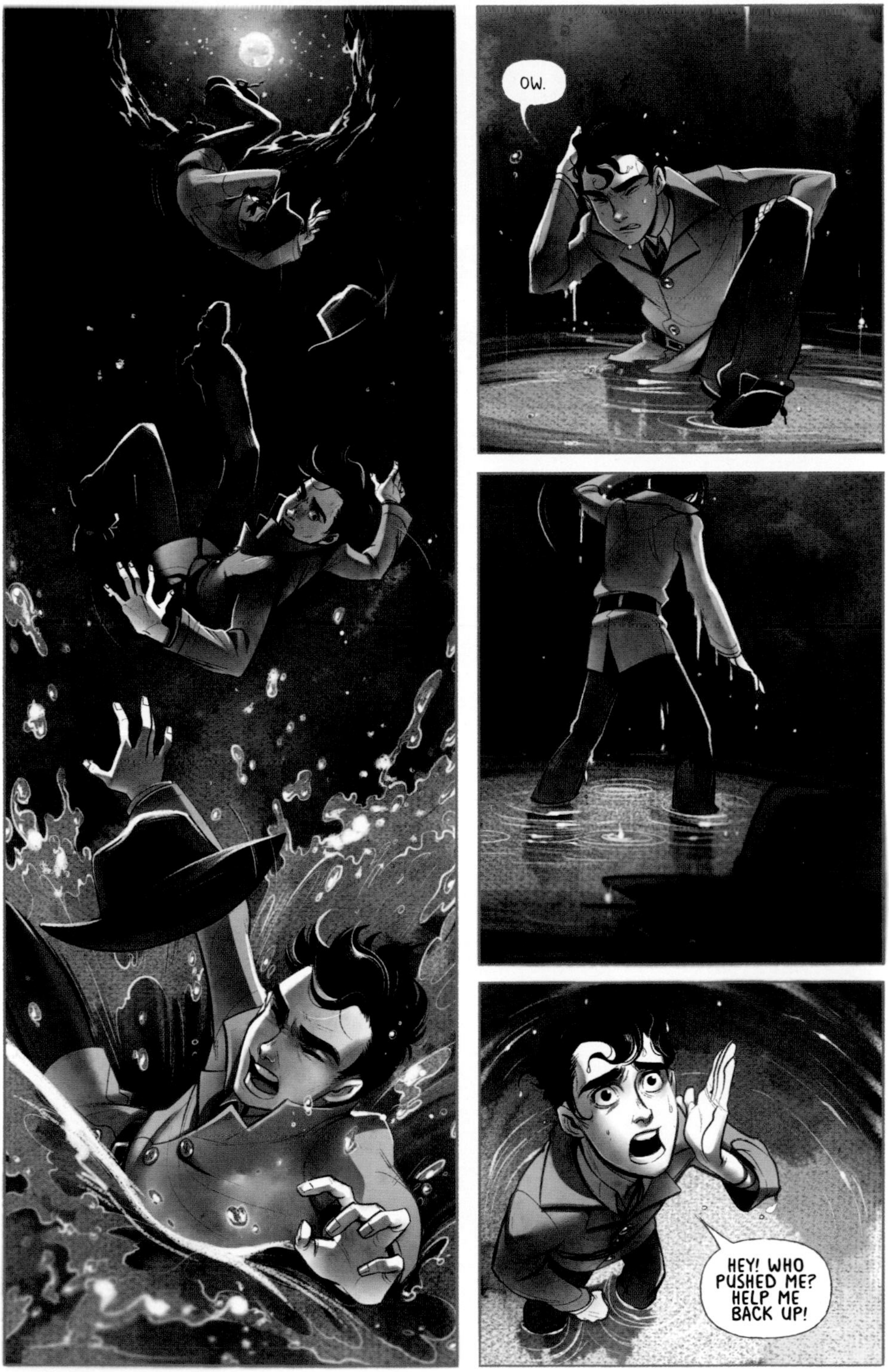
OW.
HEY! WHO PUSHED ME? HELP ME BACK UP!

...Silence...

BRRR

HELLO? IS ANYONE HERE? MY DAD IS THE SHERIFF OF BLACKWELL! SHOW YOURSELF!

SCRATCH

HELLO?

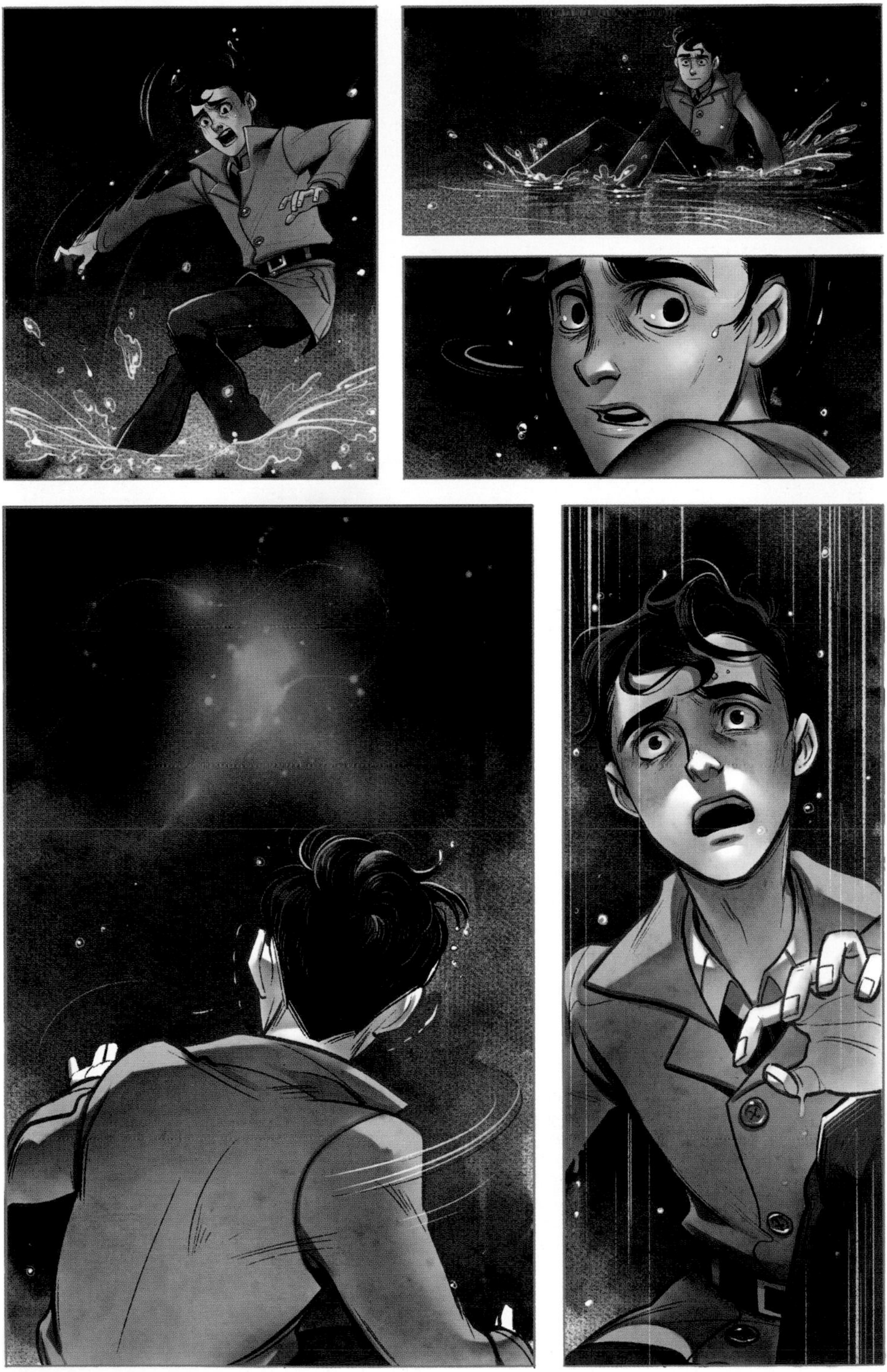

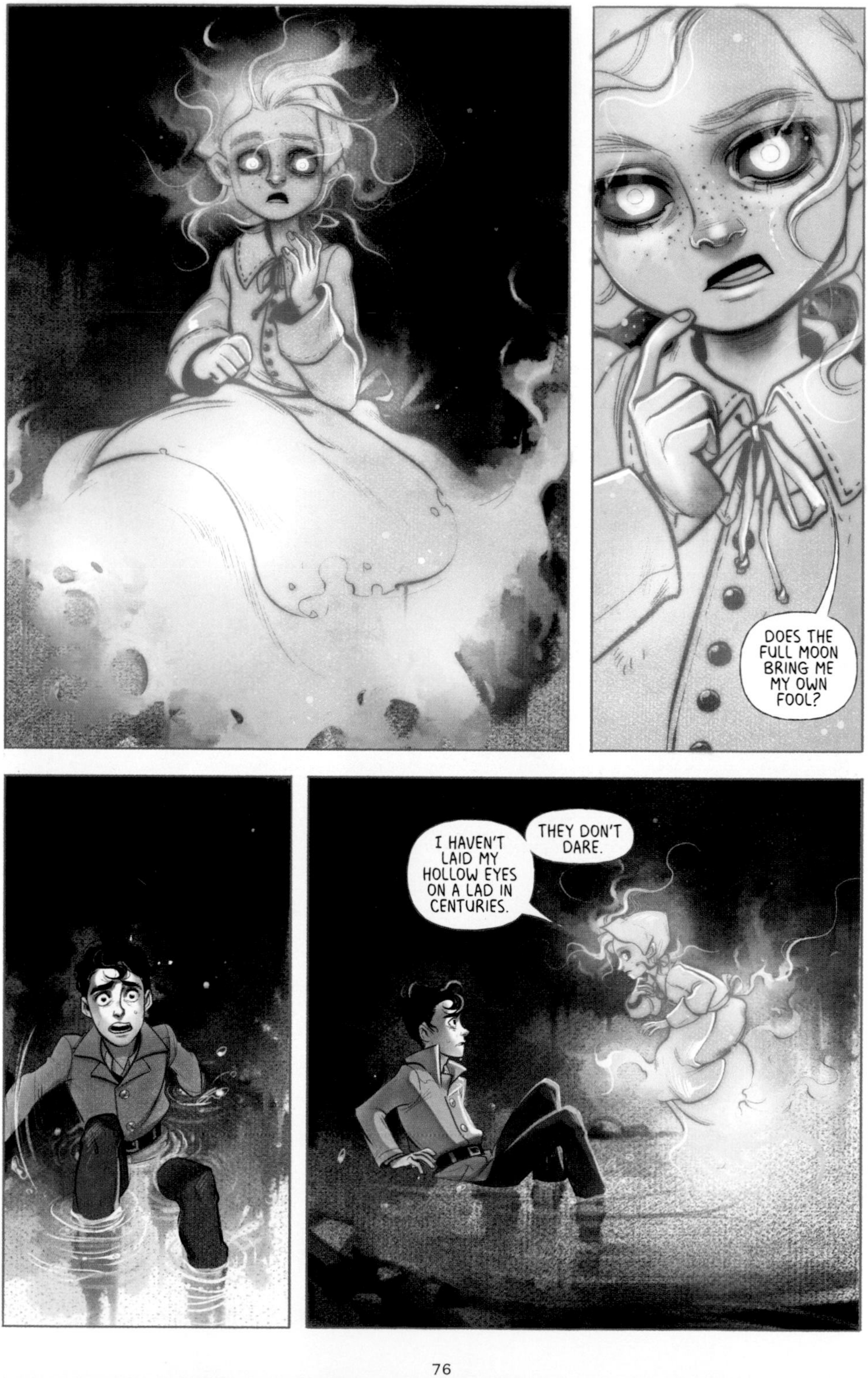
DOES THE FULL MOON BRING ME MY OWN FOOL?
I HAVEN'T LAID MY HOLLOW EYES ON A LAD IN CENTURIES.
THEY DON'T DARE.

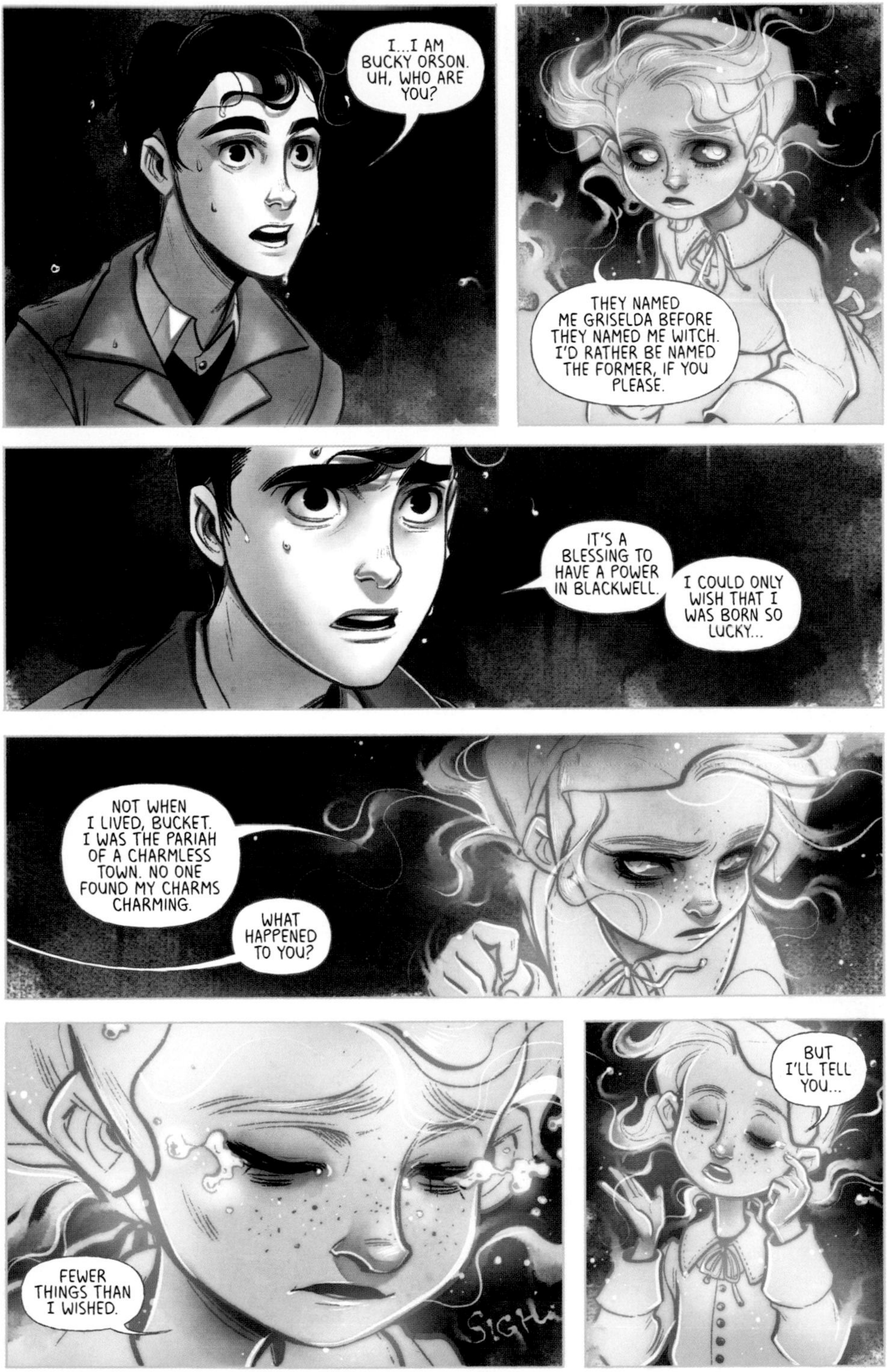
I...I AM BUCKY ORSON. UH, WHO ARE YOU?
THEY NAMED ME GRISELDA BEFORE THEY NAMED ME WITCH. I'D RATHER BE NAMED THE FORMER, IF YOU PLEASE.
IT'S A BLESSING TO HAVE A POWER IN BLACKWELL.
I COULD ONLY WISH THAT I WAS BORN SO LUCKY...
NOT WHEN I LIVED, BUCKET. I WAS THE PARIAH OF A CHARMLESS TOWN. NO ONE FOUND MY CHARMS CHARMING.
WHAT HAPPENED TO YOU?
FEWER THINGS THAN I WISHED.
SIGH
BUT I'LL TELL YOU...

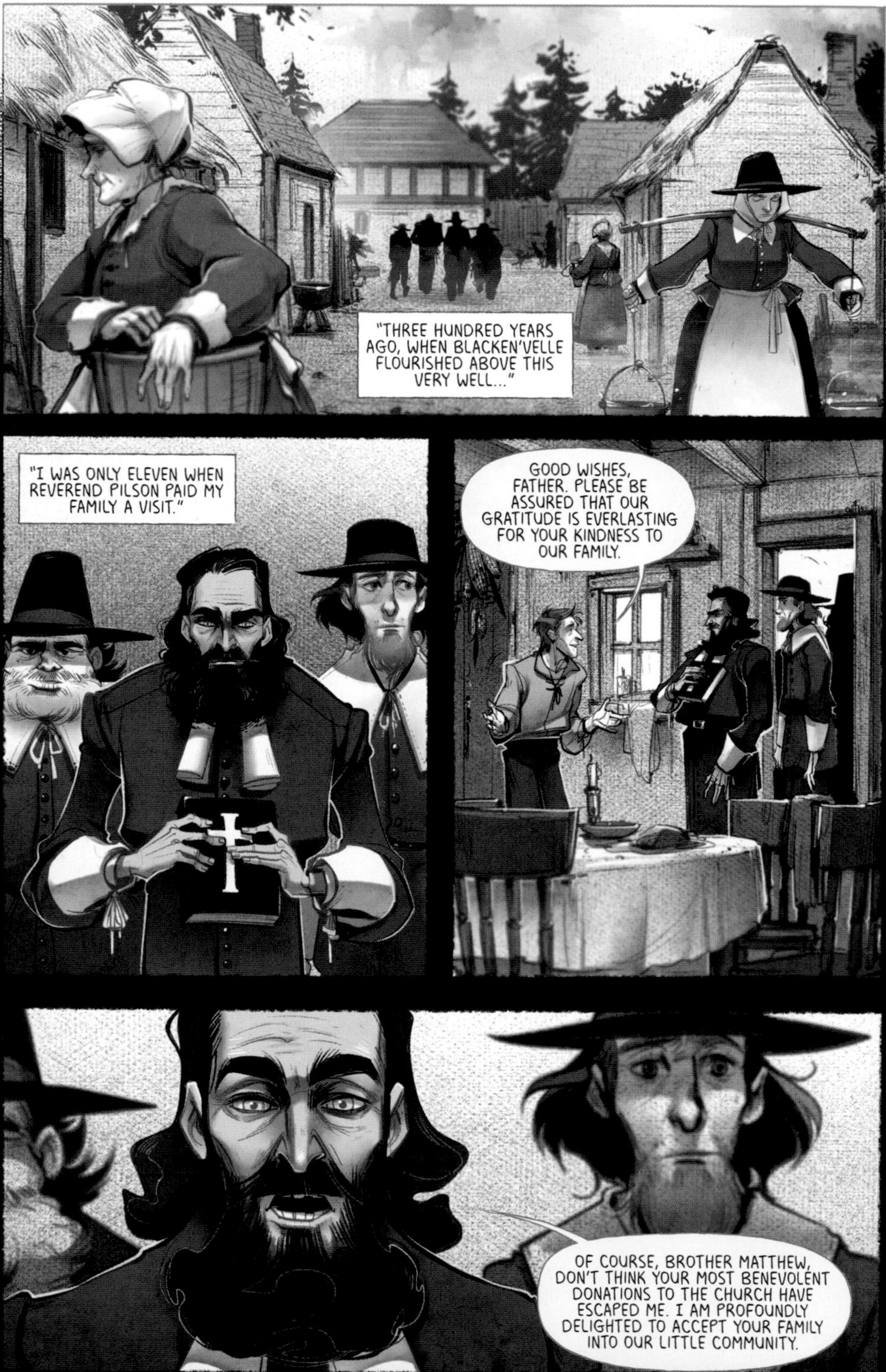
"THREE HUNDRED YEARS AGO, WHEN BLACKEN'VELLE FLOURISHED ABOVE THIS VERY WELL..."
"I WAS ONLY ELEVEN WHEN REVEREND PILSON PAID MY FAMILY A VISIT."
GOOD WISHES, FATHER. PLEASE BE ASSURED THAT OUR GRATITUDE IS EVERLASTING FOR YOUR KINDNESS TO OUR FAMILY.
OF COURSE, BROTHER MATTHEW, DON'T THINK YOUR MOST BENEVOLENT DONATIONS TO THE CHURCH HAVE ESCAPED ME. I AM PROFOUNDLY DELIGHTED TO ACCEPT YOUR FAMILY INTO OUR LITTLE COMMUNITY.

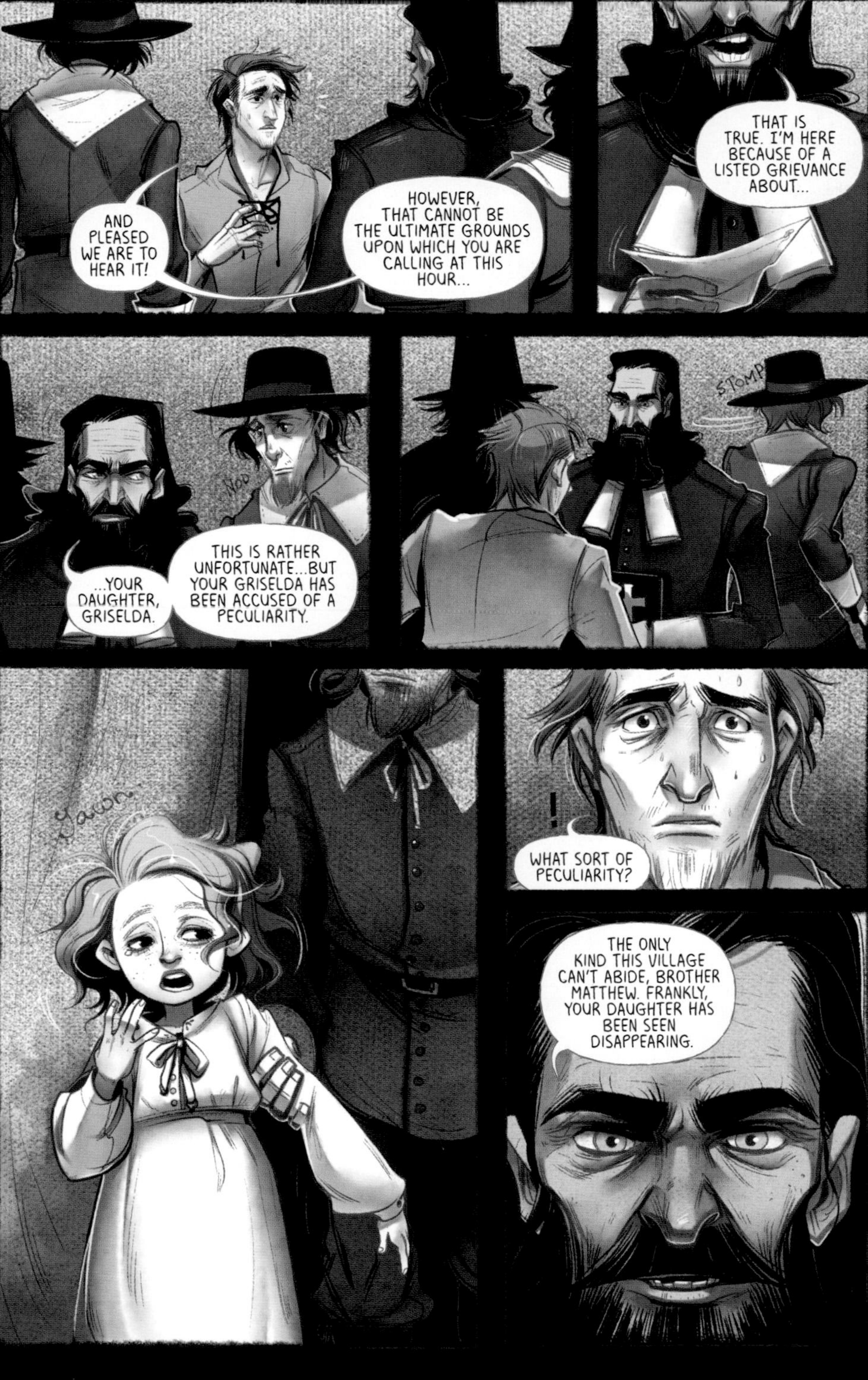
AND PLEASED WE ARE TO HEAR IT!
HOWEVER, THAT CANNOT BE THE ULTIMATE GROUNDS UPON WHICH YOU ARE CALLING AT THIS HOUR...
THAT IS TRUE. I'M HERE BECAUSE OF A LISTED GRIEVANCE ABOUT...
...YOUR DAUGHTER, GRISELDA.
NOD
THIS IS RATHER UNFORTUNATE...BUT YOUR GRISELDA HAS BEEN ACCUSED OF A PECULIARITY.
STOMP
!
WHAT SORT OF PECULIARITY?
THE ONLY KIND THIS VILLAGE CAN'T ABIDE, BROTHER MATTHEW. FRANKLY, YOUR DAUGHTER HAS BEEN SEEN DISAPPEARING.

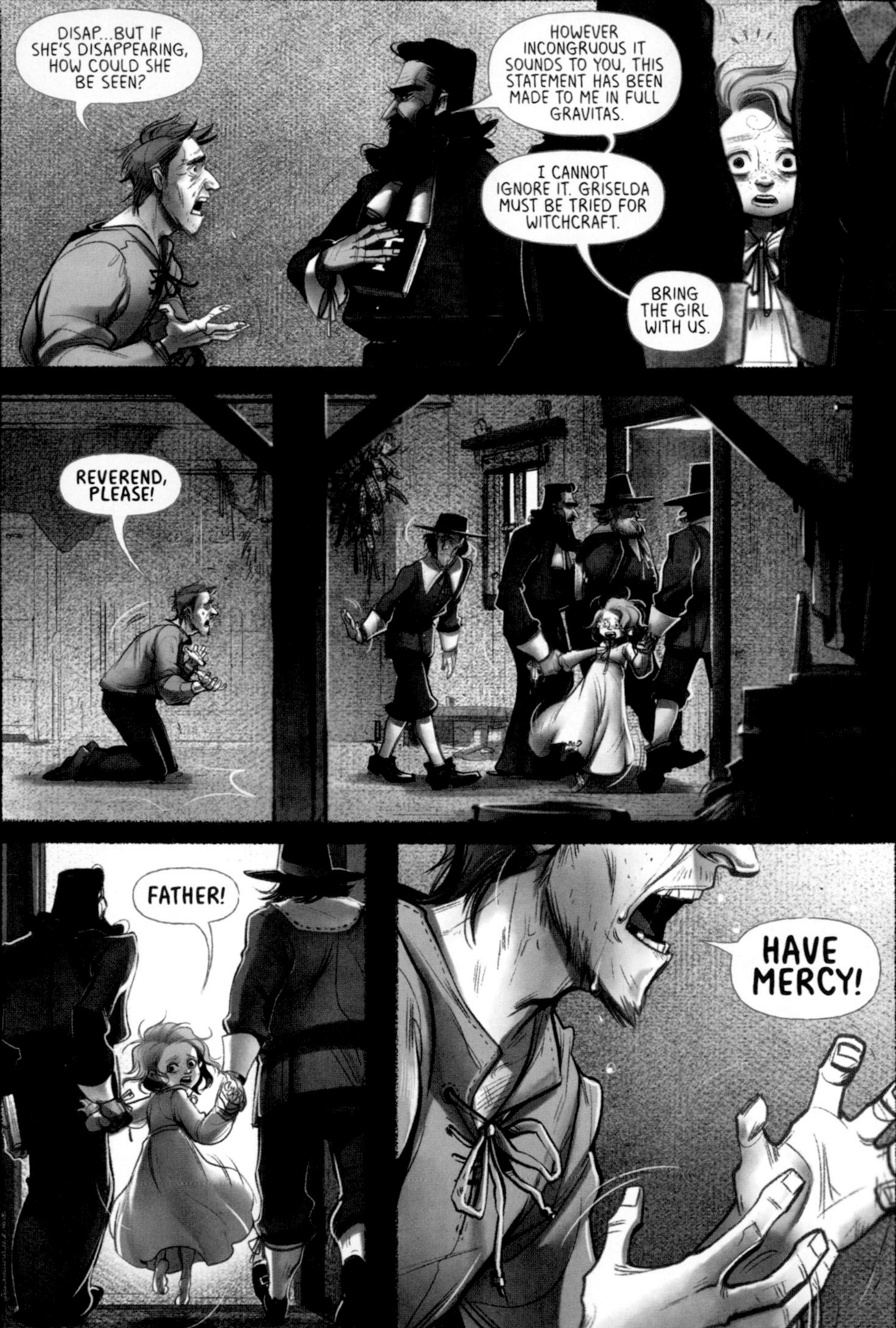
DISAP...BUT IF SHE'S DISAPPEARING, HOW COULD SHE BE SEEN?
HOWEVER INCONGRUOUS IT SOUNDS TO YOU, THIS STATEMENT HAS BEEN MADE TO ME IN FULL GRAVITAS.
I CANNOT IGNORE IT. GRISELDA MUST BE TRIED FOR WITCHCRAFT.
BRING THE GIRL WITH US.
REVEREND, PLEASE!
FATHER!
HAVE MERCY!

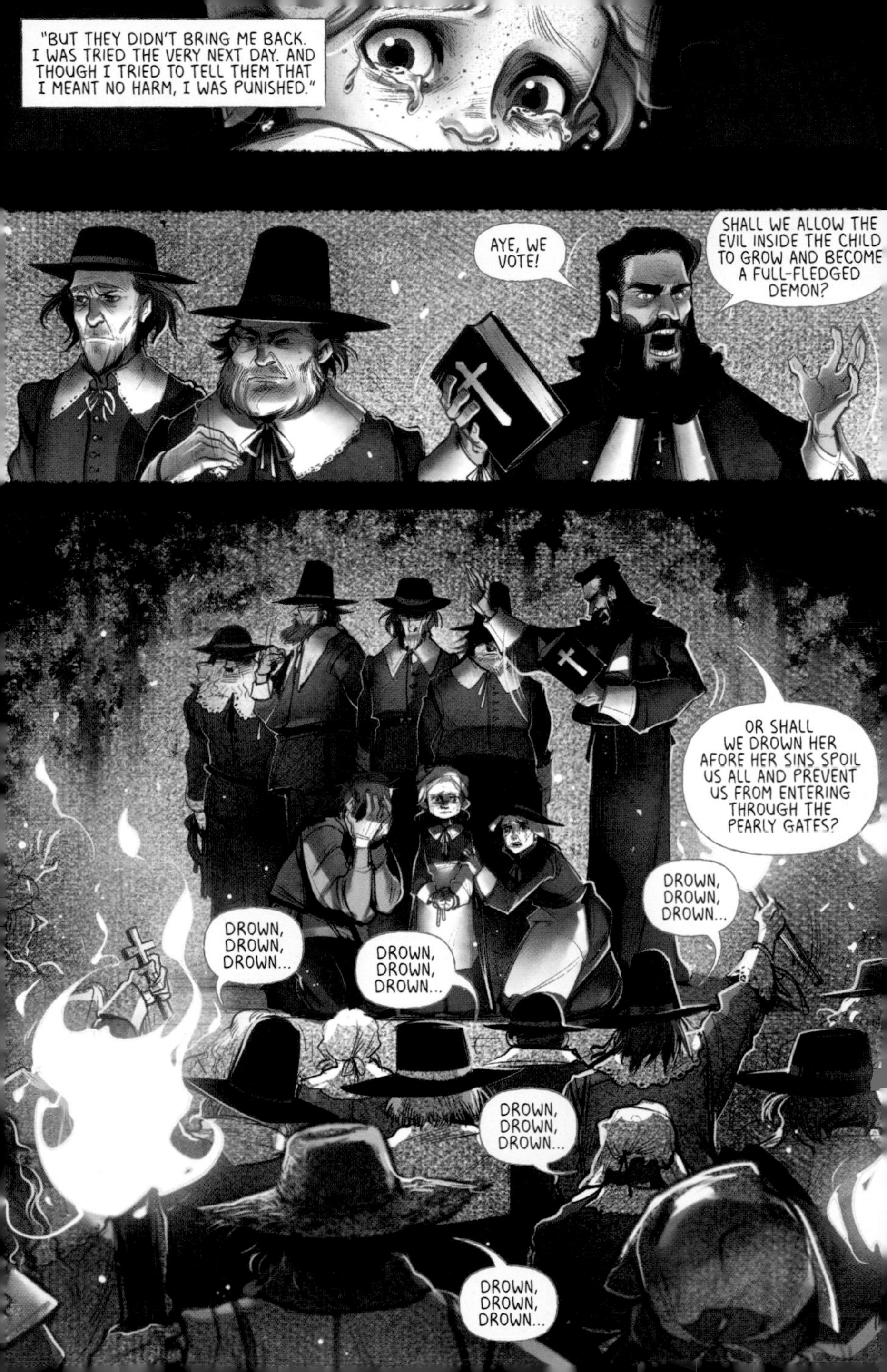
"BUT THEY DIDN'T BRING ME BACK. I WAS TRIED THE VERY NEXT DAY. AND THOUGH I TRIED TO TELL THEM THAT I MEANT NO HARM, I WAS PUNISHED."
SHALL WE ALLOW THE EVIL INSIDE THE CHILD TO GROW AND BECOME A FULL-FLEDGED DEMON?
AYE, WE VOTE!
OR SHALL WE DROWN HER AFORE HER SINS SPOIL US ALL AND PREVENT US FROM ENTERING THROUGH THE PEARLY GATES?
DROWN, DROWN, DROWN...
DROWN, DROWN, DROWN...
DROWN, DROWN, DROWN...
DROWN, DROWN, DROWN...
DROWN, DROWN, DROWN...

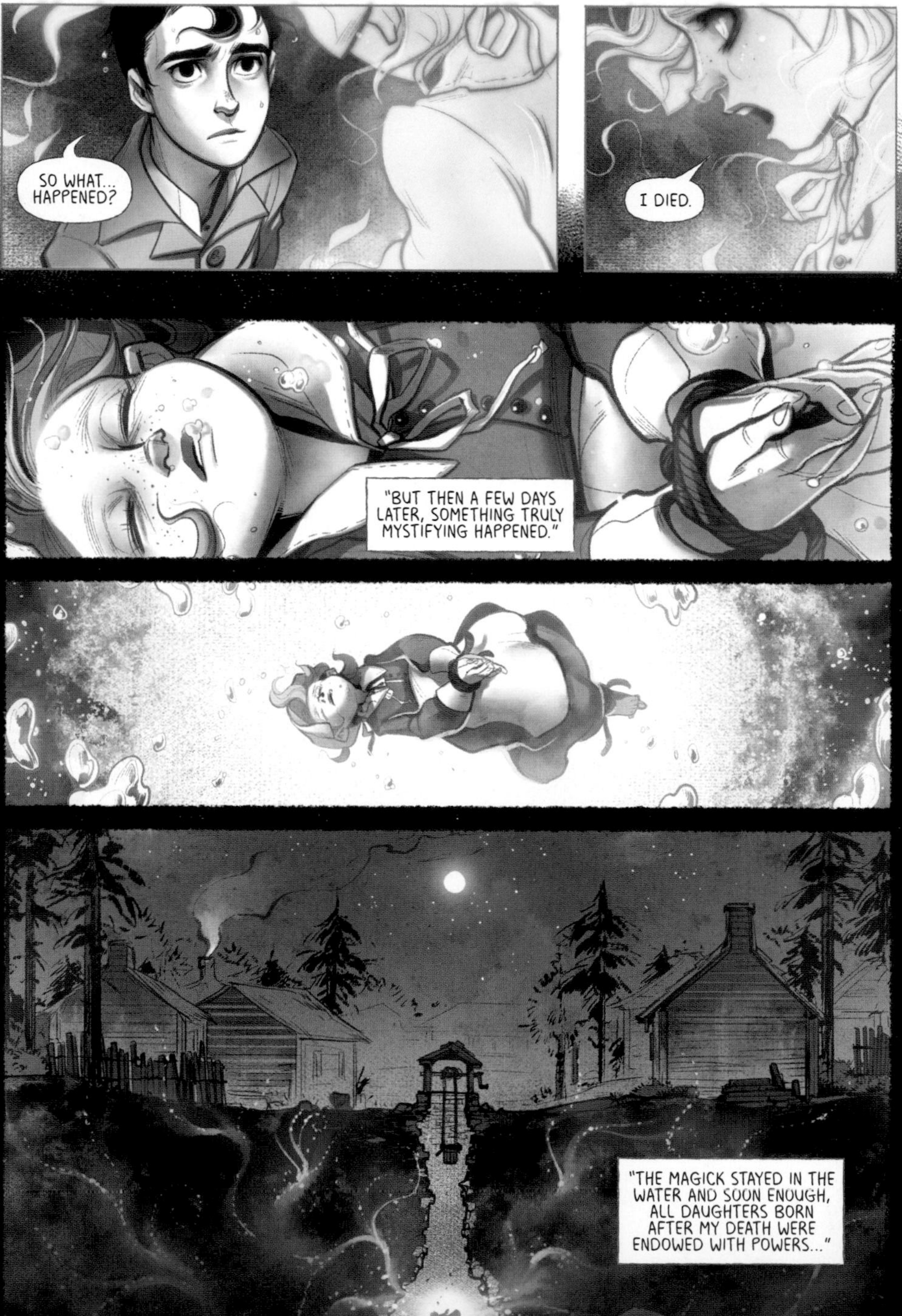
SO WHAT...
HAPPENED?
I DIED.
"BUT THEN A FEW DAYS LATER, SOMETHING TRULY MYSTIFYING HAPPENED."
"THE MAGICK STAYED IN THE WATER AND SOON ENOUGH, ALL DAUGHTERS BORN AFTER MY DEATH WERE ENDOWED WITH POWERS..."

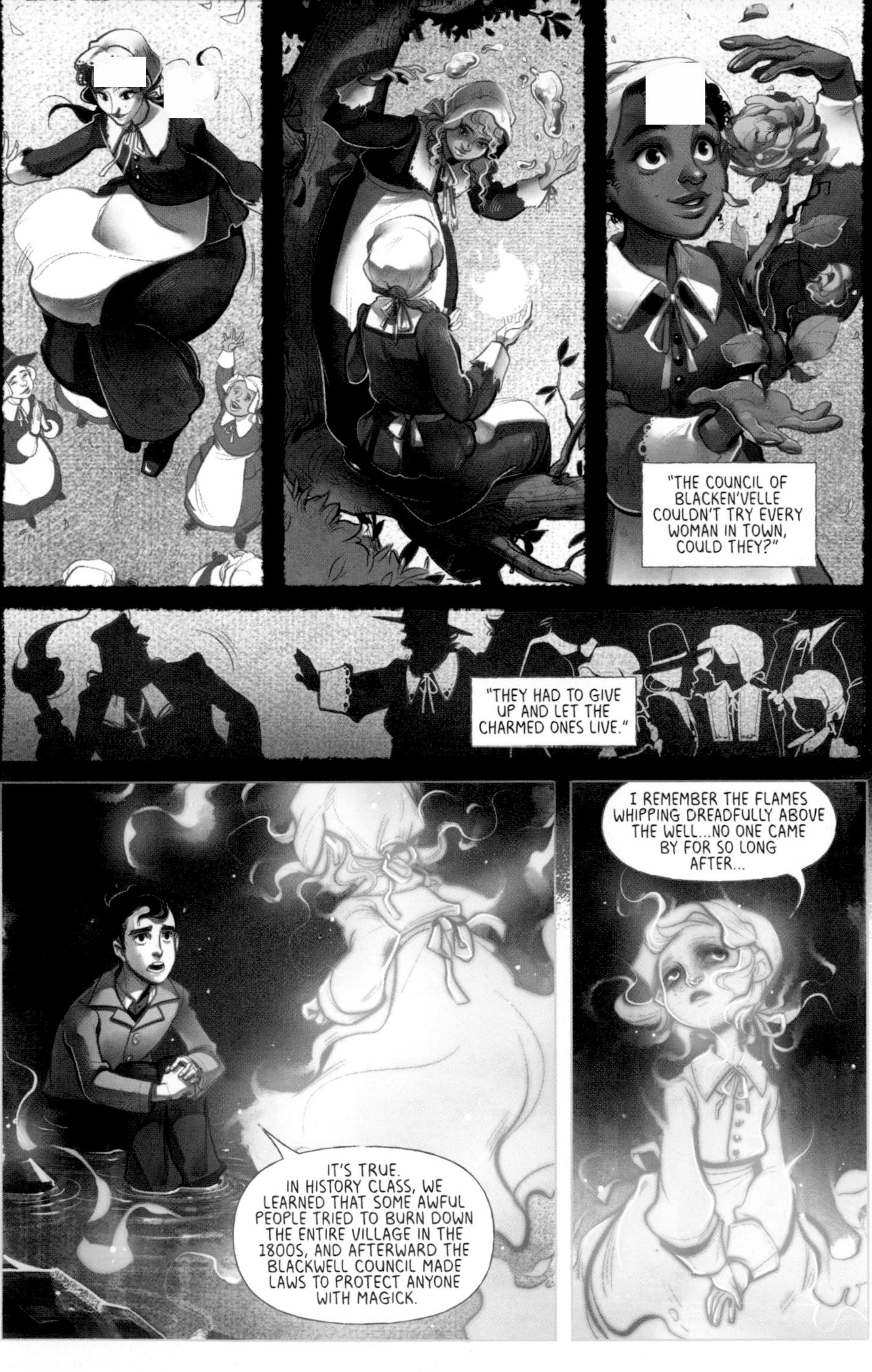
"THE COUNCIL OF BLACKEN'VELLE COULDN'T TRY EVERY WOMAN IN TOWN, COULD THEY?"
"THEY HAD TO GIVE UP AND LET THE CHARMED ONES LIVE."
IT'S TRUE. IN HISTORY CLASS, WE LEARNED THAT SOME AWFUL PEOPLE TRIED TO BURN DOWN THE ENTIRE VILLAGE IN THE 1800S, AND AFTERWARD THE BLACKWELL COUNCIL MADE LAWS TO PROTECT ANYONE WITH MAGICK.
I REMEMBER THE FLAMES WHIPPING DREADFULLY ABOVE THE WELL...NO ONE CAME BY FOR SO LONG AFTER...

I'M SORRY THAT YOU WERE ALONE, GRISELDA.

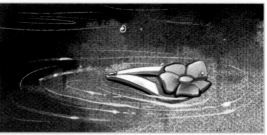

THAT'S HEIDI'S HAIRCLIP!

YOU KNOW OF HEIDI ORSON?

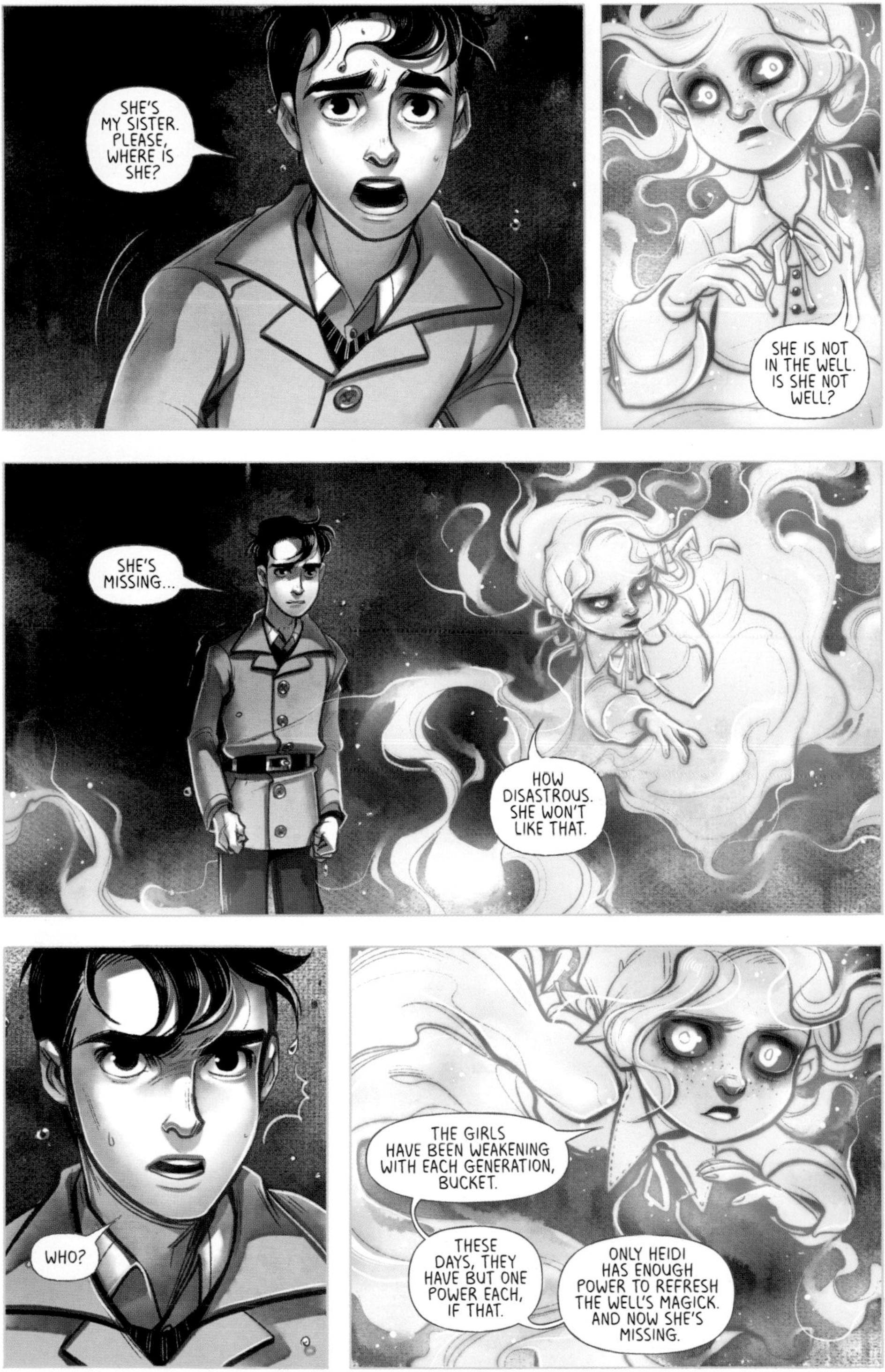
SHE'S MY SISTER. PLEASE, WHERE IS SHE?
SHE IS NOT IN THE WELL. IS SHE NOT WELL?
SHE'S MISSING...
HOW DISASTROUS. SHE WON'T LIKE THAT.
WHO?
THE GIRLS HAVE BEEN WEAKENING WITH EACH GENERATION, BUCKET.
THESE DAYS, THEY HAVE BUT ONE POWER EACH, IF THAT.
ONLY HEIDI HAS ENOUGH POWER TO REFRESH THE WELL'S MAGICK. AND NOW SHE'S MISSING.

WHO BROUGHT HER HERE? SOMEONE FROM THE COVEN OF CROWS?

I'M SPEAKING OF THE INVENTIVE ONE. MEGARA CANSI.

DESPERATE FOR A POWER SWELL, THAT ONE.

OUR BABYSITTER?

STOP HER? I THOUGHT YOU SAID YOU RESPECTED POWER.

I MUST STOP HER!

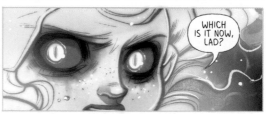

WHICH IS IT NOW, LAD?

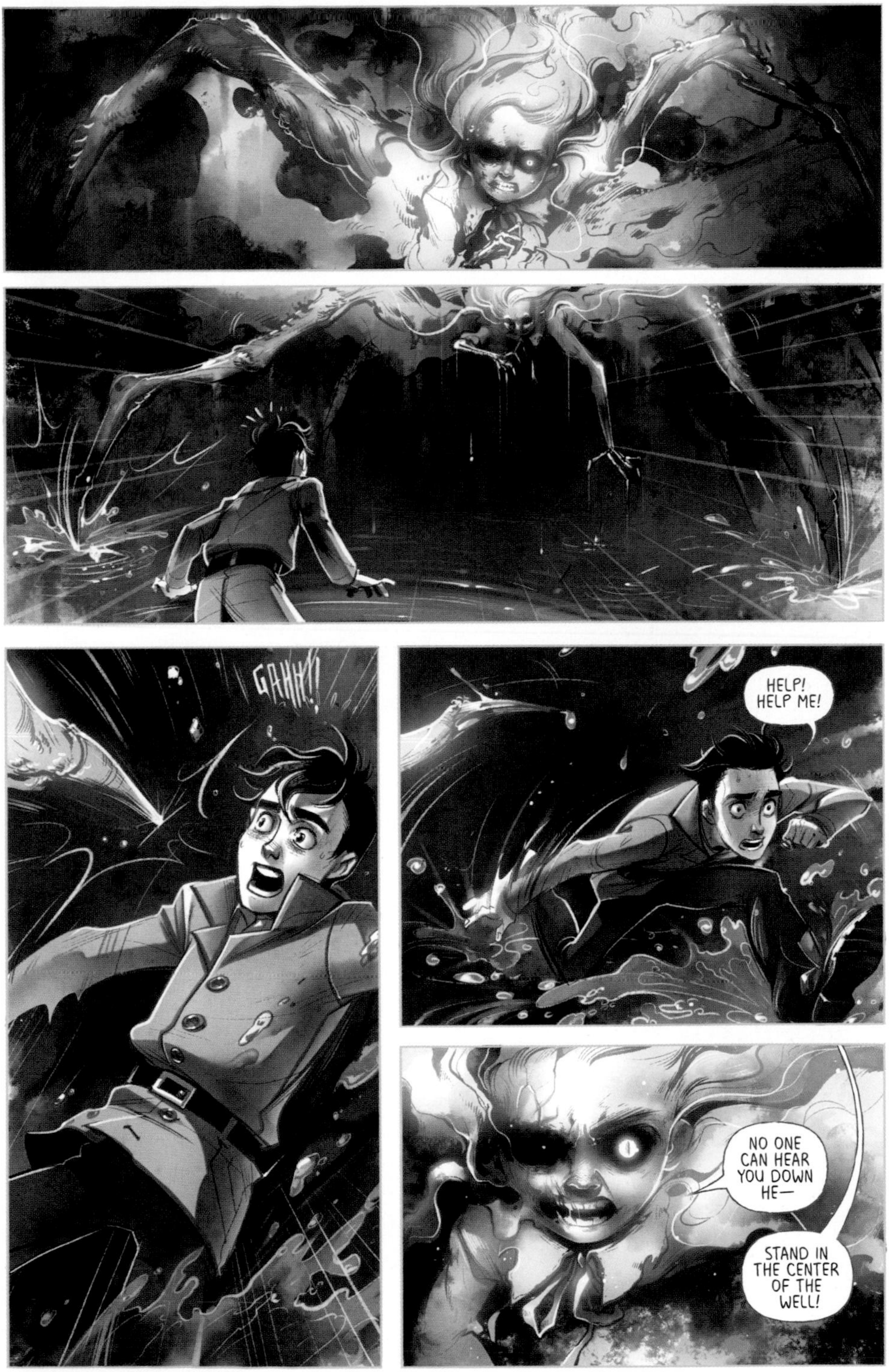
GAHH!!
HELP! HELP ME!
NO ONE CAN HEAR YOU DOWN HE—
STAND IN THE CENTER OF THE WELL!

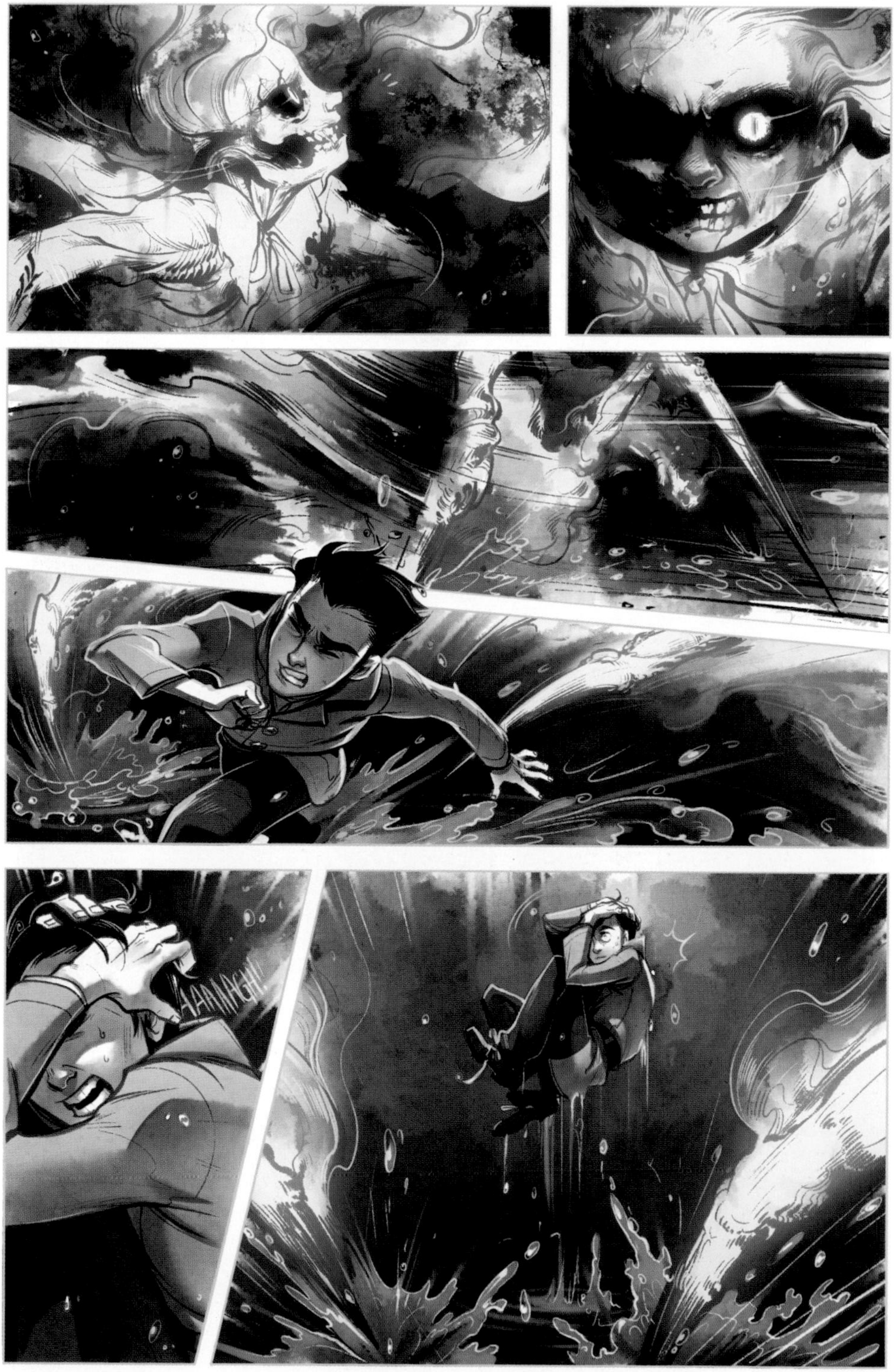
AAAHHGH!

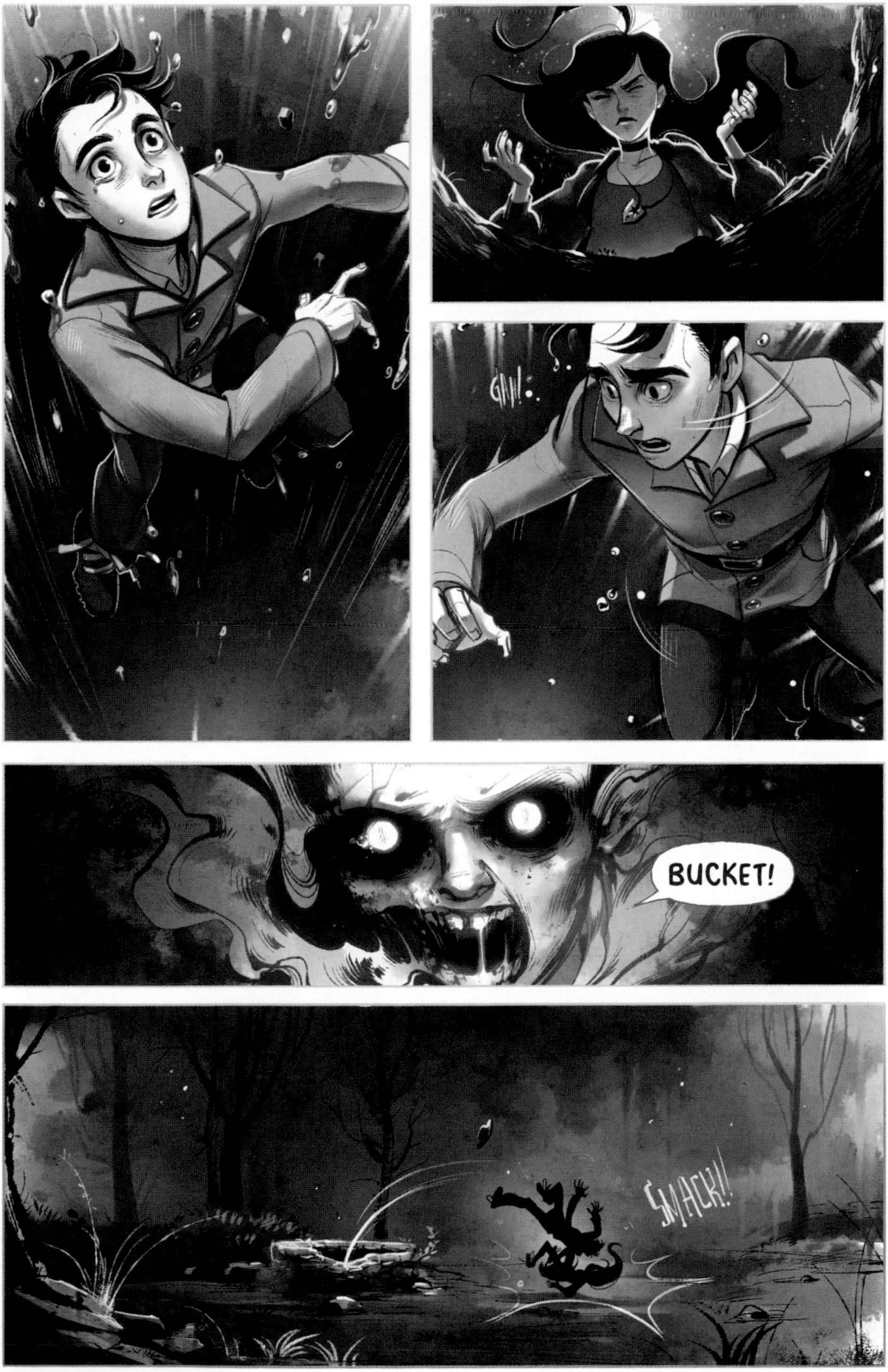
GAH!
BUCKET!
SMACK!!

CHAPTER 5

GOOSEBERRY STREET

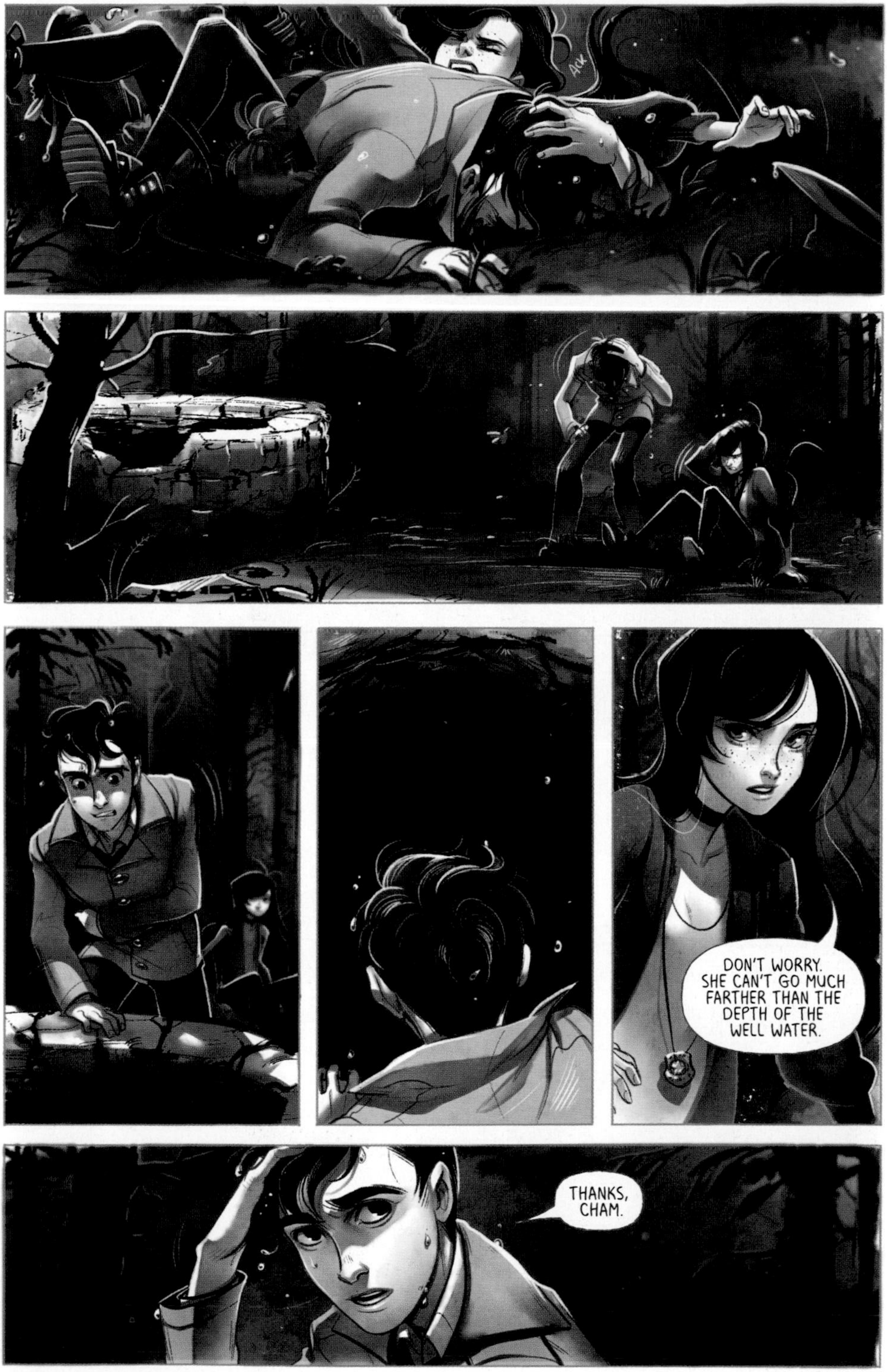
ACK
DON'T WORRY. SHE CAN'T GO MUCH FARTHER THAN THE DEPTH OF THE WELL WATER.
THANKS, CHAM.

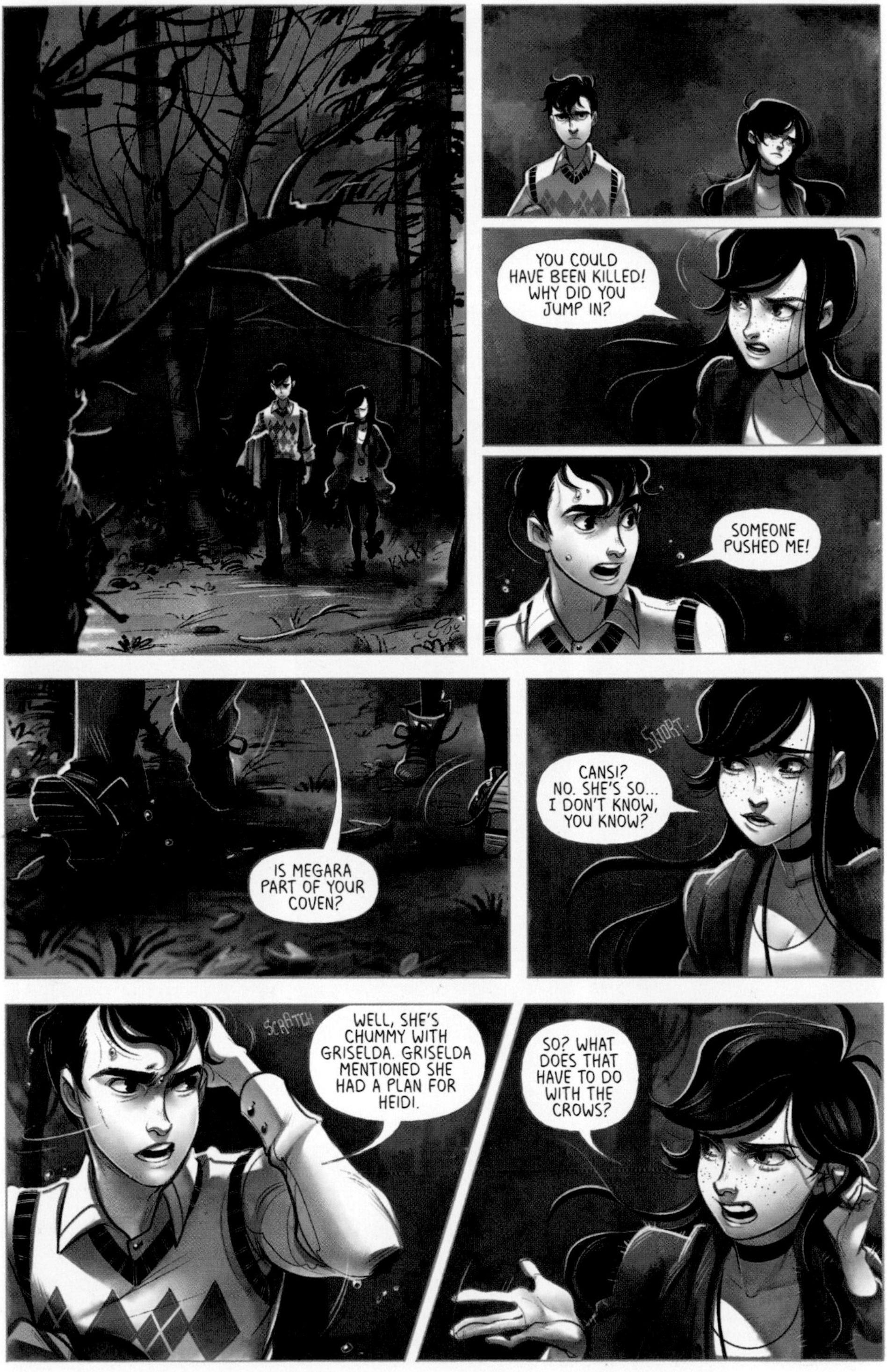
KICK
YOU COULD HAVE BEEN KILLED! WHY DID YOU JUMP IN?
SOMEONE PUSHED ME!
IS MEGARA PART OF YOUR COVEN?
SNORT.
CANSI? NO. SHE'S SO... I DON'T KNOW, YOU KNOW?
SCRATCH
WELL, SHE'S CHUMMY WITH GRISELDA. GRISELDA MENTIONED SHE HAD A PLAN FOR HEIDI.
SO? WHAT DOES THAT HAVE TO DO WITH THE CROWS?

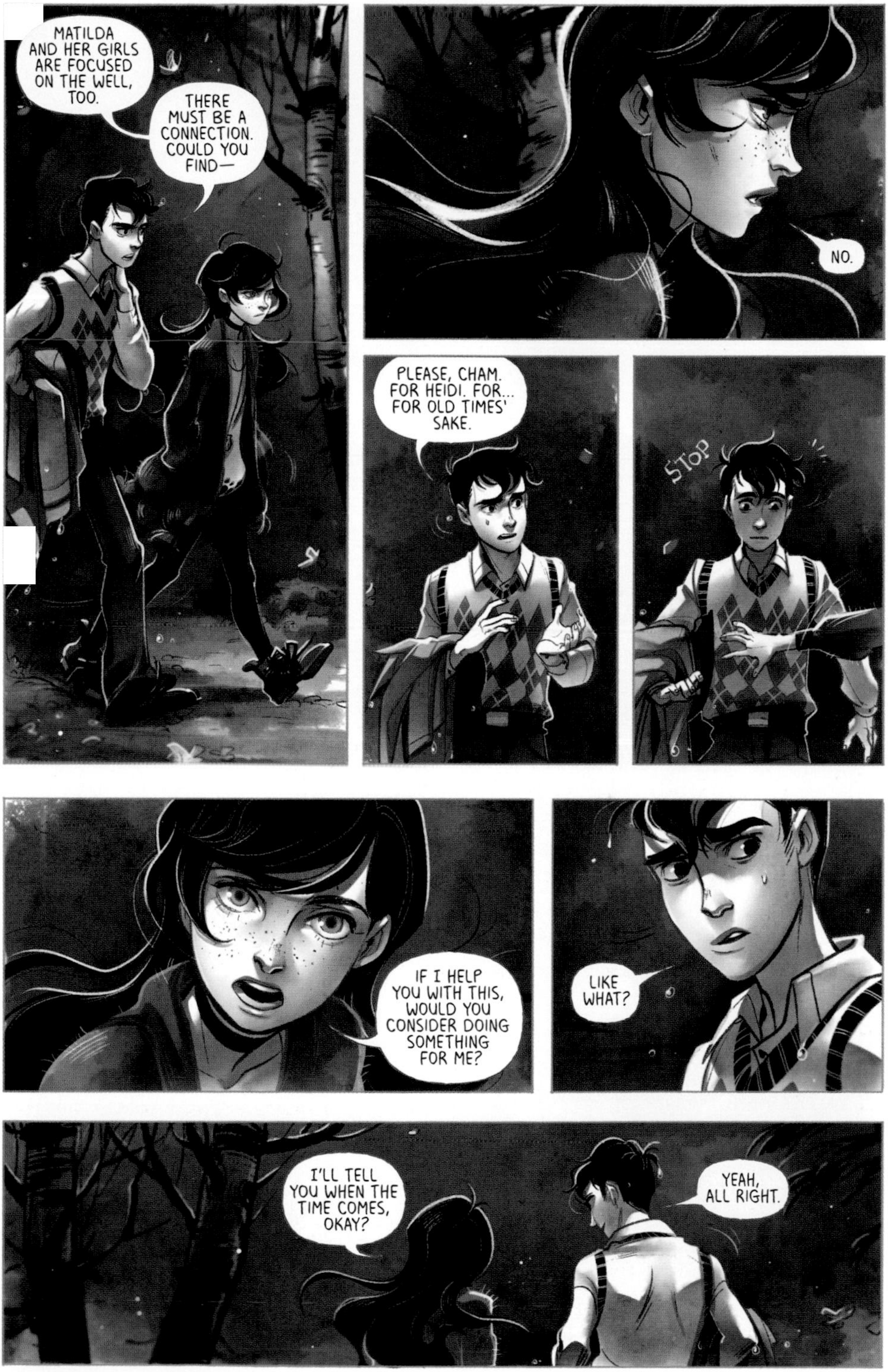
MATILDA AND HER GIRLS ARE FOCUSED ON THE WELL, TOO.
THERE MUST BE A CONNECTION. COULD YOU FIND—
NO.
PLEASE, CHAM. FOR HEIDI. FOR... FOR OLD TIMES' SAKE.
STOP
IF I HELP YOU WITH THIS, WOULD YOU CONSIDER DOING SOMETHING FOR ME?
LIKE WHAT?
I'LL TELL YOU WHEN THE TIME COMES, OKAY?
YEAH, ALL RIGHT.

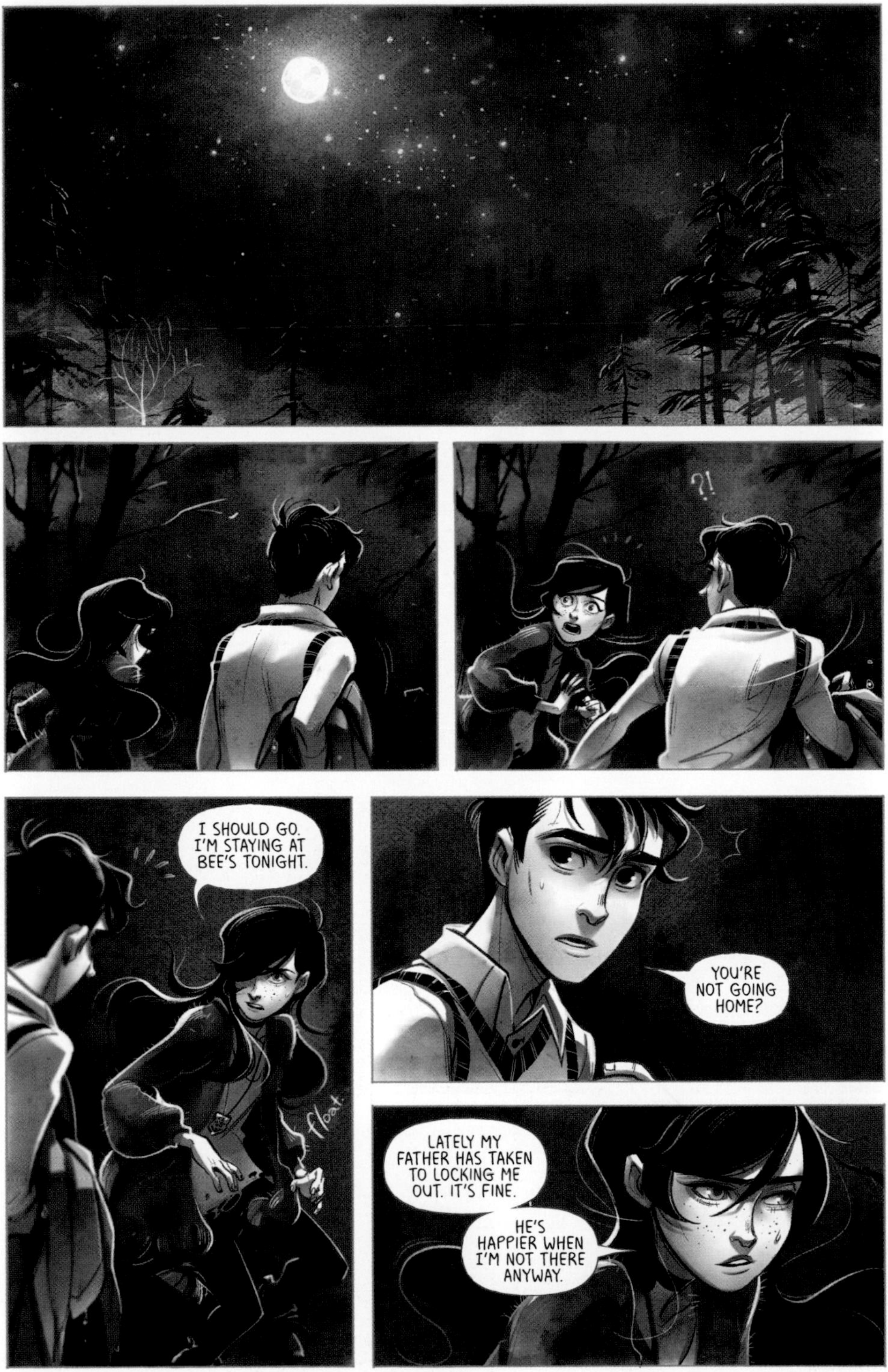
?!
I SHOULD GO. I'M STAYING AT BEE'S TONIGHT.
float
YOU'RE NOT GOING HOME?
LATELY MY FATHER HAS TAKEN TO LOCKING ME OUT. IT'S FINE.
HE'S HAPPIER WHEN I'M NOT THERE ANYWAY.

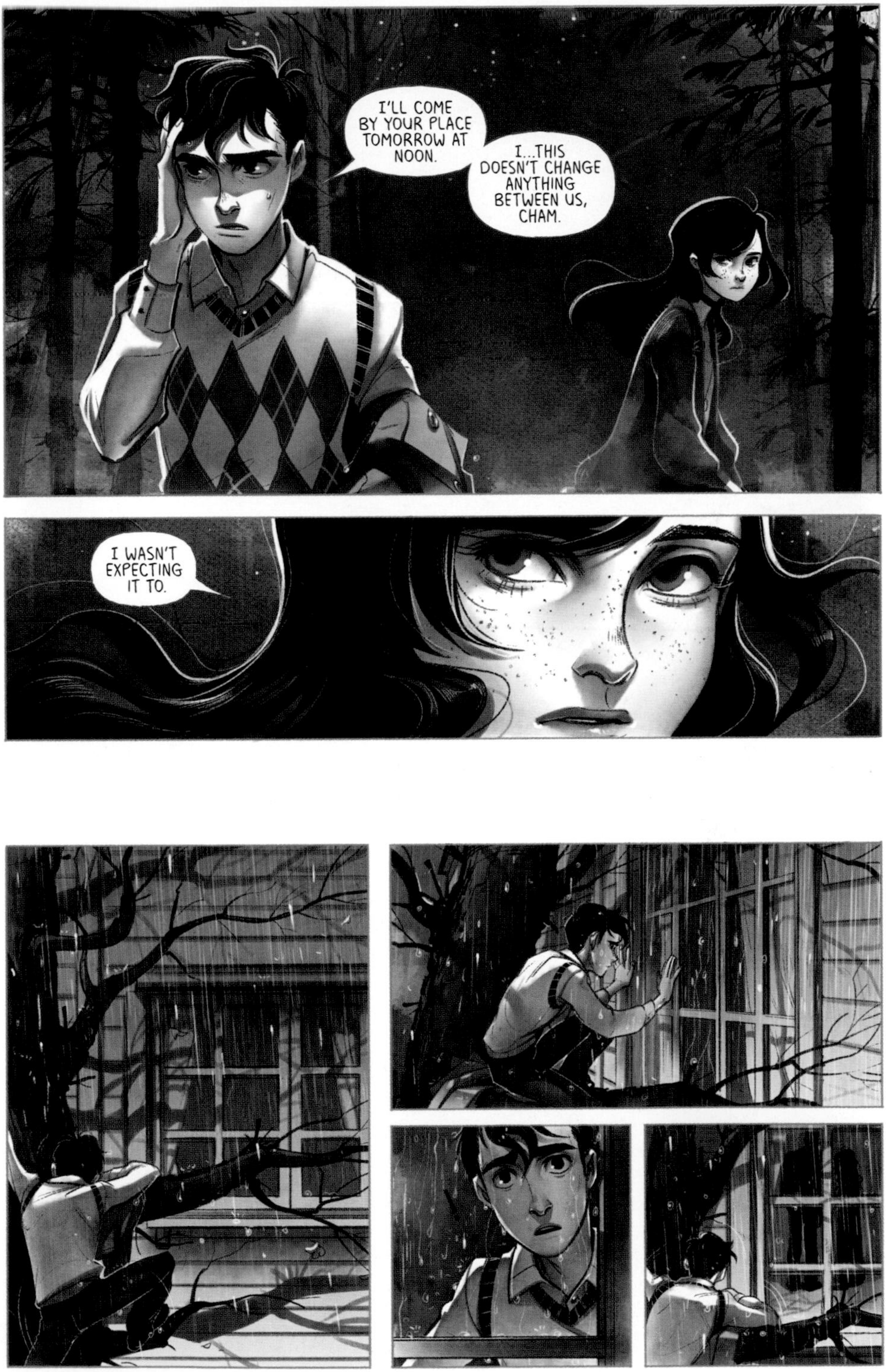

I'LL COME BY YOUR PLACE TOMORROW AT NOON.
I...THIS DOESN'T CHANGE ANYTHING BETWEEN US, CHAM.
I WASN'T EXPECTING IT TO.

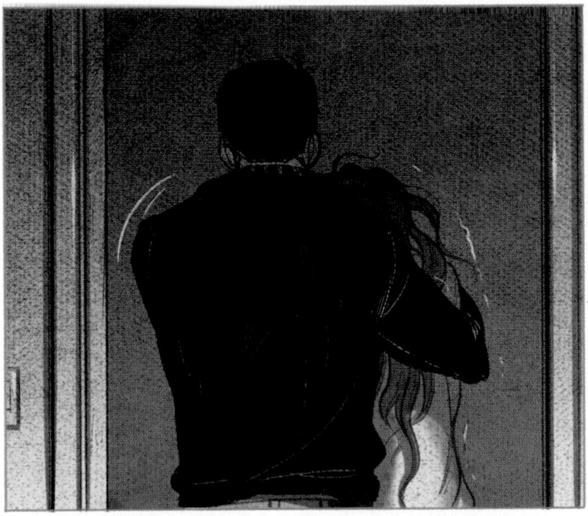

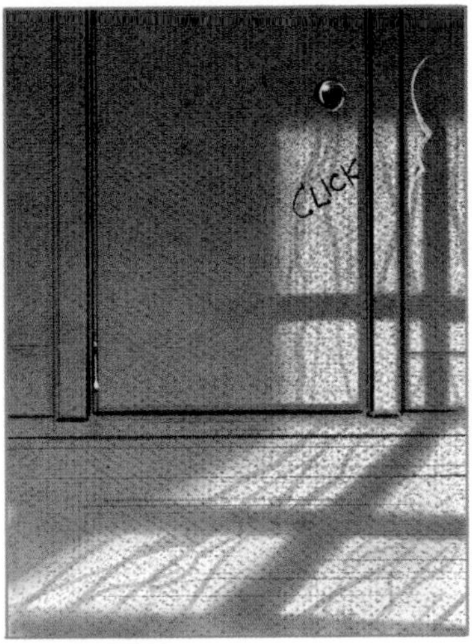
CLICK

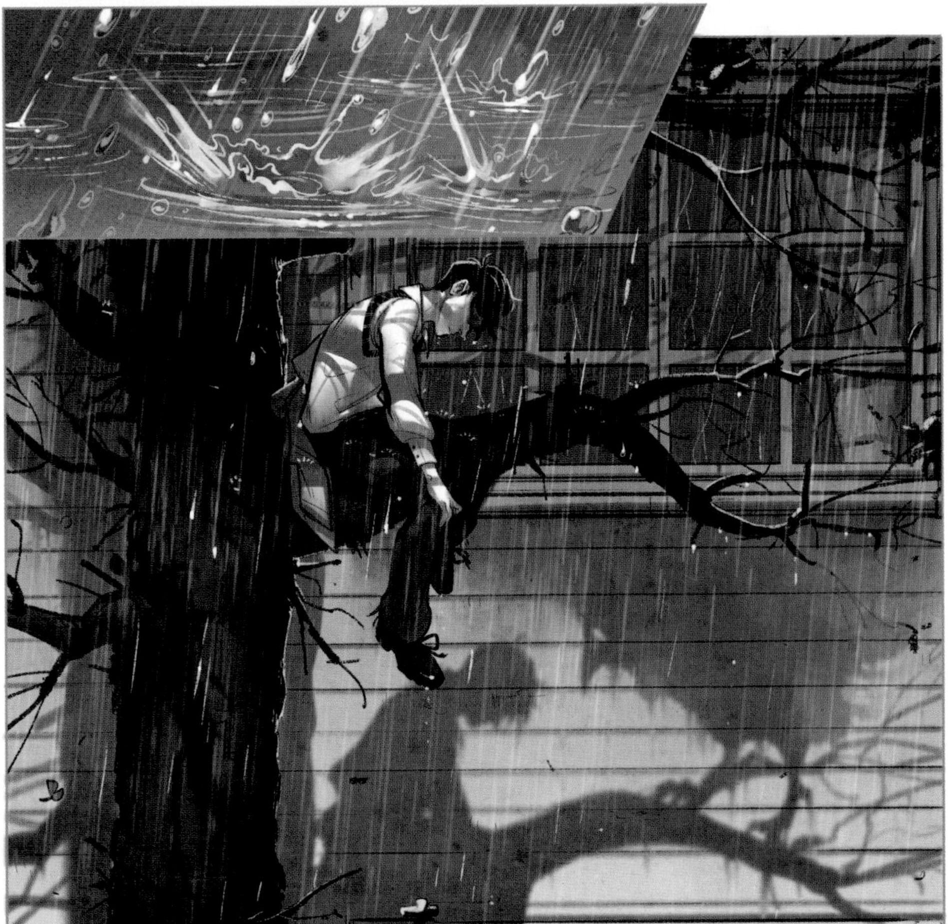

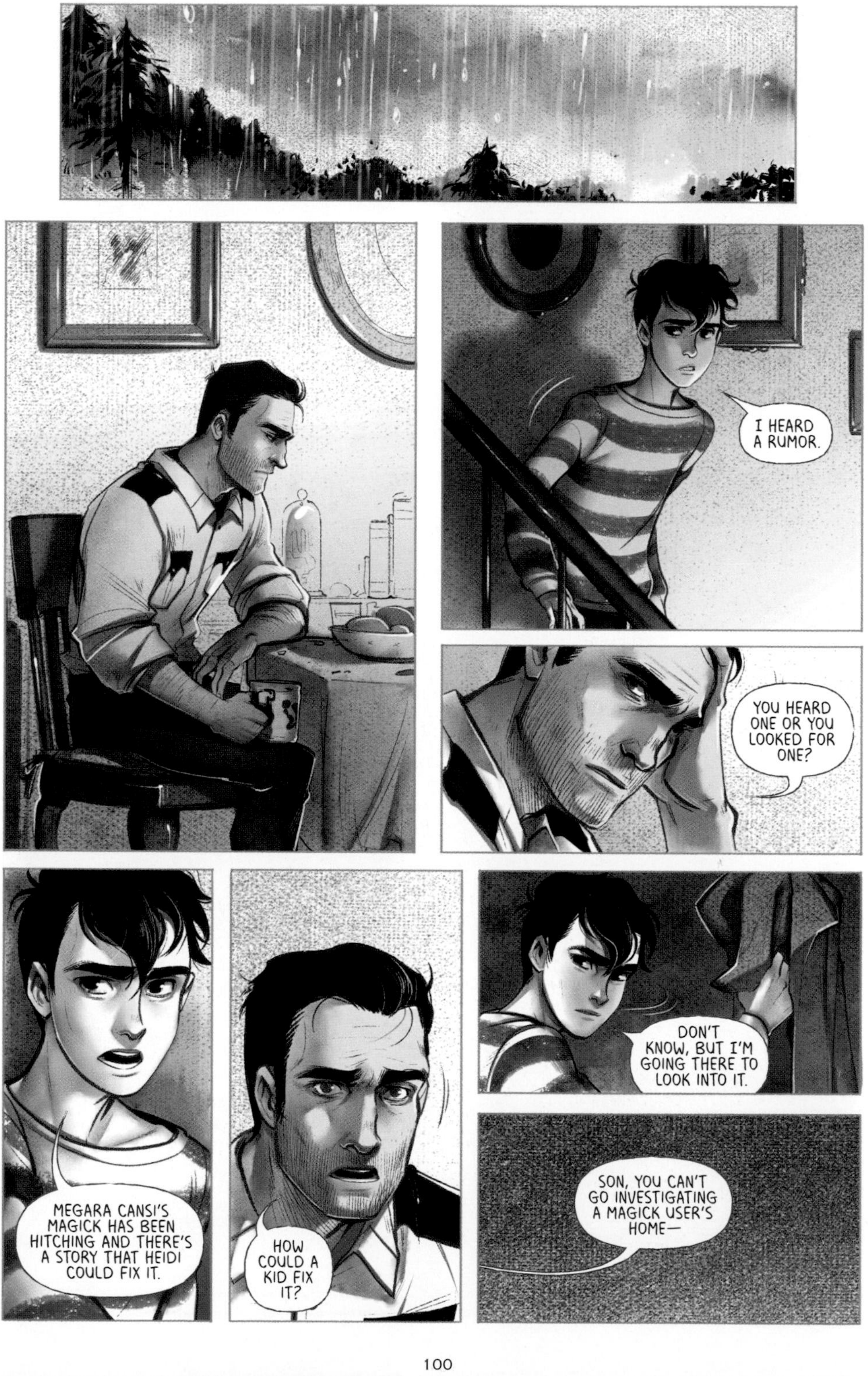
I HEARD A RUMOR.
YOU HEARD ONE OR YOU LOOKED FOR ONE?
MEGARA CANSI'S MAGICK HAS BEEN HITCHING AND THERE'S A STORY THAT HEIDI COULD FIX IT.
HOW COULD A KID FIX IT?
DON'T KNOW, BUT I'M GOING THERE TO LOOK INTO IT.
SON, YOU CAN'T GO INVESTIGATING A MAGICK USER'S HOME—

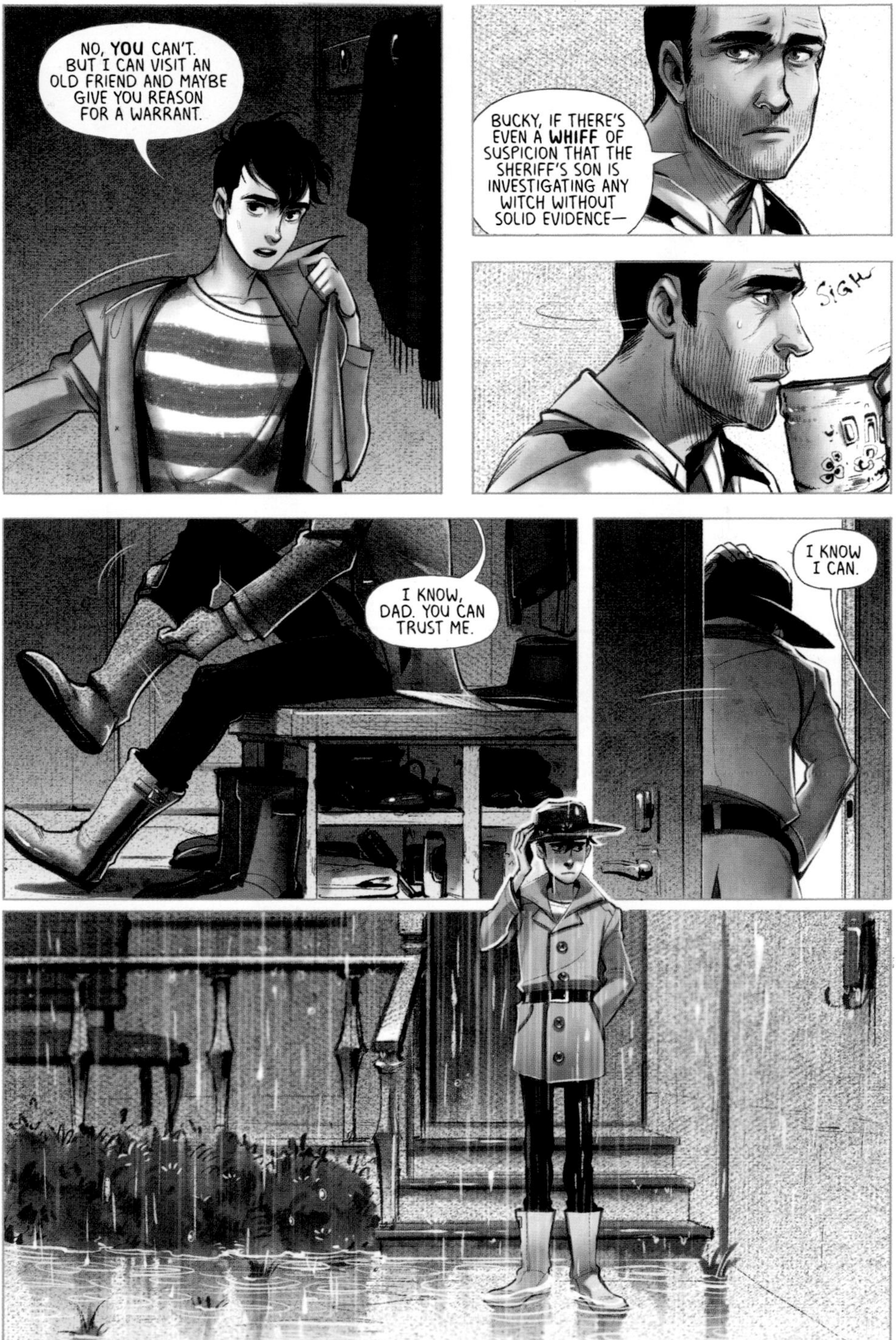
NO, **YOU** CAN'T. BUT I CAN VISIT AN OLD FRIEND AND MAYBE GIVE YOU REASON FOR A WARRANT.
BUCKY, IF THERE'S EVEN A **WHIFF** OF SUSPICION THAT THE SHERIFF'S SON IS INVESTIGATING ANY WITCH WITHOUT SOLID EVIDENCE—
SIGH
I KNOW, DAD. YOU CAN TRUST ME.
I KNOW I CAN.

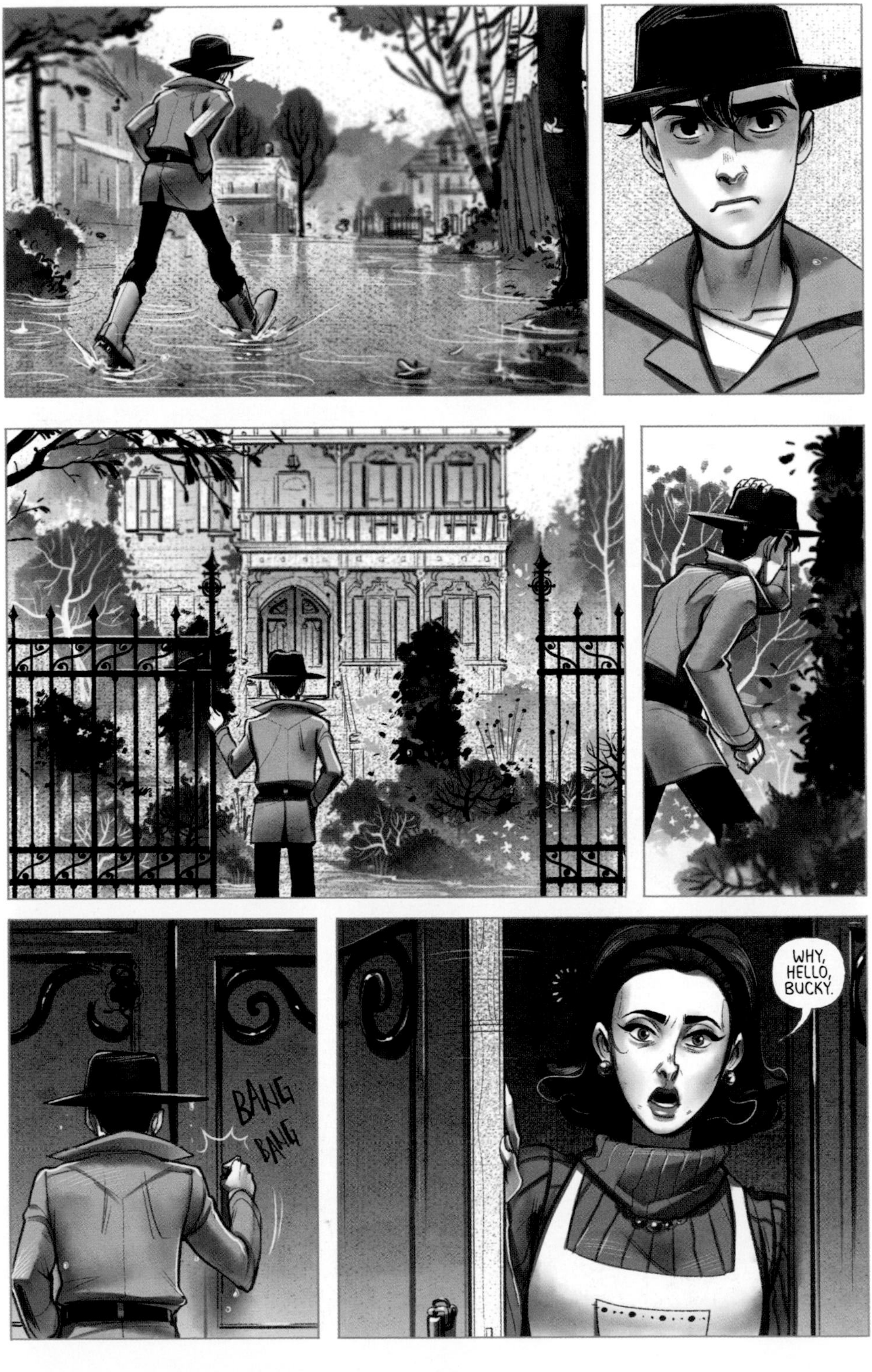
BANG
BANG
WHY, HELLO, BUCKY.

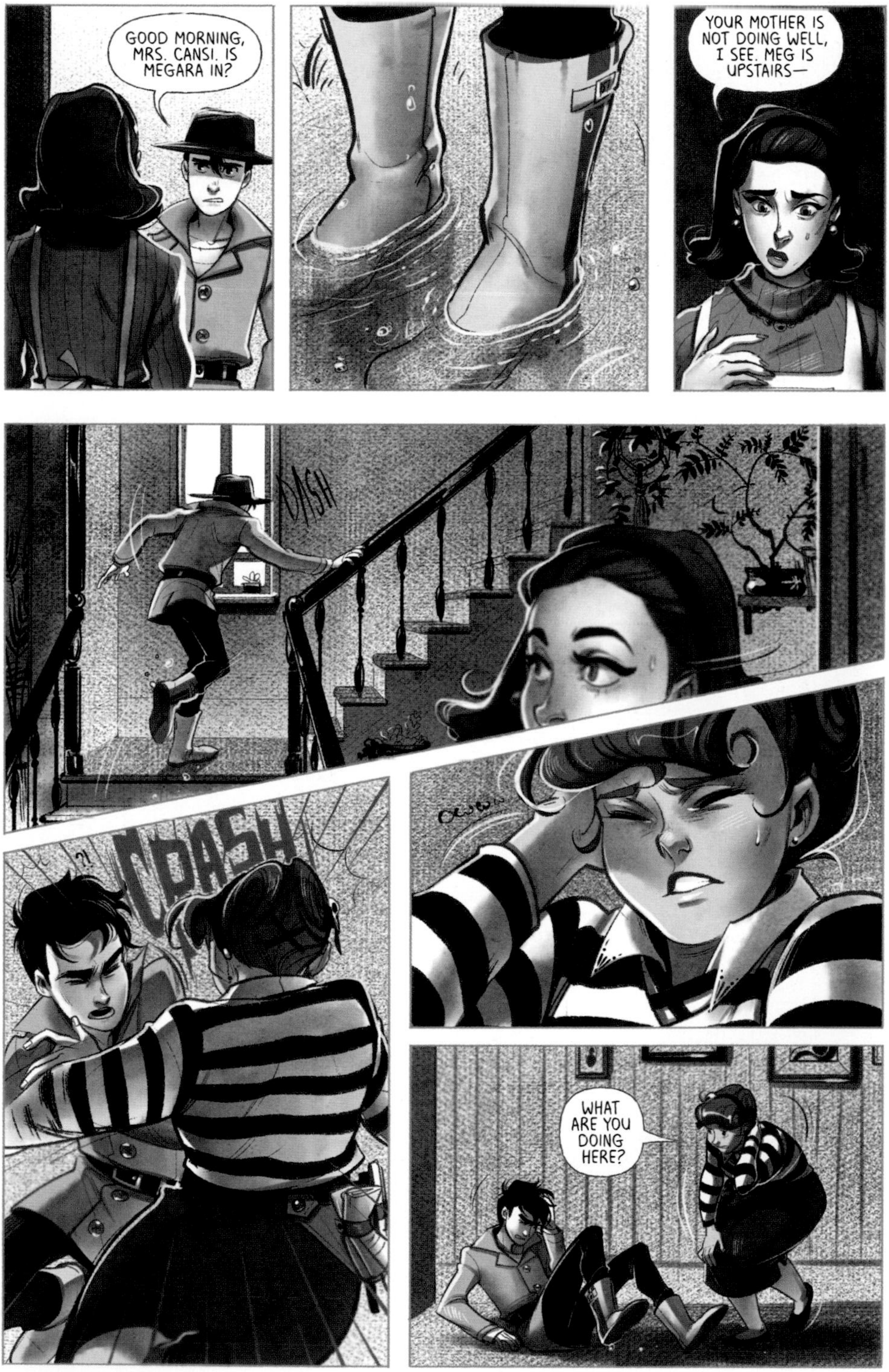
GOOD MORNING, MRS. CANSI. IS MEGARA IN?
YOUR MOTHER IS NOT DOING WELL, I SEE. MEG IS UPSTAIRS—
DASH
CRASH
WHAT ARE YOU DOING HERE?

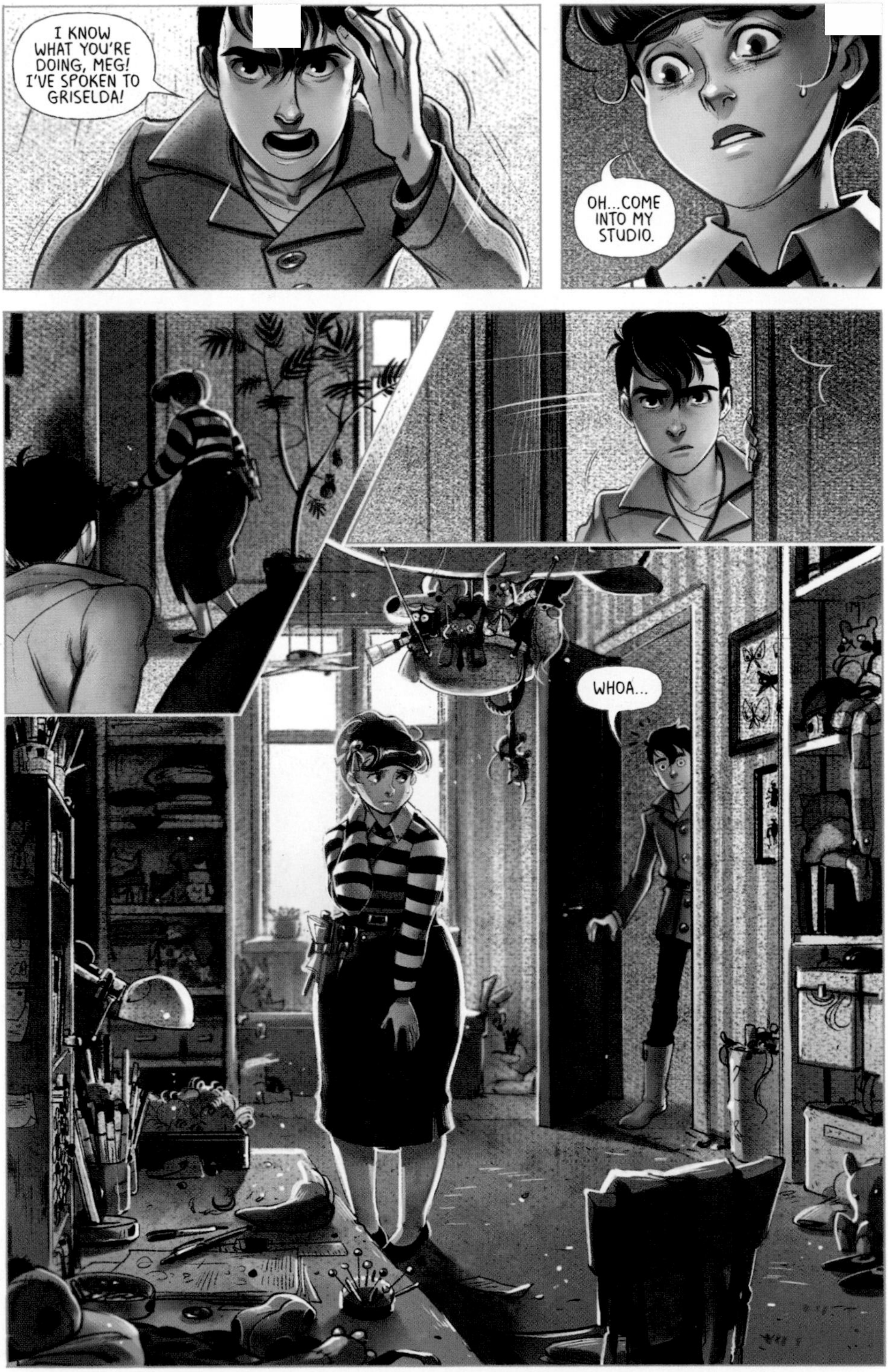
I KNOW WHAT YOU'RE DOING, MEG! I'VE SPOKEN TO GRISELDA!
OH...COME INTO MY STUDIO.
WHOA...

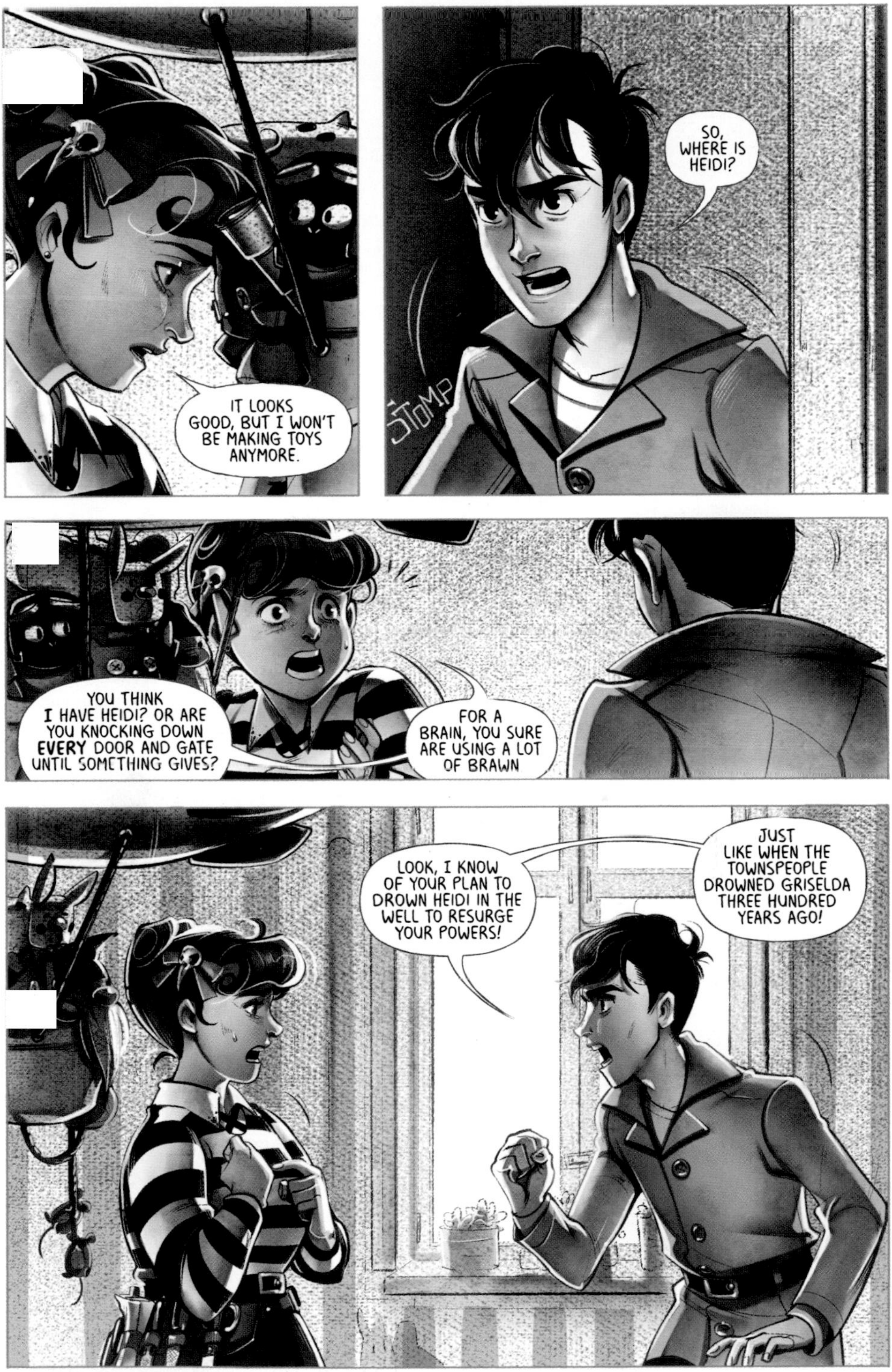
IT LOOKS GOOD, BUT I WON'T BE MAKING TOYS ANYMORE.
STOMP
SO, WHERE IS HEIDI?
YOU THINK I HAVE HEIDI? OR ARE YOU KNOCKING DOWN **EVERY** DOOR AND GATE UNTIL SOMETHING GIVES?
FOR A BRAIN, YOU SURE ARE USING A LOT OF BRAWN
LOOK, I KNOW OF YOUR PLAN TO DROWN HEIDI IN THE WELL TO RESURGE YOUR POWERS!
JUST LIKE WHEN THE TOWNSPEOPLE DROWNED GRISELDA THREE HUNDRED YEARS AGO!

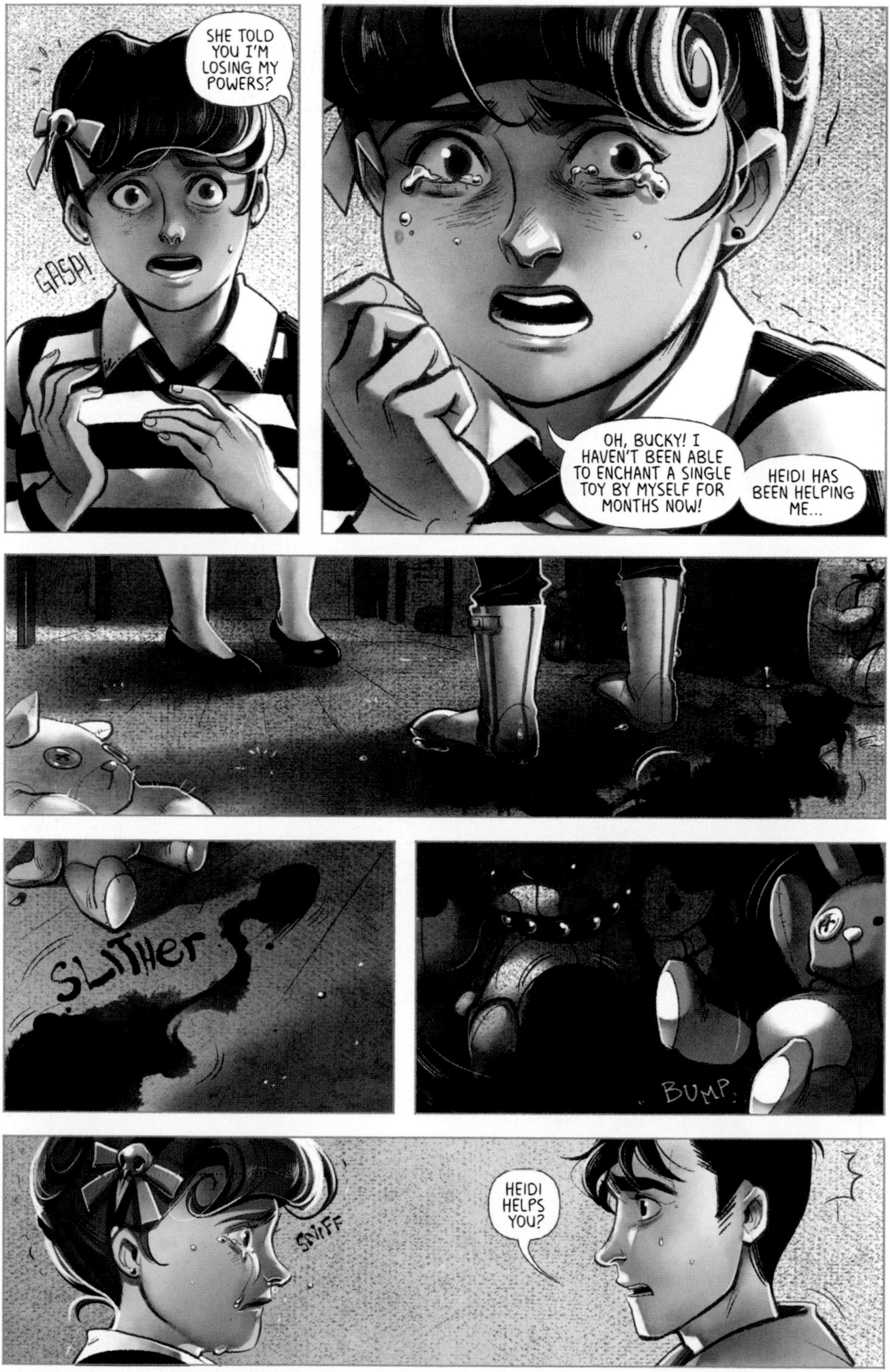
SHE TOLD YOU I'M LOSING MY POWERS?
GASP!
OH, BUCKY! I HAVEN'T BEEN ABLE TO ENCHANT A SINGLE TOY BY MYSELF FOR MONTHS NOW!
HEIDI HAS BEEN HELPING ME...
SLITHER
BUMP
SNIFF
HEIDI HELPS YOU?

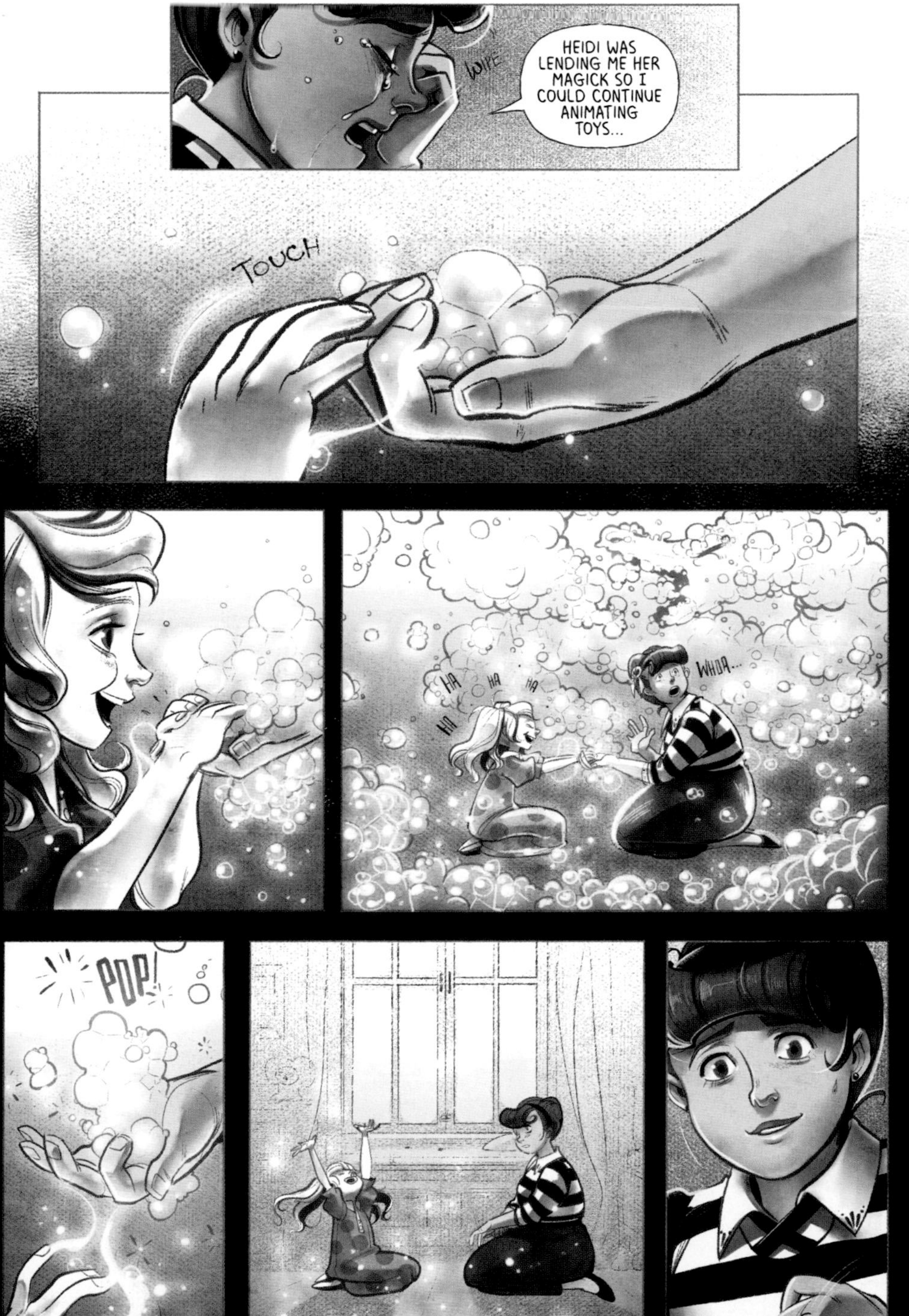
WIPE
HEIDI WAS LENDING ME HER MAGICK SO I COULD CONTINUE ANIMATING TOYS...
TOUCH
HA HA HA HA
WHOA...
POP!
POOF

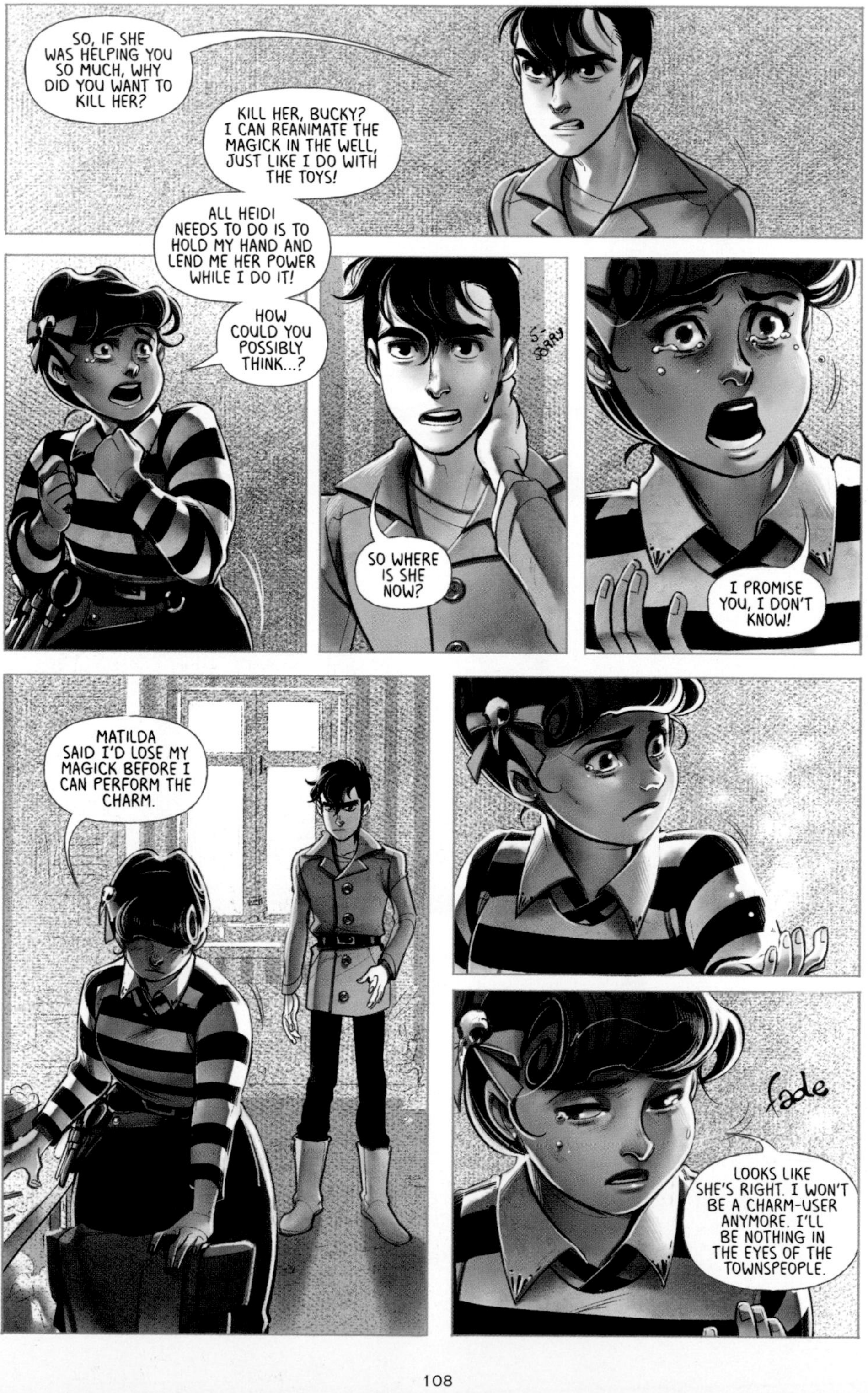
SO, IF SHE WAS HELPING YOU SO MUCH, WHY DID YOU WANT TO KILL HER?
KILL HER, BUCKY? I CAN REANIMATE THE MAGICK IN THE WELL, JUST LIKE I DO WITH THE TOYS!
ALL HEIDI NEEDS TO DO IS TO HOLD MY HAND AND LEND ME HER POWER WHILE I DO IT!
HOW COULD YOU POSSIBLY THINK...?
S-SORRY
SO WHERE IS SHE NOW?
I PROMISE YOU, I DON'T KNOW!
MATILDA SAID I'D LOSE MY MAGICK BEFORE I CAN PERFORM THE CHARM.
fade
LOOKS LIKE SHE'S RIGHT. I WON'T BE A CHARM-USER ANYMORE. I'LL BE NOTHING IN THE EYES OF THE TOWNSPEOPLE.

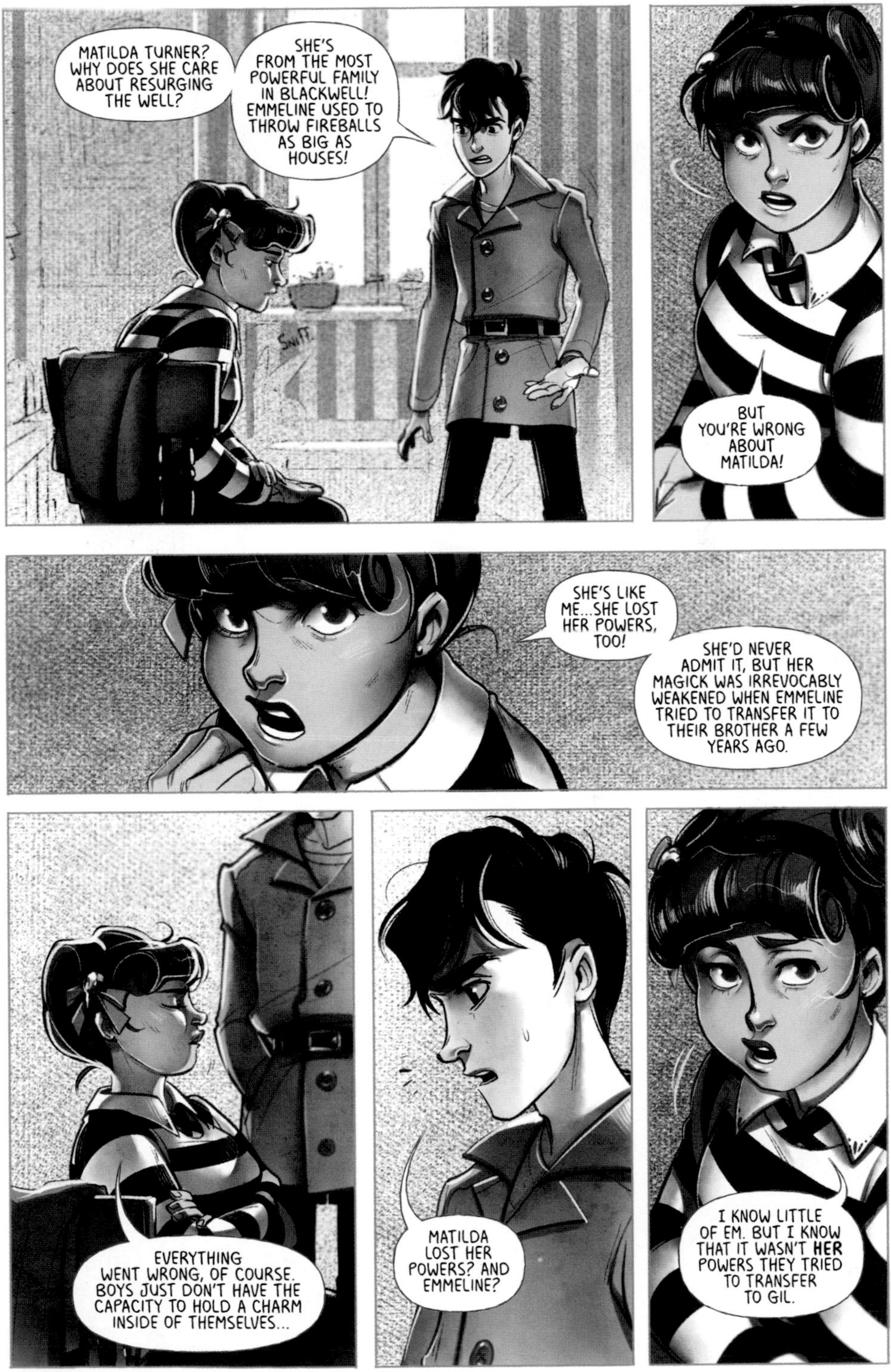
MATILDA TURNER? WHY DOES SHE CARE ABOUT RESURGING THE WELL?
SHE'S FROM THE MOST POWERFUL FAMILY IN BLACKWELL! EMMELINE USED TO THROW FIREBALLS AS BIG AS HOUSES!
SNIFF
BUT YOU'RE WRONG ABOUT MATILDA!
SHE'S LIKE ME...SHE LOST HER POWERS, TOO!
SHE'D NEVER ADMIT IT, BUT HER MAGICK WAS IRREVOCABLY WEAKENED WHEN EMMELINE TRIED TO TRANSFER IT TO THEIR BROTHER A FEW YEARS AGO.
EVERYTHING WENT WRONG, OF COURSE. BOYS JUST DON'T HAVE THE CAPACITY TO HOLD A CHARM INSIDE OF THEMSELVES...
MATILDA LOST HER POWERS? AND EMMELINE?
I KNOW LITTLE OF EM. BUT I KNOW THAT IT WASN'T **HER** POWERS THEY TRIED TO TRANSFER TO GIL.

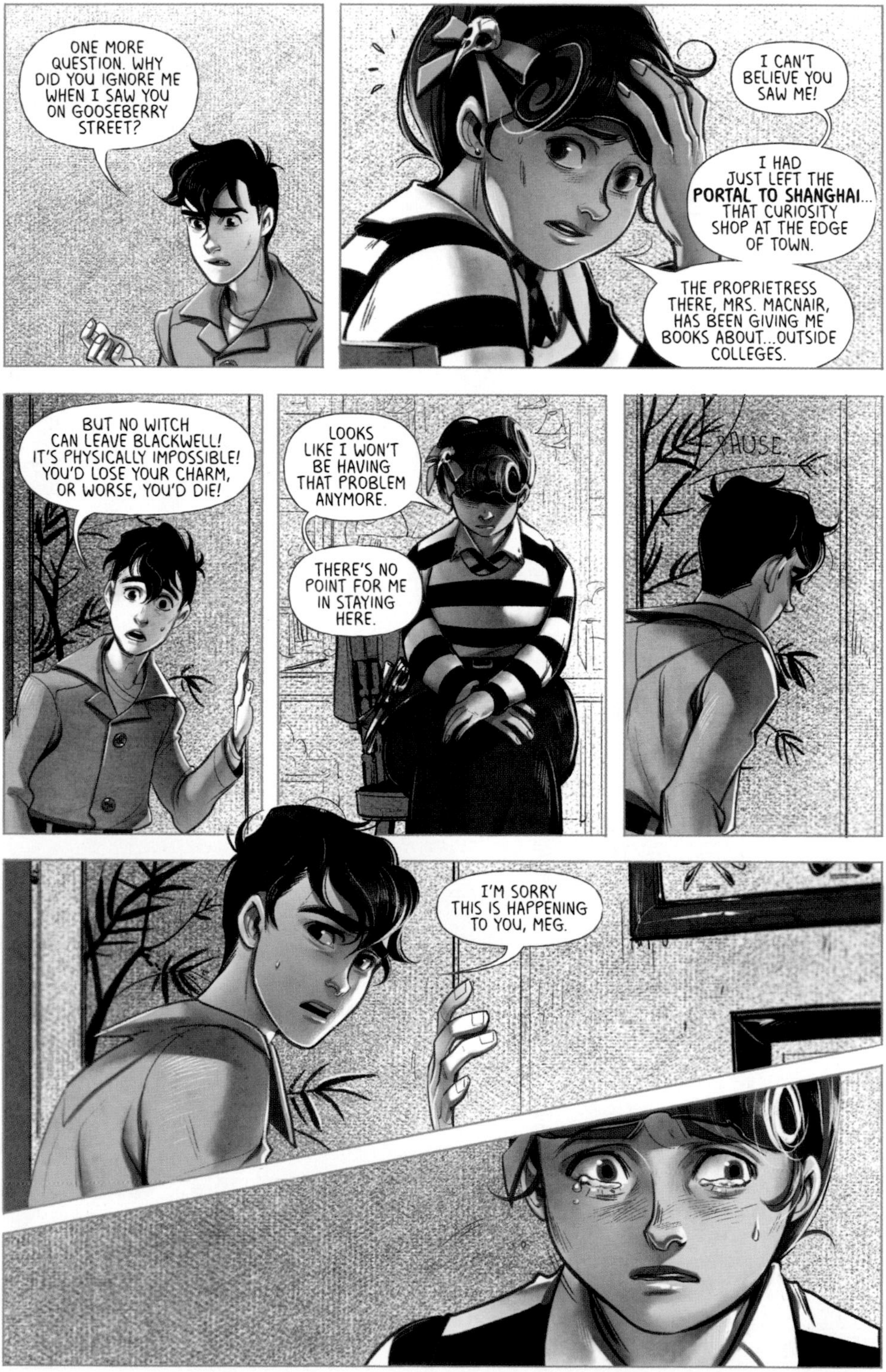
ONE MORE QUESTION. WHY DID YOU IGNORE ME WHEN I SAW YOU ON GOOSEBERRY STREET?
I CAN'T BELIEVE YOU SAW ME!
I HAD JUST LEFT THE **PORTAL TO SHANGHAI**... THAT CURIOSITY SHOP AT THE EDGE OF TOWN.
THE PROPRIETRESS THERE, MRS. MACNAIR, HAS BEEN GIVING ME BOOKS ABOUT...OUTSIDE COLLEGES.
BUT NO WITCH CAN LEAVE BLACKWELL! IT'S PHYSICALLY IMPOSSIBLE! YOU'D LOSE YOUR CHARM, OR WORSE, YOU'D DIE!
LOOKS LIKE I WON'T BE HAVING THAT PROBLEM ANYMORE.
THERE'S NO POINT FOR ME IN STAYING HERE.
PAUSE.
I'M SORRY THIS IS HAPPENING TO YOU, MEG.

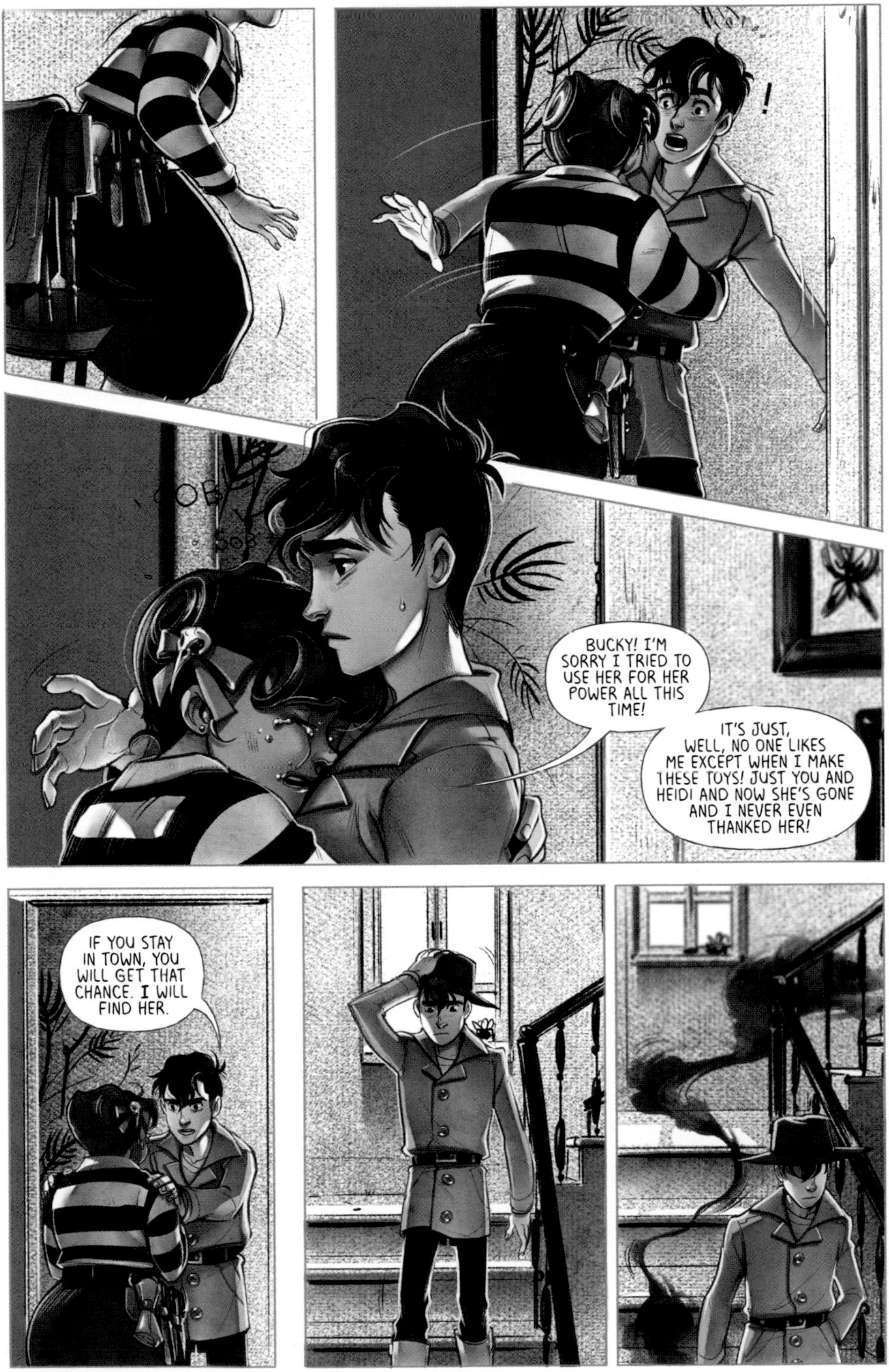
!
BUCKY! I'M SORRY I TRIED TO USE HER FOR HER POWER ALL THIS TIME!
IT'S JUST, WELL, NO ONE LIKES ME EXCEPT WHEN I MAKE THESE TOYS! JUST YOU AND HEIDI AND NOW SHE'S GONE AND I NEVER EVEN THANKED HER!
IF YOU STAY IN TOWN, YOU WILL GET THAT CHANCE. I WILL FIND HER.

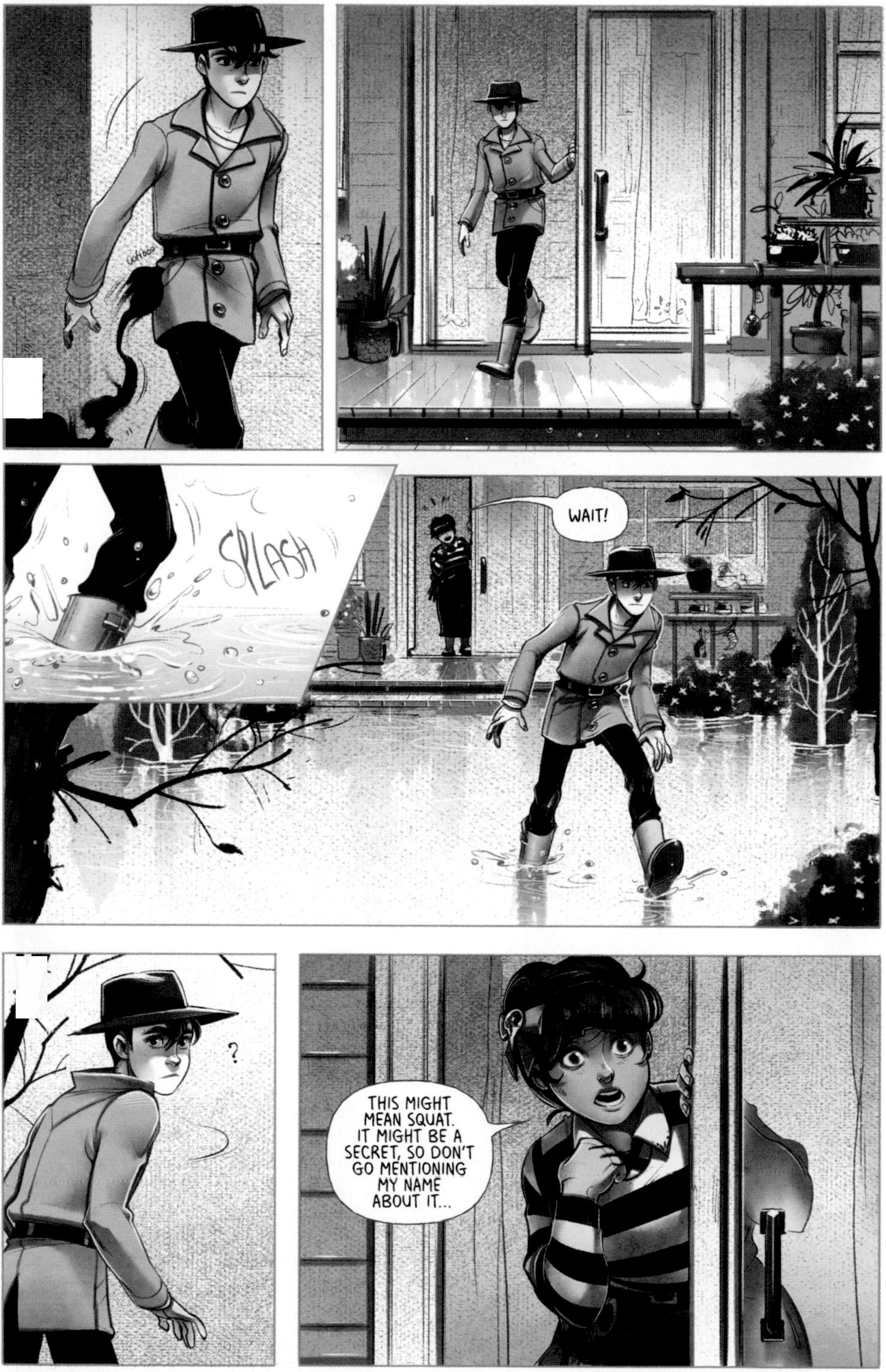
SPLASH
WAIT!
THIS MIGHT MEAN SQUAT. IT MIGHT BE A SECRET, SO DON'T GO MENTIONING MY NAME ABOUT IT...

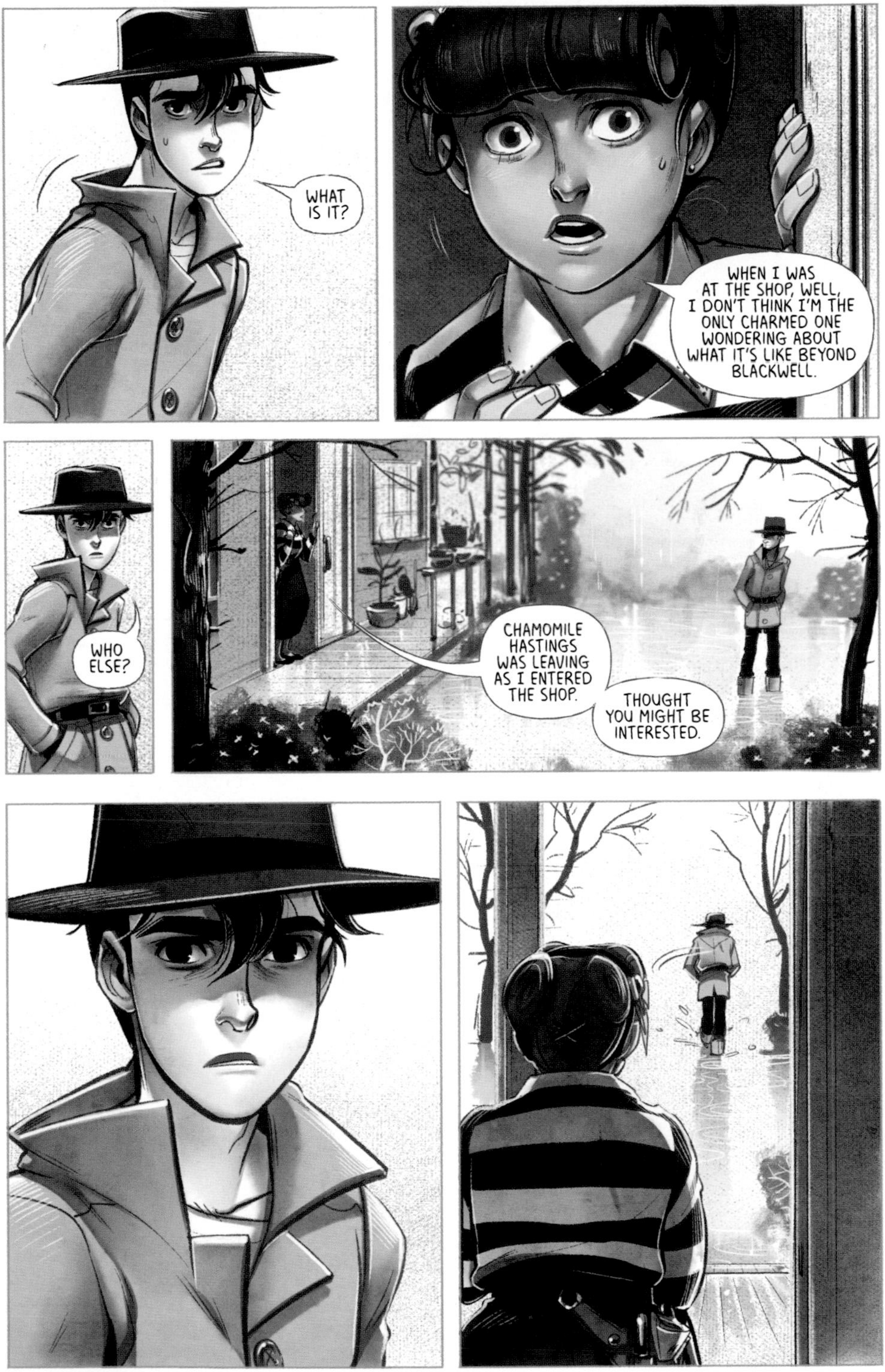
WHAT IS IT?
WHEN I WAS AT THE SHOP, WELL, I DON'T THINK I'M THE ONLY CHARMED ONE WONDERING ABOUT WHAT IT'S LIKE BEYOND BLACKWELL.
WHO ELSE?
CHAMOMILE HASTINGS WAS LEAVING AS I ENTERED THE SHOP.
THOUGHT YOU MIGHT BE INTERESTED.

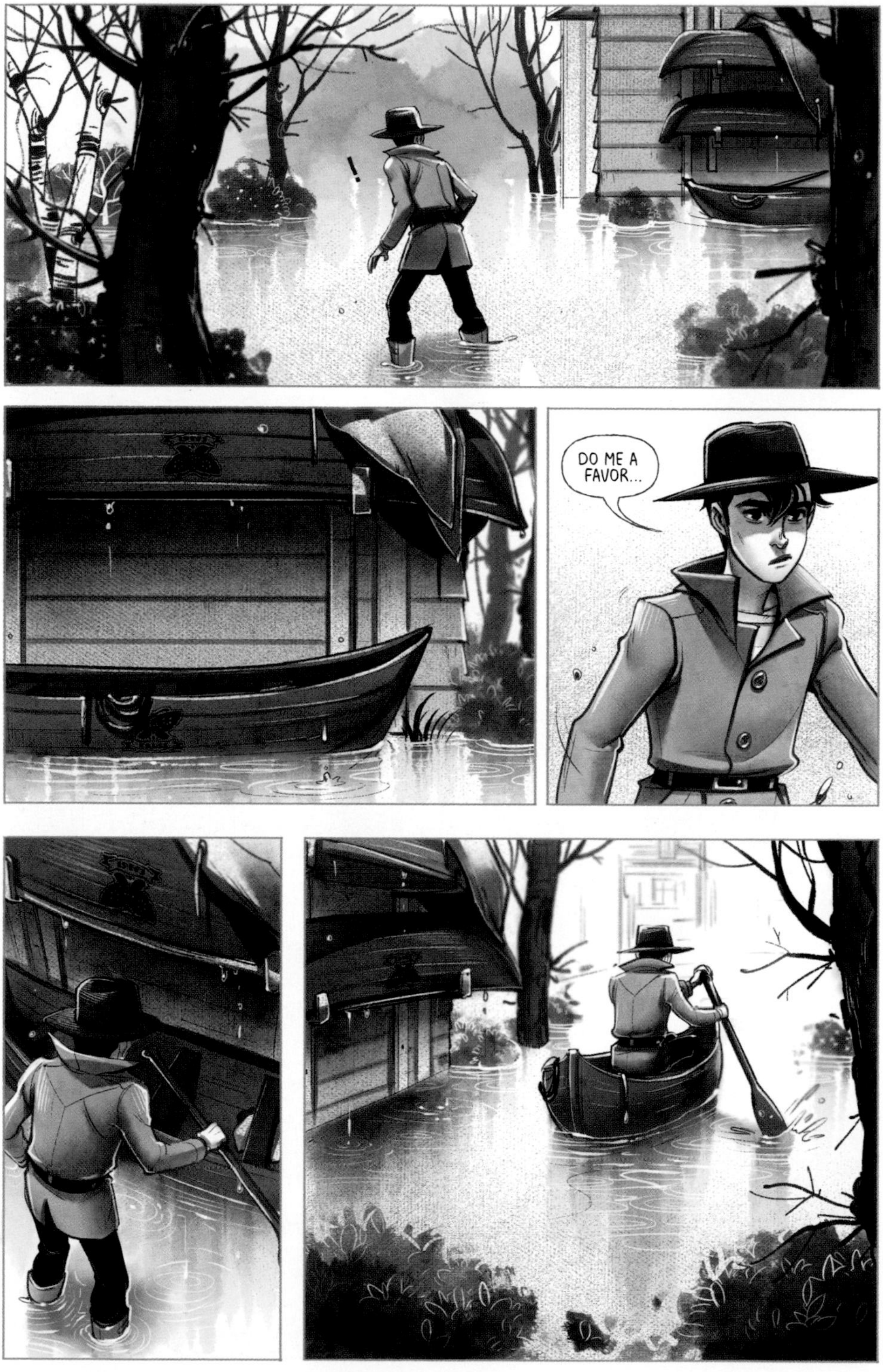
!
DO ME A FAVOR...

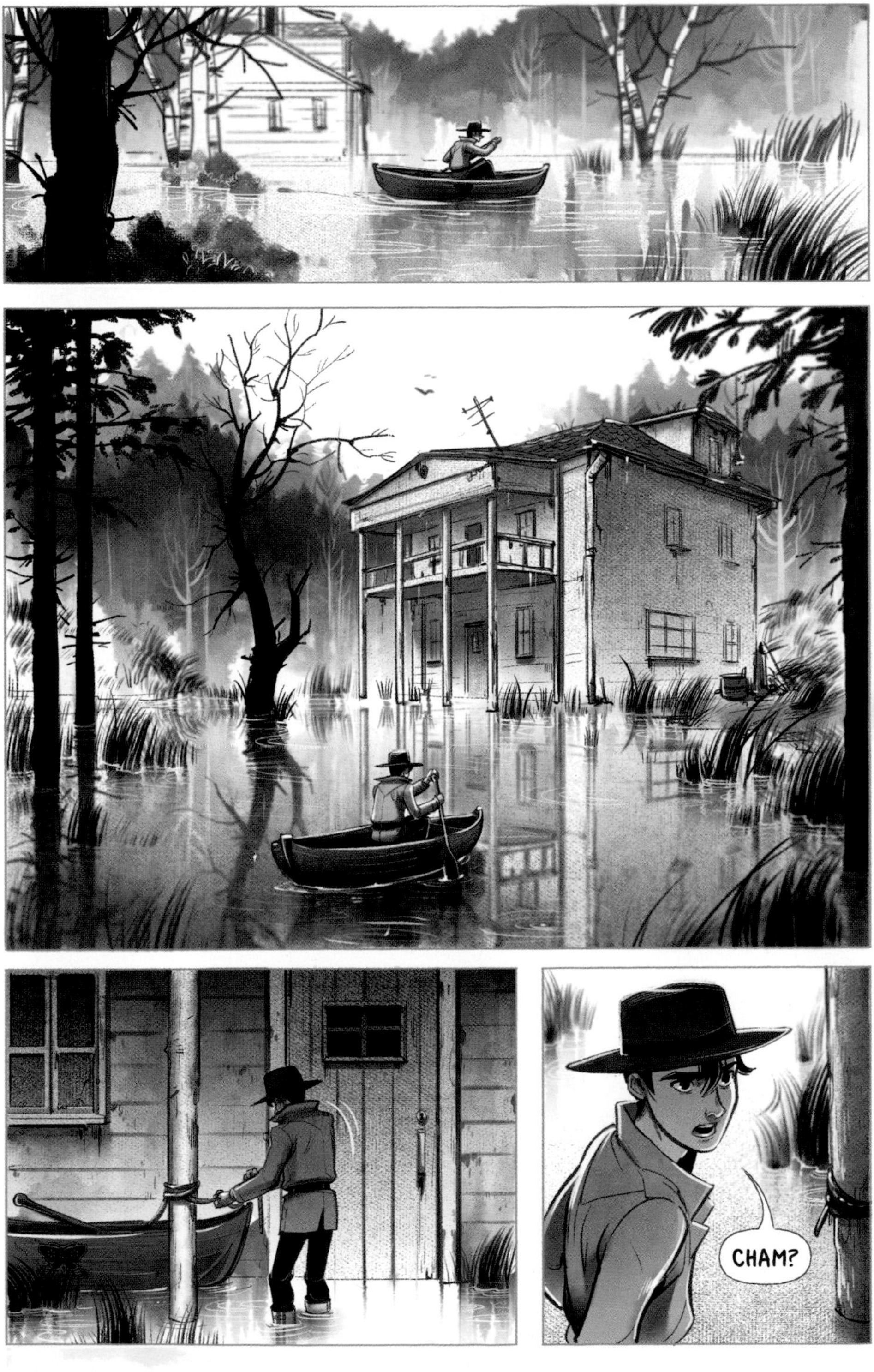
CHAM?

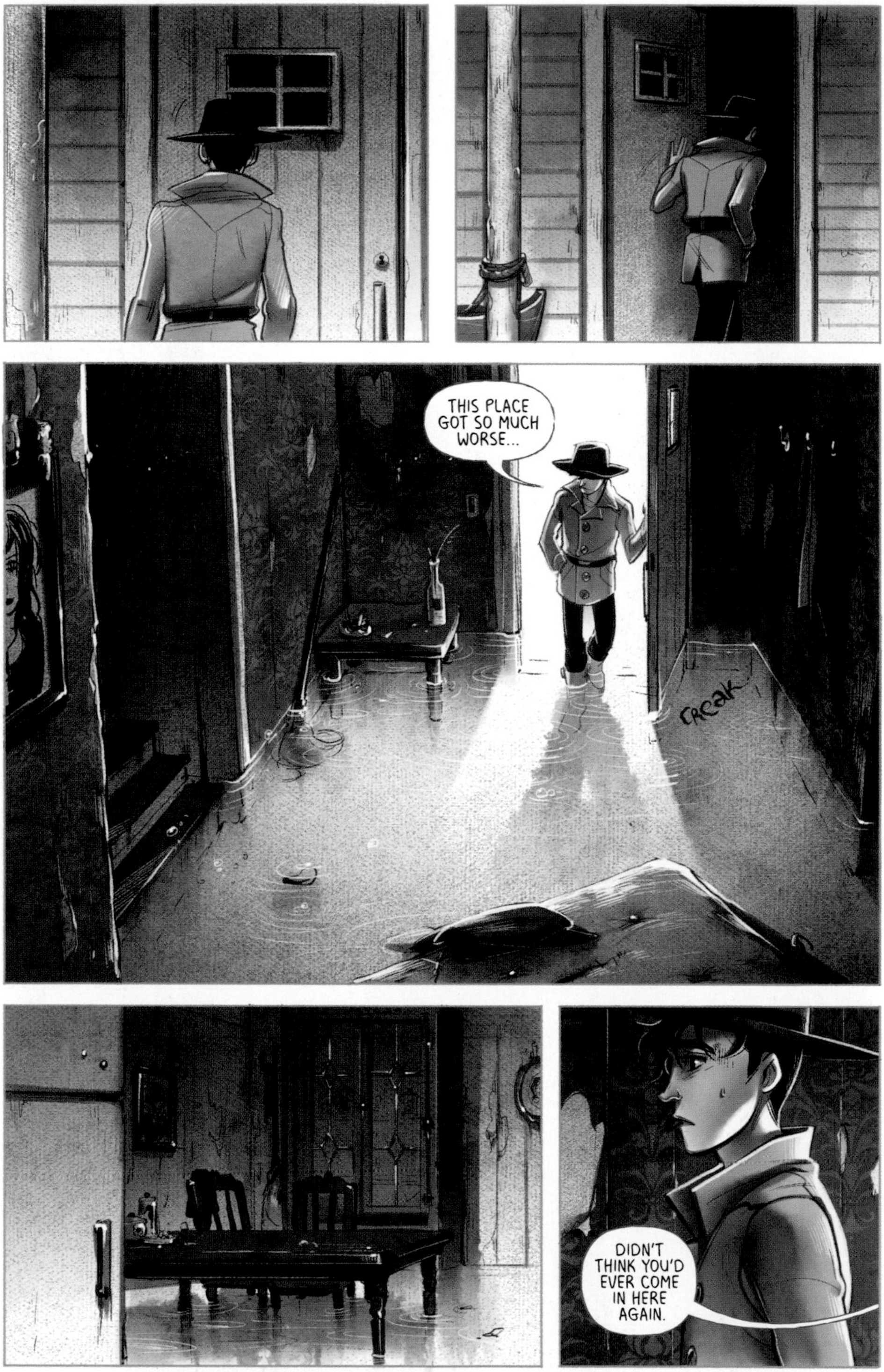
THIS PLACE GOT SO MUCH WORSE...
CREAK
DIDN'T THINK YOU'D EVER COME IN HERE AGAIN.

CHAPTER 6

IT'S A FLOOD, MY LOVE

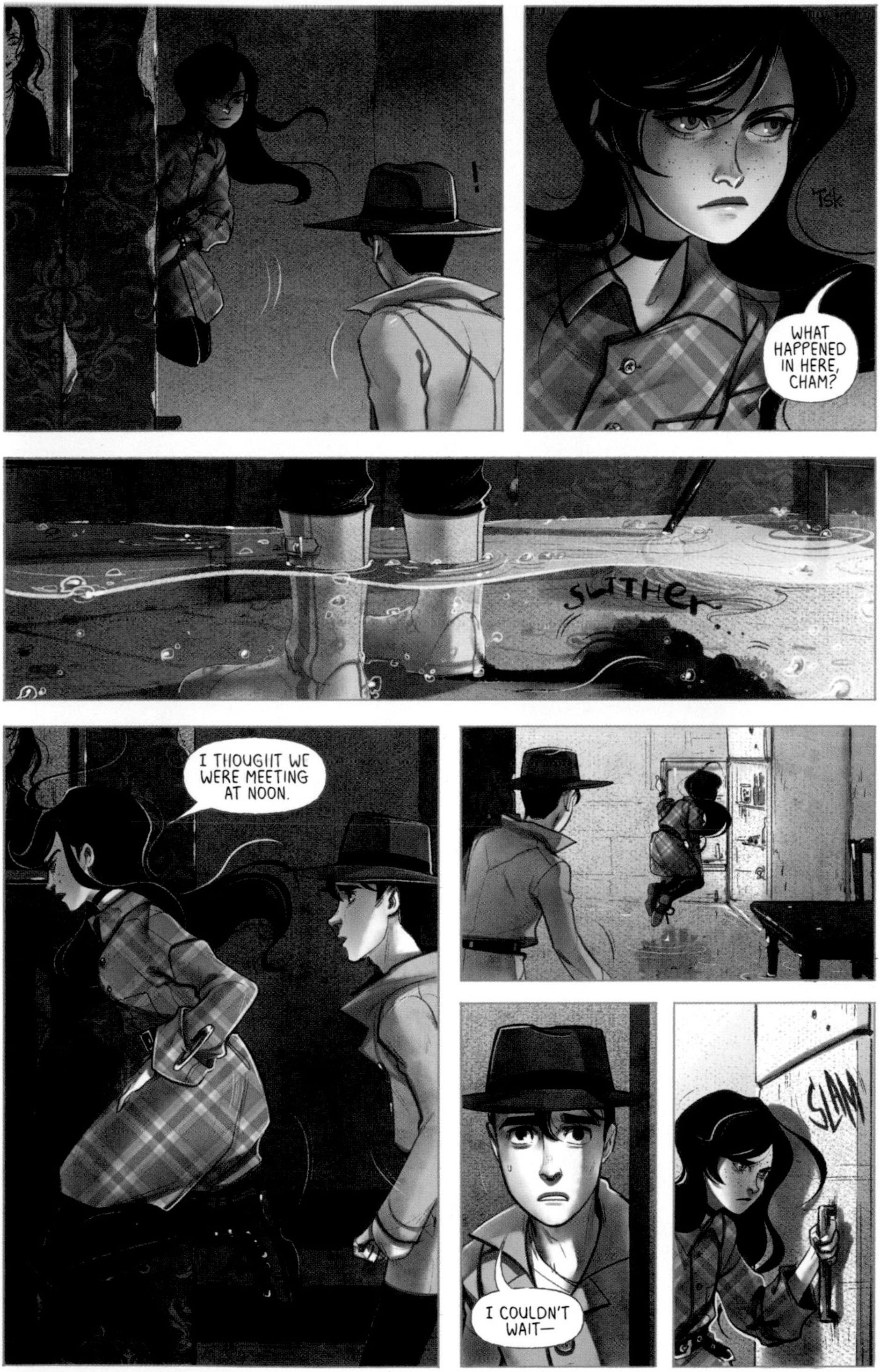
!
TSK
WHAT HAPPENED IN HERE, CHAM?
SLITHER...
I THOUGHT WE WERE MEETING AT NOON.
I COULDN'T WAIT—
SLAM

CHAM? I CAME TO APOLOGIZE.

A YEAR AGO YOU CAME TO ME TO TELL ME SOMETHING...

AND I DIDN'T CONSIDER IT. I'M SORRY.

OHH, THAT. TIMES PAST, BUCKO.

HAVE YOU BEEN LIVING HERE LIKE THIS?

PULL YOURSELF TOGETHER, PITY PARTY.

I'VE BEEN STAYING WITH THE GIRLS.

THEY'VE GOT HUNDREDS OF EMPTY ROOMS BETWEEN THEM. ALL LESS FLOODED THAN THIS ONE.

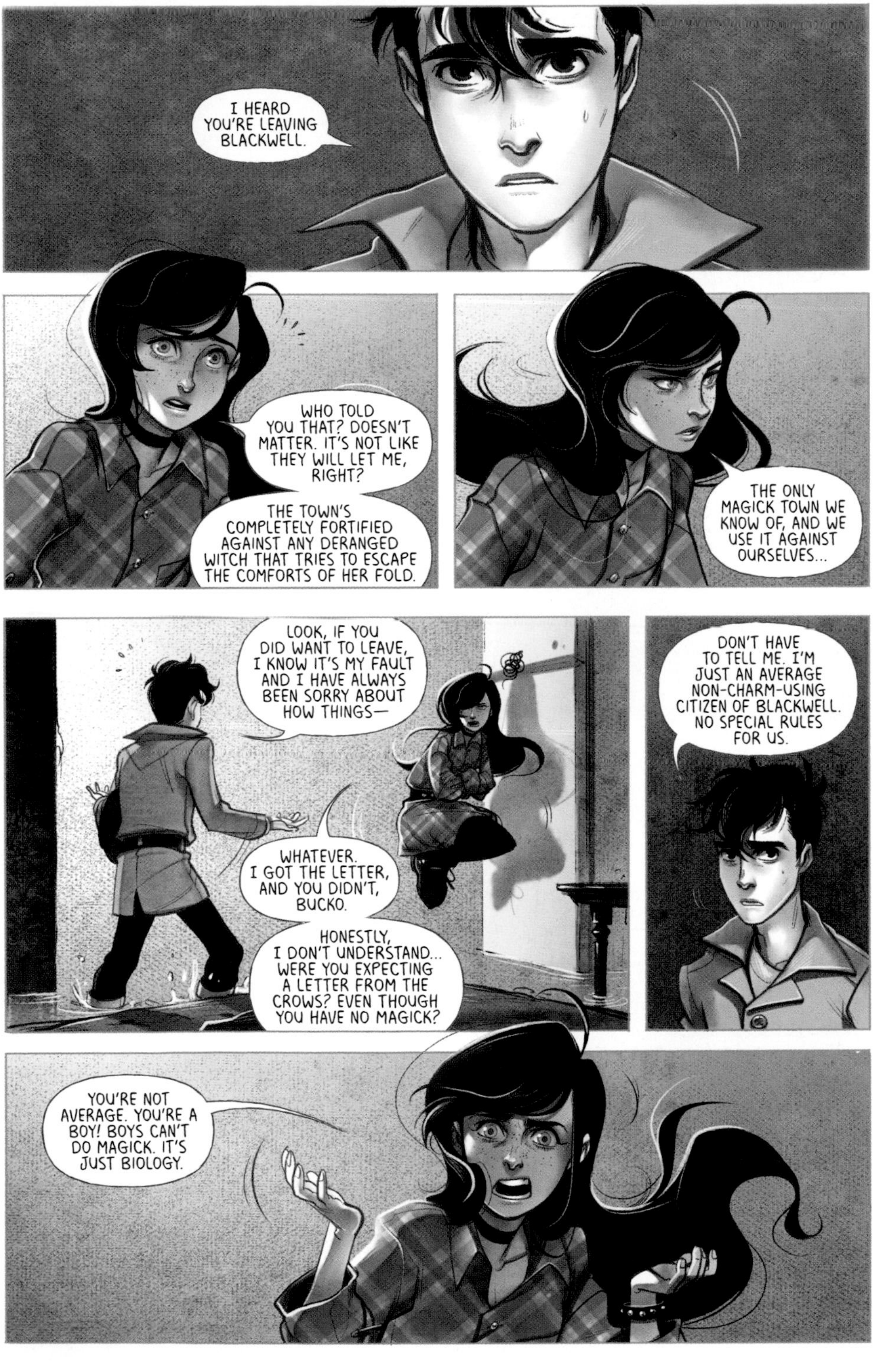
I HEARD YOU'RE LEAVING BLACKWELL.
WHO TOLD YOU THAT? DOESN'T MATTER. IT'S NOT LIKE THEY WILL LET ME, RIGHT?
THE TOWN'S COMPLETELY FORTIFIED AGAINST ANY DERANGED WITCH THAT TRIES TO ESCAPE THE COMFORTS OF HER FOLD.
THE ONLY MAGICK TOWN WE KNOW OF, AND WE USE IT AGAINST OURSELVES...
LOOK, IF YOU DID WANT TO LEAVE, I KNOW IT'S MY FAULT AND I HAVE ALWAYS BEEN SORRY ABOUT HOW THINGS—
WHATEVER. I GOT THE LETTER, AND YOU DIDN'T, BUCKO.
HONESTLY, I DON'T UNDERSTAND... WERE YOU EXPECTING A LETTER FROM THE CROWS? EVEN THOUGH YOU HAVE NO MAGICK?
DON'T HAVE TO TELL ME. I'M JUST AN AVERAGE NON-CHARM-USING CITIZEN OF BLACKWELL. NO SPECIAL RULES FOR US.
YOU'RE NOT AVERAGE. YOU'RE A BOY! BOYS CAN'T DO MAGICK. IT'S JUST BIOLOGY.

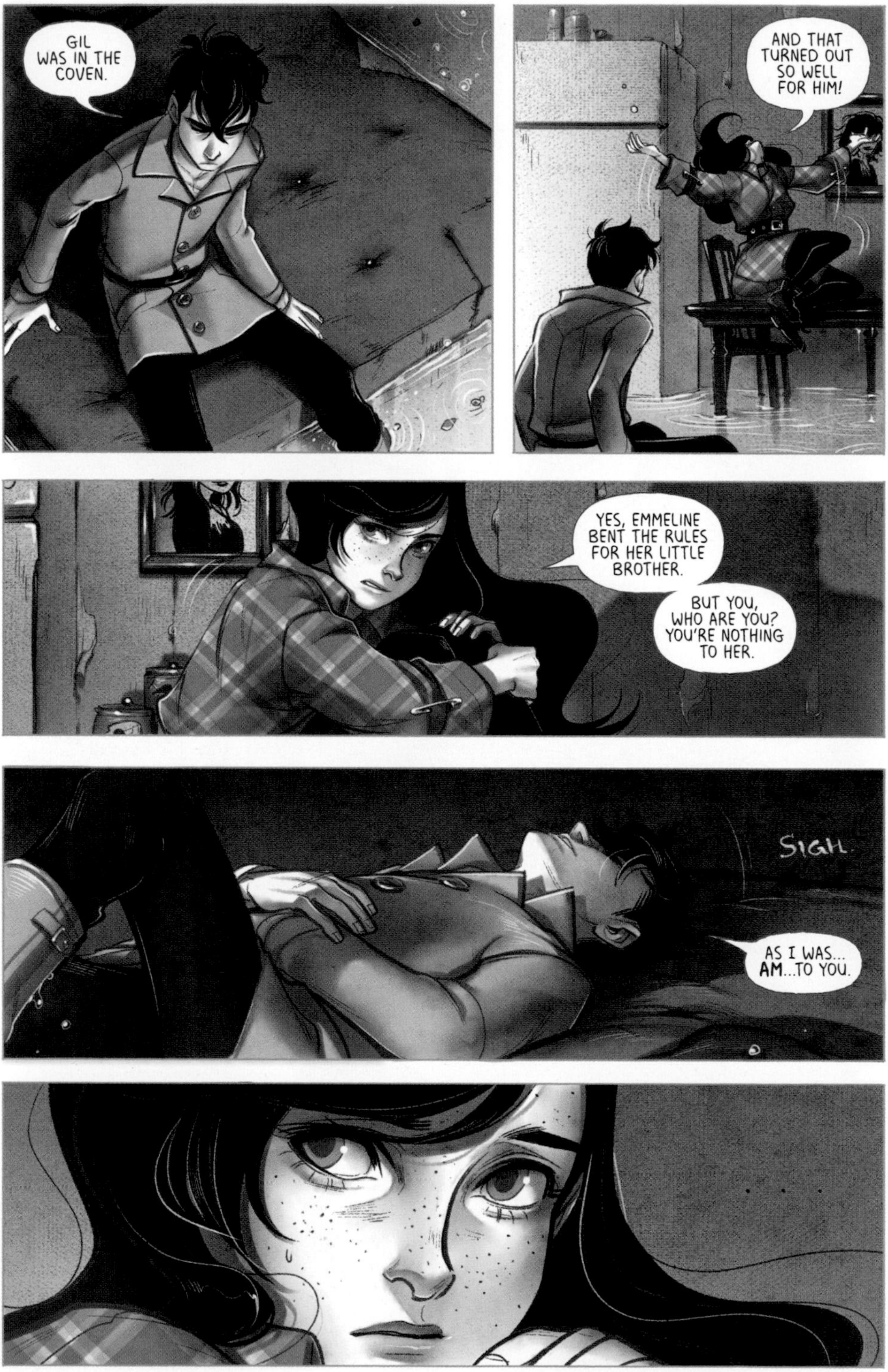
GIL WAS IN THE COVEN.
AND THAT TURNED OUT SO WELL FOR HIM!
YES, EMMELINE BENT THE RULES FOR HER LITTLE BROTHER.
BUT YOU, WHO ARE YOU? YOU'RE NOTHING TO HER.
SIGH.
AS I WAS... **AM**...TO YOU.

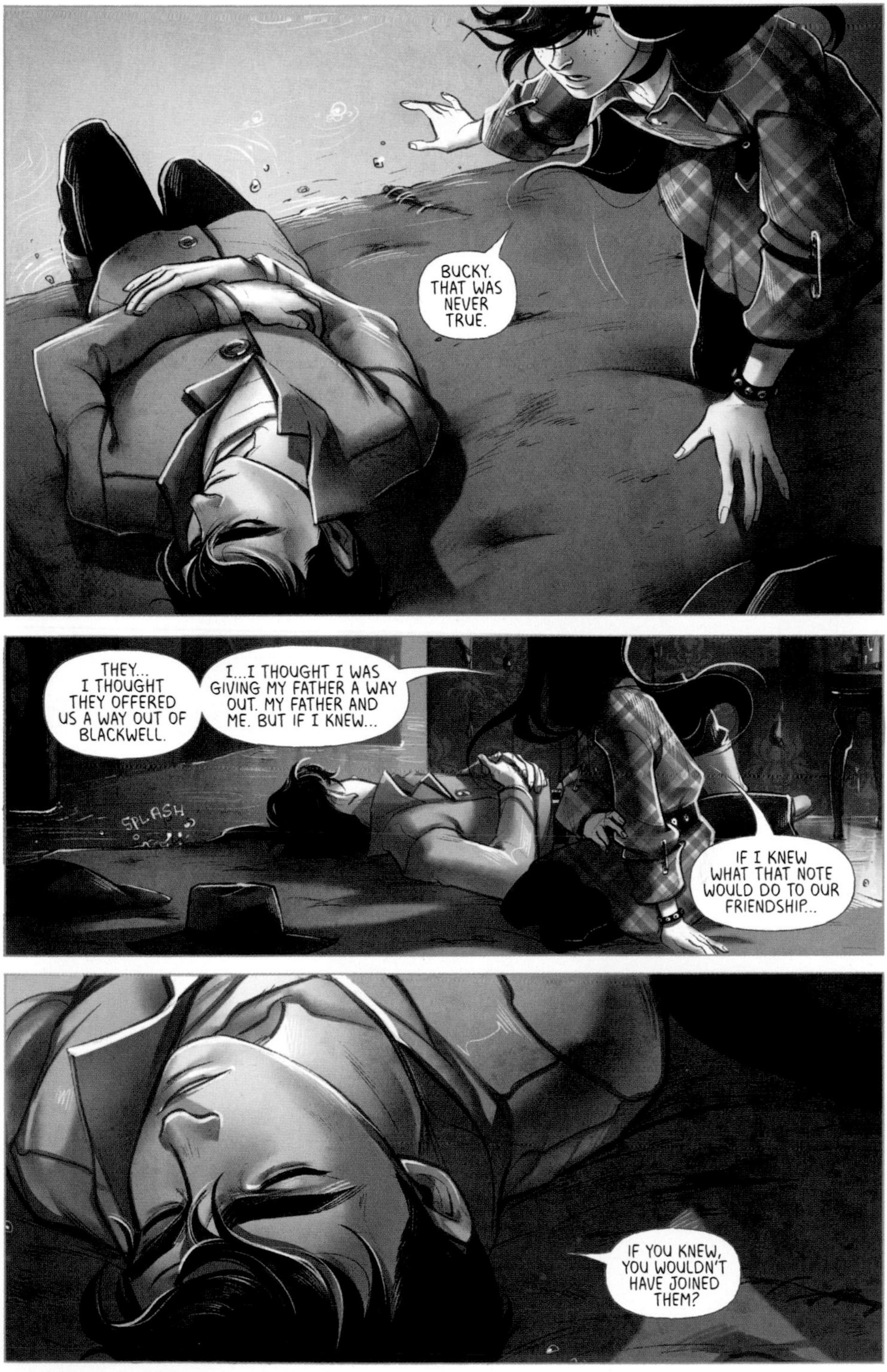
BUCKY. THAT WAS NEVER TRUE.
THEY... I THOUGHT THEY OFFERED US A WAY OUT OF BLACKWELL.
I...I THOUGHT I WAS GIVING MY FATHER A WAY OUT. MY FATHER AND ME. BUT IF I KNEW...
SPLASH
IF I KNEW WHAT THAT NOTE WOULD DO TO OUR FRIENDSHIP...
IF YOU KNEW, YOU WOULDN'T HAVE JOINED THEM?

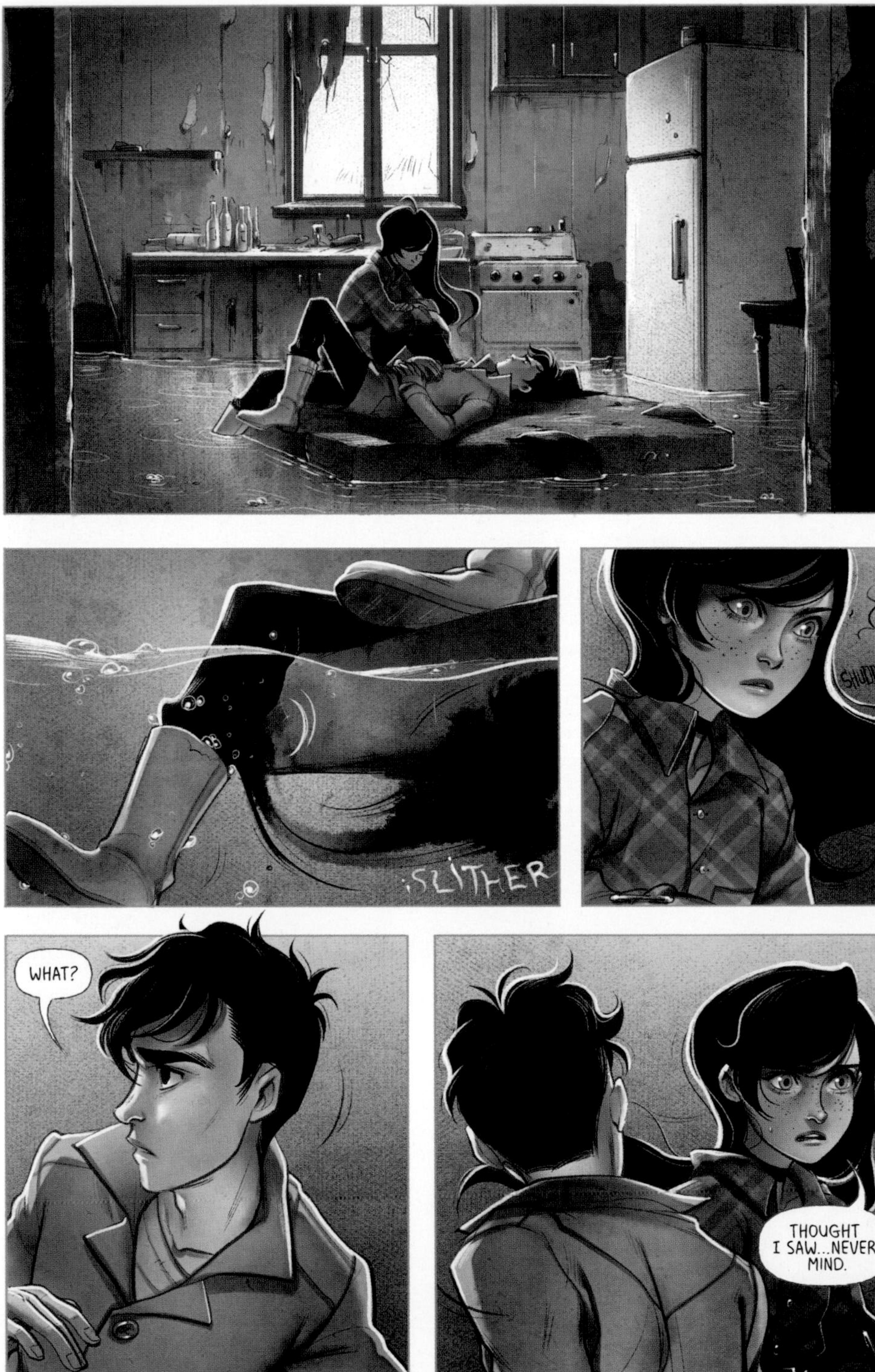
SLITHER
SHUDDER
WHAT?
THOUGHT I SAW...NEVER MIND.

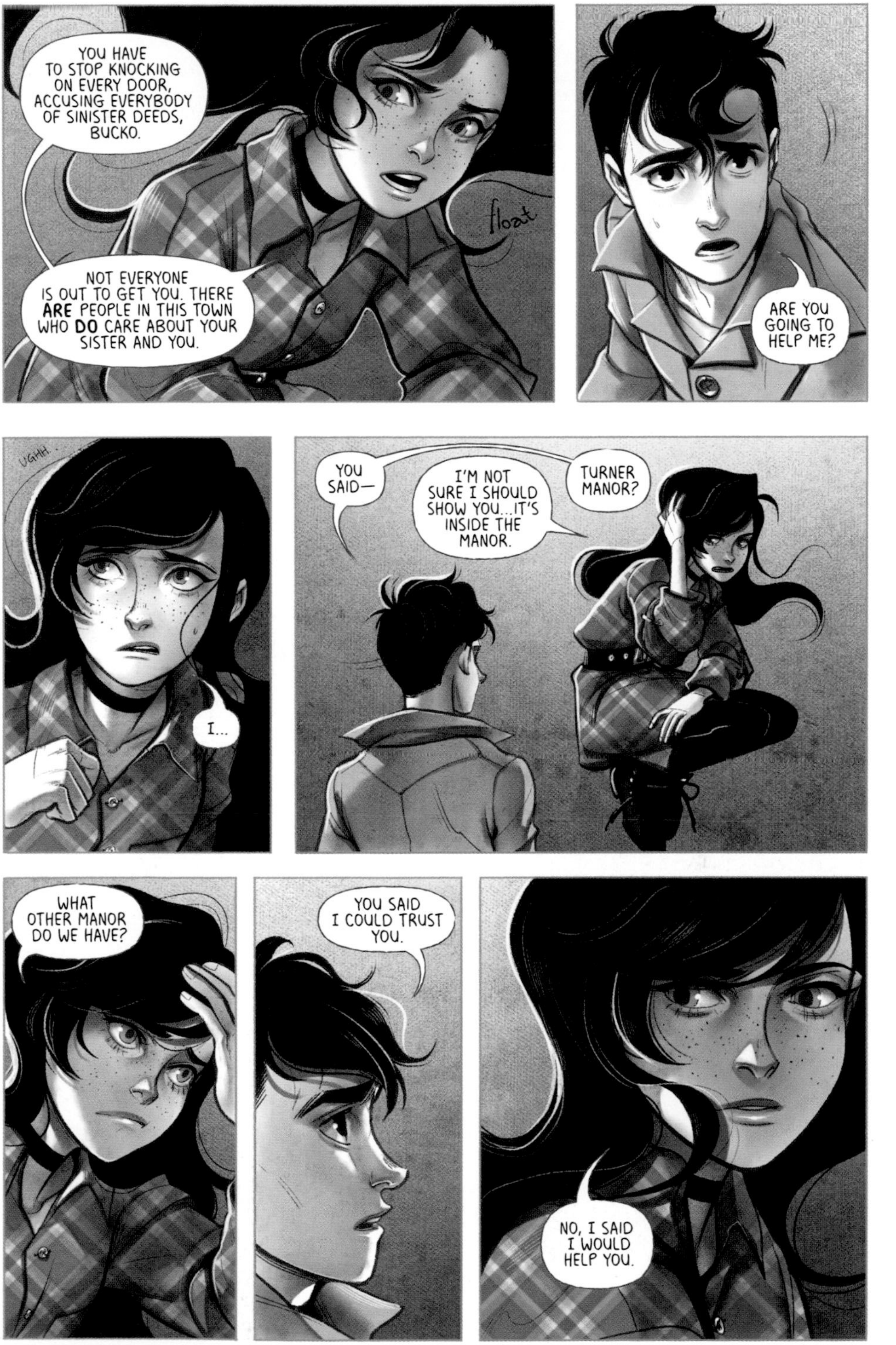
YOU HAVE TO STOP KNOCKING ON EVERY DOOR, ACCUSING EVERYBODY OF SINISTER DEEDS, BUCKO.
float
NOT EVERYONE IS OUT TO GET YOU. THERE **ARE** PEOPLE IN THIS TOWN WHO **DO** CARE ABOUT YOUR SISTER AND YOU.
ARE YOU GOING TO HELP ME?
UGHH.
I...
I'M NOT SURE I SHOULD SHOW YOU...IT'S INSIDE THE MANOR.
YOU SAID—
TURNER MANOR?
WHAT OTHER MANOR DO WE HAVE?
YOU SAID I COULD TRUST YOU.
NO, I SAID I WOULD HELP YOU.

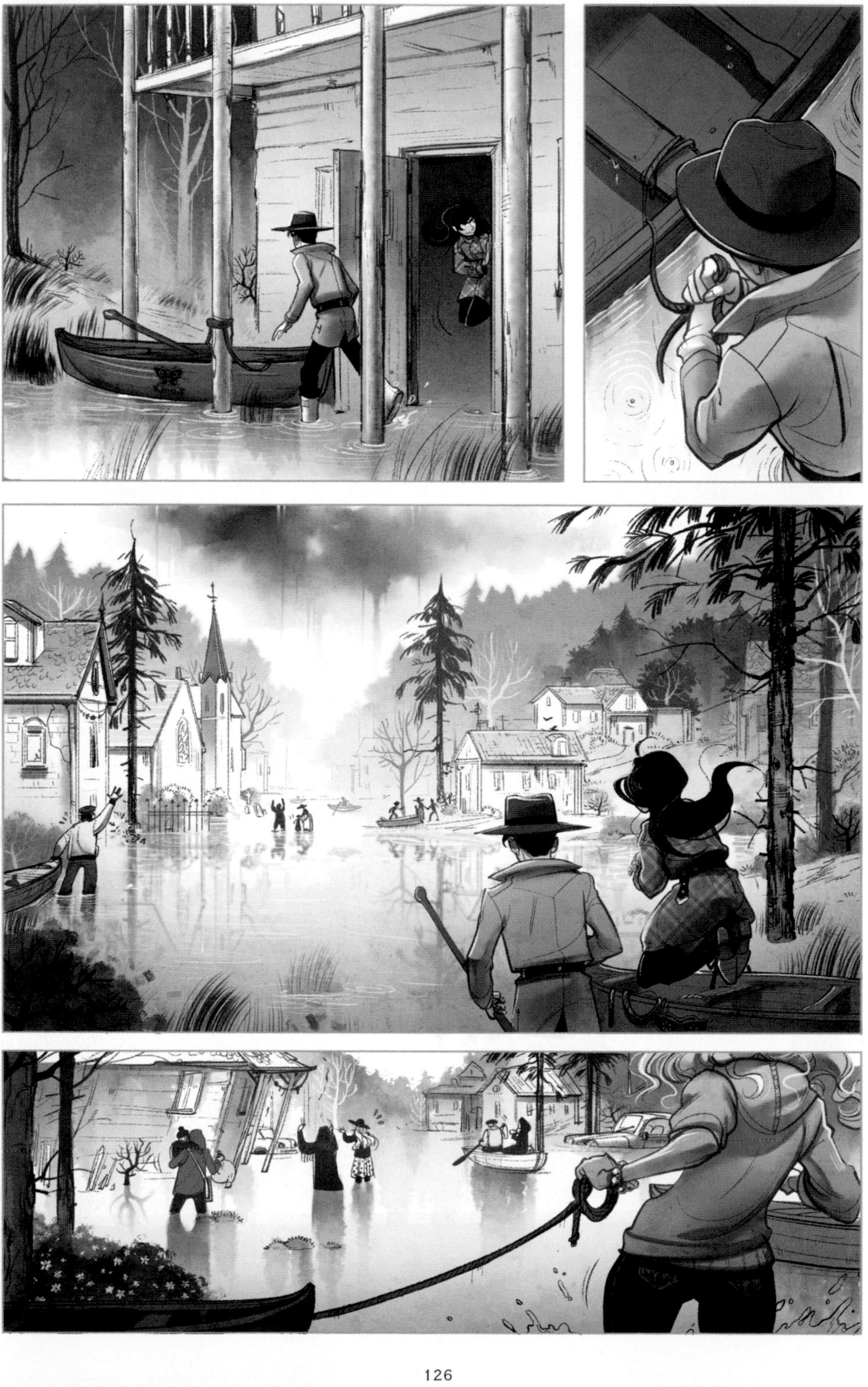

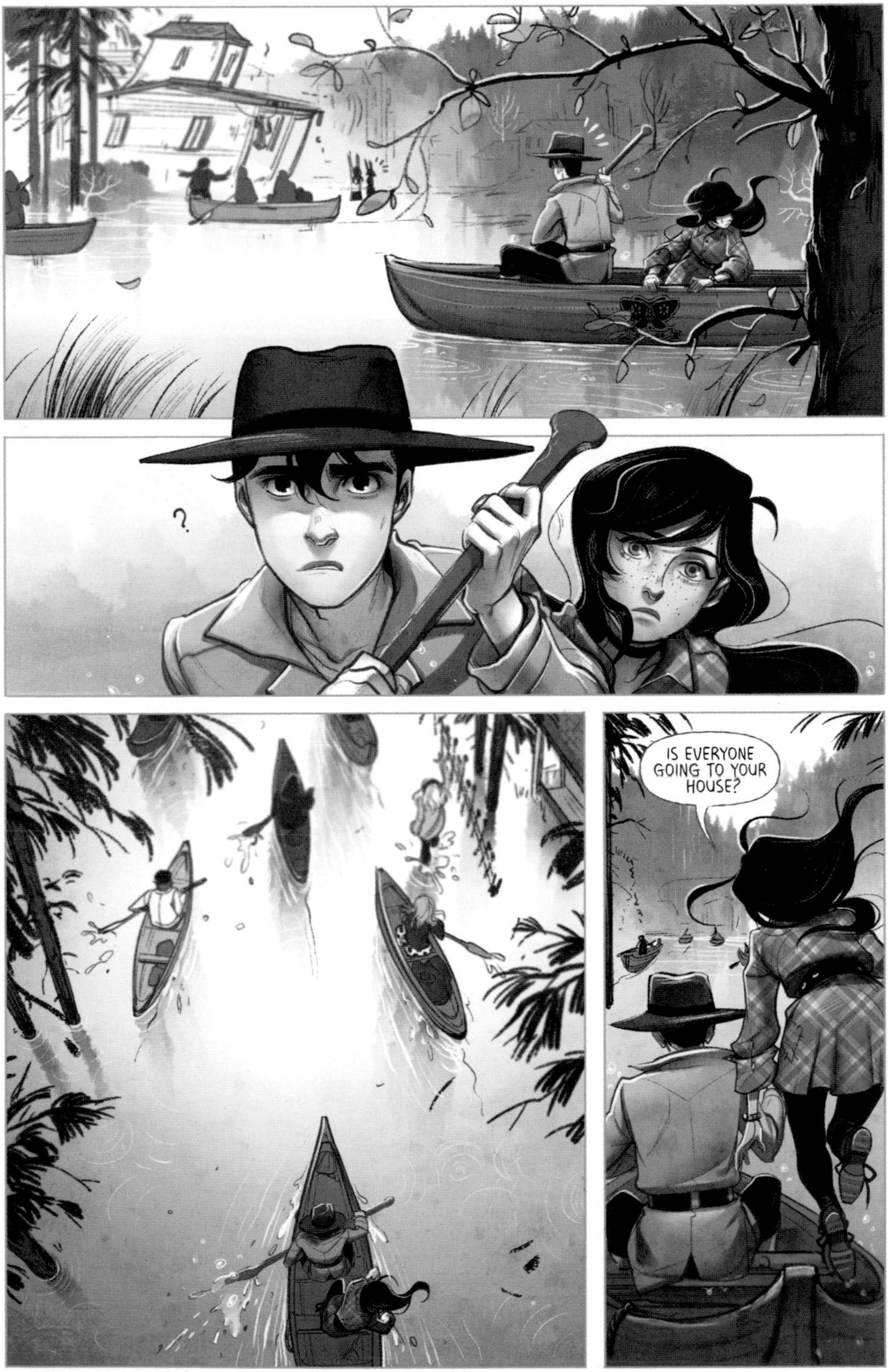
?
IS EVERYONE GOING TO YOUR HOUSE?

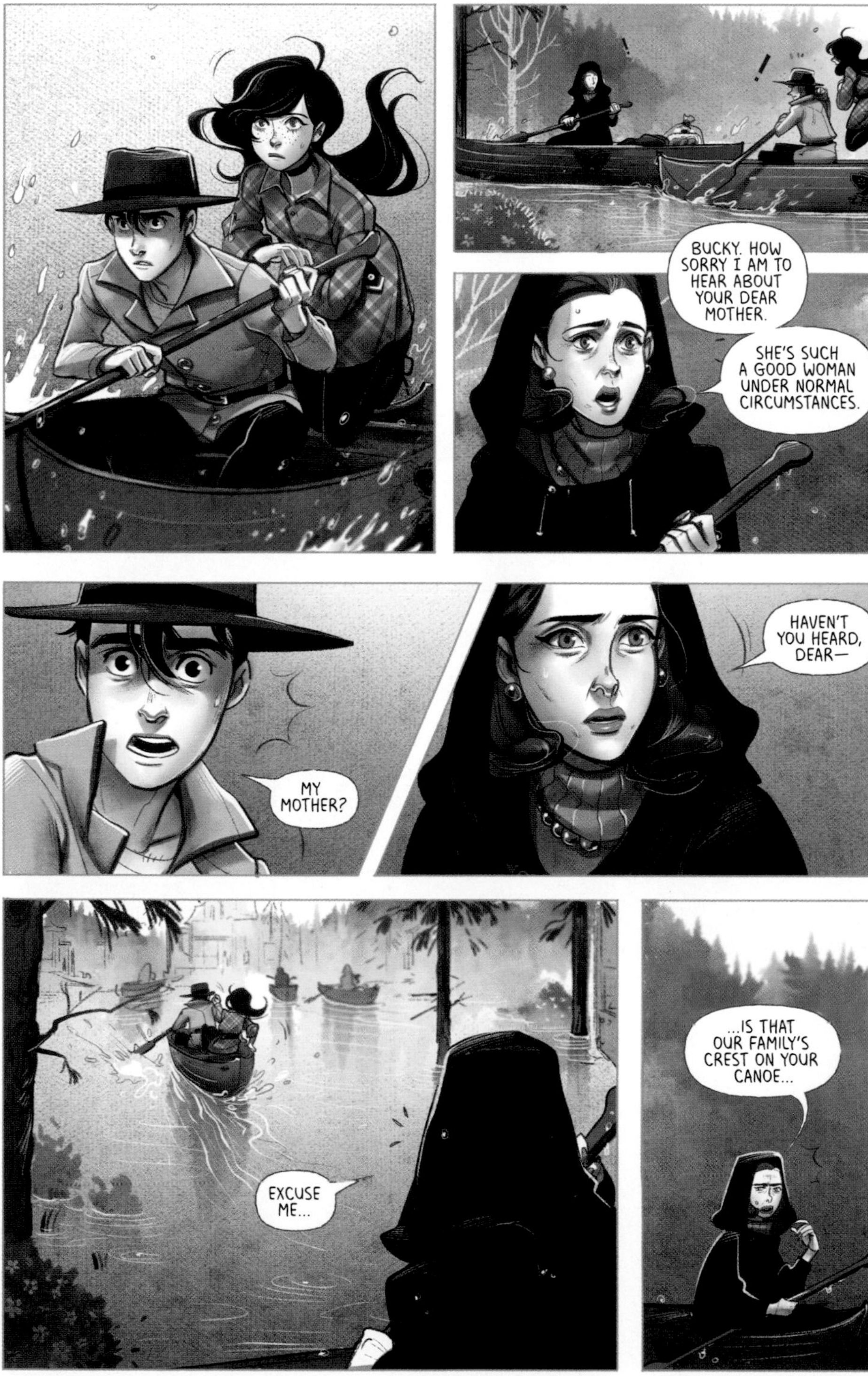
!
!
BUCKY. HOW SORRY I AM TO HEAR ABOUT YOUR DEAR MOTHER.
SHE'S SUCH A GOOD WOMAN UNDER NORMAL CIRCUMSTANCES.
MY MOTHER?
HAVEN'T YOU HEARD, DEAR—
EXCUSE ME...
...IS THAT OUR FAMILY'S CREST ON YOUR CANOE...

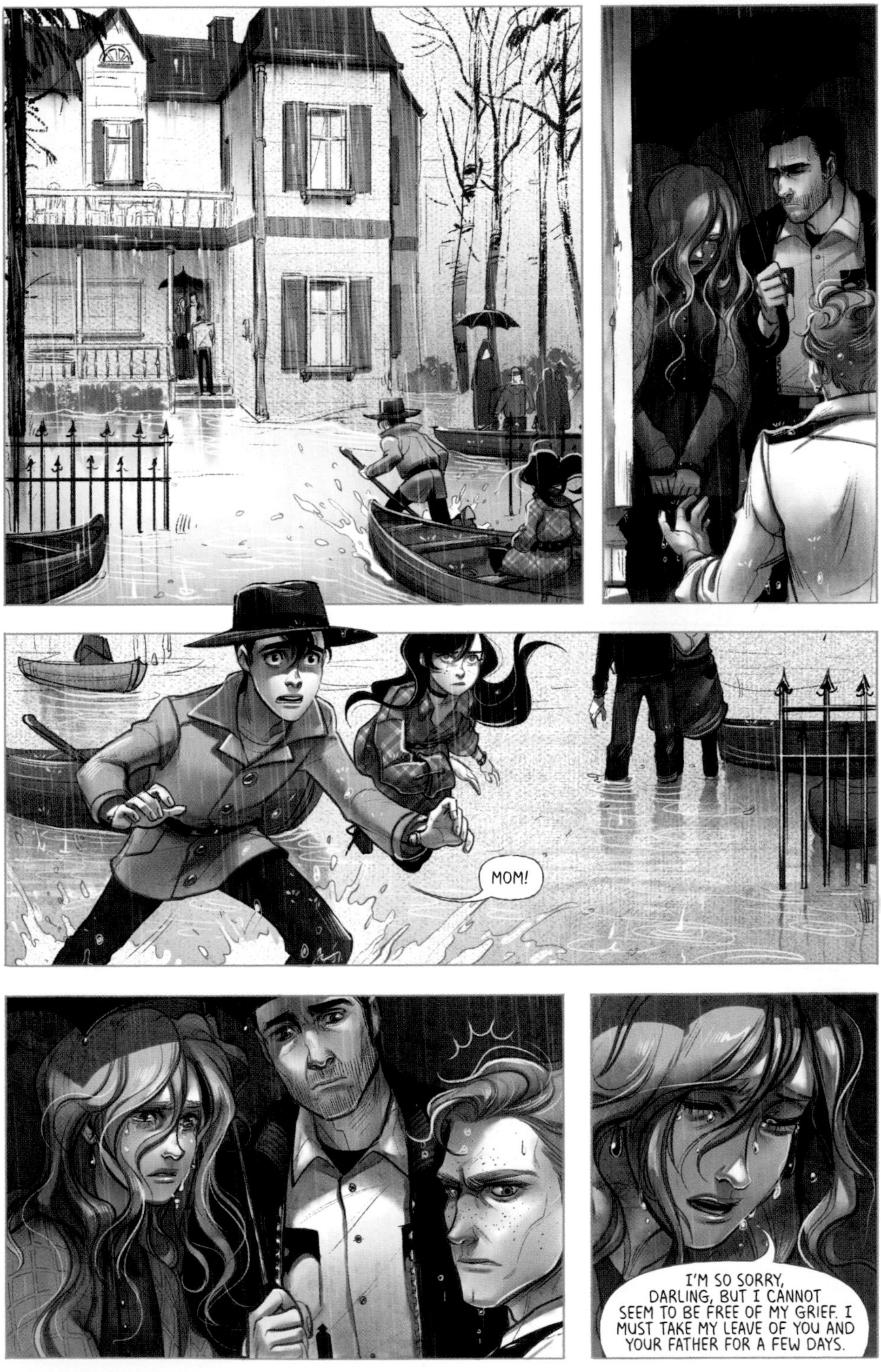
MOM!
I'M SO SORRY, DARLING, BUT I CANNOT SEEM TO BE FREE OF MY GRIEF. I MUST TAKE MY LEAVE OF YOU AND YOUR FATHER FOR A FEW DAYS.

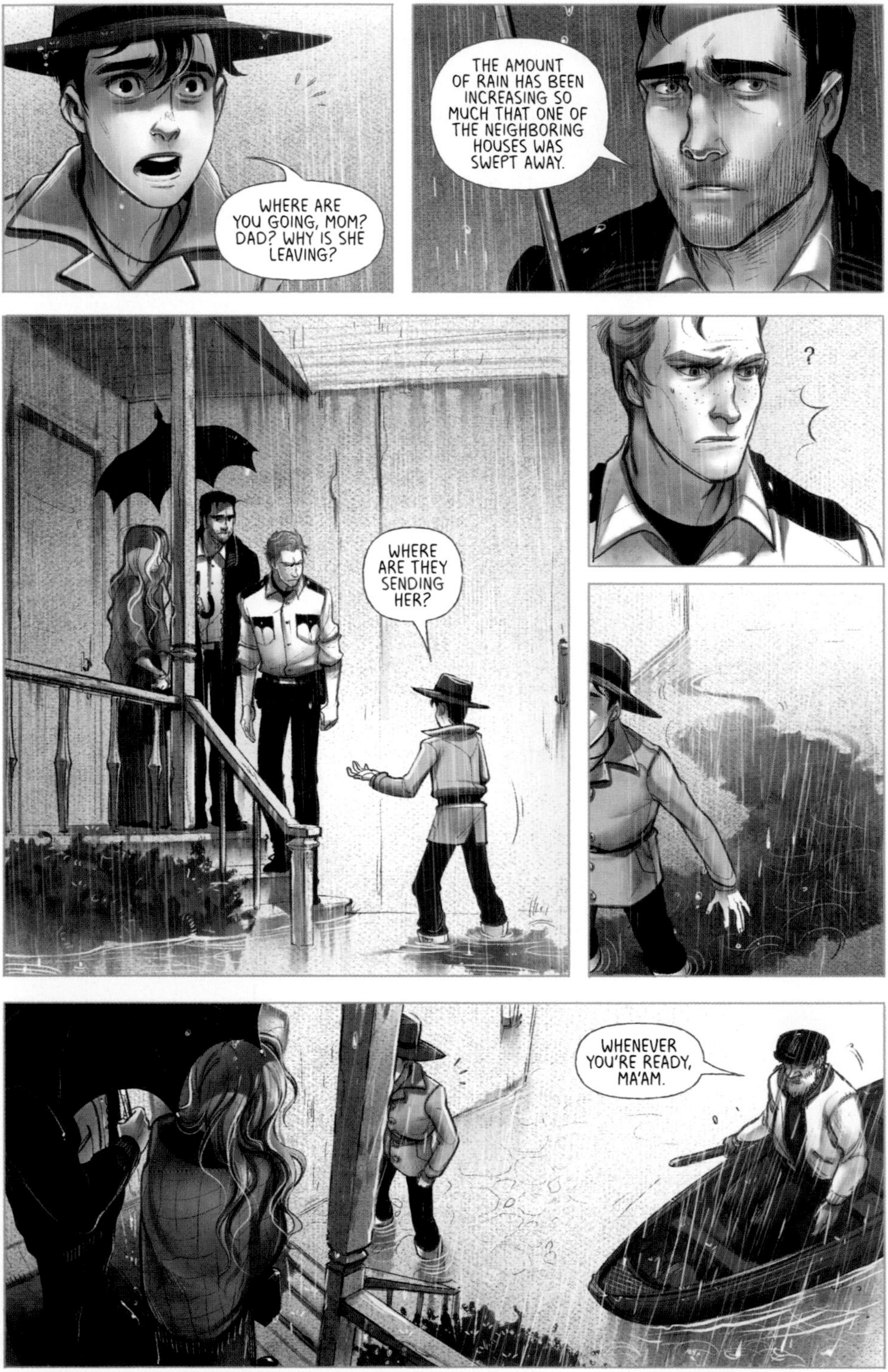
WHERE ARE YOU GOING, MOM? DAD? WHY IS SHE LEAVING?
THE AMOUNT OF RAIN HAS BEEN INCREASING SO MUCH THAT ONE OF THE NEIGHBORING HOUSES WAS SWEPT AWAY.
WHERE ARE THEY SENDING HER?
?
WHENEVER YOU'RE READY, MA'AM.

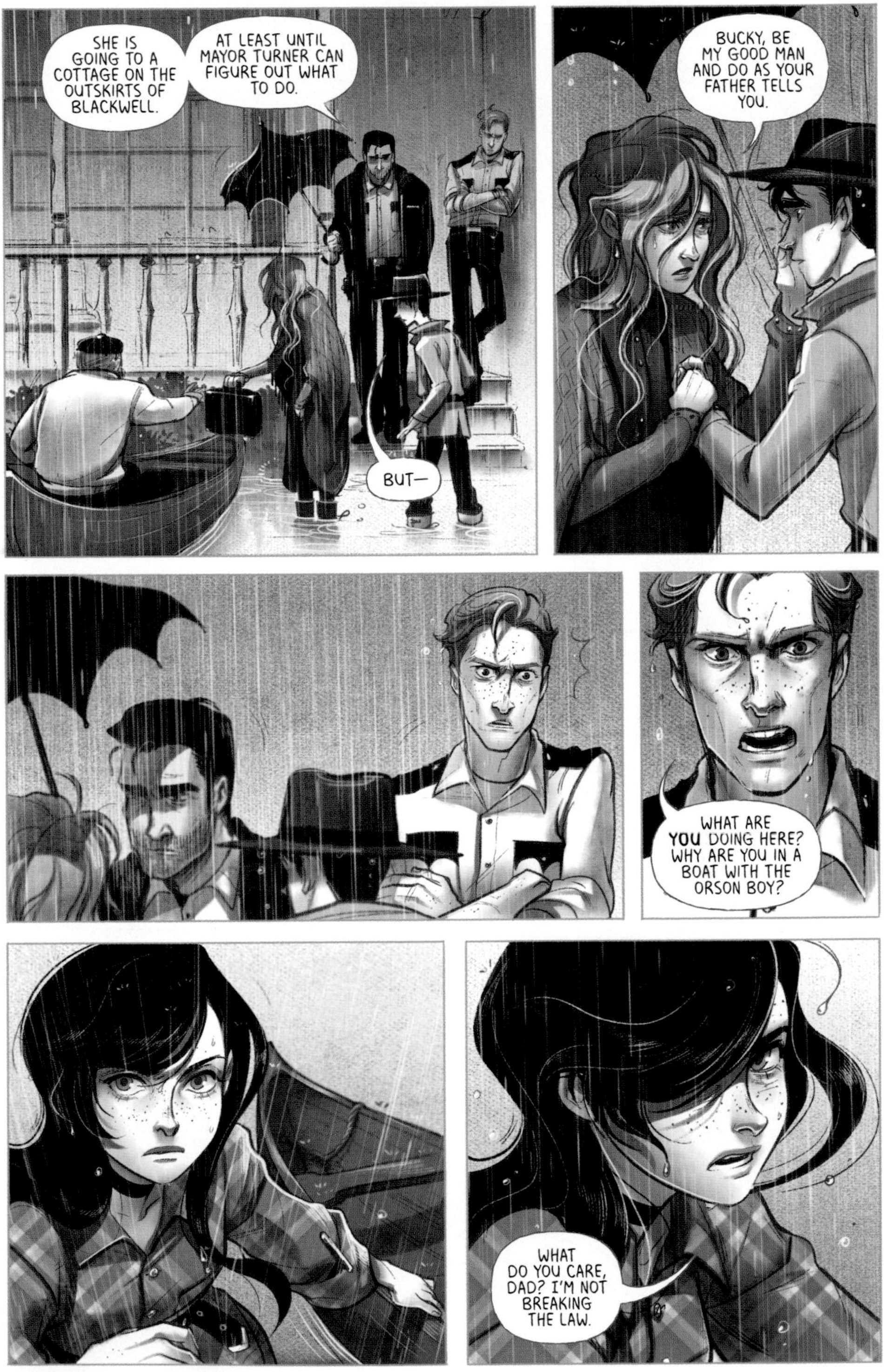
SHE IS GOING TO A COTTAGE ON THE OUTSKIRTS OF BLACKWELL.
AT LEAST UNTIL MAYOR TURNER CAN FIGURE OUT WHAT TO DO.
BUT—
BUCKY, BE MY GOOD MAN AND DO AS YOUR FATHER TELLS YOU.
WHAT ARE **YOU** DOING HERE? WHY ARE YOU IN A BOAT WITH THE ORSON BOY?
WHAT DO YOU CARE, DAD? I'M NOT BREAKING THE LAW.

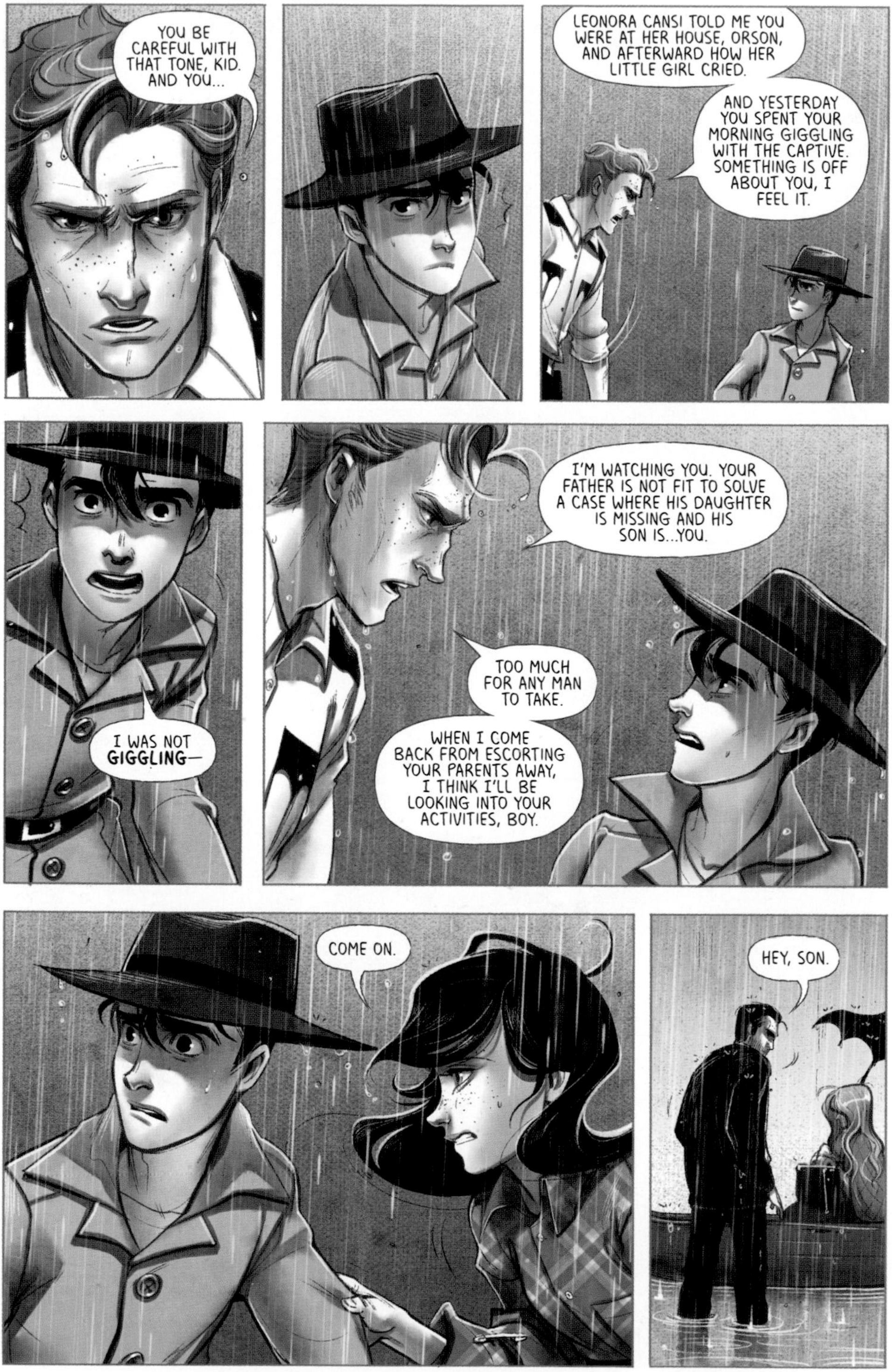
YOU BE CAREFUL WITH THAT TONE, KID. AND YOU...
LEONORA CANSI TOLD ME YOU WERE AT HER HOUSE, ORSON, AND AFTERWARD HOW HER LITTLE GIRL CRIED.
AND YESTERDAY YOU SPENT YOUR MORNING GIGGLING WITH THE CAPTIVE. SOMETHING IS OFF ABOUT YOU, I FEEL IT.
I WAS NOT **GIGGLING**—
I'M WATCHING YOU. YOUR FATHER IS NOT FIT TO SOLVE A CASE WHERE HIS DAUGHTER IS MISSING AND HIS SON IS...YOU.
TOO MUCH FOR ANY MAN TO TAKE.
WHEN I COME BACK FROM ESCORTING YOUR PARENTS AWAY, I THINK I'LL BE LOOKING INTO YOUR ACTIVITIES, BOY.
COME ON.
HEY, SON.

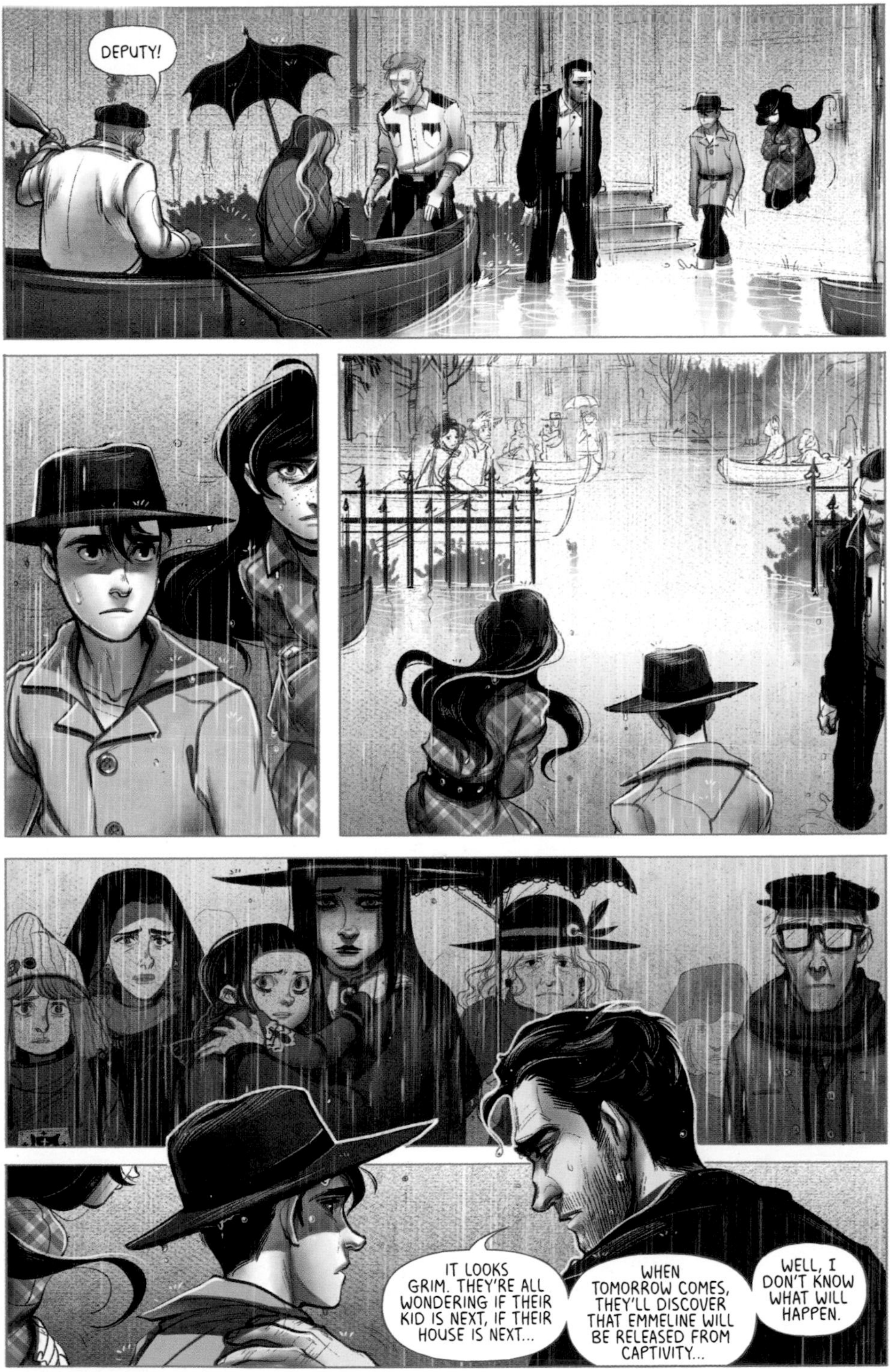
DEPUTY!
IT LOOKS GRIM. THEY'RE ALL WONDERING IF THEIR KID IS NEXT, IF THEIR HOUSE IS NEXT...
WHEN TOMORROW COMES, THEY'LL DISCOVER THAT EMMELINE WILL BE RELEASED FROM CAPTIVITY...
WELL, I DON'T KNOW WHAT WILL HAPPEN.

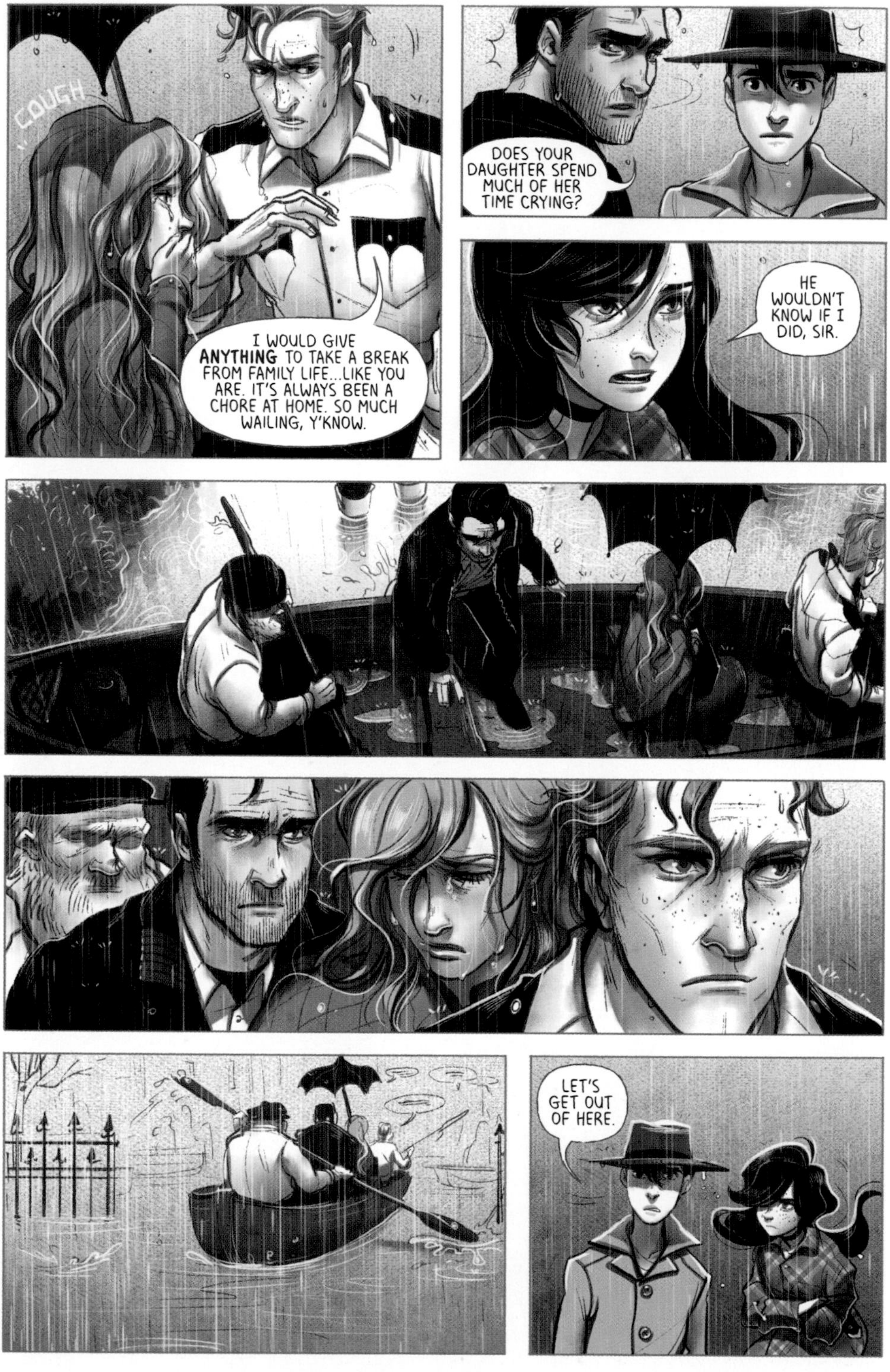
COUGH
I WOULD GIVE ANYTHING TO TAKE A BREAK FROM FAMILY LIFE...LIKE YOU ARE. IT'S ALWAYS BEEN A CHORE AT HOME. SO MUCH WAILING, Y'KNOW.
DOES YOUR DAUGHTER SPEND MUCH OF HER TIME CRYING?
HE WOULDN'T KNOW IF I DID, SIR.
LET'S GET OUT OF HERE.

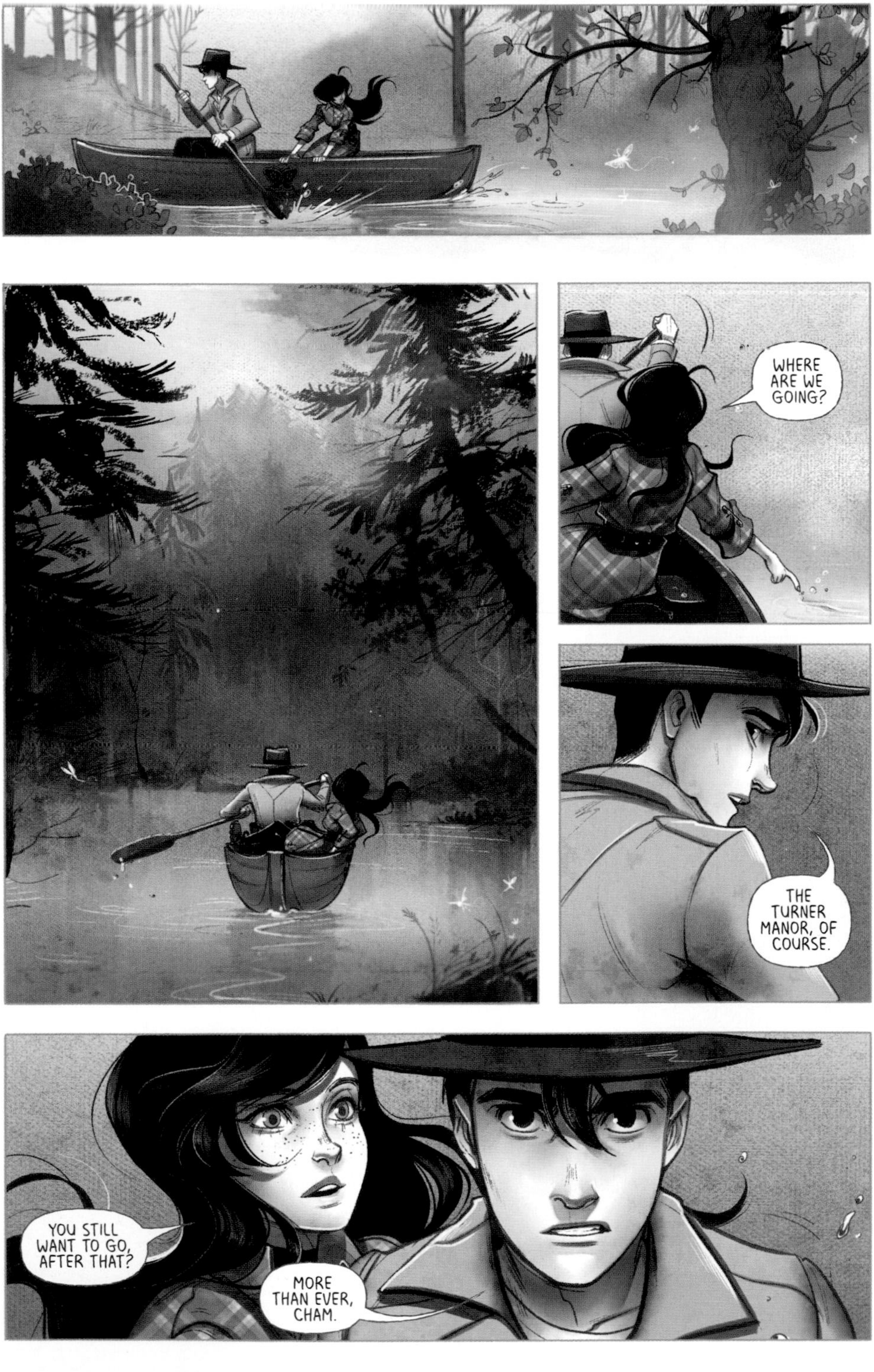
WHERE ARE WE GOING?
THE TURNER MANOR, OF COURSE.
YOU STILL WANT TO GO, AFTER THAT?
MORE THAN EVER, CHAM.

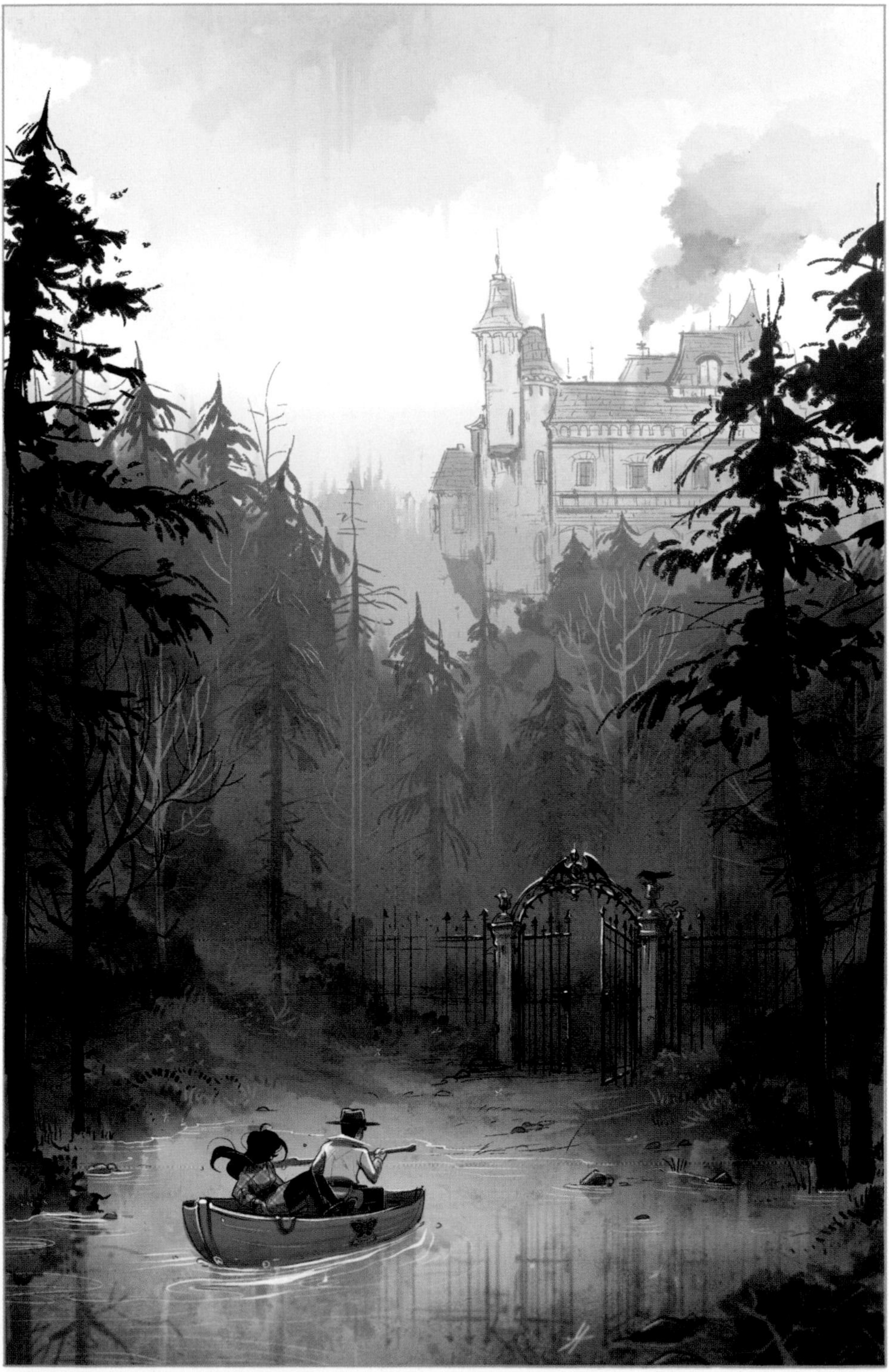

CHAPTER 7

TWO PEAS, DIFFERENT PODS

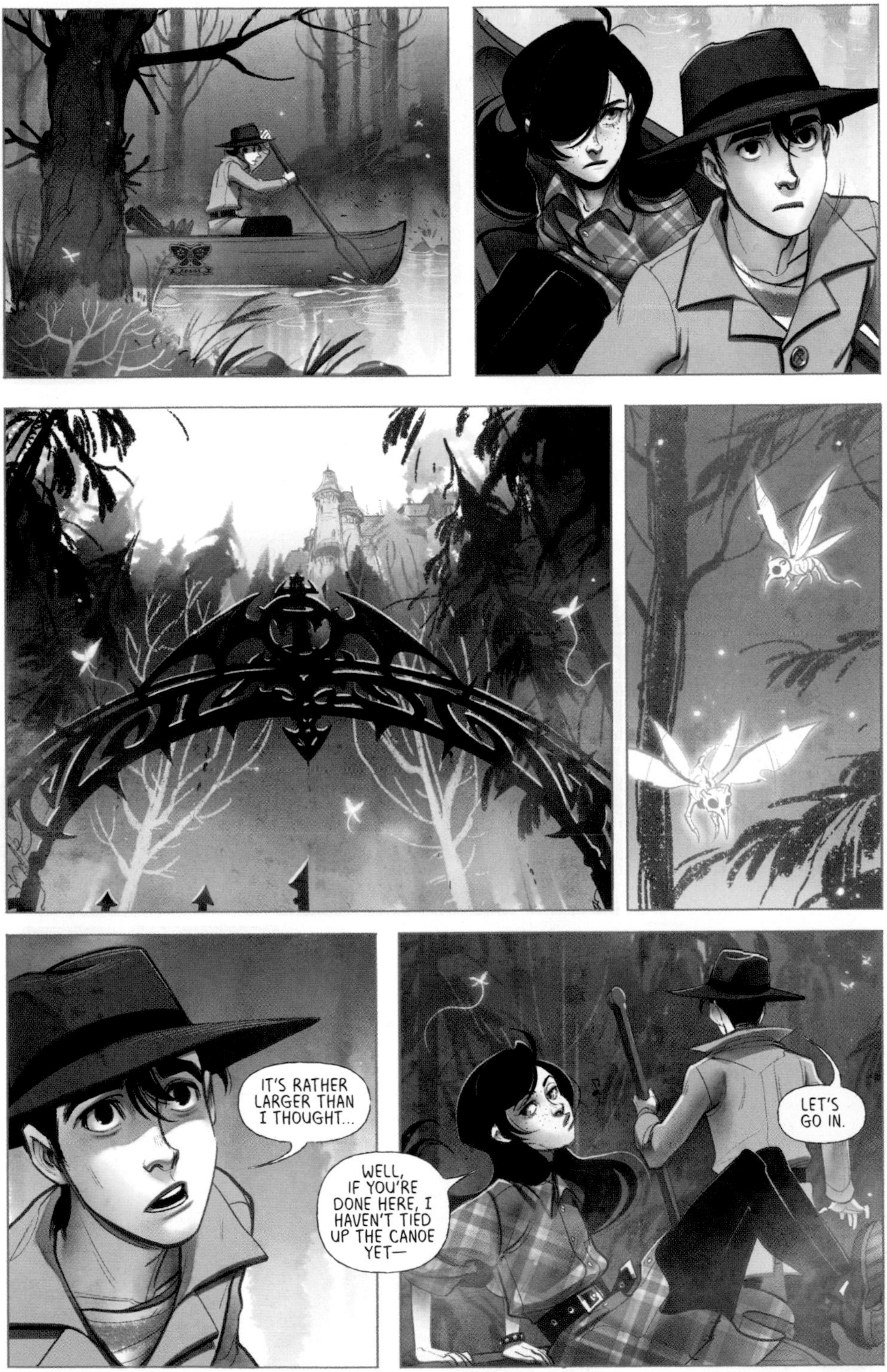
IT'S RATHER LARGER THAN I THOUGHT...
WELL, IF YOU'RE DONE HERE, I HAVEN'T TIED UP THE CANOE YET—
LET'S GO IN.

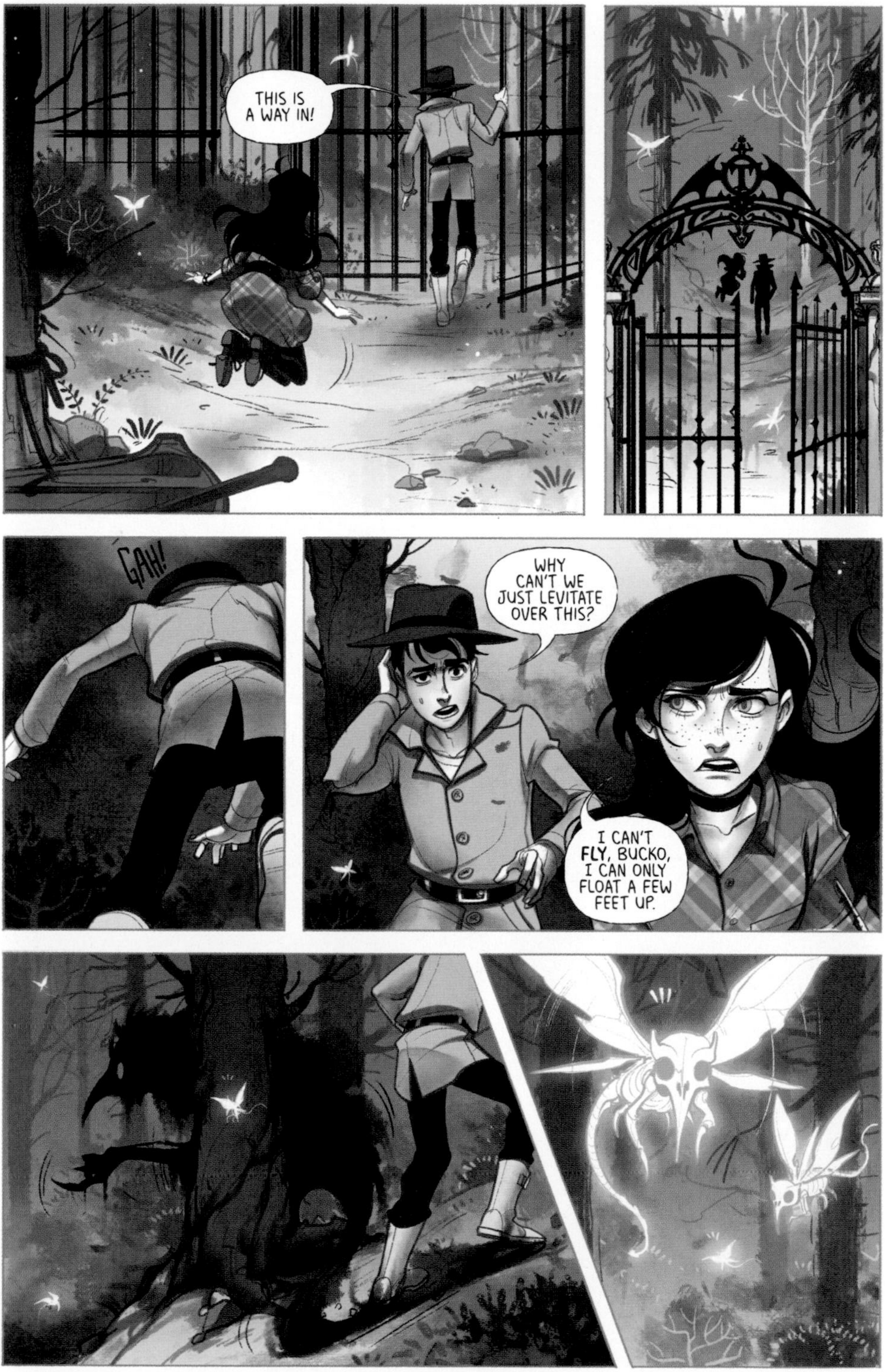
THIS IS A WAY IN!
GAH!
WHY CAN'T WE JUST LEVITATE OVER THIS?
I CAN'T **FLY**, BUCKO, I CAN ONLY FLOAT A FEW FEET UP.

GAH!

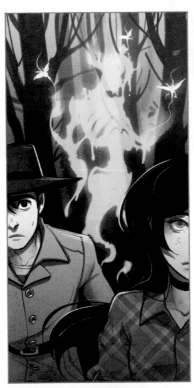

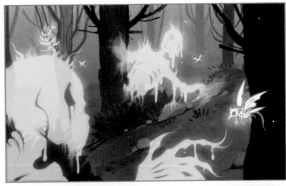

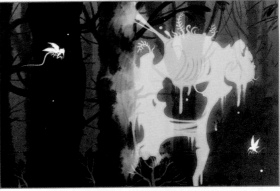

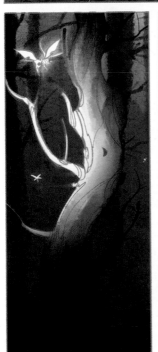

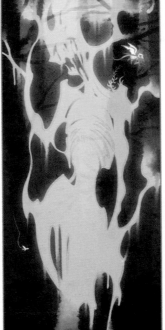

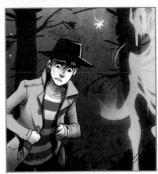

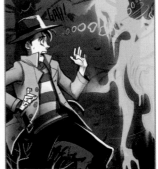

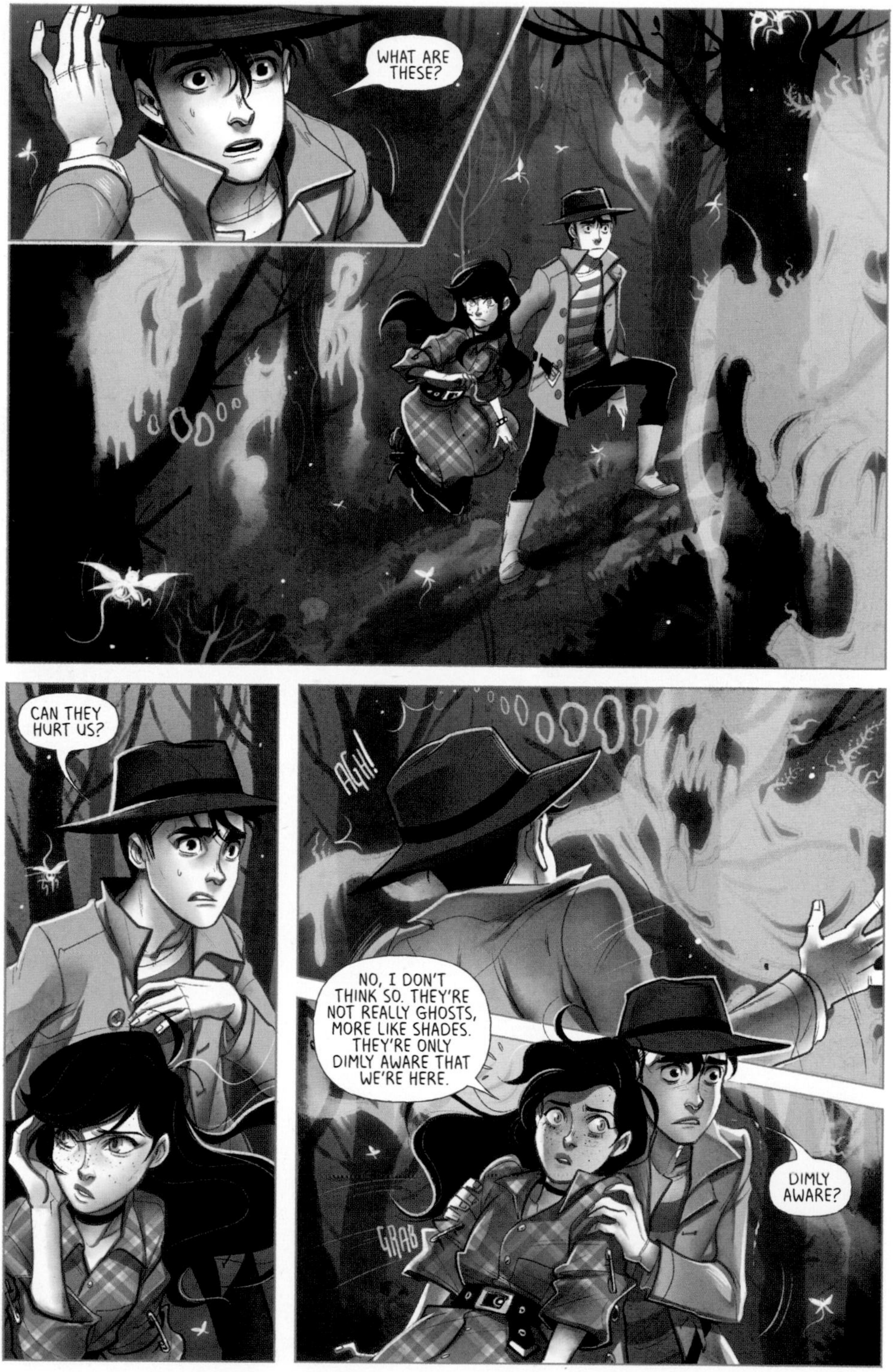
WHAT ARE THESE?
CAN THEY HURT US?
AGH!
NO, I DON'T THINK SO. THEY'RE NOT REALLY GHOSTS, MORE LIKE SHADES. THEY'RE ONLY DIMLY AWARE THAT WE'RE HERE.
GRAB
DIMLY AWARE?

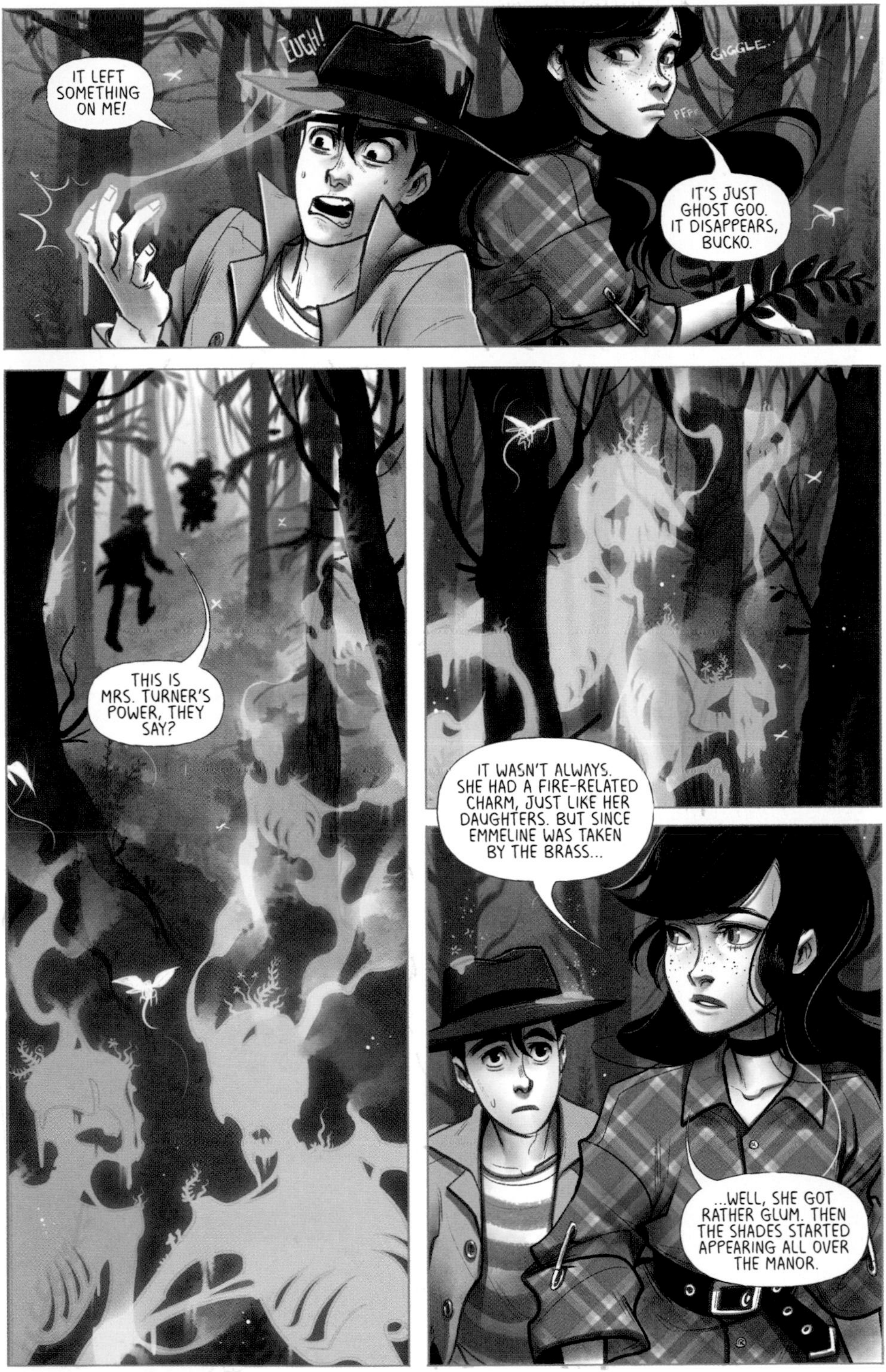

IT LEFT SOMETHING ON ME!
EUGH!
GIGGLE..
PFPF
IT'S JUST GHOST GOO. IT DISAPPEARS, BUCKO.
THIS IS MRS. TURNER'S POWER, THEY SAY?
IT WASN'T ALWAYS. SHE HAD A FIRE-RELATED CHARM, JUST LIKE HER DAUGHTERS. BUT SINCE EMMELINE WAS TAKEN BY THE BRASS...
...WELL, SHE GOT RATHER GLUM. THEN THE SHADES STARTED APPEARING ALL OVER THE MANOR.

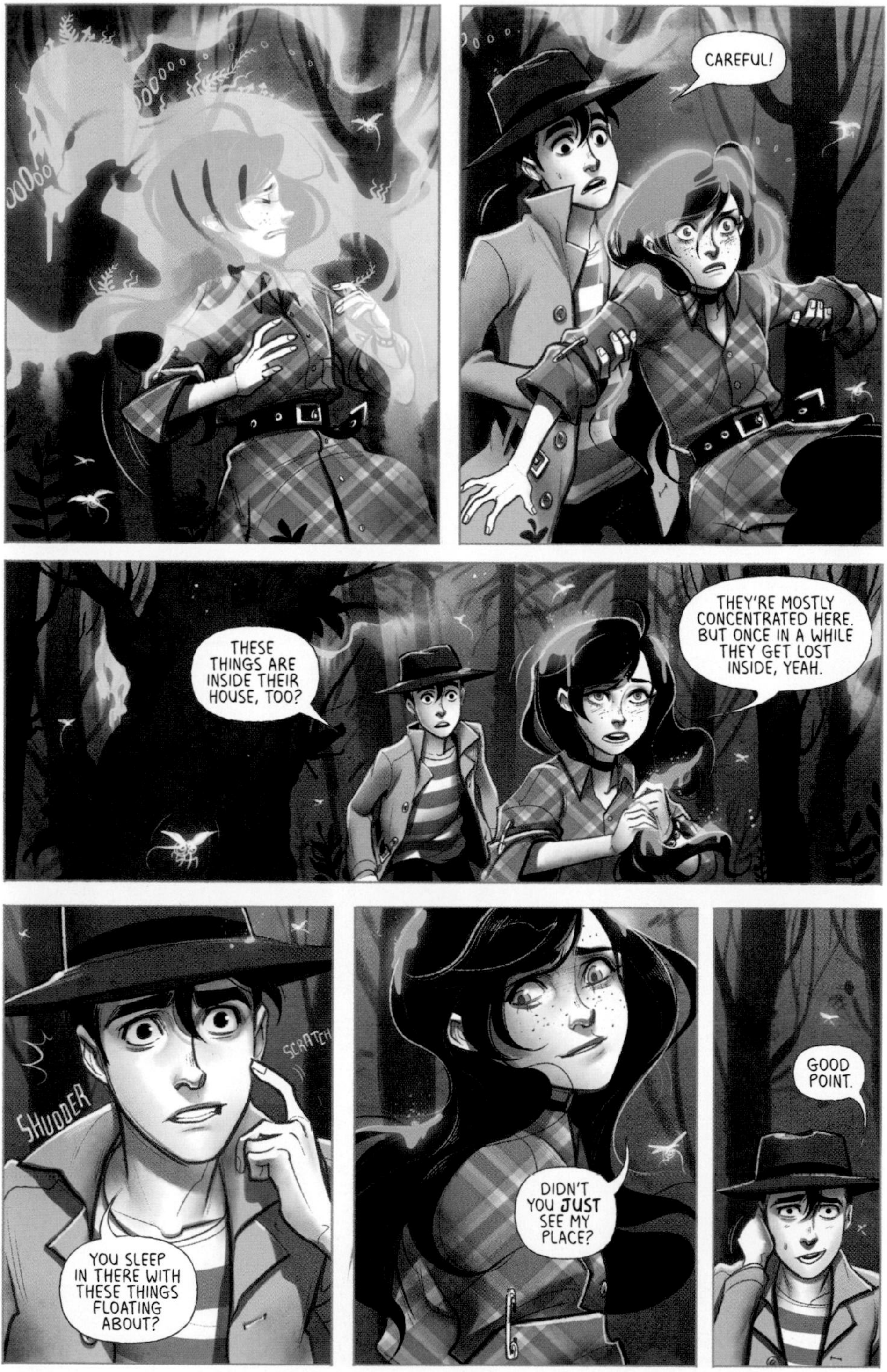
OOOOO
OOOOO
CAREFUL!
THESE THINGS ARE INSIDE THEIR HOUSE, TOO?
THEY'RE MOSTLY CONCENTRATED HERE. BUT ONCE IN A WHILE THEY GET LOST INSIDE, YEAH.
SHUDDER
SCRATCH
YOU SLEEP IN THERE WITH THESE THINGS FLOATING ABOUT?
DIDN'T YOU **JUST** SEE MY PLACE?
GOOD POINT.

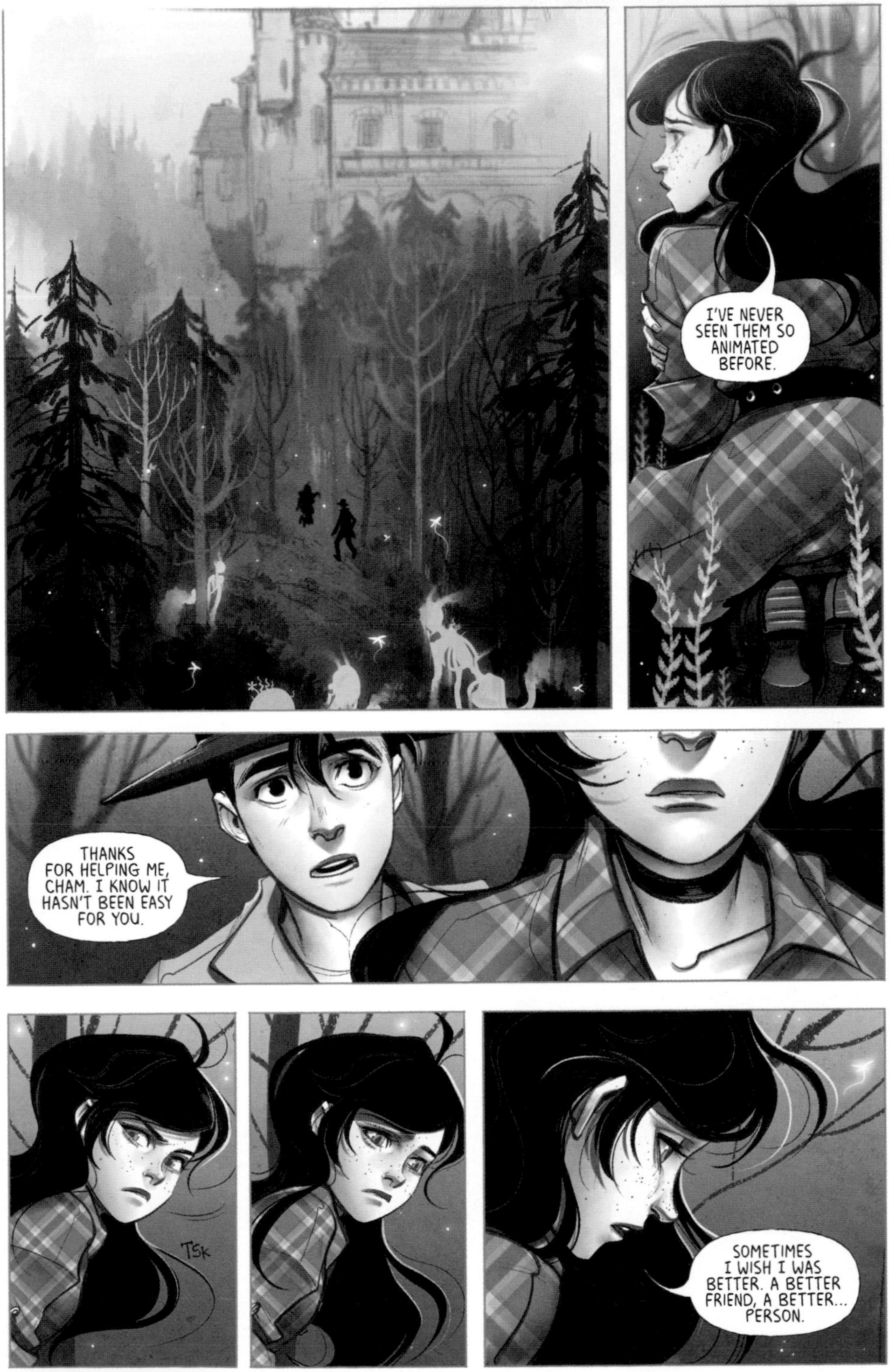

I'VE NEVER SEEN THEM SO ANIMATED BEFORE.
THANKS FOR HELPING ME, CHAM. I KNOW IT HASN'T BEEN EASY FOR YOU.
TSK
SOMETIMES I WISH I WAS BETTER. A BETTER FRIEND, A BETTER... PERSON.

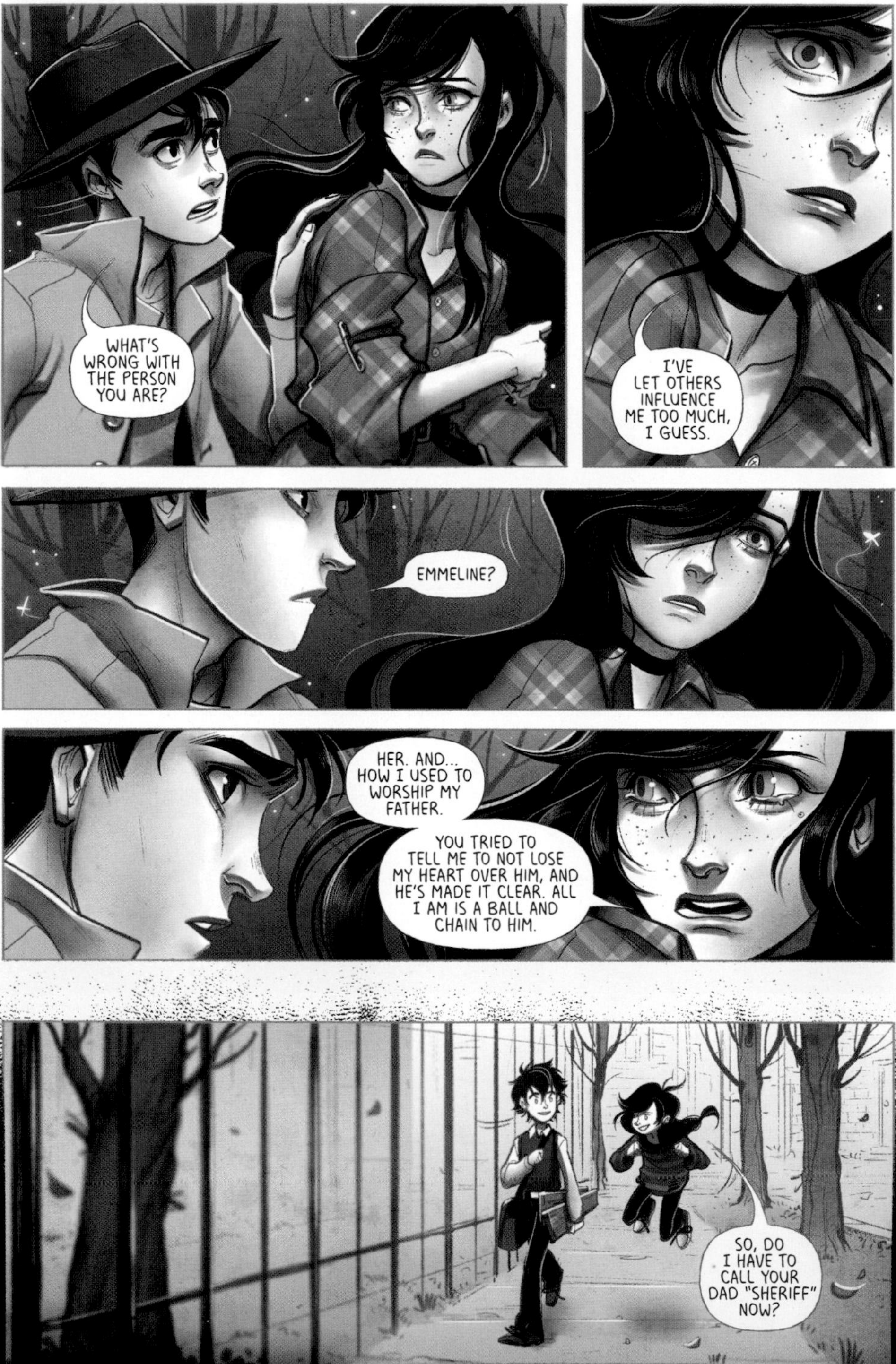
WHAT'S WRONG WITH THE PERSON YOU ARE?
I'VE LET OTHERS INFLUENCE ME TOO MUCH, I GUESS.
EMMELINE?
HER. AND... HOW I USED TO WORSHIP MY FATHER.
YOU TRIED TO TELL ME TO NOT LOSE MY HEART OVER HIM, AND HE'S MADE IT CLEAR. ALL I AM IS A BALL AND CHAIN TO HIM.
SO, DO I HAVE TO CALL YOUR DAD "SHERIFF" NOW?

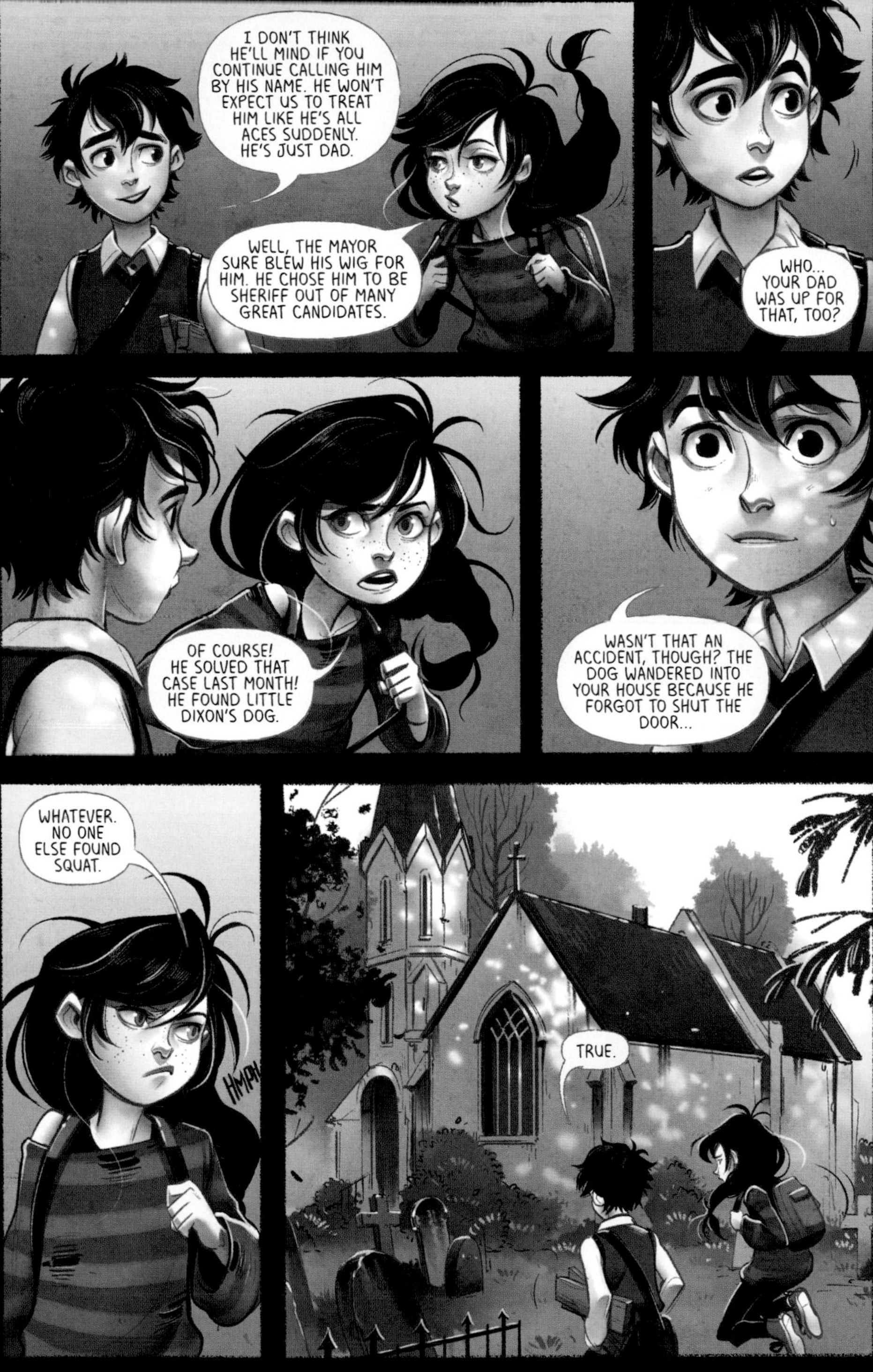
I DON'T THINK HE'LL MIND IF YOU CONTINUE CALLING HIM BY HIS NAME. HE WON'T EXPECT US TO TREAT HIM LIKE HE'S ALL ACES SUDDENLY. HE'S JUST DAD.
WELL, THE MAYOR SURE BLEW HIS WIG FOR HIM. HE CHOSE HIM TO BE SHERIFF OUT OF MANY GREAT CANDIDATES.
WHO... YOUR DAD WAS UP FOR THAT, TOO?
OF COURSE! HE SOLVED THAT CASE LAST MONTH! HE FOUND LITTLE DIXON'S DOG.
WASN'T THAT AN ACCIDENT, THOUGH? THE DOG WANDERED INTO YOUR HOUSE BECAUSE HE FORGOT TO SHUT THE DOOR...
WHATEVER. NO ONE ELSE FOUND SQUAT.
HMPH
TRUE.

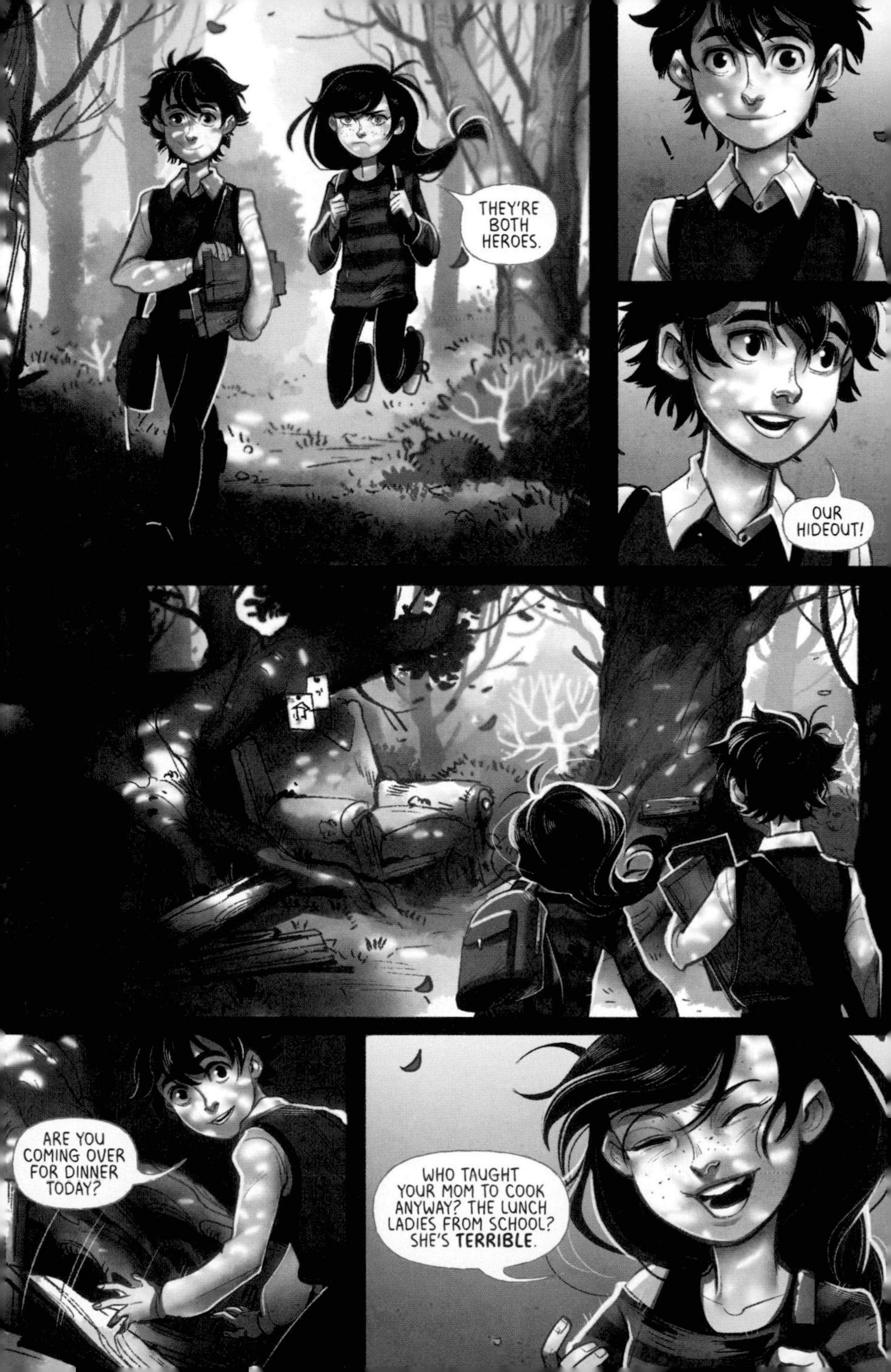
THEY'RE BOTH HEROES.
!
OUR HIDEOUT!
ARE YOU COMING OVER FOR DINNER TODAY?
WHO TAUGHT YOUR MOM TO COOK ANYWAY? THE LUNCH LADIES FROM SCHOOL? SHE'S **TERRIBLE**.

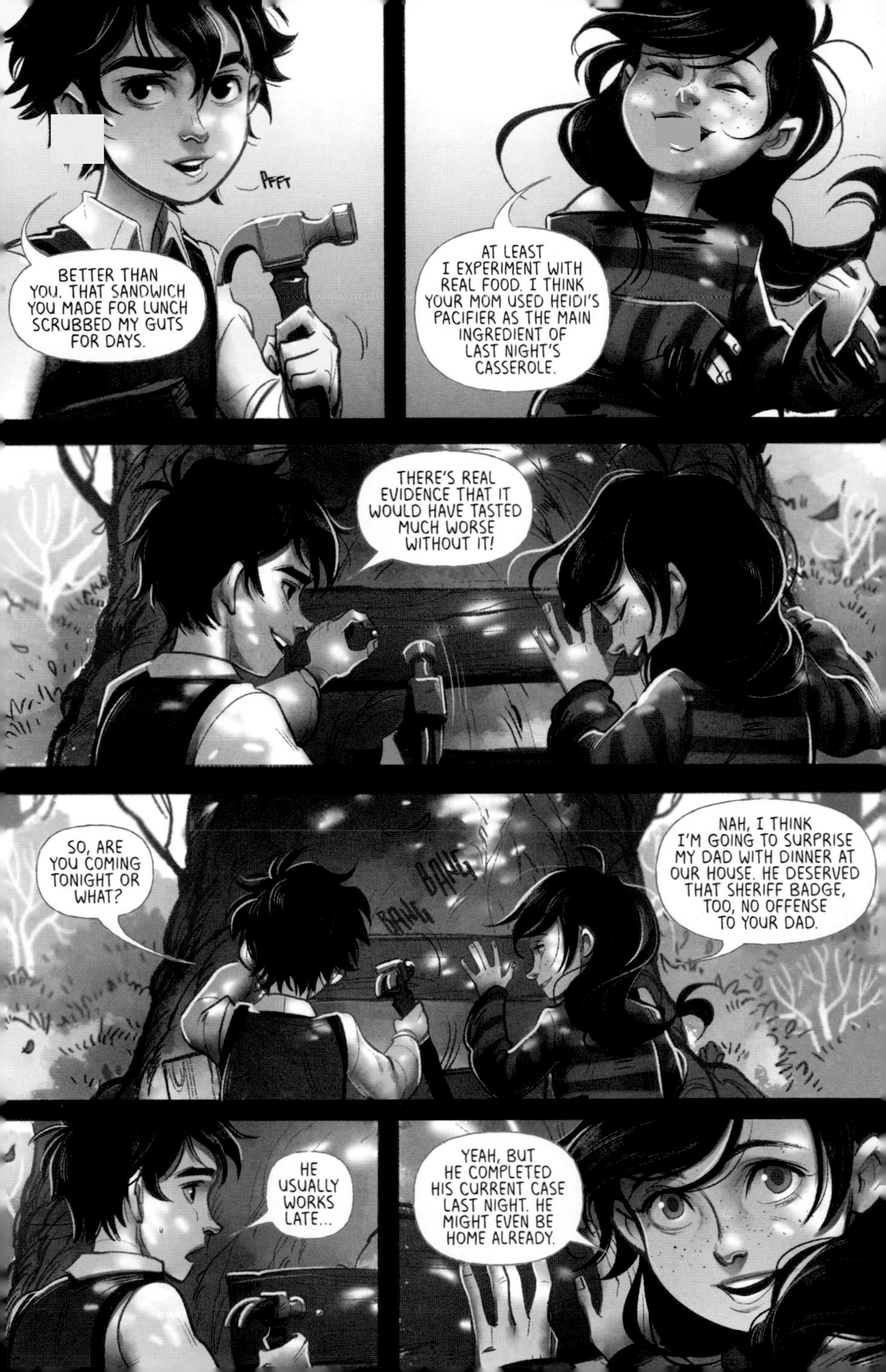
PFFT
BETTER THAN YOU. THAT SANDWICH YOU MADE FOR LUNCH SCRUBBED MY GUTS FOR DAYS.
AT LEAST I EXPERIMENT WITH REAL FOOD. I THINK YOUR MOM USED HEIDI'S PACIFIER AS THE MAIN INGREDIENT OF LAST NIGHT'S CASSEROLE.
THERE'S REAL EVIDENCE THAT IT WOULD HAVE TASTED MUCH WORSE WITHOUT IT!
SO, ARE YOU COMING TONIGHT OR WHAT?
BANG
BANG
NAH, I THINK I'M GOING TO SURPRISE MY DAD WITH DINNER AT OUR HOUSE. HE DESERVED THAT SHERIFF BADGE, TOO, NO OFFENSE TO YOUR DAD.
HE USUALLY WORKS LATE...
YEAH, BUT HE COMPLETED HIS CURRENT CASE LAST NIGHT. HE MIGHT EVEN BE HOME ALREADY.

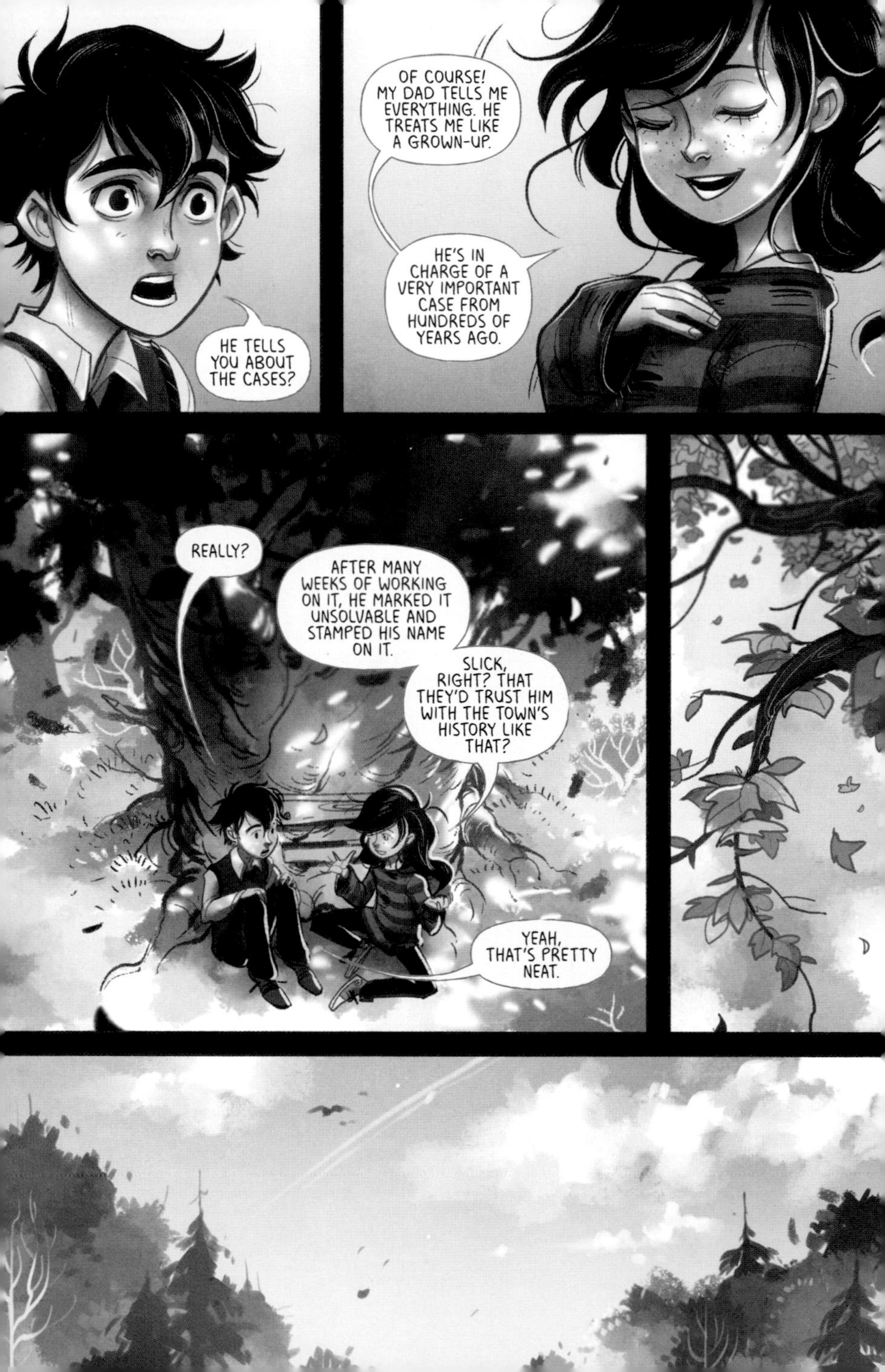
HE TELLS YOU ABOUT THE CASES?
OF COURSE! MY DAD TELLS ME EVERYTHING. HE TREATS ME LIKE A GROWN-UP.
HE'S IN CHARGE OF A VERY IMPORTANT CASE FROM HUNDREDS OF YEARS AGO.
REALLY?
AFTER MANY WEEKS OF WORKING ON IT, HE MARKED IT UNSOLVABLE AND STAMPED HIS NAME ON IT.
SLICK, RIGHT? THAT THEY'D TRUST HIM WITH THE TOWN'S HISTORY LIKE THAT?
YEAH, THAT'S PRETTY NEAT.

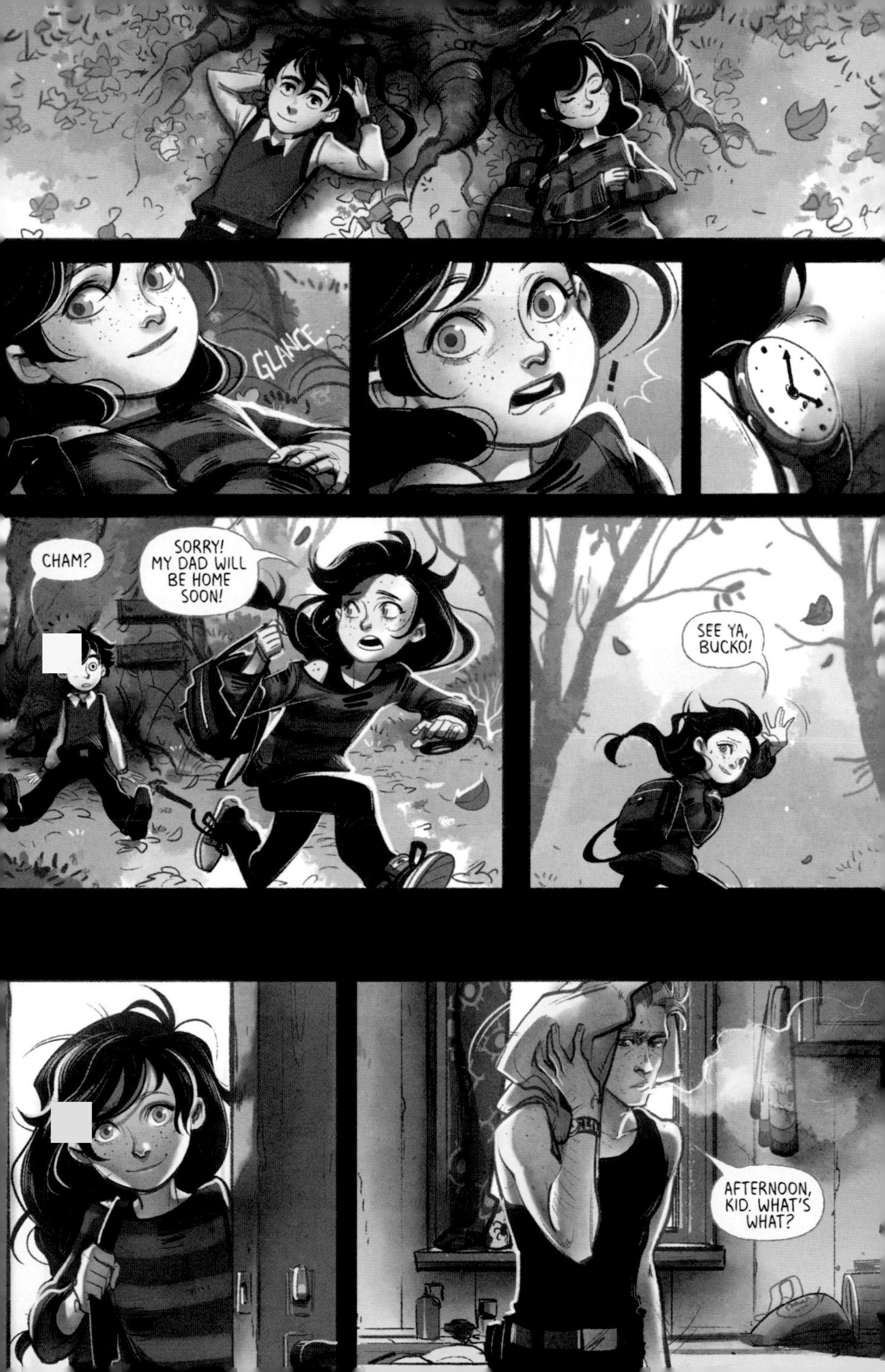

GLANCE...
!
CHAM?
SORRY! MY DAD WILL BE HOME SOON!
SEE YA, BUCKO!
AFTERNOON, KID. WHAT'S WHAT?

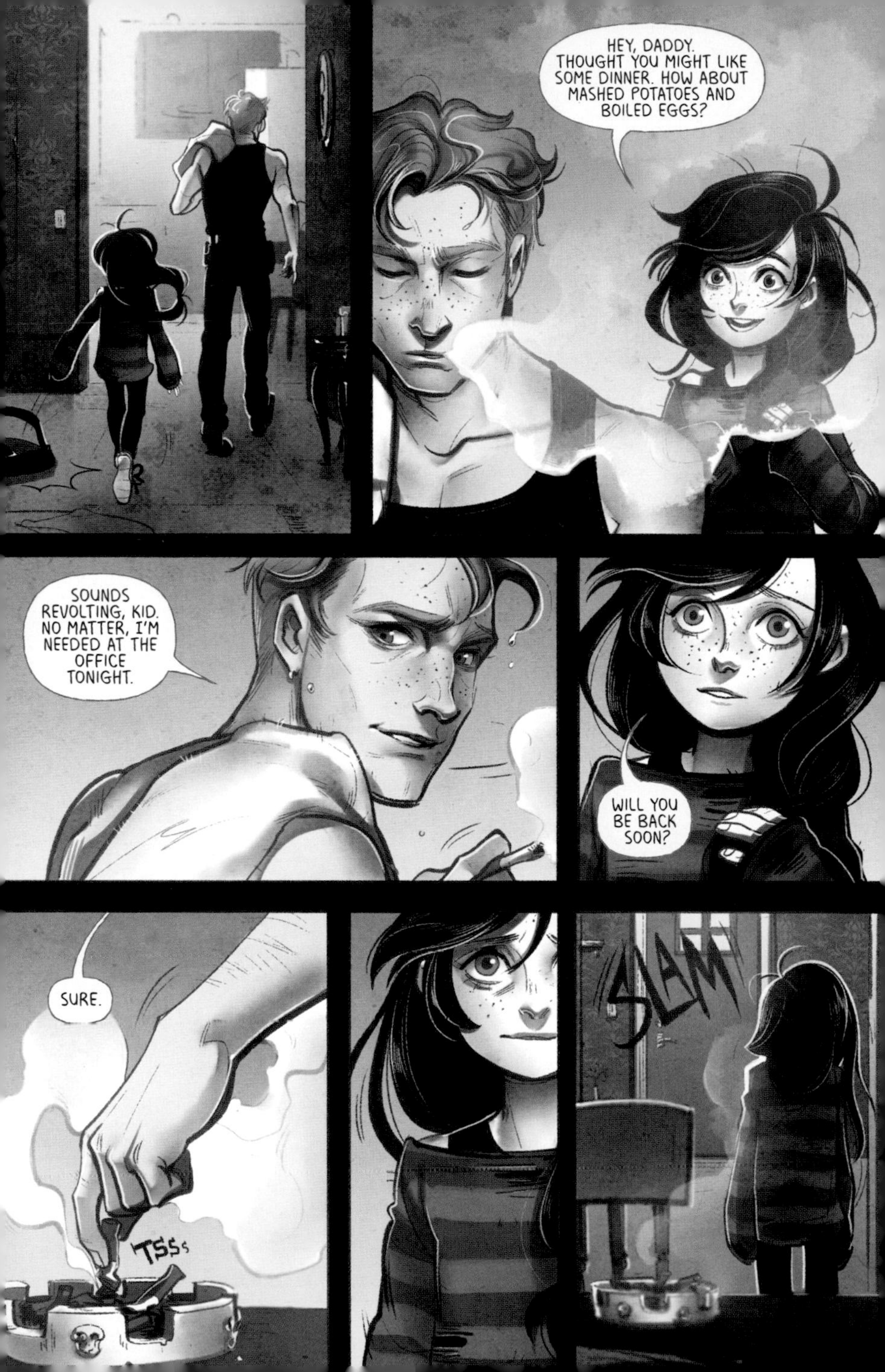
HEY, DADDY. THOUGHT YOU MIGHT LIKE SOME DINNER. HOW ABOUT MASHED POTATOES AND BOILED EGGS?
SOUNDS REVOLTING, KID. NO MATTER, I'M NEEDED AT THE OFFICE TONIGHT.
WILL YOU BE BACK SOON?
SURE.
TSSs
SLAM

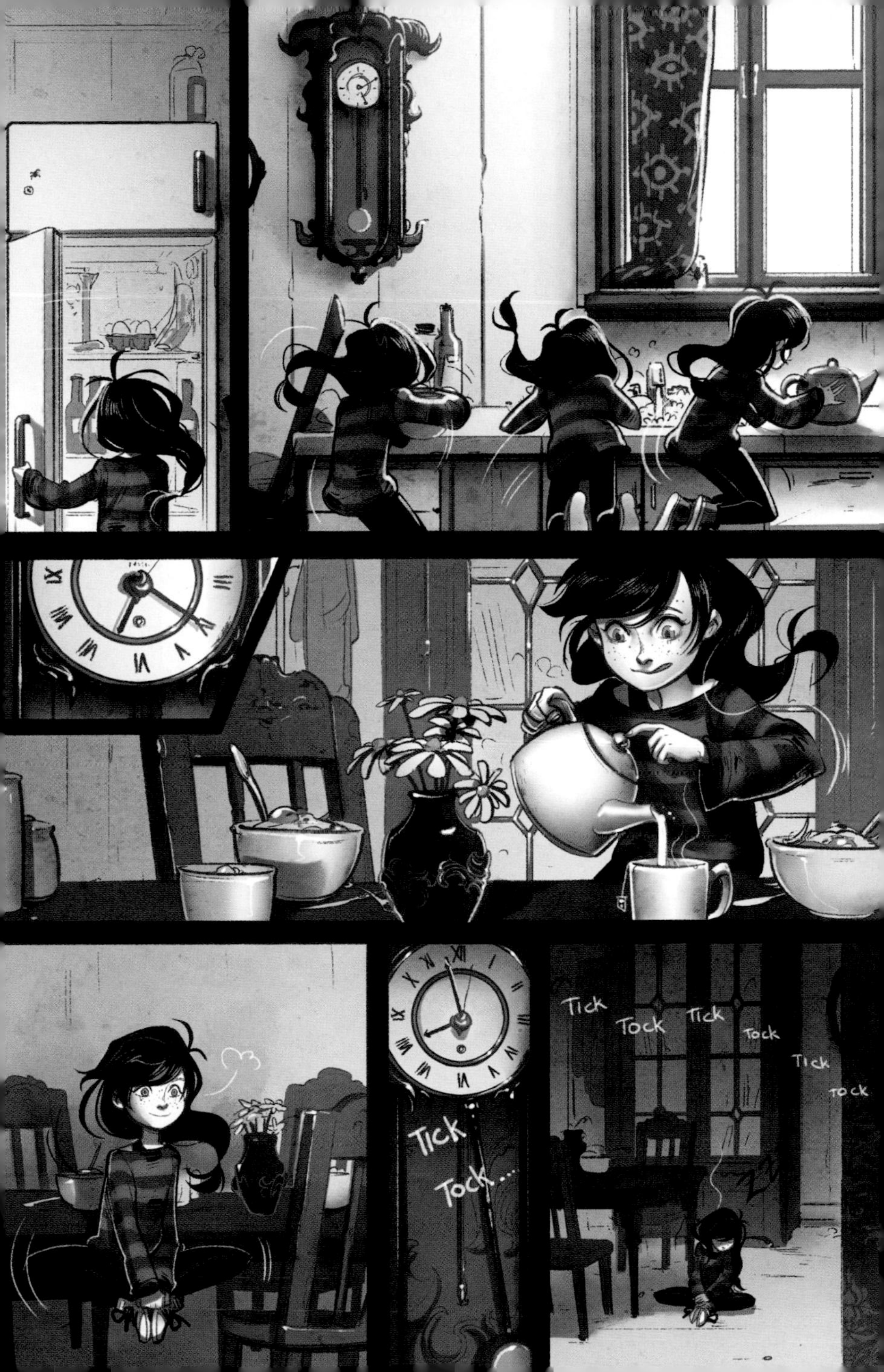
TICK
TOCK...
TICK
TOCK
TICK
TOCK
TICK
TOCK

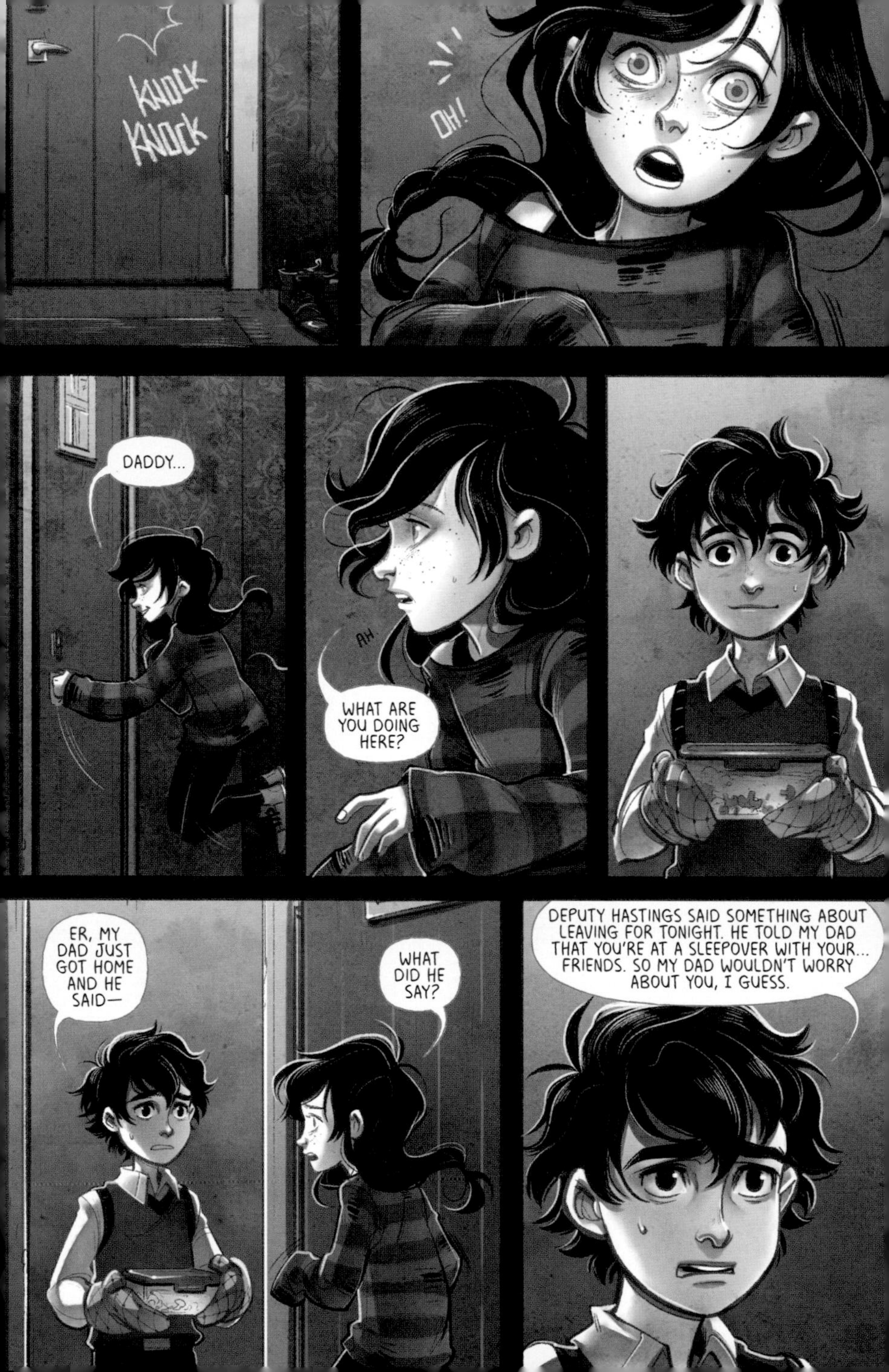
KNOCK KNOCK
OH!
DADDY...
AH
WHAT ARE YOU DOING HERE?
ER, MY DAD JUST GOT HOME AND HE SAID—
WHAT DID HE SAY?
DEPUTY HASTINGS SAID SOMETHING ABOUT LEAVING FOR TONIGHT. HE TOLD MY DAD THAT YOU'RE AT A SLEEPOVER WITH YOUR... FRIENDS. SO MY DAD WOULDN'T WORRY ABOUT YOU, I GUESS.

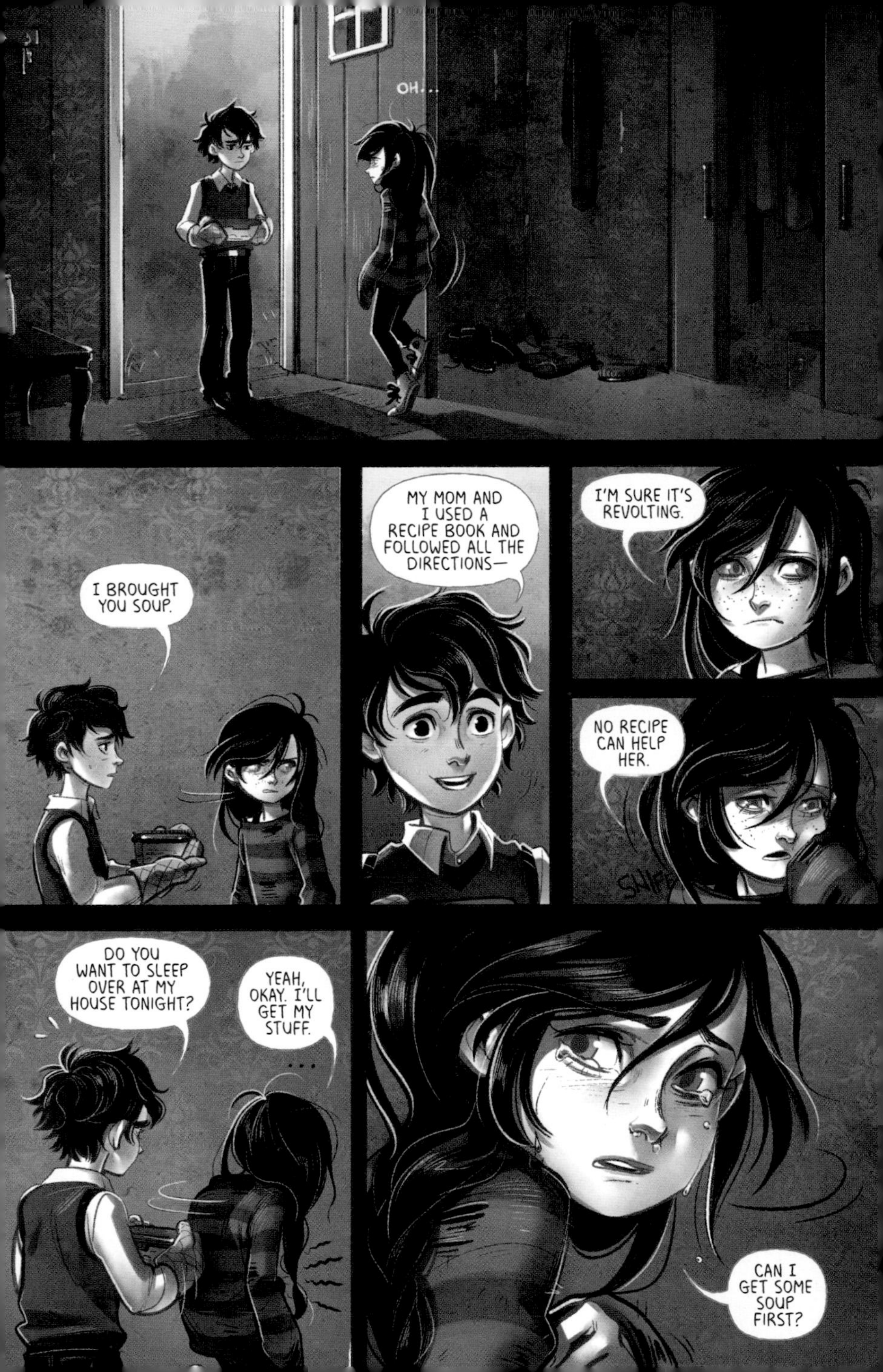

OH...
I BROUGHT YOU SOUP.
MY MOM AND I USED A RECIPE BOOK AND FOLLOWED ALL THE DIRECTIONS—
I'M SURE IT'S REVOLTING.
NO RECIPE CAN HELP HER.
SNIFF
DO YOU WANT TO SLEEP OVER AT MY HOUSE TONIGHT?
YEAH, OKAY. I'LL GET MY STUFF.
...
CAN I GET SOME SOUP FIRST?

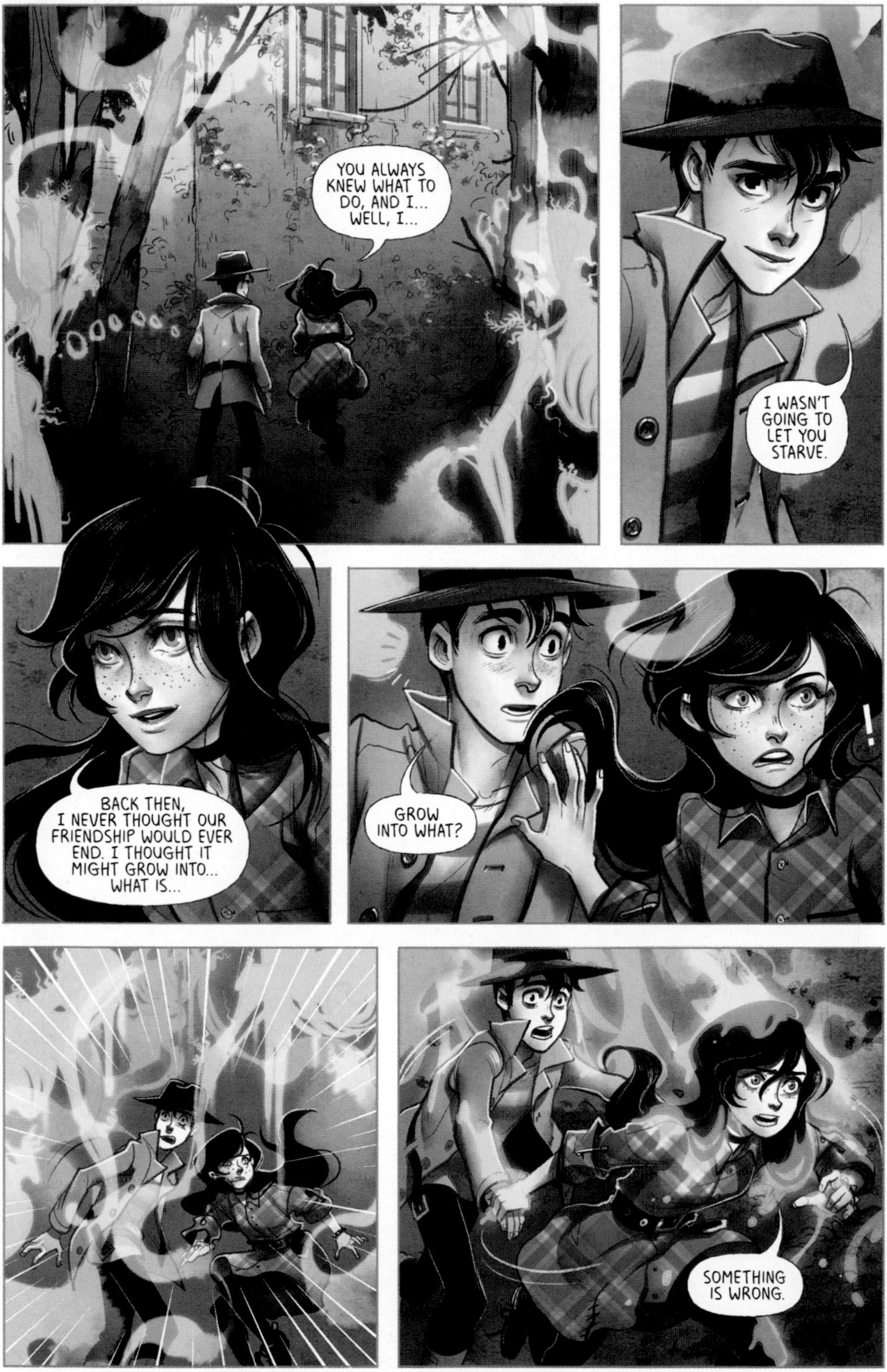
YOU ALWAYS KNEW WHAT TO DO, AND I... WELL, I...
I WASN'T GOING TO LET YOU STARVE.
BACK THEN, I NEVER THOUGHT OUR FRIENDSHIP WOULD EVER END. I THOUGHT IT MIGHT GROW INTO... WHAT IS...
GROW INTO WHAT?
!
SOMETHING IS WRONG.

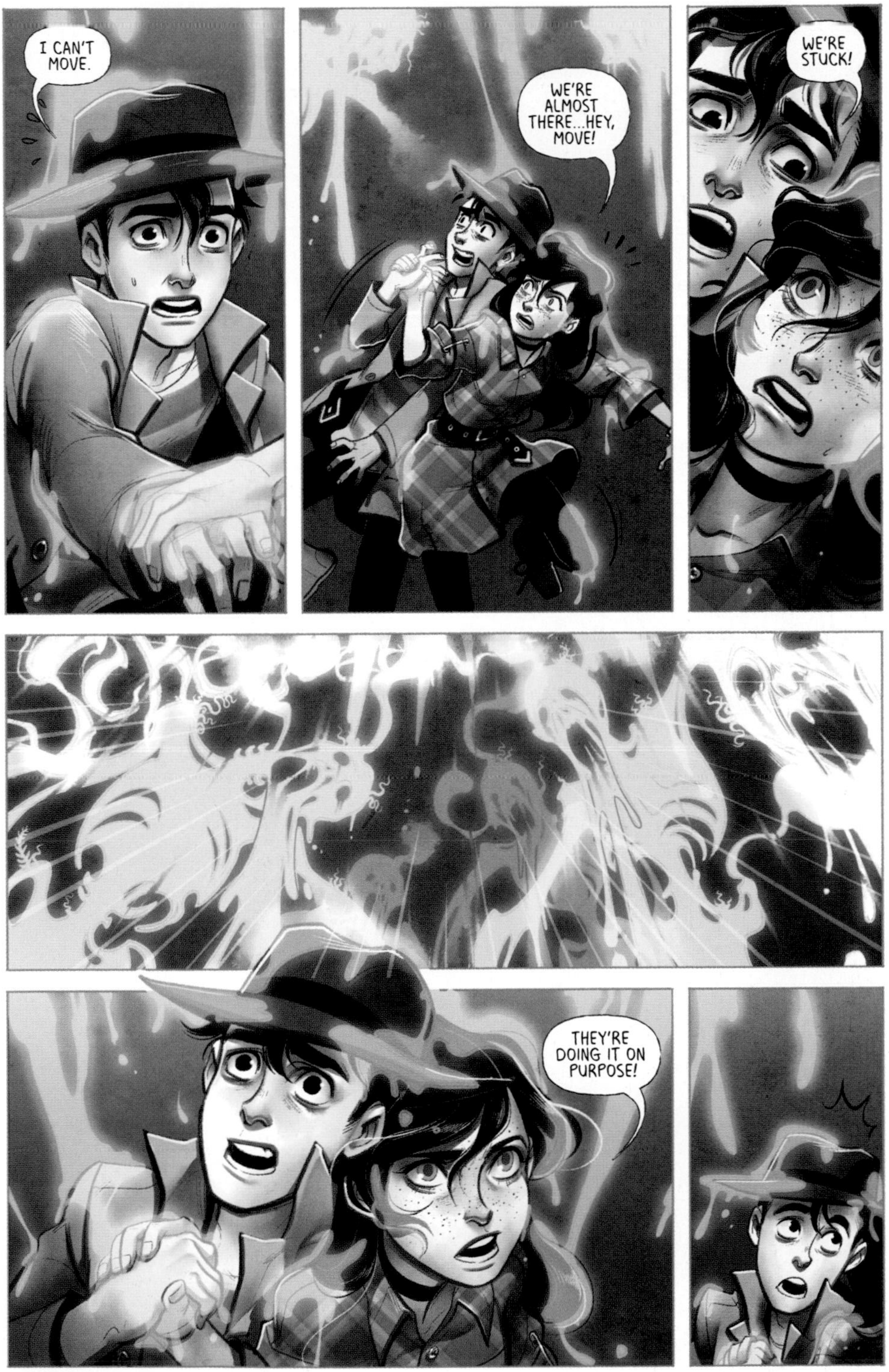
I CAN'T MOVE.
WE'RE ALMOST THERE...HEY, MOVE!
WE'RE STUCK!
THEY'RE DOING IT ON PURPOSE!

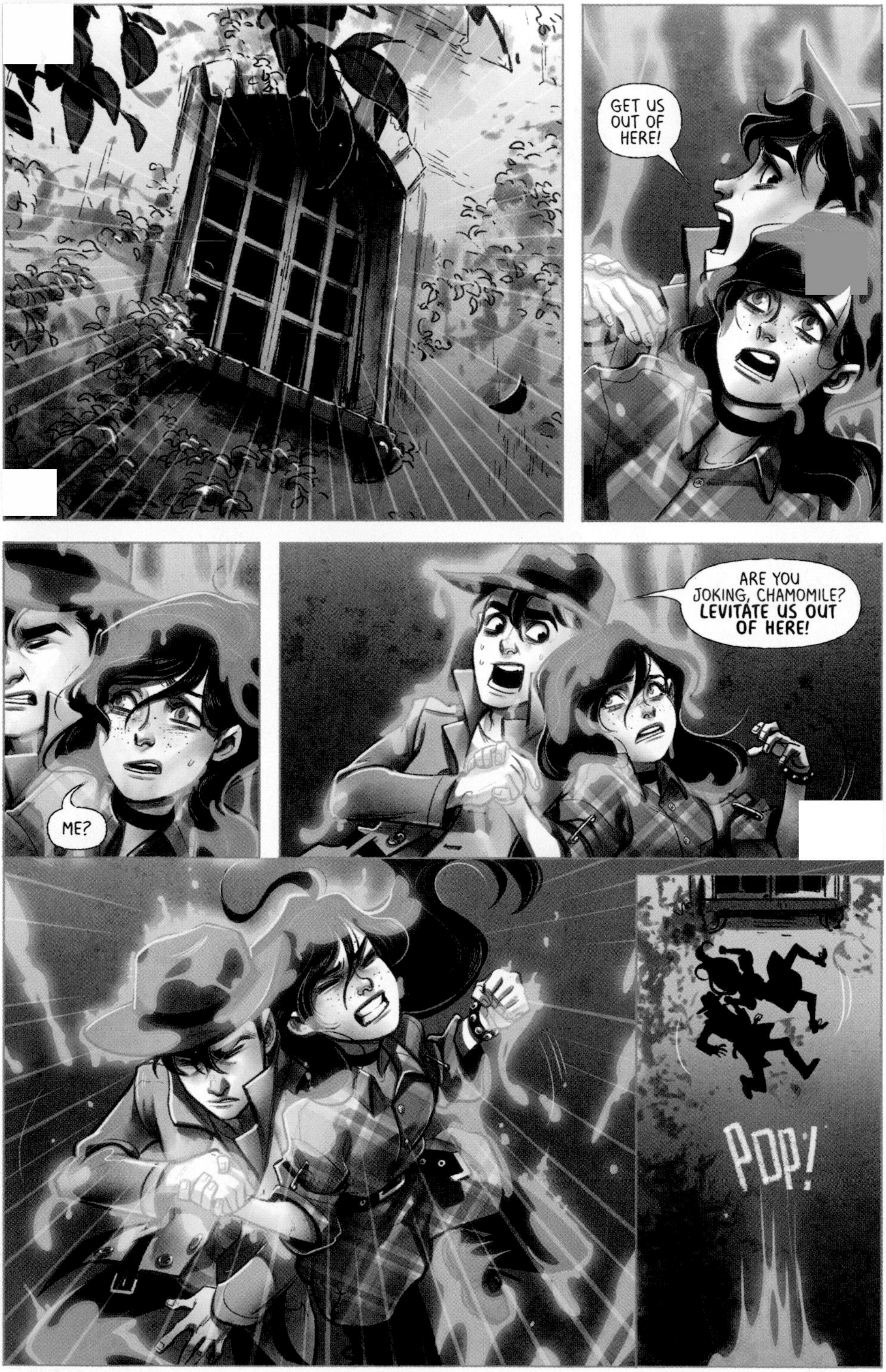
GET US OUT OF HERE!
ME?
ARE YOU JOKING, CHAMOMILE? LEVITATE US OUT OF HERE!
POP!

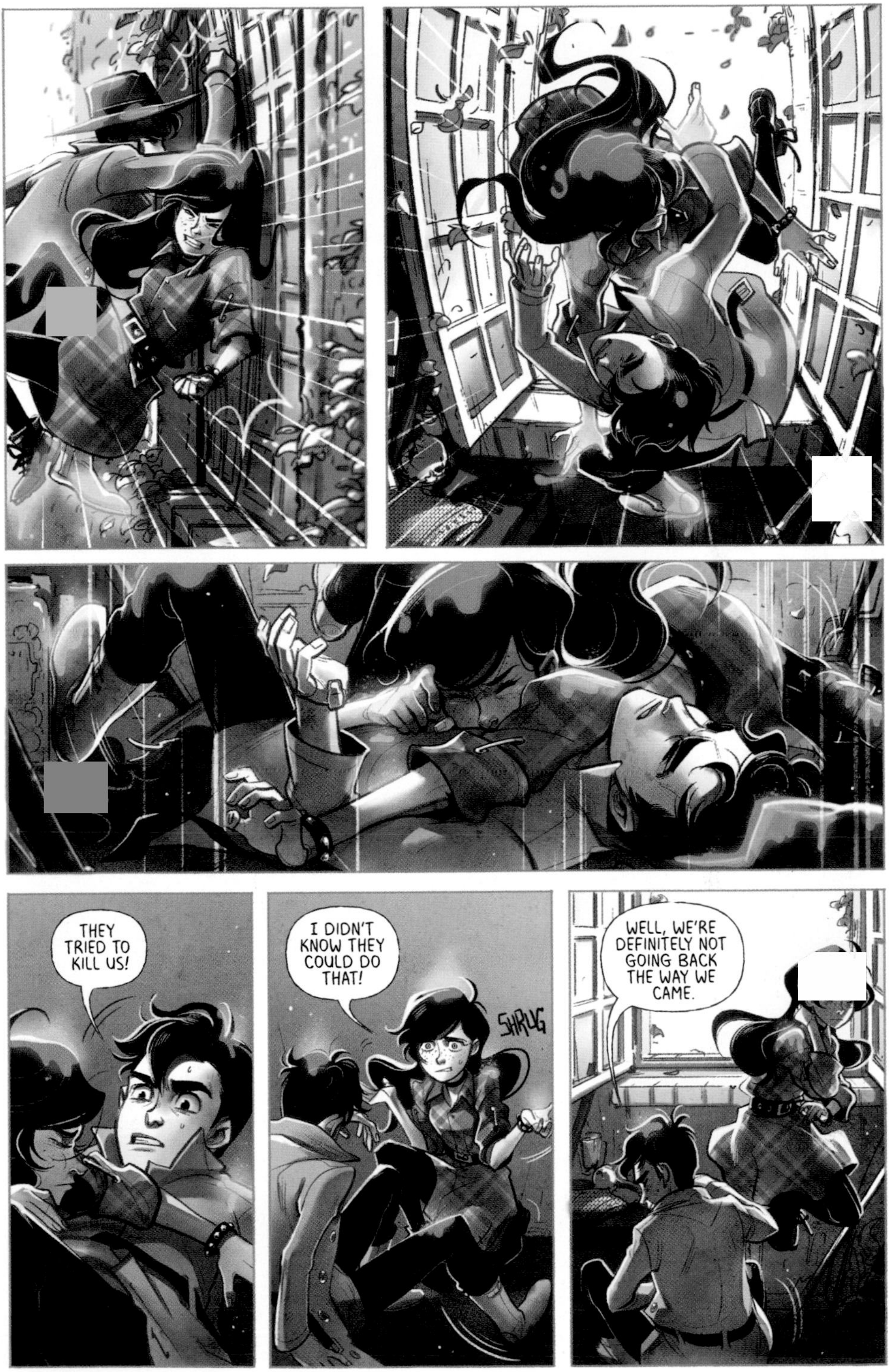
THEY TRIED TO KILL US!
I DIDN'T KNOW THEY COULD DO THAT!
SHRUG
WELL, WE'RE DEFINITELY NOT GOING BACK THE WAY WE CAME.

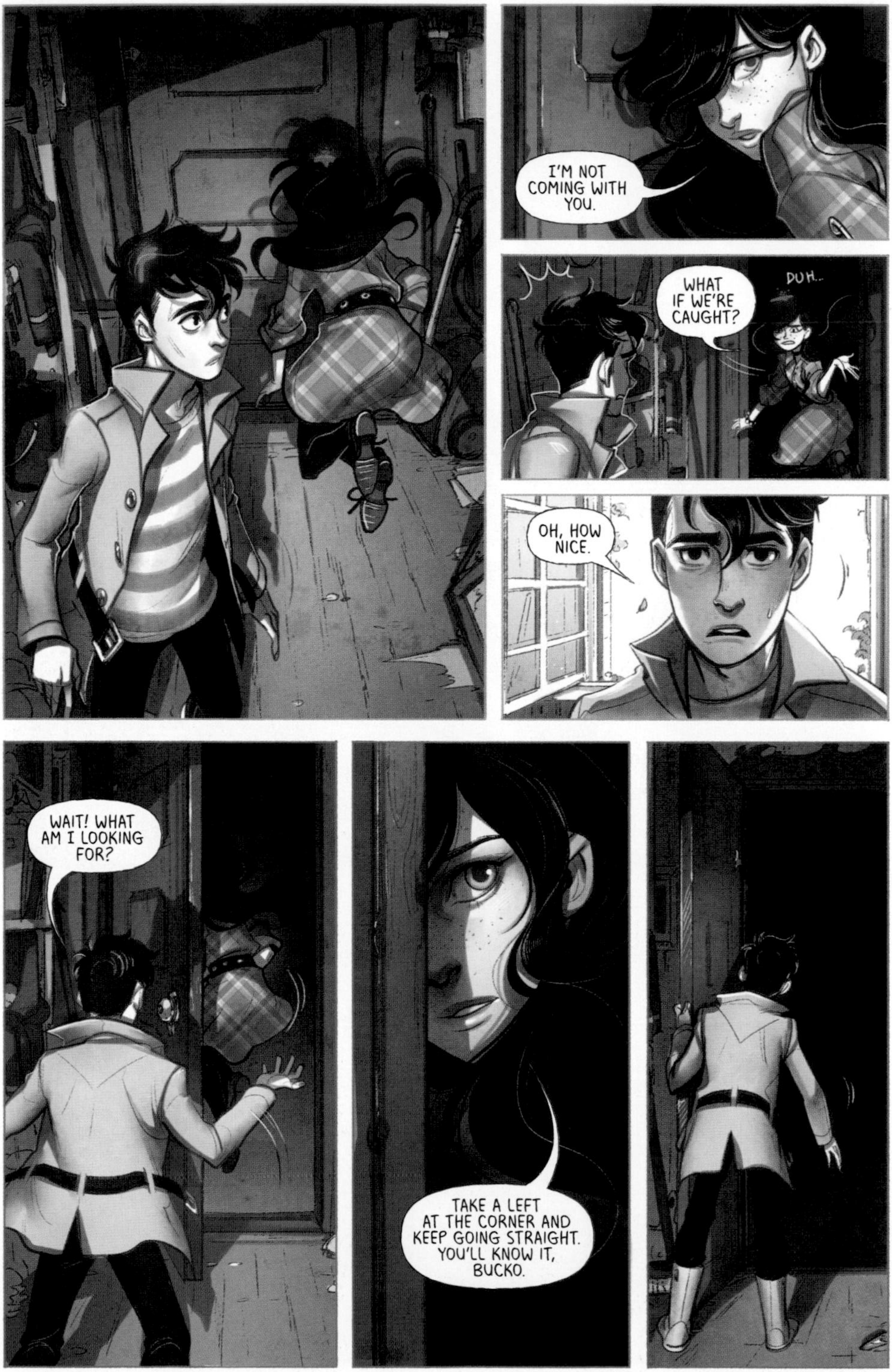
I'M NOT COMING WITH YOU.
WHAT IF WE'RE CAUGHT?
DUH..
OH, HOW NICE.
WAIT! WHAT AM I LOOKING FOR?
TAKE A LEFT AT THE CORNER AND KEEP GOING STRAIGHT. YOU'LL KNOW IT, BUCKO.

CHAPTER 8

A MAGICK TRICK

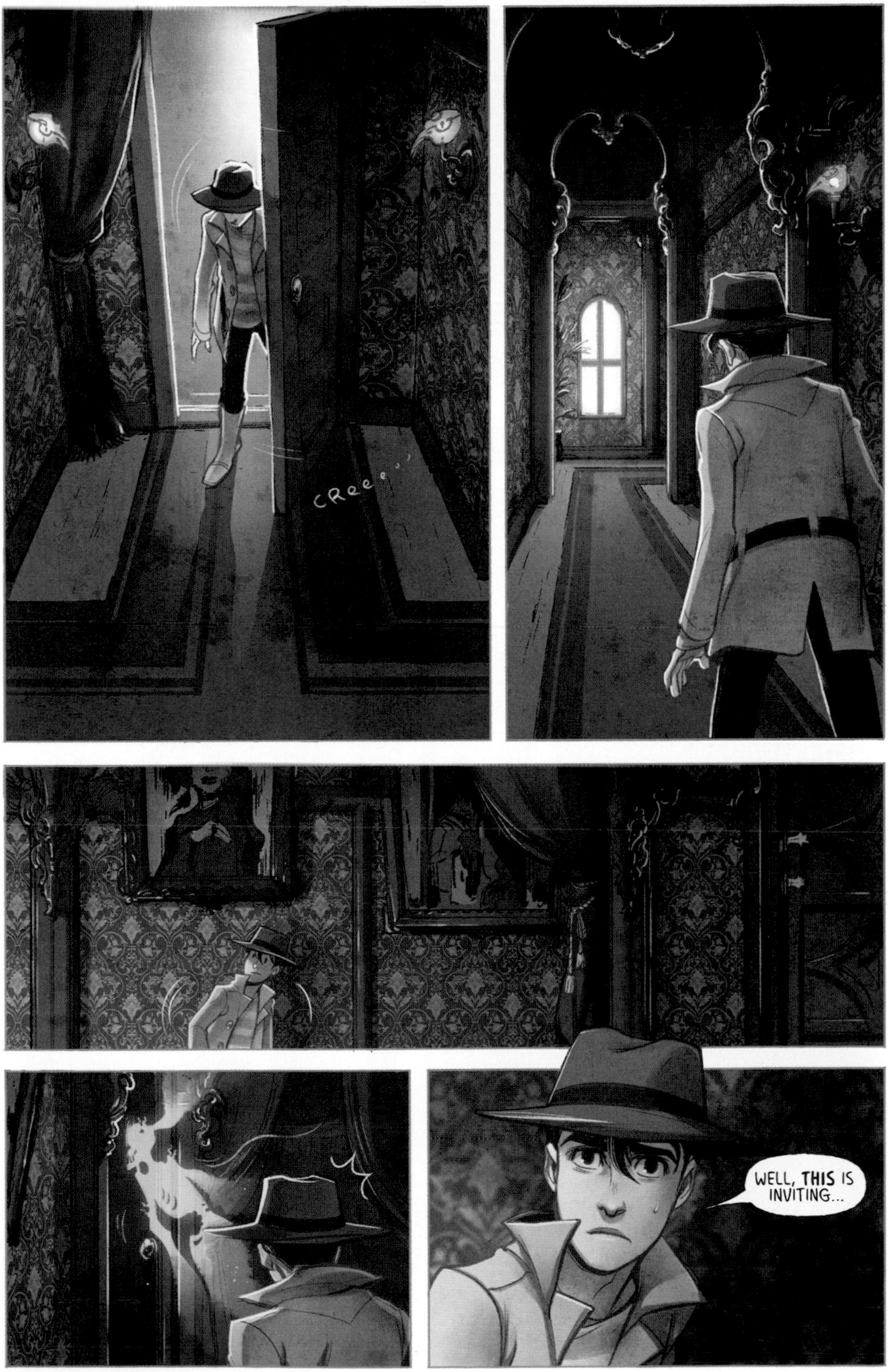
CReee...
WELL, THIS IS INVITING...

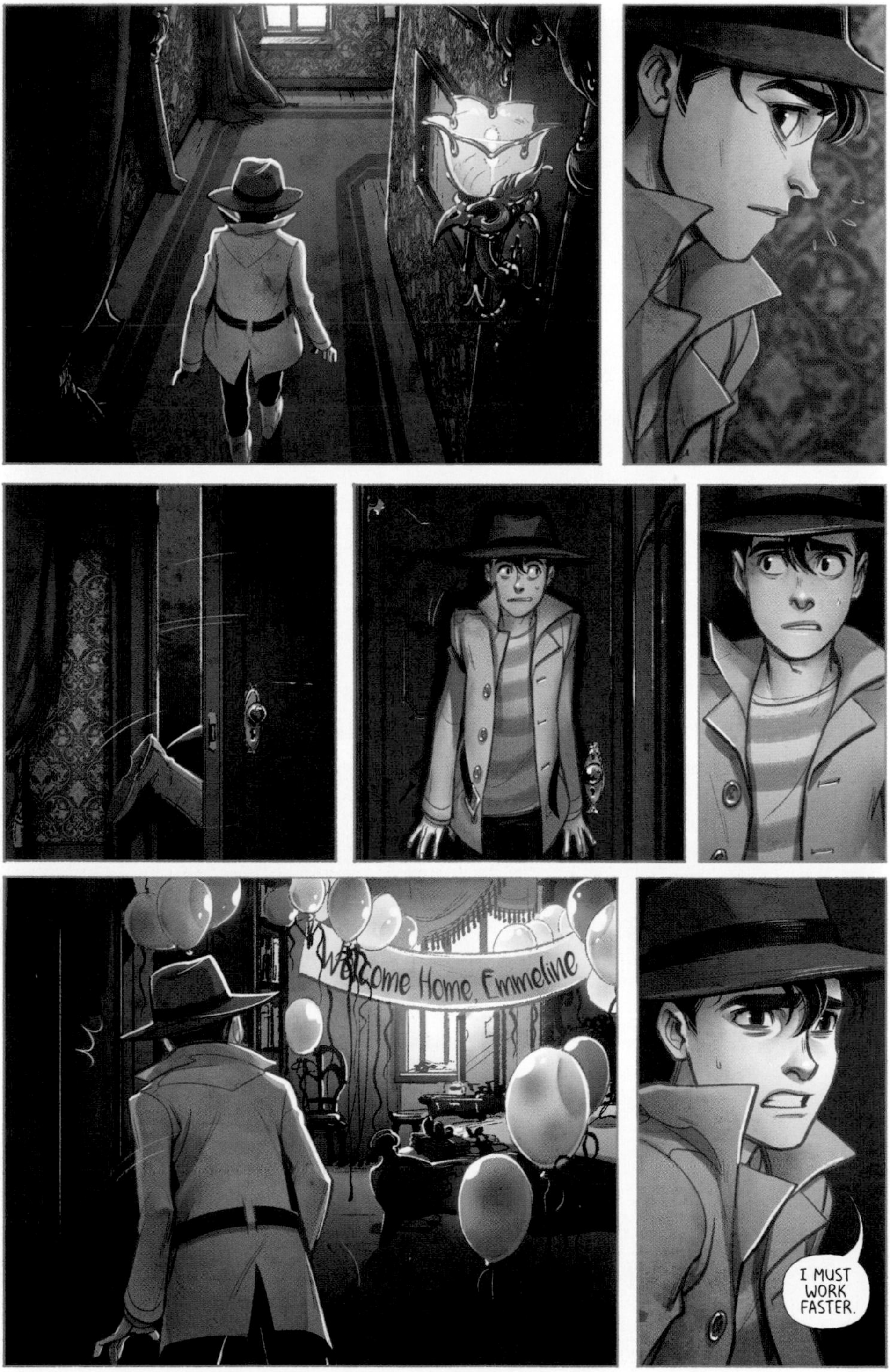
Welcome Home, Emmeline
I MUST WORK FASTER.

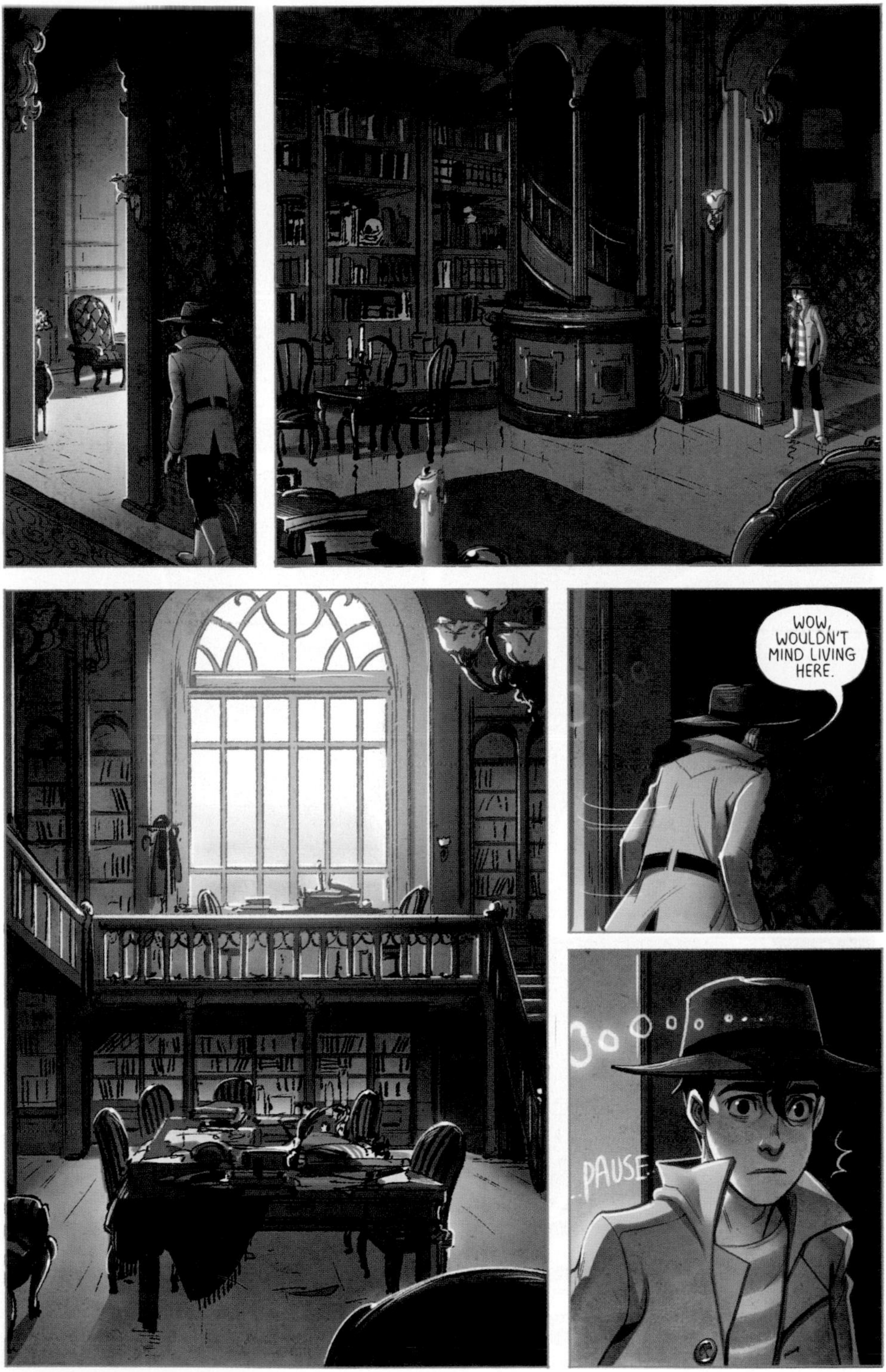
WOW, WOULDN'T MIND LIVING HERE.
OOOOO
PAUSE

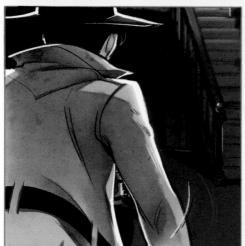

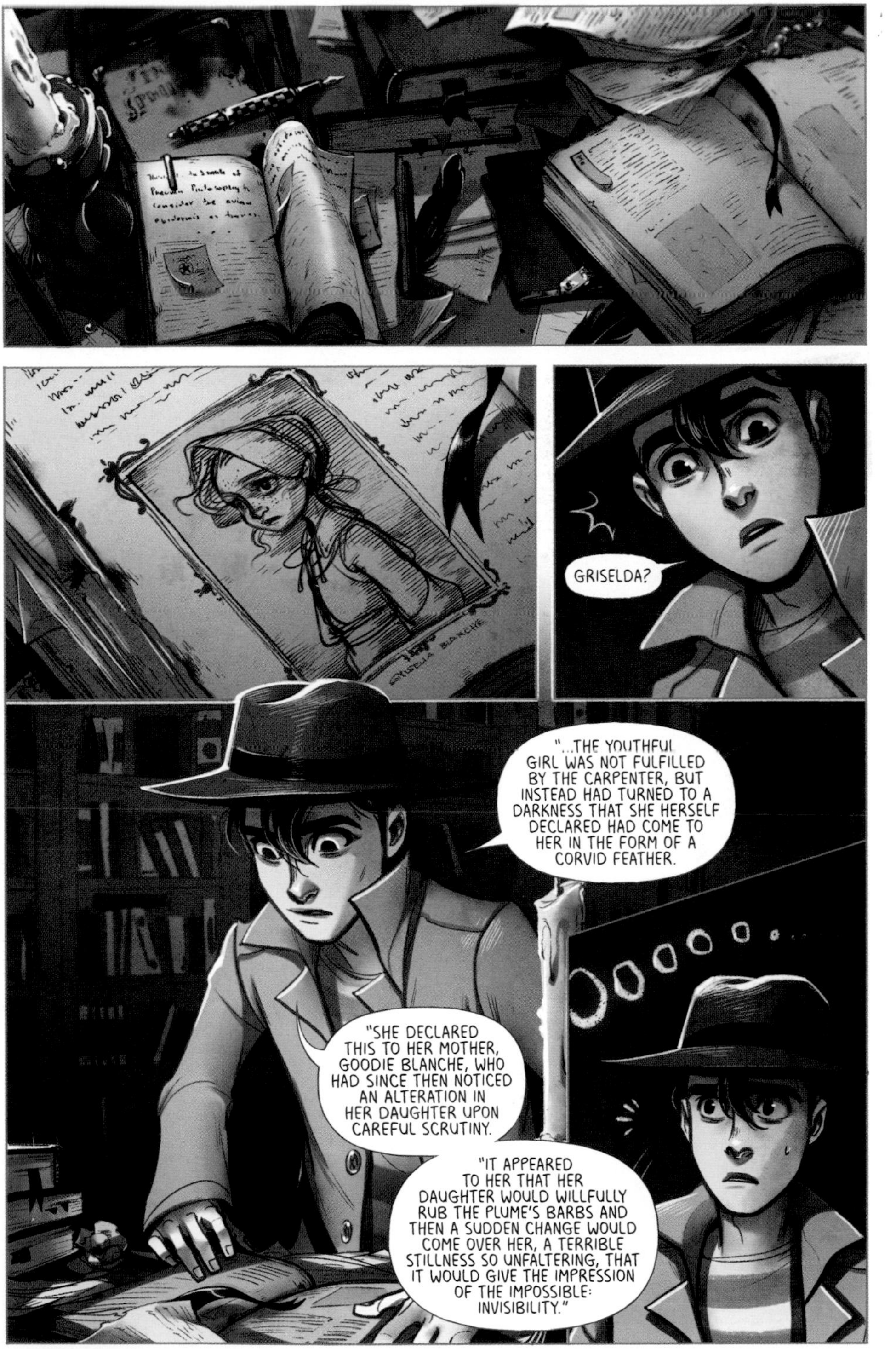
GRISELDA?
"...THE YOUTHFUL GIRL WAS NOT FULFILLED BY THE CARPENTER, BUT INSTEAD HAD TURNED TO A DARKNESS THAT SHE HERSELF DECLARED HAD COME TO HER IN THE FORM OF A CORVID FEATHER.
"SHE DECLARED THIS TO HER MOTHER, GOODIE BLANCHE, WHO HAD SINCE THEN NOTICED AN ALTERATION IN HER DAUGHTER UPON CAREFUL SCRUTINY.
"IT APPEARED TO HER THAT HER DAUGHTER WOULD WILLFULLY RUB THE PLUME'S BARBS AND THEN A SUDDEN CHANGE WOULD COME OVER HER, A TERRIBLE STILLNESS SO UNFALTERING, THAT IT WOULD GIVE THE IMPRESSION OF THE IMPOSSIBLE: INVISIBILITY."

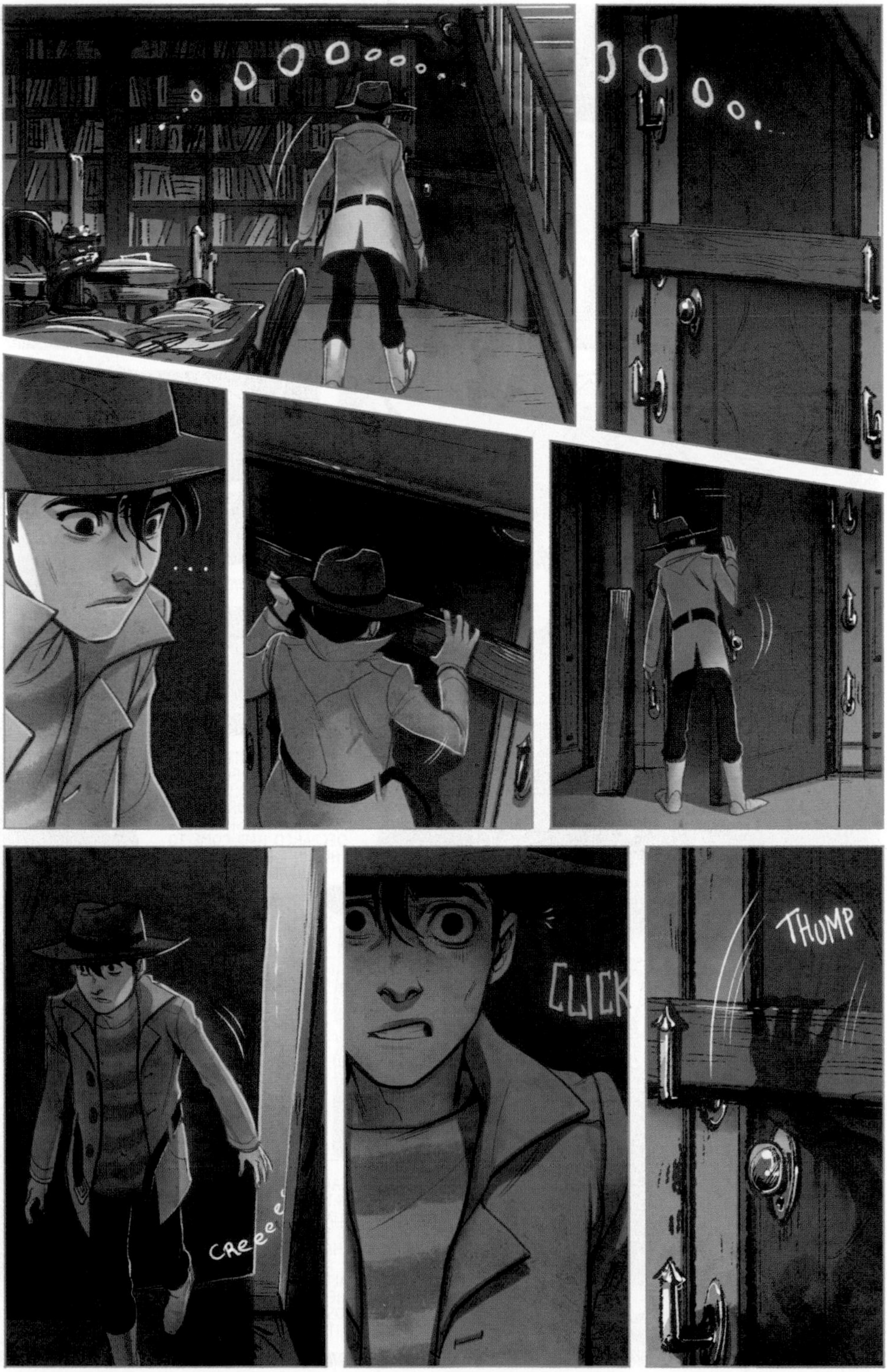
OOOooo...
OOOo...
...
CReeeee
CLICK
THUMP

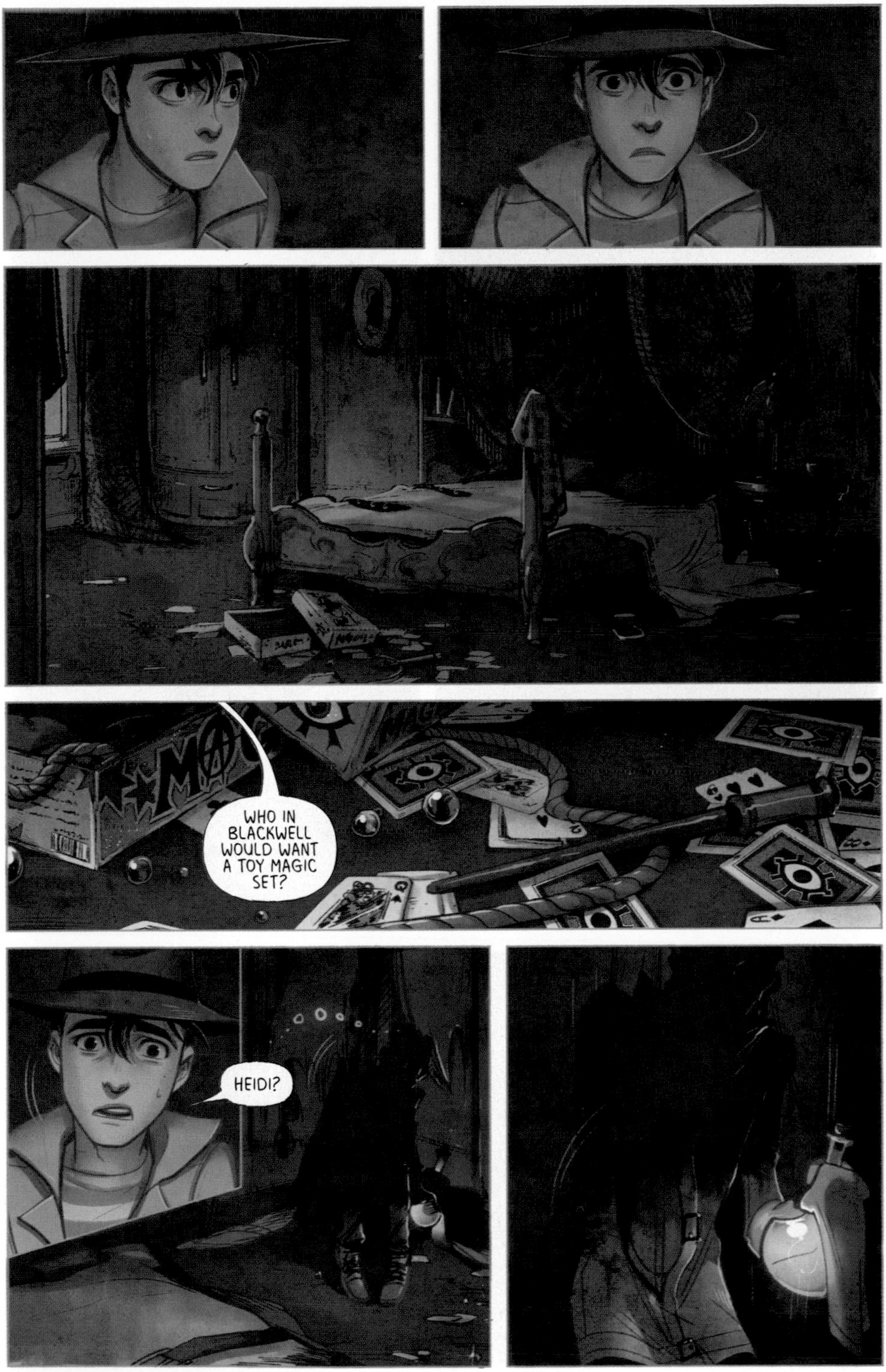
WHO IN BLACKWELL WOULD WANT A TOY MAGIC SET?
HEIDI?

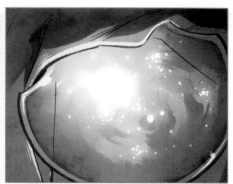

...GIL?

Hello

ER...I'M LOOKING FOR MY SISTER. DO YOU KNOW HEIDI?

SIIISTER? EMMELIIIINE?

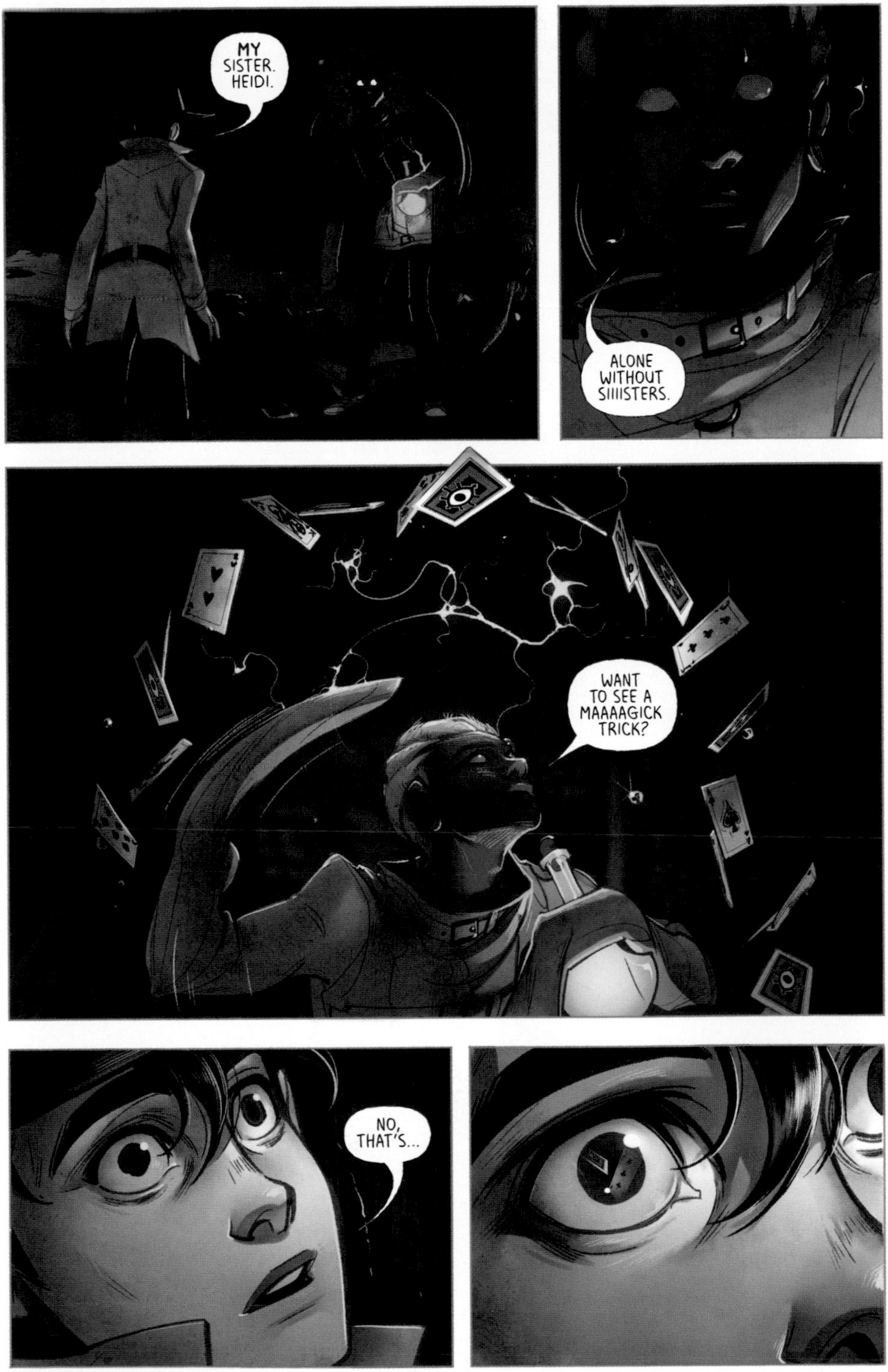
MY SISTER. HEIDI.
ALONE WITHOUT SIIIISTERS.
WANT TO SEE A MAAAAGICK TRICK?
NO, THAT'S...

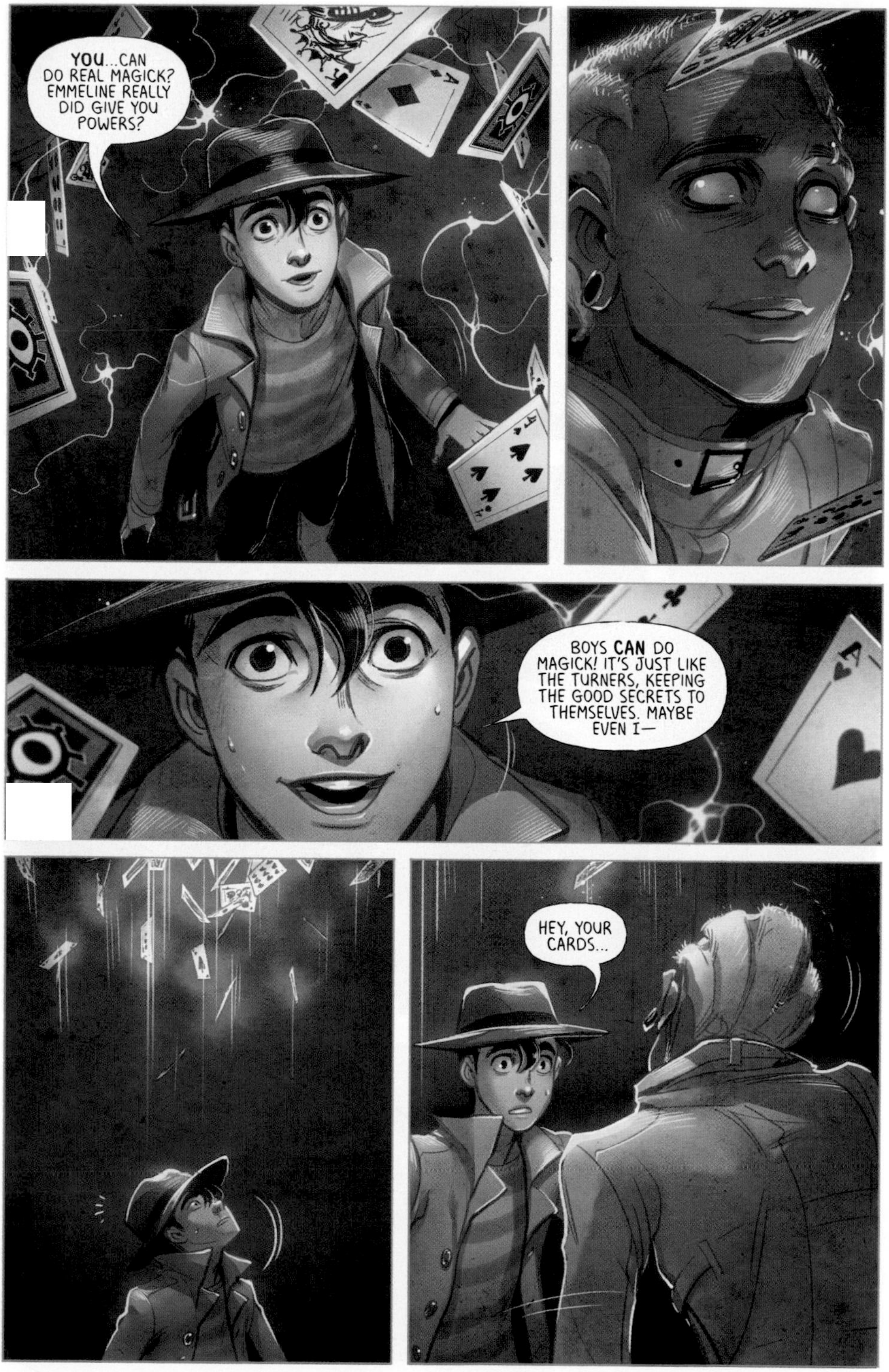
YOU...CAN DO REAL MAGICK? EMMELINE REALLY DID GIVE YOU POWERS?
BOYS CAN DO MAGICK! IT'S JUST LIKE THE TURNERS, KEEPING THE GOOD SECRETS TO THEMSELVES. MAYBE EVEN I—
HEY, YOUR CARDS...

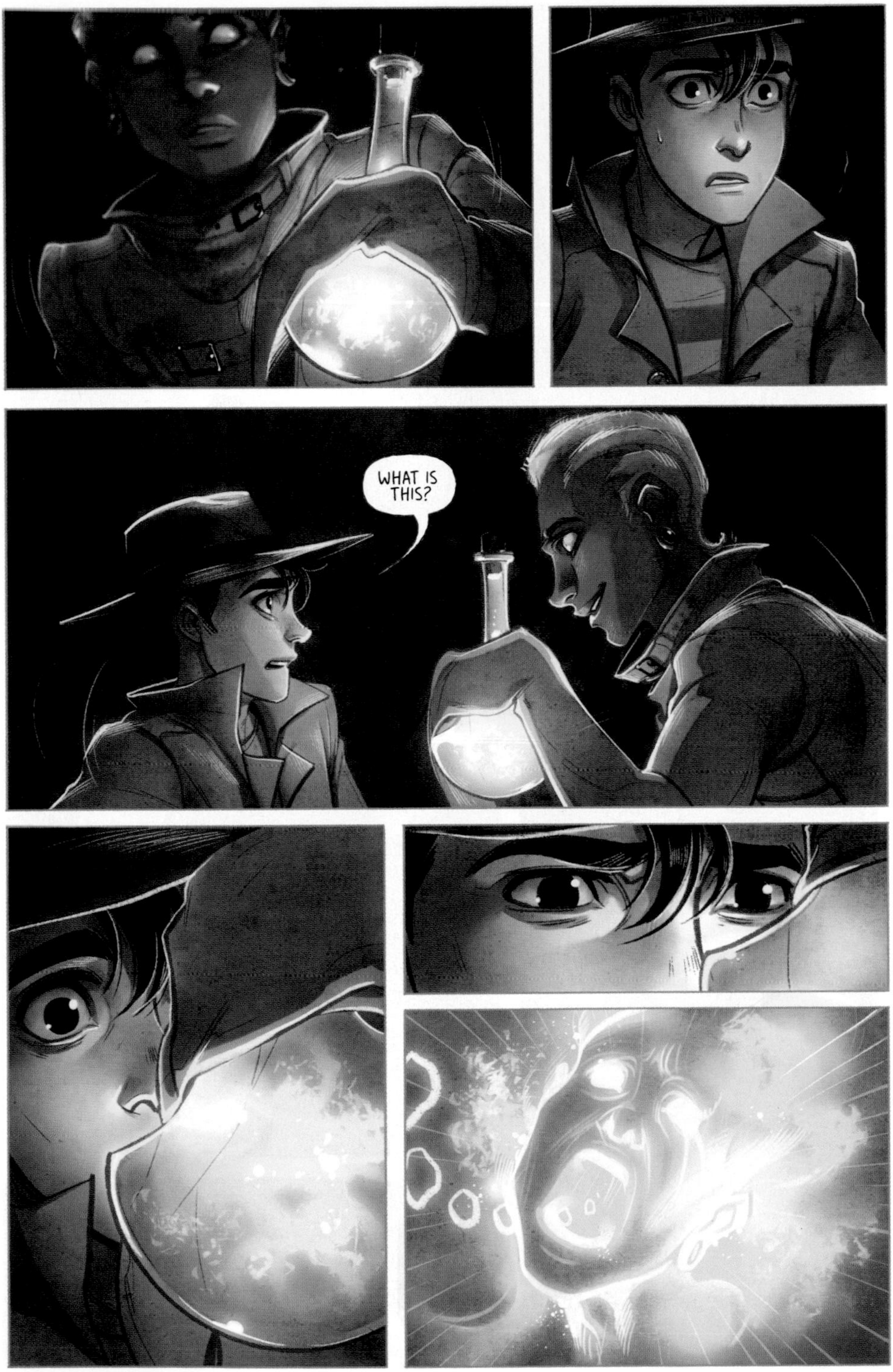
WHAT IS THIS?

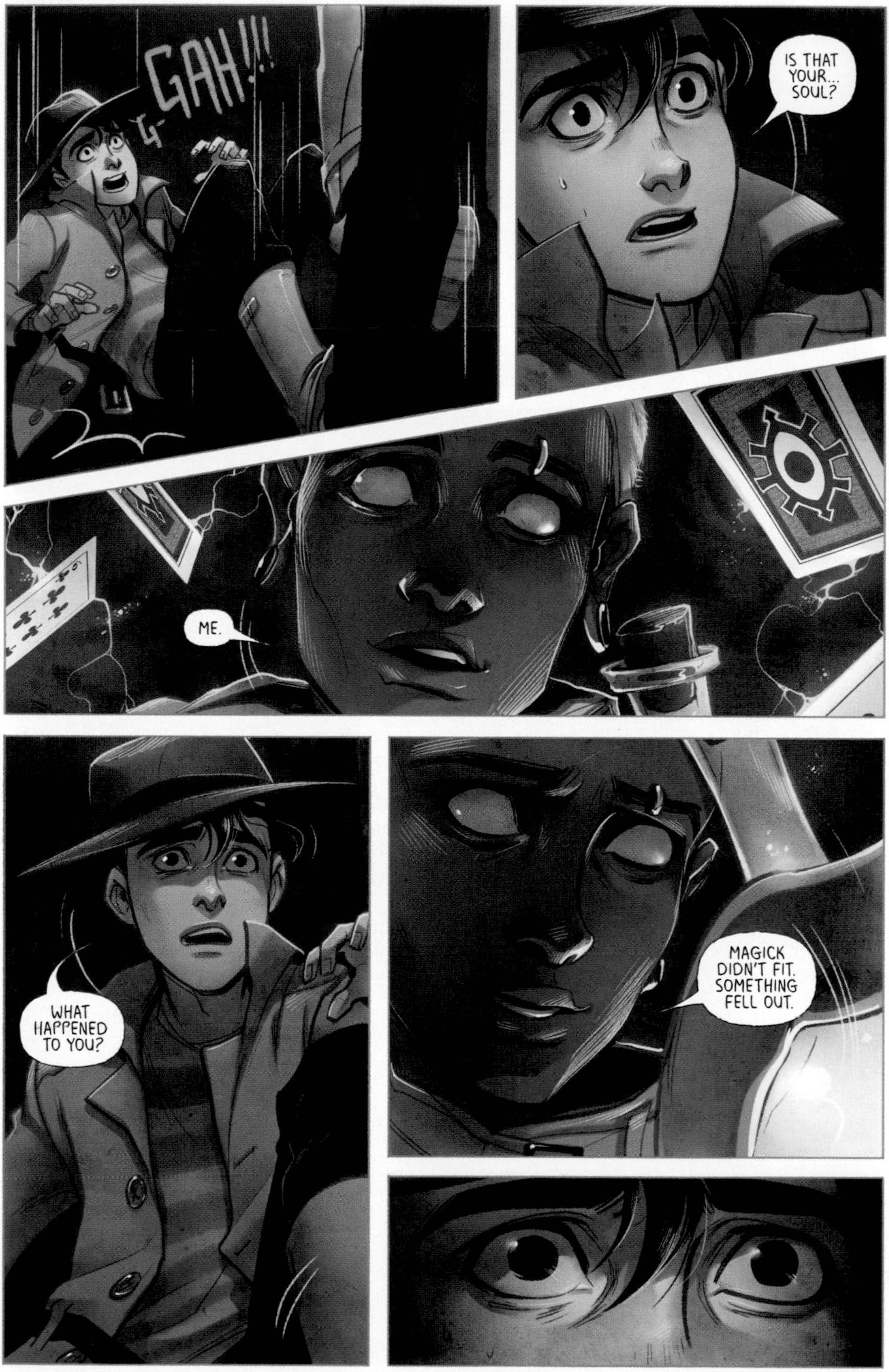
GAH!!!
IS THAT YOUR... SOUL?
ME.
WHAT HAPPENED TO YOU?
MAGICK DIDN'T FIT. SOMETHING FELL OUT.

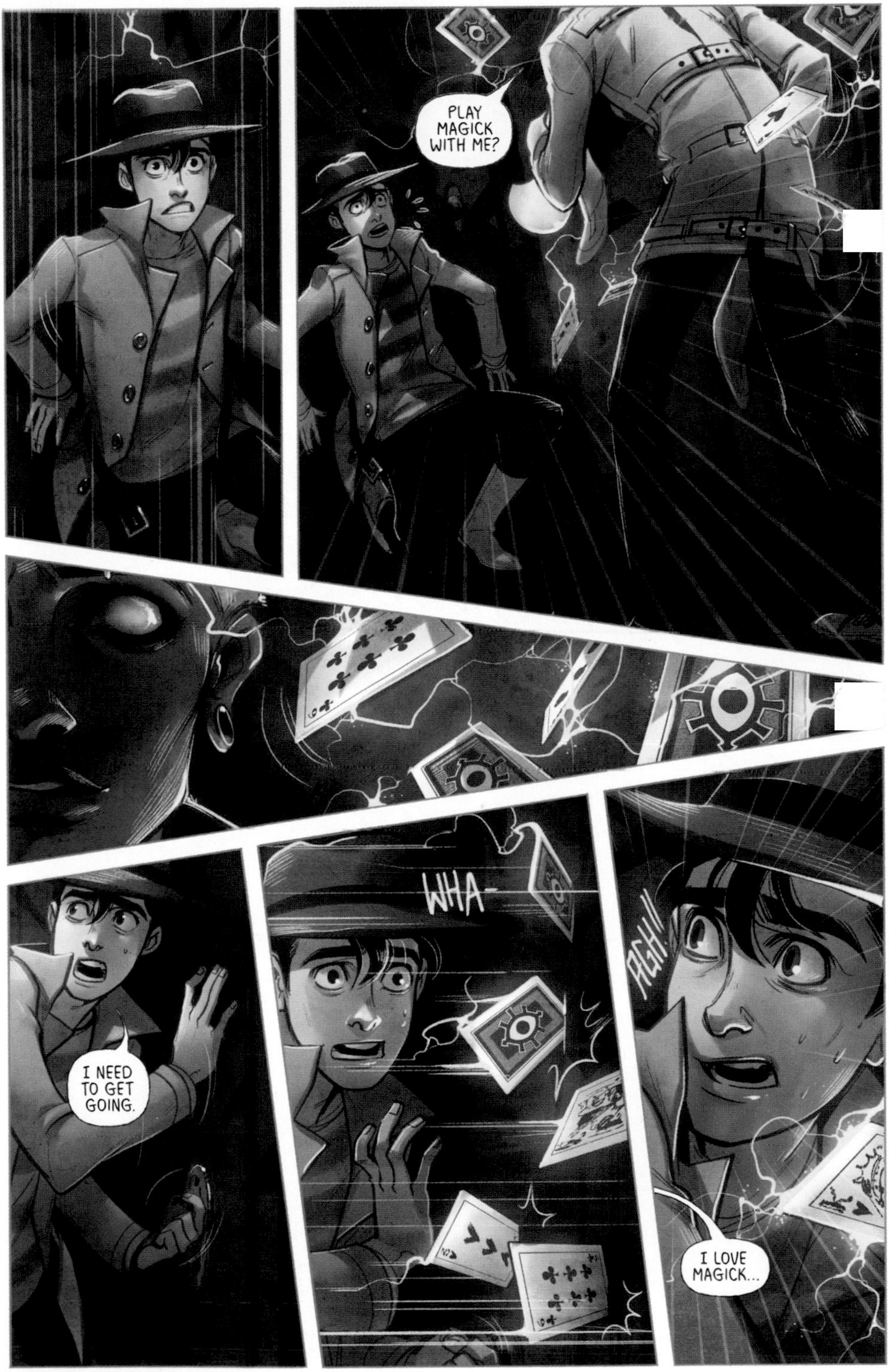
PLAY MAGICK WITH ME?
I NEED TO GET GOING.
WHA-
AGH!!
I LOVE MAGICK...

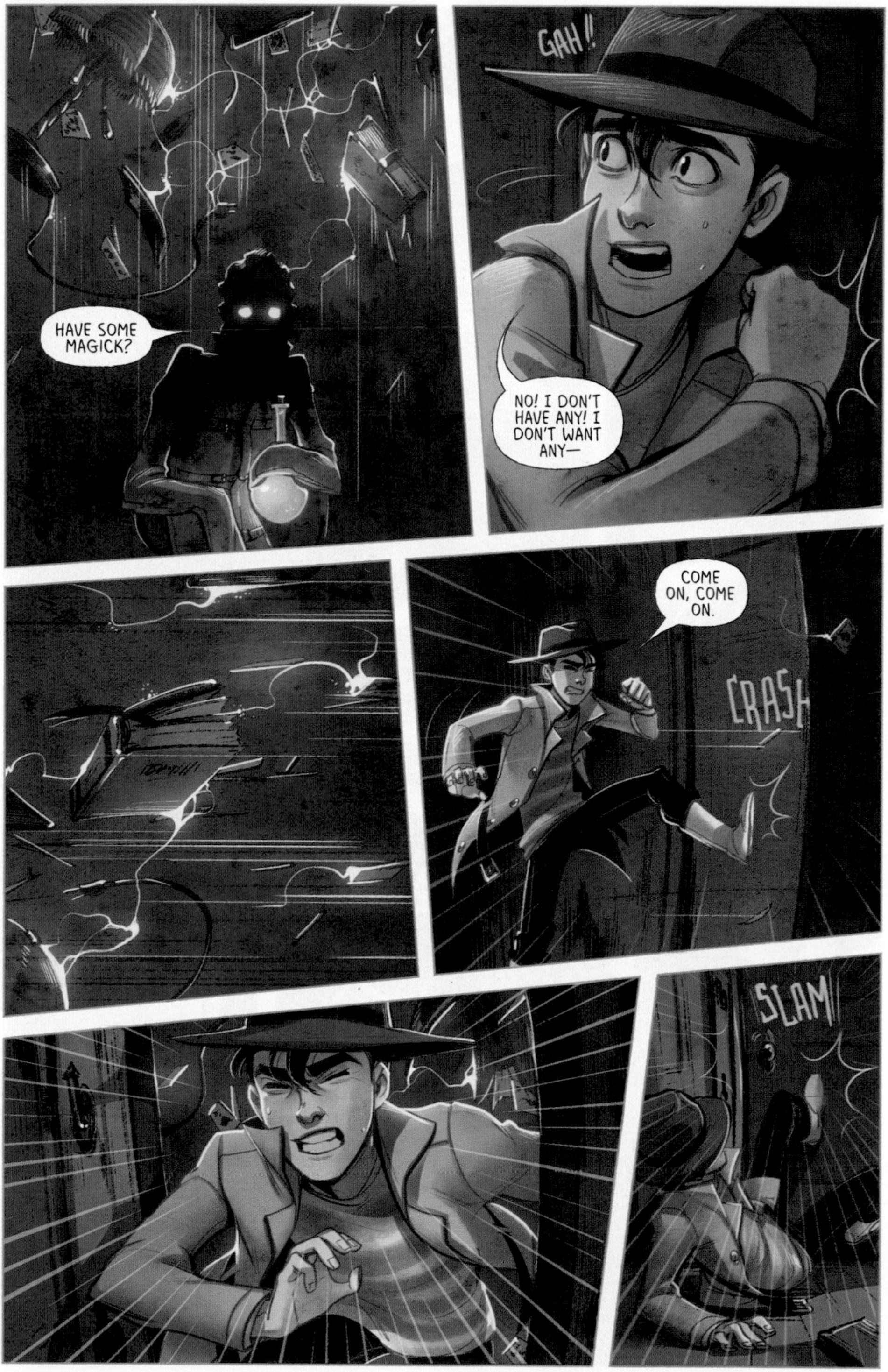
HAVE SOME MAGICK?
GAH!!
NO! I DON'T HAVE ANY! I DON'T WANT ANY—
COME ON, COME ON.
CRASH
SLAM

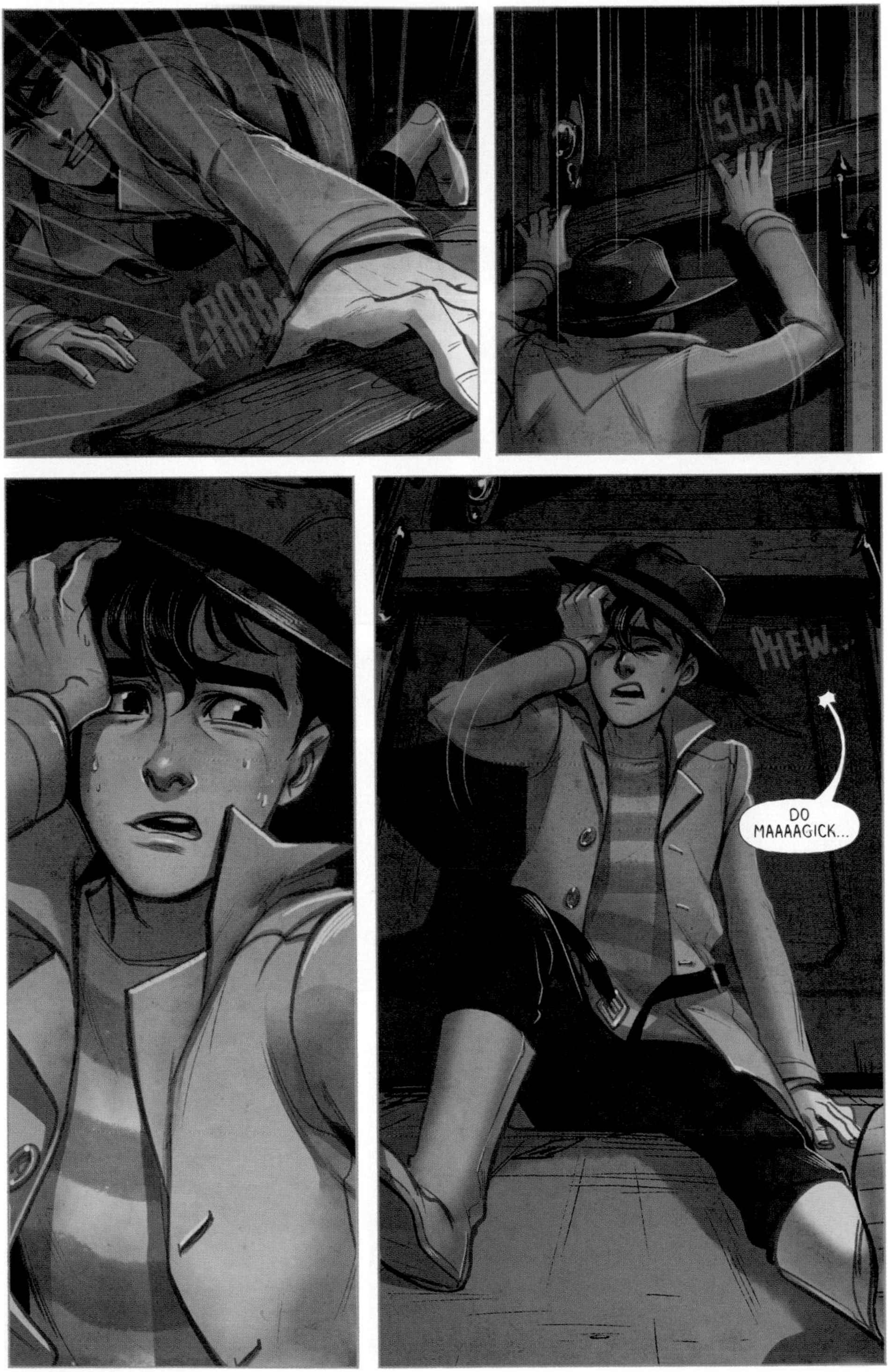
GRAB
SLAM
PHEW...
DO MAAAAGICK...

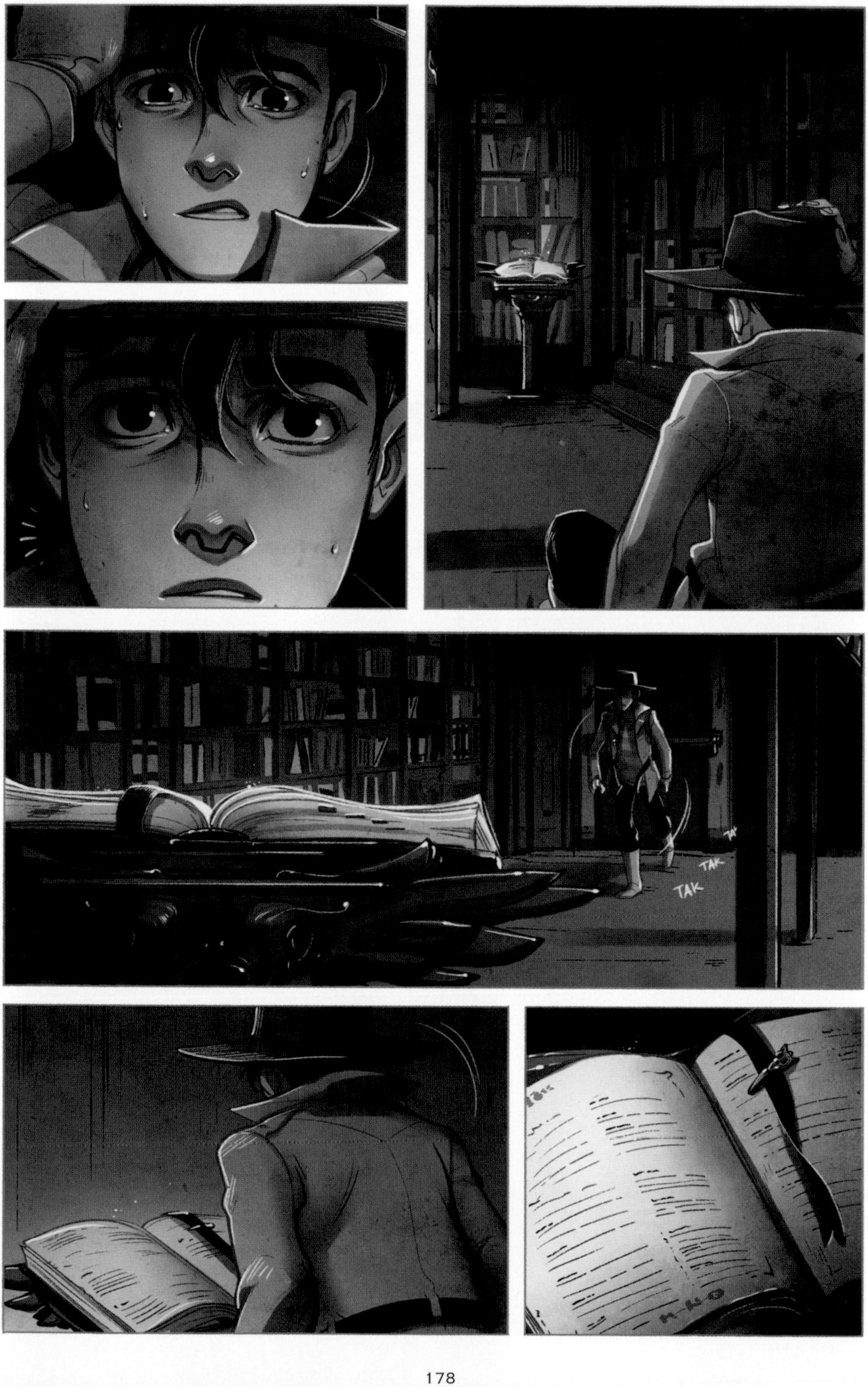
TAK
TAK
TAK

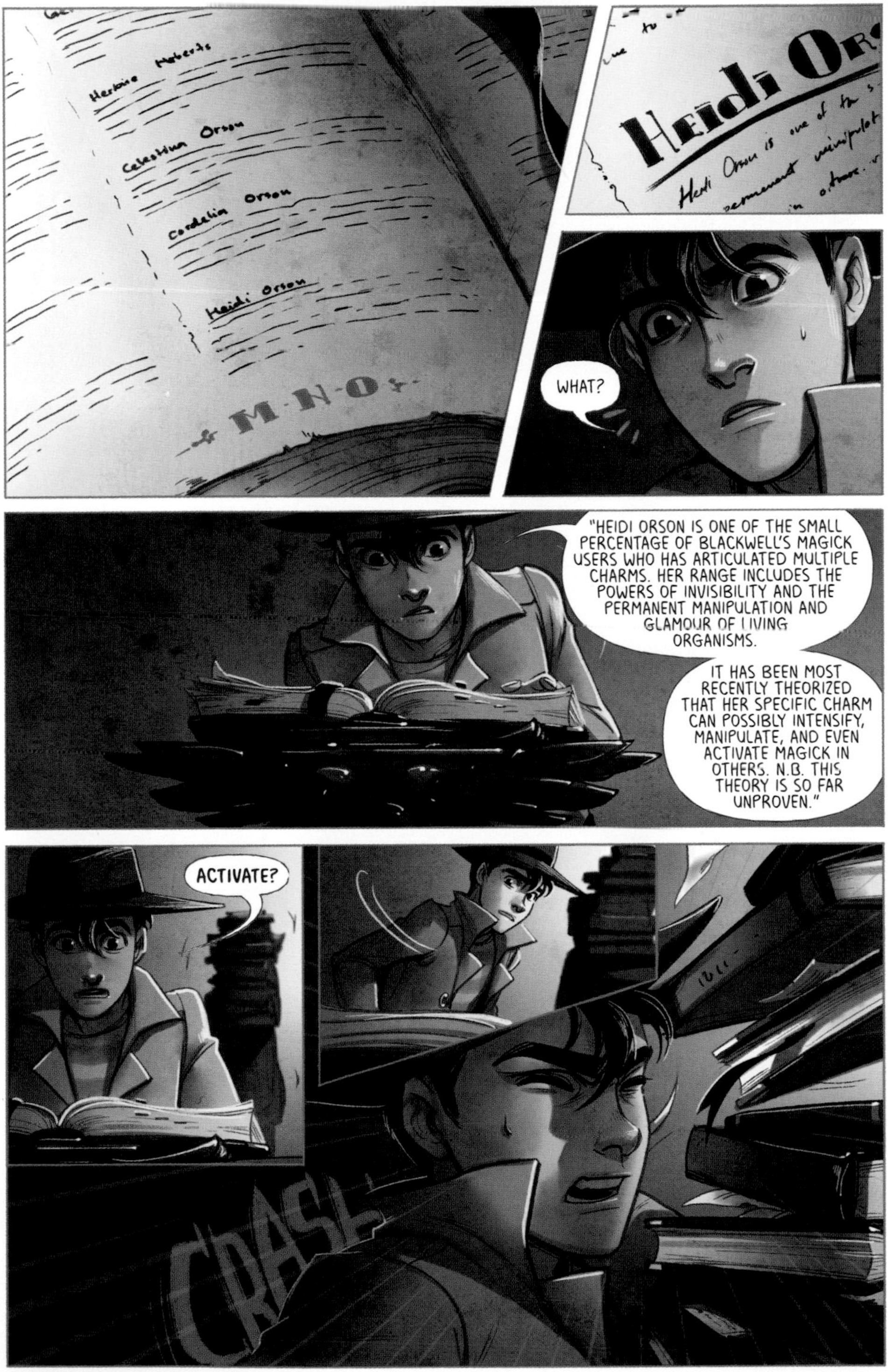
Herbie Roberts
Celestina Orson
Cordelia Orson
Heidi Orson
M-N-O
Heidi Ors
Heidi Orson is one of the
WHAT?
"HEIDI ORSON IS ONE OF THE SMALL PERCENTAGE OF BLACKWELL'S MAGICK USERS WHO HAS ARTICULATED MULTIPLE CHARMS. HER RANGE INCLUDES THE POWERS OF INVISIBILITY AND THE PERMANENT MANIPULATION AND GLAMOUR OF LIVING ORGANISMS.
IT HAS BEEN MOST RECENTLY THEORIZED THAT HER SPECIFIC CHARM CAN POSSIBLY INTENSIFY, MANIPULATE, AND EVEN ACTIVATE MAGICK IN OTHERS. N.B. THIS THEORY IS SO FAR UNPROVEN."
ACTIVATE?
CRASH

CHAPTER 9

THE BALLAD OF GRISELDA

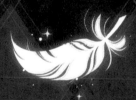

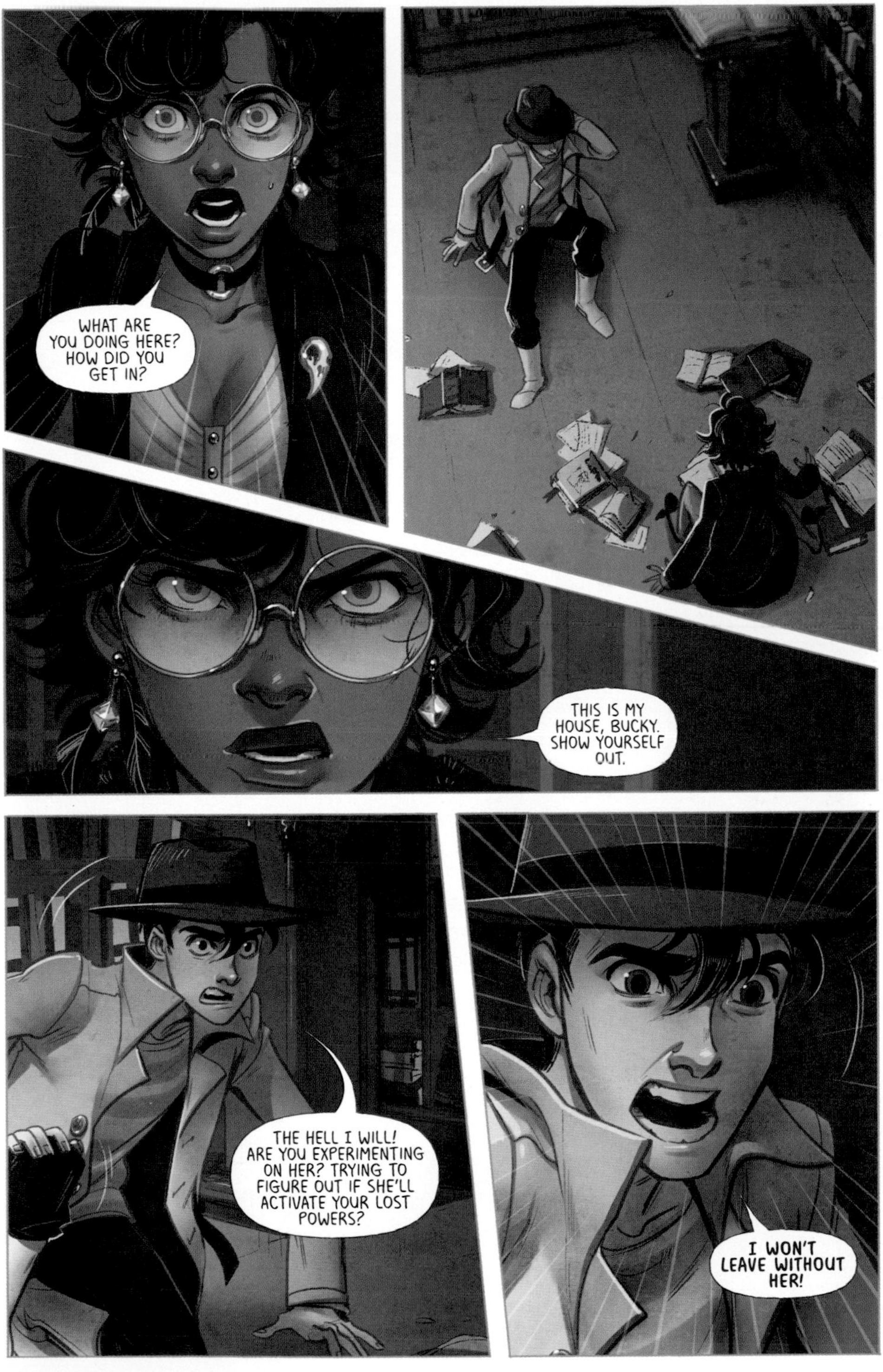
WHAT ARE YOU DOING HERE? HOW DID YOU GET IN?
THIS IS MY HOUSE, BUCKY. SHOW YOURSELF OUT.
THE HELL I WILL! ARE YOU EXPERIMENTING ON HER? TRYING TO FIGURE OUT IF SHE'LL ACTIVATE YOUR LOST POWERS?
I WON'T LEAVE WITHOUT HER!

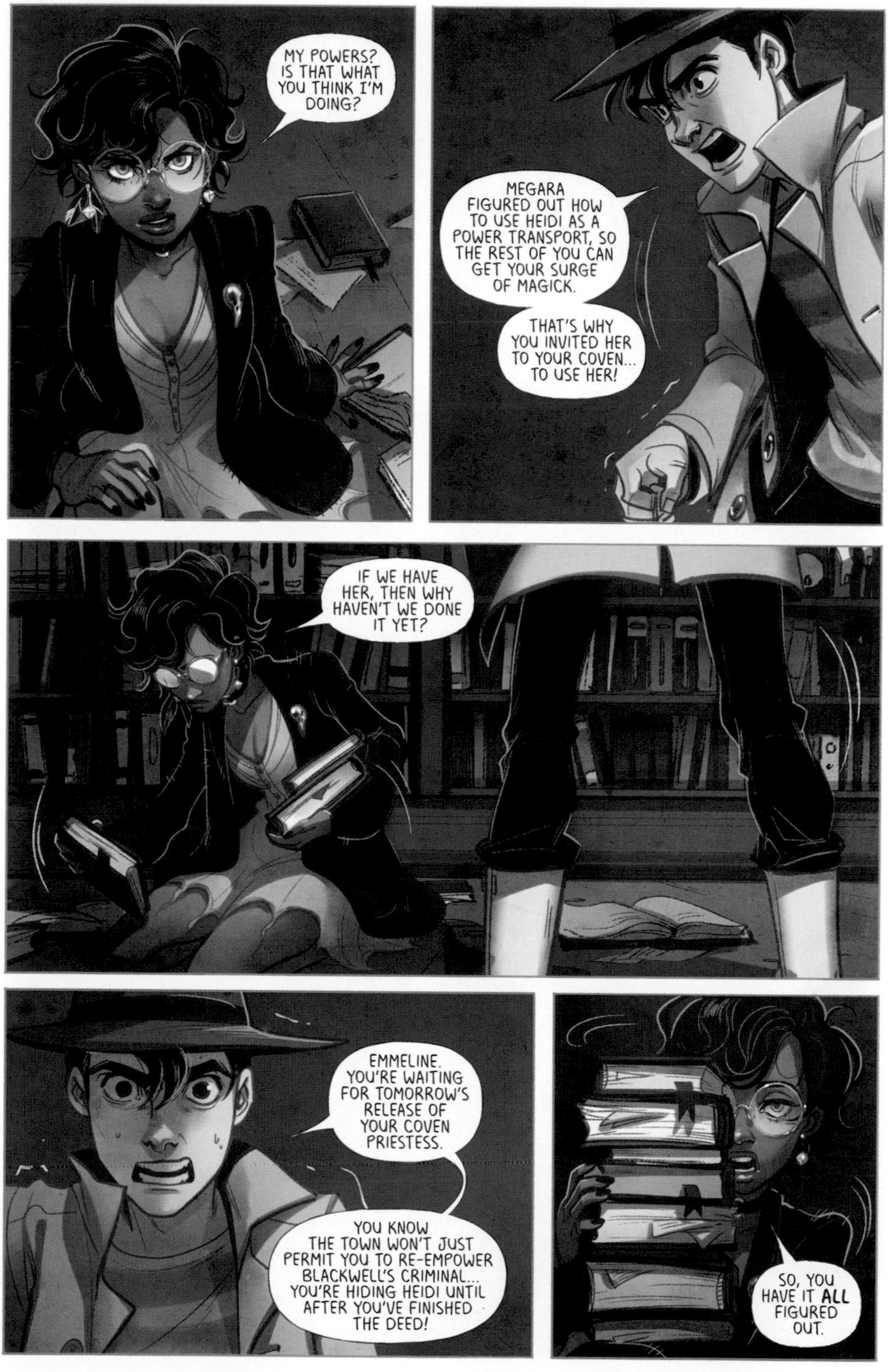
MY POWERS? IS THAT WHAT YOU THINK I'M DOING?
MEGARA FIGURED OUT HOW TO USE HEIDI AS A POWER TRANSPORT, SO THE REST OF YOU CAN GET YOUR SURGE OF MAGICK.
THAT'S WHY YOU INVITED HER TO YOUR COVEN... TO USE HER!
IF WE HAVE HER, THEN WHY HAVEN'T WE DONE IT YET?
EMMELINE. YOU'RE WAITING FOR TOMORROW'S RELEASE OF YOUR COVEN PRIESTESS.
YOU KNOW THE TOWN WON'T JUST PERMIT YOU TO RE-EMPOWER BLACKWELL'S CRIMINAL... YOU'RE HIDING HEIDI UNTIL AFTER YOU'VE FINISHED THE DEED!
SO, YOU HAVE IT **ALL** FIGURED OUT.

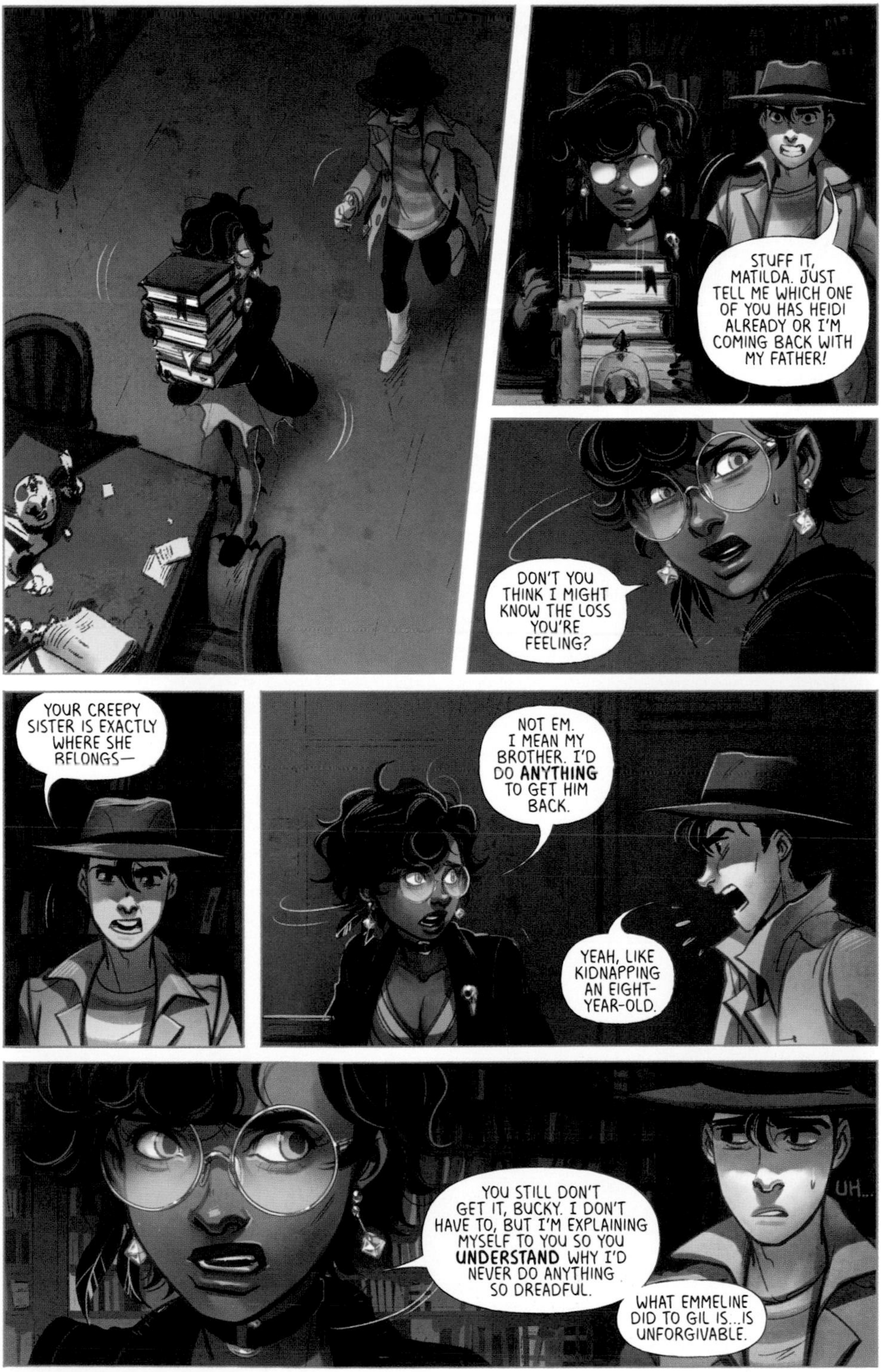
STUFF IT, MATILDA. JUST TELL ME WHICH ONE OF YOU HAS HEIDI ALREADY OR I'M COMING BACK WITH MY FATHER!
DON'T YOU THINK I MIGHT KNOW THE LOSS YOU'RE FEELING?
YOUR CREEPY SISTER IS EXACTLY WHERE SHE BELONGS—
NOT EM. I MEAN MY BROTHER. I'D DO **ANYTHING** TO GET HIM BACK.
YEAH, LIKE KIDNAPPING AN EIGHT-YEAR-OLD.
YOU STILL DON'T GET IT, BUCKY. I DON'T HAVE TO, BUT I'M EXPLAINING MYSELF TO YOU SO YOU **UNDERSTAND** WHY I'D NEVER DO ANYTHING SO DREADFUL.
UH...
WHAT EMMELINE DID TO GIL IS...IS UNFORGIVABLE.

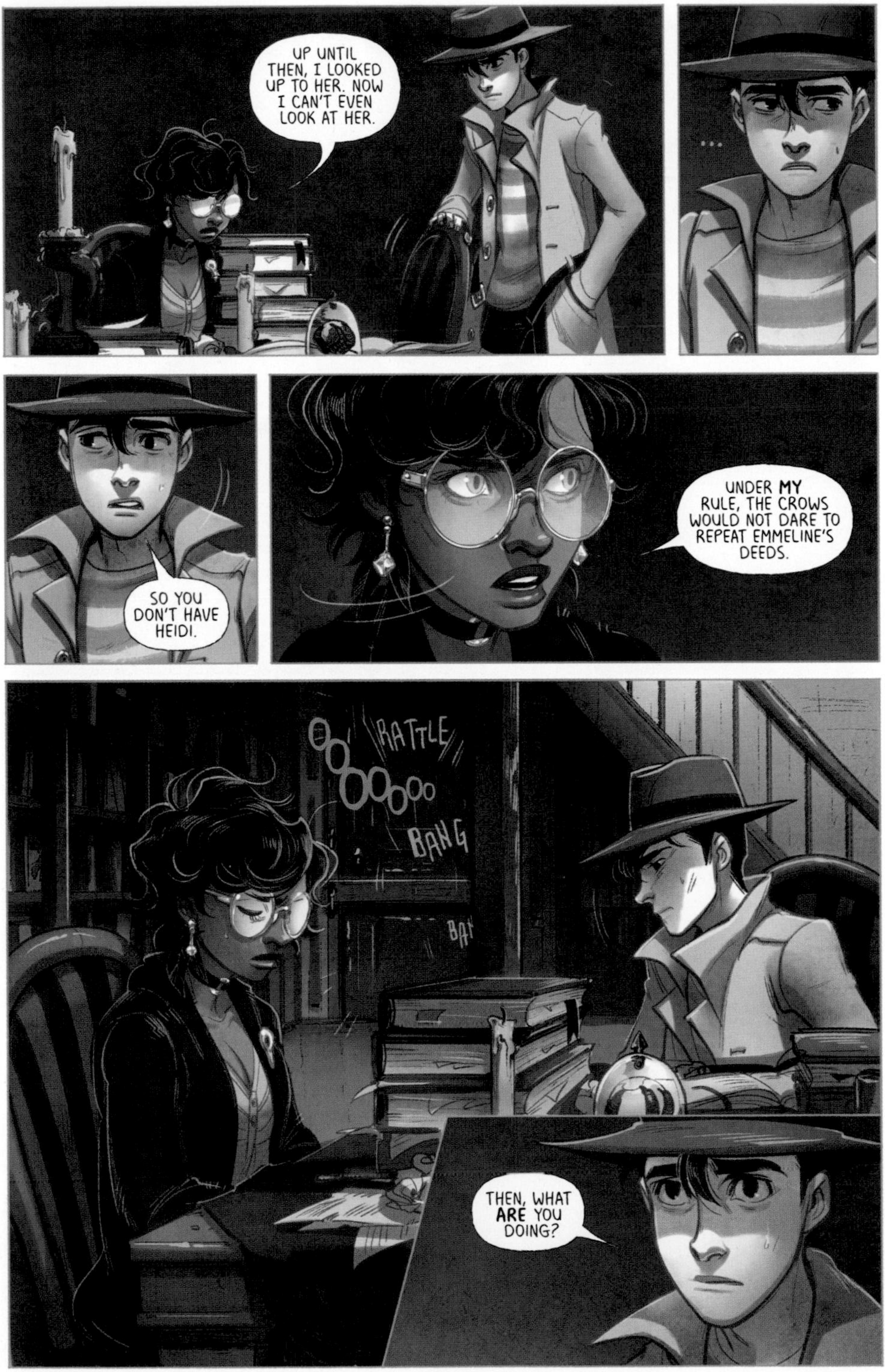
UP UNTIL THEN, I LOOKED UP TO HER. NOW I CAN'T EVEN LOOK AT HER.
...
SO YOU DON'T HAVE HEIDI.
UNDER **MY** RULE, THE CROWS WOULD NOT DARE TO REPEAT EMMELINE'S DEEDS.
OOOOOOoo
RATTLE
BANG
THEN, WHAT **ARE** YOU DOING?

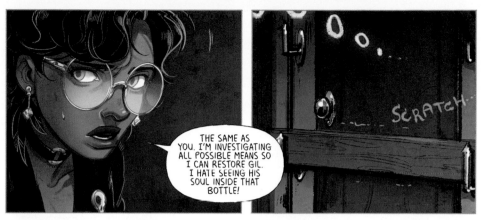

THE SAME AS YOU. I'M INVESTIGATING ALL POSSIBLE MEANS SO I CAN RESTORE GIL. I HATE SEEING HIS SOUL INSIDE THAT BOTTLE!

SCRATCH...

EVERYONE GAVE UP ON HIM. HE DOESN'T HAVE ANYONE BUT ME.

I DIDN'T KNOW, MATILDA.

DO YOU KNOW WHAT HAPPENED TO GRISELDA?

ONLY THAT SHE WAS CAUGHT DOING MAGICK AND WAS EXECUTED FOR IT.

THERE IS A BIT MORE TO THAT STORY.

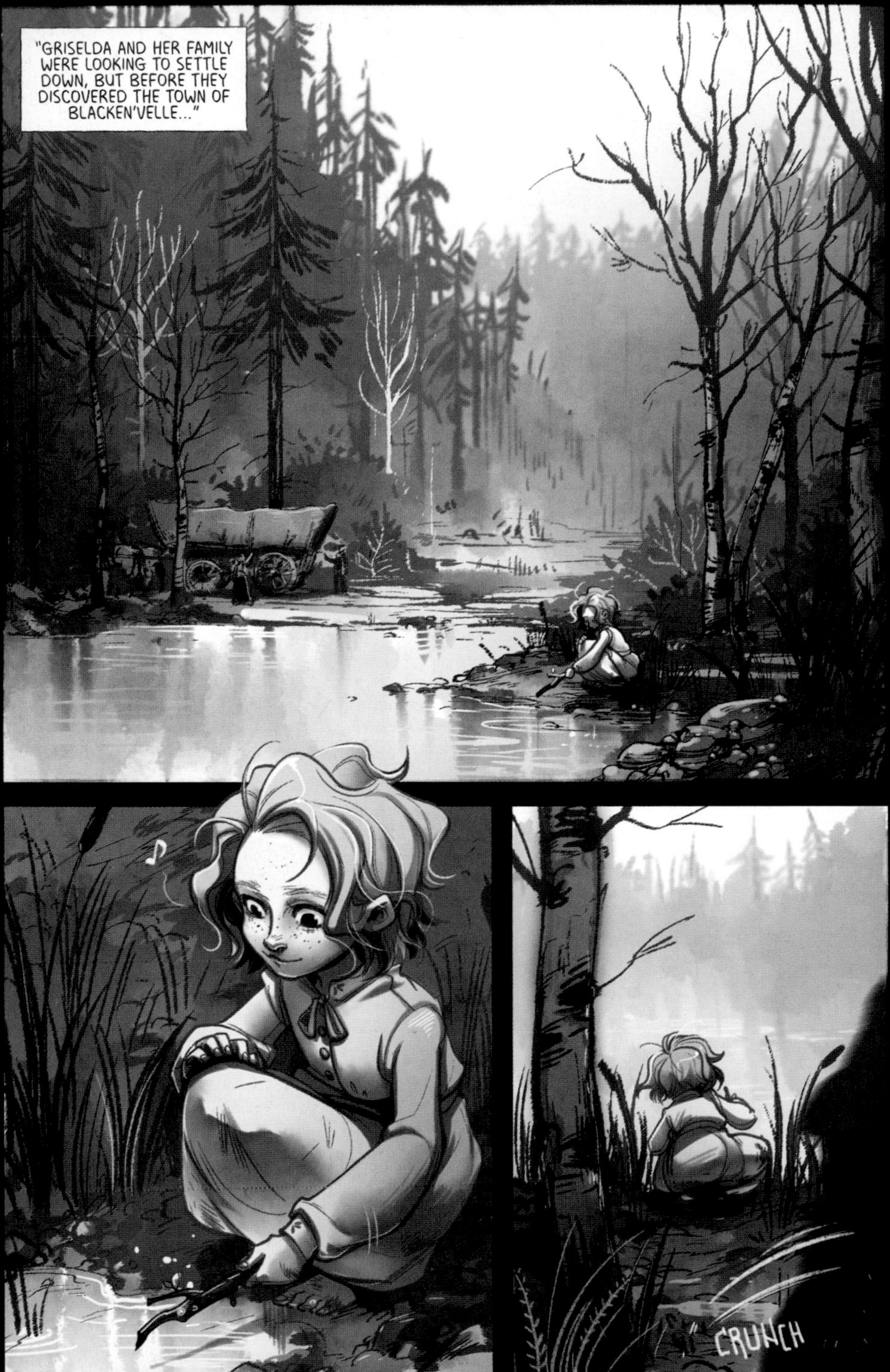
"GRISELDA AND HER FAMILY WERE LOOKING TO SETTLE DOWN, BUT BEFORE THEY DISCOVERED THE TOWN OF BLACKEN'VELLE..."
CRUNCH

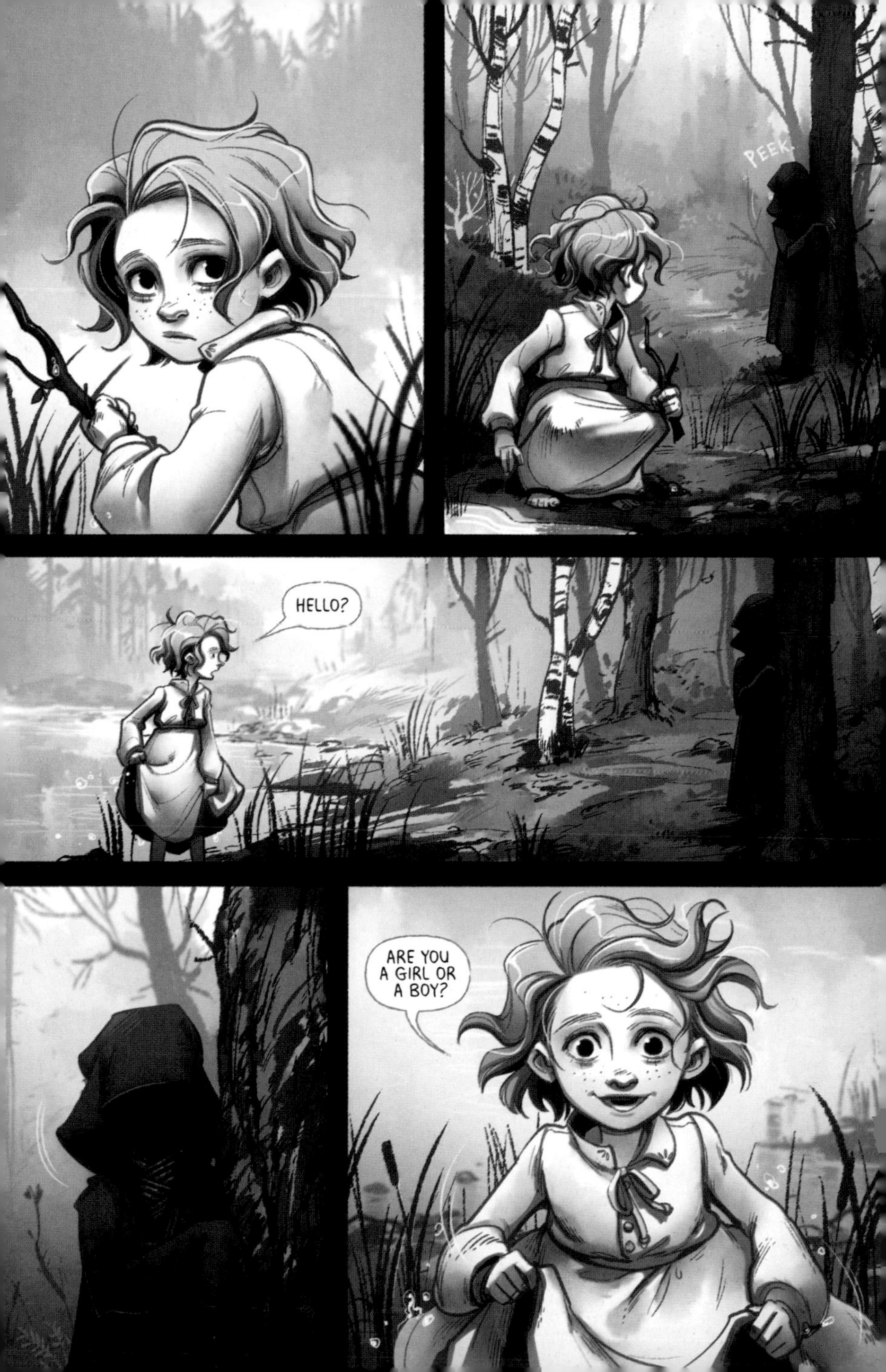
PEEK
HELLO?
ARE YOU A GIRL OR A BOY?

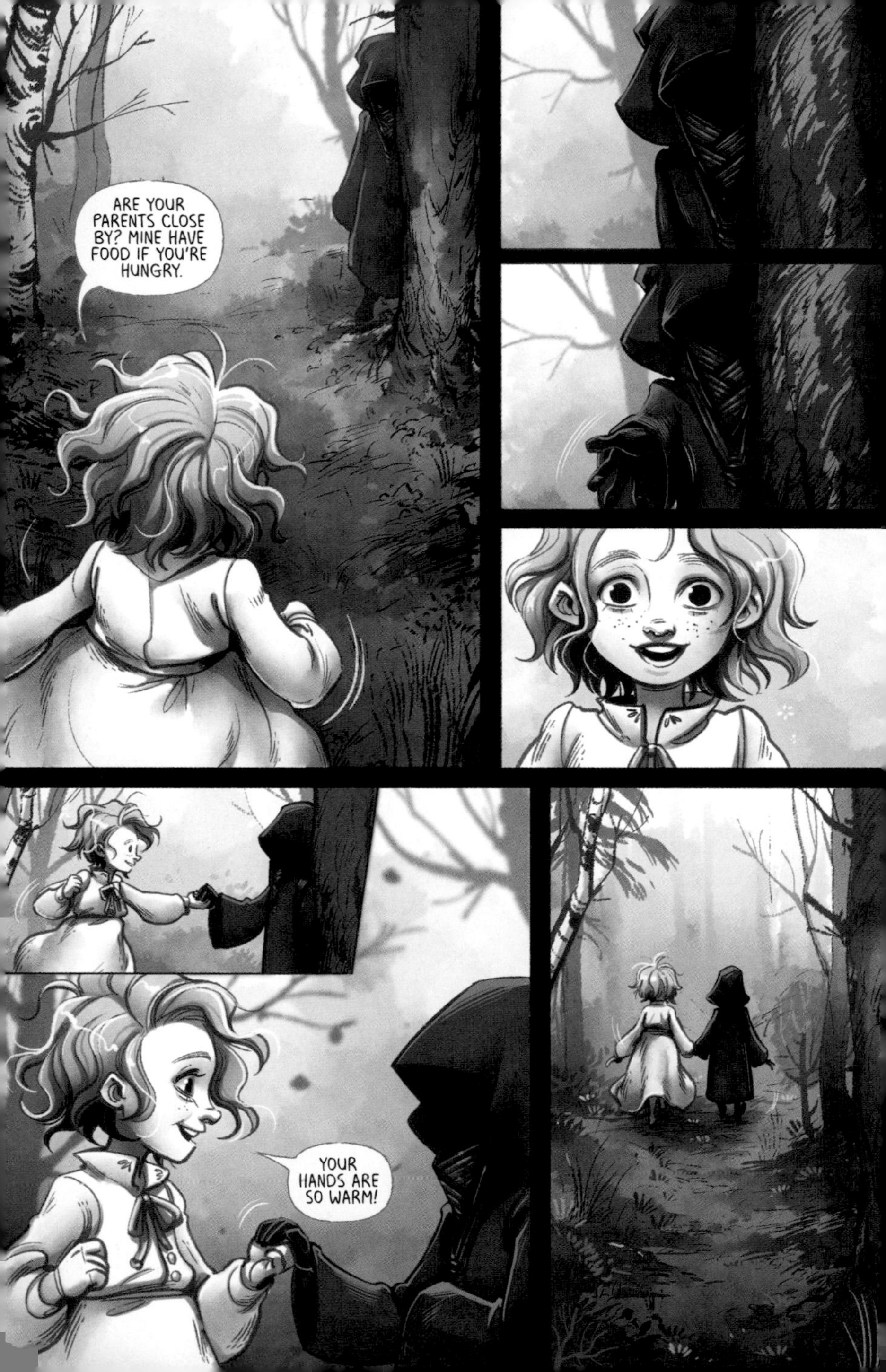
ARE YOUR PARENTS CLOSE BY? MINE HAVE FOOD IF YOU'RE HUNGRY.
YOUR HANDS ARE SO WARM!

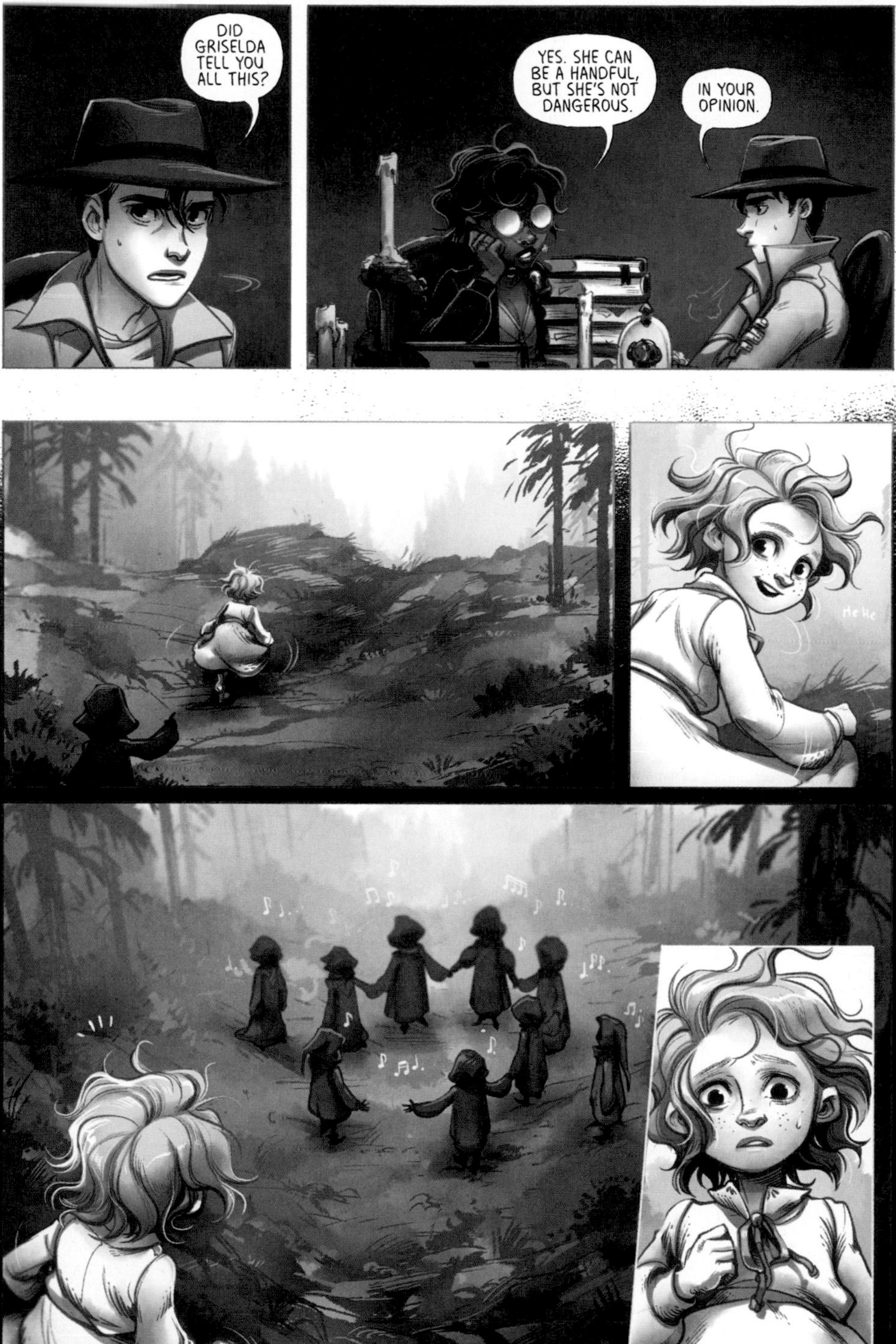
DID GRISELDA TELL YOU ALL THIS?
YES. SHE CAN BE A HANDFUL, BUT SHE'S NOT DANGEROUS.
IN YOUR OPINION.
He He

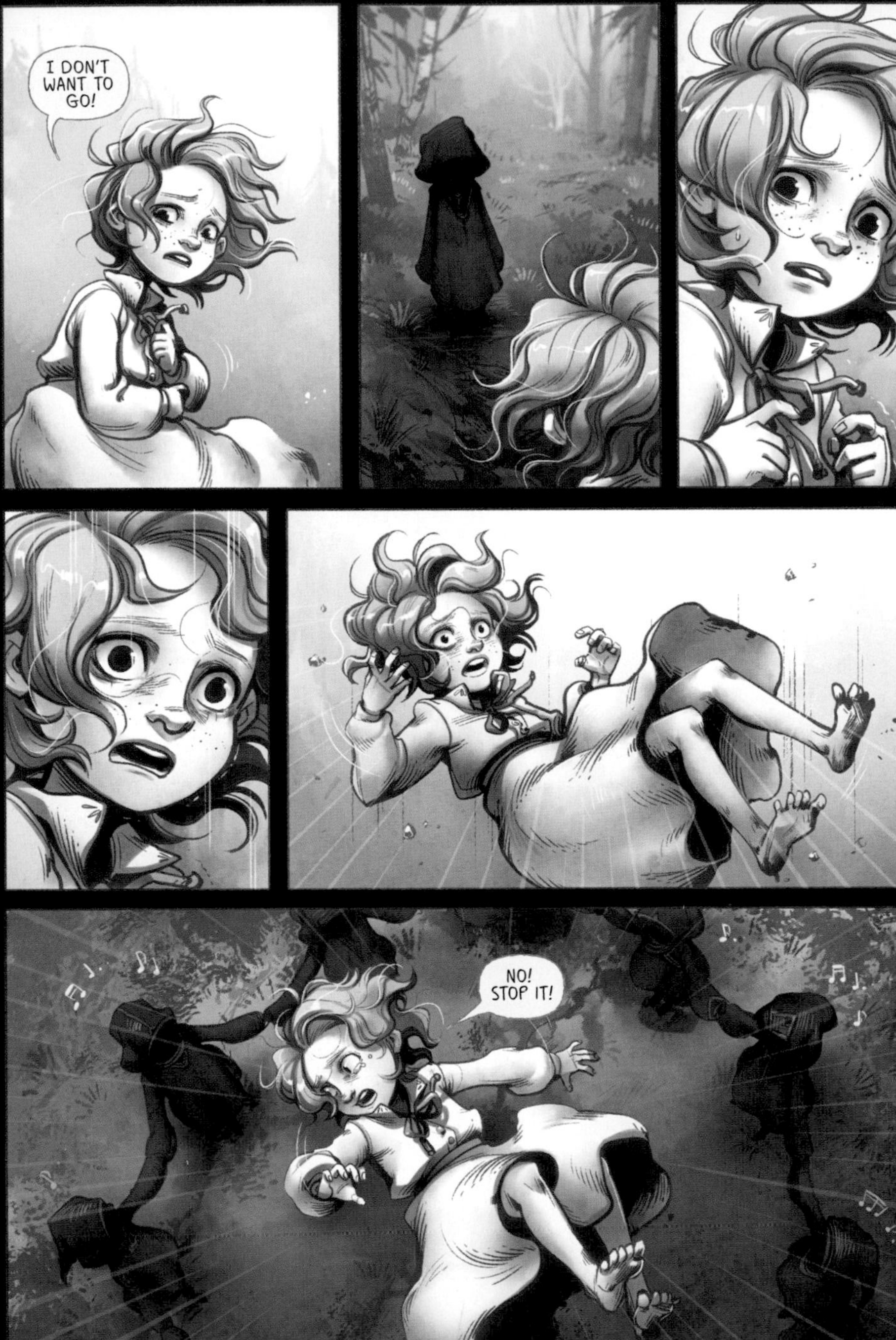
I DON'T WANT TO GO!
NO! STOP IT!

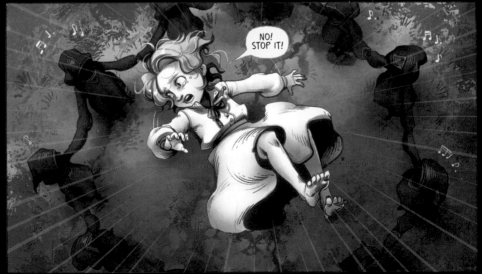

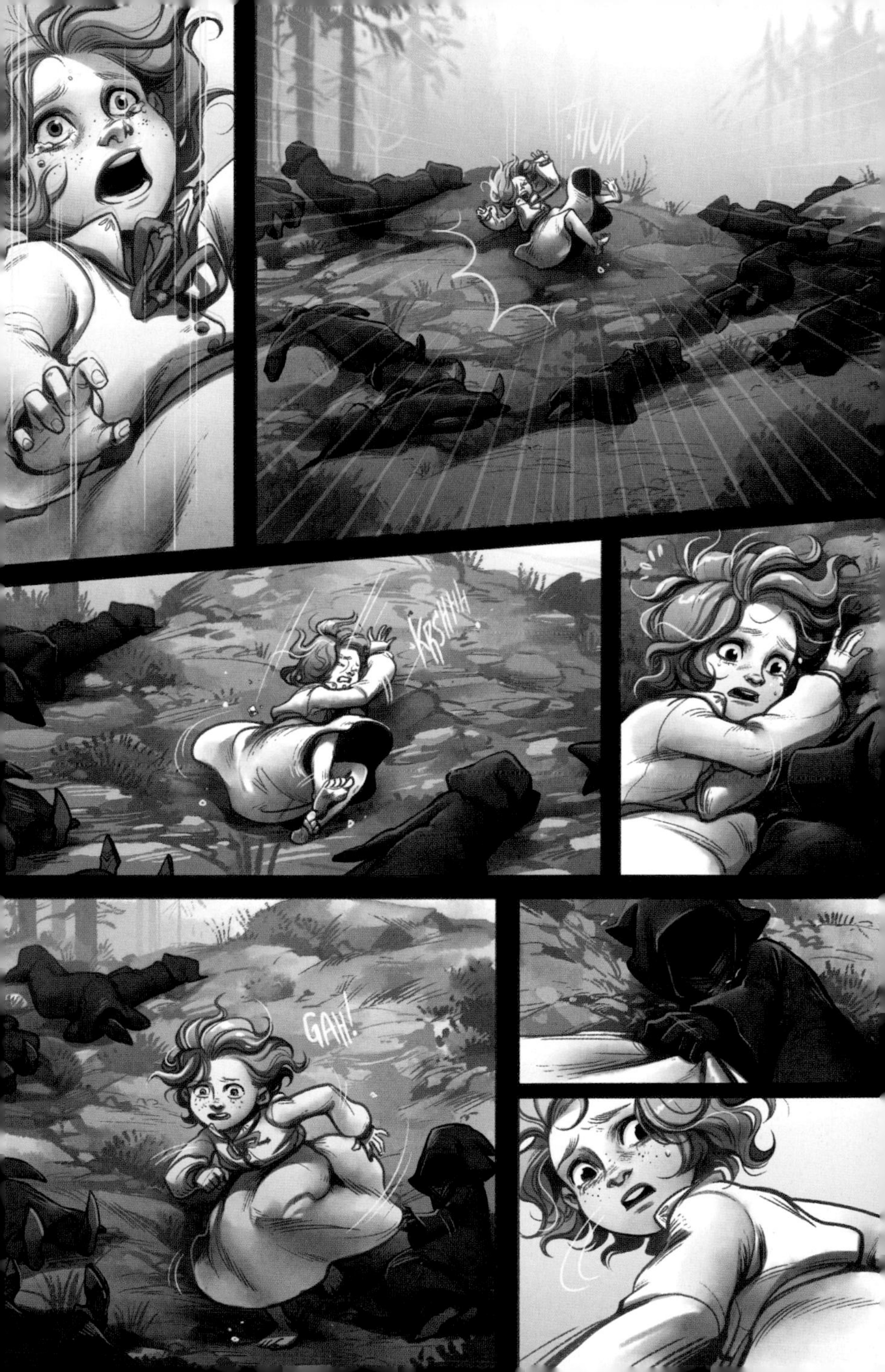
THUNK
KRSHHH
GAH!

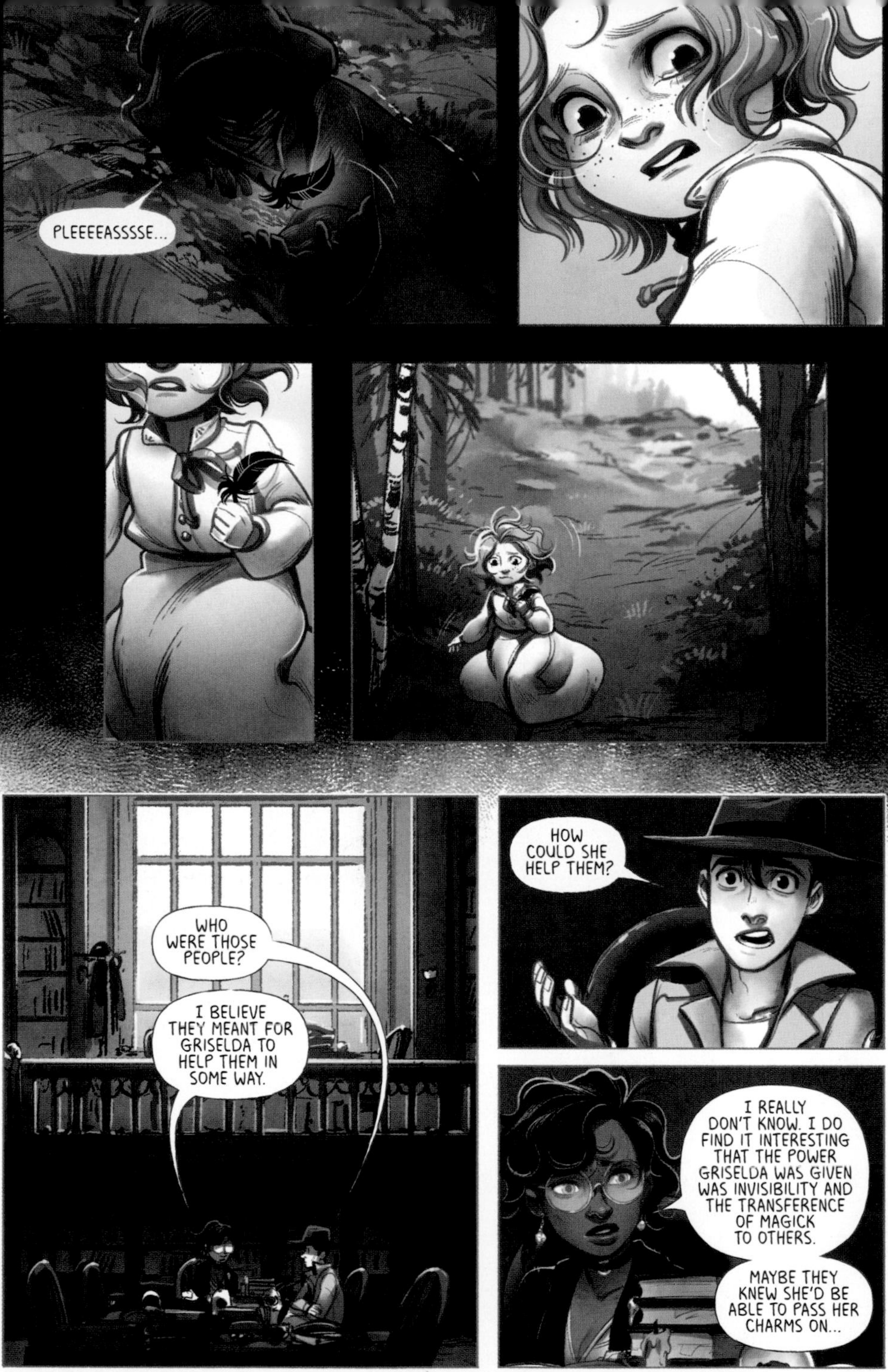
PLEEEEASSSSE...
WHO WERE THOSE PEOPLE?
I BELIEVE THEY MEANT FOR GRISELDA TO HELP THEM IN SOME WAY.
HOW COULD SHE HELP THEM?
I REALLY DON'T KNOW. I DO FIND IT INTERESTING THAT THE POWER GRISELDA WAS GIVEN WAS INVISIBILITY AND THE TRANSFERENCE OF MAGICK TO OTHERS.
MAYBE THEY KNEW SHE'D BE ABLE TO PASS HER CHARMS ON...

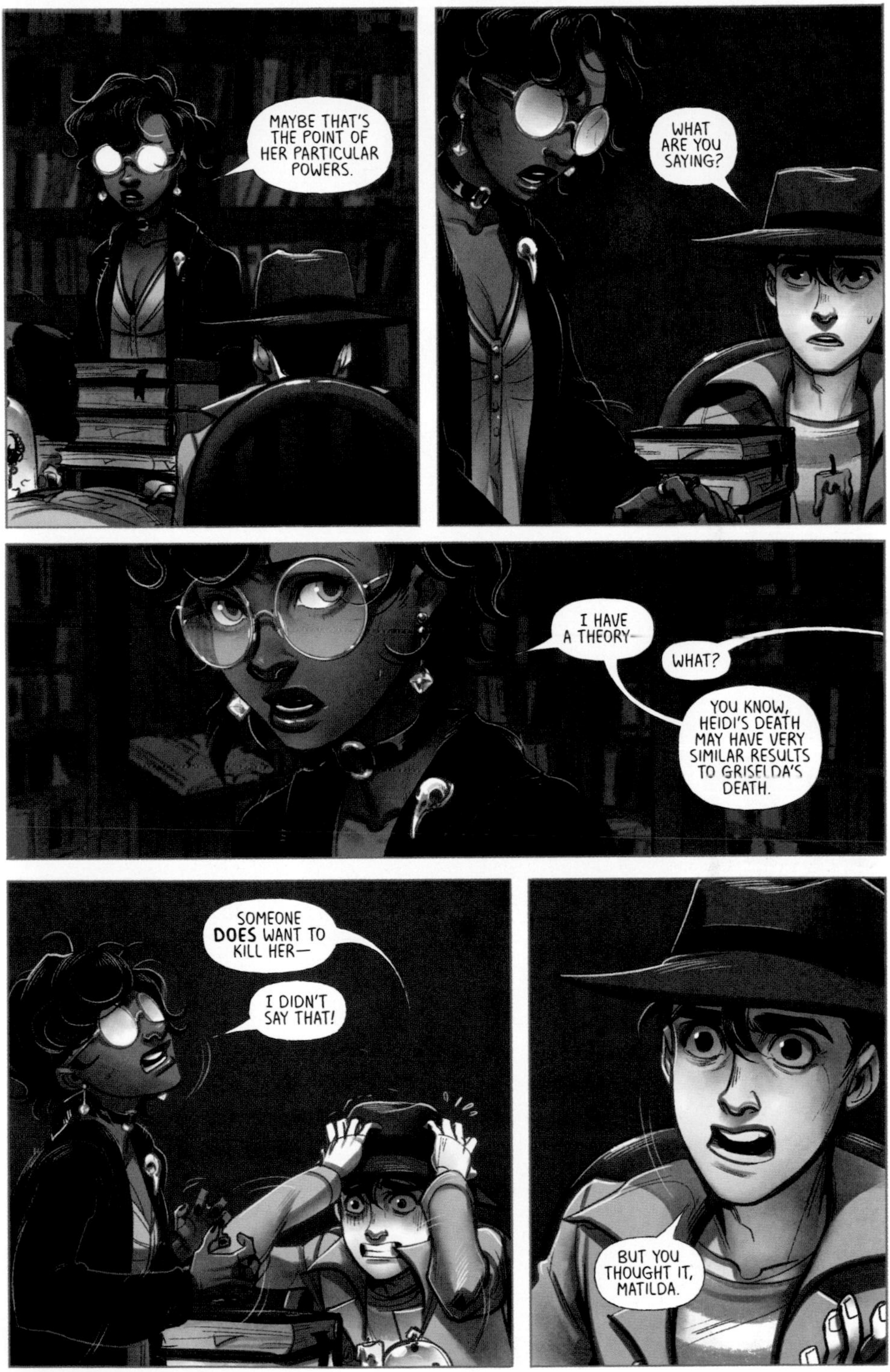
MAYBE THAT'S THE POINT OF HER PARTICULAR POWERS.
WHAT ARE YOU SAYING?
I HAVE A THEORY—
WHAT?
YOU KNOW, HEIDI'S DEATH MAY HAVE VERY SIMILAR RESULTS TO GRISELDA'S DEATH.
SOMEONE **DOES** WANT TO KILL HER—
I DIDN'T SAY THAT!
BUT YOU THOUGHT IT, MATILDA.

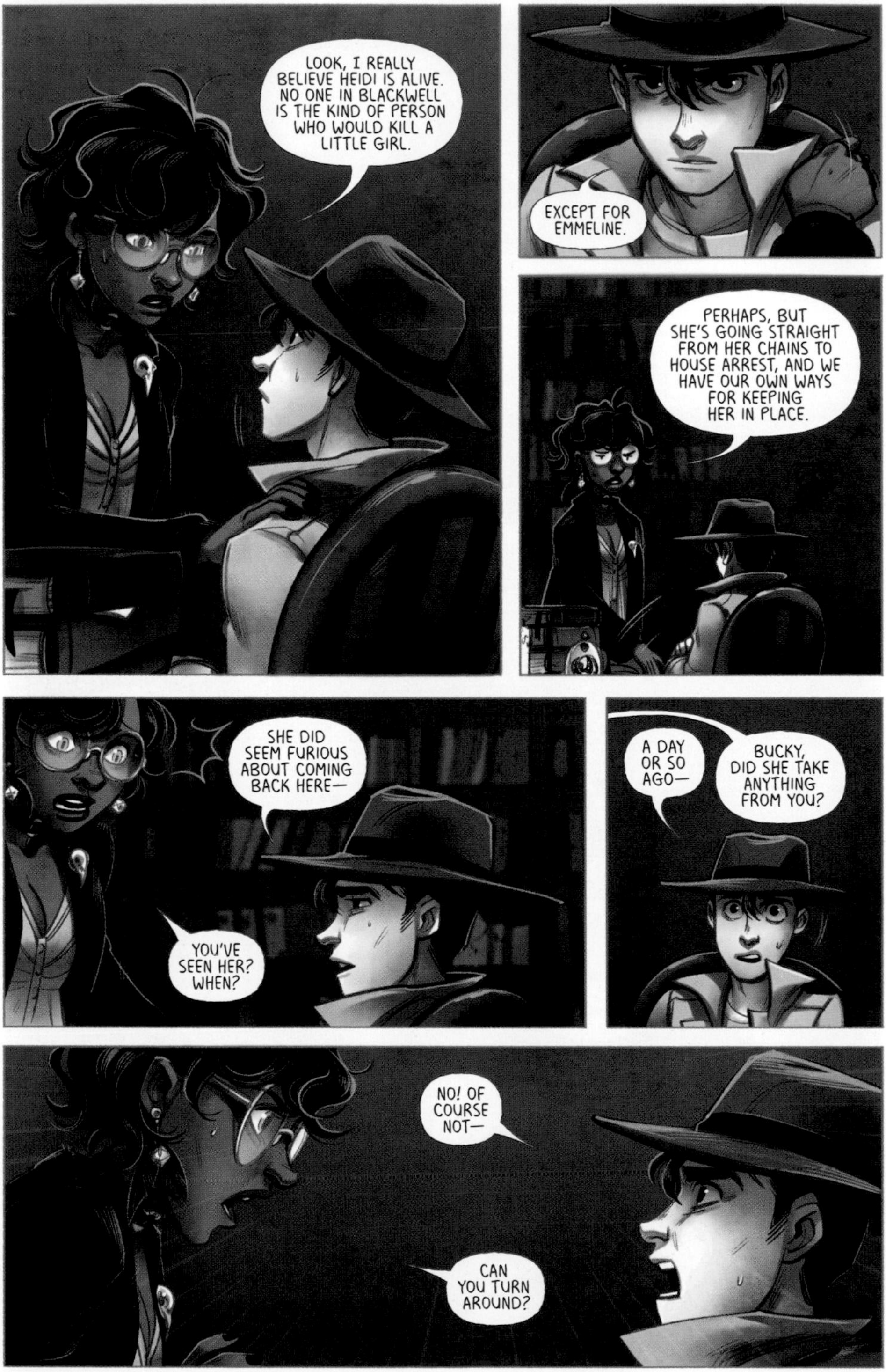
LOOK, I REALLY BELIEVE HEIDI IS ALIVE. NO ONE IN BLACKWELL IS THE KIND OF PERSON WHO WOULD KILL A LITTLE GIRL.
EXCEPT FOR EMMELINE.
PERHAPS, BUT SHE'S GOING STRAIGHT FROM HER CHAINS TO HOUSE ARREST, AND WE HAVE OUR OWN WAYS FOR KEEPING HER IN PLACE.
SHE DID SEEM FURIOUS ABOUT COMING BACK HERE—
YOU'VE SEEN HER? WHEN?
A DAY OR SO AGO—
BUCKY, DID SHE TAKE ANYTHING FROM YOU?
NO! OF COURSE NOT—
CAN YOU TURN AROUND?

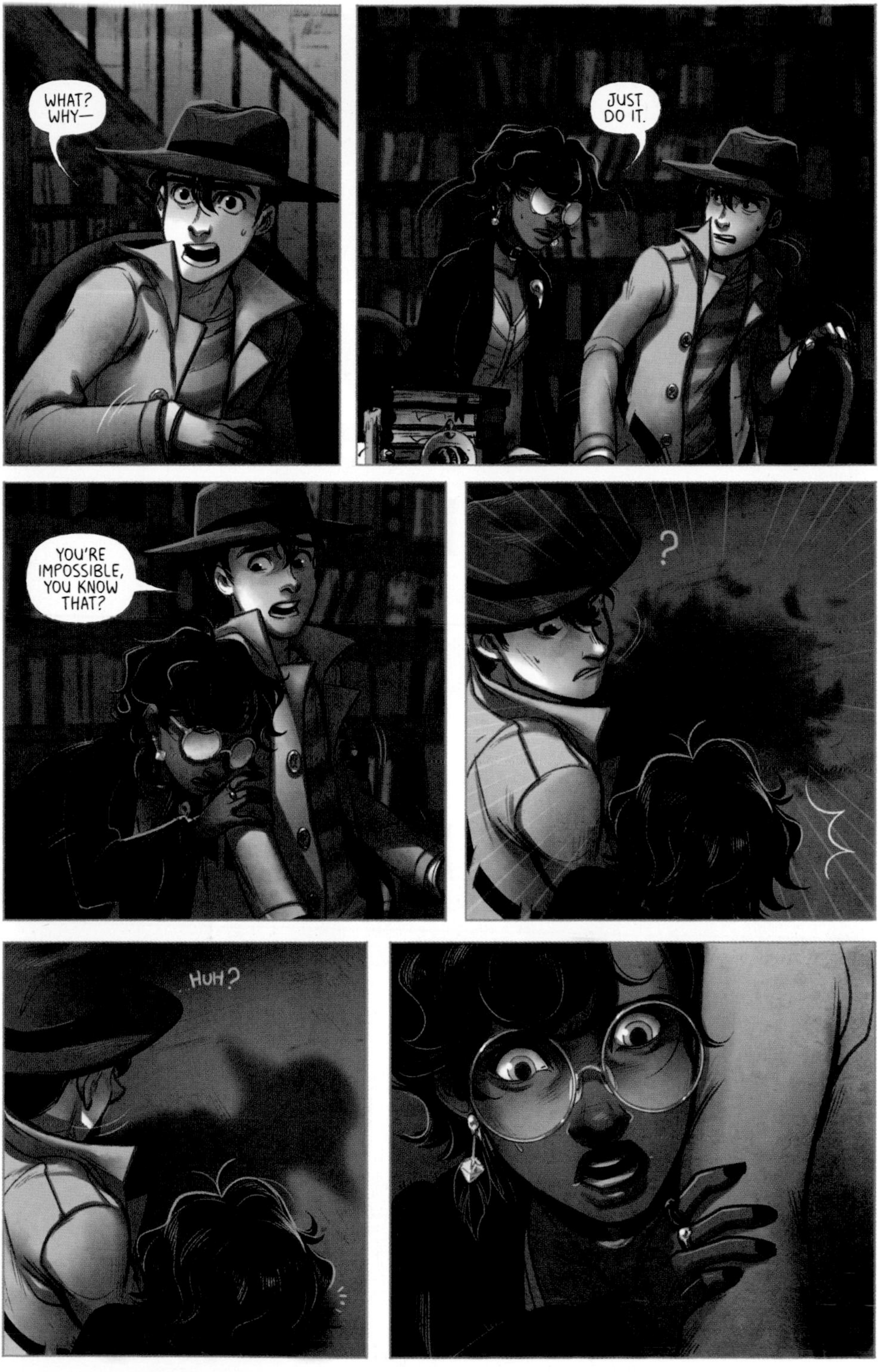
WHAT? WHY—
JUST DO IT.
YOU'RE IMPOSSIBLE, YOU KNOW THAT?
?
HUH?

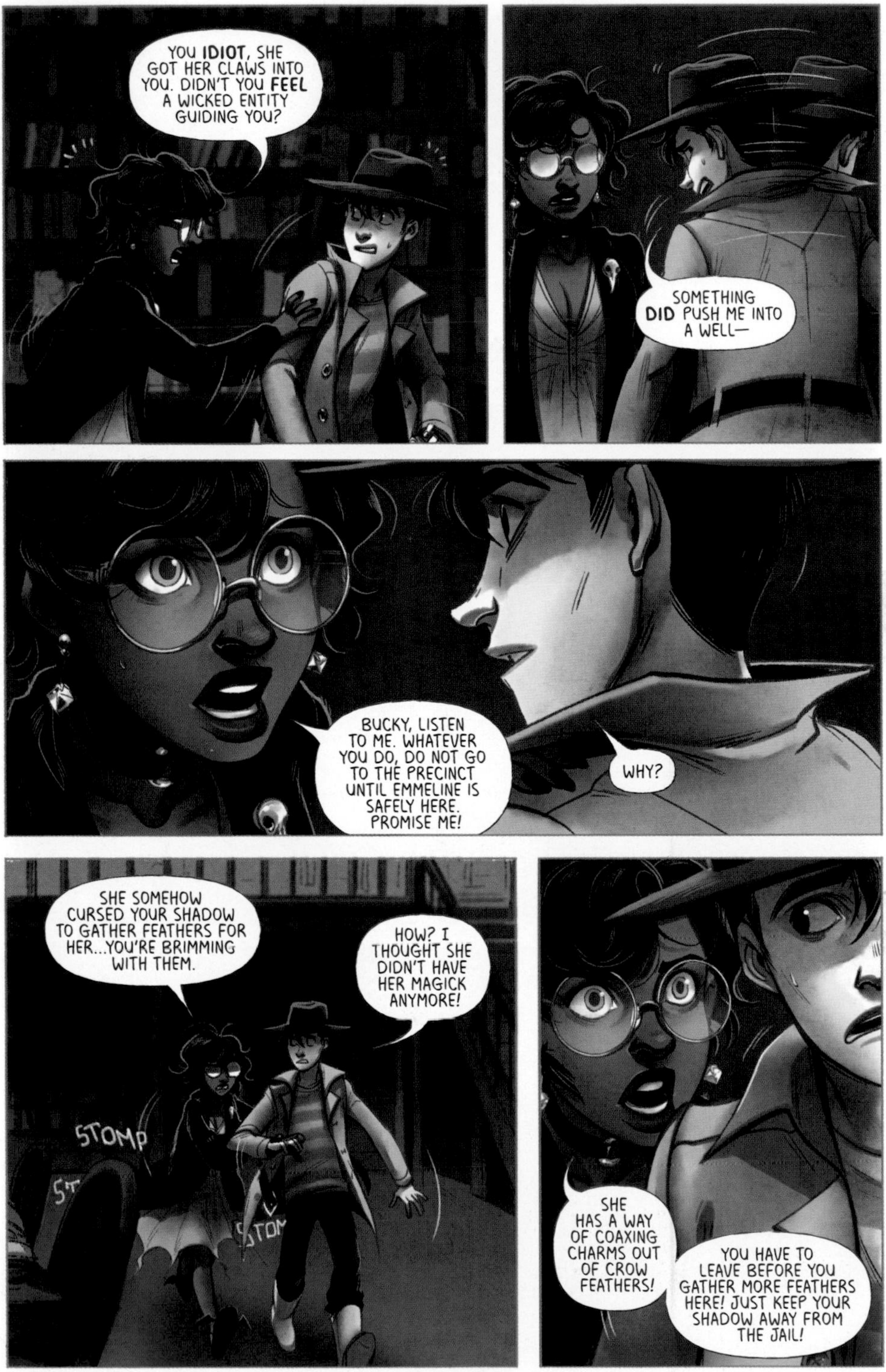
YOU IDIOT, SHE GOT HER CLAWS INTO YOU. DIDN'T YOU FEEL A WICKED ENTITY GUIDING YOU?
SOMETHING DID PUSH ME INTO A WELL—
BUCKY, LISTEN TO ME. WHATEVER YOU DO, DO NOT GO TO THE PRECINCT UNTIL EMMELINE IS SAFELY HERE. PROMISE ME!
WHY?
SHE SOMEHOW CURSED YOUR SHADOW TO GATHER FEATHERS FOR HER...YOU'RE BRIMMING WITH THEM.
HOW? I THOUGHT SHE DIDN'T HAVE HER MAGICK ANYMORE!
STOMP
SHE HAS A WAY OF COAXING CHARMS OUT OF CROW FEATHERS!
YOU HAVE TO LEAVE BEFORE YOU GATHER MORE FEATHERS HERE! JUST KEEP YOUR SHADOW AWAY FROM THE JAIL!

CHAPTER 10

SOME KIDS ARE SO EVIL

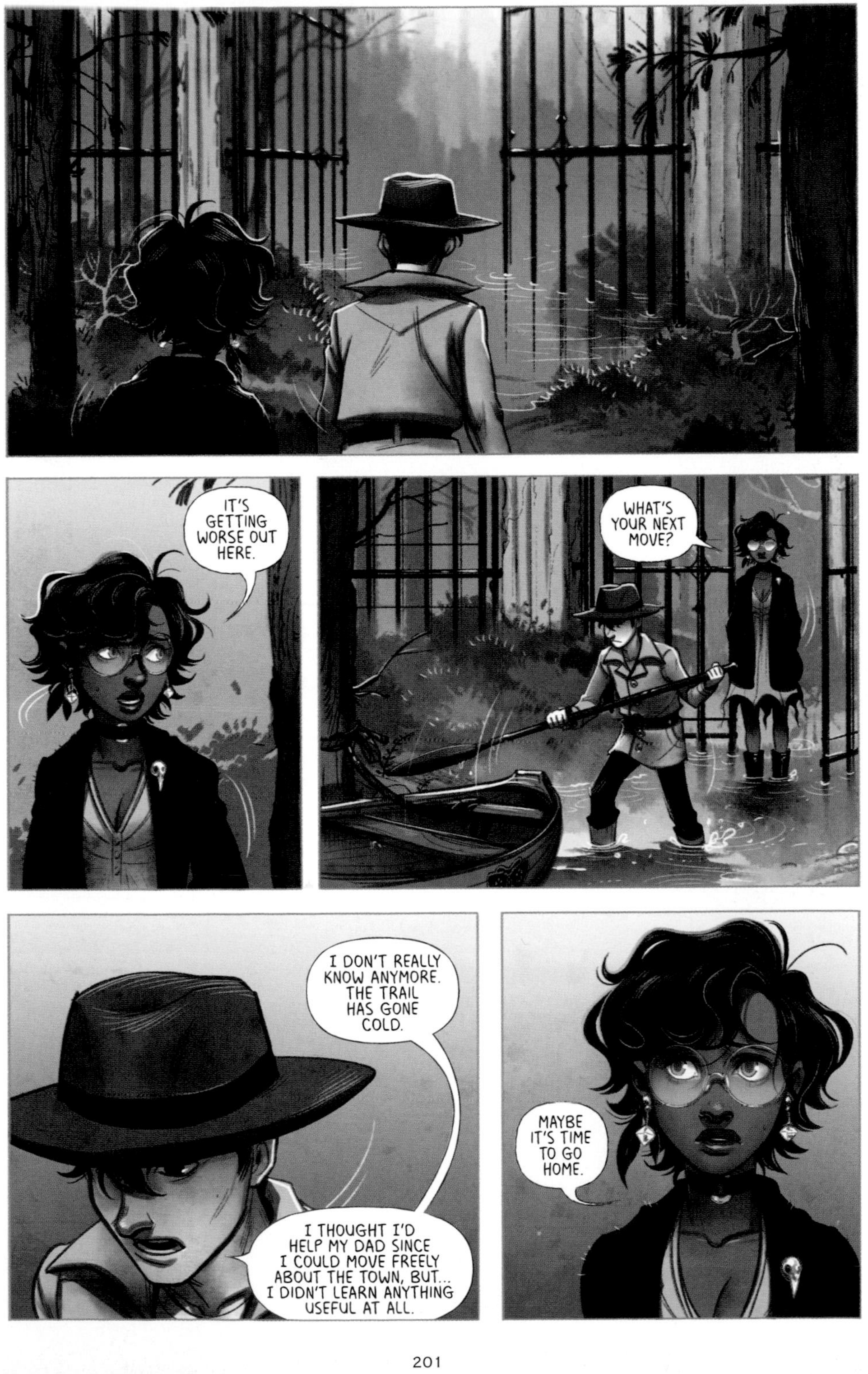
IT'S GETTING WORSE OUT HERE.
WHAT'S YOUR NEXT MOVE?
I DON'T REALLY KNOW ANYMORE. THE TRAIL HAS GONE COLD.
I THOUGHT I'D HELP MY DAD SINCE I COULD MOVE FREELY ABOUT THE TOWN, BUT... I DIDN'T LEARN ANYTHING USEFUL AT ALL.
MAYBE IT'S TIME TO GO HOME.

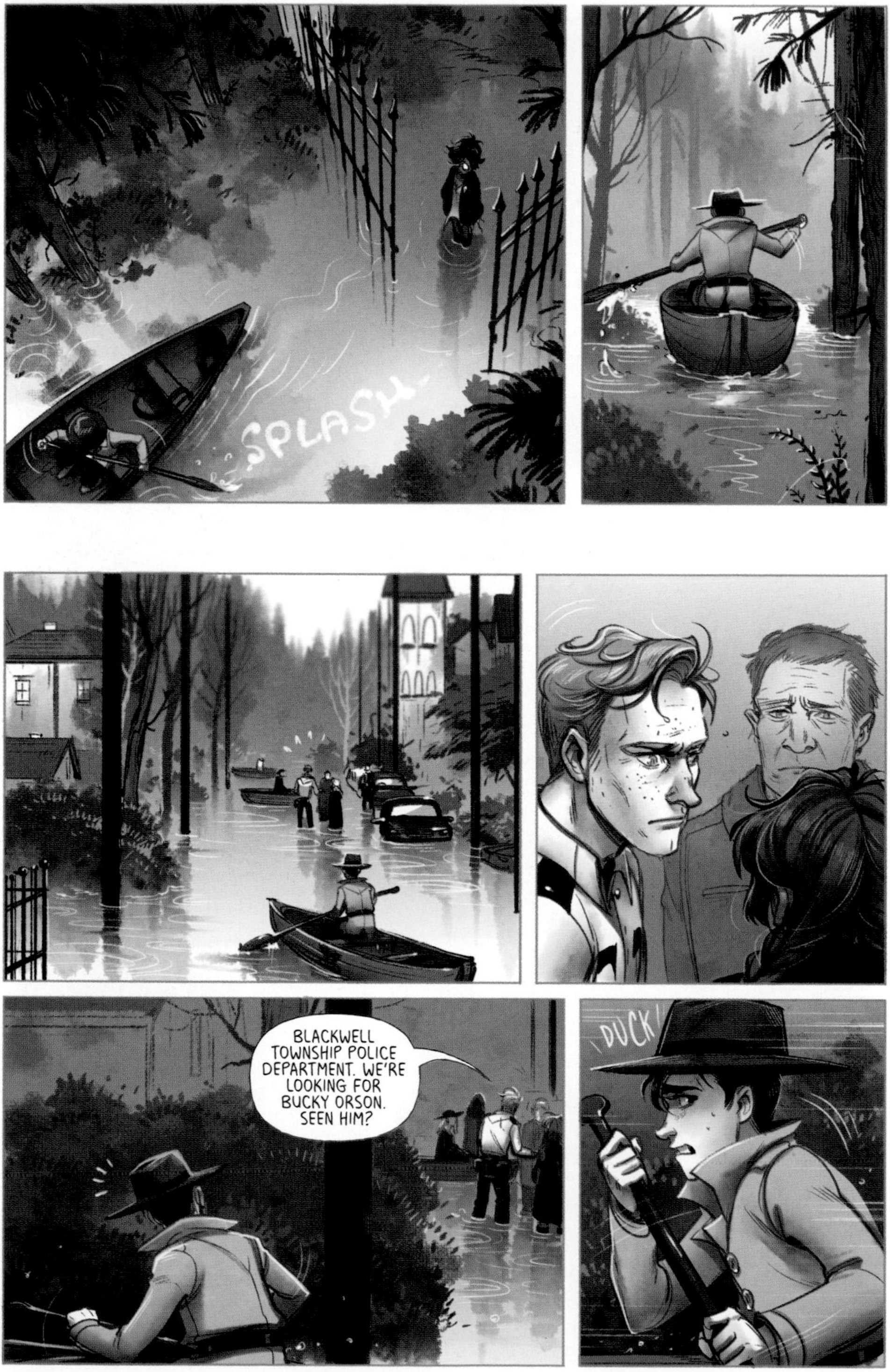
SPLASH
BLACKWELL TOWNSHIP POLICE DEPARTMENT. WE'RE LOOKING FOR BUCKY ORSON. SEEN HIM?
DUCK

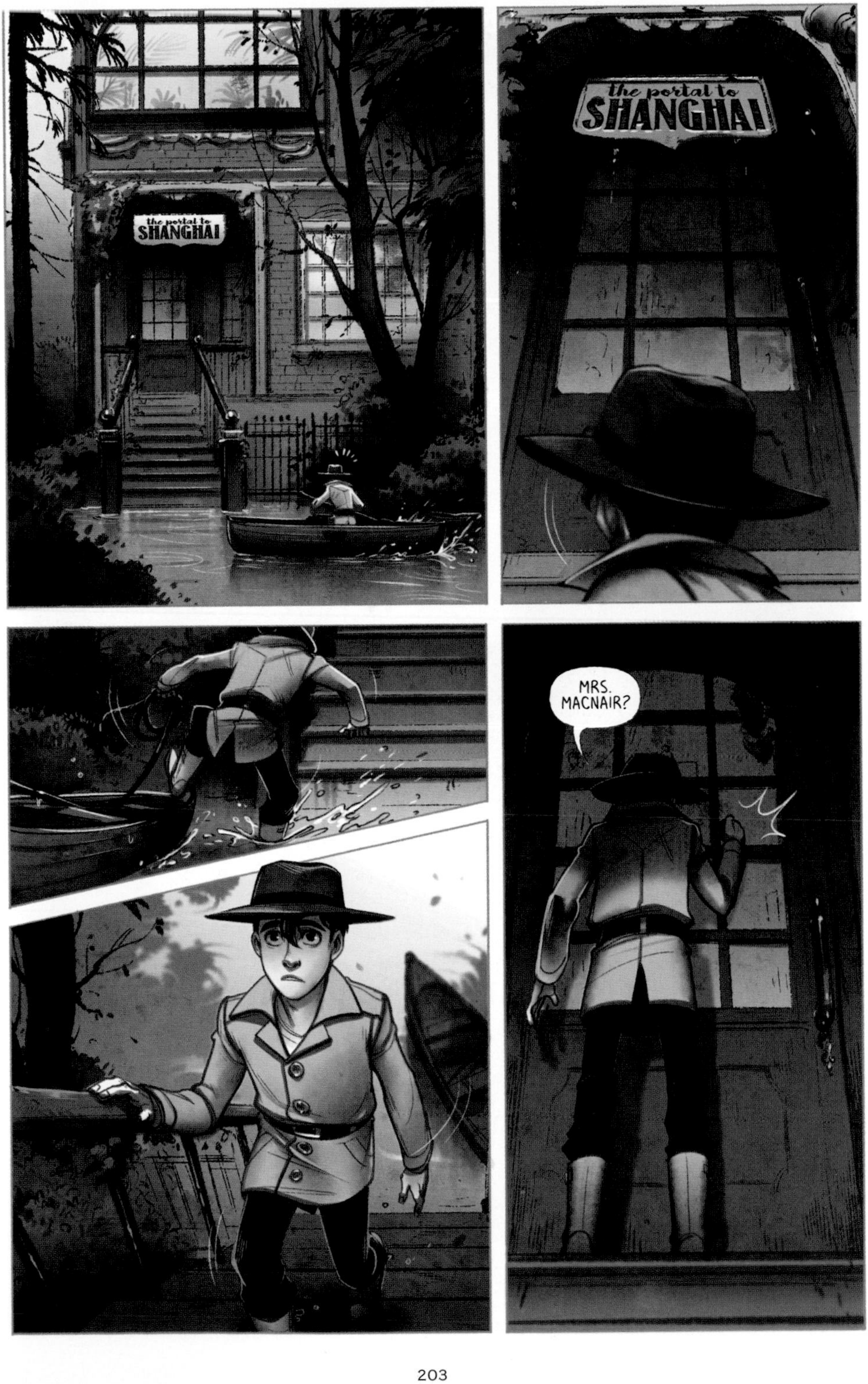
the portal to
SHANGHAI
the portal to
SHANGHAI
MRS. MACNAIR?

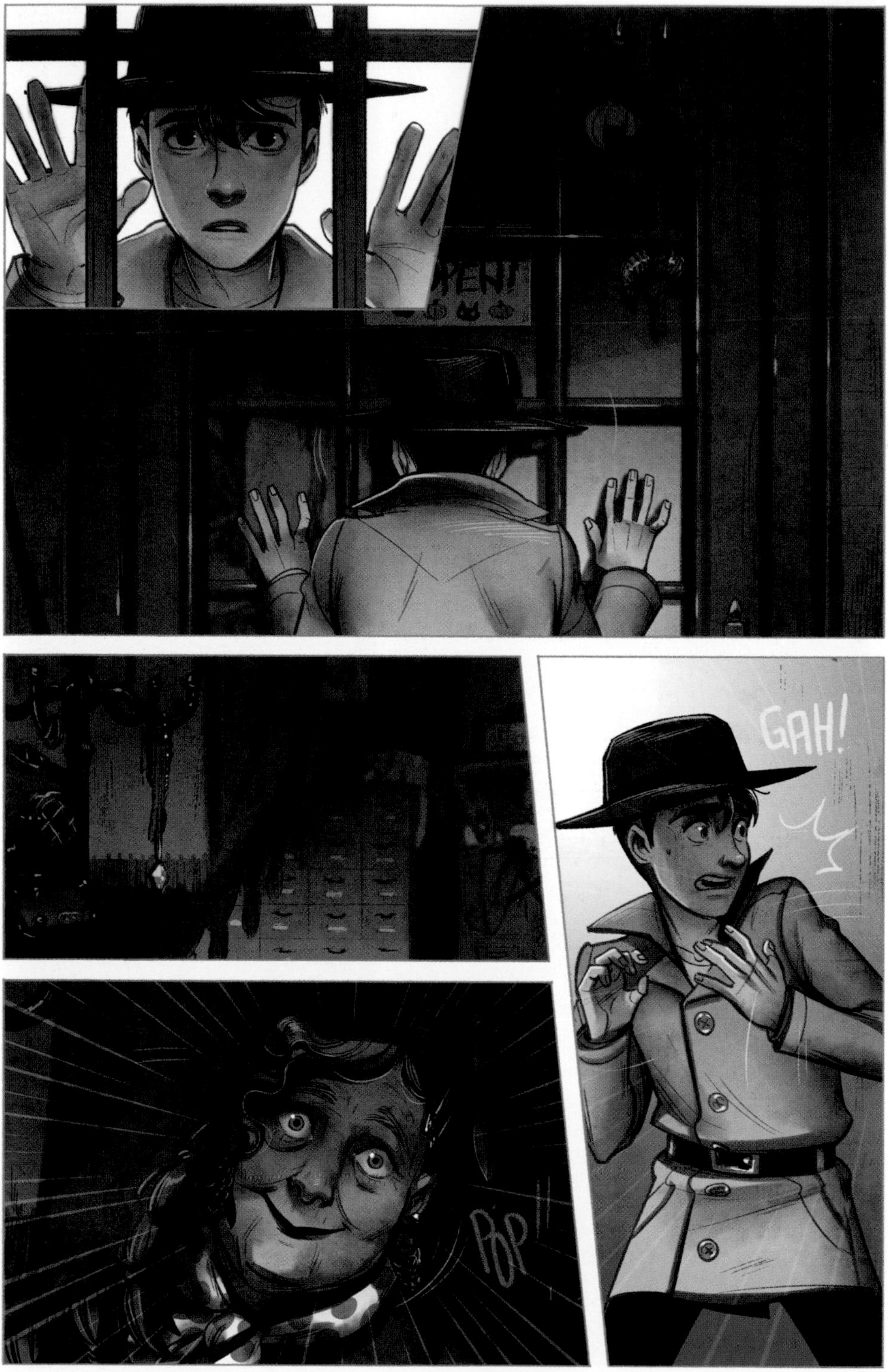
POP
GAH!

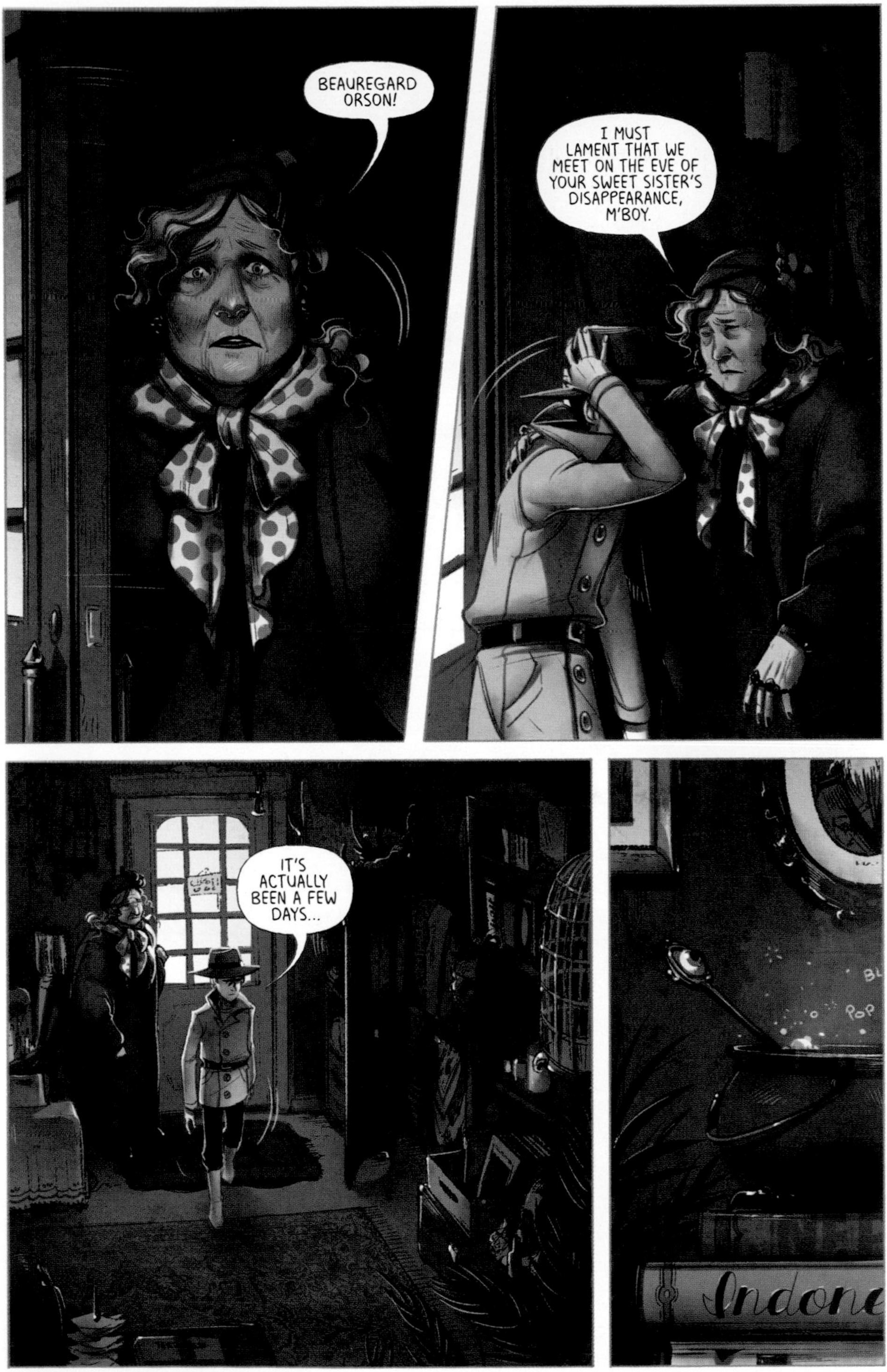
BEAUREGARD ORSON!
I MUST LAMENT THAT WE MEET ON THE EVE OF YOUR SWEET SISTER'S DISAPPEARANCE, M'BOY.
IT'S ACTUALLY BEEN A FEW DAYS...
BL
POP
Indone

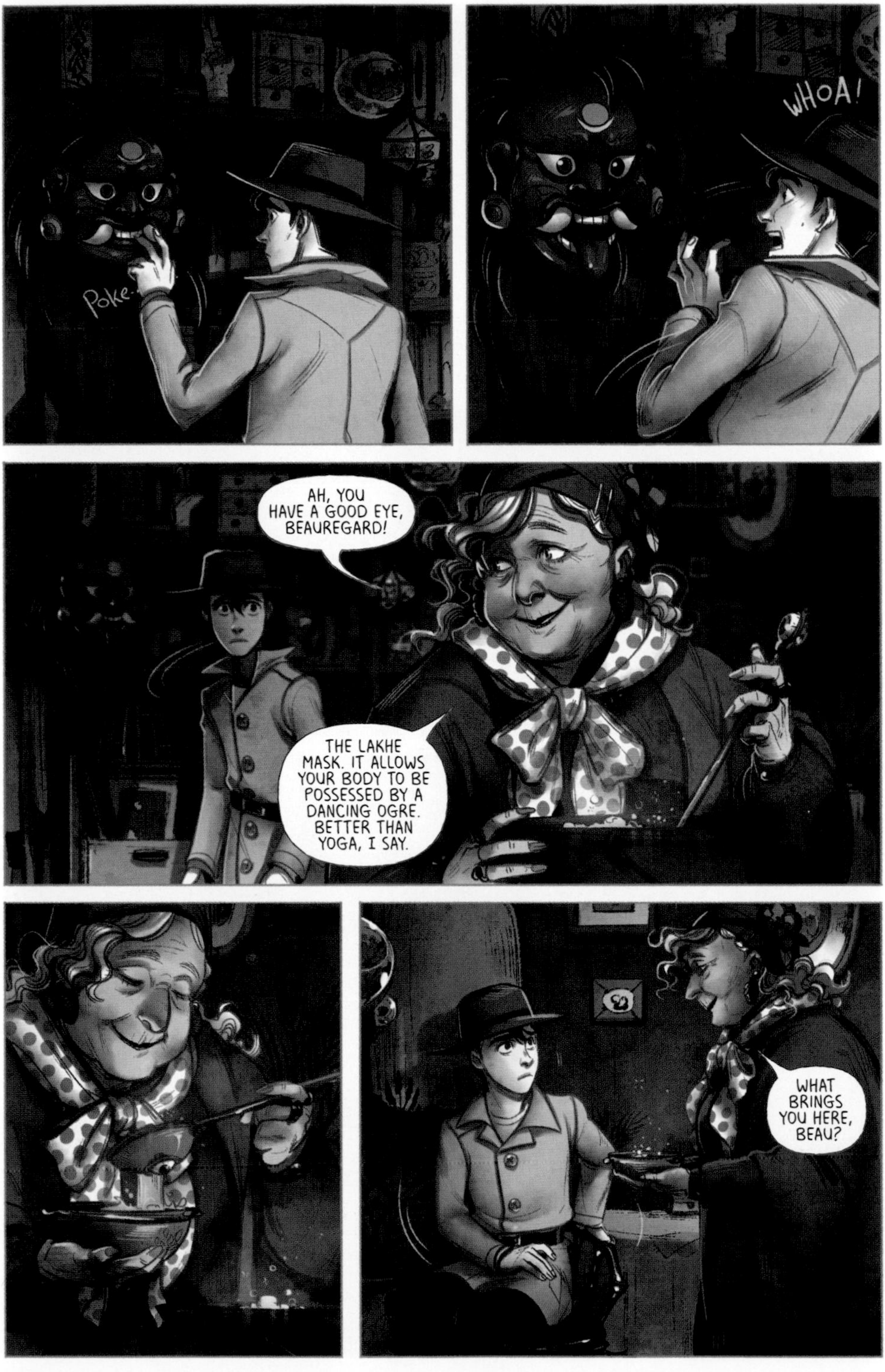
POKE...
WHOA!
AH, YOU HAVE A GOOD EYE, BEAUREGARD!
THE LAKHE MASK. IT ALLOWS YOUR BODY TO BE POSSESSED BY A DANCING OGRE. BETTER THAN YOGA, I SAY.
WHAT BRINGS YOU HERE, BEAU?

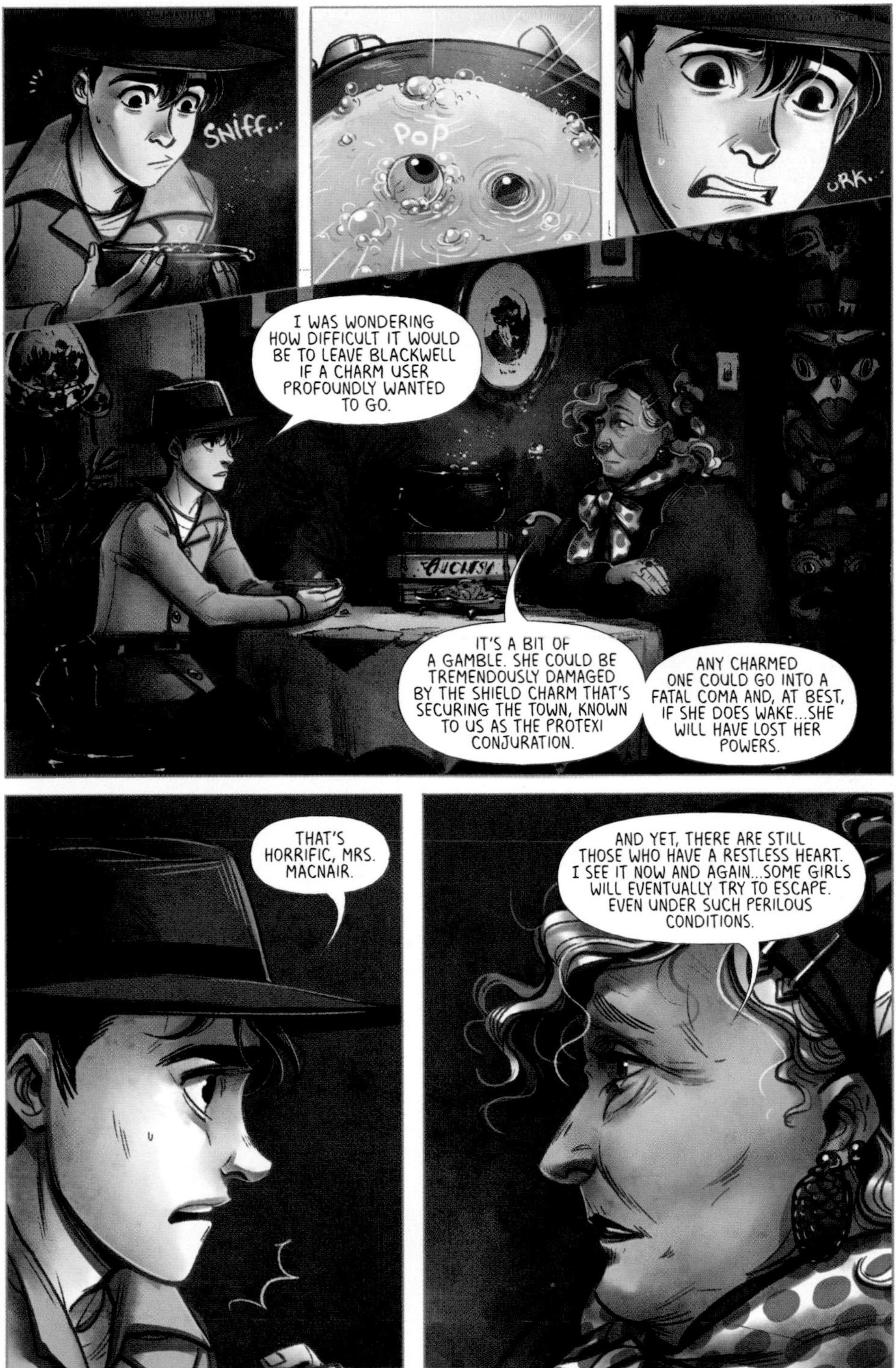
SNIFF...
POP
URK...
I WAS WONDERING HOW DIFFICULT IT WOULD BE TO LEAVE BLACKWELL IF A CHARM USER PROFOUNDLY WANTED TO GO.
IT'S A BIT OF A GAMBLE. SHE COULD BE TREMENDOUSLY DAMAGED BY THE SHIELD CHARM THAT'S SECURING THE TOWN, KNOWN TO US AS THE PROTEXI CONJURATION.
ANY CHARMED ONE COULD GO INTO A FATAL COMA AND, AT BEST, IF SHE DOES WAKE...SHE WILL HAVE LOST HER POWERS.
THAT'S HORRIFIC, MRS. MACNAIR.
AND YET, THERE ARE STILL THOSE WHO HAVE A RESTLESS HEART. I SEE IT NOW AND AGAIN...SOME GIRLS WILL EVENTUALLY TRY TO ESCAPE. EVEN UNDER SUCH PERILOUS CONDITIONS.

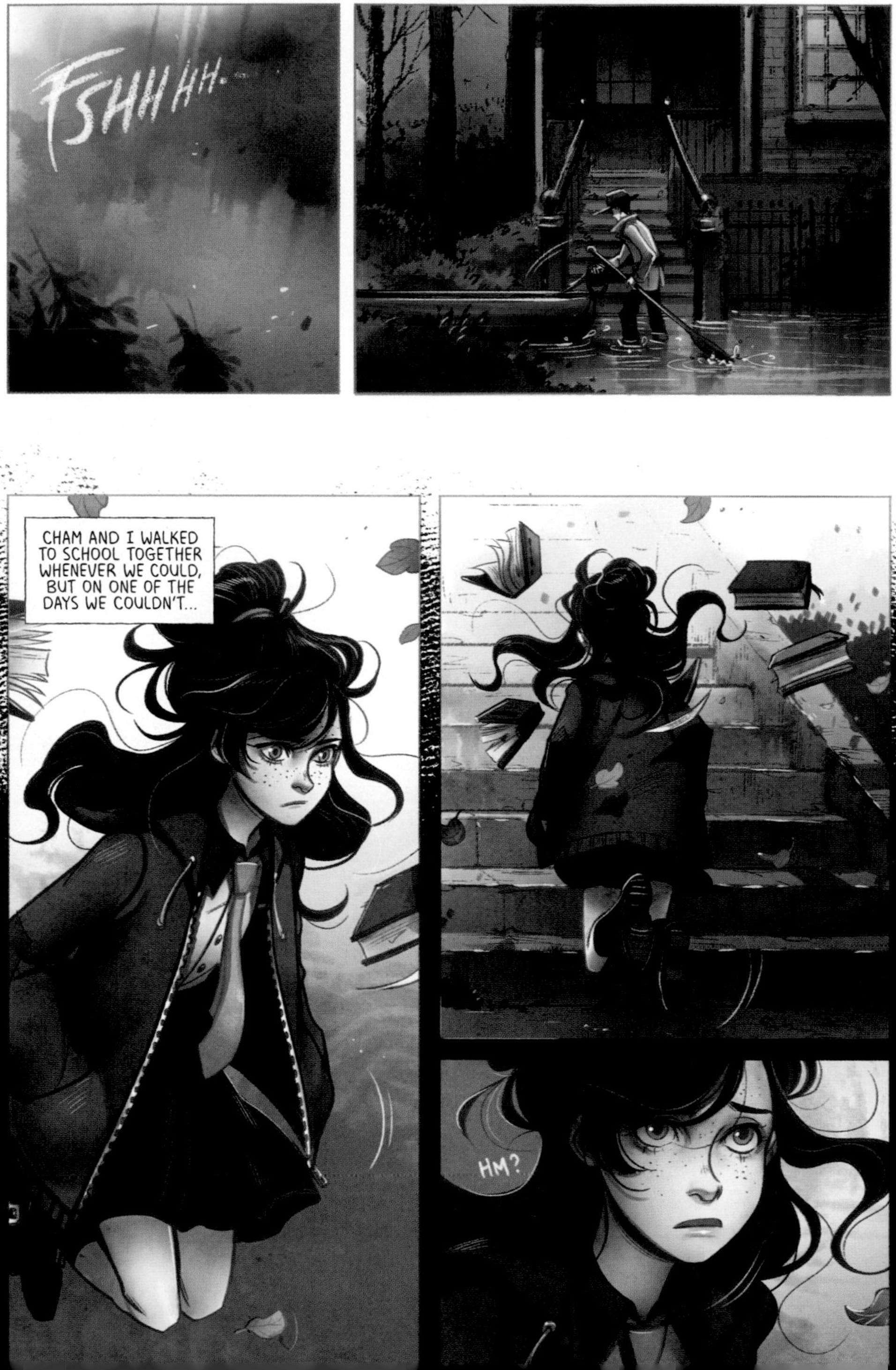
FSHHHH.
CHAM AND I WALKED TO SCHOOL TOGETHER WHENEVER WE COULD, BUT ON ONE OF THE DAYS WE COULDN'T...
HM?

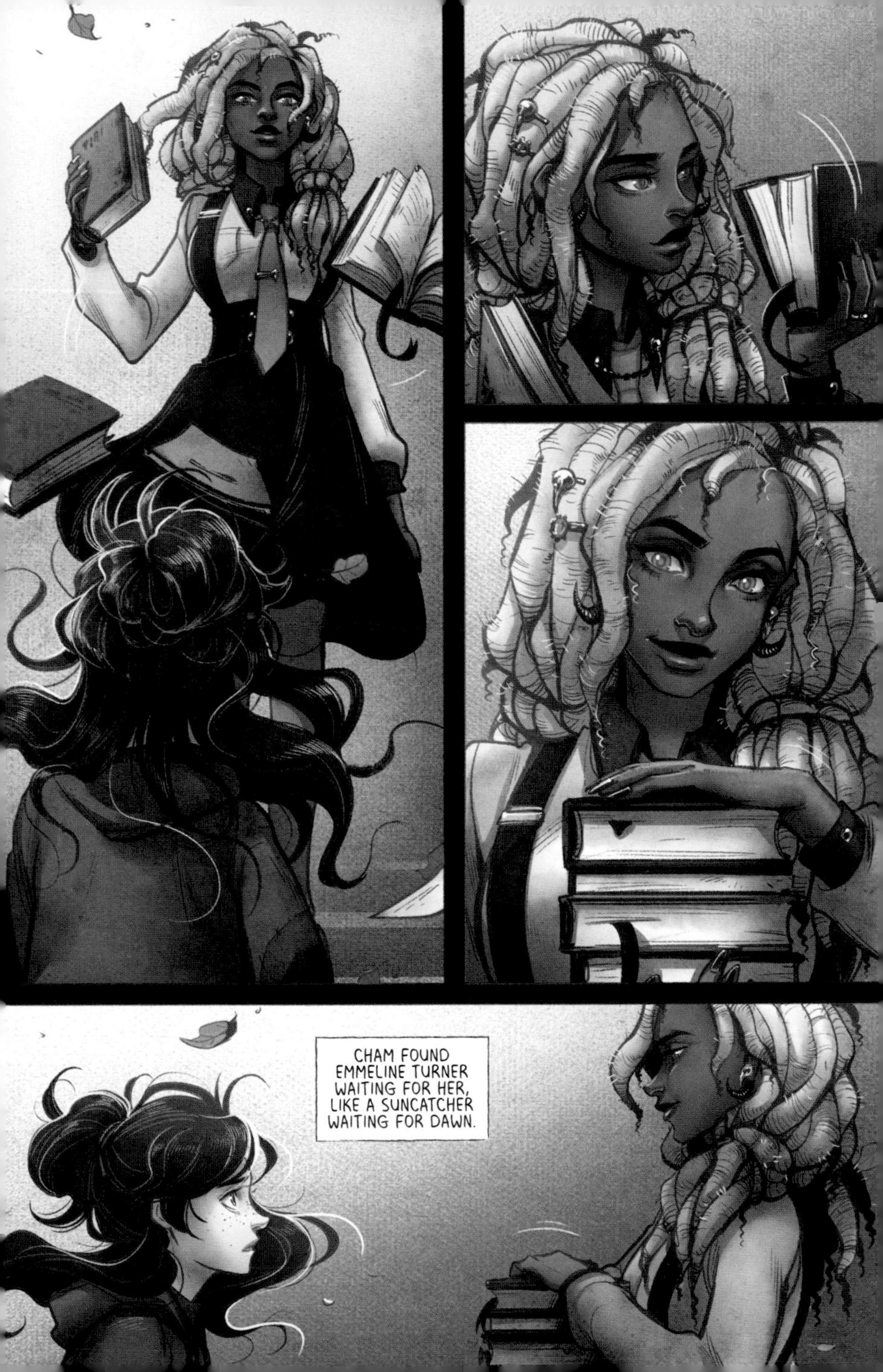
CHAM FOUND EMMELINE TURNER WAITING FOR HER, LIKE A SUNCATCHER WAITING FOR DAWN.

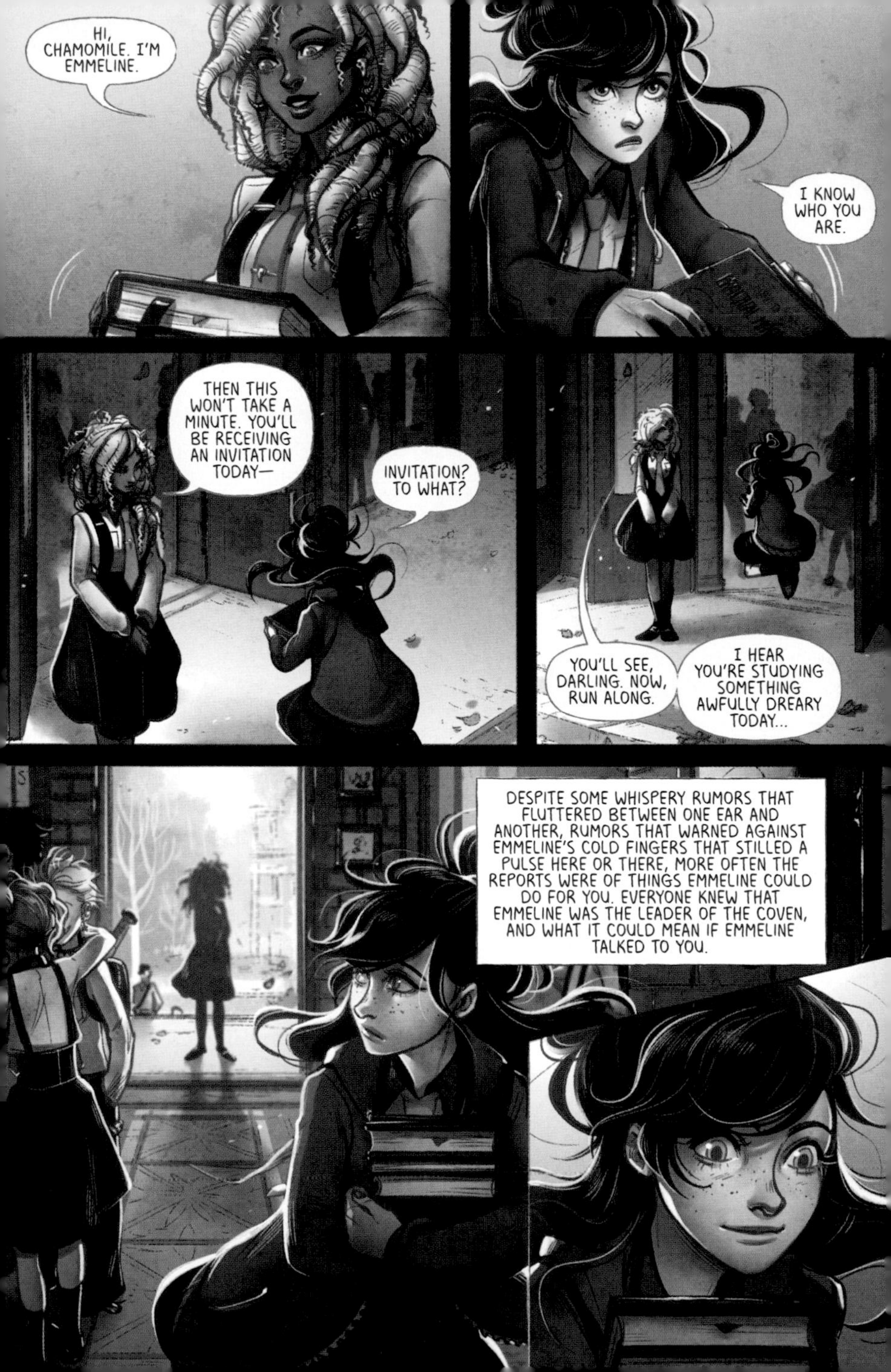
HI, CHAMOMILE. I'M EMMELINE.
I KNOW WHO YOU ARE.
THEN THIS WON'T TAKE A MINUTE. YOU'LL BE RECEIVING AN INVITATION TODAY—
INVITATION? TO WHAT?
YOU'LL SEE, DARLING. NOW, RUN ALONG.
I HEAR YOU'RE STUDYING SOMETHING AWFULLY DREARY TODAY...
DESPITE SOME WHISPERY RUMORS THAT FLUTTERED BETWEEN ONE EAR AND ANOTHER, RUMORS THAT WARNED AGAINST EMMELINE'S COLD FINGERS THAT STILLED A PULSE HERE OR THERE, MORE OFTEN THE REPORTS WERE OF THINGS EMMELINE COULD DO FOR YOU. EVERYONE KNEW THAT EMMELINE WAS THE LEADER OF THE COVEN, AND WHAT IT COULD MEAN IF EMMELINE TALKED TO YOU.

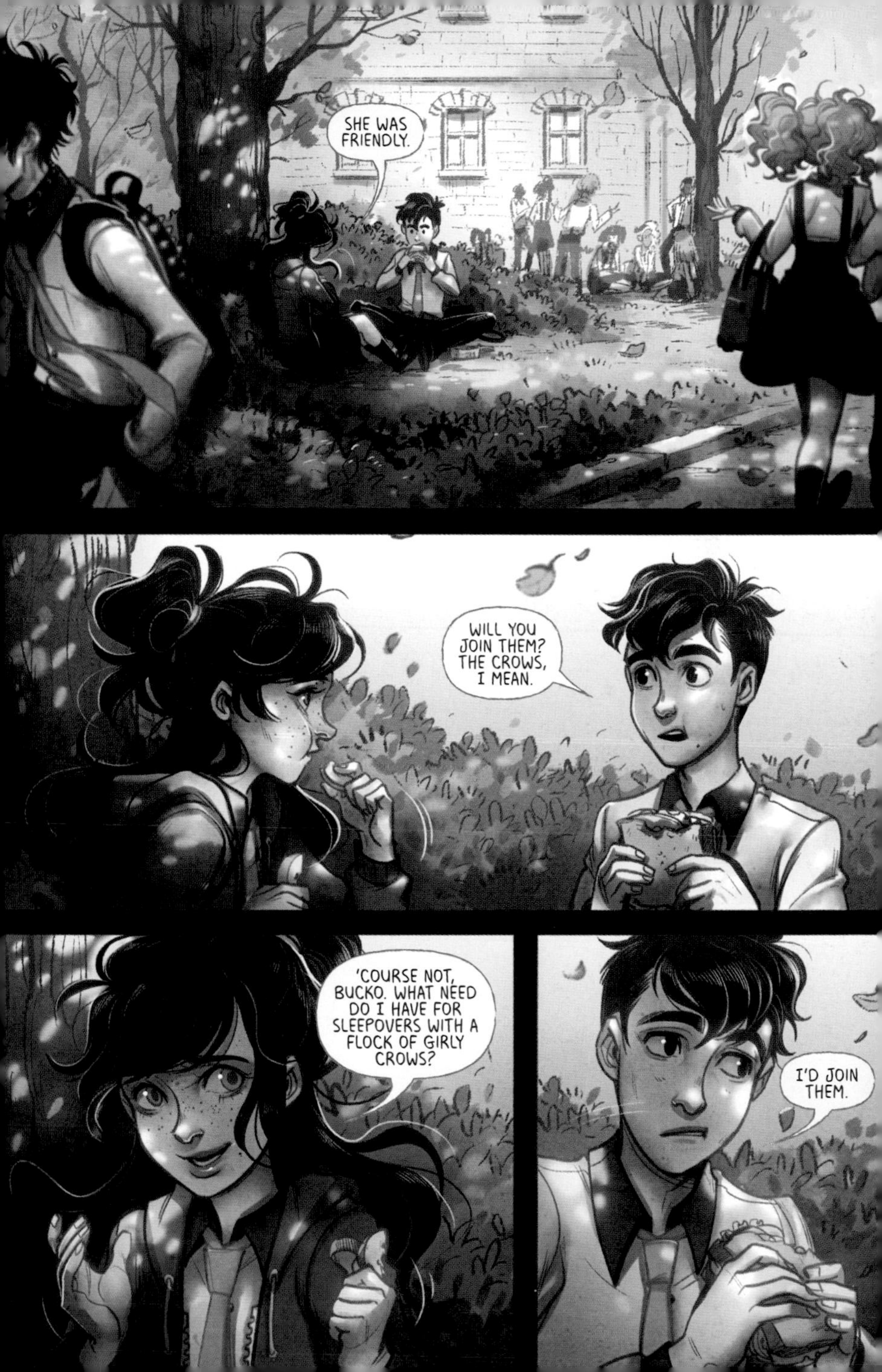
SHE WAS FRIENDLY.
WILL YOU JOIN THEM? THE CROWS, I MEAN.
'COURSE NOT, BUCKO. WHAT NEED DO I HAVE FOR SLEEPOVERS WITH A FLOCK OF GIRLY CROWS?
I'D JOIN THEM.

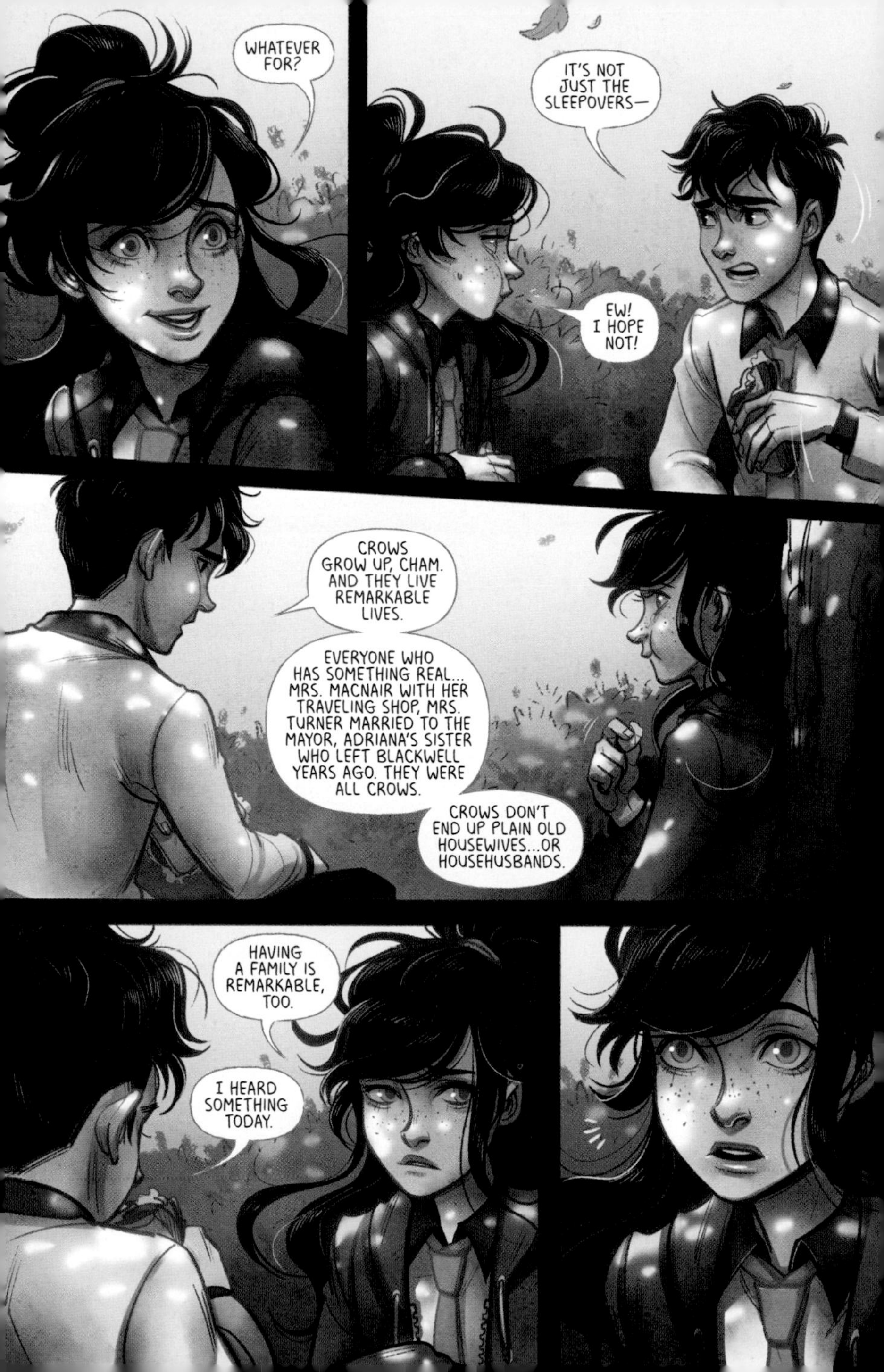
WHATEVER FOR?
IT'S NOT JUST THE SLEEPOVERS—
EW! I HOPE NOT!
CROWS GROW UP, CHAM. AND THEY LIVE REMARKABLE LIVES.
EVERYONE WHO HAS SOMETHING REAL... MRS. MACNAIR WITH HER TRAVELING SHOP, MRS. TURNER MARRIED TO THE MAYOR, ADRIANA'S SISTER WHO LEFT BLACKWELL YEARS AGO. THEY WERE ALL CROWS.
CROWS DON'T END UP PLAIN OLD HOUSEWIVES...OR HOUSEHUSBANDS.
HAVING A FAMILY IS REMARKABLE, TOO.
I HEARD SOMETHING TODAY.

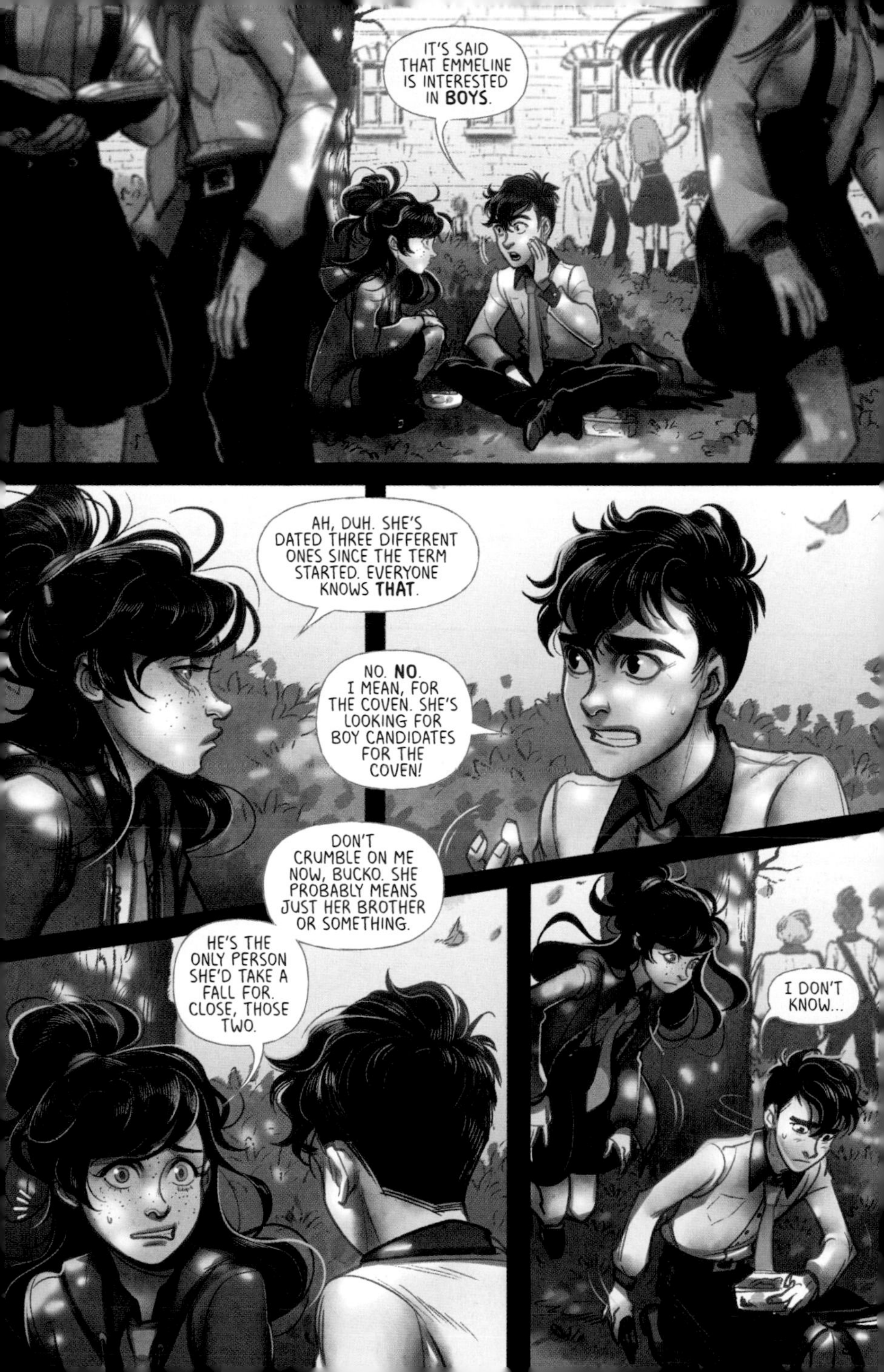
IT'S SAID THAT EMMELINE IS INTERESTED IN **BOYS**.
AH, DUH. SHE'S DATED THREE DIFFERENT ONES SINCE THE TERM STARTED. EVERYONE KNOWS **THAT**.
NO. **NO**. I MEAN, FOR THE COVEN. SHE'S LOOKING FOR BOY CANDIDATES FOR THE COVEN!
DON'T CRUMBLE ON ME NOW, BUCKO. SHE PROBABLY MEANS JUST HER BROTHER OR SOMETHING.
HE'S THE ONLY PERSON SHE'D TAKE A FALL FOR. CLOSE, THOSE TWO.
I DON'T KNOW...

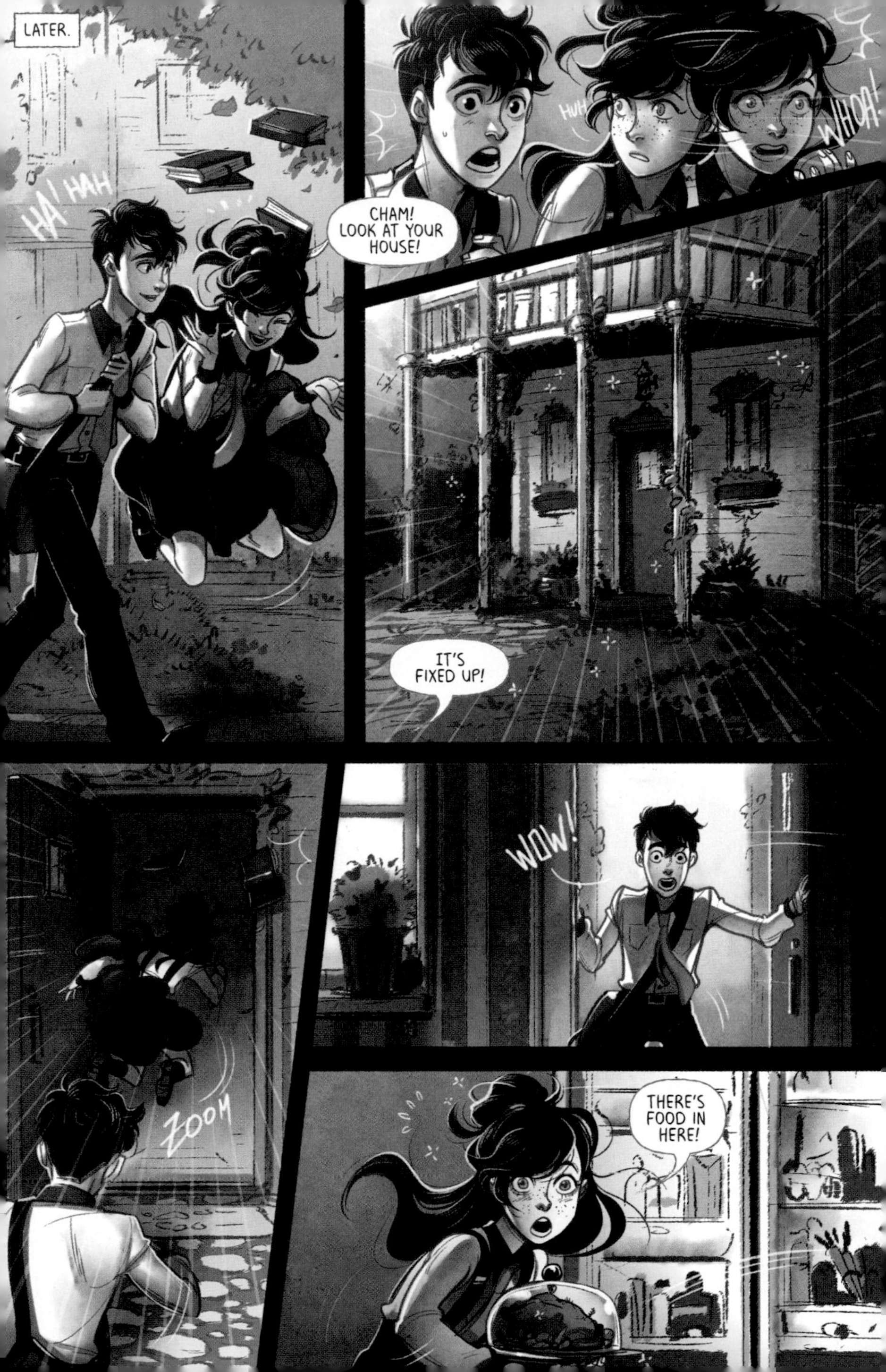
LATER.
HA! HAH
HUH
WHOA!
CHAM! LOOK AT YOUR HOUSE!
IT'S FIXED UP!
ZOOM
WOW!
THERE'S FOOD IN HERE!

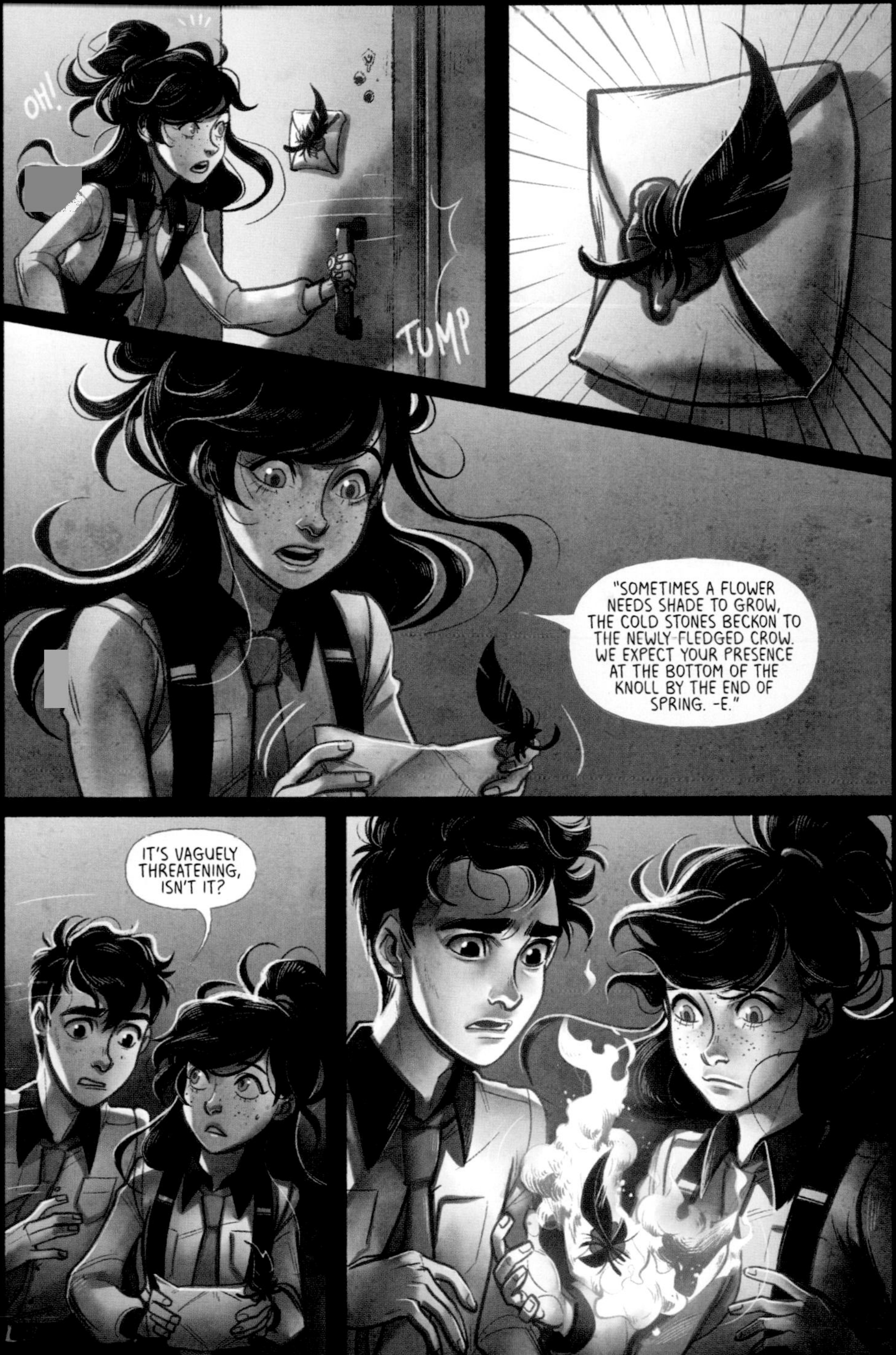
OH!
TUMP
"SOMETIMES A FLOWER NEEDS SHADE TO GROW, THE COLD STONES BECKON TO THE NEWLY-FLEDGED CROW. WE EXPECT YOUR PRESENCE AT THE BOTTOM OF THE KNOLL BY THE END OF SPRING. -E."
IT'S VAGUELY THREATENING, ISN'T IT?

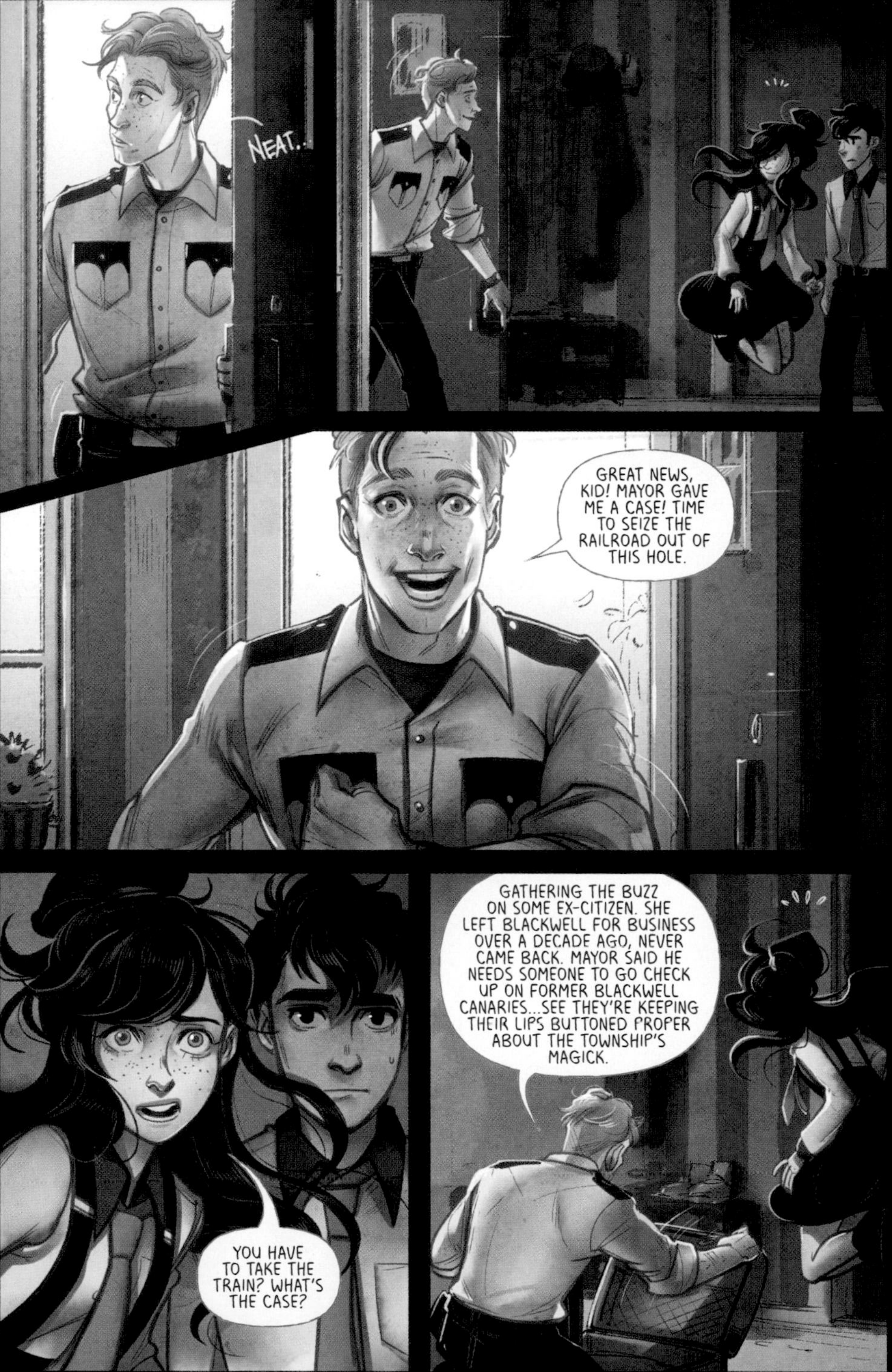
NEAT...
GREAT NEWS, KID! MAYOR GAVE ME A CASE! TIME TO SEIZE THE RAILROAD OUT OF THIS HOLE.
YOU HAVE TO TAKE THE TRAIN? WHAT'S THE CASE?
GATHERING THE BUZZ ON SOME EX-CITIZEN. SHE LEFT BLACKWELL FOR BUSINESS OVER A DECADE AGO, NEVER CAME BACK. MAYOR SAID HE NEEDS SOMEONE TO GO CHECK UP ON FORMER BLACKWELL CANARIES...SEE THEY'RE KEEPING THEIR LIPS BUTTONED PROPER ABOUT THE TOWNSHIP'S MAGICK.

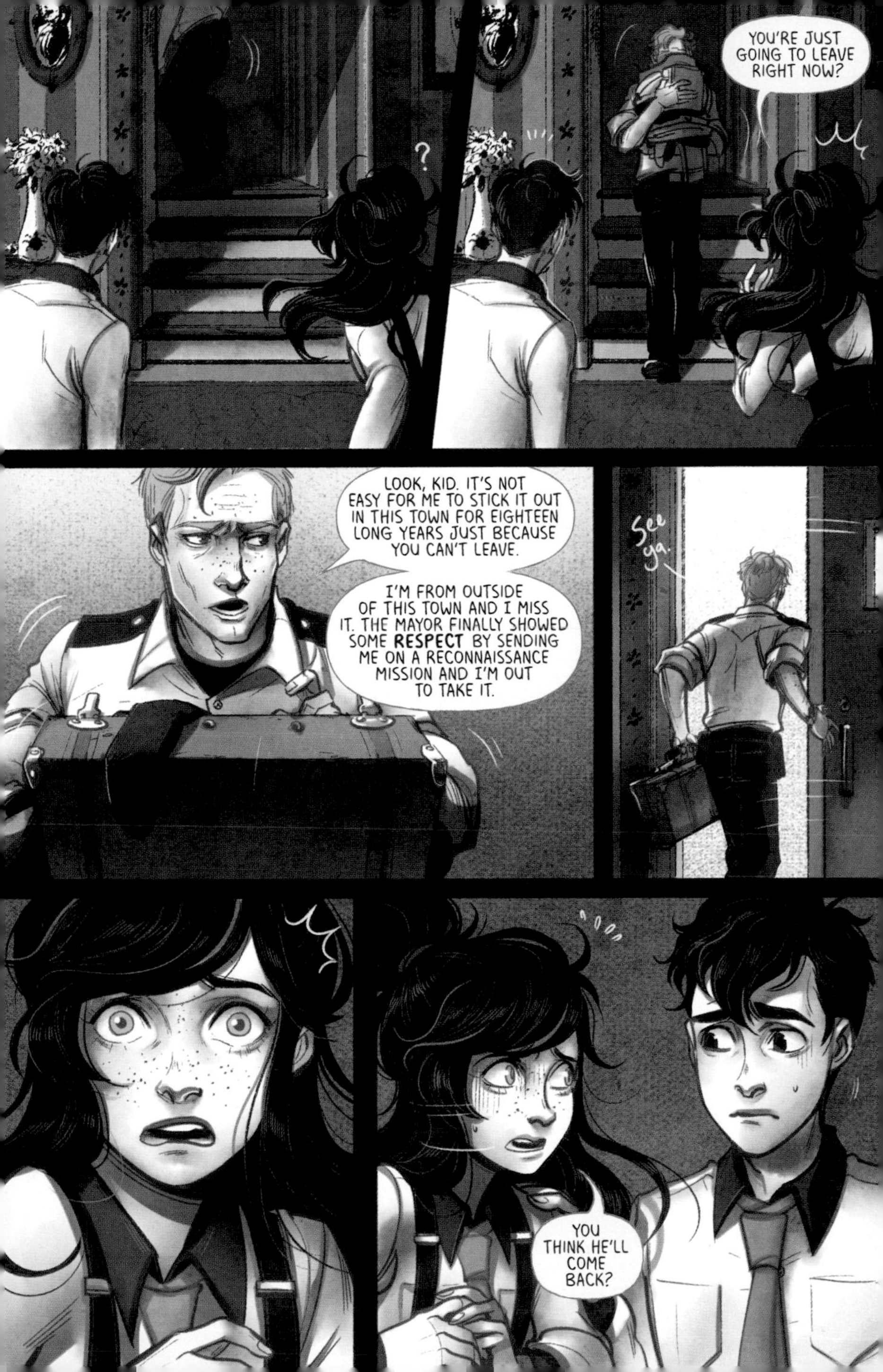
?
YOU'RE JUST GOING TO LEAVE RIGHT NOW?
LOOK, KID. IT'S NOT EASY FOR ME TO STICK IT OUT IN THIS TOWN FOR EIGHTEEN LONG YEARS JUST BECAUSE YOU CAN'T LEAVE.
I'M FROM OUTSIDE OF THIS TOWN AND I MISS IT. THE MAYOR FINALLY SHOWED SOME **RESPECT** BY SENDING ME ON A RECONNAISSANCE MISSION AND I'M OUT TO TAKE IT.
See ya.
YOU THINK HE'LL COME BACK?

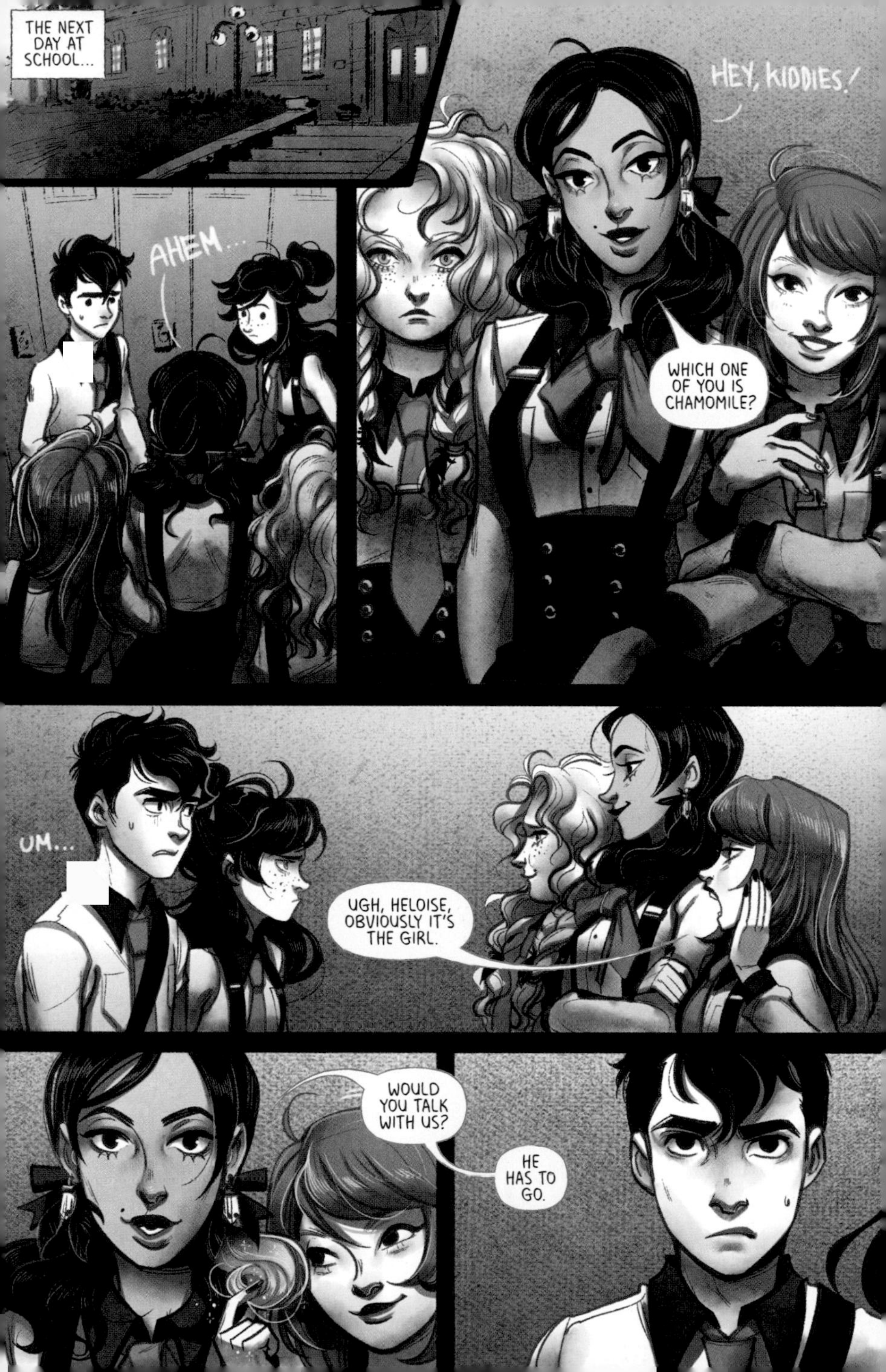
THE NEXT DAY AT SCHOOL...
AHEM...
HEY, KIDDIES!
WHICH ONE OF YOU IS CHAMOMILE?
UM...
UGH, HELOISE, OBVIOUSLY IT'S THE GIRL.
WOULD YOU TALK WITH US?
HE HAS TO GO.

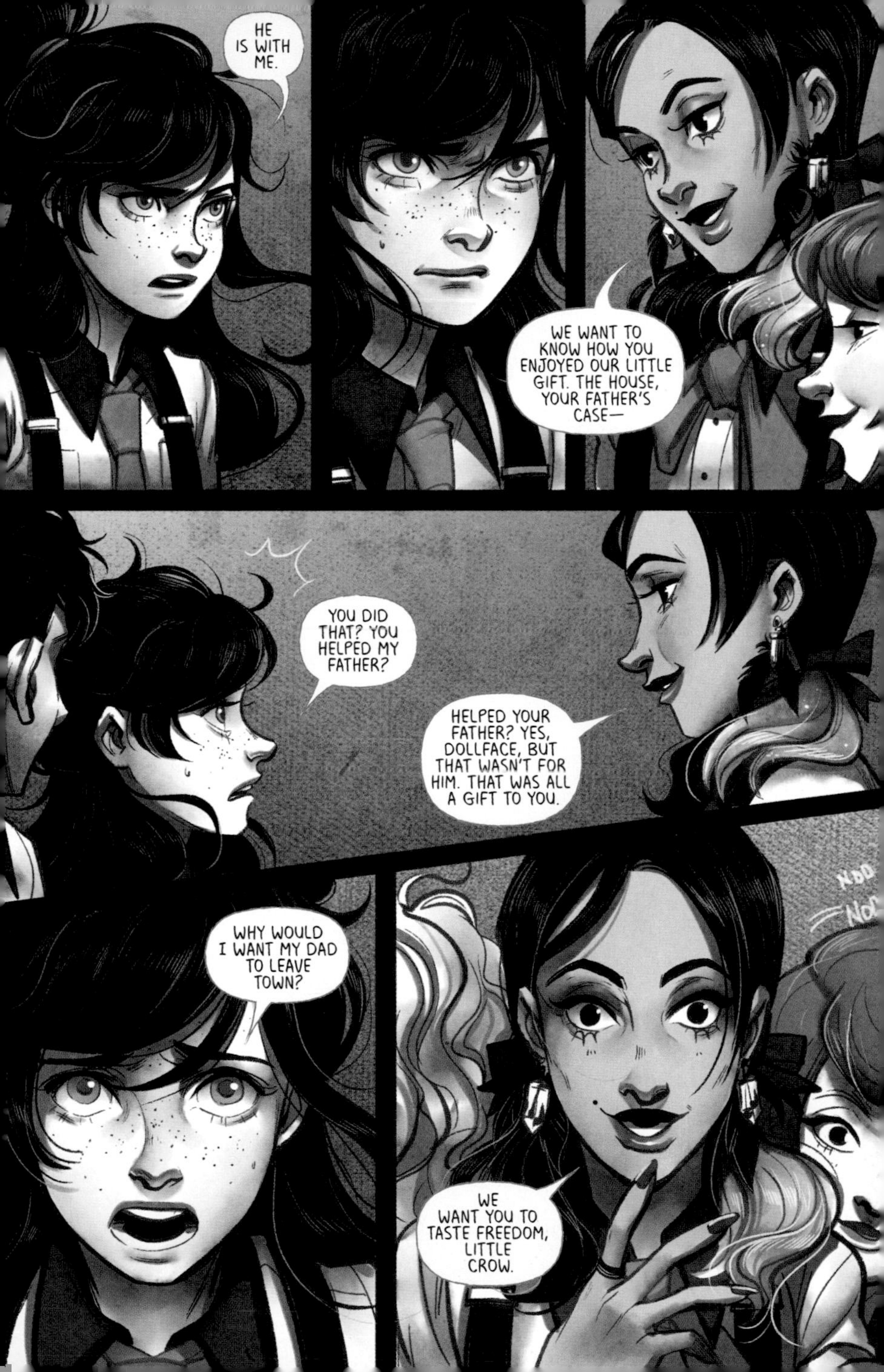
HE IS WITH ME.
WE WANT TO KNOW HOW YOU ENJOYED OUR LITTLE GIFT. THE HOUSE, YOUR FATHER'S CASE—
YOU DID THAT? YOU HELPED MY FATHER?
HELPED YOUR FATHER? YES, DOLLFACE, BUT THAT WASN'T FOR HIM. THAT WAS ALL A GIFT TO YOU.
WHY WOULD I WANT MY DAD TO LEAVE TOWN?
WE WANT YOU TO TASTE FREEDOM, LITTLE CROW.

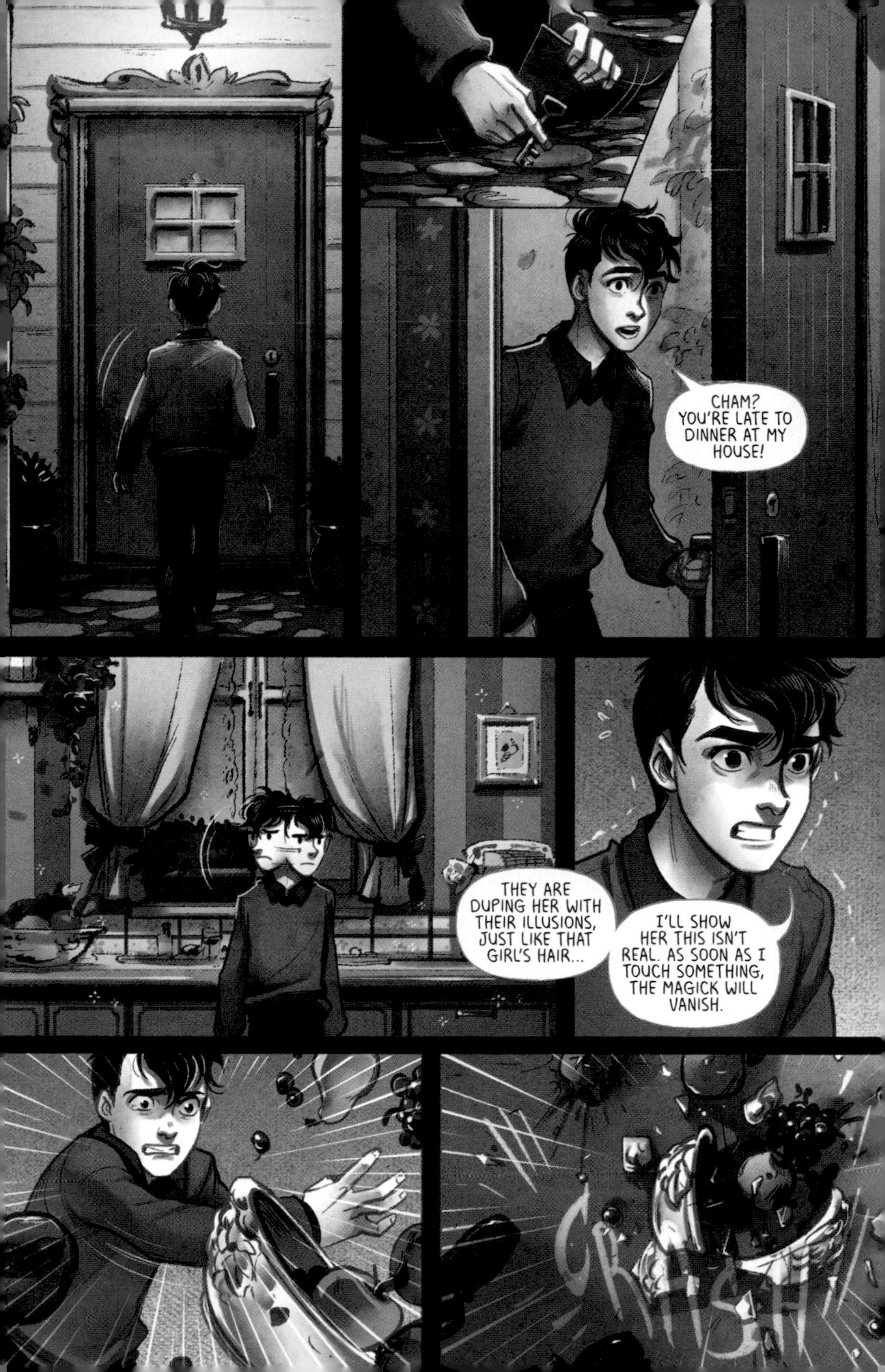
CHAM? YOU'RE LATE TO DINNER AT MY HOUSE!
THEY ARE DUPING HER WITH THEIR ILLUSIONS, JUST LIKE THAT GIRL'S HAIR...
I'LL SHOW HER THIS ISN'T REAL. AS SOON AS I TOUCH SOMETHING, THE MAGICK WILL VANISH.
CRASH!

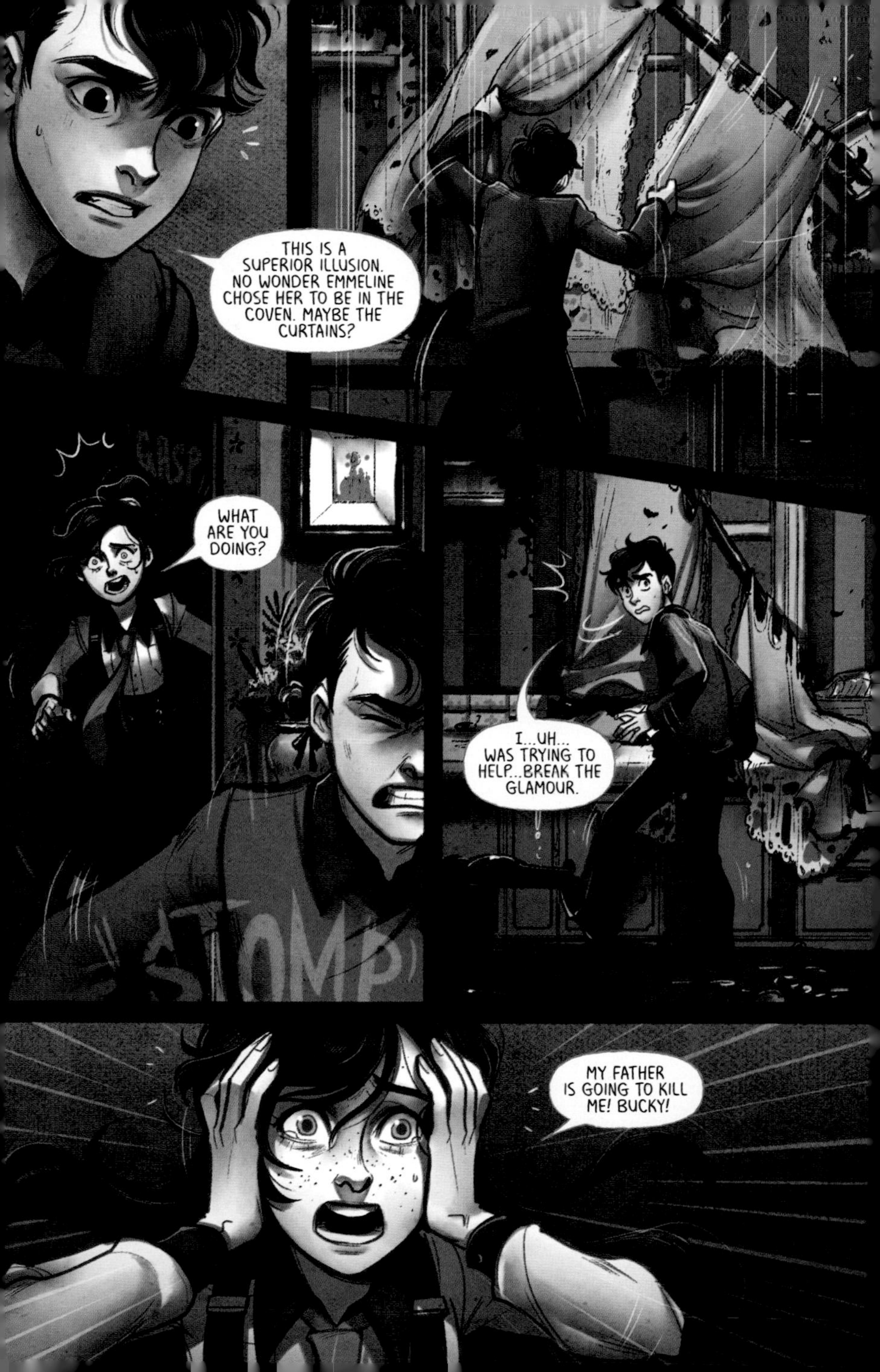
THIS IS A SUPERIOR ILLUSION. NO WONDER EMMELINE CHOSE HER TO BE IN THE COVEN. MAYBE THE CURTAINS?
GASP
WHAT ARE YOU DOING?
I...UH... WAS TRYING TO HELP...BREAK THE GLAMOUR.
STOMP
MY FATHER IS GOING TO KILL ME! BUCKY!

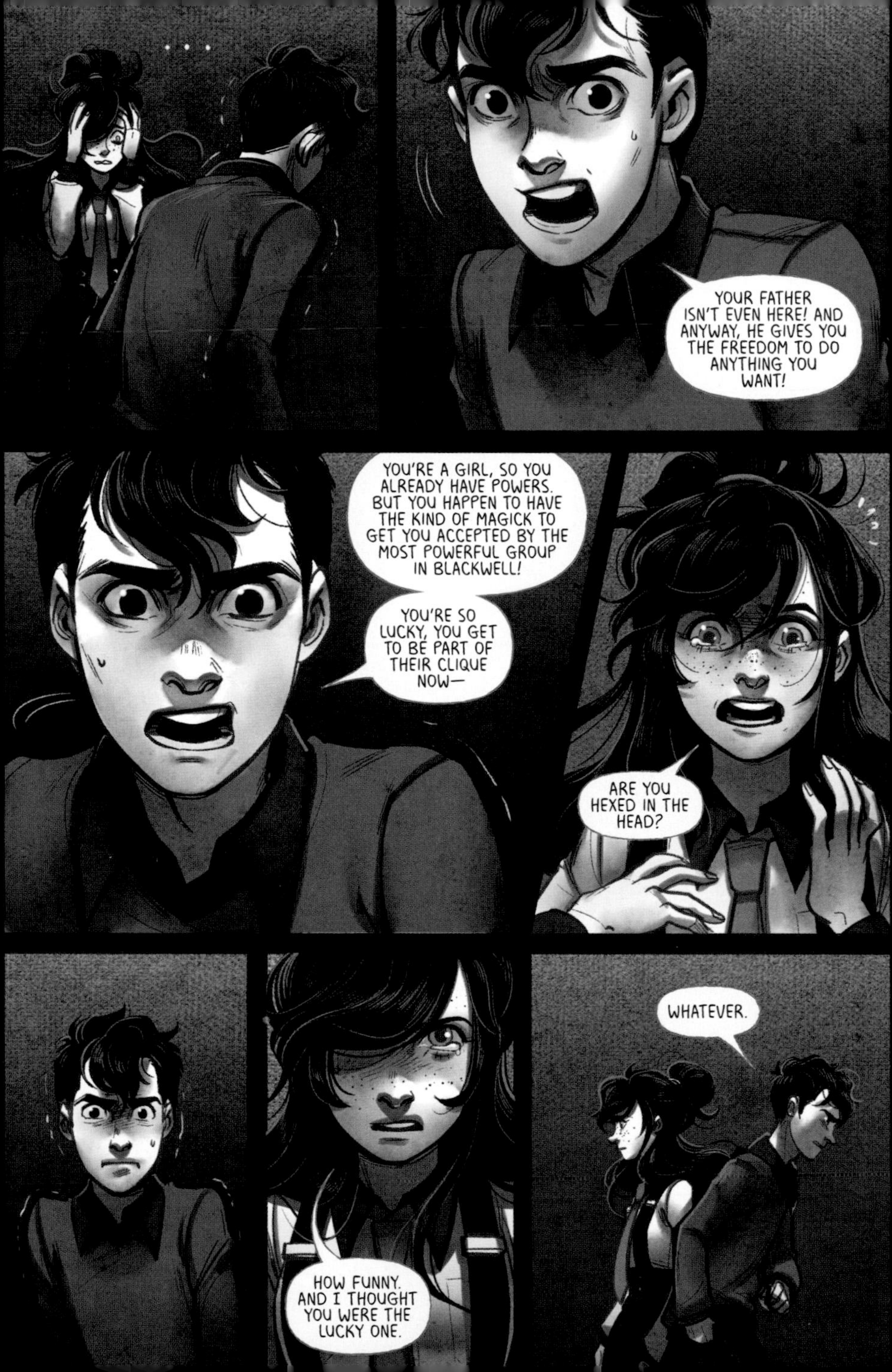
. . .
YOUR FATHER ISN'T EVEN HERE! AND ANYWAY, HE GIVES YOU THE FREEDOM TO DO ANYTHING YOU WANT!
YOU'RE A GIRL, SO YOU ALREADY HAVE POWERS. BUT YOU HAPPEN TO HAVE THE KIND OF MAGICK TO GET YOU ACCEPTED BY THE MOST POWERFUL GROUP IN BLACKWELL!
YOU'RE SO LUCKY, YOU GET TO BE PART OF THEIR CLIQUE NOW—
ARE YOU HEXED IN THE HEAD?
HOW FUNNY. AND I THOUGHT YOU WERE THE LUCKY ONE.
WHATEVER.

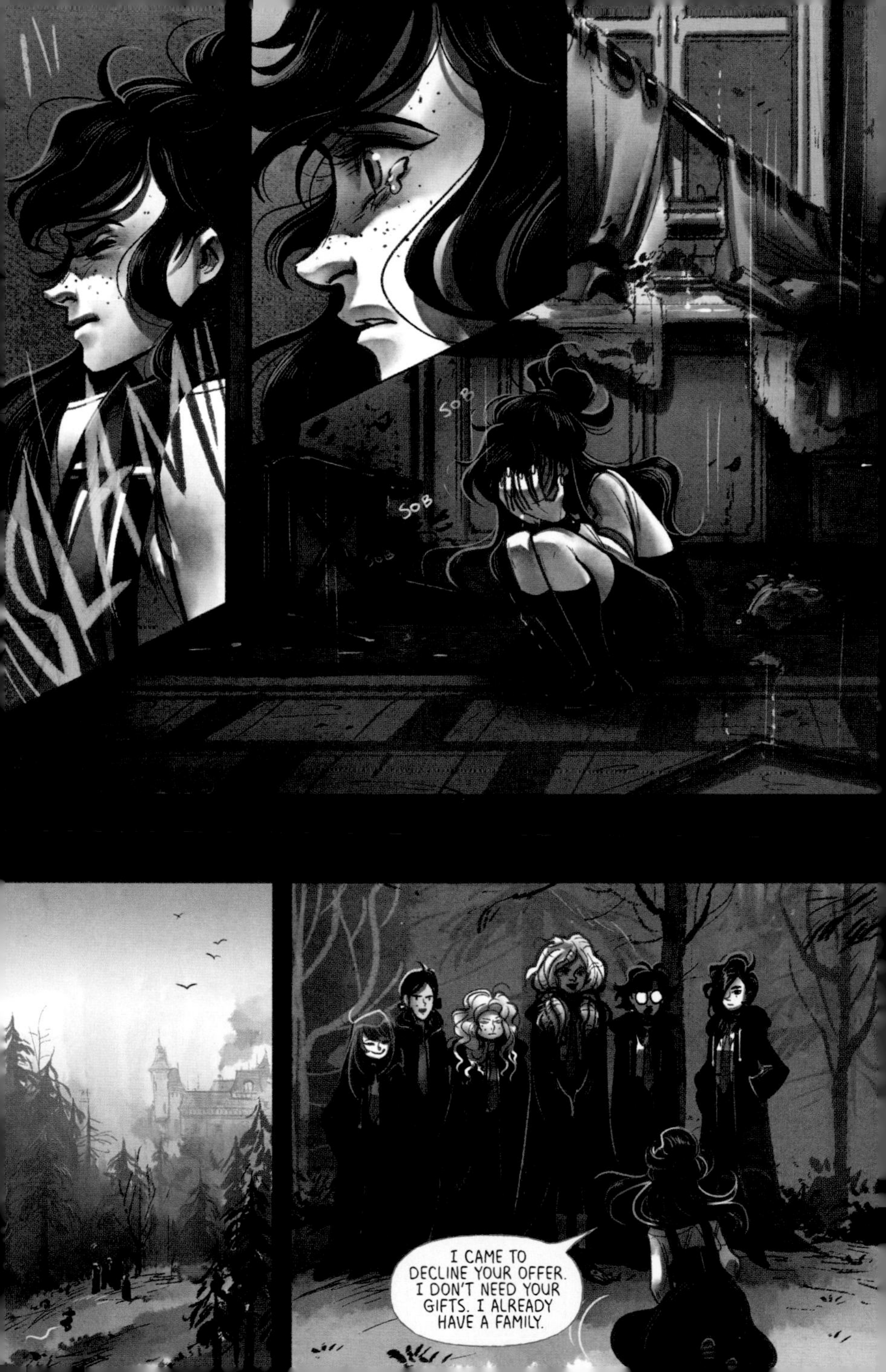
SLAM
SOB
SOB
SOB
I CAME TO DECLINE YOUR OFFER. I DON'T NEED YOUR GIFTS. I ALREADY HAVE A FAMILY.

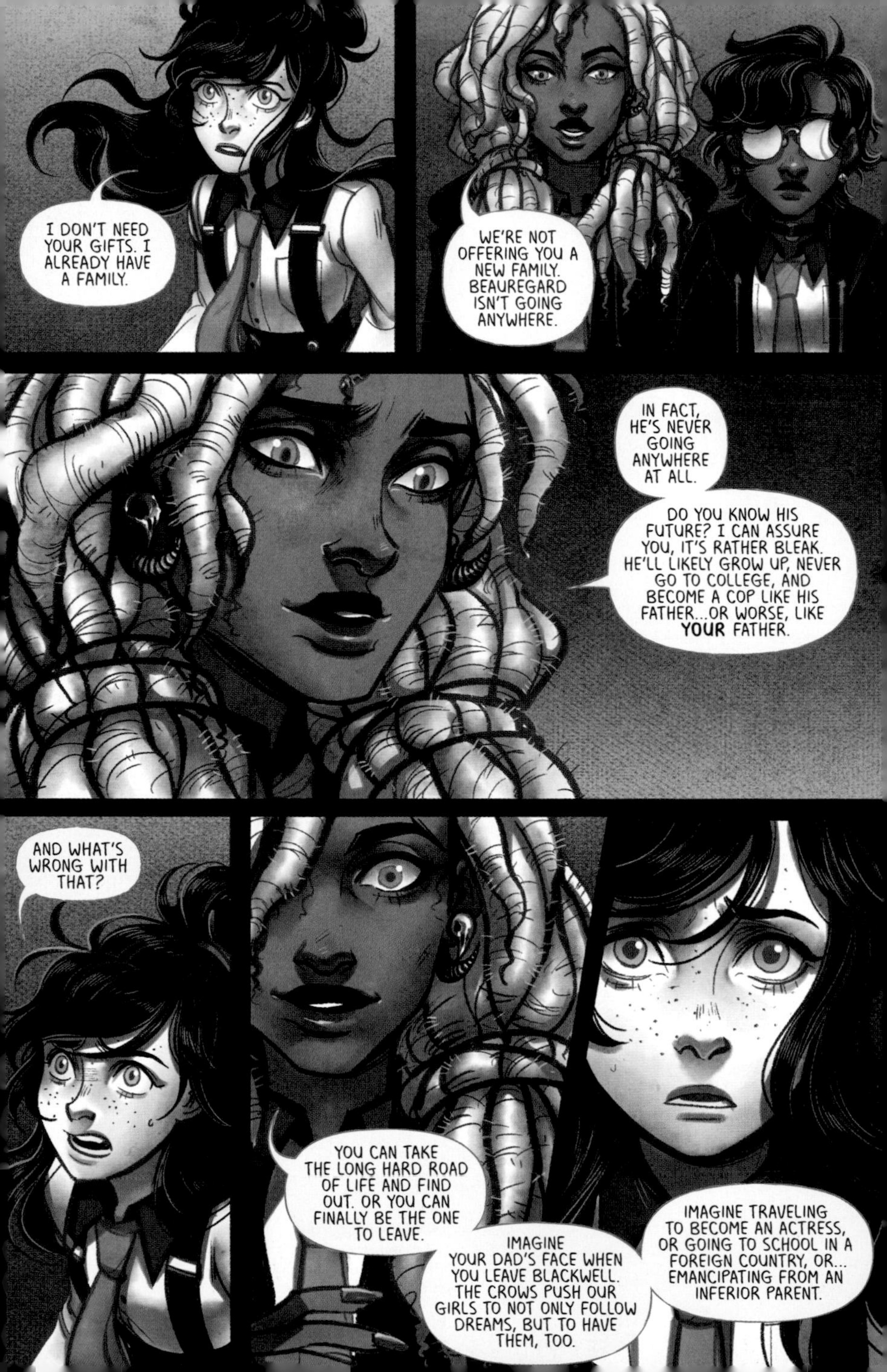
I DON'T NEED YOUR GIFTS. I ALREADY HAVE A FAMILY.
WE'RE NOT OFFERING YOU A NEW FAMILY. BEAUREGARD ISN'T GOING ANYWHERE.
IN FACT, HE'S NEVER GOING ANYWHERE AT ALL.
DO YOU KNOW HIS FUTURE? I CAN ASSURE YOU, IT'S RATHER BLEAK. HE'LL LIKELY GROW UP, NEVER GO TO COLLEGE, AND BECOME A COP LIKE HIS FATHER...OR WORSE, LIKE **YOUR** FATHER.
AND WHAT'S WRONG WITH THAT?
YOU CAN TAKE THE LONG HARD ROAD OF LIFE AND FIND OUT. OR YOU CAN FINALLY BE THE ONE TO LEAVE.
IMAGINE YOUR DAD'S FACE WHEN YOU LEAVE BLACKWELL. THE CROWS PUSH OUR GIRLS TO NOT ONLY FOLLOW DREAMS, BUT TO HAVE THEM, TOO.
IMAGINE TRAVELING TO BECOME AN ACTRESS, OR GOING TO SCHOOL IN A FOREIGN COUNTRY, OR... EMANCIPATING FROM AN INFERIOR PARENT.

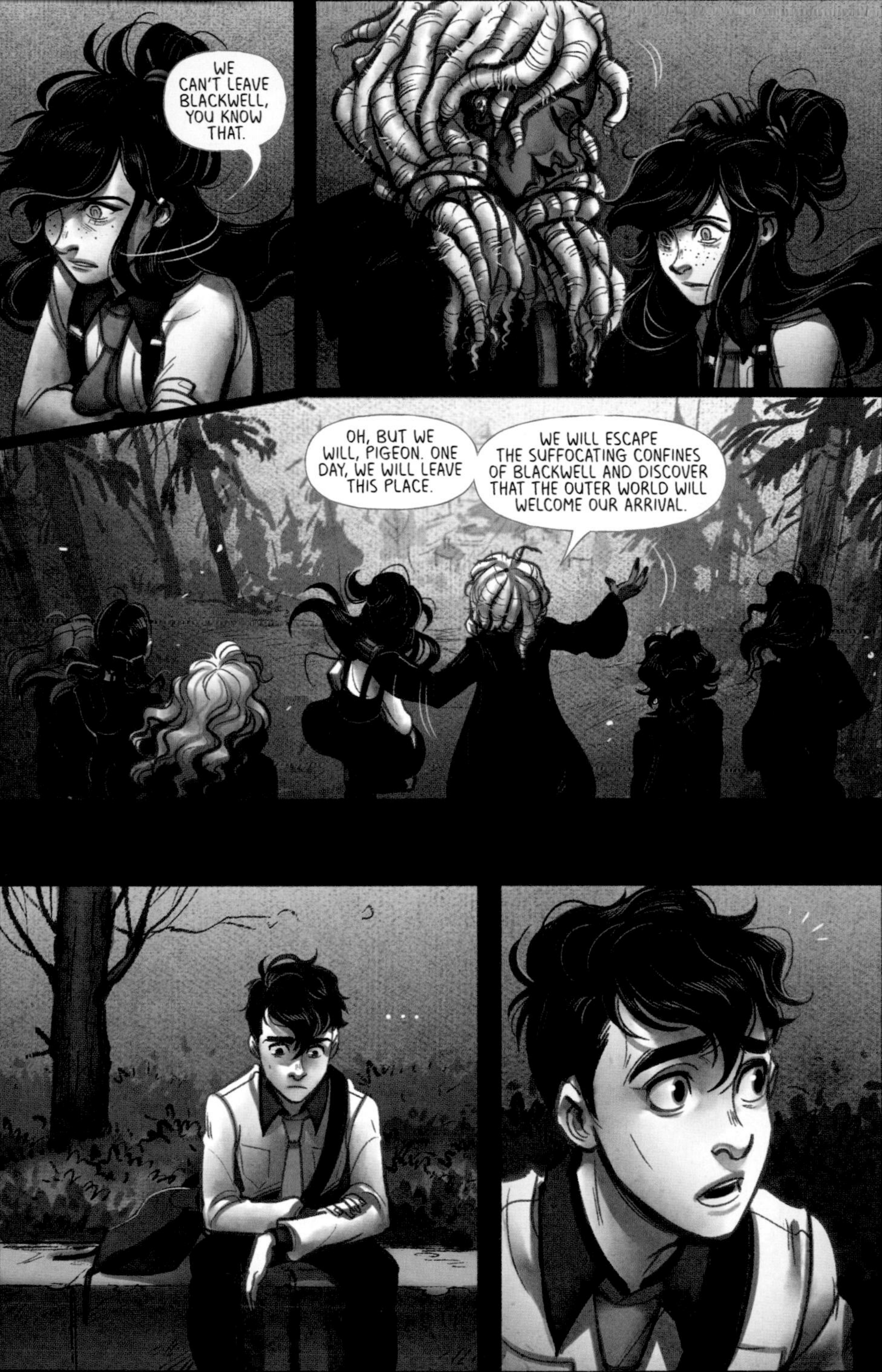
WE CAN'T LEAVE BLACKWELL, YOU KNOW THAT.
OH, BUT WE WILL, PIGEON. ONE DAY, WE WILL LEAVE THIS PLACE.
WE WILL ESCAPE THE SUFFOCATING CONFINES OF BLACKWELL AND DISCOVER THAT THE OUTER WORLD WILL WELCOME OUR ARRIVAL.
...

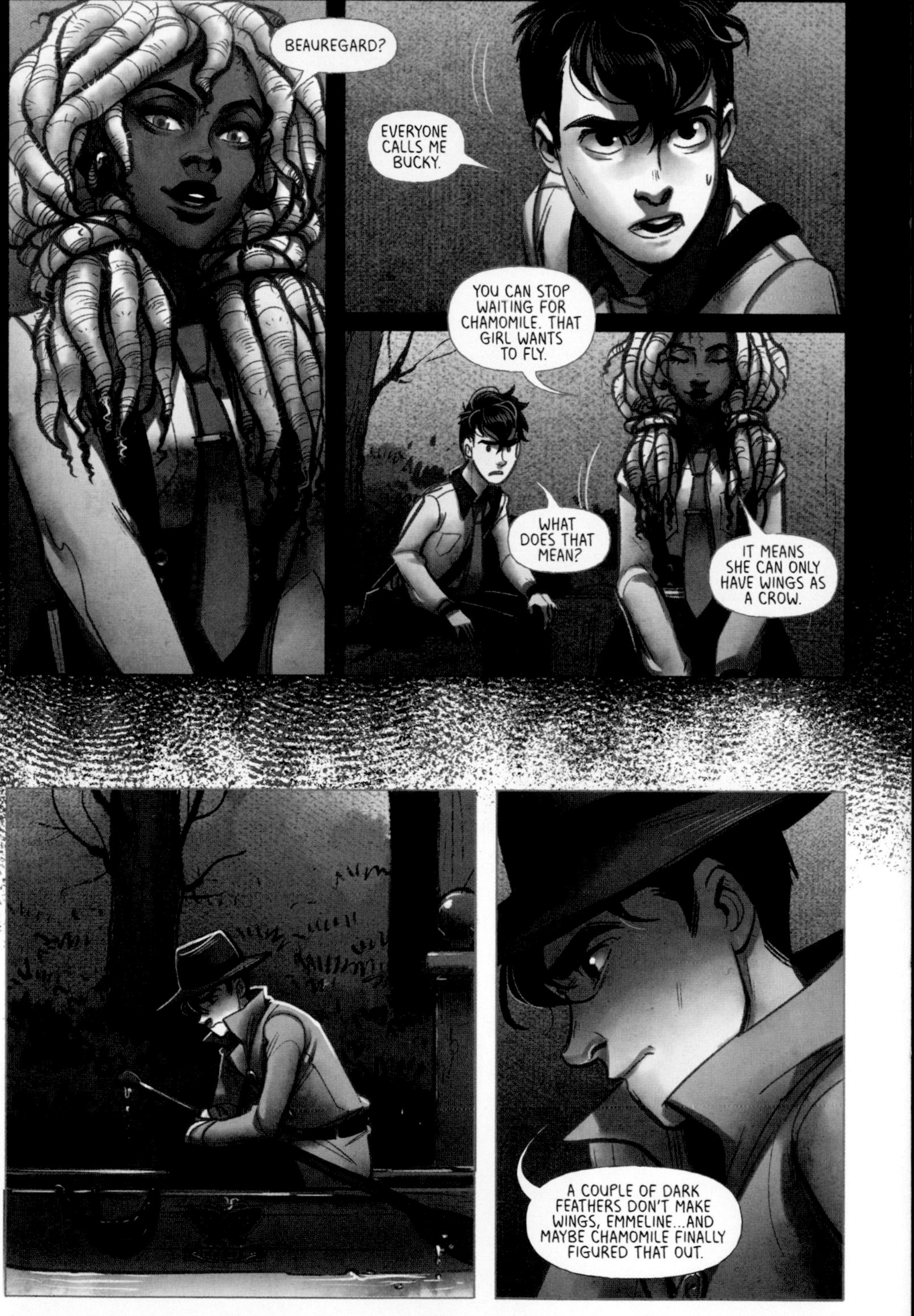
BEAUREGARD?
EVERYONE CALLS ME BUCKY.
YOU CAN STOP WAITING FOR CHAMOMILE. THAT GIRL WANTS TO FLY.
WHAT DOES THAT MEAN?
IT MEANS SHE CAN ONLY HAVE WINGS AS A CROW.
A COUPLE OF DARK FEATHERS DON'T MAKE WINGS, EMMELINE...AND MAYBE CHAMOMILE FINALLY FIGURED THAT OUT.

CHAPTER 11

THE UNSUSPECTED

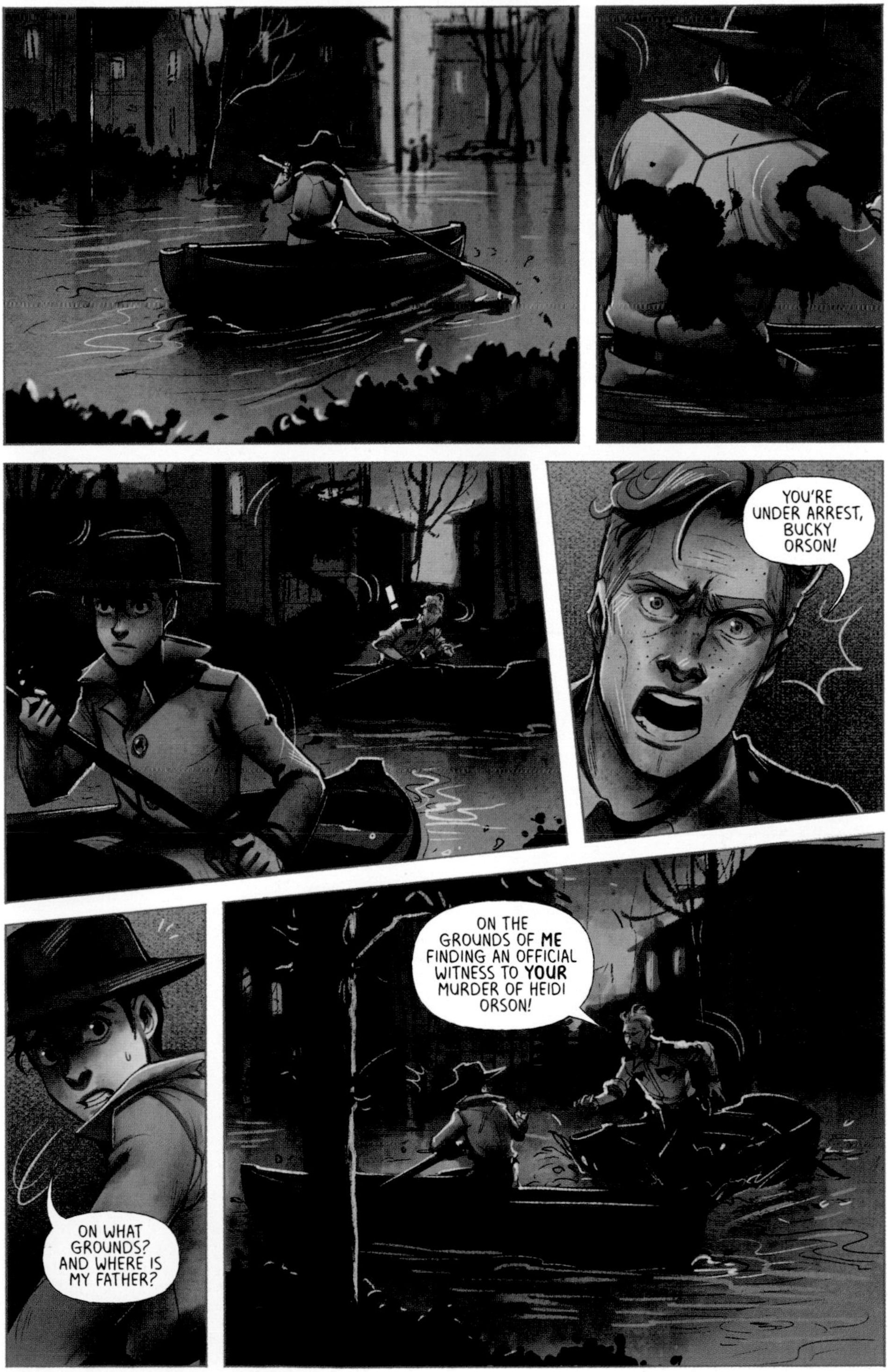

YOU'RE UNDER ARREST, BUCKY ORSON!
ON WHAT GROUNDS? AND WHERE IS MY FATHER?
ON THE GROUNDS OF **ME** FINDING AN OFFICIAL WITNESS TO **YOUR** MURDER OF HEIDI ORSON!

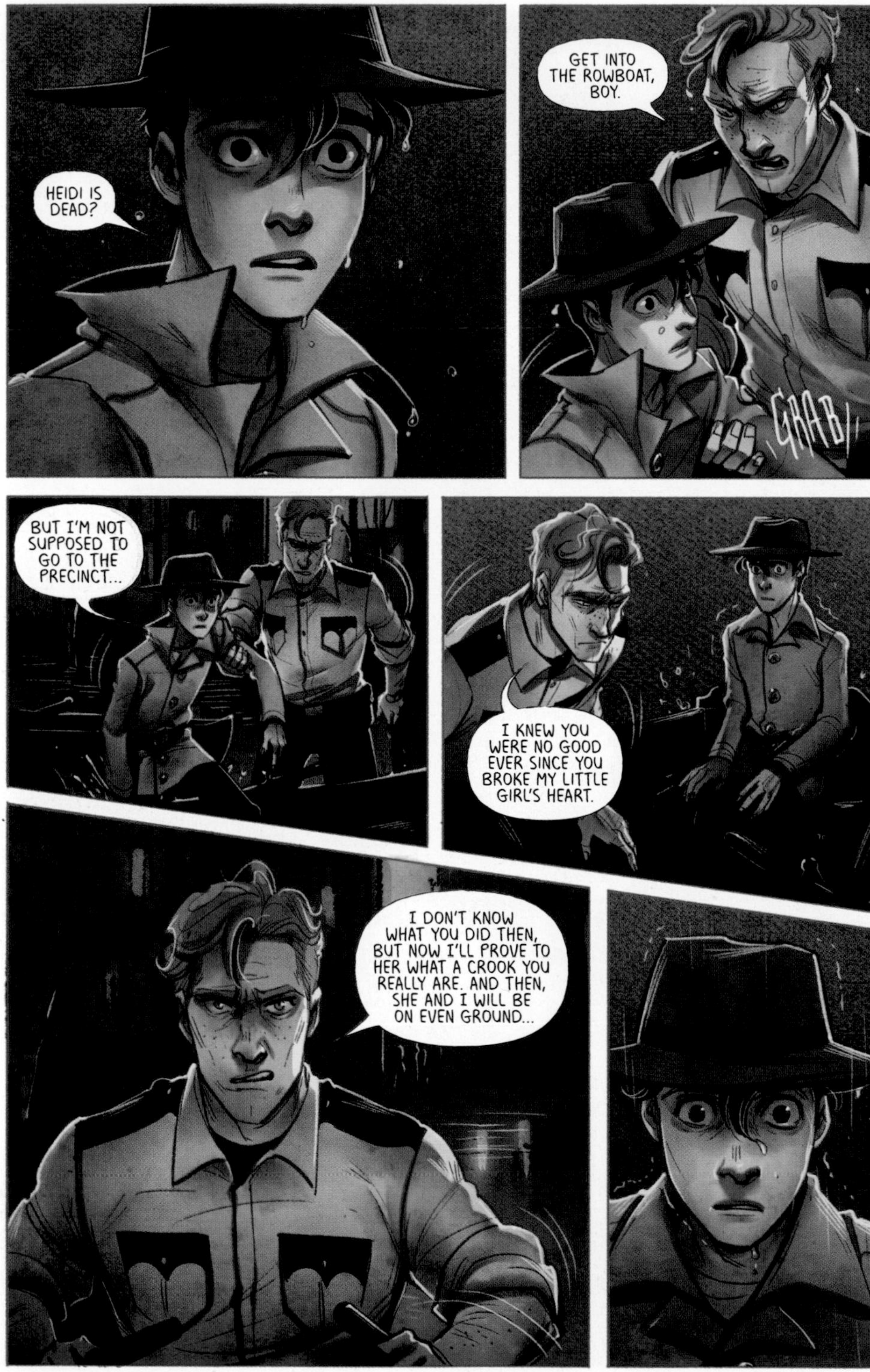
HEIDI IS DEAD?
GET INTO THE ROWBOAT, BOY.
GRAB
BUT I'M NOT SUPPOSED TO GO TO THE PRECINCT...
I KNEW YOU WERE NO GOOD EVER SINCE YOU BROKE MY LITTLE GIRL'S HEART.
I DON'T KNOW WHAT YOU DID THEN, BUT NOW I'LL PROVE TO HER WHAT A CROOK YOU REALLY ARE. AND THEN, SHE AND I WILL BE ON EVEN GROUND...

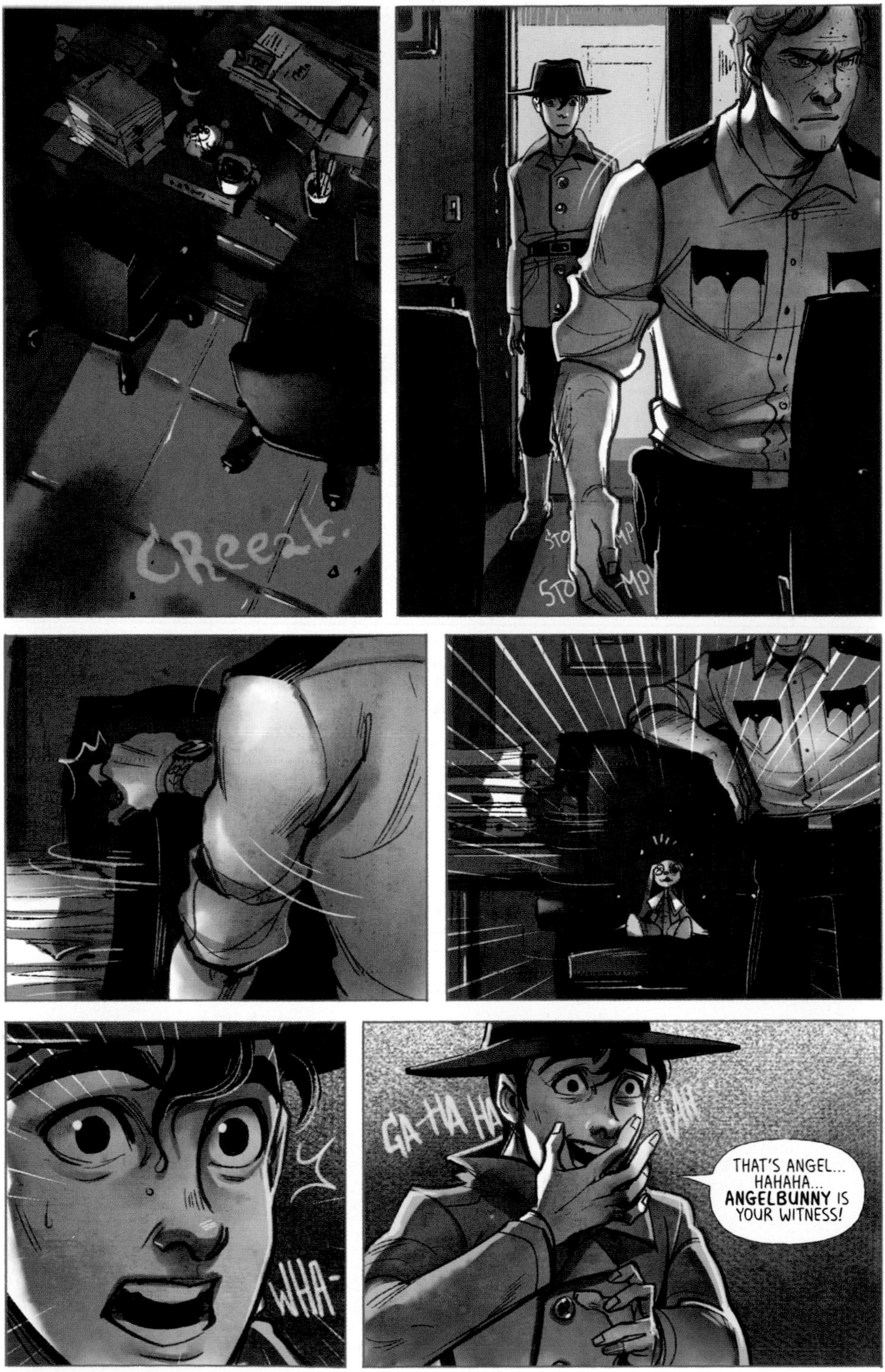
CREAK.
STOMP
STOMP
WHA-
GA-HA HA HAR
THAT'S ANGEL... HAHAHA... **ANGELBUNNY** IS YOUR WITNESS!

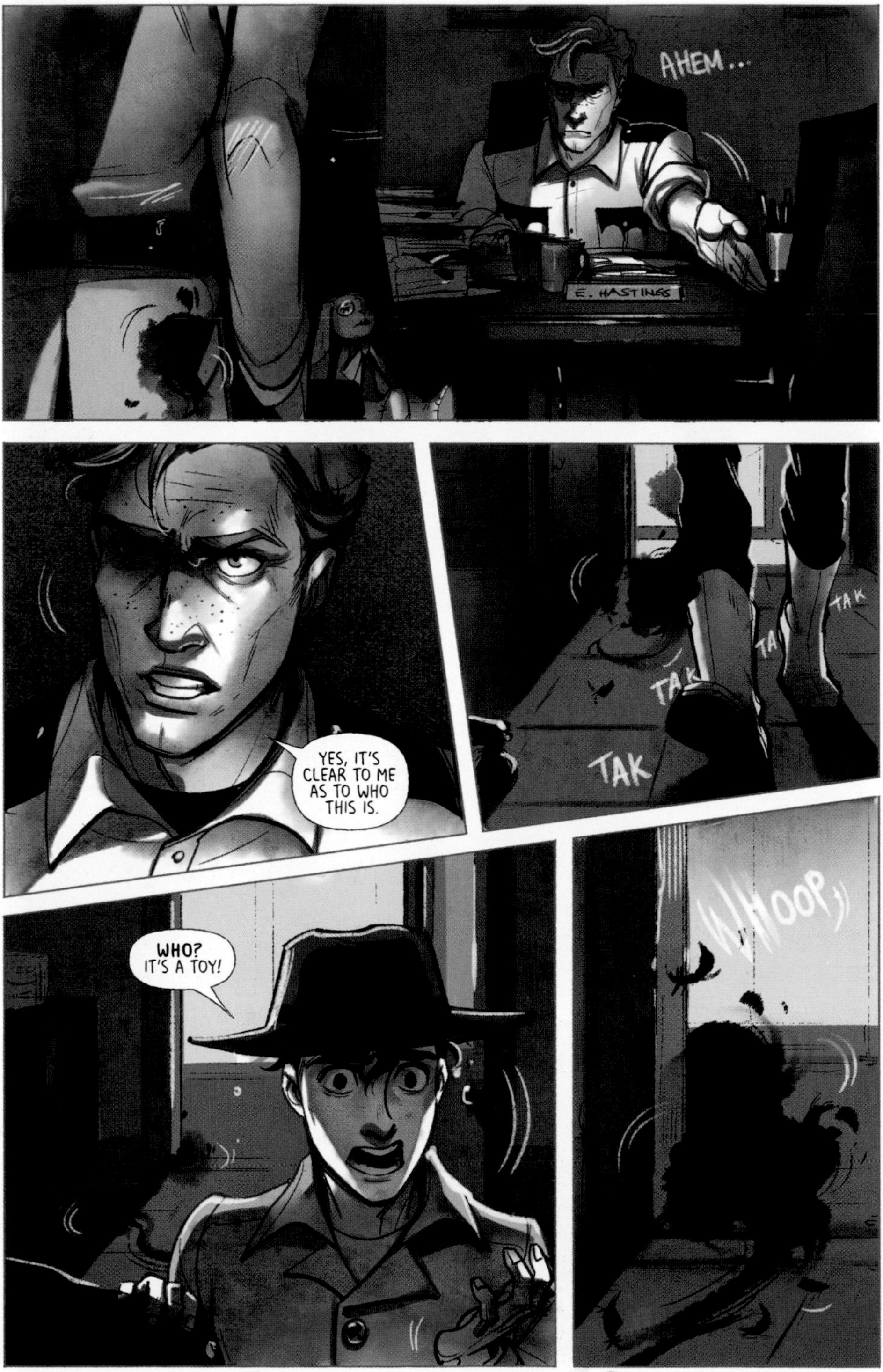
AHEM...
E. HASTINGS
YES, IT'S CLEAR TO ME AS TO WHO THIS IS.
TAK
TA
TAK
TAK
WHO? IT'S A TOY!
WHOOP

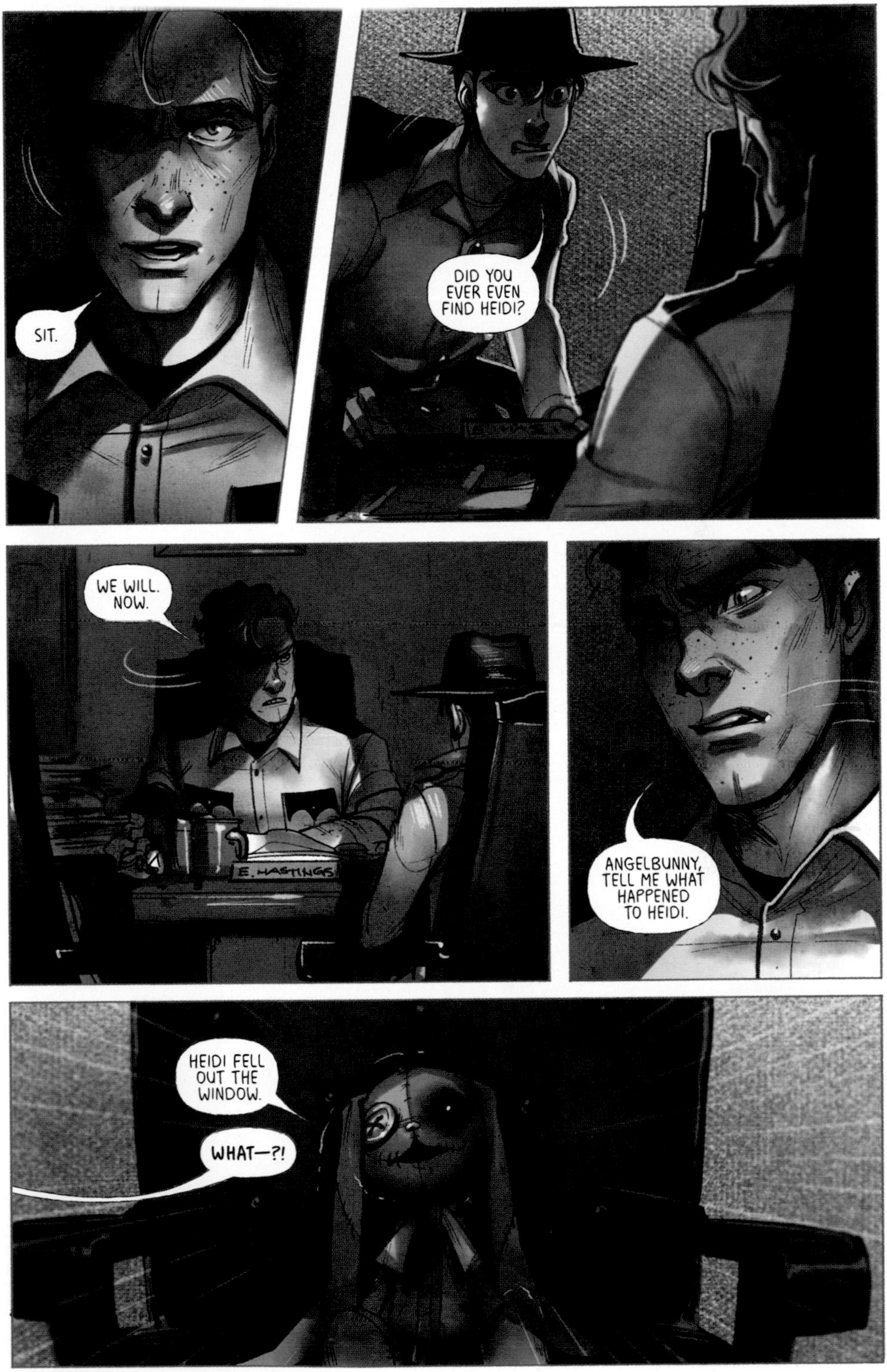
SIT.
DID YOU EVER EVEN FIND HEIDI?
WE WILL. NOW.
E. HASTINGS
ANGELBUNNY, TELL ME WHAT HAPPENED TO HEIDI.
HEIDI FELL OUT THE WINDOW.
WHAT—?!

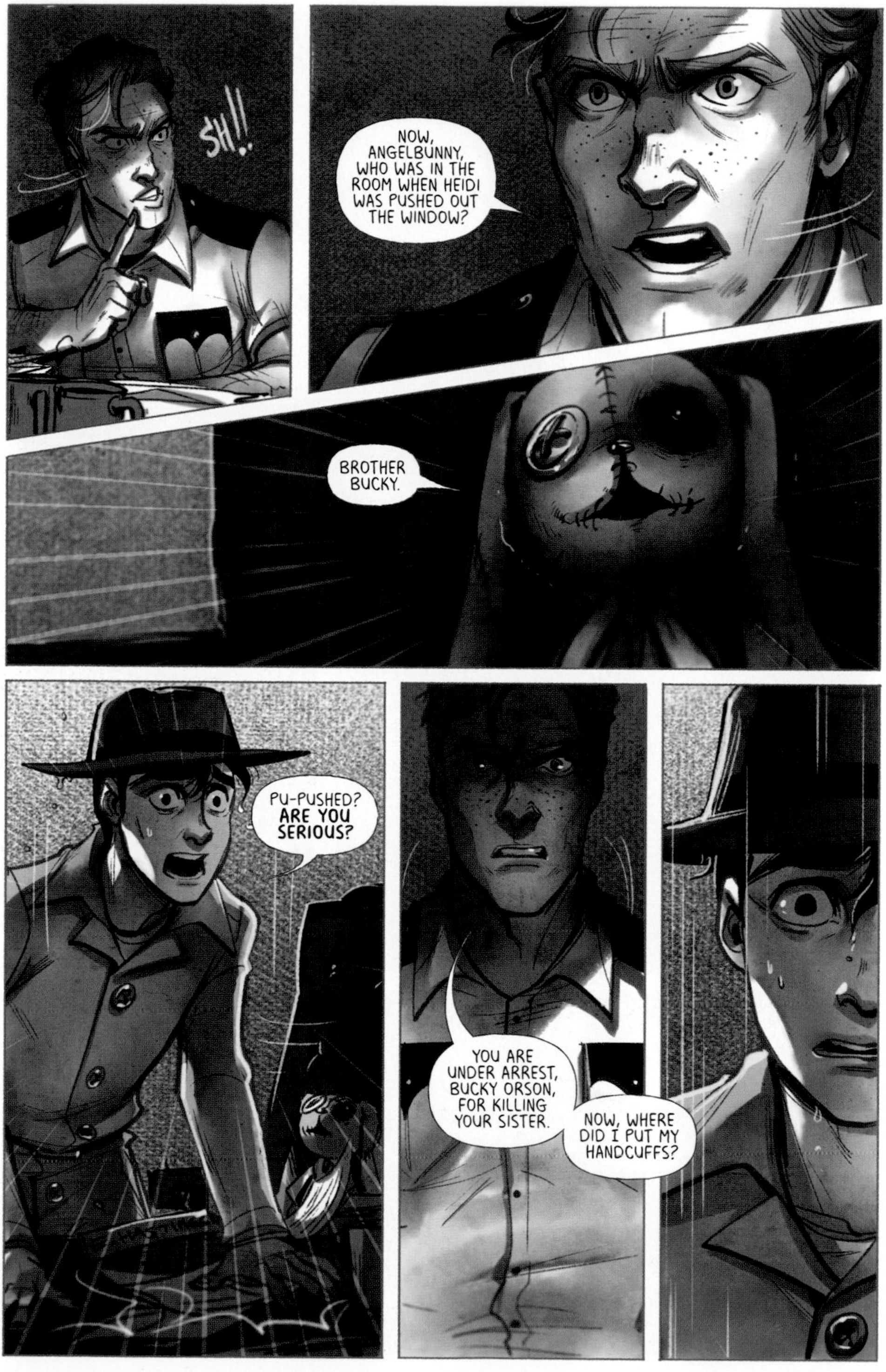
SH!!
NOW, ANGELBUNNY, WHO WAS IN THE ROOM WHEN HEIDI WAS PUSHED OUT THE WINDOW?
BROTHER BUCKY.
PU-PUSHED? **ARE YOU SERIOUS?**
YOU ARE UNDER ARREST, BUCKY ORSON, FOR KILLING YOUR SISTER.
NOW, WHERE DID I PUT MY HANDCUFFS?

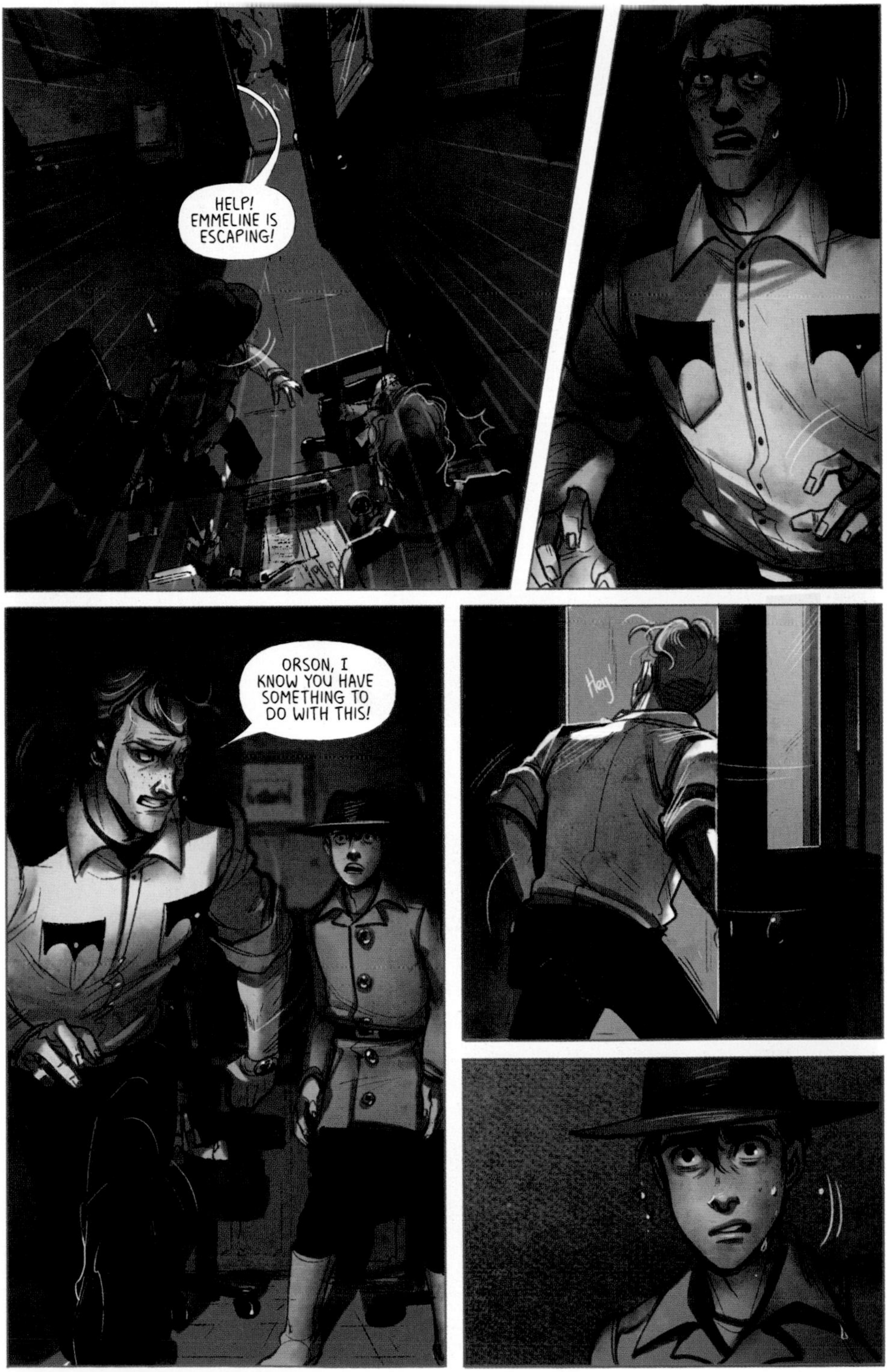
HELP! EMMELINE IS ESCAPING!
ORSON, I KNOW YOU HAVE SOMETHING TO DO WITH THIS!
Hey!

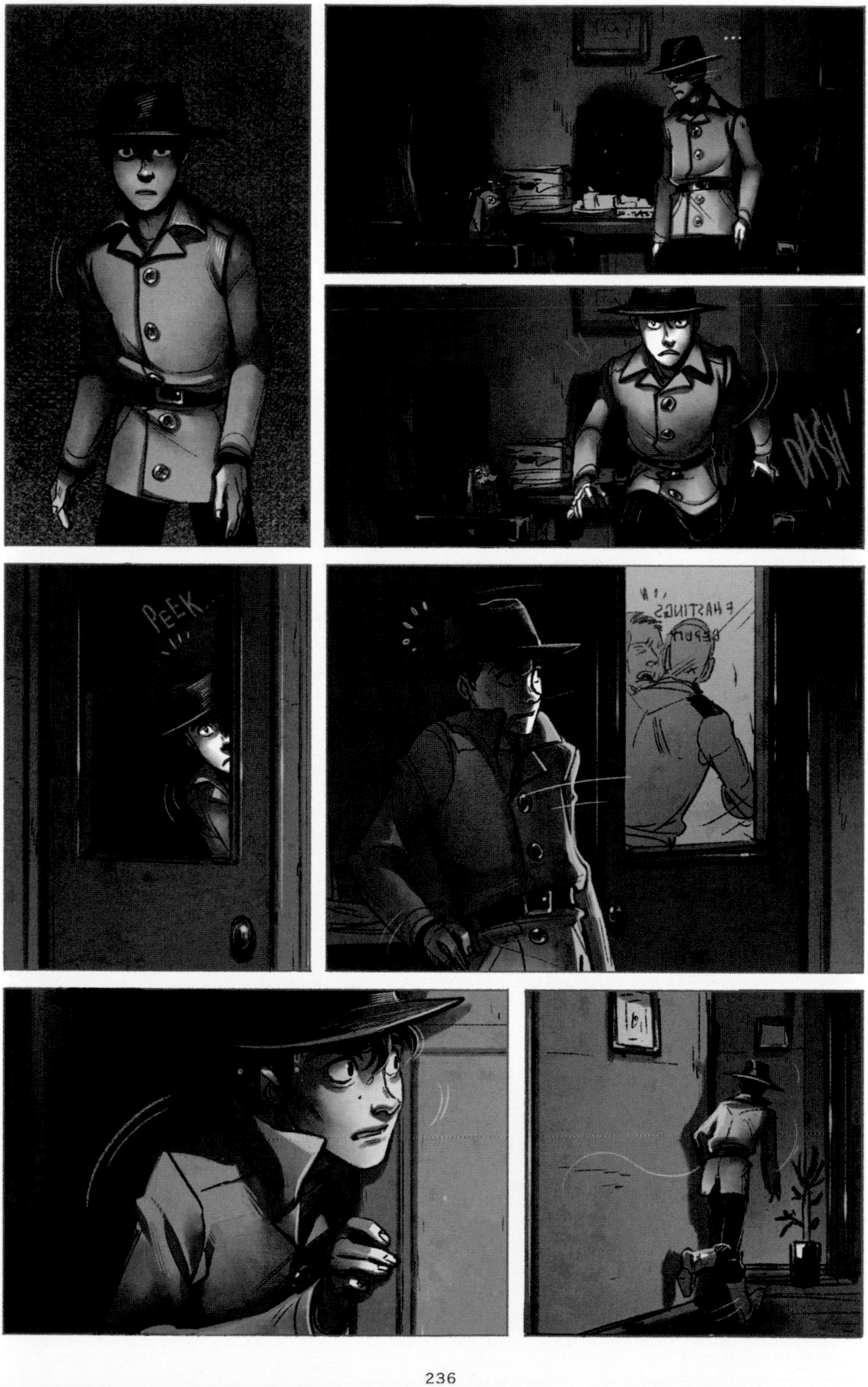
DASH
PEEK

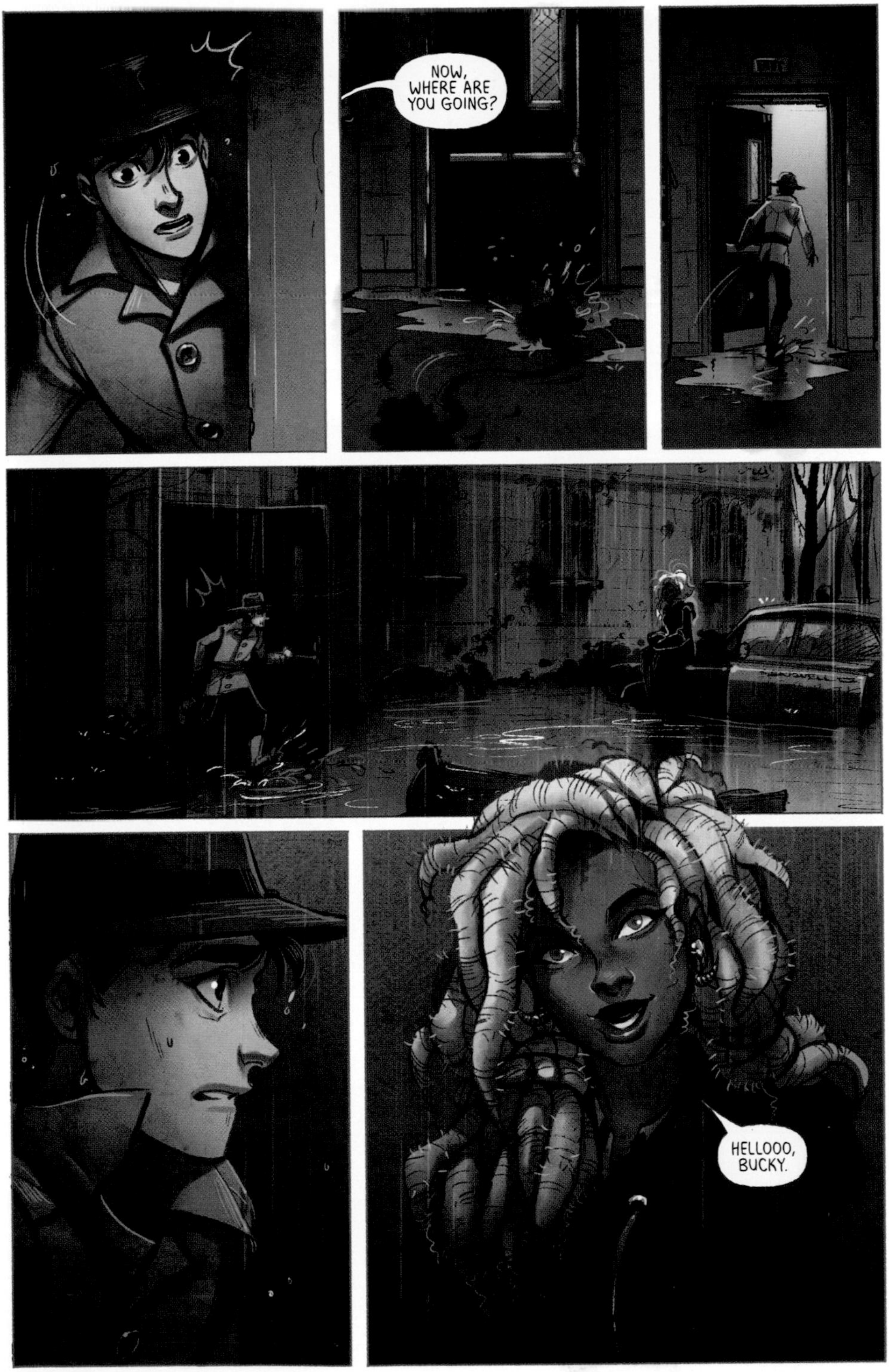
NOW, WHERE ARE YOU GOING?
HELLOOO, BUCKY.

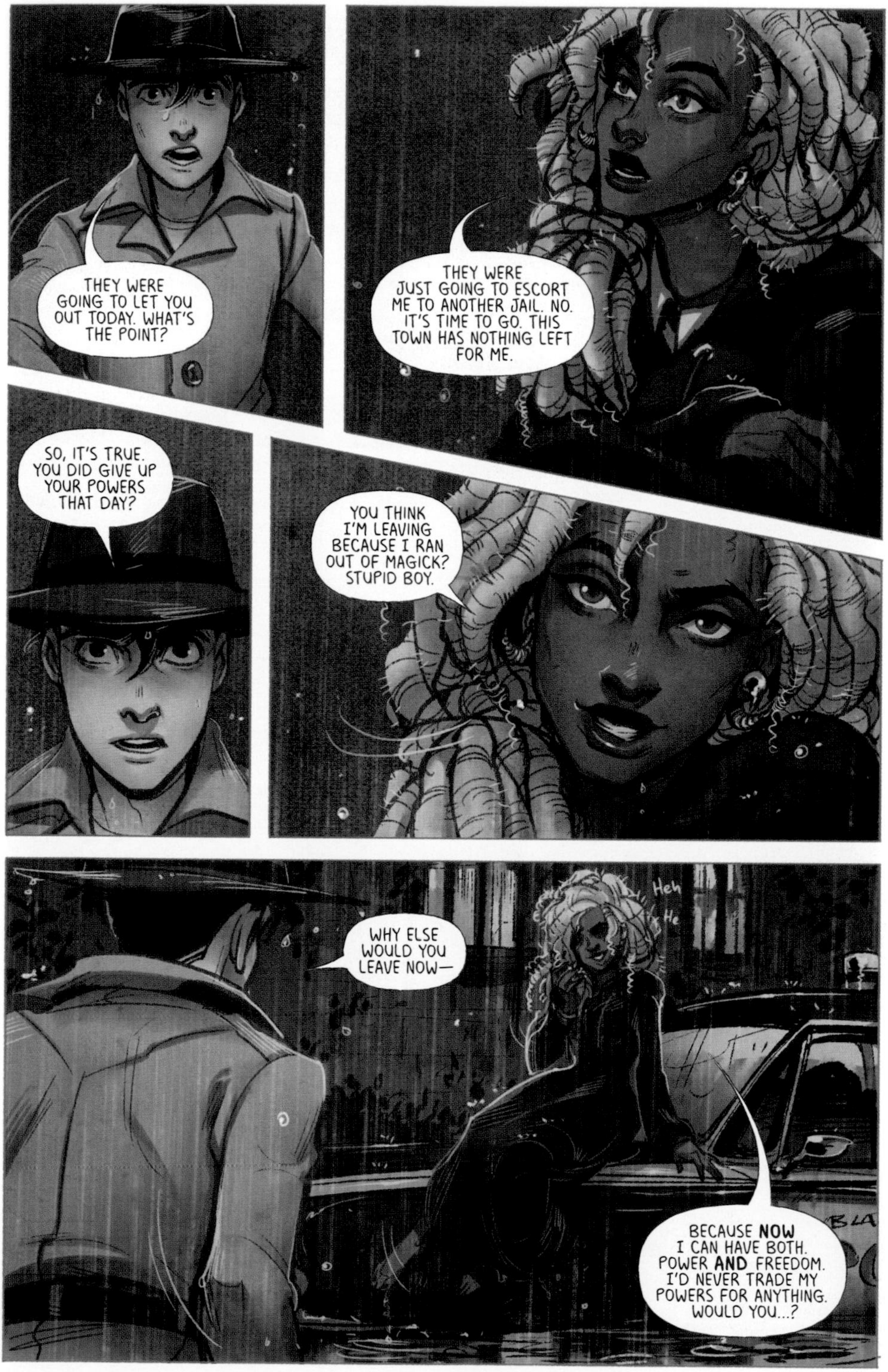
THEY WERE GOING TO LET YOU OUT TODAY. WHAT'S THE POINT?
THEY WERE JUST GOING TO ESCORT ME TO ANOTHER JAIL. NO. IT'S TIME TO GO. THIS TOWN HAS NOTHING LEFT FOR ME.
SO, IT'S TRUE. YOU DID GIVE UP YOUR POWERS THAT DAY?
YOU THINK I'M LEAVING BECAUSE I RAN OUT OF MAGICK? STUPID BOY.
Heh
He
WHY ELSE WOULD YOU LEAVE NOW—
BECAUSE **NOW** I CAN HAVE BOTH. POWER **AND** FREEDOM. I'D NEVER TRADE MY POWERS FOR ANYTHING. WOULD YOU...?

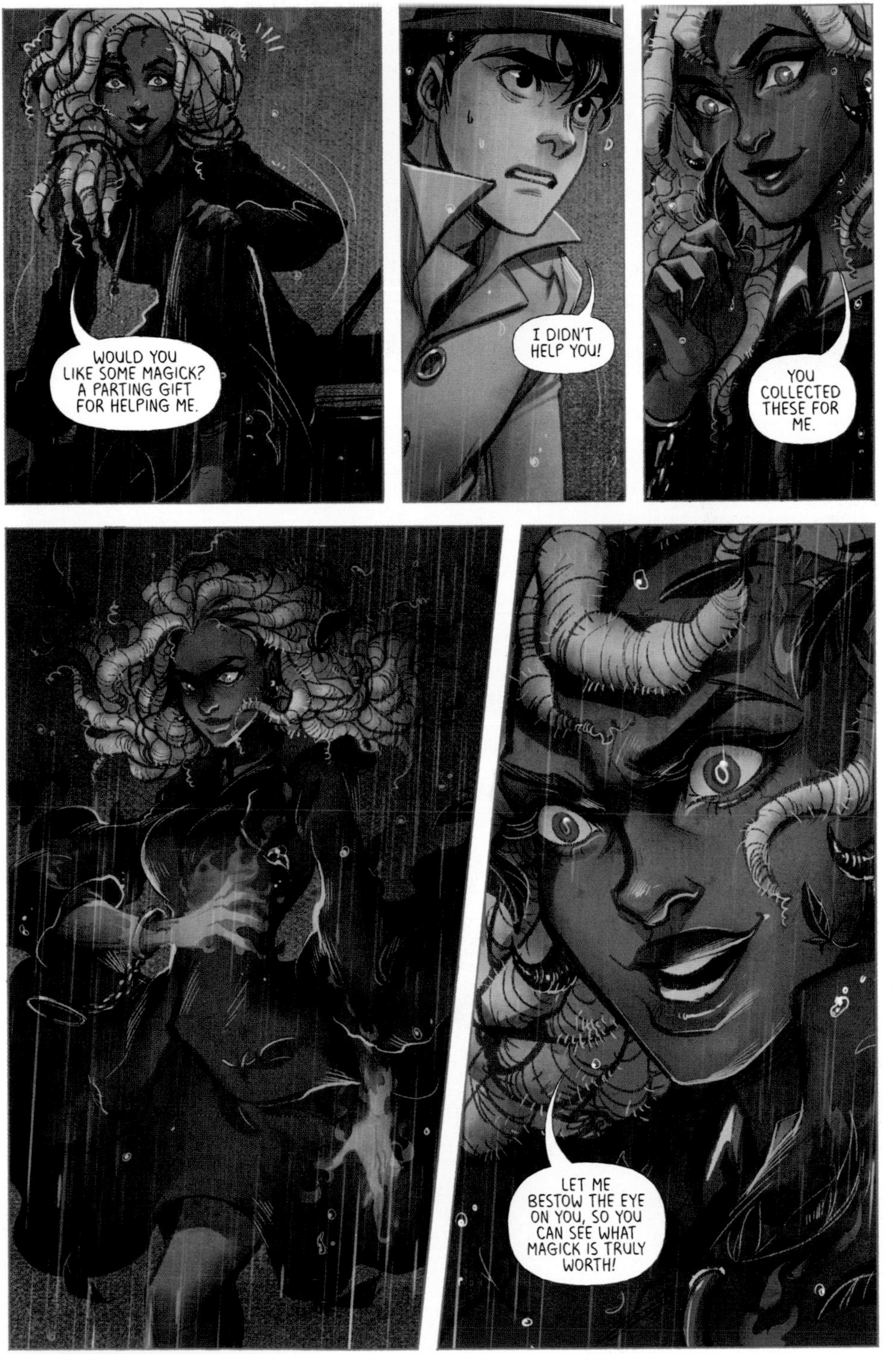
WOULD YOU LIKE SOME MAGICK? A PARTING GIFT FOR HELPING ME.
I DIDN'T HELP YOU!
YOU COLLECTED THESE FOR ME.
LET ME BESTOW THE EYE ON YOU, SO YOU CAN SEE WHAT MAGICK IS TRULY WORTH!

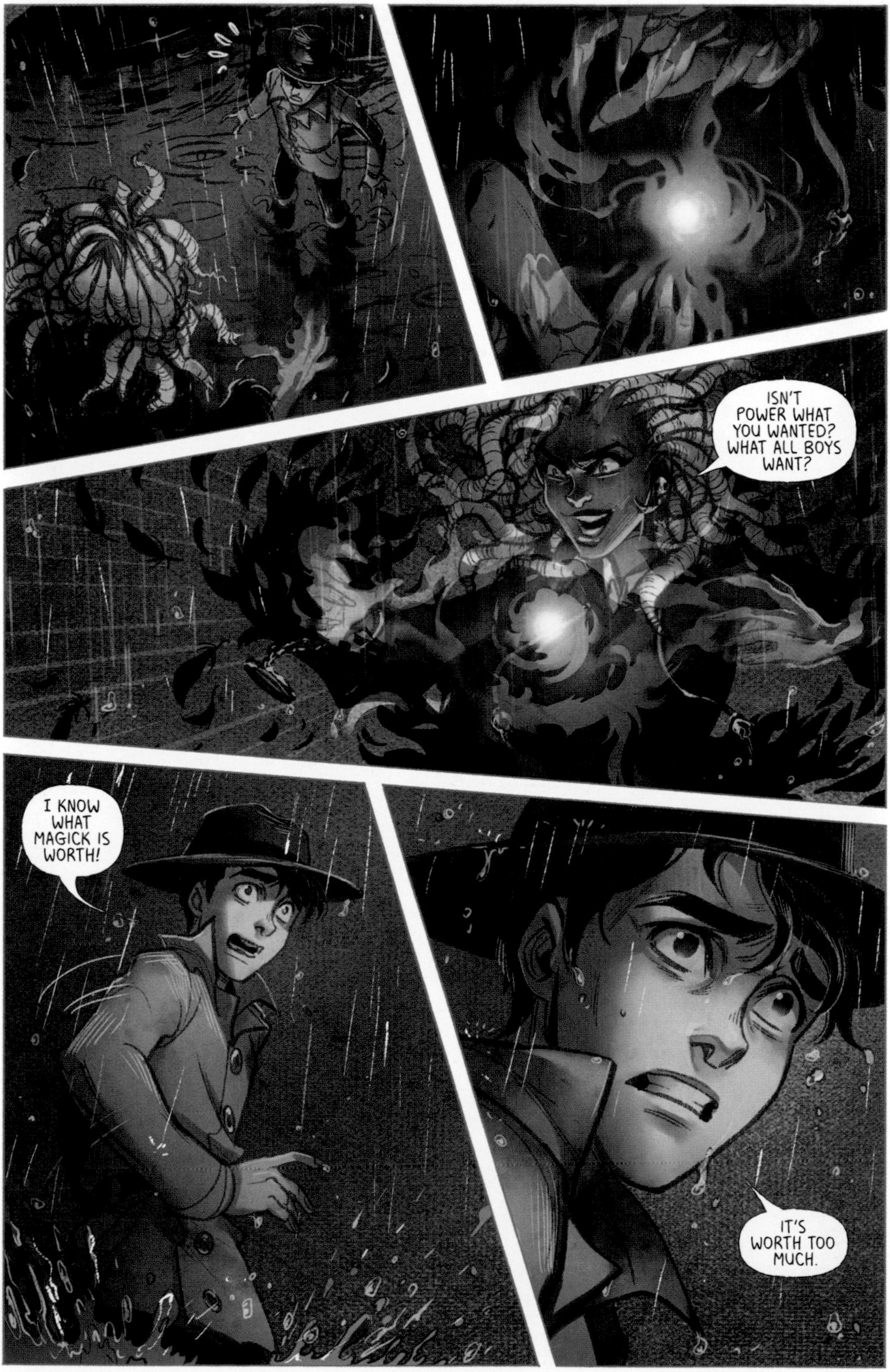
ISN'T POWER WHAT YOU WANTED? WHAT ALL BOYS WANT?
I KNOW WHAT MAGICK IS WORTH!
IT'S WORTH TOO MUCH.

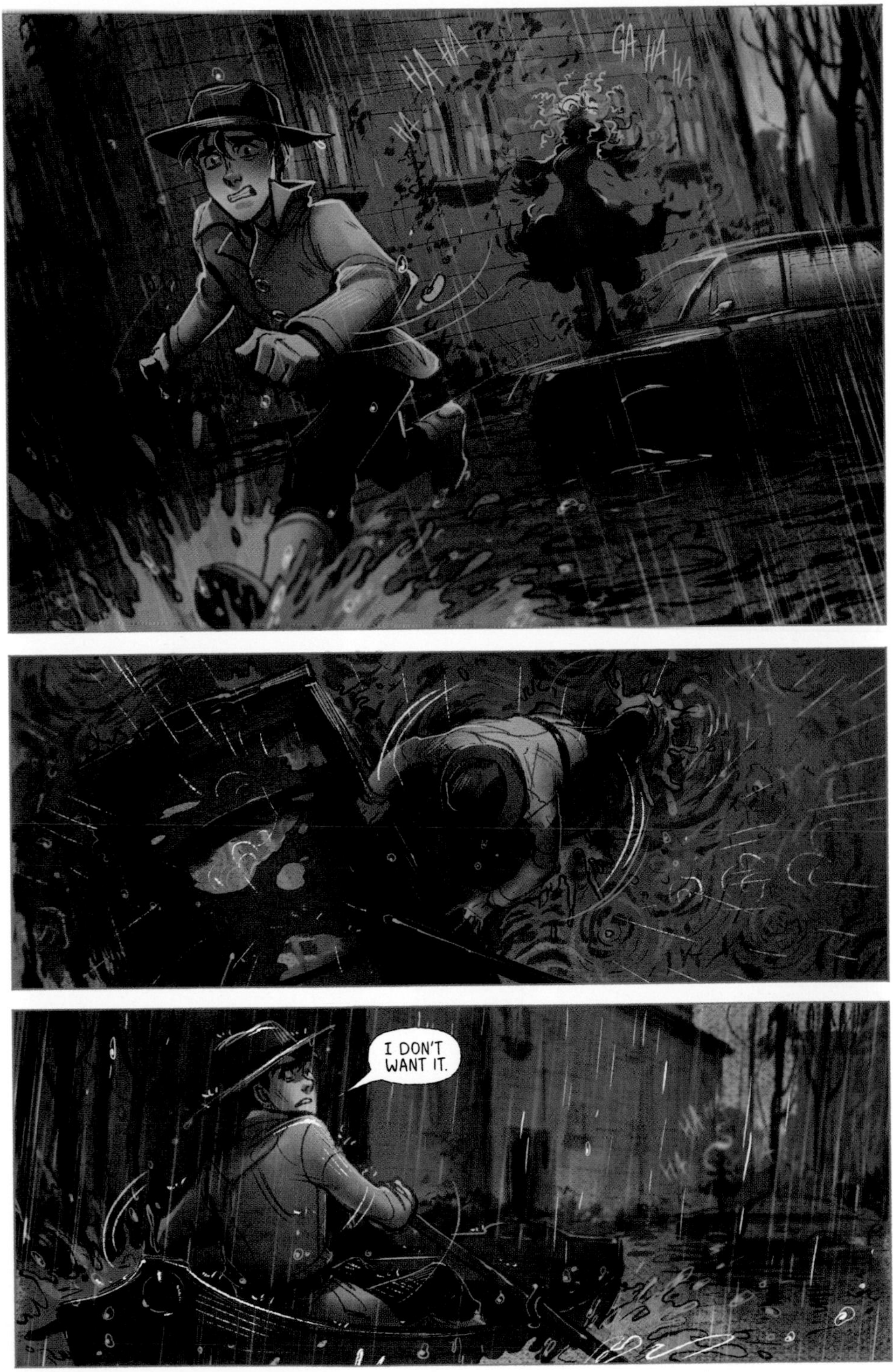
HA HA HA
GA HA HA
I DON'T WANT IT.
HA HA

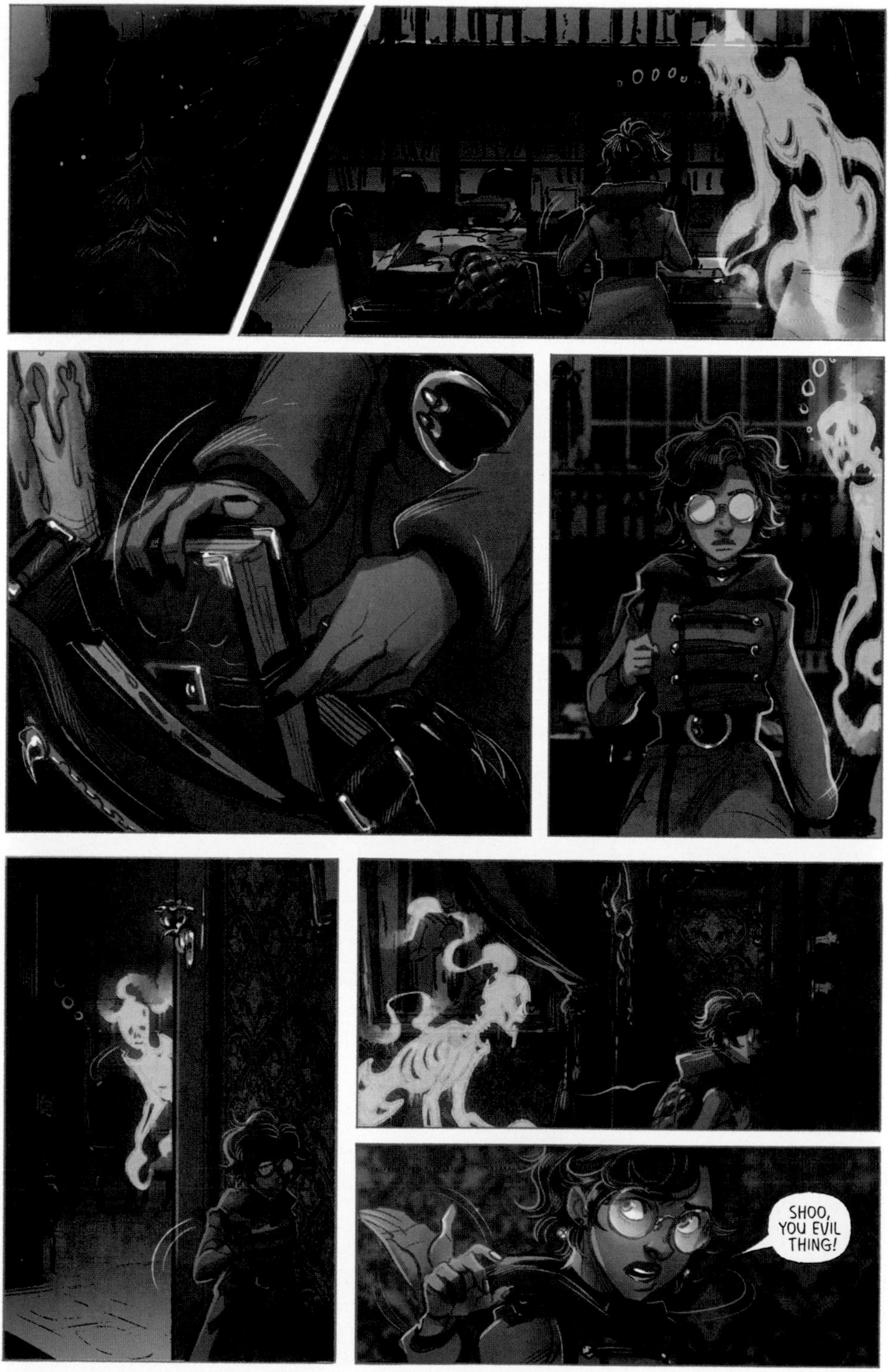
SHOO, YOU EVIL THING!

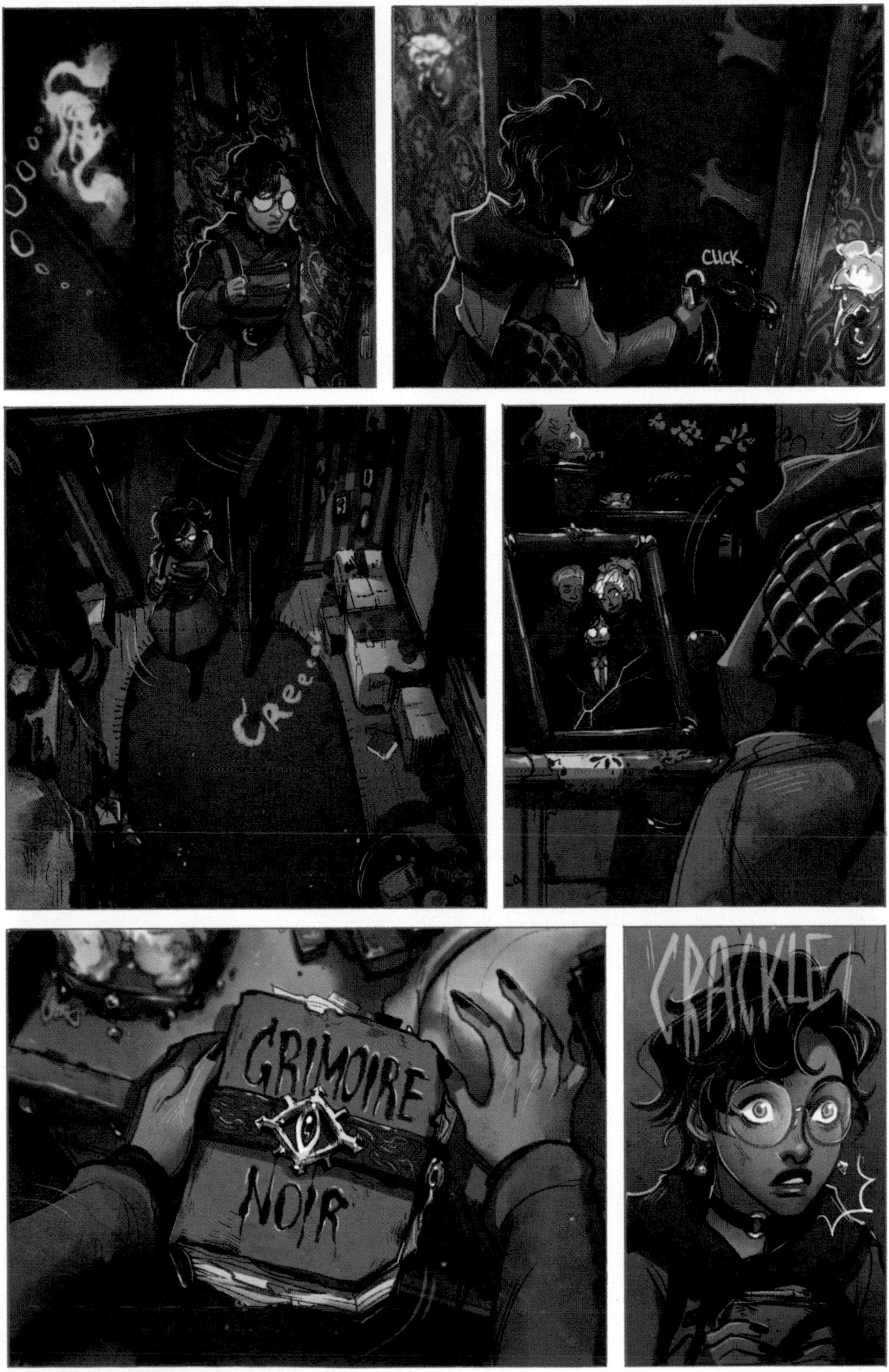
CLICK
Creee
GRIMOIRE NOIR
CRACKLE

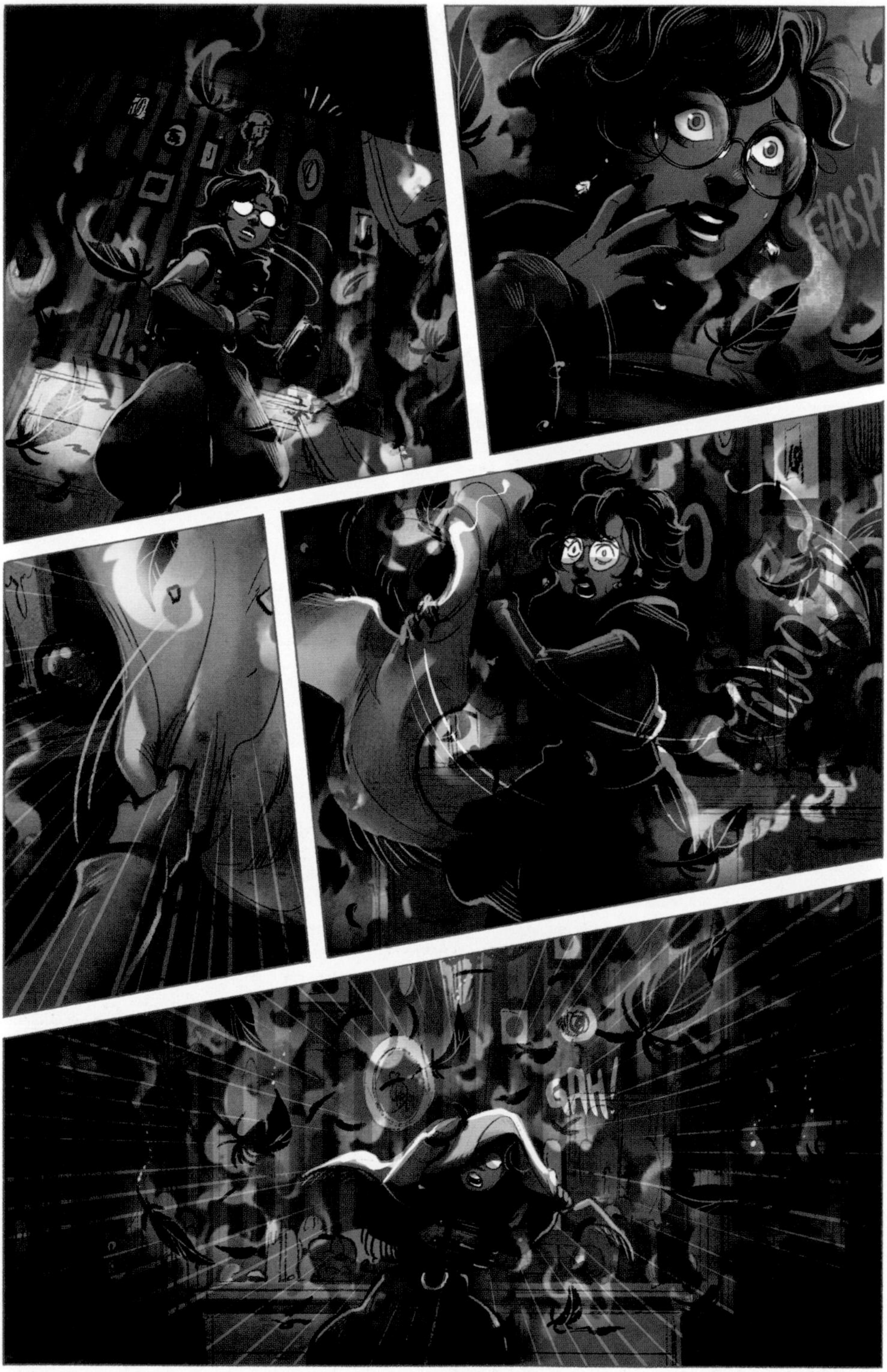
GASP!
GAH!

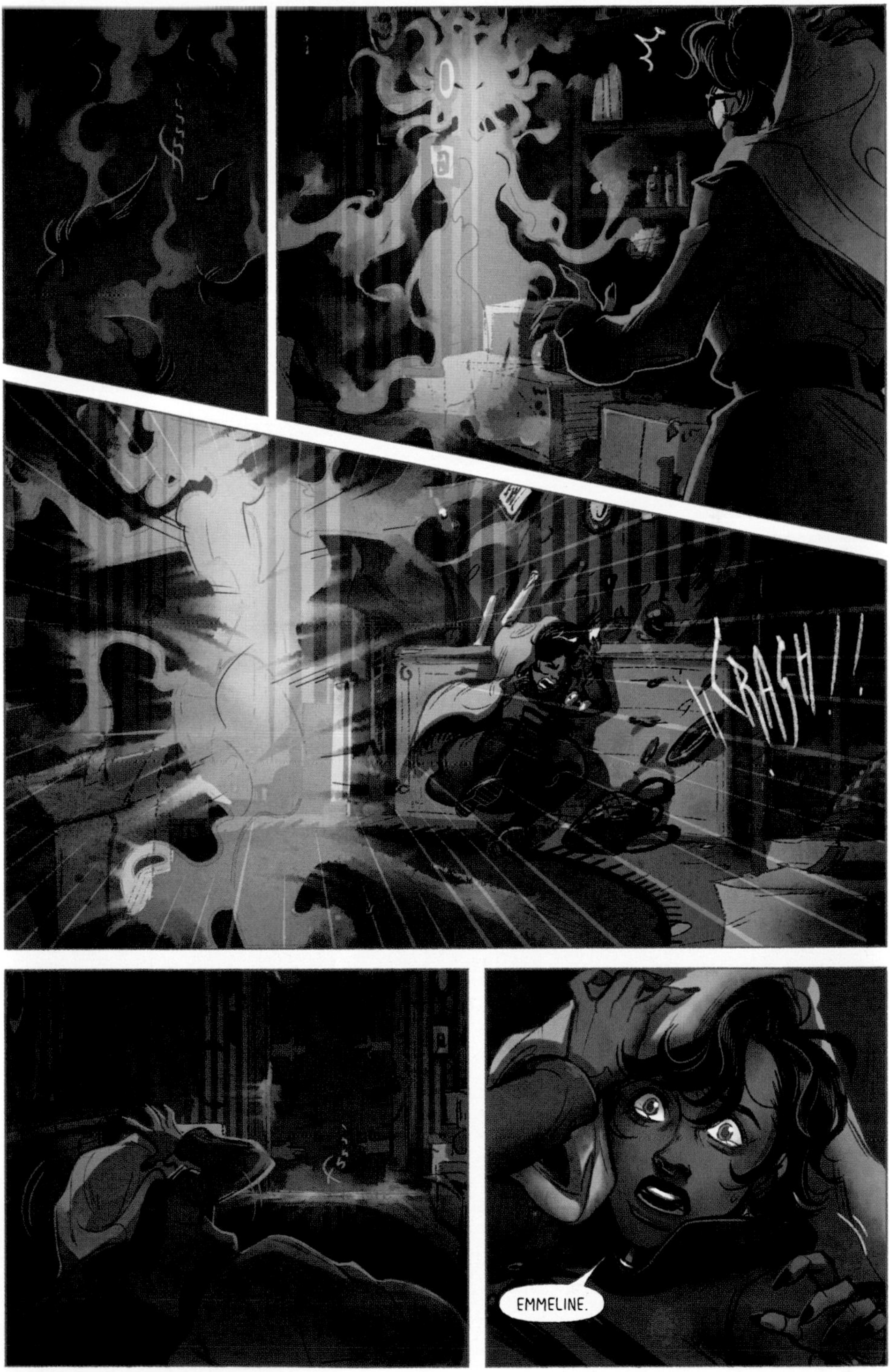

fssss
CRASH!!
EMMELINE.

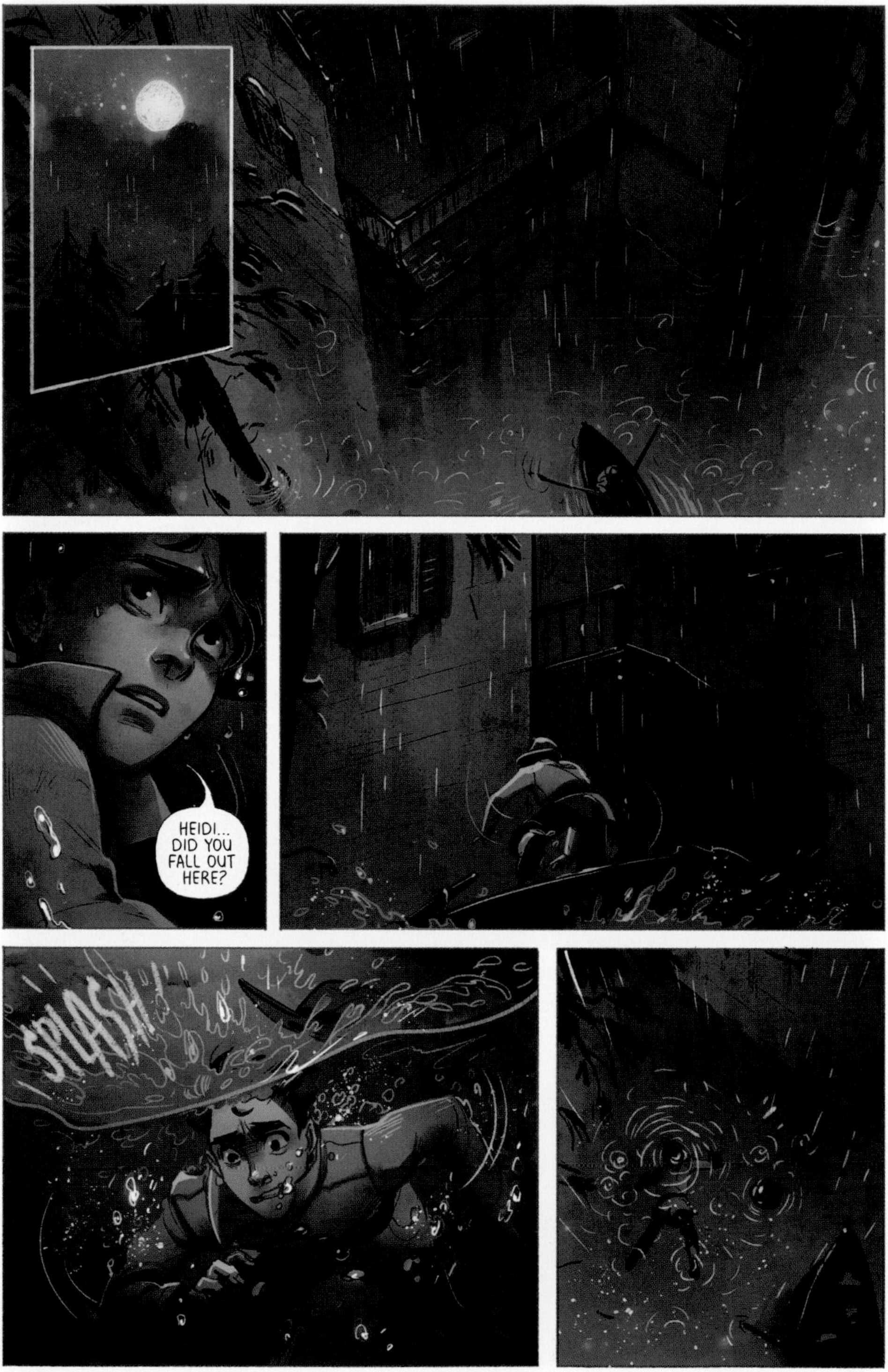
HEIDI... DID YOU FALL OUT HERE?
SPLASH!

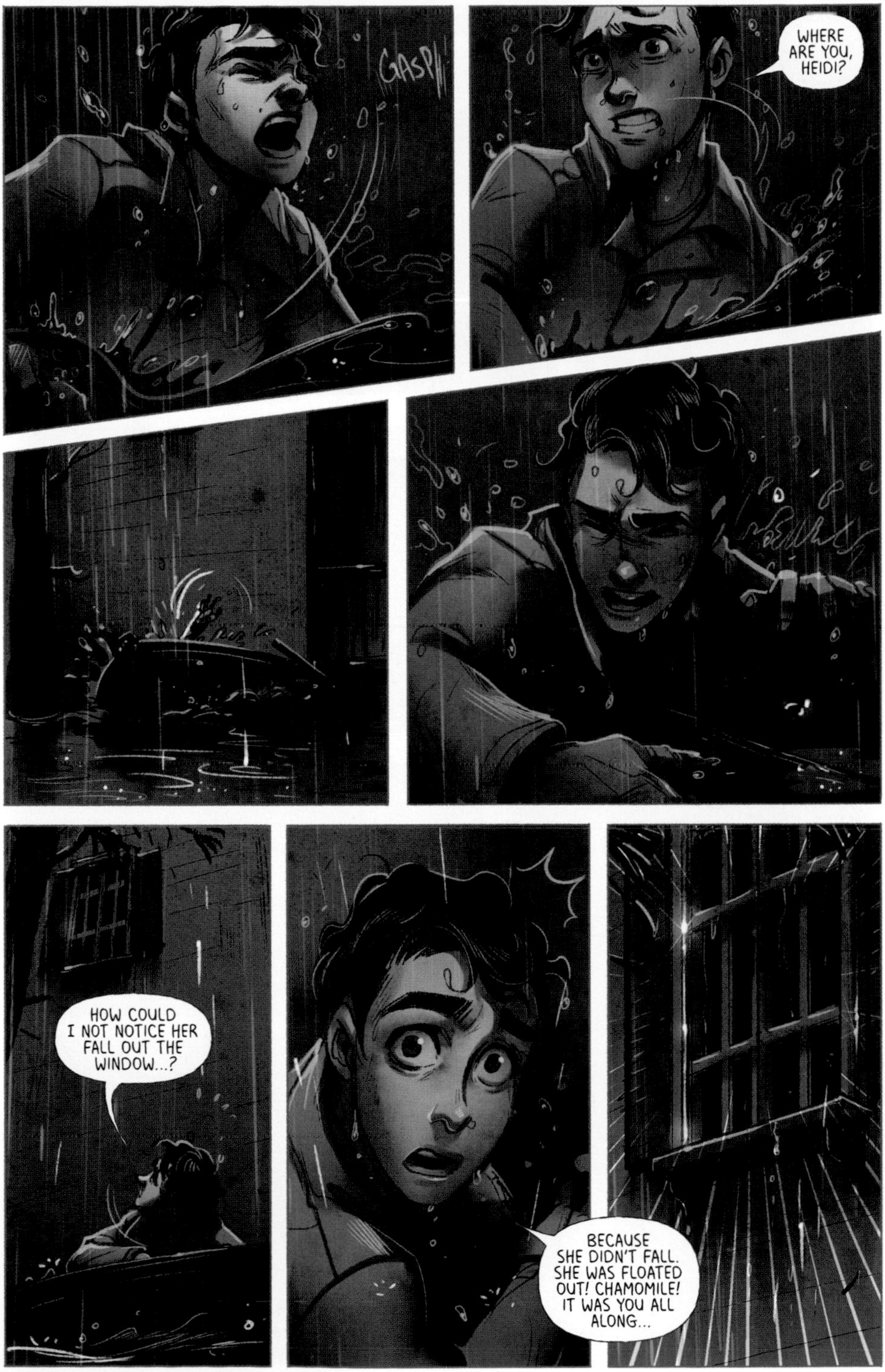
GASP!!
WHERE ARE YOU, HEIDI?
HOW COULD I NOT NOTICE HER FALL OUT THE WINDOW...?
BECAUSE SHE DIDN'T FALL. SHE WAS FLOATED OUT! CHAMOMILE! IT WAS YOU ALL ALONG...

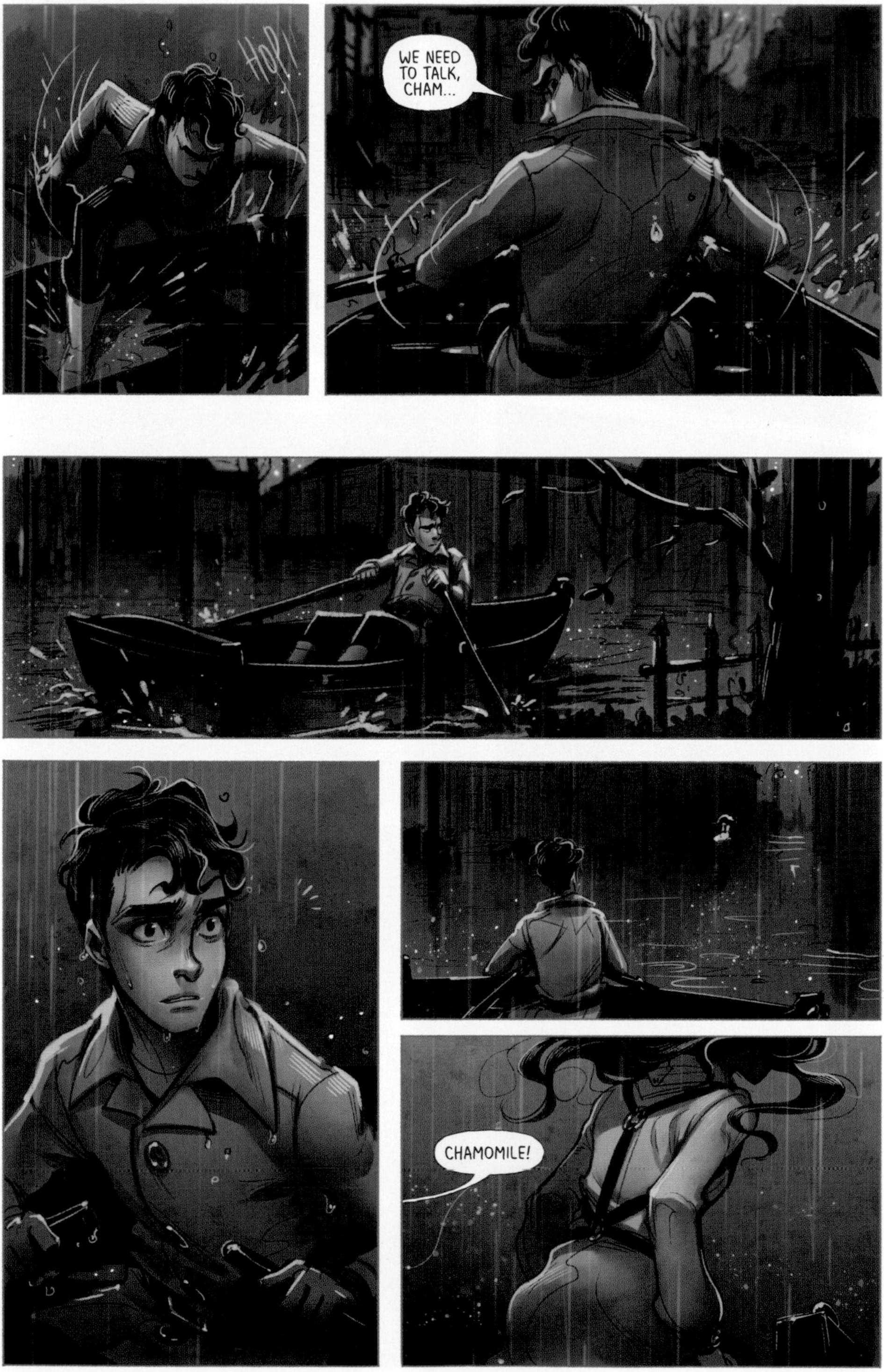
HOP!
WE NEED TO TALK, CHAM...
CHAMOMILE!

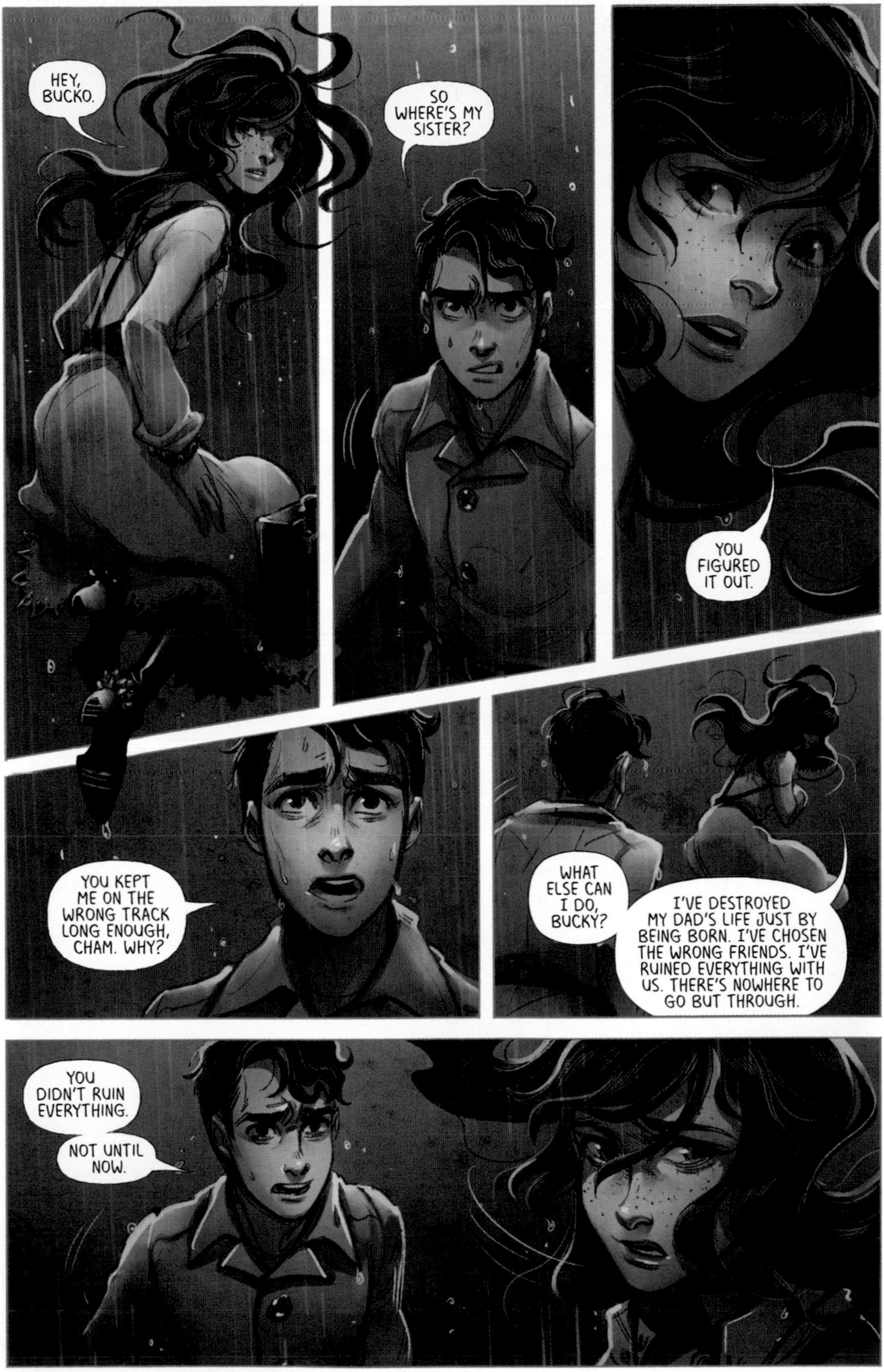
HEY, BUCKO.
SO WHERE'S MY SISTER?
YOU FIGURED IT OUT.
YOU KEPT ME ON THE WRONG TRACK LONG ENOUGH, CHAM. WHY?
WHAT ELSE CAN I DO, BUCKY?
I'VE DESTROYED MY DAD'S LIFE JUST BY BEING BORN. I'VE CHOSEN THE WRONG FRIENDS. I'VE RUINED EVERYTHING WITH US. THERE'S NOWHERE TO GO BUT THROUGH.
YOU DIDN'T RUIN EVERYTHING.
NOT UNTIL NOW.

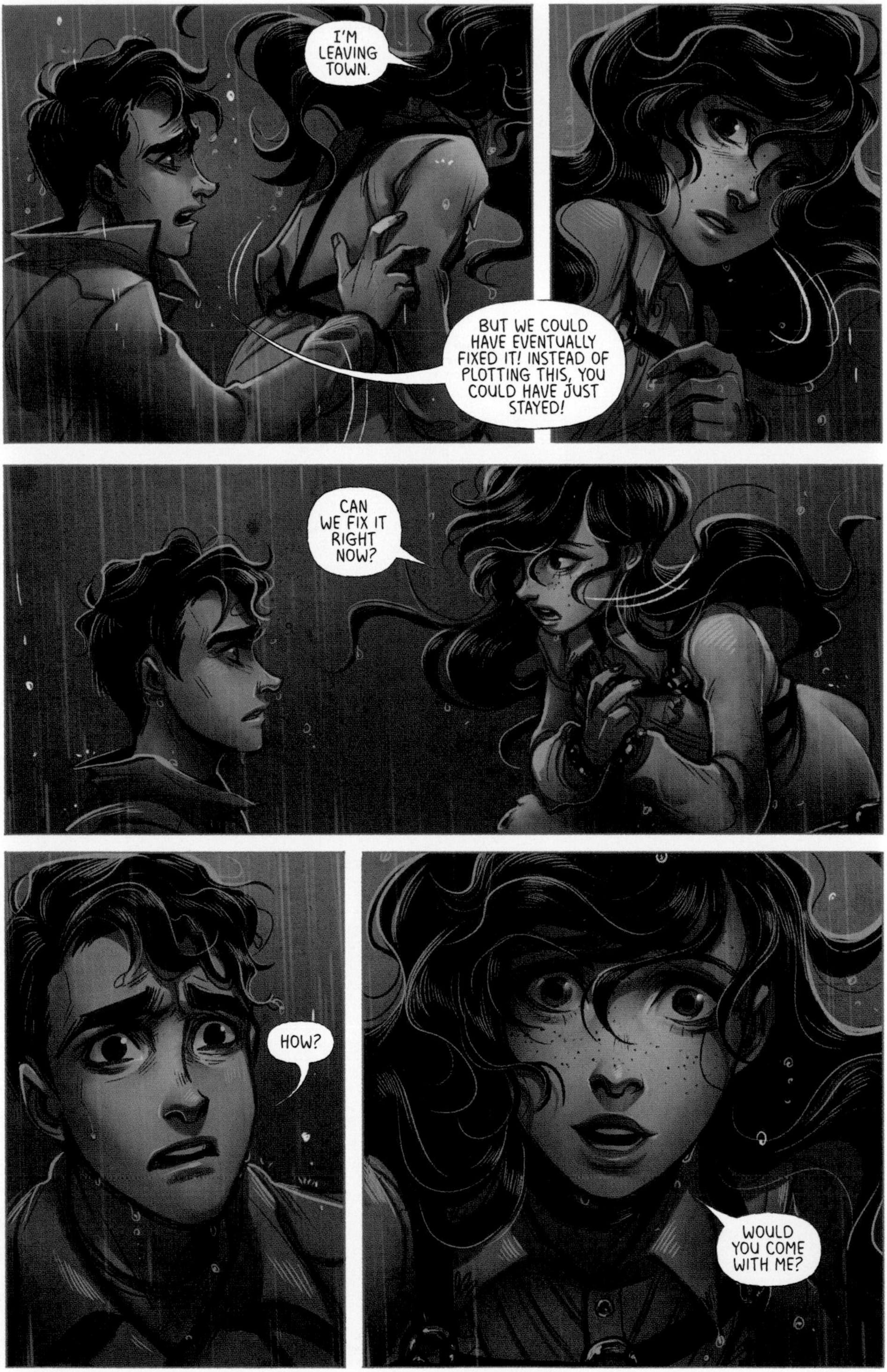
I'M LEAVING TOWN.
BUT WE COULD HAVE EVENTUALLY FIXED IT! INSTEAD OF PLOTTING THIS, YOU COULD HAVE JUST STAYED!
CAN WE FIX IT RIGHT NOW?
HOW?
WOULD YOU COME WITH ME?

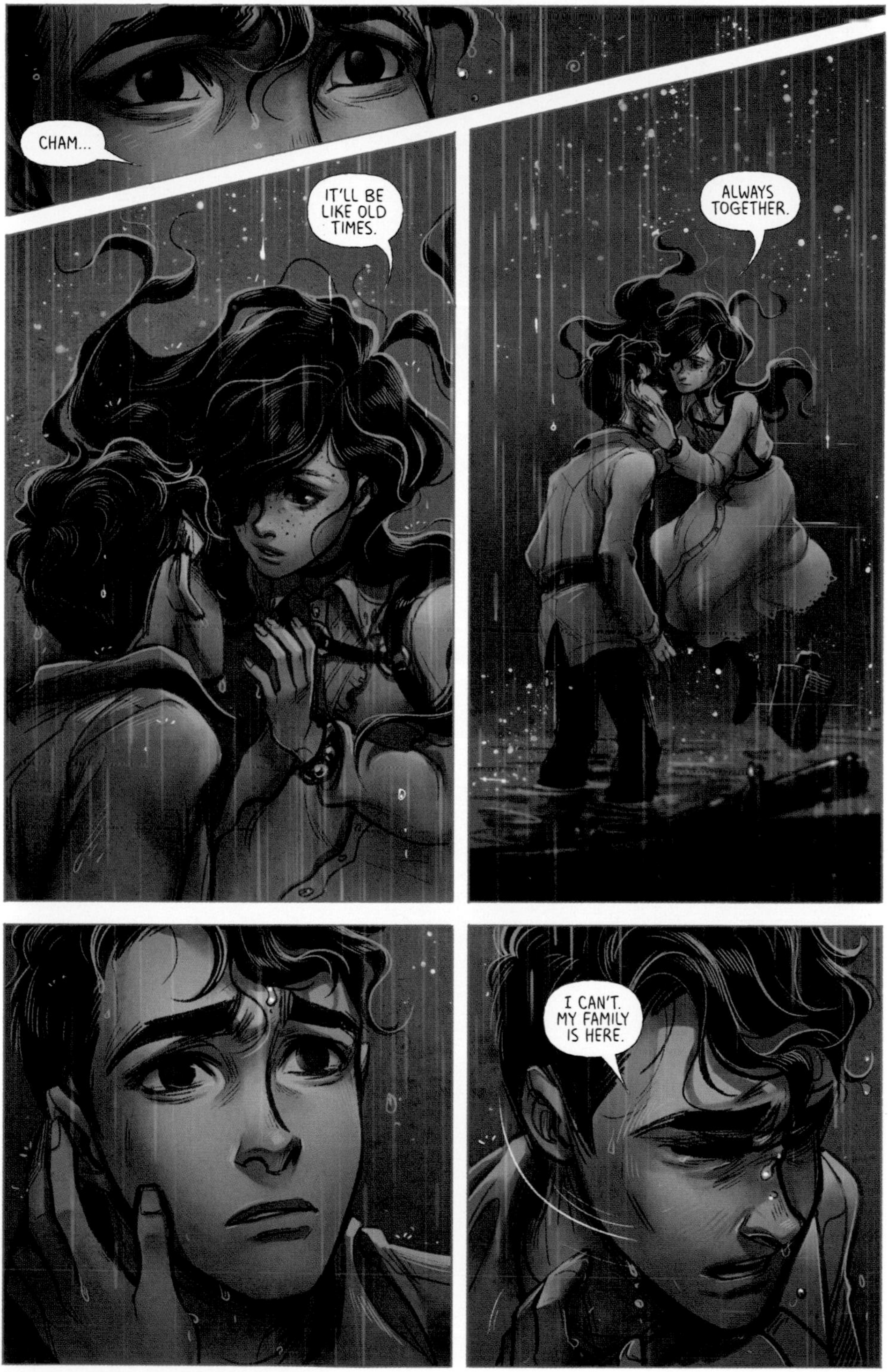
CHAM...
IT'LL BE LIKE OLD TIMES.
ALWAYS TOGETHER.
I CAN'T. MY FAMILY IS HERE.

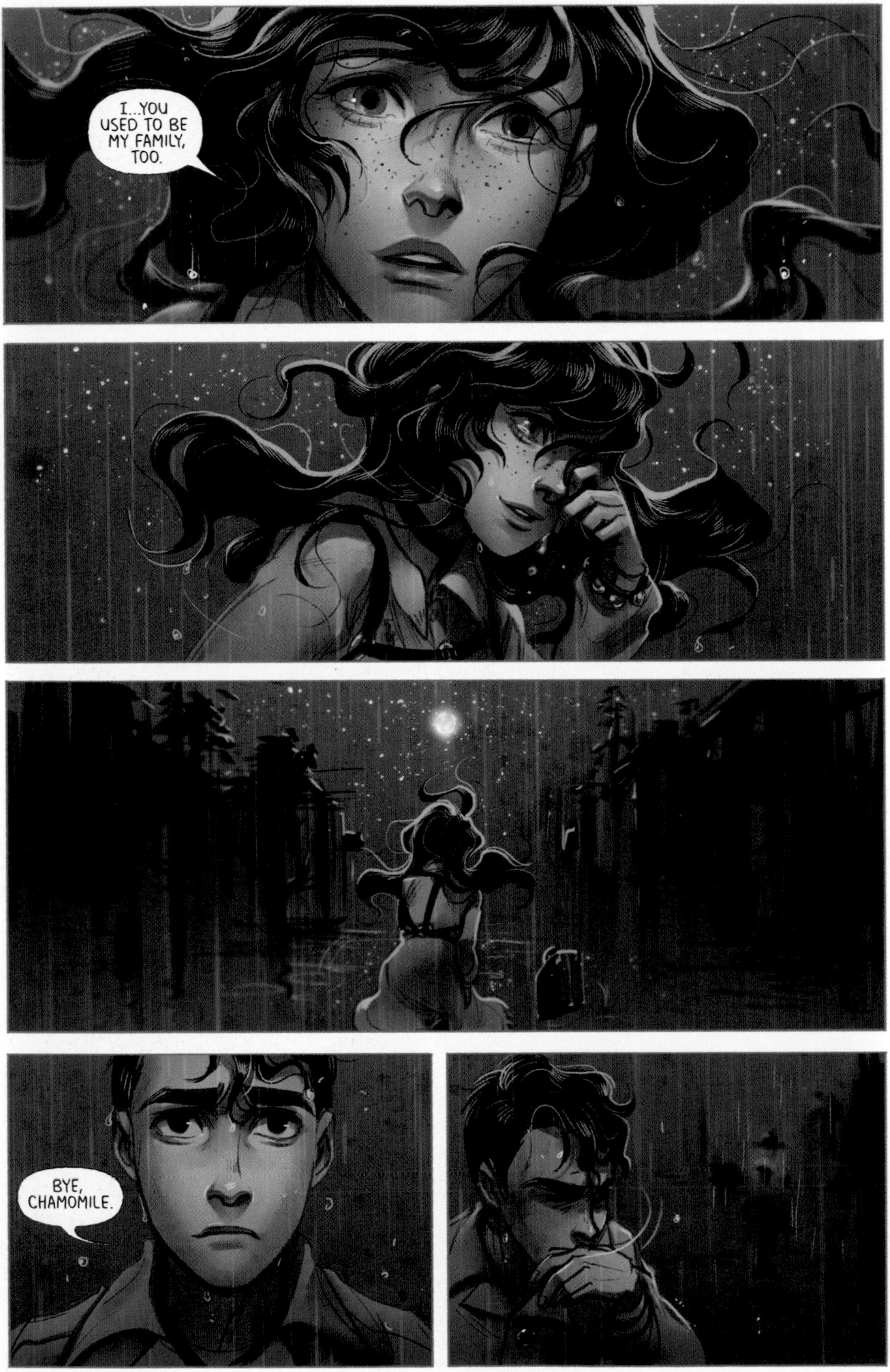
I...YOU USED TO BE MY FAMILY, TOO.
BYE, CHAMOMILE.

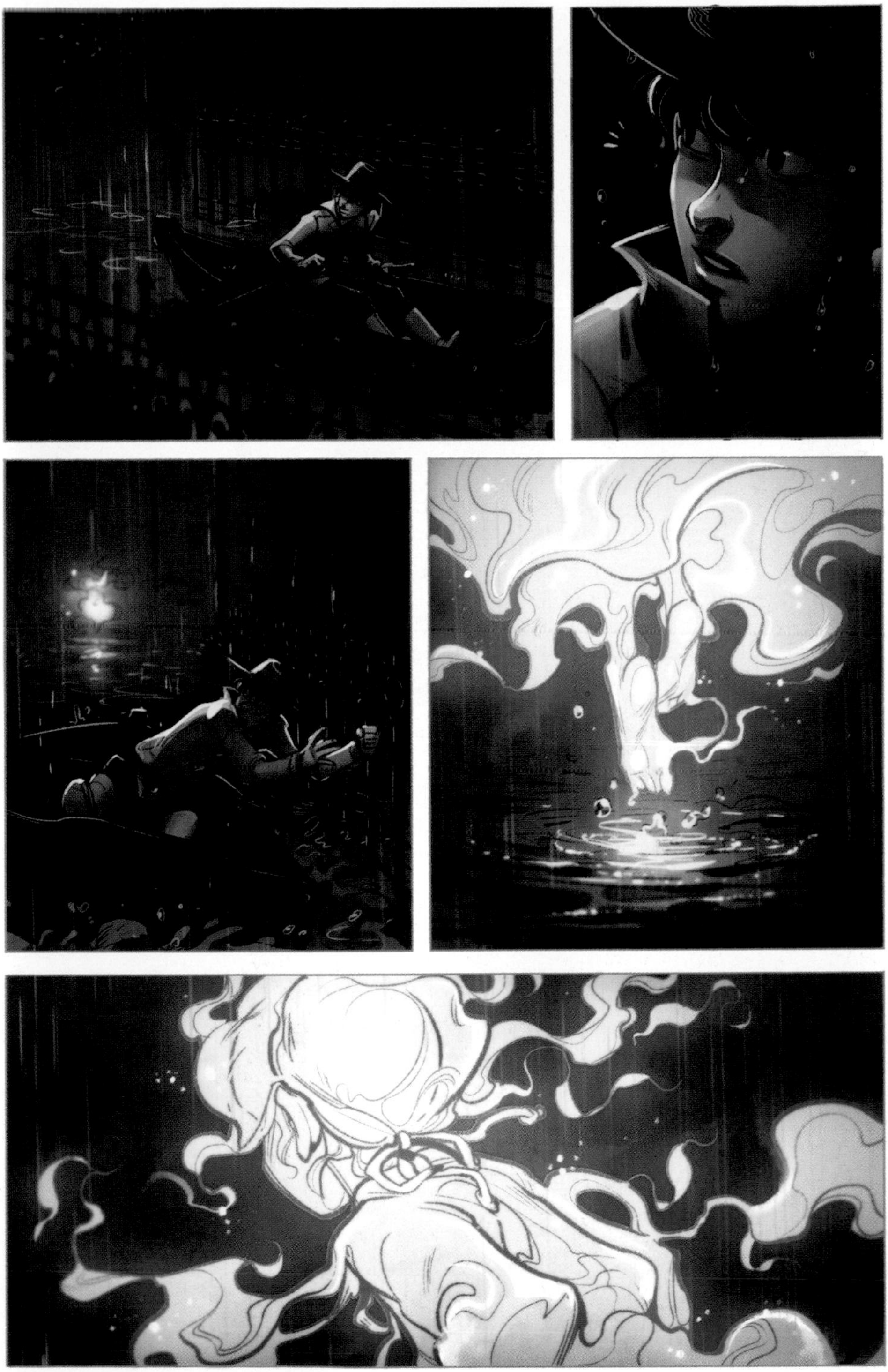

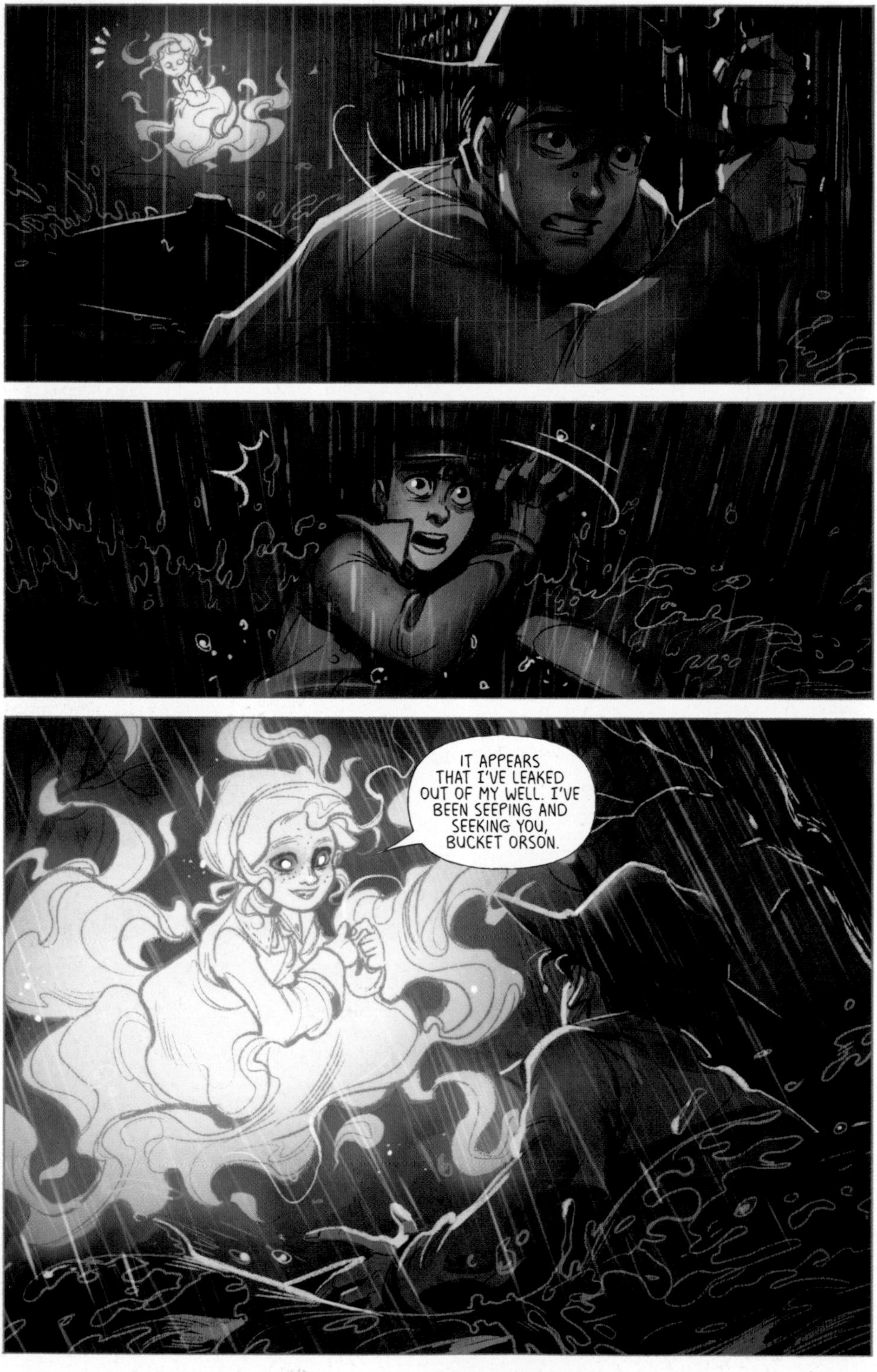
IT APPEARS THAT I'VE LEAKED OUT OF MY WELL. I'VE BEEN SEEPING AND SEEKING YOU, BUCKET ORSON.

CHAPTER 12

GRIMOIRE NOIR

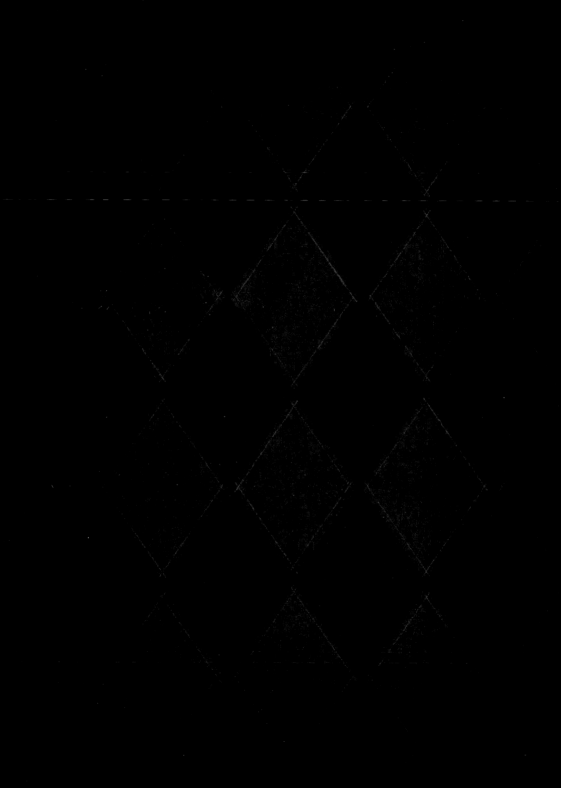

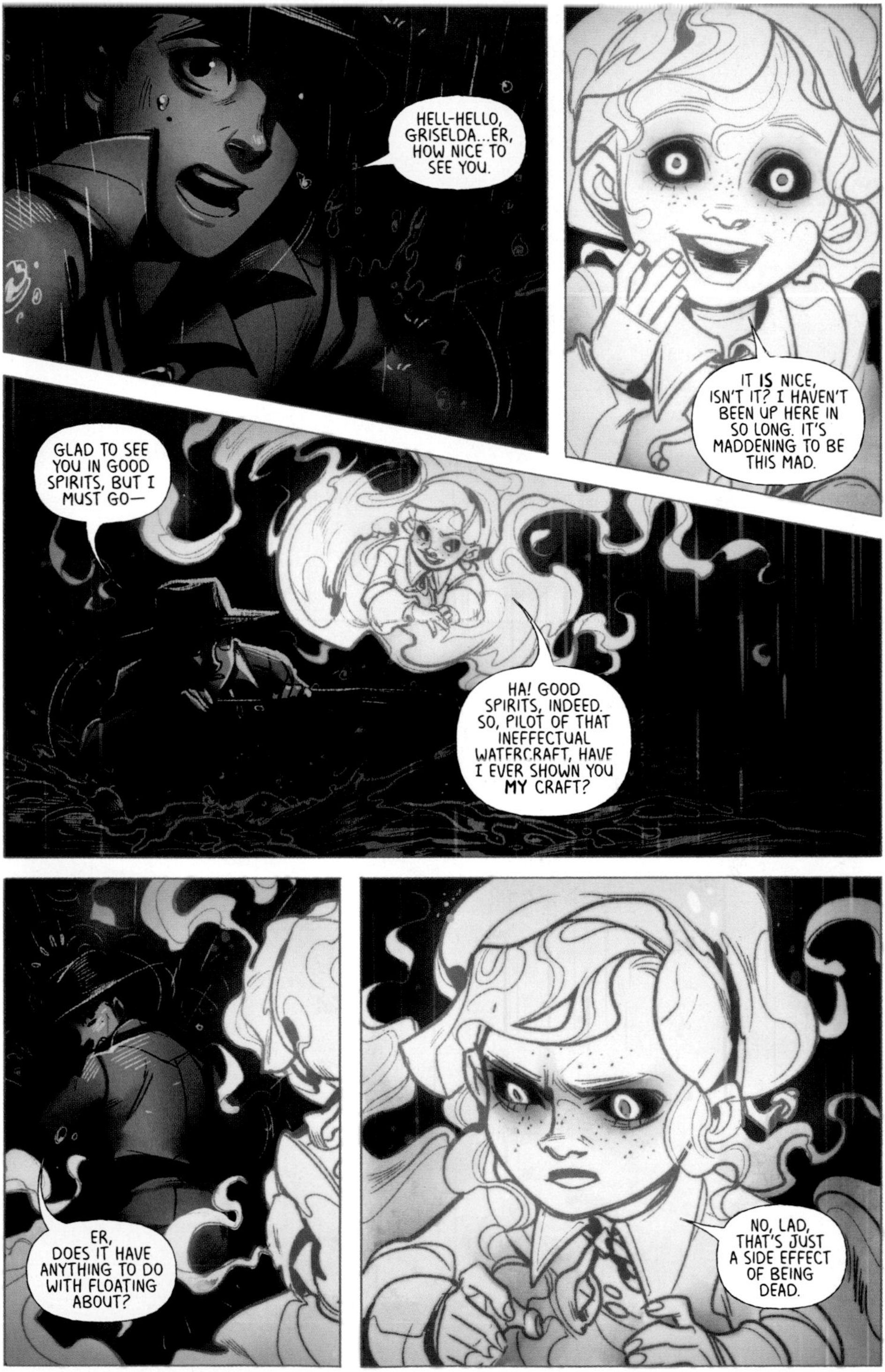
HELL-HELLO, GRISELDA...ER, HOW NICE TO SEE YOU.
IT IS NICE, ISN'T IT? I HAVEN'T BEEN UP HERE IN SO LONG. IT'S MADDENING TO BE THIS MAD.
GLAD TO SEE YOU IN GOOD SPIRITS, BUT I MUST GO—
HA! GOOD SPIRITS, INDEED. SO, PILOT OF THAT INEFFECTUAL WATERCRAFT, HAVE I EVER SHOWN YOU MY CRAFT?
ER, DOES IT HAVE ANYTHING TO DO WITH FLOATING ABOUT?
NO, LAD, THAT'S JUST A SIDE EFFECT OF BEING DEAD.

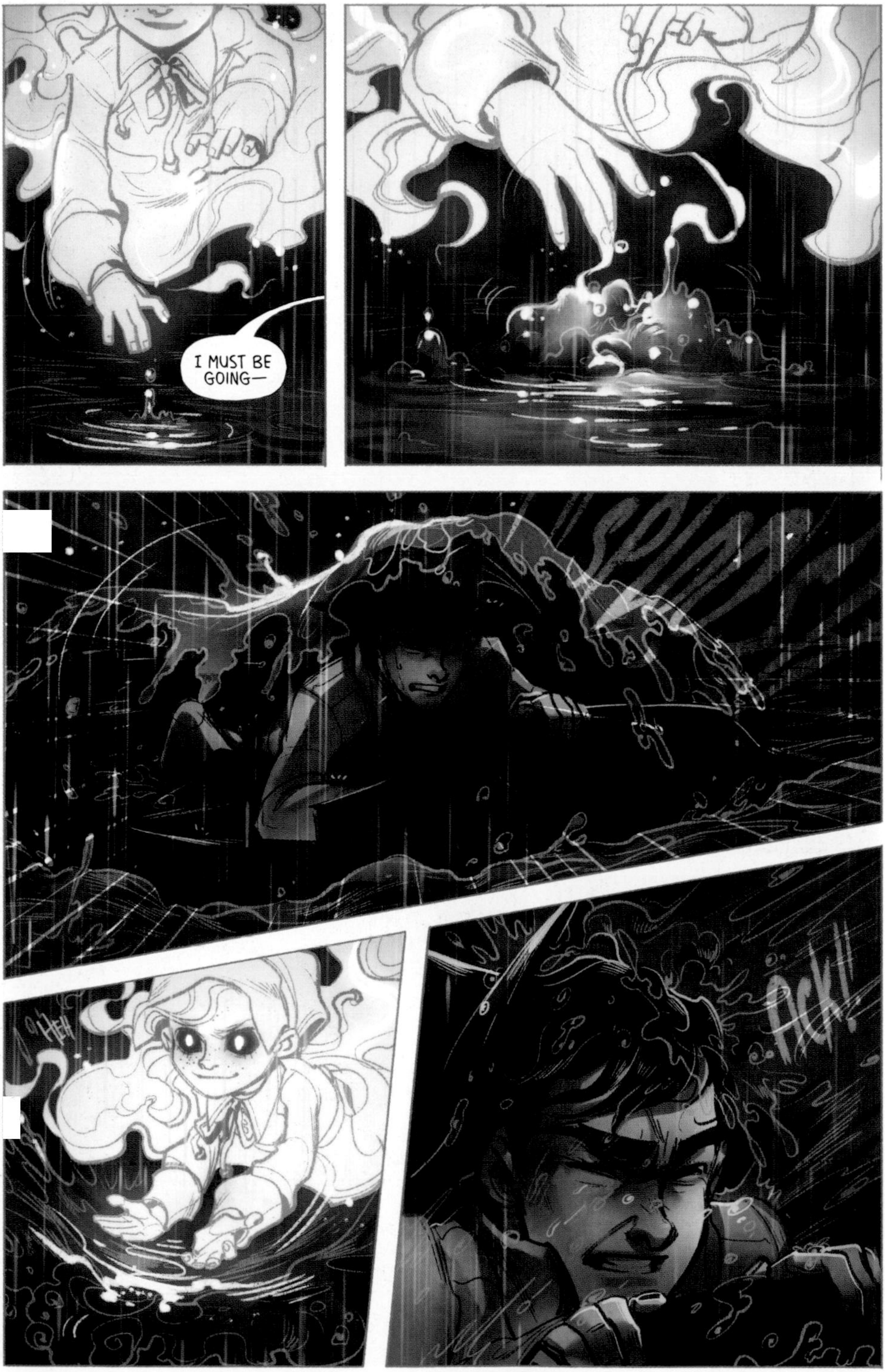
I MUST BE GOING—
HEH
ACK!

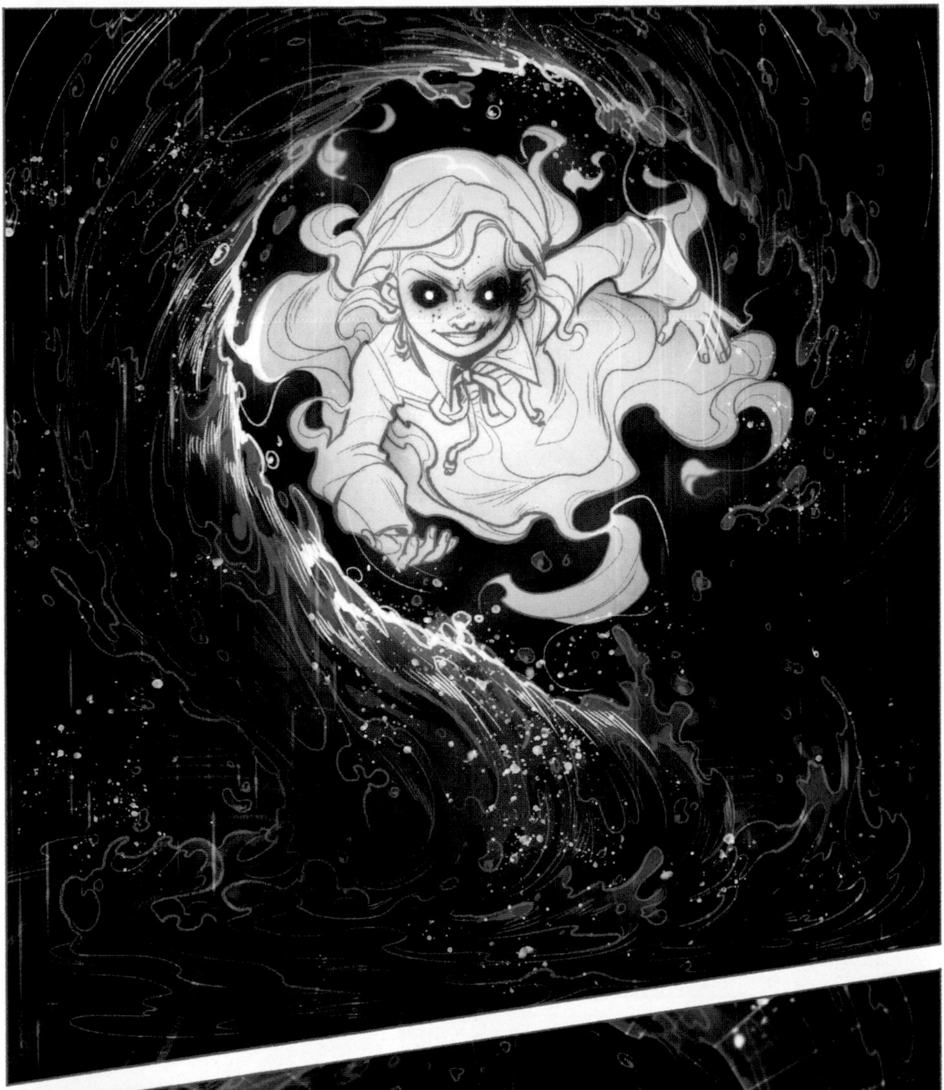

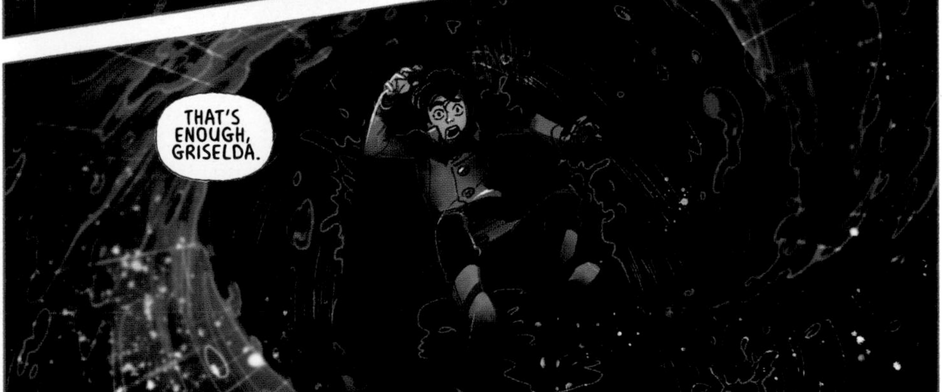
THAT'S ENOUGH, GRISELDA.

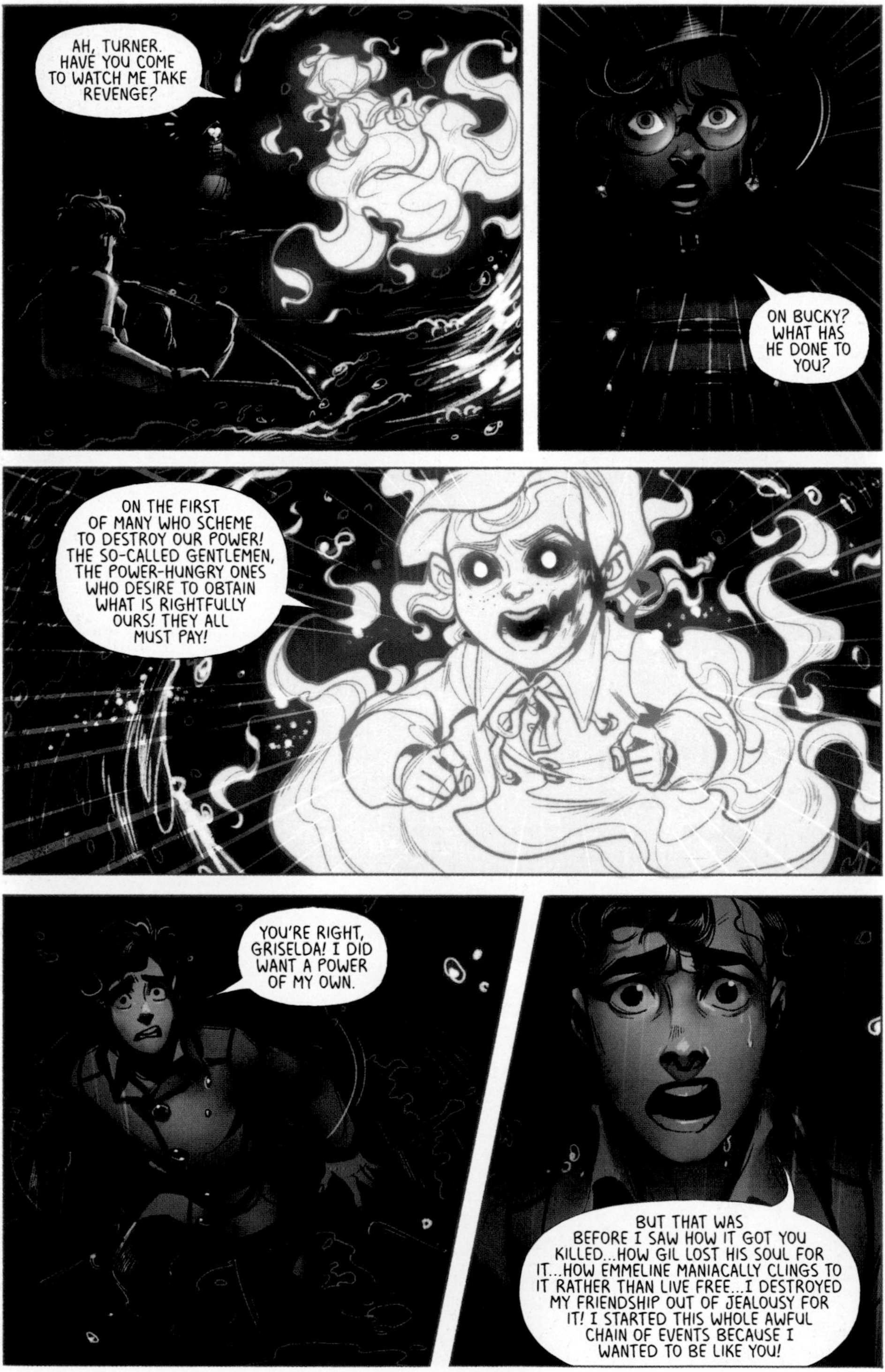
AH, TURNER. HAVE YOU COME TO WATCH ME TAKE REVENGE?
ON BUCKY? WHAT HAS HE DONE TO YOU?
ON THE FIRST OF MANY WHO SCHEME TO DESTROY OUR POWER! THE SO-CALLED GENTLEMEN, THE POWER-HUNGRY ONES WHO DESIRE TO OBTAIN WHAT IS RIGHTFULLY OURS! THEY ALL MUST PAY!
YOU'RE RIGHT, GRISELDA! I DID WANT A POWER OF MY OWN.
BUT THAT WAS BEFORE I SAW HOW IT GOT YOU KILLED...HOW GIL LOST HIS SOUL FOR IT...HOW EMMELINE MANIACALLY CLINGS TO IT RATHER THAN LIVE FREE...I DESTROYED MY FRIENDSHIP OUT OF JEALOUSY FOR IT! I STARTED THIS WHOLE AWFUL CHAIN OF EVENTS BECAUSE I WANTED TO BE LIKE YOU!

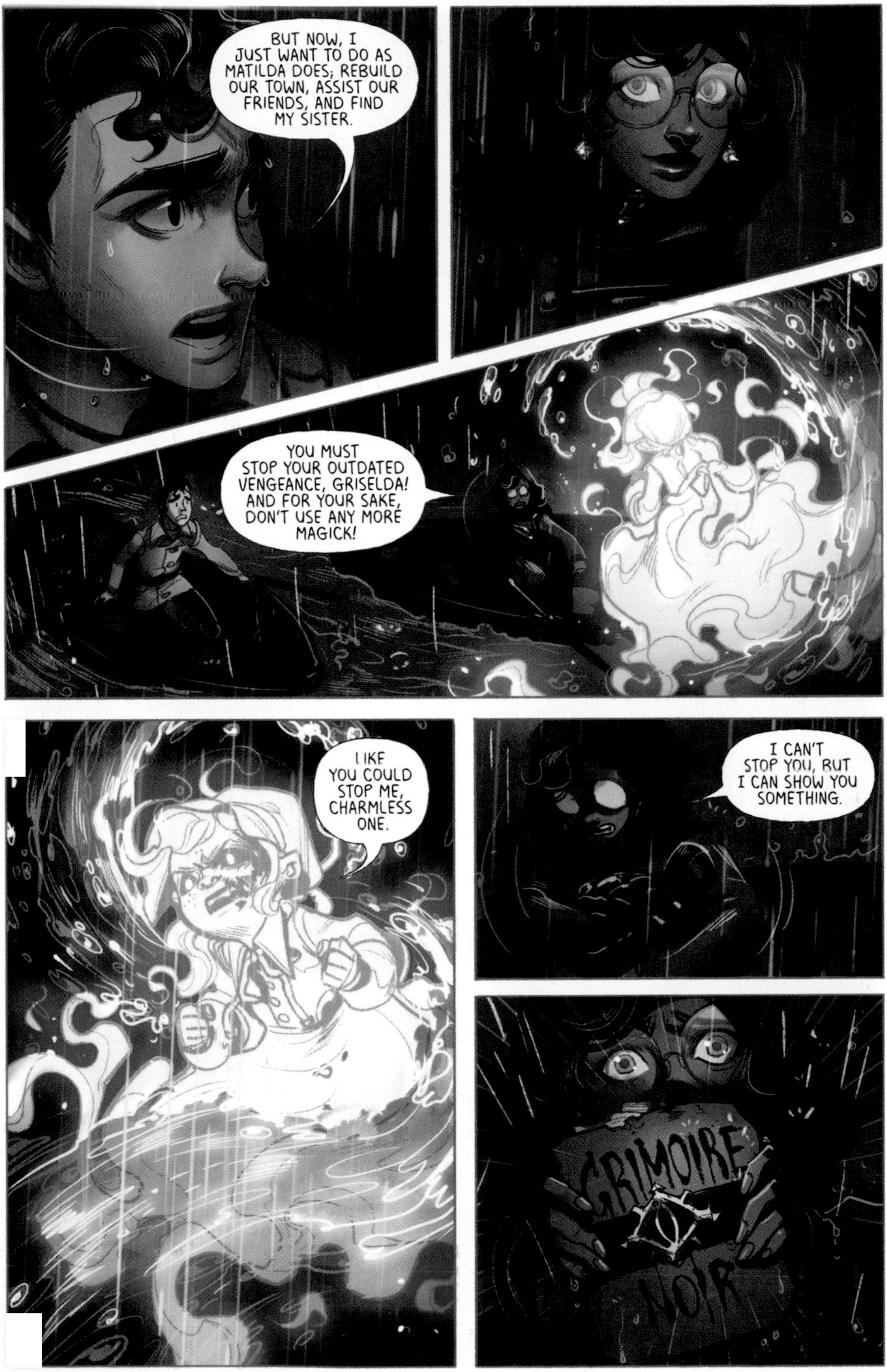
BUT NOW, I JUST WANT TO DO AS MATILDA DOES; REBUILD OUR TOWN, ASSIST OUR FRIENDS, AND FIND MY SISTER.
YOU MUST STOP YOUR OUTDATED VENGEANCE, GRISELDA! AND FOR YOUR SAKE, DON'T USE ANY MORE MAGICK!
LIKE YOU COULD STOP ME, CHARMLESS ONE.
I CAN'T STOP YOU, BUT I CAN SHOW YOU SOMETHING.
GRIMOIRE NOIR

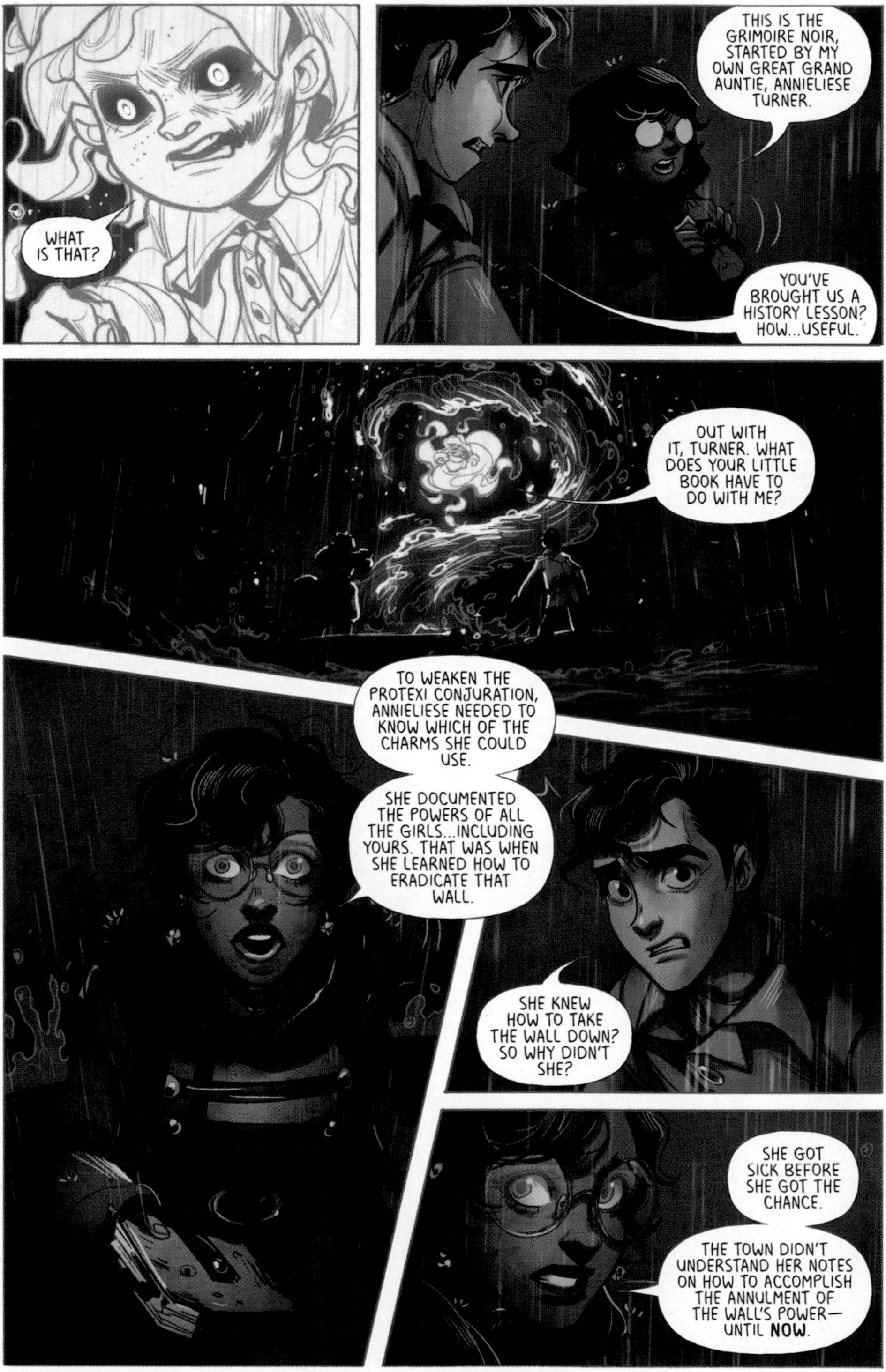
WHAT IS THAT?
THIS IS THE GRIMOIRE NOIR, STARTED BY MY OWN GREAT GRAND AUNTIE, ANNIELIESE TURNER.
YOU'VE BROUGHT US A HISTORY LESSON? HOW...USEFUL.
OUT WITH IT, TURNER. WHAT DOES YOUR LITTLE BOOK HAVE TO DO WITH ME?
TO WEAKEN THE PROTEXI CONJURATION, ANNIELIESE NEEDED TO KNOW WHICH OF THE CHARMS SHE COULD USE.
SHE DOCUMENTED THE POWERS OF ALL THE GIRLS...INCLUDING YOURS. THAT WAS WHEN SHE LEARNED HOW TO ERADICATE THAT WALL.
SHE KNEW HOW TO TAKE THE WALL DOWN? SO WHY DIDN'T SHE?
SHE GOT SICK BEFORE SHE GOT THE CHANCE.
THE TOWN DIDN'T UNDERSTAND HER NOTES ON HOW TO ACCOMPLISH THE ANNULMENT OF THE WALL'S POWER—UNTIL **NOW**.

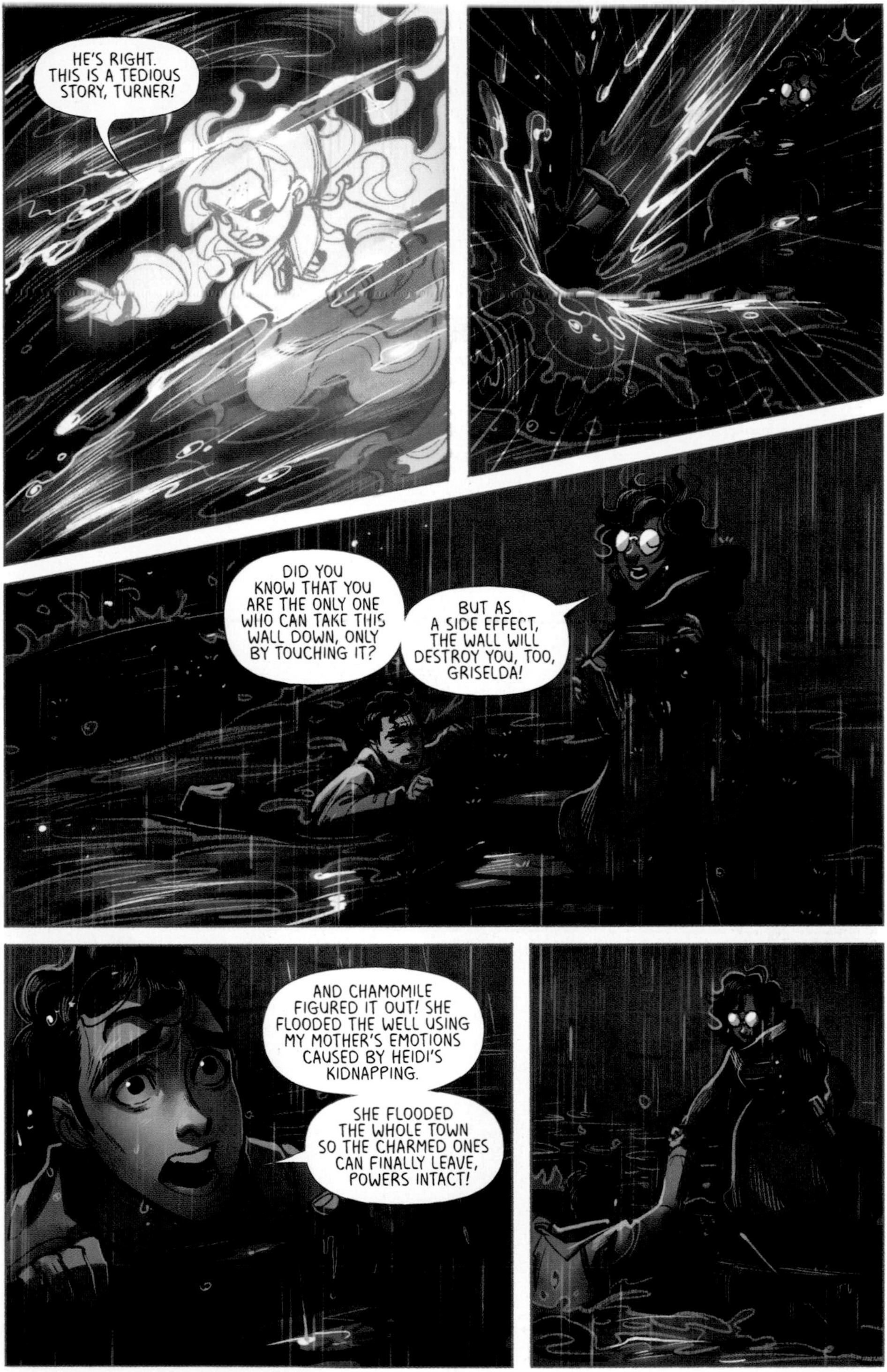
HE'S RIGHT. THIS IS A TEDIOUS STORY, TURNER!
DID YOU KNOW THAT YOU ARE THE ONLY ONE WHO CAN TAKE THIS WALL DOWN, ONLY BY TOUCHING IT?
BUT AS A SIDE EFFECT, THE WALL WILL DESTROY YOU, TOO, GRISELDA!
AND CHAMOMILE FIGURED IT OUT! SHE FLOODED THE WELL USING MY MOTHER'S EMOTIONS CAUSED BY HEIDI'S KIDNAPPING.
SHE FLOODED THE WHOLE TOWN SO THE CHARMED ONES CAN FINALLY LEAVE, POWERS INTACT!

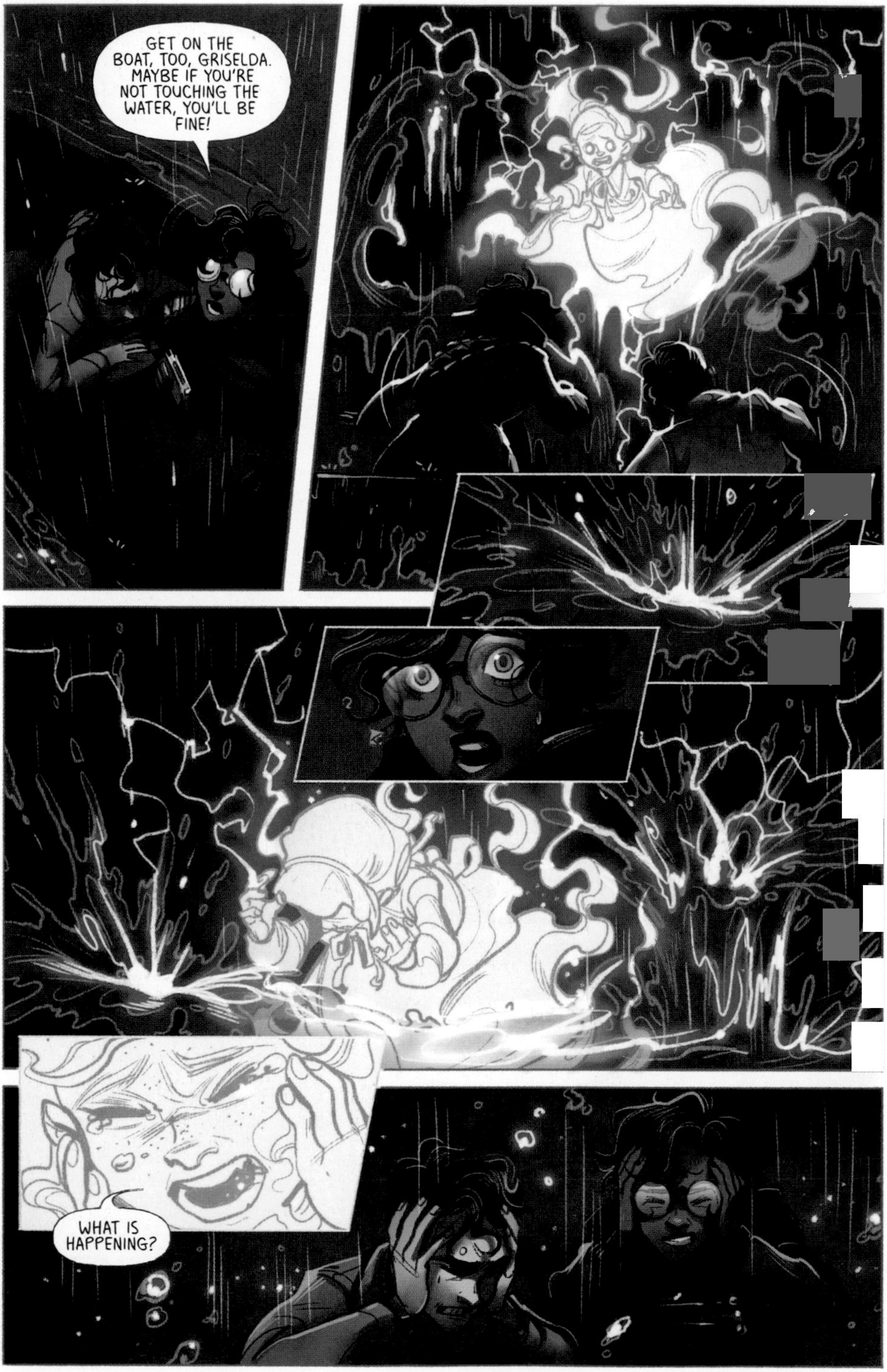
GET ON THE BOAT, TOO, GRISELDA. MAYBE IF YOU'RE NOT TOUCHING THE WATER, YOU'LL BE FINE!
WHAT IS HAPPENING?

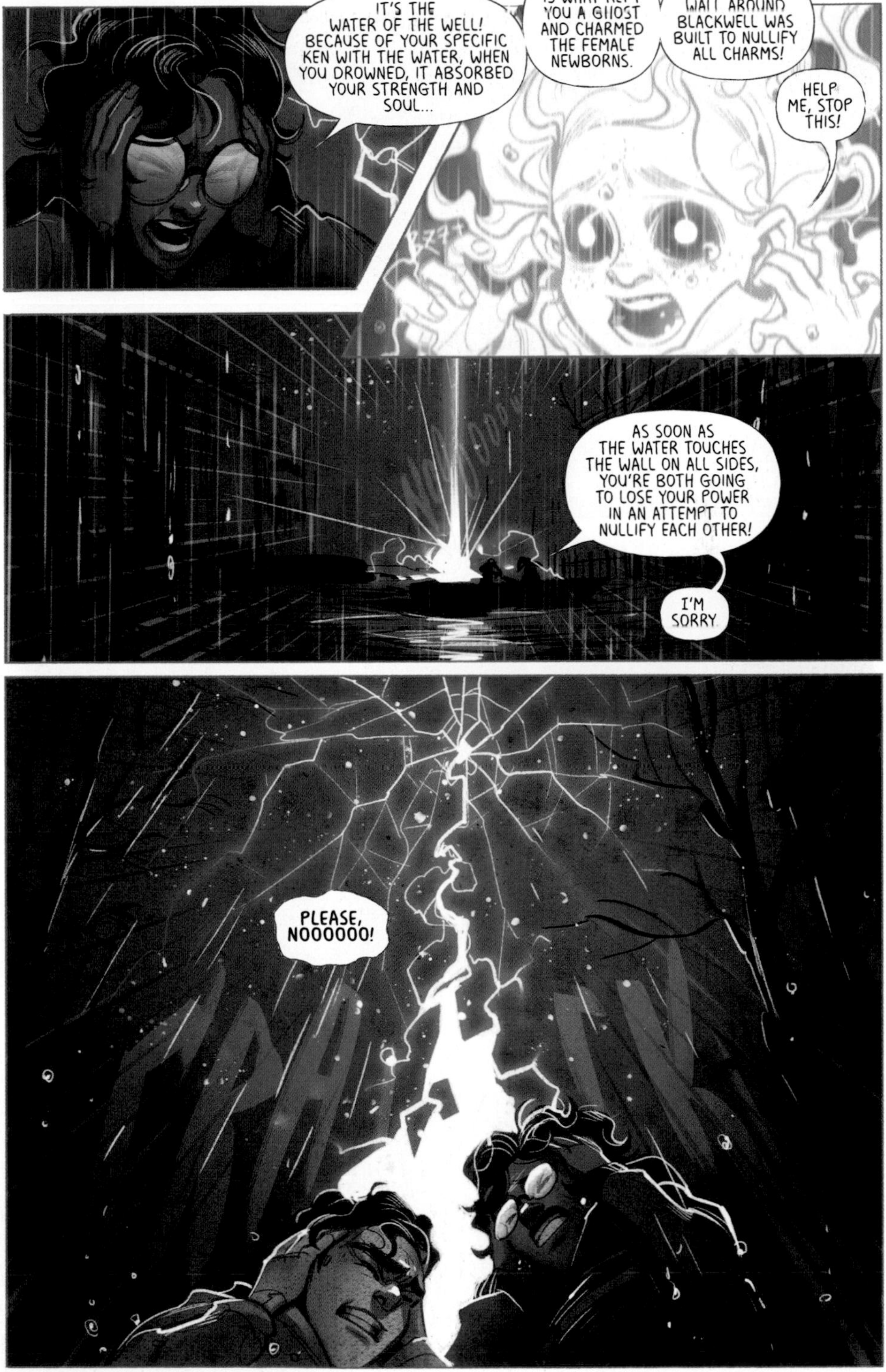
IT'S THE WATER OF THE WELL! BECAUSE OF YOUR SPECIFIC KEN WITH THE WATER, WHEN YOU DROWNED, IT ABSORBED YOUR STRENGTH AND SOUL...
...WHICH IS WHAT KEPT YOU A GHOST AND CHARMED THE FEMALE NEWBORNS.
BUT THE WALL AROUND BLACKWELL WAS BUILT TO NULLIFY ALL CHARMS!
HELP ME, STOP THIS!
AS SOON AS THE WATER TOUCHES THE WALL ON ALL SIDES, YOU'RE BOTH GOING TO LOSE YOUR POWER IN AN ATTEMPT TO NULLIFY EACH OTHER!
I'M SORRY.
PLEASE, NOOOOOO!

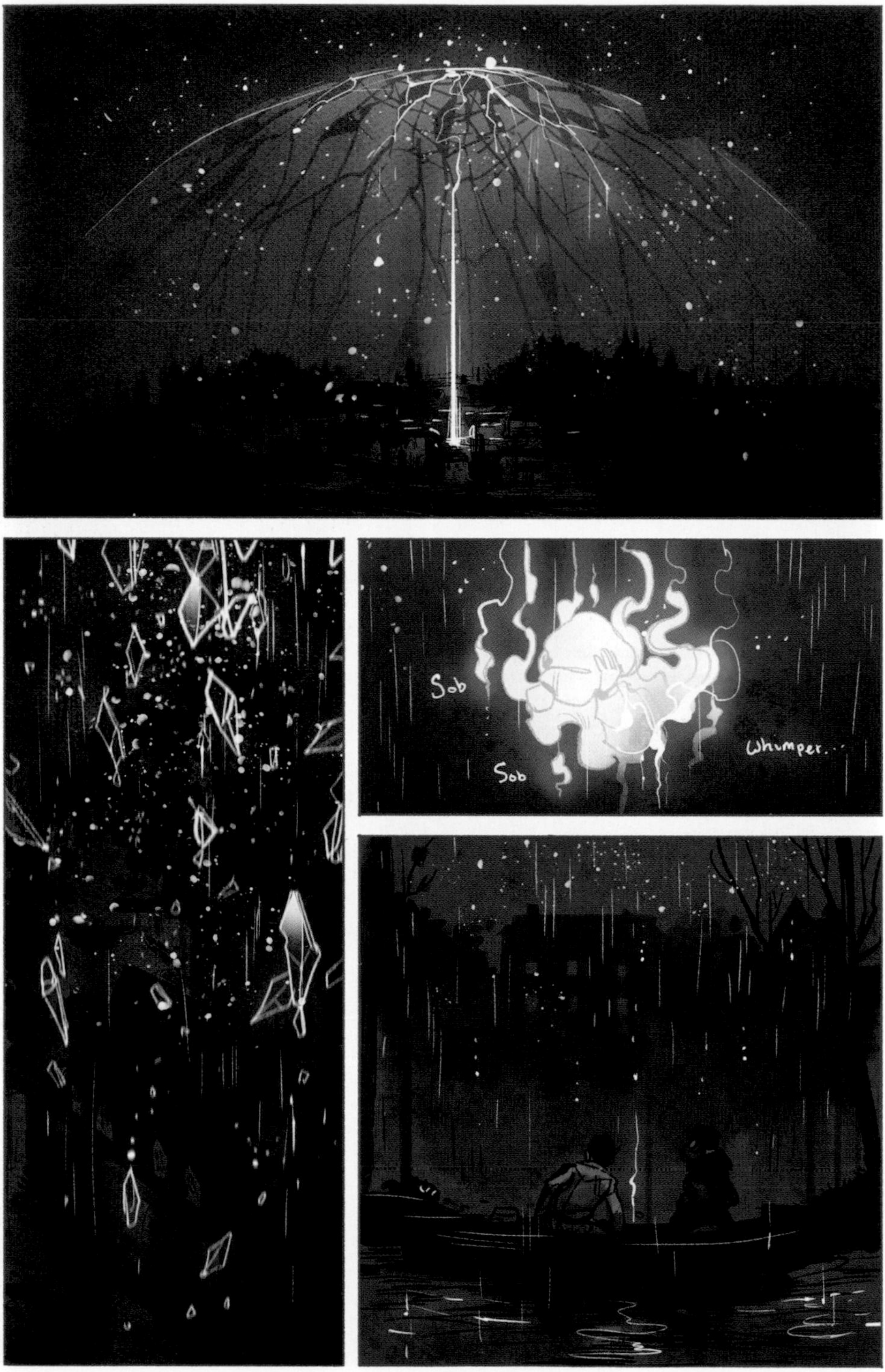
Sob
Sob
Whimper...

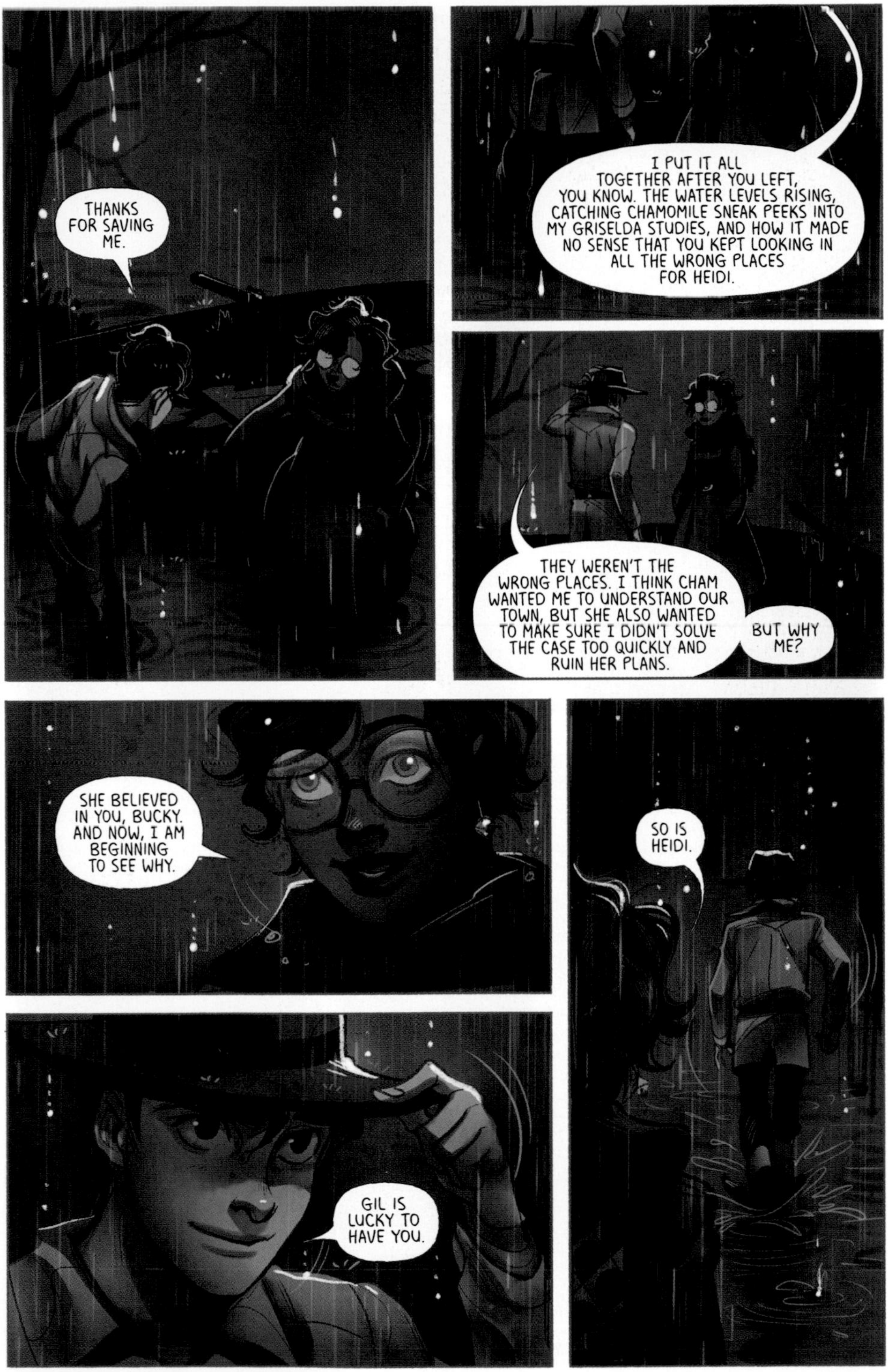
THANKS FOR SAVING ME.
I PUT IT ALL TOGETHER AFTER YOU LEFT, YOU KNOW. THE WATER LEVELS RISING, CATCHING CHAMOMILE SNEAK PEEKS INTO MY GRISELDA STUDIES, AND HOW IT MADE NO SENSE THAT YOU KEPT LOOKING IN ALL THE WRONG PLACES FOR HEIDI.
THEY WEREN'T THE WRONG PLACES. I THINK CHAM WANTED ME TO UNDERSTAND OUR TOWN, BUT SHE ALSO WANTED TO MAKE SURE I DIDN'T SOLVE THE CASE TOO QUICKLY AND RUIN HER PLANS.
BUT WHY ME?
SHE BELIEVED IN YOU, BUCKY. AND NOW, I AM BEGINNING TO SEE WHY.
GIL IS LUCKY TO HAVE YOU.
SO IS HEIDI.

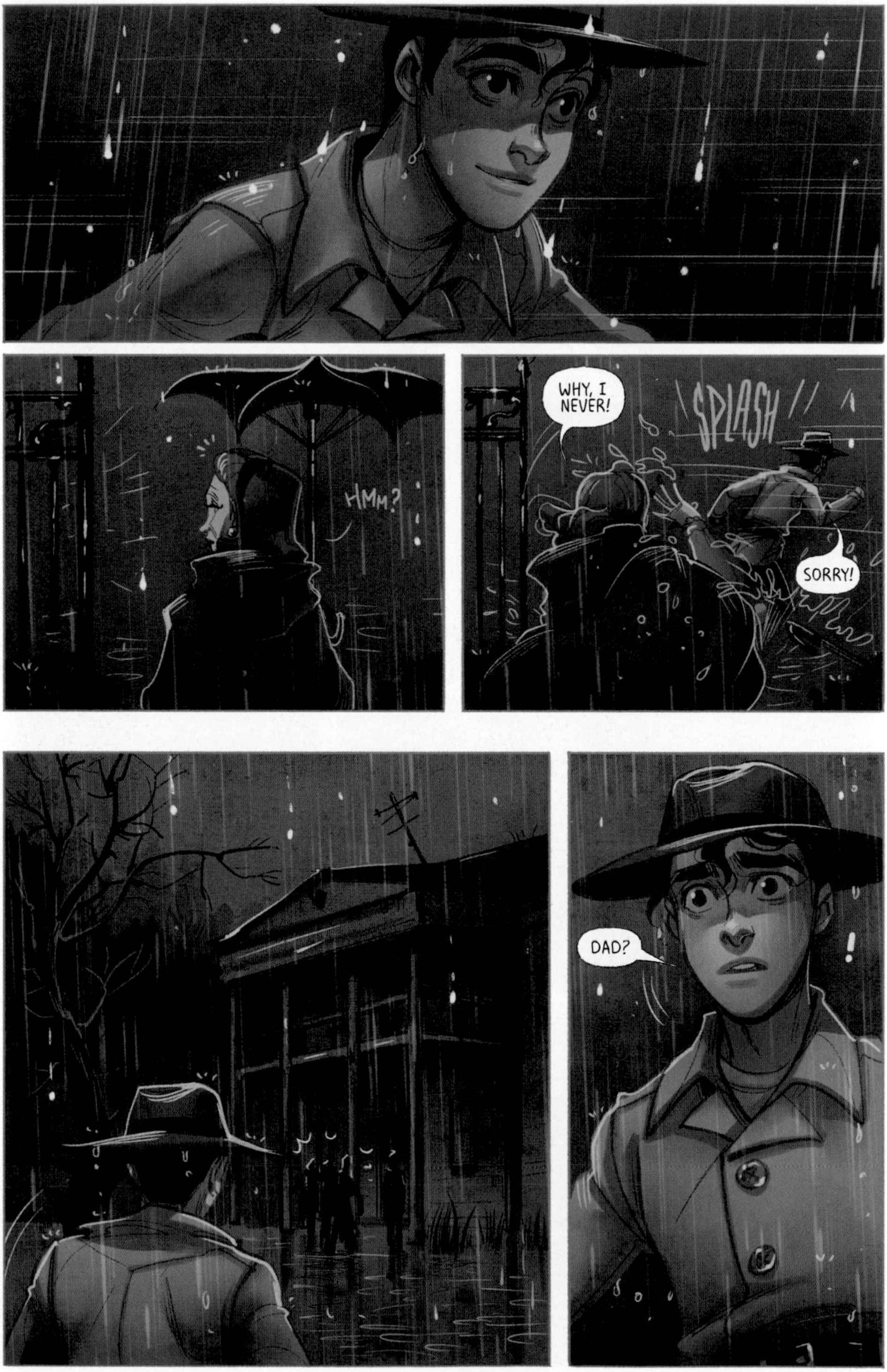
HMM?
WHY, I NEVER!
SPLASH
SORRY!
DAD?

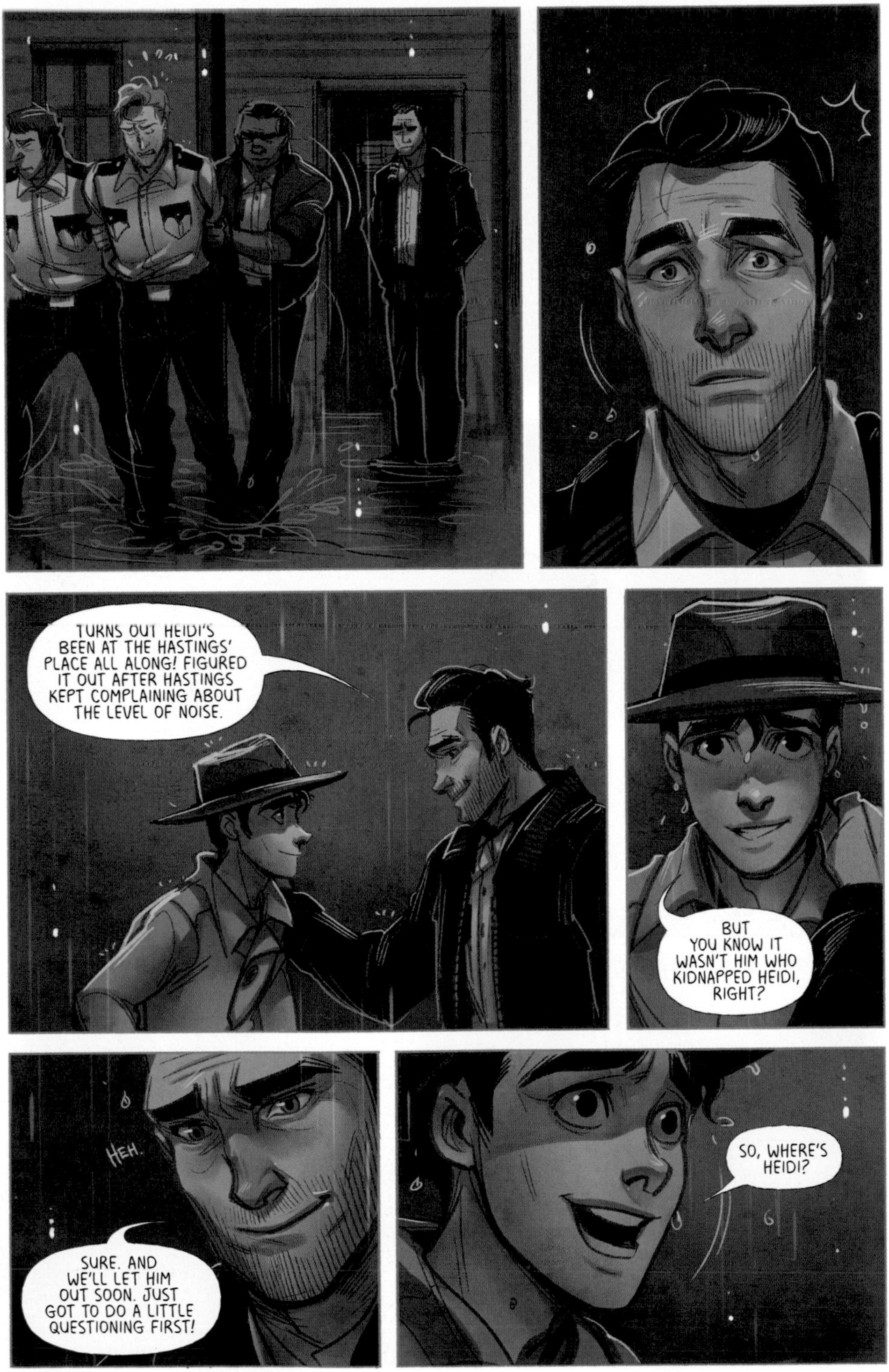
TURNS OUT HEIDI'S BEEN AT THE HASTINGS' PLACE ALL ALONG! FIGURED IT OUT AFTER HASTINGS KEPT COMPLAINING ABOUT THE LEVEL OF NOISE.
BUT YOU KNOW IT WASN'T HIM WHO KIDNAPPED HEIDI, RIGHT?
HEH.
SURE. AND WE'LL LET HIM OUT SOON. JUST GOT TO DO A LITTLE QUESTIONING FIRST!
SO, WHERE'S HEIDI?

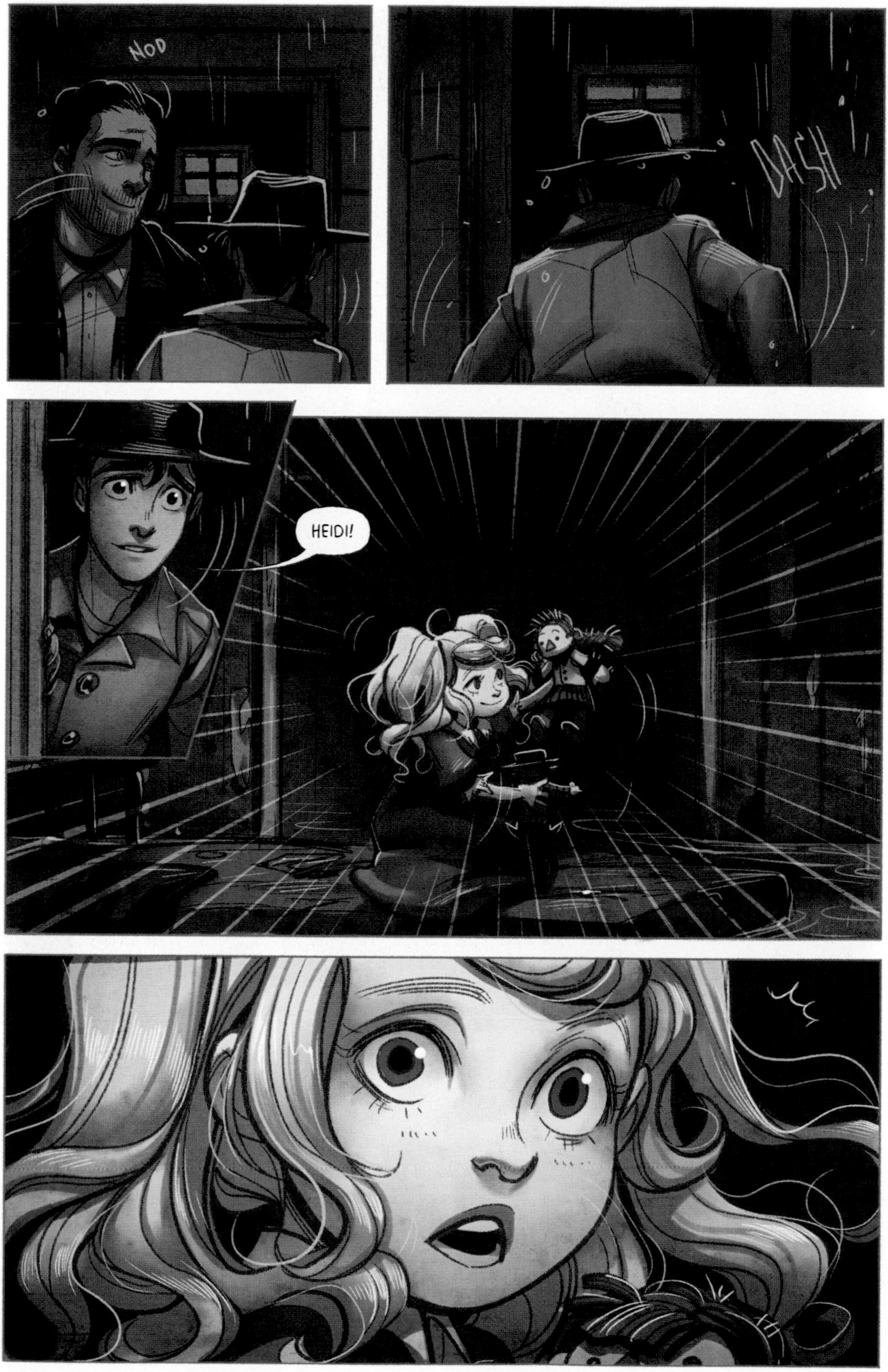
NOD
DASH
HEIDI!

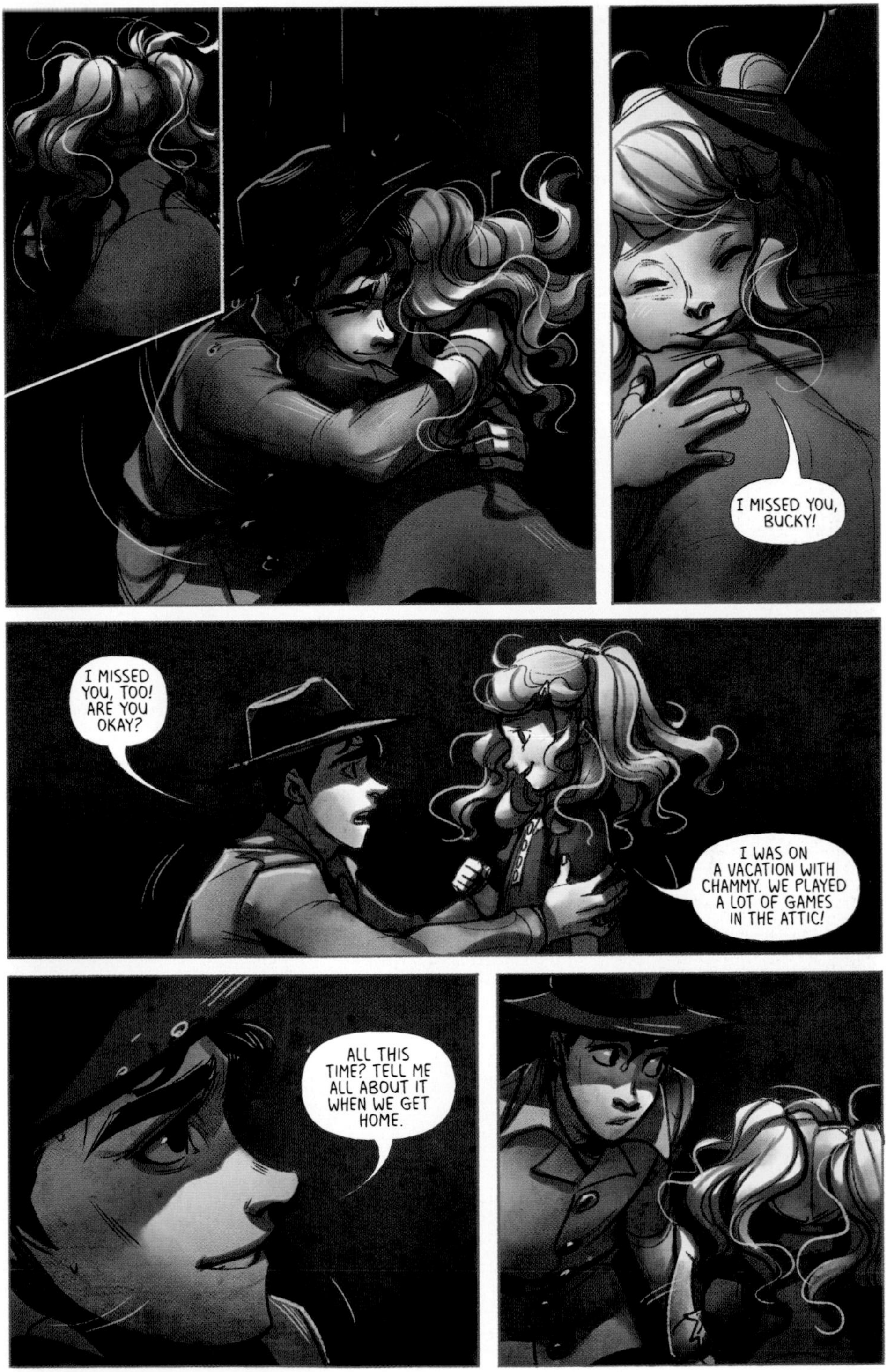
I MISSED YOU, BUCKY!
I MISSED YOU, TOO! ARE YOU OKAY?
I WAS ON A VACATION WITH CHAMMY. WE PLAYED A LOT OF GAMES IN THE ATTIC!
ALL THIS TIME? TELL ME ALL ABOUT IT WHEN WE GET HOME.

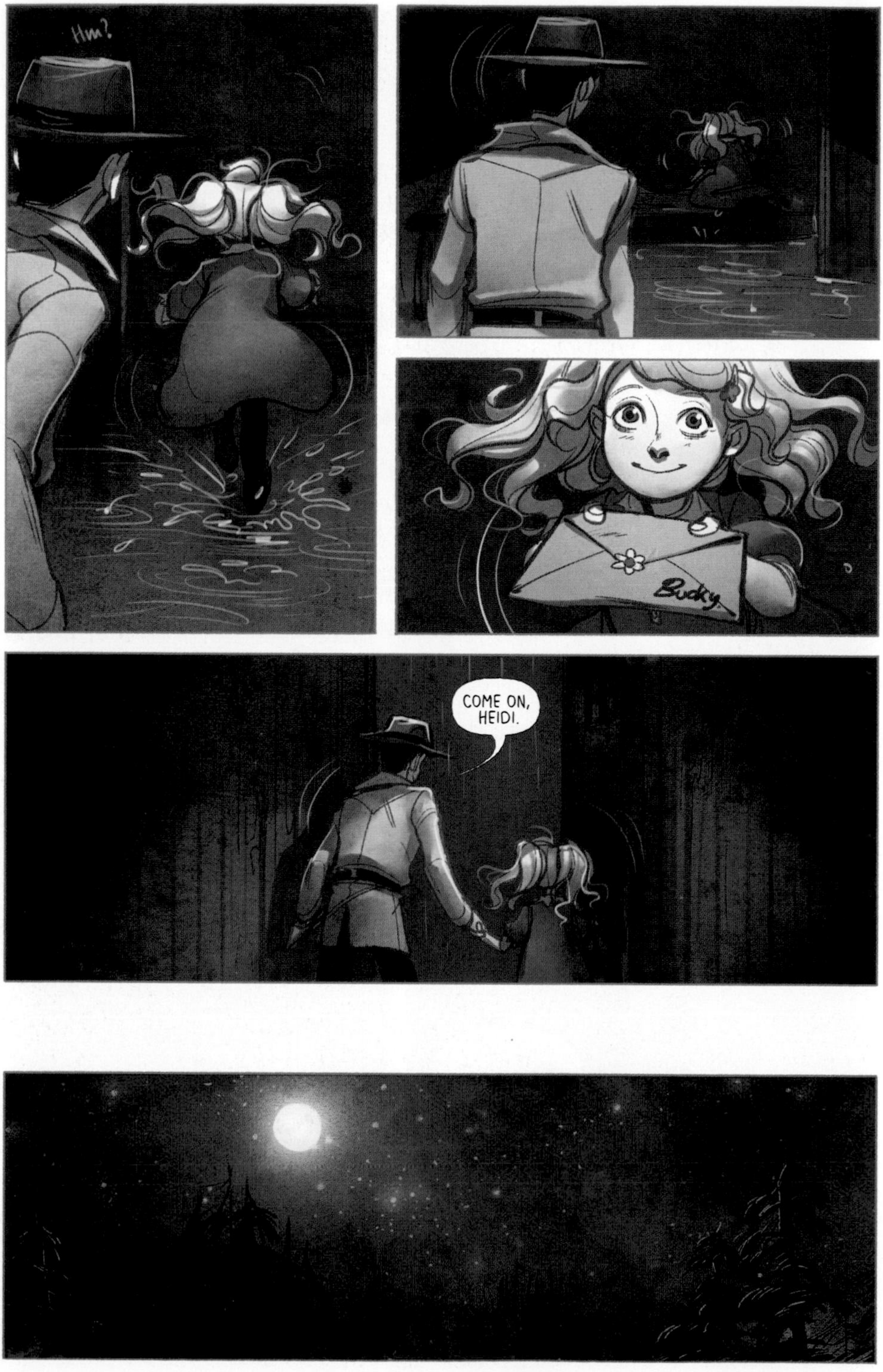
Hm?
Bucky
COME ON, HEIDI.

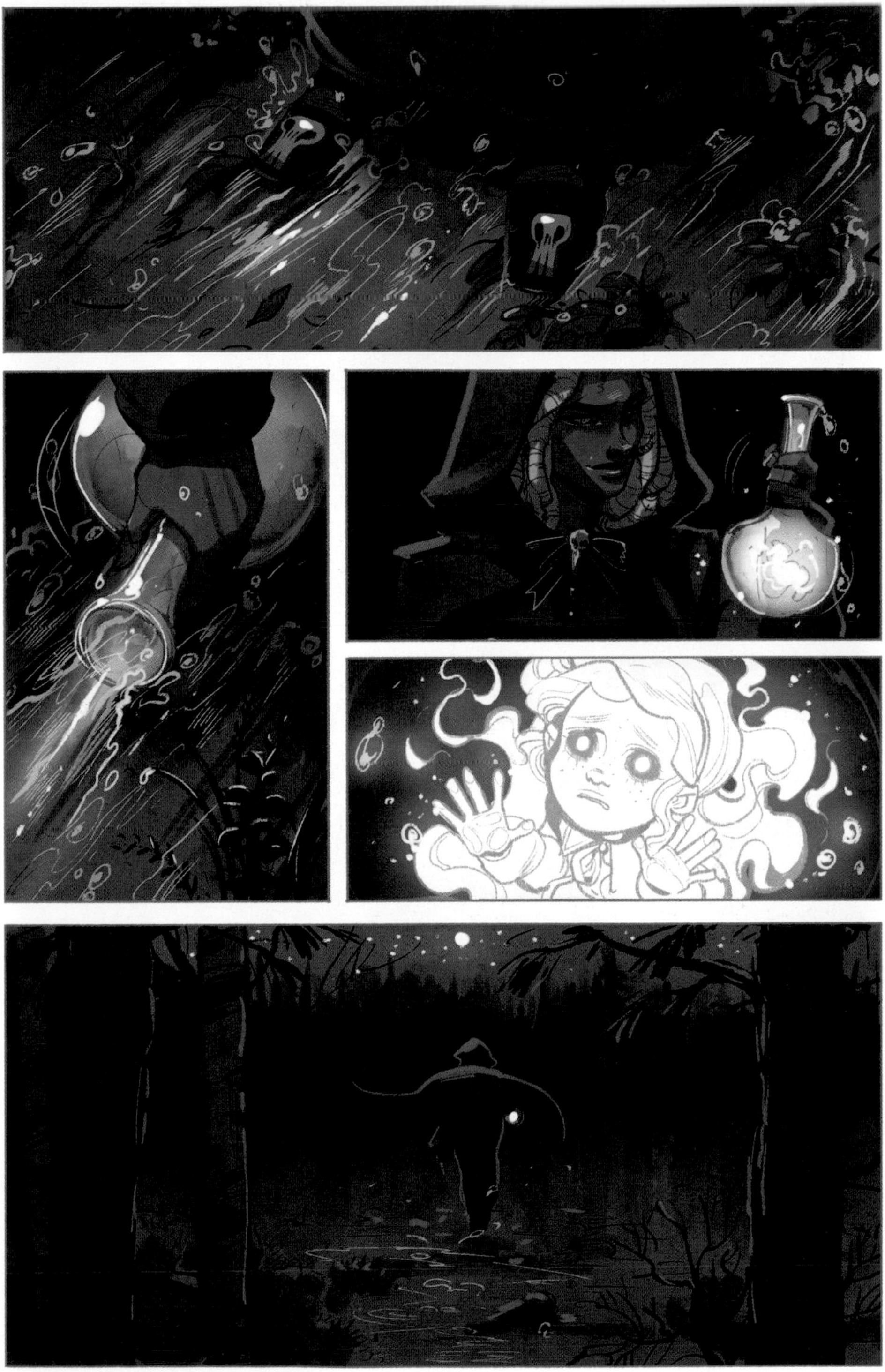

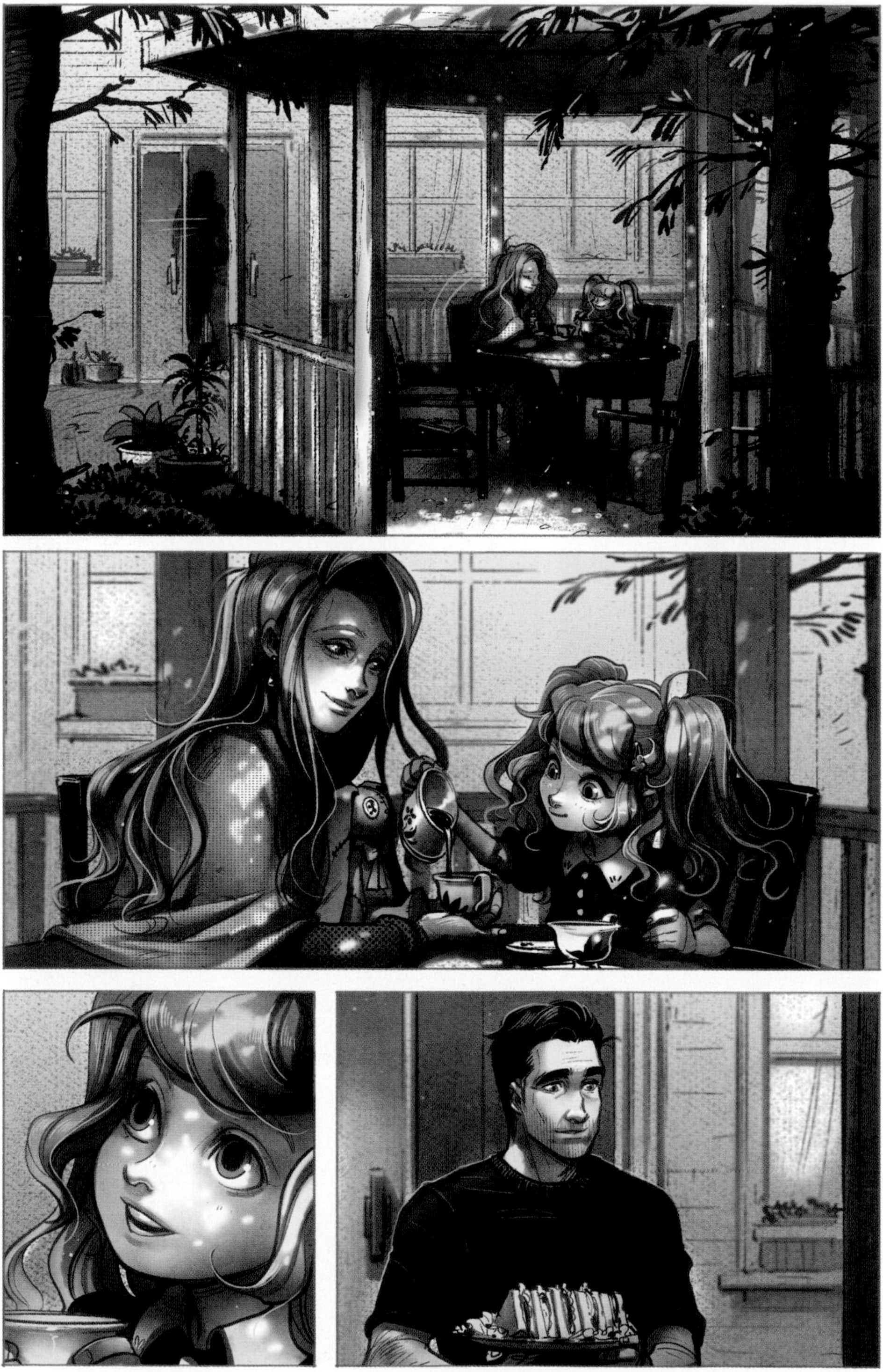

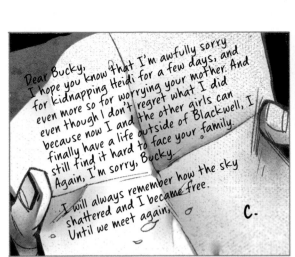

Dear Bucky,
I hope you know that I'm awfully sorry
for kidnapping Heidi for a few days, and
even more so for worrying your mother. And
even though I don't regret what I did
because now I and the other girls can
finally have a life outside of Blackwell, I
still find it hard to face your family.
Again, I'm sorry, Bucky.

...I will always remember how the sky
shattered and I became free.
Until we meet again,

C.

EXTRA
MATERIALS

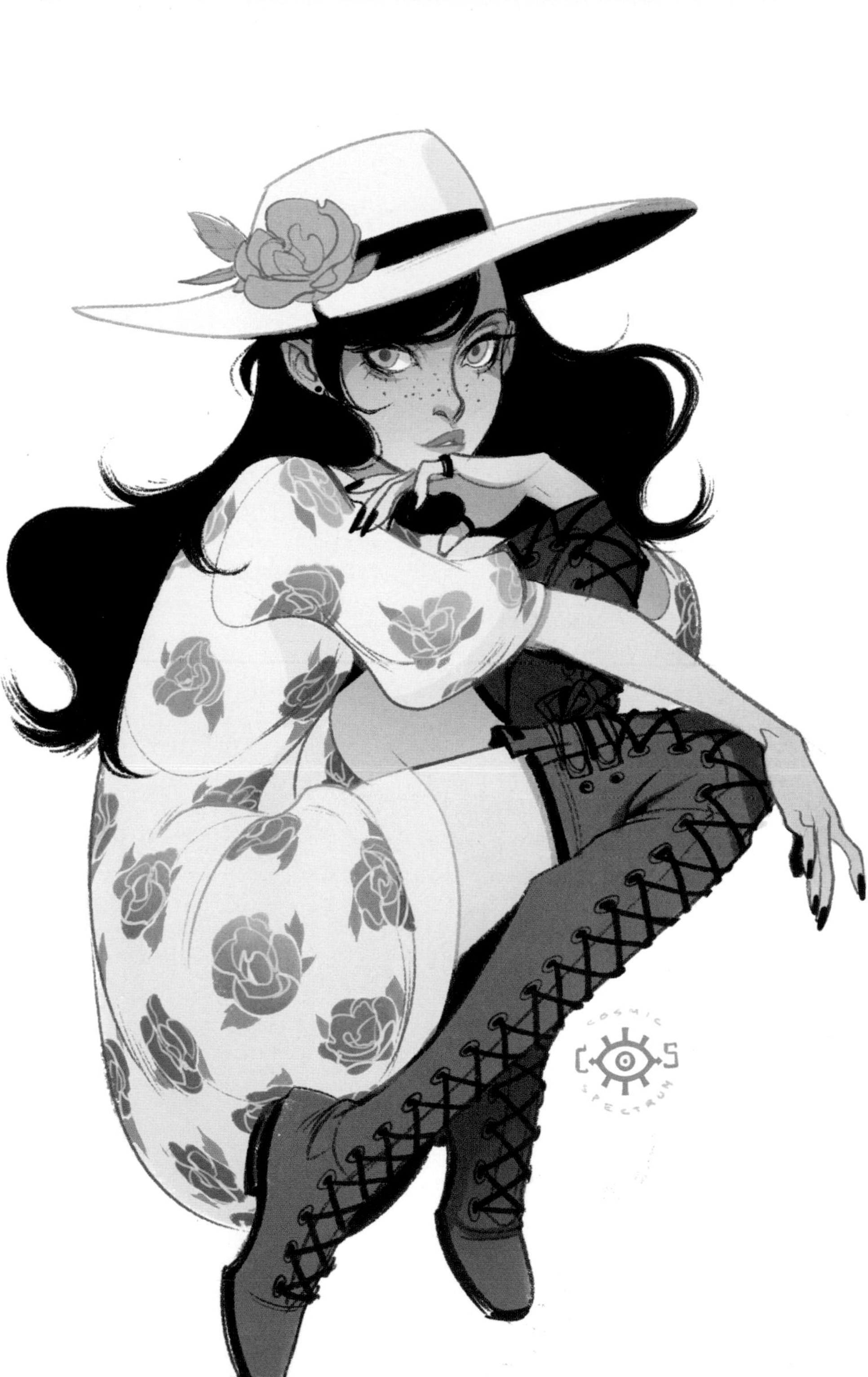
COSMIC
SPECTRUM

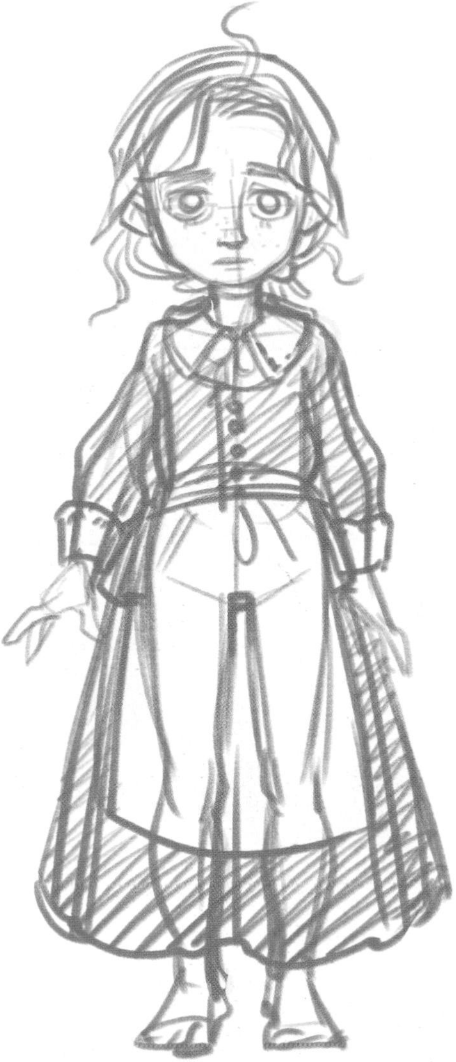
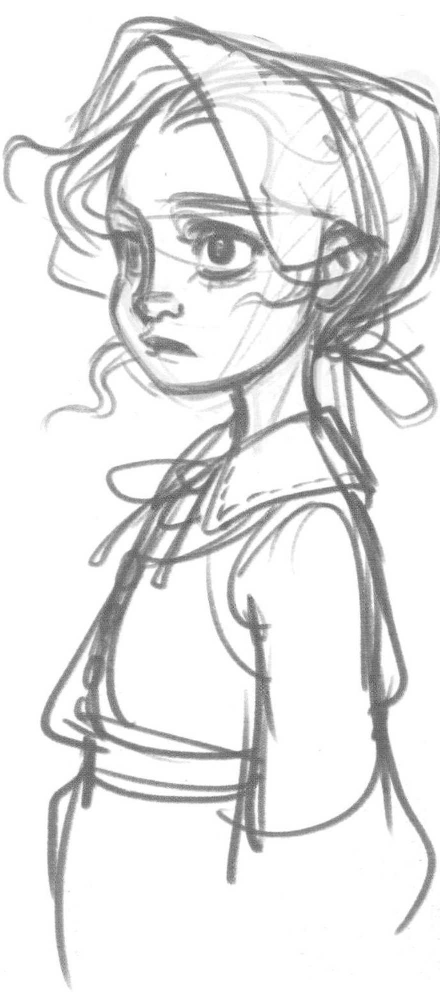

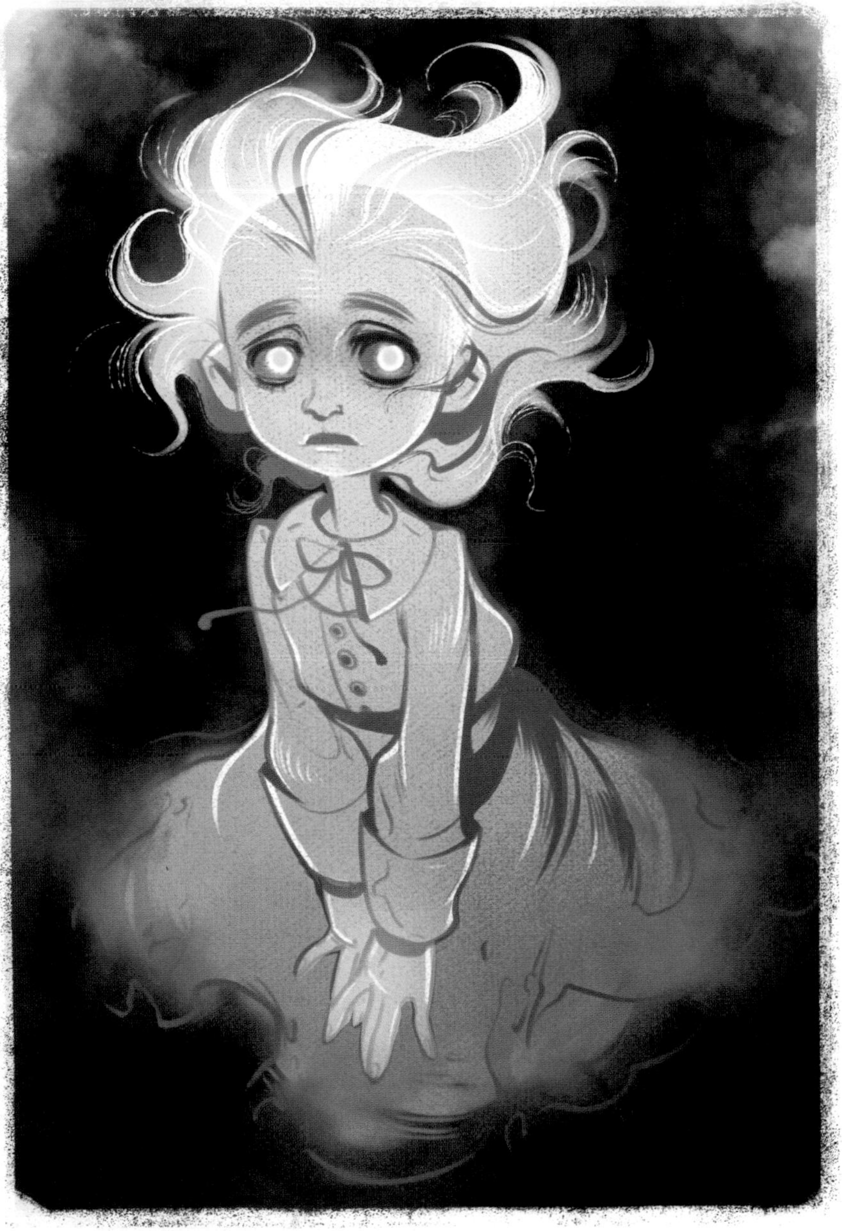

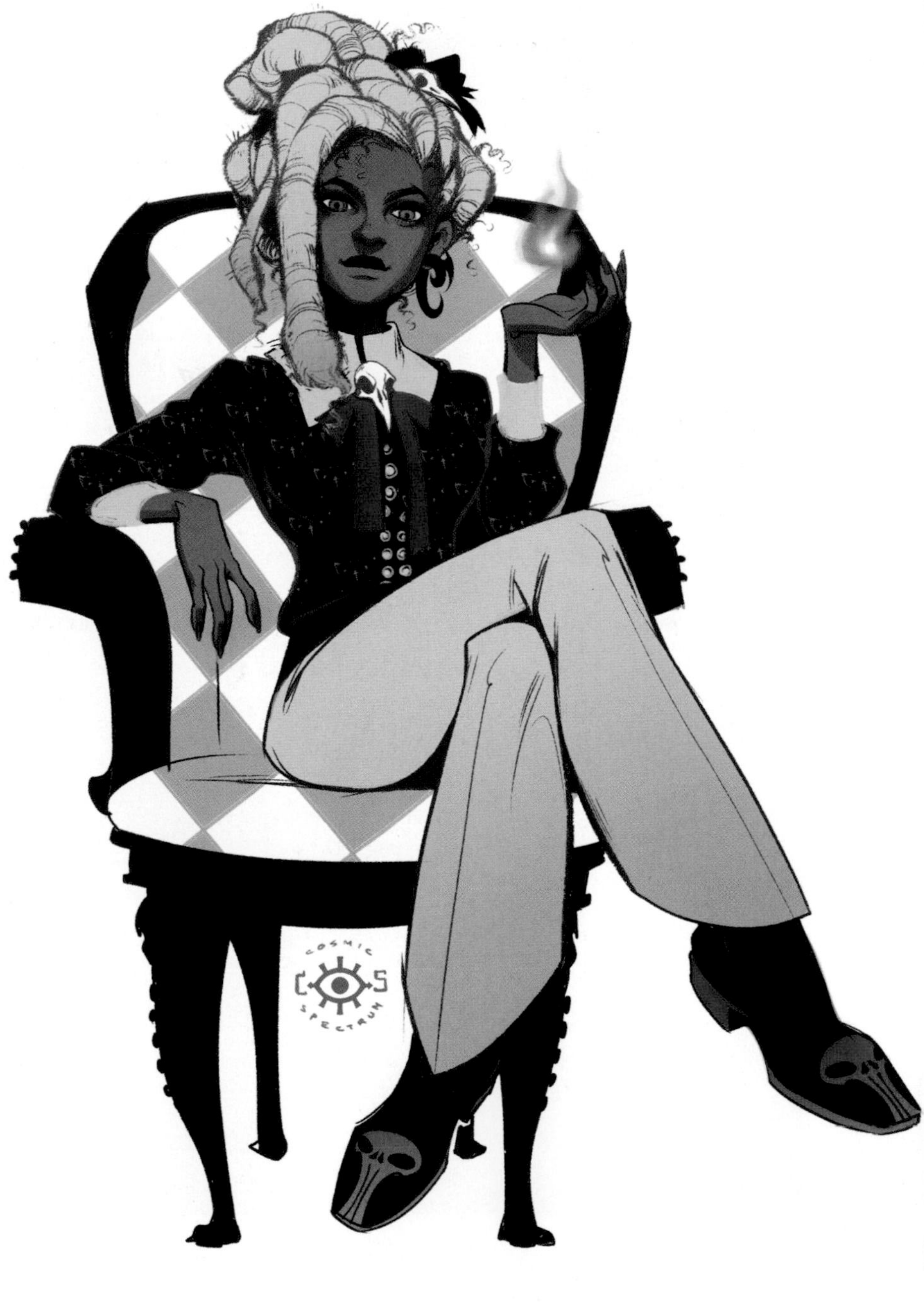
COSMIC
CS
SPECTRUM

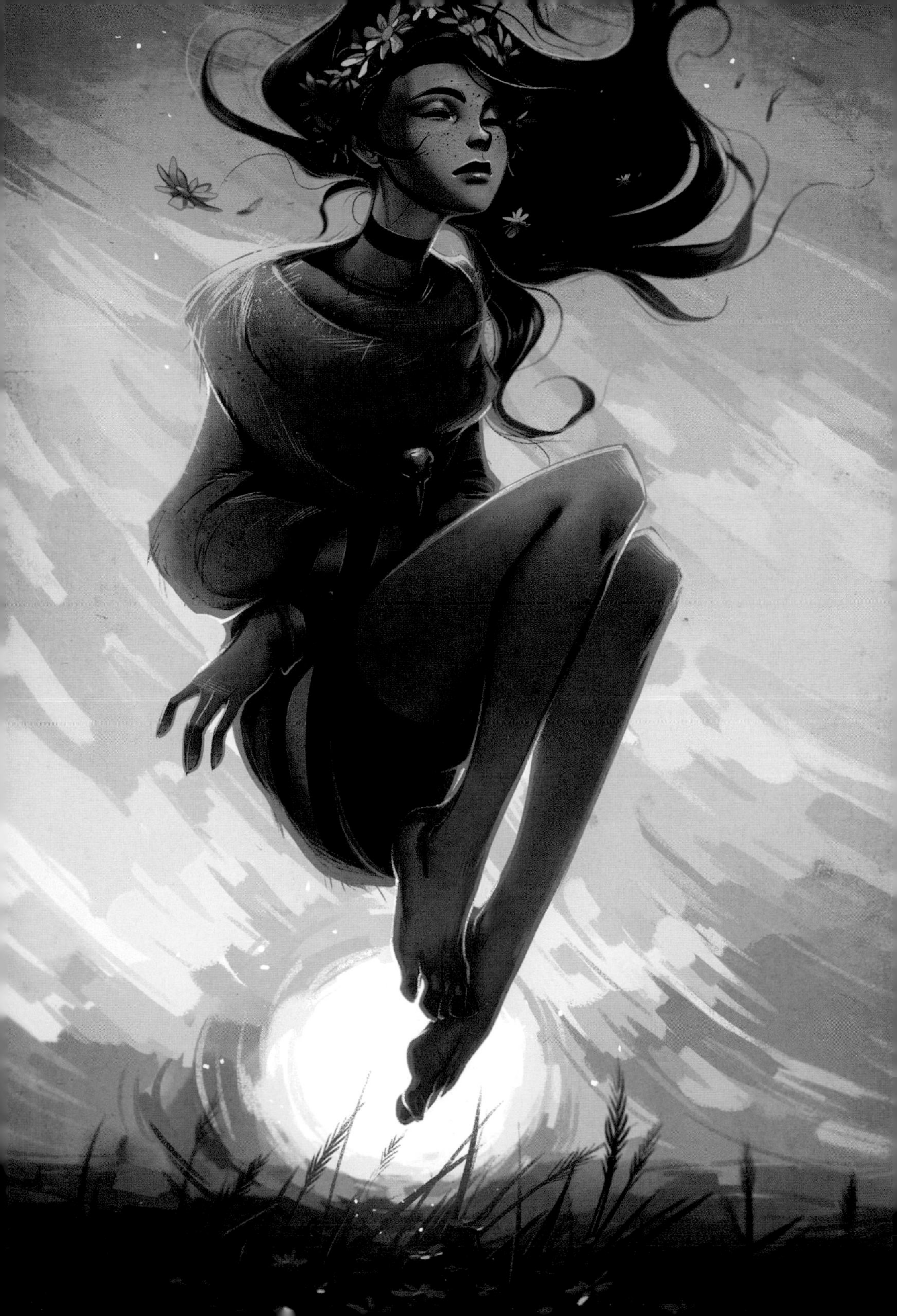

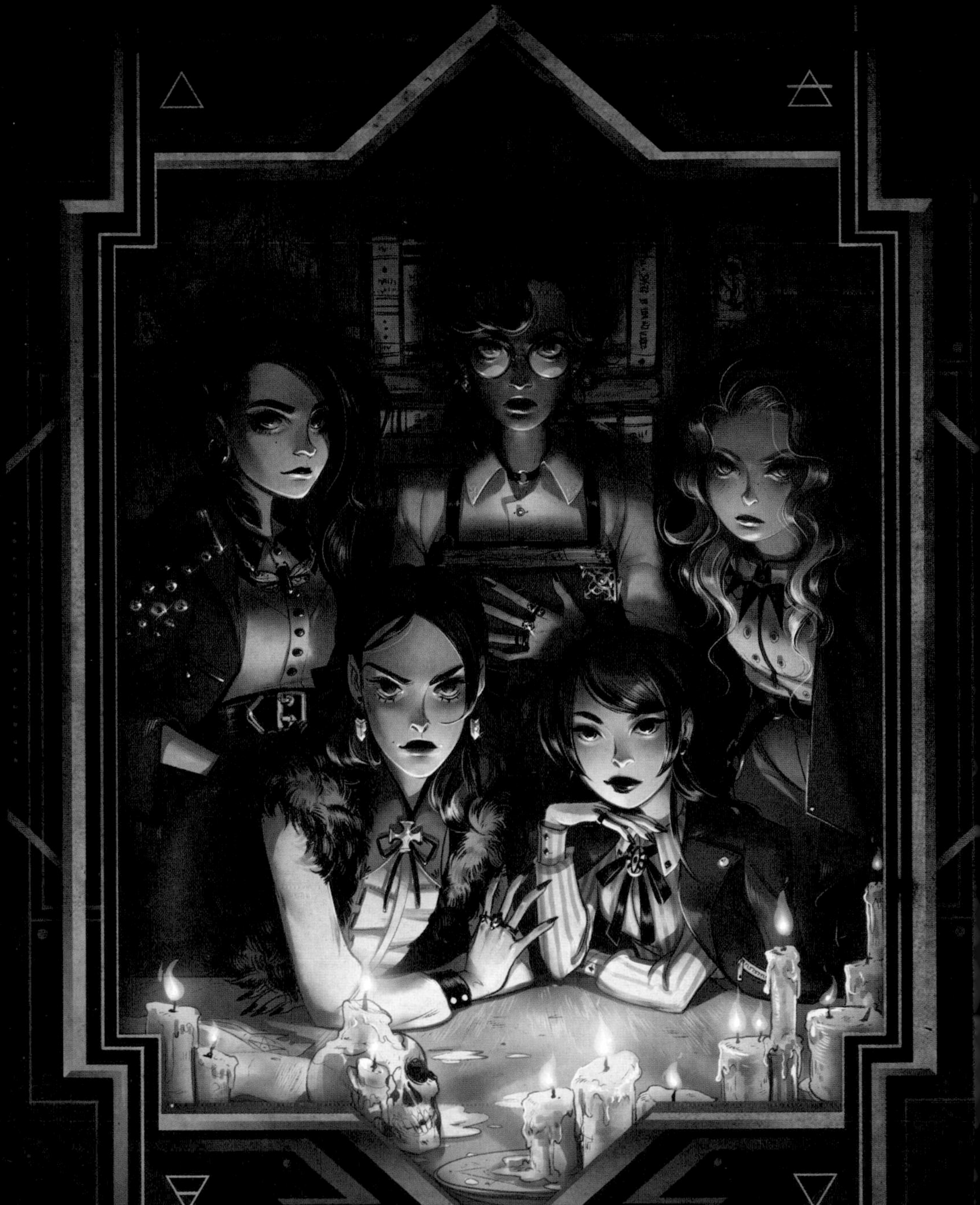

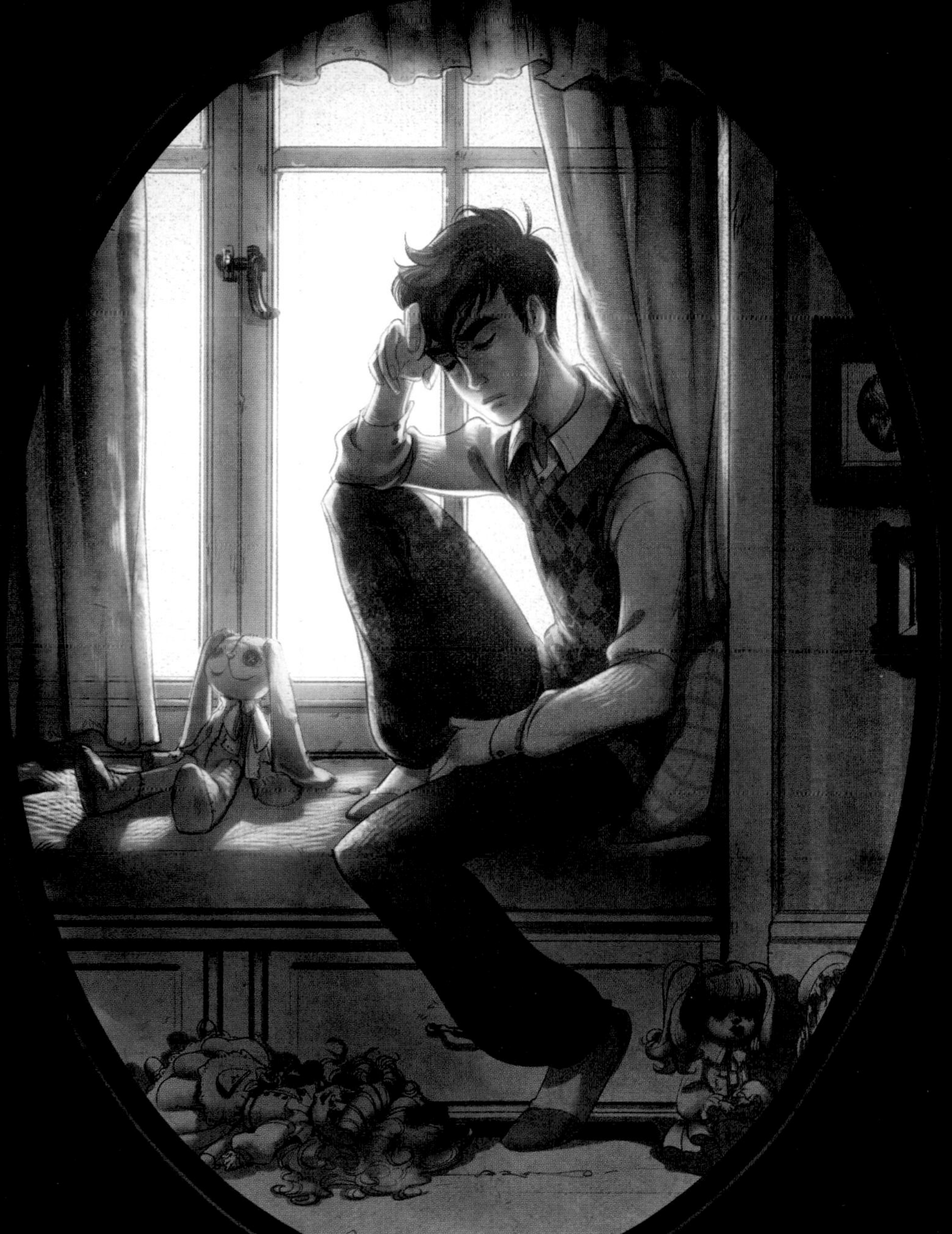

COSMIC

SPECTRUM

FOR IRINA, WHO WAS THERE AT THE BEGINNING
AND WILL BE THERE AT THE END.
—VERA

First Second

TEXT COPYRIGHT © 2019 BY VERA GREENTEA
ILLUSTRATIONS COPYRIGHT © 2019 BY YANA BOGATCH

PUBLISHED BY FIRST SECOND
FIRST SECOND IS AN IMPRINT OF ROARING BROOK PRESS,
A DIVISION OF HOLTZBRINCK PUBLISHING HOLDINGS LIMITED PARTNERSHIP
120 BROADWAY, NEW YORK, NY 10271
ALL RIGHTS RESERVED

LIBRARY OF CONGRESS CONTROL NUMBER: 2018944889

PAPERBACK ISBN: 978-1-62672-598-0
HARDCOVER ISBN: 978-1-250-30573-2

OUR BOOKS MAY BE PURCHASED IN BULK FOR PROMOTIONAL, EDUCATIONAL, OR BUSINESS USE. PLEASE
CONTACT YOUR LOCAL BOOKSELLER OR THE MACMILLAN CORPORATE AND PREMIUM SALES DEPARTMENT
AT (800) 221-7945 EXT. 5442 OR BY EMAIL AT MACMILLANSPECIALMARKETS@MACMILLAN.COM.

FIRST EDITION, 2019

EDITED BY MARK SIEGEL AND KIARA VALDEZ
LETTERING BY ADAM WOLLET
BOOK DESIGN BY MOLLY JOHANSON

PENCILED, INKED, AND COLORED ENTIRELY IN PHOTOSHOP, USING A WACOM CINTIQ 22HD.

PRINTED IN CHINA BY 1010 PRINTING INTERNATIONAL LIMITED, NORTH POINT, HONG KONG
PAPERBACK: 10 9 8 7 6 5 4 3 2 1
HARDCOVER: 10 9 8 7 6 5 4 3 2 1